HER ELEMENTAL DRAGONS

THE COMPLETE SERIES

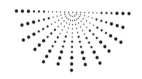

ELIZABETH BRIGGS

Cover designed by Christian Bentulan

Interior artwork by Ljilja Romanovic

ISBN (paperback) 978569337477

ISBN (ebook) 9781948456074

ISBN (hardcover) 979-8-89244-008-0

STROKE THE FLAME

HER ELEMENTAL DRAGONS BOOK ONE

1

KIRA

I crept through the forest in search of my prey, my hand tight on my bow. Heavy rain left a sheen of water on my face even with my hood covering me, and I wiped it off on my already-soaked sleeve. The storm was getting stronger. If I didn't find a deer or something else soon, I'd have to give up and return empty-handed. Roark wouldn't like that.

I made my way toward one of my traps up ahead, stepping carefully through the high brush and keeping my eyes peeled for any game. With the weather as it was, I doubted I would have any luck. All the animals in the forest had no doubt retreated once this sudden storm had come upon us. The only thing left out here would be elementals and shades—and I had no desire to confront either of those.

When I'd set out a few hours ago, the sky had been clear and bright. Only in the last hour had the storm clouds gathered overhead as if out of nowhere, or perhaps summoned by the Gods themselves. I shivered, and not just from the cold that sank into my bones through my soaked clothes.

I bent down to check the trap I'd left this morning and breathed a sigh of relief. A large rabbit had been caught inside. Tonight I'd be fed. Tonight Tash would be safe.

I tossed the rabbit into a sack and loaded it onto my shoulder. When I turned around, I wasn't alone. I dropped the sack and aimed my bow, my heart in my throat.

An old woman stood before me, her body hunched over with age, her skin pale and wrinkled. She wore a frayed traveling cloak and frizzy white

3

hair escaped her low hood. I might have heard her as she approached, but the storm drowned out all sound except for the pounding of rain in the trees.

"Can I help you?" I called out to her, as I lowered my bow and retrieved my fallen sack.

"Perhaps." She stared at me and frowned, then looked around as if confused.

"You must be lost. I can show you to Stoneham, the nearest town."

"That's kind of you."

I offered her my arm and she took it, leaning upon me. Her grip was strong, even though she seemed so frail I worried a strong gust might turn her bones to dust. I wondered how she had found herself in the middle of the forest in the first place. She shouldn't be traveling alone, especially not in this weather.

"What's your name?" she asked.

"Kira."

As we carefully stepped through the forest she gazed up at the dark sky, letting the rain wash over her face. "There's a storm coming."

I patted her wrinkled hand where it rested on my arm. "I think it's already here. But if we hurry, we can get out of it. The inn is just ahead."

"There's no escaping this storm." She turned toward me and her eyes were like steel. "Not for you."

Her words sent another shiver down my spine. "I'm not sure what you mean."

She held my gaze another few seconds, then waved her hand. "Just the ramblings of an old woman. Nothing more."

I frowned, but continued walking through the wet brush. "We're nearly there now."

"Yes, indeed we are," she said.

A rustling sound up ahead caught my attention. I dropped her arm and drew my bow. "Stay back. I'll make sure the way is clear."

I took a step forward as I peered through the brush in front of us, watching for the slightest twitch of a leaf or the dash of fur. But there was nothing other than the relentless rain.

When I turned back, the woman was gone.

"Hello?" I called out, spinning around and scanning the area for her. The storm made it hard to see anything, but there was no trace of her anywhere. She'd just…vanished.

I went back the way we'd walked, calling out for the woman, but I couldn't find her anywhere. There was no sign she'd ever been in the forest at all.

After many long minutes, with the rain pounding down on me and the wind whipping at my cloak, I reluctantly gave up my search. I told myself she must have gone ahead to the village without me, but something about that didn't feel right. It was the only explanation though, unless she was a shade. But if that were true I wouldn't still be breathing, according to the stories I'd heard anyway. I'd never actually seen a shade before, but it was said they were ghostly figures that could turn invisible, pass through walls, and suck the life right out of you. As strange as the woman was, she seemed perfectly human at least. Still, probably best for me to hurry back.

I headed toward the inn, more by instinct than sight at this point. As I left the forest, my shoes sank into the mud and the relentless wind tore the hood off my head. I tried to tug it back on, but there was no use. My hair was already soaked through and I was chilled to the bone.

Lightning flashed overhead, followed immediately by the deep rumble of thunder. I ran for the inn as fast as I could, but the wind was so strong it seemed to push me back, as if it was fighting my every step. I slipped in the mud and fell to my knees, bracing myself with my hands. The impact jolted through my bones, and for a moment I could only remain there, dazed and covered in mud from head to toe.

As I tried to stand, a bright crack lit up the sky, blinding me. Searing hot pain struck my head and I screamed as a bolt of lightning coursed through me. Electricity spread within my entire body, setting every nerve on fire and burning me from the inside out. It raced through my blood, and I thought my heart would burst from the power warring for control within me. Time stopped, and pain became the only thing I knew.

And then it was gone.

Deep, cavernous thunder sounded all around me as my sight returned. My entire body shook and trembled uncontrollably. Mud covered me completely, rain pelted my face, wind lashed at my hair, and sparks danced in my blood. As if the elemental Gods themselves had thought to strike me down, then decided to let me live after all.

I scrambled back to my feet, nearly slipping again in the slick mud. When I was steady, I grabbed the bag with the rabbit from where I'd dropped it, before stumbling to the back door of the inn. I opened the door with some effort, the wind battling me still, and then stepped inside the familiar warm kitchen that smelled of stew and baked bread. Once the door was shut, I fell back against it, breathing heavily.

I'd been struck by lightning. Yet somehow I still lived.

I quickly checked my body, searching for signs of injury, but I seemed to be physically fine, although my cloak was charred and I was in great need of a bath. The only thing that afflicted me was shock.

5

None of it made sense. Lightning usually hit the tallest thing around, and I was nowhere near that. I'd been surrounded by much better targets. The inn. The stables. The trees. Why had it hit me?

And how had I made it through without a scratch?

2
KIRA

"Kira?" a friendly voice called out. My best friend, Tash, who worked as a waitress in her father's inn and tavern. Like most of the people in the Earth Realm, she had dark skin and thick black hair, which she often wore in a braid, and with her cheerful smile she made even the drabbest apron look good. She rushed over to me and gasped. "You poor thing. You're completely soaked and look like you went mud wrestling with the pigs. Come in out of the cold and we'll get you something to warm you up."

"I'm all right," I said, but it wasn't very convincing. I'm pretty sure my teeth chattered. "Just need to change my clothes."

Tash bit her lip, but nodded. "Did you get anything?"

"Yeah." I handed her the bag with the rabbit. It wasn't much, but it would have to do. Between the elemental attacks on nearby farms and the Black Dragon's taxes, food was scarce these days. Something Roark reminded us of often.

Her face softened with relief. "Thank the Gods."

I snorted. "The Gods have abandoned us. Thank me for setting up the traps in advance."

She chuckled. "Go clean yourself up, you're tracking mud all over the kitchen. Mother's going to have a fit."

I stepped out of the kitchen and into the small room behind it, where I currently lived. Roark, Tash's father, owned this inn and allowed me to stay here as long as I caught him some game and fetched some herbs and spices from the forest. If I brought something back, I got to eat that night.

If not, I didn't. If I missed two days in a row, he'd beat Tash in punishment. Oh, originally he'd tried to beat me, but I hadn't cared. I'd suffered much worse before. He soon realized it hurt me more to beat his own daughter, my one true friend.

I'd never missed two days in a row again.

I quickly stripped off my soiled cloak, along with the rest of my hunting leathers, then changed into a simple blue dress with frayed edges. I exchanged my muddy boots for my one pair of dull slippers. Nothing could be done for my wet, crusty hair, which was more brown than red at the moment, but I tried smoothing it down anyway and wiped away the dried dirt.

Once again, I checked myself for any signs of injury, but there seemed to be no lasting damage from my brush with death. Even so, I sank onto the narrow bed and rubbed my eyes with trembling hands, willing the sense of dread to leave me. Between the old woman's words and the lightning strike, my twentieth birthday was definitely not going as I'd hoped.

After pulling myself together, I returned to the kitchen. Tash herded me into the tavern, to the lone empty table in the corner. "Sit here," she said. "I'll fetch you something to eat."

"Thanks." I gave her arm a quick squeeze before she slipped away.

The inn was packed with soldiers and travelers trying to avoid the storm, and the air had a humid, musky scent. I quickly scanned the room, but the old lady wasn't in sight. Perhaps she'd already gone to her room to rest. I ducked my eyes when one of the Black Dragon's soldiers on duty gave me a stern look. They were always watching from behind their winged helmets and scaled black armor, ready to enforce her rule. The green markings on their shoulders signaled they were in the Earth Realm division of the Onyx Army, under the command of the Jade Dragon.

At the bar, a couple travelers were speaking in hushed tones, but the word "elemental" drifted over to me and caught my attention. I leaned forward, straining to hear the rest.

"Miners dug too deep and angered those big rock elementals," a man wearing a dark green cloak said. "They smashed up the town pretty good before they were finally driven off."

"Aren't the Dragons supposed to deal with those?" another man muttered into his tankard.

A woman with a red scarf around her neck snorted quietly. "They're too busy collecting taxes and trying to stomp out the Resistance."

"I saw the Crimson Dragon the other day in the next village over," another man said, making my back stiffen. "Flying overhead like he was looking for something. Or someone."

The woman glanced warily at the nearby soldier before whispering, "I heard the Golden one was in Pebbleton a week ago."

"We never get Dragons this far from Soulspire. Why now?" the first man asked.

The second man downed his drink with a sour look. "The Black Dragon is demanding more tribute than ever before. Her Dragons are there to make sure we obey. Or else."

Cold fear gripped my throat. If the Dragons were nearby, that meant it was time for me to leave Stoneham. And soon.

I'd seen two Dragons in my life and never wanted to see one again. The screams and smell of burning flesh still haunted my dreams, but Stoneham had been safe so far. I'd been here since I was seventeen, living in the back of the inn that Tash's family owned while keeping my head down and staying out of trouble. This town was at the very edge of the Earth Realm, far enough away from Soulspire that the Black Dragon and her mates never flew out this far.

Until now.

Tash set down a steaming bowl of rabbit stew and a tankard of mead, along with a small cake she'd decorated with white frosting. "Here you are!"

"What's this?" I asked, arching an eyebrow at the cake.

"It's for your birthday, of course. You didn't really expect me to forget, did you?" She flashed me a warm smile.

"Thank you, Tash." I hadn't wanted her to make a big deal about my birthday, but I appreciated that she remembered it. She was the closest thing I had to family, after all.

She bent down and gave me a quick hug. "Happy birthday."

I hugged her back. "Hey, did you see an older woman come through here with white hair? I stumbled upon her in the forest, but then I lost her."

"No, but I've been in the kitchen all night. Father probably took her up to a room already."

"I hope so. I don't like the idea of her being out there alone." Something about the encounter tugged at my gut with a sense of wrongness, but I couldn't put my finger on it.

Tash squeezed my shoulder. "If you didn't see her out there, then she must be safe inside somewhere. Maybe she's staying with family in town."

"I'm sure you're right," I said, trying to banish my unease as I took a bite of my cake. "Mm. This is delicious."

"Of course it is." She winked, but then was called away to another table. I watched her go and sadness clenched my heart tight. I didn't want to leave Stoneham. Tash was my best friend, and more than that, she needed me. If I was gone, who would protect her from her father?

Perhaps she would come with me if I left. But no, she would never leave her mother behind. Maybe it was only a coincidence the Dragons had been spotted nearby. Maybe they would never come to Stoneham.

Maybe I didn't have to run. At least, not yet.

A commotion and a shout at the bar drew my attention. Two of the soldiers hauled the man in the green cloak off his stool and shoved him to the ground, while the woman cried out, "We were just talking! We didn't mean anything by it!"

I watched with dread, my stomach twisting at the knowledge of what would happen next. I'd seen it before, and no matter how much I wanted to help those people or stop the soldiers, there was nothing I could do. I knew how to defend myself a little, but not against two armored soldiers with swords as long as my arm. The only reason I'd made it this long was by keeping my head down and staying out of trouble. But that didn't stop me from wishing there was something I could do to stop this.

One of the soldiers grabbed the woman's wrist and dragged her off the stool too. "Sounds to me like you're part of the Resistance. Don't you agree, Ment?"

The other soldier nodded, while a cruel smile touched his lips. "That it does. And we all know how we deal with Resistance scum."

The cloaked man shook his head vehemently. "We're not Resistance! We're loyal to the Black Dragon, I swear it!"

"Tell that to the Spirit Goddess when you see her," Ment said, as he hauled the man to his feet.

Roark glared at them from behind the bar and rubbed his hands on a towel, but said nothing. The soldiers gave him a nod as they led the two struggling people out of the inn. The door shut, and the entire room froze as a howling scream tore through the sound of the rain, before it was cut short. With grim faces, the other people in the tavern returned to their meals and their conversation, including the other man who'd been talking with the doomed travelers. Maybe we were all cowards, but it was the only way to survive.

I dropped my head as shame and despair battled inside me, along with the keen realization that there was no point in running. No matter where I went, there was no escaping the Dragons or their soldiers.

3
KIRA

I had the first dream that night.

A roguishly handsome man with hair the color of autumn leaves drew a large sword, then lunged at an opponent. Both of them wore the black-scaled armor of the Onyx Army with the red shoulder markings of the Fire Realm division. A small crowd had gathered around them as they sparred, but the auburn-haired man was the only one I could see clearly. Even though I hated the Black Dragon's soldiers, I found I couldn't tear my eyes away from him, nor banish the unexpected desire he stirred inside me. As I watched, he dodged, parried, and swiftly disarmed his opponent, winning the training match without breaking a sweat. He bowed to his opponent, and when he rose up, I caught a flash of flame in his brown eyes.

When I woke my skin was so hot I had to throw the blanket off me. I was certain I'd never seen him before in my life—I would have remembered a man that attractive. I wasn't sure what the fire in his eyes meant either. The only man who could control flame was Sark, the Crimson Dragon, and that wasn't him. I'd never forget *that* monster's face.

I brushed it off as merely a strange dream, a result of my loneliness and nothing more, and forced myself to go back to sleep. But the next night, I had another dream. This one featured a different man who stood in a library wearing some of the finest clothes I'd ever seen. Clearly a nobleman of some sort, with golden hair, fair skin, and a finely sculpted face I wouldn't mind staring at for hours. He was extremely tall, but as he reached for a book on a very high shelf, his fingers barely touched it. A burst of wind suddenly swirled around him, and the book dropped into his hand.

Impossible. I'd never seen the Golden Dragon before, but somehow I knew this wasn't him. But if not, how could this man control the element of air? Only the Dragons, the representatives of the elemental Gods, were blessed with such power. Including the Black Dragon, of course—their wife and our supreme ruler.

It was nonsense, I told myself. Simply my dream brain coming up with strange images because I'd been worried about the Dragons coming for me. That was all.

But the dreams continued.

One night I encountered a ruggedly handsome green-eyed man with dark skin, a trim beard, and a broad chest. With muscular arms he hammered a sword, but when he raised it up I swore the metal bent by nothing more than the power of his mind. I had the strongest urge to run to him and bury my face in his strong chest, knowing he would protect me with his every breath.

In the next dream, I saw a black-haired man who exuded danger slip through the forest like a wraith. Rain battered against the leaves, yet somehow left him untouched. He pulled down his hood, and I caught a flash of sharp, deadly beauty. Upon awakening, my entire body was doused in cold sweat. Like the others, he filled me with a strange sense of desire and longing I couldn't understand or explain.

Every night I was visited by one of my strange elemental dream men, although they never seemed to know I was there spying on them. Soon they all began to travel, though I couldn't tell where they were headed or why. All I got were brief glimpses into their lives without any real context. Or whatever lives my mind was inventing for them, anyway—none of them were real, of course. Even if I began to secretly wish they were.

The traveling dreams were clearly a sign I should be on my way as well, yet I hesitated. A month passed. I told myself I needed more time. Time to gather my coins. Time to learn more about the Dragons' intentions. Time to make sure Tash would be okay.

But I was only delaying the inevitable.

"Heard there's a Fire Realm soldier in the tavern," the fletcher said, as I handed him my coins in exchange for more arrows.

My fingers clenched around my bow. "A Fire Realm soldier? Here?"

"That's what Brant said when he dropped off the wood. Seems like the soldier's looking for someone. Searching for Resistance members maybe?" He shrugged.

I stiffened. "None of us have anything to do with them. Everyone knows we all serve the Black Dragon loyally."

"I'm sure he's just passing through." He frowned and glanced at the door warily, where two Earth Realm soldiers could be seen patrolling the town. "Still, I'll be glad when he's on his way."

"Me too."

It had to be a coincidence. Soldiers from the Fire Realm didn't often come to Stoneham, but nothing about the fletcher's story implied the man would be the same one as in my dreams. Still, it couldn't hurt to get a look at him, just to ease my mind. I needed to head into the forest and bring back some game for Roark, but first I had to be sure.

I slipped into the back of the inn, where I found Tash and her mother Launa working in the kitchen, their eyes worried and their hands frantic, as if they needed to be doing something. Usually a clue that Roark was drinking again, although I didn't see any sign of him.

"Is everything all right?" I asked, as I removed my cloak and hung it by the door.

"There's a Fire Realm soldier in the tavern making everyone nervous." Tash tugged on her braid and gave me a concerned look. "And he's looking for someone who sounds a lot like you."

"Me?" I blinked. "What would a soldier want with me?"

"I don't know, but I don't like it."

"Perhaps you should hide," Launa said, her voice as soft as a dove's. "We'll tell him you left town."

I seriously considered it, or grabbing my things and running, like I should have done a month ago. But if this was the soldier I saw in my dreams, I had to meet him. It was the only way to find out more about this strange connection between us.

I touched Launa's arm gently. "I'll be okay."

She nodded, though her face was lined with concern. Tash gave me a hug and whispered for me to be careful, before I stepped out of the kitchen and into the tavern.

The soldier's back was to me, and the first thing I saw was his dark auburn hair, the same shade as it was in my dream. I swore my heart stopped beating as I took a step toward him, and then another. He must have heard me behind him, because he rose to his feet and turned around, his brown eyes meeting mine.

"You're her," he said.

Recognition slammed into me and I had a hard time speaking. Everything about him—from his perfectly tousled hair to his broad shoulders in a black and red military uniform—was familiar to me. I felt like I knew him already, even though we'd never met. But how was that possible? How could this man from my dreams be standing in front of me?

And did that mean the other men were real as well?

4

JASIN

A month ago I'd been on patrol in the forest and had stopped to take a piss on a tree when the Fire God, in all his blazing glory, appeared out of thin air and told me to find a woman. And trust me, when a giant made out of flames tells you to do something, you do it. Especially when he wraps a scorching hand around your neck. Except instead of burning me alive, his power became absorbed into my body, branding me as the next Crimson Dragon.

The Fire God told me my duty and gave me a name—Kira—along with a split-second glimpse of her image and one month to find her. No directions. No hints. Not even a vague idea of what Realm she was in. Just an order to find her, serve her, and protect her. Then he vanished.

It took me a day or two to wrap my head around his demand and to believe it all really happened. The Fire God didn't just appear to people, especially ordinary guys like me. Don't get me wrong, I was a damn fine soldier, but that was it. Up until that point, I wasn't even sure the Gods were real. No one had heard from them in hundreds of years, after all. Now I'd been chosen by one of them to be his representative in this world and to take the place of the current Crimson Dragon, who wasn't going to be happy about being kicked out of the role.

I'd spent the last two weeks traveling from the Fire Realm, following the persistent urge that guided me northwest, into the farthest depths of the Earth Realm. Now the woman the Fire God sent me to find stood in front of me, and she was so gorgeous it made my blood heat like never before. Her shiny red hair was tied back in a tight ponytail, and I had the strongest urge to free it and let it fall about her shoulders. Her sharp eyes were an intriguing hazel color, as if many different shades danced within them. And her body, with those fit arms, full breasts, and curvy hips... damn. Maybe being tied to one woman for the rest of my life wouldn't be such a hardship after all.

A slow grin spread across my mouth. "I had no idea you'd be so beautiful in person. Thank the Gods indeed."

"Who are you?" Kira asked, with suspicion in her voice. She stared at me as if she recognized me, but wasn't sure how. Did she not know who I was? Or what *she* was?

"Name's Jasin," I said. "I've been sent to find you."

Her eyes narrowed. "Sent? By whom?"

"By the Fire God."

She took a step back and crashed into a chair, knocking it to the ground, as fear and confusion crossed her face. "I don't understand."

Maybe she truly didn't know. Had she not been visited by the Spirit Goddess too? Did she not know about the task in front of us?

I glanced around, but the tavern was empty except for the two of us. I moved closer and lowered my voice anyway to be safe. "A few weeks ago I had a visit from the Fire God. He told me I was the future Crimson Dragon and that I had to find you—the next Black Dragon."

5

KIRA

Everyone knew the Black Dragon and the other Dragons were immortal. They'd ruled for the last thousand years, and would rule for another thousand to come. Each one was the divine representative of the five elemental Gods, hand-picked to serve them and reign over the rest of us. This man couldn't be one of them—and neither could I.

"No," I said, my head spinning. "Impossible."

"I'll prove it to you," the soldier—Jasin—said. He raised his hand and conjured a ball of flame, which danced across his fingertips.

Even with the heat from the fire, all I felt was cold terror. I turned on my heel and ran out of the inn as fast as I could while flashbacks of my parents' deaths filled my mind, their screams ringing in my ears even seven years later. There was no denying it anymore. Jasin truly was the Crimson Dragon—and a soldier for the Onyx Army—which meant I had to get as far away from him as possible.

I dashed into the forest, down the hidden paths I knew like the back of my hand, crashing through the brush with my bow clutched tight in my fingers. I ran with only instinct and fear guiding me, without a firm plan in my mind other than to escape. Not just to save myself, but to save Tash and her mother too. I couldn't let him burn them alive, like the other Crimson Dragon had done to my family.

Jasin called out, "Wait!" He chased me into the forest, and with his long legs managed to catch up to me within minutes.

When I glanced back, he was almost upon me. I stumbled and tripped over a fallen tree and he crashed into me from behind, tumbling to the ground with me. We landed together with him on top, pinning me down with his hard, muscular body.

His face was close to mine and we were both breathing heavily, our chests pressed together. "I'm not going to hurt you," he said. "It's my duty to serve and protect you."

I stared into his eyes without backing down. "Why?"

"Because you're the Black Dragon."

I let out a sharp laugh. "Hardly."

"You are. Or you will be, once you've bonded with me and the other three Dragons. Then you'll be the strongest of us all."

The Black Dragon was the representative of the Spirit Goddess and could control all the elements. She always had four male Dragons as her mates, each one representing the different elements of fire, water, earth, and air. If Jasin was correct—which he obviously wasn't—then he would be one of the men bonded to me for life as my lover, my husband, and my guardian.

The idea of sleeping with the four men in my dreams sent a rush of desire between my legs, as did the feel of Jasin on top of me. With our eyes locked together, my lips parted and raging hot lust coursed through me. Sparks of passion seemed to flare between us, and for a second I gripped his shirt and nearly pulled his mouth down to mine.

Gods, what was wrong with me?

"Get off me," I said, shoving him aside before I did something stupid. I stood up and brushed the dirt and leaves off myself. "If you're right, then where are the other three?"

"I'm sure they'll be here soon. We were given your name and told we would bond with you in the order in which we arrived. Even if the others tried to ignore it, the need to find you became almost overwhelming as more days passed." He slowly stood as his dark eyes ran up and down my body like a caress. "I'm glad I was the first though."

I tried to ignore the way his suggestive smile made me as warm as the flame he'd conjured. "If you are the Crimson Dragon, then prove it. Shift into your other form."

"I can't. I've been chosen to be the next Crimson Dragon, but I won't become one truly until I bond with you in the Fire Temple. After that, you'll be able to control fire too and I'll be able to change into a dragon at will." He shrugged. "Or at least, that's what the Fire God told me."

"How convenient." I crossed my arms, skeptical of everything he was telling me. Although he *had* summoned fire from thin air, so he wasn't completely full of lies. "You're a soldier in the Onyx Army. Why should I believe anything you say?"

All traces of amusement left his eyes and he looked away with a frown.

"I was before, yes. Not anymore. I had to leave my post to find you and I can't ever return. They won't look kindly on a deserter."

No, they wouldn't. If the Onyx Army found him, they'd assume he was a traitor working with the Resistance and make an example of him. If he was telling the truth, of course. He was still wearing their uniform, after all, though his scaled armor was nowhere in sight.

I sighed as I debated what to do. I was still wary, but something told me to listen to him. Maybe because I already felt like I knew him after seeing him in my dreams for so many nights. Years of being on my own had made it hard for me to trust anyone, but Jasin felt familiar somehow. If nothing else, I should hear more of what he had to say.

"Let's head back to the inn and talk about this over some food," I finally said.

"There's nothing I would enjoy more." He gestured toward the inn. "Lead the way."

He kept pace with me easily, and as we walked we kept sneaking glances at each other. It was hard to believe he was real, and I wondered if he felt the same way. Not to mention, he was definitely easy on the eyes. All those muscles and that cocky smile...yeah, he must be popular with the ladies.

As we emerged from the forest, I spotted the stable boy bringing in a fine white horse with a saddle decorated with what looked like real gold. Other people who frequented the tavern were gawking at it, no doubt speculating about the nobleman it must belong to.

"Nice horse," Jasin said with suspicion, his hand resting on the pommel of his sword. "Wonder who the rider is."

I remembered my dream of the man in fine clothing reaching for a book. If what Jasin said was true, the nobleman I'd seen was likely the next Golden Dragon. Assuming any of this was real and not some kind of trick or con. I certainly didn't feel like the Black Dragon, and I had no magic of my own. All I had were strange dreams that had started when I'd been hit by lightning.

I stepped inside the inn with Jasin at my heels. Inside, the beautiful golden-haired man from my dream was chatting with Tash, who hung on his every word. He immediately turned toward me, as did everyone else in the tavern, but when our eyes met it was like we were the only people in the room. His face was perfectly sculpted with sharp cheekbones and intelligent eyes, and he possessed an elegance that set him apart from every other man I'd seen before in my life. My breath hitched and desire rushed through me like a hurricane, threatening to blow me away.

"You," he said, his voice full of awe.

6

AURIC

The woman who must be Kira stood before me clutching a bow in her hand, her eyes wide with surprise, but also something like recognition. She was so beautiful it made all other thoughts vanish from my mind, leaving only an intense curiosity about my future mate. I took a moment to study her, mentally logging everything including her worn boots, dark hunting leathers, wind-swept hair, and flushed cheeks. A single leaf was stuck to her brown cloak and, judging from her state, I guessed she had just come from the forest in a bit of a hurry.

Another man stood beside her wearing the black uniform of the Onyx Army, right down to a sword at his side. His eyes ran over me in a quick, suspicious appraisal. I held my breath, waiting for him to recognize me, but all he did was touch the pommel of his sword as he moved closer to Kira, silently warning me he would protect her with his life. He must be one of the other Dragons. One of the men I would have to share her with. But which one, I wondered?

"Who are you?" Kira asked me.

A tricky question indeed. I gazed around the tavern to take in the townsfolk who were all staring at us, including the cheerful waitress. They were intrigued by me, for sure, but no one gasped or shouted my name or kneeled before me. None of them realized who I truly was.

"Can we speak alone?" I asked Kira, keeping my voice low. I was sure she had a million questions, as did I. Questions that would be better answered without the entire town listening in.

She nodded, then turned to the waitress. "Tash, is the private dining room free?"

Tash's eyebrows practically shot through the roof as she glanced between me and Kira. "It's not booked tonight. Go on in and I'll bring you three something to eat." She brushed past Kira and said, "And you better tell me *everything* later."

"I will," Kira said.

She led us into a large room off the side of the tavern which was likely used for events, celebrations, or other private gatherings, containing one long wooden table and many chairs. A painting hung on the wall featuring the Black Dragon with her four consorts flying around her, surrounded by their representative element. Each one looked terrifying and powerful, with their scaled bodies, large wings, and long tails. I'd not seen this exact painting before, but the Black Dragon demanded that one like it had to be hung in any place where people gathered. No doubt it was to remind us that the five Dragons were watching over us at all times.

I gazed at the Golden Dragon in the painting and pondered my fate, while Kira closed the door behind us. I never would have believed any of this if the Air God himself hadn't granted me his powers. I still hardly believed it, even though my draw toward Kira was unmistakable.

She turned toward me, facing me down with uneasy eyes. "I think it's time you told me who you are and what you're doing here."

I hesitated, but I wasn't quite ready to reveal who I was yet. I wouldn't lie, but I wouldn't tell them the whole truth either. Not until I knew these people better. Not until I could trust them.

7

KIRA

The golden-haired man stood up straighter, gazing down at me from his towering height. "I'm Auric. I was sent to find you by the Air God." He gave me a dramatic bow, his movements refined and graceful. "I'm here to serve the next Black Dragon."

Jasin snorted and muttered, "This guy? Really?"

I glared at him and turned back to Auric, sizing him up. His traveling clothes were simple, yet nevertheless stood out due to their fine quality and expensive fabrics. Auric was definitely not from anywhere around here. A nobleman for sure. He wasn't as obviously muscular as Jasin, but he was just as handsome in a more refined way, with the most amazing cheekbones I'd ever seen and gray eyes that entranced me immediately. He looked at me as if I was the answer to a problem he'd been trying to solve. I couldn't help but be intrigued by him, especially after watching him in my dreams for a month.

"You said you had a visit from the Air God?" I asked.

He nodded. "Exactly one month ago."

"That's when I met the Fire God," Jasin said. A flame flickered idly across his fingers. "And when I got these powers."

That was the same day I turned twenty. The same night I'd been hit by lightning.

Gods, maybe it really was all true.

I dropped into a chair as it all finally sank in. If I was the Black Dragon, what did that mean exactly? There was only one Black Dragon, and she ruled our entire world. I somehow doubted she'd be thrilled about my presence. She was a cruel empress, and she definitely wasn't the type to share power. There was no way I could replace her. This all had to be some kind of mistake.

"Are you all right?" Auric asked, as he sat beside me, his voice concerned.

"Kira?" Jasin hovered behind me, his hands gripping the back of my chair protectively.

I looked into Auric's eyes, which were the color of storm clouds. "Show me."

For a second he seemed confused, but then realization dawned across his face. A breeze began to pick up in the room out of nowhere and soon grew into a strong wind that whipped my hair around my face, making me gasp.

The door opened and the magical wind instantly died. Tash stepped inside, balancing three trays of food and drink with such skill it was almost like magic of her own. She set each one down while her eyes roamed over both men, and for a second I felt a flash of possessiveness. Which made me uncomfortable, because neither of these guys were mine, and I had no reason to feel anything but warmth toward Tash. Of course, if what these men said were true, then both of them were my future mates. Would I ever get used to the idea of that?

"Anything else you need?" Tash asked, while searching my face. Her concern for me shone through her warm eyes, and I knew she was asking if I was all right in here with these two strangers.

"We're all set, thank you," I told her with a smile that I hoped showed how grateful I was for her help. She was looking out for me, even if she had no idea what was going on.

She nodded and moved to leave the room, but was blocked by a huge, broad-shouldered man with muscular arms the size of tree trunks—the blacksmith I'd seen in my dreams. His eyes were a deep forest green, his skin was the color of tree bark, and his short beard gave him a rugged masculinity that was distinctly opposite Auric's elegant beauty and less refined than Jasin's handsome swagger. Yet I felt the same rush of desire, familiarity, and possessiveness when I looked at him as when I did the other two men.

Gods, what was wrong with me? I'd never felt this way about a single man before, yet now I felt it for *three* of them?

"Well, hello there," Tash said, staring at the new arrival with interest.

"I'm here to see Kira," the man said, his voice low and deep, like the rumble of an earthquake.

"Come inside," I said, with a nod to Tash.

As this new visitor stepped inside, Tash shook her head as if bewildered. She left us alone and shut the door, and suddenly the room seemed a lot smaller with the large mountain of a man inside.

"My name is Slade," he said, his intense eyes fixed on mine. "I've been looking for you, Kira."

"How do you know my name?" I asked him.

"The Earth God told me."

"Let me guess. He came to you a month ago, gave you powers, and sent you to find me?" When he nodded, I rubbed the bridge of my nose, so overwhelmed by it all I could hardly think straight. "That was my twentieth birthday. I was struck by lightning that night. After that I began to see all of you in my dreams."

"You knew we were coming, then?" Auric asked, his eyebrows darting up.

"No. I only caught quick flashes or vague glimpses. I didn't think any of you were real. Just figments of my imagination. I never expected you to actually turn up here. Or to tell me you're the next Dragons, whatever that means."

"We were drawn to you," Slade said. "We couldn't stay away. Even if we wanted to."

Those last words held a touch of sadness or perhaps bitterness, and I knew there had to be a story behind them. All three men had given up their entire lives because the Gods had given them a duty and told them I was the Black Dragon. If it was true, they'd each been chosen to serve me, protect me, and love me—against their will.

I stared down at my food, but I wasn't hungry. My thoughts made my stomach churn, but I couldn't deny it any longer. All three of the men had been given powers by the Gods on the same night I'd been struck by lightning, and I'd seen them in my dreams ever since. The men could control the elements, and I was strangely attracted to all of them.

Maybe I really was the next Black Dragon.

8

SLADE

I pulled out a chair and sat across from my future mate, taking her in. She was certainly beautiful, with an inner strength in her hazel eyes that made my gaze want to linger on her. That would make this situation easier, at least. I had no intention of ever giving her my heart, but if I was forced to be with her for the rest of my life, it helped I found her pleasing to look at. But was she ready for what we had to do next? Were any of us, for that matter?

"So you're the future Jade Dragon?" the soldier asked me. "Show us what you can do."

I leaned back and crossed my arms. "These powers were given to us by the Gods so we can protect people. Not to use idly."

He scoffed. "What's the point of having them if you can't have a little fun now and then?"

"Sorry, but I have to agree with Slade on this one," the nobleman said. "Our powers should be used wisely, although we need to practice with them too, of course. We can enjoy that part, at least. I'm Auric, by the way."

"Jasin," the soldier said.

So these were two of the men I'd be sharing my mate with. I shook my head at their youthful eagerness. They sat closely on either side of Kira, as if already staking their claim on her. The soldier in particular seemed impatient and overly excited, especially the way he was constantly moving, like he was full of energy he couldn't contain. The nobleman was calmer but had his head in the clouds, as evidenced when he pulled out a journal and began jotting down notes. Kira simply watched us all as though she couldn't believe her eyes. I didn't blame her.

I had probably ten years or more on all of the people at this table. It made sense that they were chosen—they were in the prime of their lives and ready to go on adventures, full of idealism and big dreams of saving the world. They likely had nothing tying them down either. Not me though. I'd already tried to help save the world and gave up on that task. Back home I had a good, stable life, one I wasn't ready to leave behind. Why had the Earth God chosen me instead of someone else? How could he expect me to just abandon everything I'd spent my entire life building up?

After he visited me, I'd struggled with my new destiny. I'd always been devoted to the Gods, and one couldn't simply turn down new powers and a divine mission. But I'd waited as long as I could to leave my home and travel here, even though it was only a day's ride away. If not for the nagging feeling in my gut, I might not have left at all.

I didn't ask for this. I didn't want this. I still wasn't sure I was the right person for the role of Jade Dragon. But even with all my doubts, I was here and I was fully committed to our mission. I would do whatever it took to serve the Gods and protect Kira.

It was my duty, after all.

9

KIRA

After Tash brought Slade a tray of food, all three men dove in while I studied them. They were each so different, yet I felt a strange connection to all of them. But there was one more man in my dreams, who must be the future Azure Dragon. Where was he now?

I took a long breath. "Okay, assuming this is all true and we are the next Dragons—which I'm not sure I believe yet—what does that mean? Why do the Gods even need another set of Dragons?"

"We're meant to overthrow the current Dragons and take their place as the protectors of the world," Auric said, his voice rather matter-of-fact considering he was talking treason.

My jaw fell open and it took a moment for me to speak. "What?"

"That's what I was told as well," Slade said.

"But why?" I asked.

Jasin shrugged casually. "Sounds like the Gods aren't happy with the way the Black Dragon and her men are ruling the world." He picked up a grape and popped it in his mouth. "Time for a change in leadership."

"Maybe they've chosen us to set things right," Slade said.

All of the men were being way too calm about this, considering what they were saying. Then again, they'd had a month to get used to the idea. Even so, I could barely wrap my mind around it. The Gods had been nothing but myth for so long that most people had stopped believing they were real at all. If the men were telling the truth—and I was starting to believe they might be—then perhaps the Gods had finally awoken and were doing something to help their people for a change. We certainly needed it.

But why me? I was a nobody. Definitely not a hero, and certainly not the kind of person who could overthrow the Black Dragon and her men. They'd ruled for thousands of years and were the most powerful beings in the world—how were we supposed to stop them?

"What are we meant to do?" I finally asked.

Auric set his fork down and met my gaze. "We must travel to each of the Gods' temples, visiting them in the order in which we arrived today. There you will have to bond with one of us, which will unlock our full powers and the dragon form. You will gain our powers as well, and once you've bonded with all of us, you'll visit the Spirit Goddess's temple to become the Black Dragon. After that, we should be strong enough to face the current Dragons."

My head spun, trying to process everything he said. "What do you mean, bonded?"

"Err…" Auric shifted in his seat a little. "You would officially take us as your mate in the most…intimate way."

Jasin flashed me a naughty grin. "What he means is that we need to have sex." He leaned back in his chair with his arms folded behind his head. "Not sure about you guys, but I for one am looking forward to all of this."

"Of course you are," I said, rolling my eyes, even as heat flared inside me at the thought of becoming intimate with all of them. "Don't get too excited, because I haven't agreed to any of this." I turned back to Auric. "So all we have to do is travel to the temples and uh, bond with each other?"

"Exactly."

I arched an eyebrow. "You seem to know a lot about this."

Auric shrugged as a small smile touched his lips. "The Air God told me some of it. The rest I learned after doing some research before I came here, although I couldn't find much information overall. I suspect if books about this ever did exist, the Black Dragon had most of that knowledge purged. I'm hoping we can uncover more on this journey."

"You make all of this sound so easy," Slade said, as his long fingers rubbed his dark beard. "What happens when the Black Dragon and the others find out about us?"

"Good point," I said. "I have a hard time seeing any of the Dragons giving up their powers willingly."

"We'll try to travel without attracting attention," Jasin said. "Keep our powers and our mission secret for as long as we can. But we should leave first thing in the morning."

"What about the last member of our team?" Slade asked.

Jasin shrugged. "He'll catch up. It's his problem he wasn't here on time."

"The Gods *did* tell us to be here in exactly one month," Auric said, his brow furrowing.

They wanted to leave tomorrow? I'd wanted to run, but not yet, and not like this. Certainly not with three complete strangers. "We're not going anywhere," I said, rising to my feet. "Not until we know more about what is going on here and what we're supposed to do next."

All three men looked like they might argue with me, but I shot them a fierce look and headed for the door. I needed some space, needed to get away from them and everything they represented. Maybe they were destined to be bonded to me, but they weren't my mates yet. I didn't know a damn thing about them, I hadn't chosen them, and I certainly wasn't going off on some dangerous quest with them.

I found Tash in the kitchen, stirring a stew with a long ladle. As soon as I entered, she spun around. "What's going on? Who are those men? Why are they here?"

Her rapid words made my head spin even more, but I had to tell someone what was going on to make sure I wasn't dreaming. I grabbed her arm and dragged her into my bedroom, then shut the door. "I'll tell you everything, but I warn you now, it barely makes sense to me."

She sat on the edge of the bed, leaning forward anxiously. "Maybe we can sort through it together."

"According to those guys, they're Dragons. Or they will be." It sounded even more ridiculous when I said it out loud. "But they already have magic."

Her brow furrowed. "How is that possible? The Dragons are immortal and there are only five of them. How does someone *become* one?"

"I don't know. But each man says one of the Gods chose him, gave him magic, and then told him to find me."

"I've never heard of such a thing." She tilted her head and frowned. "Please don't take this the wrong way, because you know I love you like a sister…but why you?"

I drew in a long breath. "Supposedly I'm the next Black Dragon."

She gasped. "What?"

"Trust me, I'm as shocked as you are." I ran my fingers through my long hair, where they got caught on the tangled ends. "Do you remember on my birthday when I came inside all muddy?"

"Of course."

"Right before that I was struck by lightning, but it didn't hurt me at all. Ever since then I've had these weird dreams of four men with elemental powers. Three of those men are now sitting in the other room, and I'm guessing the fourth will be here soon. I'm supposed to go with them to each of the Gods' temples now to 'bond' with them—and after that we'll be the next Dragons. Which I'm pretty sure the current Dragons won't be thrilled about. Especially when they learn we're supposed to overthrow them."

She stared at me as if she'd never seen me before. "Are you going to do it?"

I paced back and forth in front of her. "No way. I don't know a thing about those men. I'm not sure I believe any of this is real, anyway. It sounds even crazier now that I've said it all out loud. There must be some other explanation…"

She chewed on her lower lip as she considered. "I think you should do it."

I stopped and gawked at her. "What?"

"If any of it is true, then you have a chance to change things. You've been chosen by the Gods to make this world better and stop the Black Dragon's reign." A mischievous look entered her eyes. "Plus it means you'll be married to four very handsome men. It's hard to complain about that."

I sank onto the bed beside her and buried my face in my hands. "But I didn't ask for any of this! I don't want to change things or to go up against the Black Dragon. I just want to live a quiet, peaceful life and stay out of trouble. And I don't want four men, or even one." That wasn't exactly true, but the whole thing was far too overwhelming for me to even consider what being married to four men would mean.

She rubbed my back slowly. "It seems that's not what the Gods have in mind for you. They've chosen you, Kira. You have to answer their call."

"Curse the Gods," I muttered, then immediately regretted it. Were they watching me even now? Would they strike me with lightning again if I didn't do what they wanted?

The door suddenly burst open, and at first I thought it was the Gods coming to punish me. But it was no God, only Tash's father, who was almost as terrifying.

Roark stood in the doorway, his large hulking form completely filling it, as he glared at us. "There you are."

10

KIRA

R oark quickly took us both in with disgust written across his face. "What do you think you're doing? Lazing about while we have customers waiting! Get back to work!"

Tash scrambled to her feet. "I was only taking a short break, Father."

He grunted, then narrowed his eyes at me. "And you. It's been two days since you last brought us any game." He pointed to the door. "I have hungry soldiers out there demanding some supper. What am I supposed to tell them?"

Dread and panic shot through my blood. I'd been on my way to the forest to hunt when Jasin had shown up. "I'll go right now. I'll find something quickly, I promise."

"Too late for that." A sick grin twisted his lips as he grabbed Tash's shoulder, his meaty fingers digging into her dress until she cried out. "You know what the punishment is for slacking off."

"Father, please," Tash started, but then was cut off when he back-handed her across the face.

"Stop," I pleaded. "I'll get you whatever you want right now. Just don't hurt her."

"The two of you sitting here gossiping while the rest of us starve," he growled, before striking Tash again. "You both need to be taught a lesson."

"No!" I yelled, then launched myself at him. He was double my size if not more—as well as being both my employer and my landlord—but I couldn't let him hurt my best friend. Not again.

I tore at him with my nails, reaching for whatever I could, caught in an urgent frenzy to protect Tash. With a roar, he threw me off him in a burst of strength. I fell back, my head slamming hard on the wall behind me, before slumping to the floor in a daze of pain and darkness. *Tash, I'm sorry*.

When the black haze lifted, three silhouettes stood in the doorway.

A flash of fire danced before my eyes. A rumble shook through my bones. A burst of wind tore at my hair. Roark was thrown across the room, knocked to his knees, and surrounded by flames. My three mates moved around him, their faces filled with disgust and rage.

"You will not hurt either of these ladies again," Slade said, his voice low and foreboding.

Roark looked up at the men standing around him with both fear and hatred. "I can do what I want in my own inn. To my own women."

"Not anymore," Jasin said. The circle of flames grew hotter and danced around Roark, who yelped and shied back from it.

"Swear you won't touch them in violence again," Auric said, his voice as commanding as a prince's. "Swear on the Gods. And believe me, they're listening."

"I swear it," Roark bit out, but his eyes were full of menace.

The flames vanished. "Get out of here," Jasin said.

Roark scrambled to his feet and bolted from the room like it was still on fire. Although he seemed afraid, I doubted he would heed their warning. He would come for Tash again—he always did.

Slade knelt beside me and asked, "Are you all right?"

I nodded, though my throat was so dry I could barely speak. "Tash?"

"I'm here," she said, from behind Jasin. "I'm okay."

"Thank the Gods," I whispered, as I grabbed Slade's hand and rose to my feet. I swayed a little as a rush of pain threatened to knock me to the floor again, but he wrapped a comforting arm around me and held me steady. For a second I was distracted by his broad chest and strong arms, overcome with the urge to lean into him and let him hold me some more. He smelled good too, with an earthy, pine scent that reminded me of the forest in the morning. I took a deep breath to ground myself before pulling away from him.

"Thanks for the help, but I could have handled it," I said, as I rubbed the back of my aching head.

"He hurt you," Slade said gruffly, as if that explained everything.

"We're bound to protect you," Auric added.

"Thanks," I muttered. "And now you've cost me my job and my home, no doubt."

Jasin sheathed his sword. "We need to head out in the morning anyway."

I ignored him and moved to Tash, checking her face for injury. "Are you truly okay?"

"Yes, he didn't hit me that hard," she said, as she ran a hand over her jaw.

I glanced between her and the three men, torn between staying and leaving. Between my old, familiar life and an unknown, new one. Both seemed far too dangerous for my liking. I had no desire to leave, but after what they'd done to Roark, I couldn't exactly stay here anymore either. But who would protect Tash and make sure the inn had enough food?

"We'll talk more about this in the morning," I told the three men. "I need some time and space to gather my thoughts."

Tash wrung her hands as she addressed them. "You'll have to stay somewhere else, unfortunately. My father owns this inn."

"You sure we can't sleep in here?," Jasin asked, his eyes gleaming. "For Kira's protection of course."

"Good idea," Slade said, with a sharp nod.

"Not a chance," I said. "Like Tash said, it's better if you don't stay in this inn. I'll be fine. He won't bother me again tonight." Unless he got really drunk, anyway.

"Very well, but we'll be nearby if you need us," Auric said.

"I'll find you all someone else to board with," Tash said, leading the men out of my bedroom. They followed her reluctantly, each one glancing back at me with emotions in their eyes. Curiosity. Protectiveness. Desire.

As soon as they were gone, I changed my clothes and crumpled onto the bed, my head pounding. I had a lot to think about, but Roark must have hit me harder than I thought, because my eyes kept closing, and soon sleep carried me away.

I awoke to the sound of the door creaking open and instantly tensed, reaching for the knife I always kept under my pillow. My bedroom was completely dark except for the dim moonlight coming through the windows, which revealed two tall figures creeping into my bedroom. Fear made me immediately alert, but I held my breath and waited. I recognized Roark's broad profile and guessed the other man was his drinking buddy, Koth. Each of them reeked of alcohol, making my nose burn.

This time, my dream men couldn't save me. I was on my own.

"You're going to pay," Roark said. He reached for me, but I slashed at him with my dagger. He jerked back with a howl as it sliced through his arm, and then I pivoted on the bed, turning to ward off my next attacker. I was better with a bow, but I'd been taught a few fighting moves while living for a short time with some bandits. I hadn't fought in years, but luckily my body seemed to remember what to do.

Koth dodged my attack, while Roark grabbed my arms tightly from behind. I struggled, lashing out with my feet, as he dragged me back toward him.

"Let me go!" I yelled.

"Where are your friends now?" Roark asked, his breath hot at my ear. He tossed me to the ground hard, then moved to kick me. I tucked my arms and rolled out of the way, gripping my knife tightly. I swiped at his leg and he danced back, but I took that second to get to my feet and bolt from the room.

I ran through the dark kitchen as fast as I could, clutching my dagger in my shaking hand. Heavy footsteps pounded behind me as I reached the door leading outside, but before I could open it, someone struck me on the back of my head.

I fell against the door, momentarily dazed, even as my brain screamed at me to run and fight. Through the haze I managed to spin around and knee Roark between the legs, but Koth was there too.

His blow got me hard, right in the stomach. All the air left me in a swift whoosh and was replaced by lancing pain. Stars danced across my vision, but I wouldn't let my life end, not like this.

I stabbed the dagger into Koth's chest with one last burst of strength. Koth howled as I buried the knife deep in him, and then he hit the floor. But I wasn't safe yet.

"What have you done?" Roark asked, as he stared at his friend. When he took a step toward me, I wasn't sure how I could stop him. Not when he looked at me with murder in his eyes.

A thin knife flew across the room and landed in the wall beside Roark with a sharp *thunk*. A dark figure in a black hooded cloak stood on the other side of the kitchen, with a sword in one hand. A matching sword hung from his waist.

"Get away from her," the cloaked man said, his voice like ice.

"This is none of your concern, stranger," Roark said, glaring at him.

"I'm making it my concern."

Roark ignored the man and grabbed my arm, yanking me toward him. A blade flashed, glinting in the moonlight. A gurgling choke came from Roark's mouth. Blood sprayed across my dress.

Roark let me go and fell to the floor, his throat slashed by the cloaked man who now stood behind him. I hadn't even heard him move.

I gaped at my strange rescuer, wondering if I should be thankful or fearful. "Who are you?"

"Reven." He held up his blade and the blood flew off it in a magical swirl before he sheathed the sword. As he turned toward me, I caught a flash of dangerous blue eyes and a sharp jaw traced with dark stubble from under his hood. Familiarity crept through me and I realized who he was.

The last of my four mates had arrived.

11

REVEN

Walking in on the woman I'd been sent to find being attacked wasn't what I'd expected this evening, but it also wasn't all that uncommon in my line of work.

"Are you hurt?" I asked her, while I checked the area to make sure there were no other attackers.

She rubbed the back of her head. "A little banged up, but otherwise fine. Thanks to you."

I examined the two men on the floor—the one I'd killed, and the one with a dagger sticking out of his chest, presumably Kira's. I yanked it out, used my magic to remove the blood from the blade, then handed it to her. "Who were they?"

"Drunken fools who enjoyed hurting women," she muttered. "Problem is, one of them owns this place. Or he did, anyway."

Footsteps sounded behind us and I reached for one of my swords again, but it was only a young woman in a chemise. She paused in the doorway and gasped when she saw the bodies on the floor.

"Father?" she asked, with a slight sob.

"I'm so sorry, Tash," Kira said. "Koth and your father attacked me while I was asleep. I didn't mean for this to happen."

Another older woman ran into the room, and she let out a strangled gasp at the sight of the dead men. The other woman, Tash, was already crying, and the two women collapsed into each other's arms with a sob. Kira watched with sympathy, while I took the chance to admire her. Despite being forced into this against my will, I had to admit she was pretty easy on the eyes. Her red hair was lightly mussed and her cheeks were flushed from the attack. Her thin chemise hugged her body in ways that awakened parts of me I usually tried to ignore. She was obviously brave and quite capable, since she'd killed one of the men before I'd intervened. But none of that mattered, because I was getting out of this mess as quickly as possible.

Kira gestured for me to follow her while we left the sobbing women in the kitchen. We stepped into a back room with a small bed, which she sank onto as she covered her face with her hands. She took a long breath, then looked up at me again. "I'm assuming you're here because you're the next Azure Dragon."

"Something like that," I said, with obvious distaste.

"I get the feeling you're not pleased about that."

That was an understatement. "I'm here, aren't I?"

"Yes, you are. And a good thing too, because it seems it's time I left this town." She began pulling clothes out of a wardrobe and packing them in a bag, while I crossed my arms and leaned against the doorway.

"I assume the others are already here then," I said.

"Yes, they're staying somewhere else. It's a long story." She sighed as she shoved a pair of ragged-looking slippers in the bag. "A few hours ago I led a quiet life. Now two men are dead and four men say I have to bond with them and become a Dragon. Why is this happening to me?"

I didn't reply. It had taken me a long time to accept that the Water God had truly chosen me. I'd ignored it at first. Then I'd gotten angry. Eventually I'd tried yelling, bargaining, and even praying to get out of it. I hated the Black Dragon and her mates with every fiber of my being, but that didn't mean I wanted to get involved in some mad quest that would only end up with all of us getting killed. But no matter how much I resisted, I couldn't deny the tugging in my gut that got worse with every day that passed, until the need to find Kira became all-encompassing. So here I was.

But as soon as I could find a way to get out of this mess, I was gone.

12

KIRA

I didn't get any more sleep that night. After telling my story to the town's soldiers and trying to comfort Tash and her mother, I'd accepted it was time for me to say my goodbyes. It was clear I couldn't stay here any longer, no matter how hard it was to leave my home behind.

Roark and Koth had never been especially loved in Stoneham, but they were respected. They'd lived in the town their entire lives and were related to half the people in it. The soldiers believed me when I'd said their deaths were a result of self-defense, especially when Tash and her mother backed up my story, but the townspeople would never look at me the same way again. Especially if word got out about my new companions' strange magic. So far no one else knew about them, but how long would that last?

No, the longer we stayed, the more dangerous it was for everyone. Including Tash.

"Are you sure you'll be okay?" I asked her for the tenth time. We stood in the middle of her kitchen, with dawn's light filtering through the windows and illuminating the shadows under her eyes. Tash hadn't slept much either last night.

"I'm sure," she said, with a weak smile. Her eyes were puffy and red, but she stood tall, as if a great burden had lifted from her shoulders. "We both knew something like this would happen eventually. I'm only grateful none of us were hurt."

I took her hands in mine. "I'm sorry. I'm so sorry."

"It's all right." She squeezed my hands. "You protected me for so long, and my mother too. But it had to end someday. At least now we can live without fear, and you can fulfill your destiny without worrying about me anymore."

"I hate leaving you behind," I said. "You could come with us, you know."

She chuckled softly. "What, and travel the world with you and your four men to help overthrow the Black Dragon? That sounds fun, but my place is here. I have an inn to run, after all."

I nodded. I knew that would be her answer, but I had to ask anyway. "You're going to be amazing at it. But what about food?"

"I'm reaching out to the farmers my father made angry to see if they'll do business with me instead." A sad smile touched her lips. "Don't worry about me, I'll figure it out. Just make sure you come back and visit sometime, okay? I want to hear all about your adventures."

"I will, I promise."

"And be careful." She gave me a tight hug. "I believe in you, Kira. If anyone can save this world, it's you."

Emotion made my throat tight as I hugged her back. "I'll do my best."

We said one last tearful goodbye and then I rushed out the kitchen door and headed toward the stables. I lifted my pack up on my shoulder while wiping my eyes before approaching the four men who waited for me near their horses. The four men I was supposed to spend the rest of my life with. Starting now.

Gods, I was not ready for this at all.

Reven leaned against the stable walls with his arms crossed, his hood pulled low over his face so all I could see was his dark stubble. He'd barely said a word to the other men, so it wasn't just me he was chilly with. I got the feeling he wasn't all that excited about being here, and how could I blame him? We'd all been forced into this situation, but there was nothing to do except make the best of it somehow—and trust that the Gods had chosen us for a reason.

The other men stood apart from each other as well. Jasin rocked on his heels, his fingers resting on the hilt of his sword as if he might pull it out at any moment, while he watched for any trouble from the soldiers or other townspeople. He wore his military uniform again, which consisted of black trousers with a stiff coat over them, both trimmed with dark red to show he was from the Fire Realm division. As a former member of the Onyx Army, could I really trust him?

Slade stood inside the stables, saddling a large brown horse with gentle eyes. He had a calm way about him, perhaps because he was a few years older than the rest of us. I had no doubt he was loyal to our cause, and I couldn't forget the way it had felt to be held in his arms for even a brief moment, but I had the sense something was holding him back too.

Auric peered at a map and took notes in his journal while the wind tousled his golden hair. His clothes were finer than the rest of ours and I wondered how he felt about being stuck with a girl like me, so below his station. I got the feeling he saw our mission as a chance to uncover hidden knowledge, but was that all he cared about? Could he ever care about me?

Would any of these men?

Not Reven, for sure. Slade was just as distant. Jasin maybe, though I got the feeling he'd be willing to bond with just about any woman.

"We need to make a plan," Auric said, snapping me out of my thoughts.

I drew in a breath as I stared at his map, which was more elaborate and finely made than any I'd seen before. Done in different colors, it depicted the four Realms, each one converging in the center at the capital, Soulspire, where the Black Dragon and her mates resided near the Spirit Temple. The Earth Realm, where we were now, was located in the north, with the Air Realm to the east, the Water Realm to the west, and the Fire Realm to the south. The map had each Realm's capital labelled, along with some other major cities, rivers, lakes, mountain ranges, and—most importantly—the five Gods' temples.

"We have to visit the temples in the order in which we arrived," Auric said. "That means the Fire Temple is first."

"Why can't we go to the Air or Earth one first?" I asked. "They're both closer."

"Because that's what the Gods decreed," Slade said.

Jasin flashed me a suggestive grin. "Definitely fine with me."

"I suspect they made that rule to keep it fair and to encourage us to find you faster," Auric said, with a shrug. "Either way, we need to head to the Fire Realm first."

For the next few minutes, Auric, Jasin, and I plotted a course to the Fire Temple, with a few helpful comments from Slade, while Reven ignored us entirely. Once that was done, the men's horses were brought out, each one as unique as their riders. I didn't have a horse, and certainly didn't have the money to buy one. Not that there were any for sale in a town as small as Stoneham anyway.

"You'll have to take turns riding with one of us," Auric said, from atop his elegant white horse with the gold-trimmed saddle.

"She can ride me any time." Jasin winked. "I mean, ride *with* me."

"I'm sure that's what you meant." I rolled my eyes and threw my pack on the back of Auric's horse. Jasin was a little too eager, and the other two were keeping their distance from me, so Auric it was.

Auric offered me his hand and I climbed onto the horse behind him. A jolt of surprise and desire shot through me when I pressed against his back, along with the realization of how close we were. It had been years since I'd been this close to a man, but in the next few days I'd have to sit with all of the men like this. Of course, if they were really my mates, I'd be doing a lot more than just riding a horse with them soon.

I hesitated, then slid my arms around Auric, trying not to focus on the feel of his strong chest or his clean, fresh scent that made me want to get even closer. He sucked in a breath at my touch, but then rested his hand over mine and gave it a quick squeeze.

"Ready?" he asked.

I cast one last glance back at the town that had been my home for the last three years, then turned to gaze at my other companions. Each one was staring at me, waiting for me to give the signal to leave. Reven, on his swift black steed, looking broody and bored. Jasin, impatiently twitching on his dark stallion that looked like it was no stranger to combat. And Slade, on his large chocolate brown horse, waiting with a steady, calm demeanor.

"Let's go," I said.

My arms tightened around Auric as the horse began to move. It had been three years since I'd ridden a horse and I had the feeling it would take some time to get used to it again. By the time we stopped, I'd probably be sore all over.

As we rode out of town, the soldiers watched us with stony glares and a few people stepped out of their houses to gawk at our strange procession, but no one seemed all that sad to see me leave. I'd killed Koth, and might as well have killed Roark too. They weren't the first men I'd killed and likely wouldn't be the last, but their deaths still weighed heavily on me. Taking a life never got easier, nor did seeing a dead body, even if the person deserved it. I only hoped Tash and her mother would be okay.

I gazed at the forest where I'd gone hunting every day for the last few years. I'd promised Tash I would return someday, but it was hard to know what lay ahead of me, or how different I would be if I did return. Would I truly be the Black Dragon then? I'd never seen the current Black Dragon before, but I knew she was immortal, could control all four elements, and turned into a great winged beast with huge talons and glowing eyes. Was that my fate as well?

And what would the Black Dragon do when she learned I was like her?

13

AURIC

Kira was quiet as we left Stoneham and traveled on the road alongside the edge of the forest, but I was constantly aware of her presence. Not only were her arms wrapped tight around my chest, but her feminine curves were pressed against my back in a way that was hard to ignore. Especially since I wasn't used to anything like this. I spent my time with books and...well, that was about it. I certainly wasn't very good with women and didn't know what to say to them. Now I was put in a position where I desperately wanted to get to know my future mate better, but was also unsure how to talk to her. I bet none of the other men had that problem.

"Is your head okay?" I asked her.

She pressed a hand to the back of her head. "Surprisingly it is. No pain at all, actually. They must not have hit me as hard as I'd thought."

"That's good." I paused. "Are you comfortable?"

"As comfortable as can be expected, considering I haven't ridden a horse in years." She shifted behind me, making her breasts rub against my back, a sensation that made my trousers suddenly tight. "How long do you think it will take to reach the Fire Temple?"

"I estimate it will take about eight or nine days, depending on how long we stop and if we have to go out of our way to avoid any problems."

"Is that all?" she asked, her voice hollow.

Was she nervous about this too? "I believe we've mapped out the most efficient route, but if you'd like to go slower or stop somewhere along the way I'm sure it won't be a problem."

"No, it's fine," she said, then drew in a long breath. "Eight or nine days is simply not a lot of time to get to know all of you, before we…"

"Before we become mates."

"Yes."

I understood her concern all too well. "None of us want to rush you. Take as much time as you need." I hesitated, glancing over at the Fire Realm soldier, who looked at ease on his horse. "You might want to spend extra time with Jasin though, since you'll have to bond with him first."

"Probably. But your temple is second."

"True." I cleared my throat at the thought of what that meant. "You'll have a lot more time to get to know Slade and Reven before we arrive at their temples, at least."

"I suppose so," she said. "What else can you tell me about all of this?"

"Not much, I'm afraid. I scoured the library in Stormhaven for any information after the Air God visited me, but found very little of interest. What I did find, I picked up from various different texts that otherwise seemed to have nothing to do with the Black Dragon or the Gods. One was on geography, one was on fashion, and one was on food. I suspect the Black Dragon had the rest destroyed."

"Probably," Kira said. "She didn't want anyone to be able to challenge her."

"That seems likely. I'm hoping I might be able to uncover more during our travels. I'd like to record all of this too, for future generations. Assuming we survive and the Black Dragon doesn't destroy my writings too."

"So you're a scholar?" she asked. "And a nobleman, I assume, judging from your clothes."

I tried not to react to her question and chose my words carefully. "Yes, I'm a member of House Killian, but I spend most of my days in the library. Or I did before all of this, anyway."

"House Killian? Does that mean you're related to the royal family of the Air Realm?"

"Yes," I replied hesitantly. I didn't want to lie to her, but I didn't feel comfortable divulging the full story yet. "But I'm no one of consequence." There, that was true enough.

"Maybe not to you, but I guarantee your life has been very different from mine and the other men. You grew up in luxury and never had to worry about where your next meal would come from or whether you could afford to repair your shoes."

I wondered what she had gone through before we arrived in her village. She wasn't wrong either. Gods, she must think I was pathetic, and if she only knew the full truth, she'd definitely think the worst of me. Now

I really couldn't tell her. "That is true. I grew up in privilege and have little to complain about."

"I didn't mean what I said as an insult," Kira added, with the slightest brush of her hand against mine. "I was only pointing out the differences between all of us."

"I understand." I tilted my head as I considered. "Perhaps the Gods chose the four of us to be your mates for the sheer reason that we *are* all so different from one another."

"That could be. The Air God didn't give you any hint of why he picked you?"

"No, not at all. He was pretty vague about everything though. Of course, I was also pretty shocked at the time, so I didn't get to ask him as many questions as I would have liked."

"What happened? I know you all supposedly met the Gods, but I don't know the details."

My hands tightened on the reins as I thought back to what occurred a month ago. "I've always been an early riser, and I like to take breakfast outside in the garden at dawn, usually with a book or two. That morning it was unusually windy outside and I could barely read because the pages kept turning. I nearly went inside, but then he appeared. The Air God."

"What did he look like?" she asked.

"Like a giant made out of a tornado. He was composed of swirling wind and lightning, and his voice was like thunder. As he spoke to me, everything around me floated in the air. My books. My breakfast. The bench I'd been sitting on." I shook my head, remembering how shocked and confused I'd been. "He told me I'd been chosen to be the next Golden Dragon and that I had to find you so we could take the place of the current Dragons. Then he sent a rush of air through me, lifting me up into the sky, and I thought I would surely plummet to my death. Instead I floated back down, but he was gone."

"It sounds like something from a dream."

"Yes, it does. I questioned everything that happened, sure that I'd been imagining it all, but then I began moving things without touching them, and one night woke up floating in the air. Not to mention, I had this overwhelming urge to head northwest to find you."

"What did your family think of all that?" she asked.

"I didn't tell them anything. The Air God warned me not to speak of this with anyone except you and your other mates. Of course, it was difficult to hide my powers from my family, but people are often willing to believe there was a sudden gust of wind or a strange breeze instead of magic."

"Were they okay with you leaving?"

"I informed them I was traveling to Thundercrest to visit the library there, but once I was on the road I escaped my guards and came here." I frowned as my guilt at deceiving my family returned. "I left them a note telling them I was all right, but they're probably looking for me now. I hope they're not too worried."

She shifted again behind me, as if trying to get comfortable. "Are you close with your family?"

"Yes. For the most part." Talking about my family would be tricky without revealing more about who I truly was, so I changed the subject. "What of you? I'm guessing those people back there were not your family."

"No, my family is long gone."

I heard something in her voice that made me think this wasn't something she cared to elaborate on, and I fell silent. I could understand not wanting to talk about some things about our pasts. None of that mattered anyway. Our old lives were over. What mattered now was the journey ahead of us.

14

KIRA

We traveled along the road with the forest all around us, Jasin in the lead to make sure the way was clear, while Slade and Reven rode behind to guard our backs. On any other day I would be heading into the forest right now and trying to find some game for Roark to make sure that Tash would be safe and that I would be fed tonight. Now I was sitting behind this man I'd just met, with three other strange men around me, and together we were supposed to save the world. I still didn't know how I had gotten involved in this, and wondered if it was all a big mistake. Maybe the men were supposed to find some other girl. Maybe the Gods chose wrong.

Even if I ignored the whole "overthrow the Black Dragon" goal, which was so far-fetched it was laughable, the thought of bonding with all the men was hard to swallow. We would be mated for the rest of our lives, with the four of them sharing me forever. It was hard to believe they would be okay with that. I could barely fathom it myself, although I had to admit I didn't hate the idea either. I had to give the Gods credit, they'd certainly found me four men who made my mouth water.

I supposed the only thing to do now was to get to know my future mates better. I'd made some progress with Auric, and over the next few days I'd learn what I could about the other men as well. Especially Jasin. In less than two weeks I'd be expected to sleep with him, and I barely knew a thing about him.

At midday, we stopped beside a small stream for a break and to have a quick meal, but none of us felt like chatting much. I intended to ride with Jasin next, but then I caught him casting fire, moving it from hand to hand like a juggling ball, and fear crept down my spine. Even though he wasn't the one who'd killed my family, I'd had a fear of fire ever since that day.

I decided to ride with Slade, whose solid, quiet presence soothed me as we rode east through the Earth Realm. He was so large and muscular it was a pleasure to hold onto him and feel all that contained strength under my arms, even if he had no interest in making conversation.

When the sun touched the horizon, Jasin called for us to halt. "This looks like a good place to camp for the evening."

He'd chosen a spot in a small clearing near a freshwater stream. Thick trees sheltered us on either side, filled with the sounds of birds chirping as they found their resting spots for the night.

As I eased off Slade's horse, I let out a pained groan. Every muscle in my body seemed to hurt, especially my thighs and back. If I was this sore after only a few hours of riding, how would I make it through nine or ten days of this?

"Are you all right?" Slade asked, resting one of his large hands lightly on my shoulder.

I stretched my back, trying to ease the aches in it. "Just sore. I haven't ridden in some time."

"You'll get used to it," Jasin said. "I've seen plenty of soldiers get broken in. Try to stretch and walk around, that will help."

"Sitting behind one of us can't be helping either," Slade said.

Jasin nodded. "We should get her a horse when we can."

"With what money?" I asked.

"Money isn't an issue," Auric said.

I blew out a long breath. "Maybe not at the moment, but we have a long journey ahead of us."

Reven stayed silent the entire time, almost as if he wasn't there at all. He removed his things from his horse, then spread his bedroll out on one side of the clearing. The rest of us followed his lead, quickly setting up camp while the sky darkened.

I grabbed my bow and headed into the forest before the men could stop me. Tash's mother had been kind enough to pack us some rations, but they would only last so long if we didn't supplement them with fresh food. Besides, we would need to keep our energy up for the journey ahead. We could stop in an inn every few days, but that wasn't possible every night.

The Spirit Goddess must have been smiling upon me, because I managed to take down a large gray hare almost immediately. Maybe she had chosen me after all, although I didn't remember a visit from her.

Wait. The old woman I'd found in the forest. Could that have been her? If so, why hadn't she given me more information? Or some powers, like the guys had gotten from their Gods?

I pondered this as I made my way back to the clearing, where Jasin had started a small fire in the center. Slade and Reven were tending to the horses, while Auric was studying the map. I got to work skinning the hare, but then Jasin took over cooking duties.

"I've got this covered," he said, with a cocky grin.

"Be my guest," I said, stepping back.

He pulled out some herbs from his packs and tended to the hare, then strung it up over the fire. I moved my bedroll farther away from the flames, then sank down onto it, remembering the last time I'd traveled like this. Back then I'd been alone and terrified, searching for somewhere safe to lay low for a while. At least now I had four men with me who seemed like they could handle themselves in combat, even without their new powers.

When the food was ready, the others settled in around the fire. I pulled out some of the cheese and fruit from Tash's mother, while Jasin sliced pieces of the hare and served it to us. The tempting aroma had all of us digging in immediately, and it didn't disappoint.

"This is really good," I told Jasin. "Where did you learn to cook?"

"From my mom, but also in the army. You pick up all sorts of skills there. I'm not bad with a sewing needle either. But food is my second love, so I made a point to learn to make some decent meals after choking down the other soldiers' terrible grub."

"What's your first love?" Slade asked.

Jasin smirked. "Women, of course."

"Of course." I rolled my eyes, while Slade chuckled and Auric shook his head. Reven just looked bored, which seemed to be normal for him.

Once we finished eating, I leaned back on my bedroll and stretched my aching limbs, feeling exhausted but not yet tired enough to go to sleep. "I'd like to get to know you all a little better. Maybe you can each tell me something about yourselves, like where you're from, or what your life was like before you met a God."

"Makes sense," Jasin said. "Guess we better get to know each other, since we're going to be bound together for the rest of our lives. Not just Kira, but all of us."

"Not me," Reven said, his voice cold.

"What do you mean?" Auric asked.

"I'm not going to be one of you."

Slade gave him a steely look. "We were selected for a purpose. The Water God chose you for a reason."

Reven broke a branch in half with a sharp *snap*. "Then he can choose another."

"Why are you even here then?" Jasin asked.

"I didn't have much of a choice," Reven said. "I couldn't deny the urge to reach Kira, same as all of you. But as soon as I find a way out of this mess, I'm gone. I have no desire to be a Dragon or to be anyone's mate."

Jasin's eyebrows drew together and he looked furious, and both Auric and Slade looked like they might respond, but I held up a hand.

"It's fine," I said. "None of us chose this. I understand if you don't want to be here. Gods know I don't want to be a part of this myself." I glanced between all of them, watching the fire's glow flicker on their masculine faces. "If there is a way out of this, you're all welcome to take it. I won't hold it against you. But at the moment we need to work together to get through this." I turned to Reven. "Can you do that?"

He gave me a cold look. "For now."

I supposed that was the best I'd get from him. "This isn't easy for me either. I never expected to suddenly have four men show up in my village and claim me as their mate, but here we are. Right now we're all strangers, but I'm hoping we can change that."

For some time, the only sound was the popping of the fire, but then Slade spoke up. "I'm from Clayridge, a town on the western side of the Earth Realm. Lived there my entire life working as a blacksmith, like my father. Not much more to tell really."

I was certain that wasn't true, but I didn't blame him for not wanting to spill all his secrets to what were effectively a bunch of strangers he'd only met yesterday. At least he was trying.

"Ever been in a fight?" Jasin asked him.

"A few," Slade replied.

Jasin nodded, and everyone looked to him next. "My turn, I guess." He gestured at his uniform. "Pretty sure you've all guessed what I did before this. I come from a military family actually. Everyone in my family has served at one time or another. Grew up in the Fire Realm, but I've been all over as part of the Onyx Army."

"Are you still loyal to the Black Dragon?" Reven asked, his tone deceptively casual. I instantly tensed, worried the question might cause a problem, even if I'd been wondering the same thing. It was something no one would ever ask out loud, and something no one would ever deny. *Of course* we were all loyal to the Black Dragon. Everyone was, unless you wished to be cut down by her soldiers or her mates.

Jasin looked caught off guard, but then he stared into the flames with his jaw clenched. "I was, once. Not anymore."

I wanted to ask him what occurred to make his loyalties shift, but I wasn't sure now was the time. Was it being chosen by the Fire God? Or did something happen before that?

Auric cleared his throat. "Guess I'll go next. I'm from Stormhaven. I'm a…scholar, I guess you could say. I have a special interest in history, culture, geography, and religion. All of which might come in handy now, I hope."

Jasin snorted. "You're a nobleman. That much is obvious."

"Well, yes." Auric straightened up, raising his chin. "Is that a problem? If you doubt my usefulness in combat, I've been trained in sword fighting since I was a child."

"Ceremonial sword fighting, no doubt," Jasin muttered. "Maybe we should be asking *him* about his loyalties. All the noble families serve the Black Dragon too."

Auric narrowed his eyes at Jasin. "I'm loyal to this mission. Can the rest of you say the same?"

"That's enough," I said, feeling even more exhausted after listening to them bicker. It was a bad sign if they were fighting already. "No one is questioning anyone's loyalty." I turned toward Reven. "I assume you must be from the Water Realm then. What did you do before you were chosen?"

He leveled his dark gaze at me. "I killed people for money."

We all froze, staring at him as if to check that he was serious. Yes, he definitely was. An *assassin*. I supposed that explained all the black clothing and the way he'd killed Roark with silence and ease. But why would the Water God choose such a man for me?

Jasin forced a grin and broke the awkward silence. "Well, at least we know he'll be good in a fight."

15

JASIN

I coaxed a small flame to life on each of my fingertips. Even after a month with these powers, they never ceased to amaze me. I doubted having magic would ever get old. After all, who wouldn't want to be able to control fire?

The sun had only just breached the horizon, its light filtering through the thick trees around us. My companions were still asleep, but it was my turn on watch and I'd been passing the time playing with fire. Literally.

I'd moved to the other side of the stream, far enough from the camp that I wouldn't spook the horses or accidentally set fire to anything important, but close enough to keep an eye on my companions and watch for any threats. I summoned a ball of flame between my palms, making it hotter and hotter, until it burned blue underneath my fingers. I threw it as if it were a rock, aiming it at a cluster of large stones in the middle of the stream. The fiery ball flew across and hit the stones with a burst of embers and the hiss of steam.

A twig snapped behind me and I turned quickly, but it was only Kira. Her long red hair was messy from sleep and her eyes were huge, as if startled. I glanced around, but didn't see any signs of danger. Then I realized she was staring at the spot where I'd thrown the fire.

"Everything all right?" I asked.

She blinked and seemed to shake herself out of it. "Fine. Just half asleep."

I nodded, but I got the feeling there was more to it than that. Was she nervous about all of our powers? Or just mine?

"Should we wake the others?" I asked, glancing back at the other men. I wasn't sure what to think about any of them. Slade seemed like a decent enough guy, even if he didn't talk much. Auric was a useless nobleman who shouldn't even be on this journey. And Reven? I didn't trust him at all. I planned to keep my eye on him so none of us ended up with a knife in our backs.

Kira, on the other hand, was everything I could have hoped for. I'd never thought I could ever settle down with just one woman, but the second I'd met her, that worry had vanished. Sharing her with the other guys though... I wasn't sure I'd ever be okay with that. Sure, I'd shared women with other soldiers before for a night or two, but that was different. None of those women were mine. Not like Kira would be.

She moved beside me, leaning against the same thick tree trunk that had been my backrest for the last hour. "We'll give them another few minutes to sleep. Were you practicing your magic?"

"I have to, since my new powers didn't come with any kind of training lesson or manual on how to use them. Good thing I seem to be immune to fire now, or I'd be dead many times over, or at least a whole lot crispier." I flashed her a grin. "The barracks I was living in? Not so lucky. But after a lot of practice over the last month, I'm learning to control what the Fire God's given me. Mostly."

She shivered and wrapped her arms around herself, even though it wasn't that cold. "Probably a good idea. Just be careful."

"Always," I said, conjuring another fireball over my open palm.

She flinched back, her eyes fixed on the flickering flame like it was a live snake. Maybe she wasn't scared of our magic—she was scared of fire. I closed my hand over the flame, dousing it immediately, and her shoulders relaxed.

"You don't need to be afraid," I said. "I'd never hurt you, Kira."

"I'm not afraid of you." She tore her gaze away and stared into the forest, then drew in a breath and faced me again. "Tell me about your encounter with the Fire God."

"It was pretty incredible. A giant made out of flames came to me in the middle of the forest and told me to find you. At first, I thought maybe I'd eaten one of those weird mushrooms in the forest again. Last time that happened I saw pink dancing water elementals for two days and had a raging headache for a week." I winked at her and she gave me a smile that made my heart beat faster. "But there was no denying this was all real and not a hallucination—not after I accidentally set my bed on fire."

"No wonder you're practicing," she said. "Is that when you left the Onyx Army?"

"Pretty much. Once I accepted that I really had been chosen by the

Fire God I knew I had to quit. That turned out to be a lot harder than I expected. The Onyx Army wasn't exactly happy about one of their finest soldiers up and leaving for no real reason." *Not when he was so good at hunting the Resistance,* I mentally added. "But as the days went on, the tugging in my gut told me there was no other option. This was my destiny and I had to find you, no matter what. I escaped the army and became a deserter, even though it cost me everything. My job. My friends. Probably my family too."

"I'm sorry." She frowned as she glanced back at the camp. "It seems none of us want to be here on this journey."

"That's not true. Yes, I had to give up my previous life, but I do want to be here."

She sighed. "You might be the only one."

"Nah. We've all been ripped from our normal lives and given this larger-than-life destiny to fulfill with four strangers we're now stuck with, possibly forever. It's going to take some getting used to for all of us." I reached out and pushed back a stray piece of her red hair, smoothing it on her head. "But we'll get there, I promise."

"Thanks. I appreciate your confidence."

"Confidence is my specialty," I said, giving her an arrogant grin. She laughed, and the sound was so perfect I knew I'd do whatever it took to make her laugh like that again. How was it possible we'd only met yesterday?

"You're such a flirt," she said. "I bet you woo all the women you meet."

"I was quite popular with the ladies, it's true." I leaned against the tree and gazed into her eyes. "For good reason, I assure you."

She cocked her head. "Let me guess. You have a lover or two in every town you've visited, who are now all pining away, awaiting your return."

"Not quite. And every woman who shared my bed knew I wasn't making any promises."

An eyebrow darted up while her smile dropped. "Is that what I should expect as well?"

"No," I said quickly. "My past is behind me. From now on, I'm yours and yours alone. Assuming you want me as your mate, of course."

Our eyes locked and heat passed between us, but then she quickly looked away. "We should probably get ready."

She straightened, brushed herself off, and headed back to the main part of the camp. I watched her go, checking out her behind in those tight hunting leathers she wore, then sighed. I'd ruined the moment with my stupid mouth, and now she doubted my loyalty. Sure, I'd slept with lots of women, but that was before I'd met her. She couldn't hold that against me now.

I made another flaming ball, the frustration fueling my magic and making it especially large, and then I hurled it at the stones with extra vigor. Unfortunately, I missed. The fire hit the grass on the other side of the stream, instantly setting it alight. Panic rose in my throat as the flames spread to a nearby tree, but I was too horrified to do anything. Gods, what had I done?

Water leaped up from the stream and covered the fire, dousing the flames with a loud sizzle. I turned and saw Reven standing in the shadow of the tree. He gave me a sharp look, before turning away. How long had he been there, spying on us?

Worst of all, Kira stood behind him. And she'd seen it all too.

16

KIRA

Once our camp was packed up, we continued traveling along the main road toward the Air Realm in the southeast. I rode with Reven first, needing some space from Jasin, especially after that last fireball. Thank the Gods Reven had put it out quickly before the flames took over the entire forest. How was I supposed to bond with Jasin when fear spiked through me every time he used his powers? Better yet, how was I supposed to face the Fire God? And after I did that, I'd be able to conjure fire myself—did I even want that?

Did I have a choice?

I tried to put the thoughts out of my head by focusing on the man sitting in front of me, but he wasn't exactly one for conversation. Our last exchange had gone like this:

"So, you're an assassin?" I'd asked Reven, after we'd been on the road for fifteen minutes.

"Yes," he'd said, his voice showing no emotion at all.

"How did you get involved in that kind of work?"

"It's a long story."

I'd waited for him to go on, but he seemed content to leave it at that. Giving up, I'd sighed and turned back to gazing at the forest and the mountains in the distance instead. Good thing the Water Temple was last, because I had a hard time seeing the two of us getting intimate anytime soon. Assuming Reven would even stick around that long.

We stopped for lunch in another clearing and then it was time for me to ride with Jasin, who still wore his military uniform. Even though I would never admit it out loud, it was a good look on him, complementing the red highlights in his hair and enhancing his broad shoulders. There was something about a man in uniform, and Jasin looked commanding, dangerous, and incredibly sexy.

"Don't you have something else you can wear?" I asked, as he helped me up onto his war horse. Unlike the others, he had me sit in front of him, and the solid presence of him behind me made my heart race.

He took the reins in front of me, his arms brushing against mine. "Not really. I only grabbed a few things when I left, and since I was traveling alone I figured it would be safer if I was in my uniform."

"Maybe, but it might draw attention now. It'll be hard to explain why you're traveling with the four of us. Plus a lot of people don't look fondly on the Onyx Army around here."

I felt him shrug. "It'll have to do for now. I can take the coat off when we enter a village."

"That could work, and once we get to a larger town we can see about getting you some other clothes."

He snorted. "Make sure to get some for Auric too then. He sticks out more than I do."

I cast a glance over at Auric, who sat straight on his white horse wearing clothes that looked more suitable for going to a ball than for traveling. "You have a point there."

We continued for another few hours through a bit of road that had thick trees on either side of it, cutting out a lot of the light. I nearly dozed off, with the horse moving rhythmically underneath me and Jasin's very warm body behind me. I almost leaned back and rested my head against him, but managed to restrain myself. My body was comfortable with him already, even if my mind wasn't yet.

As the hour grew late, we decided to stop at a village up ahead for the night so we could get supplies and feed the horses. But as we approached, it was immediately clear something was wrong.

We walked our horses slowly into the center of the village, their steps the only sound we could hear. The stone buildings around us had all been turned to little more than rubble, with huge pieces missing or crumbled to the ground. It seemed fairly recent, since the nearby forest hadn't taken over the ruins yet, but there was no sign of anyone still living here.

"What happened here?" Auric asked, as we spun around to take it all in.

"An elemental attack, most likely," Slade said, his tone grim. "The people must have abandoned the village afterward."

"I heard about a town that was attacked by rock elementals a month ago," I said, remembering the doomed travelers' words. "This could be the same place, or one that suffered a similar fate."

"If so, where are the elementals now?" Jasin asked, his hand on his sword as he glanced around.

"Perhaps the Dragons took care of them," Auric said, with a shrug.

"Unless the Jade Dragon is the one who did this," Slade said.

"It doesn't matter what happened," Reven said. "No one is here now. We should look around for any supplies they might have left behind and find a place to sleep for the night."

The thought of staying here in this abandoned town made my stomach twist. "What if the elementals return?"

He met my eyes. "Then we'll deal with them."

I still didn't like it, and the other men seemed wary as well, but they nodded and dismounted their horses. We did a quick search through the crumbled buildings, with Slade moving the stone so we could look for supplies or any sign of what had happened. We found very little, which made me think we weren't the first people to pick through these ruins.

We found a small building that was mostly intact except for one missing wall and decided to sleep there for the night. As I pushed aside the debris and laid out my things, I wondered what the building had once been used for before. A small house? A shop? It was hard to tell. I picked up a dusty old doll with only one leg and shuddered, before tossing it aside.

Between exhaustion and the eeriness of the place, none of us spoke much that night before we took to our beds. I fell asleep almost instantly, but it seemed as if only minutes had passed before Reven's voice woke me.

"Wake up," he said in a low voice. "We've got company."

I rose to a sitting position and blinked back sleep as his words settled over me. Reven had taken the first watch, and now he stood over the four of us with only the moonlight illuminating his dark frame. Outside, the night was silent. Maybe too silent.

Jasin jumped to his feet instantly. "What kind of company?"

"Not the friendly kind," Reven said.

"How many?" Slade asked.

Reven glanced through the missing wall, though I couldn't see anything out there. "Seven at least. Bandits, most likely. They're surrounding us now."

Jasin swore under his breath. "They must have been watching this town. Waiting for us to go to sleep so they could attack."

Yes, that was definitely their plan. I remembered as much from my short time living with a group of them myself.

"Can we get our horses and outrun them?" Auric asked, as he quickly pulled on his boots.

"Not likely," Reven said.

"Especially not with Kira sharing a horse," Jasin said. "But we could try."

"Run or fight?" Slade asked, turning his green eyes to me. The others waited for my answer too.

I swallowed. All my life I'd stayed in the shadows and kept to myself, trying to draw as little attention as possible. I wasn't used to being a leader and wasn't sure I liked this new role. What if I made the wrong decision and one of them was injured, or Gods forbid, worse? How could I live with that?

I went over everything they'd said. We were surrounded and couldn't outrun the bandits, not with me riding with one of them. We didn't know the land around here, and the bandits probably did. No matter what we chose we were at a disadvantage.

"Fight," I said, praying I'd made the right decision and wasn't leading my men to their deaths. I'd only known them for a few days, but I was already terrified of losing them.

"So be it," Jasin said, flashing a bloodthirsty smile. "I do love a good fight."

"We have to be careful not to use our powers though," Auric said. "We can't let anyone know who or what we are."

"Or we need to make sure no one is alive to speak a word about us," Reven said, pulling his hood over his head again.

With that grim thought, we quickly prepared ourselves and left the ruined building, since there was no room to fight inside it. As we stood in the center of the village, the men all drew their weapons and I gripped my bow tight. Jasin clutched his large sword, while Auric held a long, thin blade with elaborate carvings. Slade lifted his huge axe, his stance wide, like nothing was getting through him. Reven disappeared into the shadows or maybe onto a nearby roof, I wasn't sure.

Dark figures crept out of doorways and blades glinted under the starlight, but my rapid breathing was the only thing I could hear.

Auric raised his sword. "Here they come."

"Protect Kira," Slade told the others.

Jasin gripped his weapon tighter. "With my life."

"I can protect myself," I told them, readying my bow. I prayed to the Gods it was true.

17

KIRA

As dark figures approached from all around us I nocked an arrow, my heart pounding in my chest. We were outnumbered and would soon be surrounded. What if I'd made the wrong decision?

When the first bandit came within range, I released my arrow. It struck the man in the chest and he hit the ground. I grabbed another arrow immediately, but by then the attackers were already upon us.

Thin knives appeared from the rooftops above us, landing in the throats of two of the bandits, killing them instantly. Thrown by Reven, no doubt. He leaped off the rooftop and his twin blades sliced through another bandit as he landed. He then launched himself at the next attacker in a blur of movement.

Slade swung his axe at a man wearing a gray hood, while Auric's long blade clashed with a curved sword wielded by a woman. Jasin moved in front of me, meeting two bandits with his heavy sword, his movements swift and powerful. He spun and slashed between the two of them, keeping them at bay.

Everything happened so quickly it was hard to tell who was friend or foe in the darkness, and I hesitated to release my arrow while wishing I could be of more help in the fight. When Auric narrowly dodged a blow from the woman with the curved sword, I saw my chance and let my arrow fly, taking her down with a well-placed shot in the chest.

The two men fighting Jasin pushed him back against a wall and I saw a burst of blood under the moonlight. Panic shot through me and I readied another arrow to help defend him, but then a woman lunged at me with a dagger. Auric let out a shout and blasted a gust of wind toward her, sweeping her off her feet—and me along with her.

I hit the ground hard on my back, all the air knocked from my chest and my head smarting from the impact. The bandit woman recovered faster and grabbed her dagger off the ground, already getting back to her feet. I sucked in a breath and lifted myself up, but I wasn't quick enough in reaching for my own knife from my boot. She raised her dagger, but then a barrage of rubble slammed into her, courtesy of Slade I assumed.

Only problem was the rocks went wide and smashed into Jasin and Auric too. Flames lashed out from Jasin's hands at the two bandits in front of him, setting them both on fire, along with everything around them. In an instant, the nearby brush was alight and blazing with heat.

Behind me, Reven swore under his breath and conjured a downpour of water over the flames like he'd done this morning, except on a larger scale. A *much* larger scale. Suddenly we were up to our knees in a flash flood of muddy water, which swept two of the bandits away into the forest. I grabbed onto a nearby piece of rubble to steady myself as the water rushed around me.

Within seconds, all our attackers were either dead or gone. I wasn't sure if any of them had escaped or not. If they did, then our secret would be out.

A body floated up beside me and I shuddered, while our nearby horses stomped their feet in the rising water. I lifted my bow above the water and each of my men looked somewhere between stunned and exhausted, which was about how I felt too. We were all soaked through, covered in mud and blood with a few cuts and bruises, but at least we were alive.

"Is everyone all right?" I asked.

Jasin touched his neck, which was still bleeding. "Nothing serious."

"I'm fine," Auric said.

Reven regarded the ruined village like he still expected trouble to emerge from its dark doorways. "We should get moving."

"No kidding," Jasin said, as he trudged through the knee-high muddy stream. "Think you summoned enough water here?"

Reven's eyes narrowed at him. "I wouldn't have had to use my powers at all if you hadn't set the entire place on fire."

"That wouldn't have happened if Slade hadn't attacked me with a pile of rocks," Jasin snapped.

"That was an accident," Slade said.

"We all made mistakes," Auric said, glancing at me. "I'm sorry I hit you also."

"We're still alive," I said. "That's what matters. We just have some things to work on, that's all."

"That's an understatement," Jasin muttered.

We made it to the horses and began packing up quickly, all of us eager to get away from this wretched place. But then Slade stopped just before mounting his horse and moved to rest his hand against a large rock nearby. All of us paused to watch him, wondering what he was doing. He closed his eyes and stood there, his palm pressing on the smooth stone, before finally pulling away. "There's a cave nearby. We can camp there tonight."

"Now you tell us," Jasin said, throwing up his hands.

"I didn't feel its presence before." Slade frowned. "Actually, I didn't know I could do that until now."

"Fascinating." Auric said. "I suspect we'll all discover new uses of our powers the more we use them."

Reven mounted his horse in one quick movement. "Let's go."

As Jasin pulled me up onto the horse behind him, he flinched a little. His neck was soaked in blood from the wound he'd received earlier. The wound he'd gotten defending me.

I lightly touched his neck, inspecting the gash. "We should take care of this."

"I'm fine," Jasin said, as he flicked the reins of his horse. "Just a scratch."

"We should at least clean it and wrap it." As we left the abandoned village behind us, I covered his wound with my hand, trying to stop the flow of blood. It was the only thing I could do while we were riding. Warmth flared as we touched, making my fingertips tingle against his skin.

"It's not so bad, really. I've had worse while shaving." Despite his words, he rested his hand over mine, like he didn't want me to pull it away. I became acutely aware of how close we were, with my fingers on his neck and my other hand on his hip. But I didn't pull away either.

I ran my thumb slowly along his skin. "I just hate seeing any of you hurt."

"Ah, so you do care about me."

"You may be growing on me a little," I admitted.

"I knew it." He flashed me a roguish grin over his shoulder.

"Don't get—" I started, but then I pulled my hand away to check the flow of blood and the rest of the words caught in my mouth. Jasin's neck was not only no longer bleeding, but it didn't seem to be injured at all anymore. How...?

"What is it?" Jasin asked, twisting on the saddle to look back at me. Auric glanced over at us, his brow furrowed, while Slade stopped his horse.

"Your neck," I said, running my fingers over it, not believing my eyes. "The wound. It's gone."

Jasin touched the area where he'd been cut with a frown. "Gods, you're right."

"Kira must have healed it," Auric said.

"Me?" I asked. "I didn't do anything."

Slade shrugged. "You're the representative of the Spirit Goddess and the next Black Dragon. It makes sense you would have some powers of your own."

Jasin stretched his neck, but he didn't seem to be in any pain anymore. "Incredible."

Auric examined Jasin closely. "I've heard rumors that the Black Dragon can heal her mates. I should have realized that would apply to us as well."

I stared down at my hand, which was still coated in Jasin's blood. "When I touched Jasin my hand felt warm, but he's always warm so I didn't think much of it. Maybe that's how I did it?"

"Is anyone else injured?" Auric asked.

Slade shook his head, and we turned to Reven, who'd been watching the entire conversation in silence. When all eyes fell upon the small cut on his forehead, he sighed. "Fine, you can heal me."

I slid off of Jasin's horse and climbed up behind Reven. I was even more hesitant to touch him than Jasin, but I braced myself and lightly rested my hand over Reven's forehead. While Jasin was comforting and warm, like sitting near a hearth on a cold night, Reven was cool and sooth-ing, like diving into a refreshing lake on a hot day. That same tingling feeling returned to my fingertips, and when I pulled my hand away, the cut on his forehead had vanished.

"Praise the Gods," Slade said quietly.

I stared at my hand. Even though I hadn't been given any direction by the Spirit Goddess, it seemed she'd given me a gift too. Praise the Gods indeed.

18

KIRA

As the moon climbed the sky, Slade guided our horses through the forest toward the mountains and the cave he'd sensed. The entrance to it was so small that none of us could squeeze inside, but he used his powers to push some of the stones away so we could enter.

We spread out around the cave and Jasin started a fire, while Auric created a breeze so the smoke would travel outside. Slade made a circle of stone, which Reven filled up with water, allowing us to wash ourselves and our clothes as best we could to get the mud and blood off. I took care of the horses, rubbing them down and giving them a few slices from an apple. They all butted their heads against my hand, wanting my attention. No surprise, really. Animals had always liked me. A coincidence, or because I was the representative of the Spirit Goddess? I wasn't sure.

After washing our clothes, we hung them on rocks near the fire so they would dry by morning. I'd donned one of my fraying dresses, while Jasin had opted to go shirtless, wearing only trousers after claiming he was hot. I tried not to stare at his naked chest and failed horribly. Who could blame me, with all those muscles on display and that intriguing trail of dark hair going down into his pants? He smirked at me, like he knew I was enjoying the show, and I swallowed and forced myself to look away.

None of us were ready to sleep yet after a fight like that, even though we were all exhausted. Instead we spread out around the fire and ate some of the dried meat, bread, and fruit we had stored in our packs.

"Let's admit it," Jasin said, as he leaned back on his bedroll in a way that flaunted his well-developed chest. "Tonight was a disaster. We got lucky, but it could have gone another way easily."

Auric smoothed back his blond hair, which looked darker since it was still wet. "We simply need more training. Not just on our own, but as a team."

"You should practice fighting against each other too," I said. "And then once you're all masters, you can teach me. Since supposedly I'll be inheriting these powers soon." I couldn't decide if I was excited about the idea or nervous. The guys could barely control their powers with just one element and I was supposed to master all four somehow. Including fire. I shuddered just thinking about it. But until I got those powers, I'd be at a disadvantage too. I was pretty good with my bow, but my fighting skills were a bit rusty otherwise.

"At least you can patch us up when we get injured," Slade said.

"Hopefully that won't happen too often, but I suppose I need to practice that also. Or even just figure out how I did it." I sighed and wiped bread crumbs off my lap. "You each fought well earlier. Maybe you could teach me some tricks too."

"I'd be happy to teach you lots of things," Jasin said, with a naughty grin that made me shake my head, even though I was secretly a little bit tempted.

"Training with each other is a good way to pass the time while we're in camp," Auric said. "We have many nights ahead of us while we travel to the different temples."

"I have something we can use to pass the time tonight." Slade reached inside his bag, then pulled out a large dark bottle.

"What's that?" I asked.

"Whiskey. Finest in the Earth Realm." He chuckled softly. "Okay, that's not true, but it was cheap at least."

Slade poured us each a bit of whiskey and we all relaxed as we took a sip. After a few minutes, even Reven looked less tense than usual. With the alcohol warming me from the inside out, I felt more comfortable around the guys than I had before. Even though things had gone wrong tonight, we'd fought together, bled together, and all had each other's backs. That kind of experience created a bond like nothing else could. Or maybe that was just the alcohol talking.

As Slade poured me a refill, he said, "Last night you asked us about where we're from and what we did before this. I think it's time you told us more about yourself, Kira."

My fingers tightened around my cup. "What do you want to know?"

"Everything," Auric said with a warm smile. "Did you always live in Stoneham?"

My past was not something I liked to talk about. Even Tash knew very little about my life before I showed up in her inn looking for a job. But these men were supposed to be my mates. I had to tell them something, and maybe someday I'd feel comfortable enough to tell them more. "No, I only lived there for the last three years or so. Before that I traveled around a lot."

"Where were you from originally?" Slade asked, as his fingers ran through his dark beard in a very distracting way. "Somewhere else in the Earth Realm?"

"I grew up in the Water Realm, actually. A small town on the coast called Tidefirth." Thinking back to those happy years made my throat tighten with emotion. "But I've lived in all of the Realms at some point or another, for a short while at least."

"Sounds like you were on the run from something. Or someone." Reven gazed at me from under his dark hood with those brooding blue eyes that seemed to peer deep into my soul.

I looked into Jasin's eager brown eyes next, then Auric's intelligent gray ones, and Slade's calm green ones. Each man stared at me, but none of them pressured me to reveal more about my past. But I would have to take a leap at some point. Might as well be now.

I drew in a breath. "My family was killed by the Crimson Dragon when I was thirteen." My hands wrung together in my lap, while I forced the next words out. "He burned down our entire house with my parents still in it. The memory has haunted me for my entire life."

Jasin reached over and grabbed my hand. "I'm so sorry."

"That must have been horrible," Slade said.

"It was." I shuddered as I remembered the flames, the smoke, the screams, and worst of all, the smell. "I only survived because my parents made me hide, after warning me that the Dragons would kill me if they ever found me. I didn't realize it at the time, but I think they were part of the Resistance. They knew the Dragons would come for me too because of that. I've been laying low ever since."

Auric took my other hand and gave it a squeeze. "Could your parents have known what you are?"

"I doubt it," I said. "How could they have known? Even I didn't know until the four of you showed up. Did any of you think something like this would happen?"

"Not a chance," Reven muttered.

Slade shook his head. "I still barely believe it."

"What did you do after your parents were killed?" Auric asked.

"I was so terrified that I fled my home as soon as I could. Hitched a ride with some traveling merchants at first. I moved around a lot after that until I landed in Stoneham." There was more, of course, but I'd already mentioned my parents' deaths. I didn't need to drag up any other bad memories tonight.

Before they could ask me any more questions, I downed the rest of my whiskey. "I'm exhausted. I think I'll hit the sack."

"Need some company?" Jasin asked, sitting up and drawing my eyes back to his naked and very appealing chest.

"Not a chance," I managed to say.

He shrugged, with a sinful smile on his lips. "The offer is always open in case you'd like to practice before we arrive at the Fire Temple."

I ignored him as I prepared for bed, although I wondered if practicing wasn't a bad idea. But the other three men were all watching us, and I knew they'd heard what he'd offered. Would they be jealous when Jasin was the first to bond with me? Or grateful it didn't have to be one of them?

19

REVEN

With my arms crossed, I kept a wary eye on Jasin as he threw streams of fire toward the wall of the cave. I'd already had to put out his flames twice yesterday. I wouldn't be surprised if I had to do it again now. The man was reckless and out of control, although I had to admit he was a skilled fighter. I wouldn't want to face him in combat, but I didn't trust him not to get us all killed either.

Outside the cave, Slade lifted small pebbles and tossed them at Auric, who blasted them away with a strong gust. A blacksmith and a nobleman. I had little in common with either one and no desire to know them better. I got the feeling they were both hiding something too, but then again, who among us wasn't?

On the other side of the cave, Kira was packing up the last of our camp so we could get back on the road soon. I caught myself staring at her as she straightened up and threw her bag over her shoulder, admiring the curves of her body in that thin dress and the way her hair brushed against her graceful neck. I turned away with a frown. I shouldn't be looking at her like that. Not when I had no plans to make her mine.

"Are you going to practice your magic too?" she asked, as she walked over to me.

"I'm fine." I didn't plan on keeping these powers much longer either.

She tilted her head and examined me. "I suppose you don't need magic to stay safe anyway. Where did you learn to fight like that?"

I gave her the side-eye. Once again, she was trying to learn about my past. If only she knew how similar our childhoods had been. But I never talked about that. "Here and there."

She sighed and began to turn away. "I get it. You don't want to talk to me."

Something ached in my chest at the disappointment in her voice. No doubt because of this stupid magical connection between us, nothing more. It made me desire her and care for her, even if I didn't want to. Gods, I couldn't wait for this spell to be broken.

"My father taught me," I reluctantly said. "He was a great swordsman."

She paused and considered me again. "Do you think you could teach me as well? I'd like to be able to fight better at close range."

"I can do that." If we were training, I wouldn't have to talk about my past or think about how much I wanted her. I drew both of my swords and handed one of them to her.

She examined the finely crafted blade, which was black and carved with elaborate designs. "This is beautiful. Your father's?"

"They were, yes." I gripped the matching blade in my hand. "How much do you know about sword fighting?"

"I've been trained in the basics before and I'm pretty good with a dagger." She got into position, holding the blade out as if ready for an attack. "Maybe you can give me some tips and help me practice."

"First of all, you'd be better off holding the sword like this." I moved close and adjusted her fingers on the hilt. As we touched, the connection between us snapped into place, like when she'd healed me yesterday. I jerked my hand away and stepped back quickly. "See if that's better."

She swung the sword and nodded. "I think so."

"Let's see what we're working with." I lunged toward her, moving slower than I normally did. She raised her blade to meet mine with some hesitation, her movements a bit jerky. I swung again and she managed to dodge, then sliced toward me. I parried her, but with each second, I could tell her confidence was growing as she remembered how to use a sword. She'd clearly had some training before, but she was out of practice and still had a lot to learn.

"Not bad," I said. "Where did you learn to fight?"

"The merchants taught me a little, and the rest…" Her face paled and she looked away. "I'd rather not say right now. We all have things in our past we'd prefer not to discuss."

"That we do." I gestured for her to attack me again.

We did another round, and by the end of it she was breathing quickly, her chest rising and falling in a way that made it hard not to stare at her full breasts. I couldn't deny she was beautiful, or that I wanted her in my bed. That would be true even without the damn magic tugging me toward her. It simply made it harder to resist her. But I'd lived my entire life exercising control over myself and my surroundings, and I wasn't about to let a pretty face and alluring body ruin all of that.

As I stared at her, she managed to catch me off guard and almost landed a blow. "Aha!" she said, laughing.

I scowled at her. "I let you get that one to boost your confidence."

"Of course you did," she teased.

We were about to go again, when Auric suddenly let out a pained sound, and we both turned toward him. Kira rushed out of the cave, with me right at her heels and Jasin a step behind us. I was instantly alert, worried the bandits had returned. Or worse, that the elementals had found us.

Auric was on the ground, nursing a cut on his cheek. "It's nothing. Slade nicked me with a rock."

Slade offered Auric his hand to help him up. "Sorry about that."

"It was my fault, I missed that one," Auric said, as he stood up and brushed himself off.

Kira moved close to Auric, inspecting his face. "I suppose it gives me a good excuse to practice healing you."

She brushed her fingers against the gash on his cheek, while he stared at her with lovesick eyes. Pathetic. Except as she caressed his face, jealousy boiled up in me. I wanted her to touch me like that, not him. Gods, now I was the pathetic one.

She pulled back and smiled at Auric. "All fixed."

"My thanks." He took her hand and pressed a kiss to it. "You're truly amazing, Kira."

Jasin grinned at her. "Now we're going to get injured just so you have an excuse to touch us."

She shook her head with an amused smile. "Please don't."

A strange sound came from the east, overhead. A huge gust of wind. The flap of large wings. The rustle of many trees.

I knew that sound.

"Get in the cave!" I grabbed Kira's arm and dragged her inside before she could protest. "Hurry!"

"What is it?" Slade asked, as the others rushed inside behind us.

"A Dragon," I said.

"What?" Kira's eyes went wide, but she didn't pull away from me, and I didn't release her arm. I didn't trust these other guys to protect her the way I could. None of them knew the danger that was coming for us, not the way I did. Kira knew, though. She understood all too well what the Dragons could do.

"Quick, cover the mouth of the cave," Auric told Slade.

Slade gestured and some of the large rocks moved in front of the cave entrance, though they left a small enough opening for us to peer through. We each crowded around it and watched as the dragon appeared over the forest, his large wings spread wide, casting huge shadows on the trees. Dark blue scales flashed under the sun, and even from this distance his sharp talons were visible, as was his long tail.

The Azure Dragon circled overhead twice, as if looking for something, before finally moving on. The cave was entirely silent while we watched him, as if we were each holding our breath, and only when he disappeared from sight did we all take a collective exhale.

"Was he looking for us?" Kira asked, her voice barely above a whisper.

"No way," Jasin said. "How would he know about us?"

Auric frowned as he gazed at the sky. "Some of the bandits might have gotten away and started spreading rumors about people with magic. Maybe he heard them somehow."

"Or maybe it was a coincidence and he's looking for someone else," Slade said.

I realized I was still holding Kira close even though the danger had passed. I quickly released her. "It doesn't matter. We need to get moving anyway."

I glanced back at the sky, at the spot where the Azure Dragon had soared over us. That was supposed to be me one day.

Not if I could help it.

20

KIRA

W e stayed off the road as much as we could, eager to remain out of
sight between the bandit attack and the Azure Dragon flying over
us. I mentally shuddered remembering his dark wings soaring through the
sky and that long tail stretched behind him.

I'd seen him once before when I was fourteen. He'd come to a village
in the Air Realm I'd been visiting with the traveling merchants. I'd
wandered off to pet some kittens in the inn's stables when the Azure
Dragon, Doran, swooped down and landed in the center of the town. I'd
peered through the wooden slats of the stables as he changed back into a
tall man with blond hair that hung past his shoulders. I was terrified he
was going to flood the entire village or drown someone, but all he did was
talk to one of the merchants briefly before casting his gaze in the direction
of the stables. His eyes were cold and piercing, and I had the horrible
sense that he would find me and finish the job the Crimson Dragon had
started. But then he turned away, shifted back into his dragon form, and
flew off without a word.

Just to be safe, I'd left the village that night on my own. The merchant
family had treated me well, almost like another daughter, and I hated
abandoning them without a word, but the memory of my parents' deaths
convinced me they would be safer without me around. Later I decided I'd
been paranoid, that it was a mere coincidence that the Azure Dragon had
shown up while we were there. He had no reason to look for me.

Now I wasn't so sure.

None of us seemed to feel like chatting much throughout the day, and

71

we made good progress toward the Air Realm without encountering any danger. When night began to fall we paused near a larger town, and Auric pulled out his map.

"We should stop there for the evening," he said. "According to this map it's a town called Rockworth and should be large enough for us to buy some new clothes."

Reven frowned. "It would be safer if we avoided towns entirely."

"The horses need to eat and rest," Jasin said. "And so do we."

Slade rubbed his dark beard. "We should stock up on supplies too if we're going to be avoiding towns in the future. Especially since we didn't get anything from that village yesterday."

I gazed at the wooden roofs of the town, barely visible over the stone wall surrounding it with a small moat, likely to protect it from elementals. "Let's stop for the night, but be especially cautious while we're there. Auric, maybe you can borrow clothes from Reven or Slade so you don't stand out as much."

The men grumbled, but we stopped in the forest so they could change their clothes. I was already wearing one of my ragged dresses with my cloak over it. Jasin kept his black trousers from his uniform but donned a plain gray shirt from his pack. Auric's fine silk clothes went in his bag, and Slade gave him a pair of brown trousers, while Reven reluctantly let Auric use one of his black shirts. They didn't fit Auric perfectly, but they were good enough for now.

Once we all looked like any other group of weary travelers, we headed for the town. I rode with Auric, breathing in his clean, fresh scent as I held onto his back. Of all the men, I felt the most comfortable with him so far, which surprised me. On the surface we had little in common, but something about his cool, logical mind put me at ease. I also appreciated that he wanted to learn as much about me as he could, and the way he flattered me with his attention. And unlike Jasin, he seemed to want me for more than just sex.

Auric's horse led us to the open gates, where the Onyx Army had guards posted to inspect everyone who went in or out. They regarded us suspiciously and I grew nervous they'd stop us. Reven slipped some coins into their palms as if he'd done it a hundred times before, and then they let us go through with barely a second glance.

Rockworth was more than double the size of Stoneham and many other horses and carriages filled the road, along with people walking along the side of it. We passed a bustling market with men and women selling their wares, before stopping at the first inn we saw.

The inn was called the Knight's Reprieve and was crowded with dozens of travelers in the tavern grabbing some supper. Slade and Auric arranged for us to get the last two rooms, before we headed into the tavern ourselves. The room smelled faintly of warm food and was loud with the sounds of eating, talking, and music from a man playing fiddle in the corner. Reven slipped through the crowd easily and managed to grab us the last free table, but it only had four chairs.

"It's fine," Slade said. "I'll sit at the bar and see if I can get any information from the other travelers."

"Good idea," Auric said.

As Slade took a stool at the bar, Jasin pulled out a chair at the table for me, before immediately claiming the one to my right. Auric got a journal out of his bag and began jotting down some notes, while Reven sat against the wall, his arms crossed as he eyed everyone in the tavern with suspicion.

A waitress with a low-cut dress that probably got her a lot of tips came over to our table, and her face lit up when she saw the man at my side. "Jasin! What are you doing here?"

Jasin flashed her the same charming grin he often gave me. "Just stopping in for a night."

"Is that so?" She leaned close, accentuating her ample cleavage. "I'm so happy you're back in town."

"It's good to see you, Minda. How've you been?"

"Good, but even better now that you're here," she said, batting her eyelashes. "My sister will be excited to know you're back too."

"Tell her I said hello," he replied, while my fists clenched under the table. That familiar possessiveness rose up in me again, and this time it was harder to push down. Jasin and the others were supposed to be my mates and all, but even ignoring that, I'd spent the last few days traveling with them, sleeping near them, and fighting alongside them. Maybe I had a little bit of a right to be possessive at this point.

"I will." She trailed a hand lightly along his shoulders and her voice turned sultry. "And if you need a room tonight, ours is free."

He cleared his throat, glancing at me. "Thanks for the offer, but I've got a room."

"Too bad. We had a lot of fun last time. Let me know if you change your mind." She removed her hand, casting me a quick, appraising look. "I'll get you all some food."

After she walked away, I turned to Jasin, my blood boiling. "You slept with *both* sisters?"

"I did, yeah." His eyebrows darted up. "Long before I met you. Is that a problem?" He gestured at the other men. "And should you really judge me when you're going to sleep with all four of us?"

"I'm not judging, I'm just—" The words died on my mouth and I looked away, still seething.

73

"What? Jealous?"

"No!" My cheeks flushed, because that's exactly how I was feeling.

He gave me that infuriatingly sexy grin. "I told you my bed's always open to you."

"Me and every other woman, it seems." I jumped to my feet, making the guys glance up at me with worried expressions. "I just need a moment. Feel free to start eating without me."

I headed out the front door of the inn, then walked around the side of it until I was near the stables and away from everyone else. My heart raced, and I felt like I couldn't breathe. Gods, why was I so upset? I'd only met Jasin a few days ago and we'd never made any promises to each other. What he did in the past—or even now—wasn't any of my business. He'd already admitted that he liked women. Lots of women. Which was fine, really. I didn't have any real claim over him, just some weird magical bond drawing us together. Without that, we would be strangers. So why did it hurt so badly when I saw him flirting with that woman?

"Kira, are you okay?" Auric asked.

I turned toward him, trying to keep my face blank. "I'm fine. Just needed some fresh air."

He moved closer, making me keenly aware of his height. "This situation is strange and overwhelming for all of us, but especially for you, I'm sure. It makes sense you would need to take a break from it now and then. But I just want you to know I'm here if you ever need to talk about it."

"Thank you. I appreciate that." I ran a hand through my hair and sighed. "I'm not sure it's possible to take a break from it either. This is my life now, and for better or worse, I'm stuck with the four of you. And you're all stuck with me."

Auric touched my cheek, his stormy eyes locked on mine. "I don't know about the other guys, but I'm glad I'm stuck with you."

"You are?" I asked, resting my hand over his. I remembered the moment we'd shared this morning when I'd healed him, and my eyes dropped to his mouth. I'd wanted to kiss him then, but the other guys had been watching. Now we were alone.

"I know you think none of us want to be here, but I do. Everything about this feels right." He lowered his head, his fingers tracing my lips. "Including this."

With one hand on my jaw he pressed his mouth to mine, while his other hand slid to my lower back to pull me against him. Sparks flashed between us as he teased my lips open, before stroking me slowly with his tongue. With a soft gasp, I wrapped my arms around his neck, wanting even more. It had been way too long since anyone had kissed me, but my body seemed to remember how to respond. Or maybe it was Auric who did that to me.

At first, I'd thought Auric might be snobbish or distant with his fine clothes and his head always buried in a book, but his kiss was anything but. He took his time with my mouth, learning what I responded to most, and soon he made me forget everything I'd been upset about. All I could think about was this rush of desire that swept through me at his touch, and how I wanted more.

"What the..." Jasin's voice said from behind me, interrupting the moment.

Auric and I broke apart, although he kept his hand on my back as we turned to face Jasin. My soldier looked stunned and maybe a little angry, but he was still mouth-wateringly handsome. That would never change, I supposed. And with lust already coursing through me thanks to Auric's kiss, it was hard not to want Jasin too. An image flashed in my head of being pressed between them with both their hands and mouths on me that sent heat straight to my core.

"Jasin." I wasn't sure what else to say. I didn't know if I should feel guilty for kissing Auric or not. Soon I'd be kissing all of them, if everything went according to plan, but I still had no idea how to handle this or how to juggle the feelings of four men. Or my overwhelming attraction to each of them.

"Could we have a moment alone?" Jasin asked Auric.

Auric glanced at me. "Are you all right with that?"

I nodded. "Yes, I'm fine. Thank you for making sure I was okay."

"Any time." He brushed his lips across mine, then straightened and gave Jasin a smug look before heading into the inn. I could practically feel the tension crackling in the air between them, and this new development would only make it worse.

Jasin swallowed, and my eyes couldn't help but linger on his strong neck dusted with stubble. "You kissed him."

"What? Jealous?" I asked, throwing his earlier words back at him.

"I am, yeah." He looked down at the ground, with a strand of hair falling over his forehead that I itched to brush away. "I thought I would be the first."

My heart softened at the vulnerability in his voice. "You're going to be the first in other things."

"I know. And I'm sorry about what happened in there. I swear, all of that is in the past. Nothing is going to happen with Minda or her sister or any other woman." His words warmed my chest, but then he blew out a breath. "But seriously, *that* guy?"

And now my heart hardened again. "What's your problem with Auric?"

"He's a stuffy nobleman!" Jasin's eyes flared, his jaw clenching. "Although maybe you like that sort of thing. He is rich, after all."

I propped my hands on my hips. "I like him because he's smart and kind and attentive, not because of his money. I don't care about any of that. And if you want to stay in this group, you're going to have to find a way to get along with him too."

I brushed past him as I made my way into the inn, my whole body flushed with both desire and anger. I'd never understand how Jasin could be so damn sexy while driving me crazy at the same time. And I was supposed to bond with him in only a few days? Not likely.

21

SLADE

I sat on the windowsill and observed the empty town lit with only moonlight and a few torches. I'd been on guard duty for an hour, but everything had been quiet so far. Nevertheless, I would remain vigilant to protect Kira and her other mates from any possible threats for the next few hours, when Auric would take my place.

Kira rose from the bed beside me and silently headed into the wash-room. Jasin slept in the other bed, face down and completely out. He was a true soldier, able to fall into sleep the second his head touched the pillow and instantly alert the moment he got up. I had no doubt if I woke him now he'd be ready to fight on a second's notice. The boy was a hothead, but I never once doubted his loyalty to Kira or his willingness to do what-ever it took to keep her safe.

The other two, I wasn't so sure. Auric seemed a decent fellow, but I was wary of him due to his background. I didn't have any great love for noble-men, but he was smart, I'd give him that. He seemed to be interested in Kira as well, but was it for the right reasons? Or did he only want to be a part of this for the knowledge and power he could uncover along the way?

And Reven? I didn't trust him at all, but he could have walked away a hundred times already, and he hadn't. I planned to keep an eye on him, but I didn't think he would put Kira in danger, not after how he'd defended her from the bandits. Even though he was distant now, I had a feeling he would come around eventually. If not, I'd be happy to show him the door. We had no room on this team for people who weren't committed to our mission.

ELIZABETH BRIGGS

As I watched through the window, something caught my eye outside the stone fence. An air elemental. It glided along the perimeter of the town and looked like a swirling tornado with arms and glowing eyes. I'd seen a few elementals before, mostly rock and water ones, but never an air type.

Elementals were immune to their own element, so Auric would be useless against this one, but they were weak against the others. The Dragons were supposed to keep us safe from them, but elemental attacks were common enough that people had learned how to defend themselves from them. Of course, that hadn't helped the village we'd visited last night. They'd clearly been unprepared for whatever had hit them and had fled the village instead of fighting back. But larger towns like this one were well fortified against elemental attacks. Other than the stone wall and the small moat, they also had a line of kindling next to a brazier they could easily light. I had no doubt that the guards were all trained in how to handle elementals as well, but I kept watch on the one below anyway.

We were just lucky it wasn't a shade. They were even more rare than elementals, but deadlier—and very little could stop them.

When Kira returned from the washroom, she spotted me and paused. She wore her one chemise, which was thin enough to show off her curves and the outline of her pale breasts, though I forced myself not to stare. If I looked at her like that I might start feeling things I had no desire to feel.

"Can't sleep?" I asked, my voice low so it wouldn't wake Jasin.

She shook her head as she sat beside me on the windowsill. "How's guard duty?"

"Quiet so far, although now we have a visitor." I pointed at the air elemental as it hovered outside the wall.

Her eyes widened as she caught sight of it. "Should we be worried?"

"Not yet. It seems to be alone, and it can't get through the town's wall. If it did, the guards could probably handle it. But I'm keeping an eye on it in case I need to help fight it off."

She nodded. "Let's hope it's just the one."

I leaned back and let my gaze linger on her a little longer. Her long red hair hung about her shoulders and a frown touched her lush lips. She'd worn that frown ever since she'd run out of the inn earlier tonight. I had a feeling Auric and Jasin were involved, judging by their similar expressions, but I wasn't sure if it was any of my business. Still, I didn't like seeing her upset.

"You seem troubled," I said.

"Is it that obvious?" She sighed. "Auric kissed me, Jasin's an ass, and Reven won't talk to me. You're the only one I can stand to be around at the moment."

"I'm honored," I said, with a low chuckle.

78

She took a piece of her hair and began idly twirling it as she looked out the window. "I don't know how to do this. I wasn't prepared to be involved with one man right now, let alone four."

I couldn't stop staring at her. She was too damn beautiful, and she made my resolve to keep my distance from her crumble. "You'll figure it out."

"I have to, I suppose." Her bright eyes found mine again in the darkness. "Do you ever wonder why we were chosen and not someone else?"

"Every damn day," I muttered.

"Me too. I can't stop questioning it all. Was I chosen for all of you, or were you chosen for me? What if the Gods chose wrong?"

"I've considered that too, but we must trust that they have a plan for us."

Her lips quirked up slightly. "Your faith in them is inspiring."

I shrugged. "I need to believe, otherwise I question everything too. Especially my place in this. I'm a simple blacksmith, nothing more. I don't belong here."

"Do you want to leave?" she asked softly.

"No. Not at all." I shook my head. "I'm sorry if I made it sound that way. I'm loyal to you and to our mission. Have no doubt about that."

"But you don't really want to be here."

"It's not that." I ran a hand along my beard as I considered my words. "It's more that I had a life I was content with already. A life I had no desire to leave behind."

"I see." She said, her voice quiet. "Did you leave someone behind?"

My chest clenched and at first, I couldn't respond. "No," I finally said. "There was someone once, but it's over."

Outside the window, the air elemental began moving toward the hills, leaving the town alone. My shoulders relaxed as he drifted out of sight. I didn't want to fight anyone unless it was absolutely necessary, even an elemental.

"It's gone," I said, turning back to Kira. "And you should head back to bed."

"I don't know if I can sleep."

Before I could stop myself, I said, "I can help. Turn around."

She shifted on the windowsill so that her back was to me. I took hold of her luxurious red hair and considered wrapping it around my hand and pulling her head back so I could claim her mouth, but I restrained myself and simply moved it over her shoulder. Over the chemise, I rested my hands on her upper back, immediately feeling the tension in it. Her upper body was strong, probably from her skill with a bow, and I smoothed my hands across her, slowly kneading her muscles. She tipped back her head with a breathy sigh that made me instantly hard.

"That's it, relax," I said, my breath close to her ear.

"I'm the one who is supposed to be healing you," she said.

"This is a different kind of healing." My hands moved up to her shoulders and she let out a soft groan as I worked the muscles there. I hadn't touched a woman like this in so long, and I hated to admit that I was enjoying it as much as she was. Compared to my large size she was so small and feminine, with soft skin and an inner strength that made her even more irresistible.

She relaxed against me and I trailed my fingers up the back of her graceful neck and into her hair. As my hand slid along her scalp, she leaned back against my chest and turned her head toward me. I caught her chin with my other hand, my eyes falling to her lips, which were open slightly and very inviting.

I stopped myself with my mouth only an inch away from hers. Gods, what was I doing? They'd surely put some kind of spell on me to make me desire her so. It took every ounce of self-restraint I had to release her. I quickly stood up and put some space between us before I could reach for her again.

She opened her eyes and looked at me with obvious disappointment. "Are you okay, Slade?"

"Fine," I said tersely, while trying to gain control of myself again. "That should be enough to help you sleep."

She rose to her feet and straightened her chemise. "Thanks for your help. I'll see you in the morning."

I pointedly looked away, my heart hammering in my chest. "Glad I could be of assistance."

She slipped back into bed and I forced myself to sit back down and look outside again, when all I really wanted to do was crawl in bed beside her. I'd wrap my arms around her and keep her close to me all night, making sure she was safe and happy. I'd gladly do more too, if she wanted it.

I shook my head, disgusted with myself. I'd loved someone once, and I would never go down that path again. Especially not with a woman whose heart would be divided between four of us. I knew where that would lead, and it was nowhere good.

From now on, I had to keep my distance from Kira.

22

KIRA

I n the morning we had a quick breakfast at the tavern, where I tried to ignore the way Minda looked at Jasin, before we headed to the market to get supplies and some new clothes. We passed by dozens of covered stalls with people yelling about their goods, from stoneware to cloth to fruits and vegetables. Reven, Jasin, and Auric all went separate ways, while Slade stayed by my side for protection, though he didn't say much to me. We'd almost kissed last night and I'd felt a real connection with him finally, but then he'd erected even more walls between us. Now his face was as hard as the stone he could control.

We passed by a stall selling weapons, and Slade took a moment to compliment the owner on their fine craftsmanship. I eyed a sword that would be the perfect size for me, and even held it in my hand briefly to feel its weight, before I put it back and turned away with a heavy heart. I longed for a sword of my own to be able to defend myself better, but I only had a few coins to my name and didn't want to abuse Auric's generosity.

As we continued through the market to pick up the supplies we needed, I tried not to get off track, though it was hard not to be tempted. There were dozens of things I wanted, including some new clothes and a horse, but the more frugal we were now the longer the money would last us.

After Slade and I picked up all the supplies we needed, we found Auric at a stall selling old books, which made me smile. Where else would he be, after all?

"Find anything?" I asked.

Auric closed the book he was flipping through. "Not here, unfortunately. I did get some new clothes, and I bought you a present as well."

He handed me a long, heavy package, and I immediately knew what it was. I tore the paper open and found the sword I'd been looking at earlier. The blade shone under the bright sunlight, while the hilt was simple and black, but it was exactly what I wanted. Auric had also gotten me a new sword belt made of black leather, which I couldn't wait to strap onto my waist.

"Thank you so much," I said to Auric. "But this is too much, really."

"Nonsense. I saw you admiring the sword earlier and knew you had to have it, for your own protection if nothing else." He slid his hand around my waist, drawing me close as his eyes gazed into mine. "If things were different, I'd buy you everything you could ever want. Gowns of the finest silks. Jewels to complement your beauty. An entire library full of books, or a whole arsenal of weapons, if that was more your style. But unfortunately, none of those things are practical right now, so this will have to do."

"I love it." I slid my arms around his neck. "Thank you, Auric."

He brought his lips to mine, while Slade crossed his arms and looked at everything except us. I pulled away from Auric quickly, feeling awkward about kissing one of my mates in front of another. I wasn't sure any of us were ready for that yet.

Slade cleared his throat. "We should get back on the road soon."

We returned to the inn and found Reven waiting outside by the stables, looking impatient and bored. I couldn't tell if he had bought anything or not.

"Have you seen Jasin?" I asked.

"He's upstairs, first door on the right," Reven said, with distaste. "Might want to knock first though."

"Thanks." I headed inside to find our wayward soldier while the other men loaded our supplies onto the horses. The place had cleared out since last night, and I didn't see any sign of Jasin anywhere. My stomach sank as I realized what he must be doing. And with whom.

"Jasin?" I called out, as I rushed up the stairs.

I knocked on the first door, but then threw it open with a burst of anxious energy. Jasin stood inside without a shirt on, while Minda, the waitress from last night, sat on the bed with a smile. My jaw fell open and I could only glance between the two of them, completely speechless. Even though I'd suspected this was what he was doing, it was still so much worse seeing it in person.

"It's not what you think," Jasin said quickly. But I'd already turned on my heel and walked out of the room.

He rushed after me into the hallway, then caught my arm to pull me back to him. He moved close, his naked chest only inches away. Muscles rippled across his skin, showing all the contained strength and power in his body. I swallowed as I forced my gaze up to his face, but that wasn't any better because he was so handsome he made my chest ache. Especially when I thought of him with that other woman.

"Her brother is about my size and I was trading my clothes for his," Jasin said. "Getting rid of my uniform, like you suggested. That was all. Nothing happened, I swear it."

"She was watching you change!"

"I was trying on a shirt to make sure it fit. She saw nothing more than you're seeing now."

I glanced down at his words, taking his body in again. He was so warm I could feel the heat radiating off him, and he smelled good, like a bonfire on a cool night. I had the strongest urge to press myself against him, tilt my head up to his, and ask him to give me some of that warmth too. But then Minda walked out of the room and gave us a smirk before heading down the stairs back to the tavern, and jealousy and hurt rose up in me again. I pulled away.

"Kira?" Jasin asked.

"It's fine," I said. "I just came to tell you we're leaving soon."

"No, it's not." He took my hand and led me into the room, then shut the door behind us. "I can tell you're upset. What can I say or do to make it better?"

"I have no right to be upset. What you do with other women is no business of mine. We've never made any promises to each other and I know you didn't choose this life with me."

His dark eyes were intense and serious as he gazed into mine. "Kira, I'm yours and yours alone. There's nowhere else I'd rather be but by your side."

Gods, how I wanted that to be true, and how I wanted to believe him. But no matter how much I desired him and wanted him for myself, I wasn't sure I could trust him. I pressed my back against the door, my heart racing. "You don't need to say that. You don't even know me."

Jasin placed his hand on the door by my head, leaning close. "I want to know you. In every sense of the word."

A rush of desire flared inside me at his words. He caged me against the wall, and though I could easily step away from him, I didn't dare move. "Me and every other woman, it seems."

"Not anymore. The moment I met you I knew the Fire God had chosen me for a reason, and that reason is you." He used his free hand to cup my face, and I sucked in a breath at his warm touch. "The only woman I want is right in front of me."

"And I'm supposed to believe you'll be loyal? Or happy with one woman for the rest of your life?" I gazed up at him defiantly, even though he was making me melt. "You admitted you've slept with lots of women."

"I have, yes. But that's all in the past." He arched an eyebrow. "You don't honestly believe the other guys have all been waiting for you to come along, do you? I doubt any of them are strangers to a woman's bed either."

My cheeks flushed. "No, of course not, but you're the one I have to bond with first. And I've never...ah..." I tried to duck my head, embarrassed as soon as the words slipped from my mouth, but he caught my chin and made me look up at him.

"Never?" His eyes flared with obvious desire, and then his gaze dropped to my lips. "Then it's a good thing I'm well versed in the arts of pleasing a woman."

His mouth captured mine, while his strong body pushed me back against the door he leaned against. With dominant hands he tilted my head up to his and gave me the most sensual kiss of my life, teasing a soft moan from my lips. His naked chest pressed against my breasts, and even through my dress I felt how firm his body was. I was suddenly overcome with the need to touch him and placed my hands on his waist, pulling him closer. I needed to claim him as my own in the same way he was claiming me.

His mouth moved to my neck, leaving a trail of light kisses that made me moan again, while my hands smoothed across his hard chest and strong arms. His powerful fighter's body was solid under my fingers, and as his lips skimmed across my collarbone, all I wanted was to feel more of it. Forget the Fire Temple, I was ready to bond with him right now. Or at least get some of that practice in.

But then he straightened up and stepped back, making me instantly miss his warmth. I nearly pulled him back to me, but somehow regained control of myself. Except there was no denying I'd kissed him back as hard as he'd kissed me. And if he kissed me again? I wouldn't stop him.

He ran his thumb slowly along my lower lip. "That's only a taste of what's to come. But first, I'm going to convince you that the only woman I want is you."

Without another word, he grabbed his clothes off the bed and walked out of the room, still shirtless. Leaving me breathless and dazed and wondering what exactly just happened.

23

KIRA

Another day of travel passed by without incident, except that I was forced to ride with Slade and Reven for long hours while trying to ignore the feel of their strong bodies against mine as they pointedly did not make conversation. I loved my sword, but I really should have asked Auric for my own horse.

At least I wasn't sore anymore. Like my head injury from Roark, my body had recovered quickly from the aches and pains of riding. It made me wonder if my new healing powers were working on myself as well.

After so many days on the road, we were all exhausted by the time we stopped to make camp in the forest. I set my bedroll as far from the fire as possible like I did every night, and both Jasin and Auric rushed to put theirs on either side of mine. Not that Slade or Reven seemed to care about being close to me anyway. Reven was brooding in the shadows as far away from me as possible, and Slade turned away from me when I glanced at him. How was I ever supposed to get close to them if they kept their distance like this?

On the other hand, maybe Slade and Reven were the least of my problems. Jasin and Auric had been glowering at each other all day, and as Jasin walked past me, he bumped into Auric hard and obviously on purpose. Auric muttered a word under his breath that sounded a lot like, "Barbarian."

I couldn't take it anymore. I got to my feet and glared at all of them. "I need a few minutes alone. Don't follow me."

"Stay close," Jasin said.

"I'll be fine," I snapped.

I headed into the dark forest, shoving branches out of my way and kicking at rocks under my boots. But even once I was out of sight, I could still hear their low male voices behind me, though I couldn't make out the words. I moved deeper into the woods, with the bright moon guiding my steps, until I found a large rock to sit upon. I listened carefully. Silence. Blissful, sweet silence.

It was the first time I'd been truly alone with my thoughts for days and I relished it. I'd gotten used to being in solitude for most of my life, and it was hard to adjust to suddenly being around four men all day every day. Even if I enjoyed their presence—when they weren't being obnoxious males, that was. It felt right with all of them at my side, but I realized I still needed some alone time now and then too.

The male voices grew louder, intruding on my quiet moment. Arguing about something, it sounded like. Probably related to me. Maybe I should feel honored they were fighting over me, but I had a feeling it would only get worse as I got closer to each man. Would any of them ever be comfortable sharing me with the others?

Would I?

The idea of sleeping with Jasin didn't make me as nervous as it once did, not after his mind-blowing kiss. But I had also kissed Auric only hours before and enjoyed it just as much. And then there was Slade, who I'd nearly kissed. Not to mention Reven, who I'd definitely *wanted* to kiss, if only because he was so gorgeous in his deadly, dangerous way.

How could I have feelings for all four men? It didn't make sense. Lust, I could understand. Friendship as well. But I felt more than that for all of them. Not love, not yet, but the potential that I could love each of them someday. It had to be the magical bond pulling us together and nothing more, right?

I covered my face in my hands, feeling overwhelmed by it all. That's when I heard something moving in the bushes near me.

I jumped to my feet and rested my hand on the hilt of my sword as I scanned the woods. Something was out there.

I was about to call the guys, when the leaves swept aside and the old woman I'd met on my birthday stepped forward.

"Hello there," she said, as if it was perfectly normal for her to run into me in the middle of the nowhere. "Kira, isn't it?"

"You," I said, my mouth hanging open. "Are you the Spirit Goddess?"

She let out a low laugh. "Gods, no. Why would you think that?"

My heart sank and I sighed. "You were outside Stoneham on my birthday, and now you're here. How?"

The old woman shrugged. "I get around."

"Are you following me?" I asked, my eyes narrowing.

"Not exactly."

She settled in on a rock opposite mine and I slowly sat back down since I sensed she wasn't a threat. She looked exactly as I'd seen her before, down to the same hooded robe. How had she wound up here, in the middle of the woods? We weren't anywhere near a town this time and she was alone, without even a horse.

"You can call me Enva," she said, as she folded her hands in her lap. "Let's just say I have a special interest in you."

"Do you know who—what—I am?"

"I do, and I might be able to help you." She cocked her head. "I'm sure you have some questions."

"Hundreds of them," I said. "Is it true? Am I the next Black Dragon?"

"Yes, you are. Assuming you live long enough to claim that title." She shrugged. "None of the others have ever made it that far."

My mouth dropped open. "There were others?"

"Of course," she said, as if it were obvious. "You didn't think you and Nysa were the only ones, did you?"

Nysa, the Black Dragon. Even hearing her name sent shivers down my spine. "I wasn't sure. I've never heard of any others."

"Because she kills them all before they become a threat."

I swallowed the lump in my throat. "But not me."

"She doesn't know about you. Yet. Best thing to do is to keep it that way as long as you can."

I nodded slowly. "We'll do our best."

"See that you do." Enva examined her fingernails on one of her wrinkled hands. "Any other questions? I don't have all evening."

She was mighty pushy, considering she was the one who'd visited me. "Why did the Gods choose me?"

She let out a sharp laugh. "They didn't."

I blinked at her. "I…I don't understand."

"The others were chosen. You were born."

My mouth fell open as I absorbed this bit of information. "How?"

She gave me a sardonic look. "I'm pretty sure you know how that happens. I should hope so, or you're going to be in for a big surprise when you reach the Fire Temple."

I bit back a frustrated response and asked, "Did my parents know about what I was?"

"Yes."

I nodded slowly as everything I knew about my past realigned. The Dragons had been looking for me all along. My parents really were killed because of me. "But there was never anything special about me. I never had any powers or anything. Not until now."

"Animals have always been drawn to you. You've always had a way with plants and herbs as well. Those are all gifts from the Spirit Goddess."

"What about the healing? That only started recently."

She nodded. "You came into your powers on your twentieth birthday, although you still have a long way to go. After you bond with your mates you'll be able to take on their powers as well." With those words she stood up. "I think that's enough for one night. I'm sure we'll meet again. If you live that long."

She gave me a short nod before stepping back into the forest. I called out, "Wait!" but she had already disappeared. Literally. Leaving me with a few answers, and even more questions than before.

24

KIRA

When I returned to camp I told the guys about my strange visit from Enva, but none of them had any further insight into what she'd said or who she was. For now, she remained a mystery.

And thanks to her, I was stuck with four overprotective men who kept telling me not to wander off by myself again. The tension between them was still there, but they were united under a new purpose: keeping an eye on me at all times. Needless to say, I wasn't thrilled.

"Where are you going?" Slade asked me the next morning, as I walked toward the forest. He was already jumping to his feet and grabbing his axe as if to follow me.

I gave him an exasperated look. "I need to relieve myself. Could I get a tiny bit of privacy?"

Jasin looked up from where he was sharpening his sword. "You shouldn't go anywhere alone."

"For once I agree with Jasin," Auric said. He was jotting notes down in his journal, likely recording everything that had happened yesterday. "One of us should be with you at all times."

I propped my hands on my hips. "Seriously, I'm fine. First of all, I wasn't even in any danger last night, and second of all, I can protect myself."

"We know you can, but it's our duty to protect you," Slade said, his brow furrowing.

Auric nodded. "Exactly. We don't know who or what Enva was. Your encounter with her proves there are forces at work we don't understand, whose interests might not be aligned with ours. We won't know until we learn more."

"Don't follow me. I mean it!" I snapped, before storming into the forest without looking back to see if they listened. If my infuriating men wanted to chase after me, that was their problem. I couldn't live my entire life making sure one of them was guarding me at all times.

I took care of my business quickly, just in case they *were* watching, then headed back toward camp. I caught sight of Reven standing in front of a stream, making the water rise and fall in front of him, almost like it was dancing.

I sighed. "Did they send you to keep an eye on me?"

"Hardly." The water stopped moving immediately as he turned toward me with a scowl.

I gestured toward the stream. "Good to see you're practicing. You should train with the others too sometime."

He gave me a scathing look. "No thanks. I have no interest in keeping these powers."

I blinked at him. "Are you still planning to leave?"

"I am."

I'd thought he had changed his mind after all we'd been through. And with everything else already frustrating me, this was the last straw. I gestured into the forest angrily. "Why don't you go then? No one's stopping you."

"None of you would survive a day without me." He shook his head with disdain. "Besides, I can't leave. The Gods saw to that. But I'll find a way."

"Good luck with that," I tossed over my shoulder as I stomped off through the woods, even more annoyed than I'd been before. I didn't even glance at the other men when I entered camp again, just grabbed my bow and quiver and stalked back into the forest. Target practice. That's what I needed.

Once I was in place, I pulled the bow taut and released an arrow. It flew true and struck the tree in exactly the spot I'd intended, a little round knot in the trunk. As the arrow vibrated against the wood, I drew another one and prepared to shoot again.

"Not bad," Jasin said, as he approached me through the trees.

I arched an eyebrow at him, then released my arrow without even looking at my target. It struck the tree in nearly the same spot. "Not bad?"

"You're definitely good, I'll give you that."

"You think you can do better?" I asked.

With a cocky smile, he pulled his own bow off his back and drew an arrow. With lightning fast movements, he fired into the tree, his own red-tipped arrow nearly on top of mine. As I watched, he fired three more times, forming a circle around my own arrows. What a show off.

Not to be outdone, I released my own volley, splitting each one of his arrows in half with my own. I turned to him with a wry smile.

"Let's call it a draw," he said, with a wink.

"If you insist," I said, shaking my head.

He gestured at my waist. "How's that new sword? You any good with it?"

"Getting there." I put my bow down on a tall rock and drew my blade. It fit perfectly in my hand and the weight was ideal for my size, although it was much smaller than Jasin's.

He drew his own sword. "Let's see what you've got."

I lunged for him, but he was fast, even with his heavier weapon. Our blades clashed, the ringing of metal echoing through the forest as we exchanged blows. I was sure he was holding back, especially knowing how strong he was, but it was good practice for me anyway. And as we fought, my tension and frustration slowly melted away.

"You favor your right side," he said. "Be careful of that."

I nodded and made a mental adjustment, then slashed out at him. He did a quick swirling maneuver and the next thing I knew my sword was sticking out of the ground a few feet away. Then he grabbed me from behind, his free arm across my chest, holding me tight against him. I nearly fought back, but then his lips were on my neck, and all the fight left me.

"So easy to let down your guard?" he asked, as his teeth nipped at my earlobe. "Or maybe you wanted me to catch you?"

I stomped on his foot and pushed away from him, but all he did was laugh. Breathing heavily, I used his moment of distraction to knock his sword away. Then we were fighting hand to hand, blocking each other's blows, although he was so much more experienced than I was that it was hardly a fair fight.

He knocked me off my feet, but I brought him down with me onto the forest floor. We tumbled over until I found myself on top of him, staring down at him as he laughed again.

"If you wanted to get on top of me, there are easier ways," he said, as his hands rested on my waist.

I gazed into his eyes, my heart beating fast, and not just from our fight. "Don't read too much into this."

"No? This is the second time we've been on the ground together. Although last time I was on top. You'll have to tell me which position you prefer."

I pushed on his chest to stand up, but he caught my wrists and pulled me back to him. The anger from before quickly turned to passion as our mouths found each other for a smoldering kiss. All I could think about was his firm body beneath mine and the way his arms circled my back to hold me against him like he never wanted to let go.

"Kira?" Auric called out from somewhere in the distance.

Jasin broke off our kiss and released me. "As much as I'd like to continue this, I think our companions are calling us."

Reality came crashing back in and I sat up, feeling dazed. I brushed leaves off myself. "Right. We should get going."

Jasin rose to his feet and offered me a hand, then pulled me close for one more kiss. "We'll continue this later."

The other three men were already on their horses and gave us looks that showed they knew exactly what we were doing. I tried not to let it get to me. Jasin would be the first to have me, and there was nothing I could do about that. Only Auric was even trying to stake his claim, so what did Slade and Reven have to be upset about?

I decided to ride with Slade, hoping it would stop some of the jealous looks. As usual, his quiet, calm strength made me feel better, as if just being near him soothed all the anxious thoughts swirling in my mind. I also found it easy to talk to him, much more so than any of the others.

"Slade, is there a magical bond tying you to me now? Or could you leave if you wanted?" I asked, as I remembered Reven's words.

"I don't know," he said, in that low, grumbly voice I found so sexy. "Originally, we had this overwhelming urge to find you, but that passed once we met. I suspect any of us could leave now, but maybe not after we're officially bound together."

I nodded slowly. If Slade was right, then Reven could have left at any time. He was simply using the magic as an excuse. Maybe a tiny part of him wanted to be here after all.

As we rode, the landscape began to change. The forest thinned out around us, the trees becoming sparse and the ground becoming harder. I'd heard much of the Air Realm was a desert, but we wouldn't go very far into it, luckily. At least not yet.

To avoid the border crossing—where the Onyx Guard soldiers might give us trouble—Jasin had us go out of our way over some steep hills that our horses were not happy about in the slightest. The off-road terrain slowed us down and it felt like we were making no progress at all, until we were officially in the Air Realm.

Slade's horse threw a shoe only a few minutes later, and we were forced to stop at the first village we found. None of us thought it was safe to do so, but we didn't have much choice, and luckily the place was small enough that there were few soldiers in it. Slade immediately took the horse to the local blacksmith, while the rest of us went to find rooms for the evening.

The inn was mostly empty and much smaller than the one we'd stayed in the other night, which suited us fine. The fewer people who saw us, the better.

"We'd like a room for the evening," Jasin said to the innkeeper, a stout man with a moustache.

"Of course. We have many rooms available. How many will you need?"

Jasin glanced back at Auric, who said, "Two, I think."

The innkeeper nodded as he scanned our group. But then he paused and his eyes widened. He suddenly dropped to one knee, bowing his head. "Your highness! I'm sorry, I didn't recognize you at first. Please forgive me, Prince Tanariel."

I stared at him in confusion, until I realized who he was addressing.

Auric.

25

AURIC

I knew we should never have stopped in the Air Realm.

I cleared my throat, trying not to show my panic. "You must be mistaken. I'm not Prince Tanariel, I simply bear a passing resemblance to him. Please stand up."

The innkeeper slowly rose to his feet and lowered his voice. "Of course. Your secret is safe with me, your highness."

I pinched the bridge of my nose. "Please don't call me that."

"My apologies." He clapped his hands together and smiled at the group. "Now then. You'll have the finest rooms available, and I'll make sure some food and wine is brought up for you. Is there anything else I can do for you?"

"That will be great, thanks," Jasin said, as he glared at me. He already hated me, and now he had even more reason. Not that I was particularly fond of him either, but I didn't want to fight with him, for Kira's sake at least.

And Kira... she gaped at me like she'd never seen me before. My gut twisted with guilt and shame from deceiving her, even if I had a good reason for keeping my identity hidden. Now that my secret was out, would she look at me differently, knowing who I truly was?

The innkeeper showed us to two of his best rooms, which meant they were slightly larger and cleaner than the others, before apologizing again and promising to have someone bring up some refreshments. I pressed a coin into his hand and assured him all was well.

The second he was gone, Kira turned to me with narrowed eyes and asked, "You're a prince? I thought you said you were only a distant relation!"

I sighed. "I said I was no one of consequence in the family, which is true."

"I don't think being fifth in line to the throne of the Air Realm counts as inconsequential," she snapped.

"I can explain everything," I said quickly.

"Better get started, Auric," Jasin said, crossing his arms. "Or should we call you Prince Tanariel? Is Auric even your name?"

I pinched the bridge of my nose. "It's my middle name. No one calls me Tanariel. That was my grandfather, not me."

"So you really are a prince," Kira said.

I met her eyes. "Yes, I am."

"I'm surprised none of you recognized him," Reven said from the corner, where he was flipping one of his knives.

"You knew who he was all along?" Kira asked, growing visibly more upset. "And you never thought to mention he was a prince at any point?"

Reven shrugged. "Not my problem."

"It's all of our problems," Jasin said. "Auric was going to be recognized sooner or later, which puts all of us at risk. He should have told us long before we got to the Air Realm."

"Yes, he should have," Kira said.

Before I could respond she threw open the door and stomped out. Silently cursing myself for being an idiot, I started to follow after her, but Slade blocked me in the doorway.

"What's going on?" he asked, sounding weary.

"Auric is a prince of the Air Realm," Jasin explained in a low growl.

Without waiting for Slade's response, I darted after Kira, who had slipped into the other bedroom reserved for us. I closed the door behind me and faced her. "Kira, I know you're upset, and you have every right to be. But please let me try to explain."

"You lied to me," she said, in a way that made my heart twist.

"I didn't lie, not once. Everything I told you was true, I simply... omitted certain things."

She sat down on the edge of one of the beds. "Some really big things. Things you should have told me."

I sat beside her. "Probably, yes. But you have to understand that when this started I had no idea who you or the others were. I didn't know if I could trust any of you. Telling people I'm a prince is like putting a target on my back. Not to mention, people treat me differently once they know who—what—I am. I didn't want that to happen with you, Kira. I wanted you to get to know me as you would any other man, not as a prince. And after everyone's reaction to me being a nobleman, can you blame me for being hesitant to reveal the truth?"

"I understand why you didn't tell me at first, but don't you trust me now?" she asked.

"I do, yes. And I was going to tell you at the right moment, I promise."

She raised an eyebrow. "When was that going to be?"

"Um." I swallowed the lump in my throat. "Before we reached the Air Temple, for sure."

She sighed. "I just don't know how I can trust you anymore."

"I'm sorry I kept this from you, but please try to understand. I'm the youngest prince, with enough older siblings to make sure I'll never be king. In my family, I'm the odd one out who was always in the library instead of attending balls and dealing with politics. I never cared about any of that and so to them I've always been inconsequential. So yes, I am a prince, but at the same time, nothing about me has changed."

She nodded slowly. "Are you hiding anything else from me?"

"Not exactly," I said. "There's nothing I am *hiding*. Simply things I haven't chosen to share yet. Surely you can understand that. There are lots of things you haven't told us either, and I don't see you getting upset with Reven for not sharing all the details of his past. But in time, I'll be willing to open up completely."

She blew out a breath. "Okay, I see your point."

"Thank you. I truly had no wish to deceive you, I just wanted to make sure my place in the group was more stable before I told everyone."

"Why wouldn't it be stable?"

I cleared my throat and looked away. "I've been reminded many times that I don't fit in with the rest of you."

"Ignore the others." She leaned against my side. "I want you to stay, and that's all that matters."

"You do?" I took her hand in mine. "Because I have no desire to leave either. This is my life now." I slowly ran my thumbs along her knuckles. "That's another reason I didn't mention I was a prince. In my mind, I no longer am one. I gave up that life and that title when I left home to find you."

"Do you regret leaving all of that behind?"

"Not one bit. I'm your mate and one day I'll be the Golden Dragon. That is more than I ever dreamed of, and all I could ever want."

She melted into my embrace and our lips found each other easily. Kissing Kira was the most amazing thing I'd ever experienced. When we touched, sparks danced between us, but when we kissed, our connection flashed like a burst of lightning. I could only imagine what it would be like after we'd officially bonded.

Her hand rested on my thigh as she moved even closer, and the sensation shot straight to my groin. I groaned as I pulled her flush against me, my fingers digging into her hips as I took the kiss deeper. This woman, Gods. She was gorgeous, but that wasn't why I cared for her so much already. It was her intelligence, her kindness, and her inner strength that had won me over. Even now, she accepted me for who I truly was, despite my mistake of not telling her the truth sooner. How had I gotten so lucky to end up as one of her mates? When I met the Air God again, I'd be sure to thank him for choosing me.

Her hands stroked my jaw, but she finally pulled away. "Come on. Let's go calm the others down."

When we went into the other room, she held my hand, even though the other men eyed me warily. "All right," Kira said, as she glanced between them. "Auric was a prince once, but he's one of us now, and that's all that matters."

Jasin frowned and looked away, while Reven shrugged as if he couldn't care less. Slade said, "Fine with me."

"I know this isn't easy for any of us, and I can't expect all of you to get along, but please try at least." She looked between me and Jasin. "For me."

"Fine," he muttered.

"Of course," I said, squeezing her hand.

A knock sounded on the door, and the innkeeper and a young woman brought in large trays of food with two bottles of wine. If nothing else, at least we'd be well fed tonight. I still wasn't thrilled my true identity had been revealed this way, but at least the weight had been lifted off my shoulders and I didn't have to keep it from Kira anymore. Of course, once we got closer to the Air Temple, I'd have to reveal some of the other things I was afraid to admit—but hopefully she would accept those parts of me too.

26

KIRA

As we continued through the rolling hills of the Air Realm, passing a few farms but little else, I thought back on what had happened the night before. Auric was a *prince*. Even now it was hard to wrap my head around the idea. It was even harder to accept that he had given all that up to be with me.

I wasn't happy that he'd kept something this huge from me, but I also didn't blame him. I understood his reasons, even if I didn't like them. And it's not like the other guys were all that forthright about their pasts either. Nor was I, for that matter. But I was beginning to think the only way we'd get through this was if we started trusting each other.

Easier said than done, of course.

My thoughts were interrupted when I began to smell smoke. We were moving through a large field of wheat, and I noticed black smoke rising in the distance to our left. A bonfire? I hoped that was all it was, but we didn't really have time to stop, especially when it was probably nothing.

A piercing, inhuman shriek tore through the air, one I hadn't heard in seven years. I was suddenly doused in pure terror, as if a bucket of ice water had been dumped over my head. My arms tightened around Reven's chest as he pulled our horse to a stop and reached for one of his knives.

"What was that?" Auric asked.

"A Dragon," I whispered.

Then it appeared. Through the black smoke, the beast rose up on his giant, blood red wings. Sark, the Crimson Dragon. The monster who had haunted my nightmares for much of my life.

The others tensed, but there was nowhere we could run—we were out in the open, too far from anywhere we could hide. If we had to fight Sark with our weapons and our magic, would we even stand a chance?

But Sark didn't even glance our way. With a great flap of wings that sent the smoke billowing away, he cast one last breath of fire on whatever was below him before flying off toward the west, his tail whipping behind him. Within seconds, he was only a dark speck in the sky, and then he was gone.

Reven suddenly kicked his horse into action and charged us forward, toward the smoke. I was torn between telling him to run the opposite direction and yelling for him to hurry. The others followed right at our heels as we made it through the wheat field and burst out onto a farm. The smoke was stronger here, and soon I spotted flames flickering up ahead.

A small house in the middle of the farm was completely on fire. Many of the flames had already begun to spread to the surrounding fields as well. Reven immediately summoned water and doused the field to stop it from being engulfed, then leaped off his horse and called forth even more water to work on the house.

I tumbled off the horse as well, but all I could do was stare at the flames in horror. There was no screaming, but the air smelled of burnt flesh, just as it had when I was a child. I was trapped inside my bleakest memory and my worst nightmare and there was no escape.

When the others arrived, I could only wrap my arms around myself and shake as they tried to stop the fire too. Jasin managed the flames as best he could and tried to coax them to die down. Auric calmed the wind and sucked the air from the fire. Slade covered the house in dirt and soil. But it was Reven who did the most, as he called down wave after wave to douse the raging inferno.

I wished there was something more I could do, but at the same time I was relieved that I didn't have to get any closer. Seeing this happen again was bad enough. Getting near the flames would have been impossible. Even standing at a safe distance, I was trembling and struggling to breathe, and not just from the smoke. How was I supposed to bond with Jasin, knowing it would turn him into a dragon like Sark? Or that it would give me these dark powers too?

I wasn't sure how long it took for the men to put out the fire, but it seemed like an eternity. By the time they were done, the house was little more than a charcoal ruin, and if anyone had been inside, there was no way they could have survived. Bile rose up in my throat at the thought of charred, blackened bodies, like my parents had once become. No matter how hard I tried, I would never be able to scrub that image from my brain.

One by one the men returned to my side, all of them covered in black soot with sweat running down their faces, looking as haunted as I felt.

"Why would he do this?" Auric asked with a weary voice.

Slade leaned against his horse and wiped his face. "This is what the Dragons do to anyone suspected of being in the Resistance."

"Were there people inside?" I asked, though I almost didn't want to know the answer.

Jasin dropped his head. "We were too late to save them."

I nodded, as tears pricked my eyes. I tried to blink them away, but it was no use. Another family had been snuffed out by Sark. Jasin moved close and tried to wrap an arm around me, but I pushed him away.

"Don't touch me," I said, stepping back. "You're going to be the Crimson Dragon soon. The same as him."

"I'm nothing like Sark," Jasin said in a rush. "You have to know that."

I shook my head. I knew I wasn't making sense, but all I could think about was Jasin summoning flames like Sark. Flames which could be used to destroy lives, like they had done today. Like they had done to my family all those years ago.

"Just leave me alone," I said, as I stumbled into the wheat field.

Memories of my family's death crowded my head as I ran. The flames. The screams. The smells. Oh Gods, the smells. The same smells that lingered in the air now.

I had to get away.

27

REVEN

"I'm going after her," Jasin said, already charging forth into the field.

Slade caught the soldier's shoulder. "Don't. You're the last person she wants to see right now."

Jasin's brow furrowed. "But why? I'm not the one who set that house on fire. I would never do anything like that!"

"She knows that, but she's not thinking clearly right now. Just give her some space."

"Fine," Jasin said, slumping against a broken cart. "I just hate seeing her upset."

"We all do," Auric said.

While they stood around moping, I slipped between the trees, needing space of my own. Like Kira, the sight and smell of that fire, plus that cursed dragon in the sky, had brought back a lot of painful memories. Now I wanted nothing more than to get away from this place and wash the soot and ash off my hands and clothes.

I'd tried my best to put out the fire. I'd done what I could to save the people inside. But I'd failed. Just like I'd failed when I was a child and couldn't save my family from Sark's fire. Except now it was worse, because I could summon water. But my magic still wasn't enough.

It was a stark reminder that I shouldn't be here. I was no hero. Most of my life I'd been a villain. That wasn't going to change. The sooner I left, the better it would be for everyone.

I spotted Kira ahead of me, crumpled on the ground, and found myself making my way over to her even though I knew it was a bad idea.

Not only because she needed some space, but because I didn't want to get involved with her. I had to keep my distance so I could easily leave when the time came. But I couldn't ignore the sight of her back hunched over in the dirt, knowing she was in as much pain as I was.

She looked up with a start as I emerged from the wheat beside her, then let out a sad laugh. "You're the last person I would have expected to come find me."

I crossed my arms. "Don't get the wrong idea. I'm not here to comfort you."

She wiped at her eyes. "Then why are you here?"

"I couldn't stand to listen to your boyfriends bicker anymore so I went for a walk. I just happened to stumble across you here."

"I see," she said, although she didn't sound convinced. She was no longer crying though, and instead regarded me with a curious expression on her face. "You could have kept walking."

I gave a casual shrug. "I like this spot."

The slightest hint of a smile crossed her lips. "Me too."

For the next few minutes she wiped at her soot-streaked face and stared off into the fields, while her breathing slowed and her shoulders relaxed. I stood near her in companionable silence, though I had to fight the urge to wrap my arms around her and tell her everything would be okay. She didn't need my pity or my comfort, anyway. She was already strong and brave and didn't want someone to save her. She simply needed a few moments to remember all that.

When she rose to her feet, she was steady again. "Thank you."

"For what?" I asked.

"For being here with me." She moved close and pressed a hand against my black leather jerkin, looking up at me with those intriguing eyes. "For letting me have a moment to calm down while still showing me I wasn't alone."

"You're reading way too much into my actions." I should really move away. I didn't.

"Maybe so," she said, but then she slid her arms around my chest.

My entire body stiffened at her touch. It took me a moment to realize she was *hugging* me, of all things. Gods, when was the last time someone had hugged me? I couldn't even remember. Was it my parents, before the Crimson Dragon had taken them from me? Or was it Mara, before she was killed?

My throat grew tight as emotions I tried to keep tramped down suddenly flooded me. My grief and pain at seeing the burning house and the Crimson Dragon must mirror Kira's own, and maybe on some level she sensed that. Though I couldn't talk about it, and wasn't sure I would ever be able to, I understood more than anyone what she was going through.

My arms came up of their own will and circled her, pulling her tighter against my chest. She breathed out a light sigh and softened into my embrace, resting her head on my shoulder. Time melted away as we held each other, and a terrible yearning filled me as I slowly ran my fingers through her hair. For a few seconds, I imagined what it would be like if I let myself become one of her mates and could hold her like this anytime.

Startled by that train of thought, I pulled away abruptly and stepped back to put some distance between us. I'd let myself feel too much, but that was over now. I locked all those emotions away in the dark recesses of my mind, until I was calm and cool again, like ice.

"We should head back before your boyfriends start to miss you," I said.

I turned away and began walking toward the others before she could open her mouth and make me stay with the slightest word. She made me feel too much, and that was dangerous. Caring for people made you vulnerable, and emotions made you weak.

I knew that all too well.

28

KIRA

On our seventh day of traveling we finally made it to the Fire Realm. According to Jasin, there was no way to avoid the border crossing here. This part of the Fire Realm was walled off as far as the eye could see, and the only way through was at one of the gates, which were all manned by the Onyx Army.

Jasin donned his black and red uniform, which he still had packed away, and led us to the gate. Onyx Army soldiers in full armor with red markings on their shoulders scrutinized us as we approached. Archers stood on the walls, ready to strike us down if we made a run for it.

A soldier wearing a helmet with red dragon wings on it stepped forward and held up a hand for us to stop. "What is your business in the Fire Realm?" he called out.

"I'm escorting these people to Ashbury," Jasin said.

The soldier removed his helmet. "Jasin, is that you?"

"Gregil?" Jasin flashed him a smile. "Good to see you. What are you doing out here?"

The soldier chuckled softly. "Stuck on border duty for this quarter. You know how it goes."

"That I do." He gestured to the rest of us. "I'm just taking some friends and family to Ashbury to visit my parents."

Gregil nodded. "That shouldn't be a problem, although we need to search through your things."

Jasin groaned. "Do you really? We're in a bit of a rush, and you know me, after all."

"Sorry, General's orders. Shouldn't take long."

We were asked to dismount and step aside, while four soldiers took our horses and began going through all of our things. Every muscle in my body turned into a tight knot as I watched them, though I couldn't think of anything suspicious we might be carrying. As they searched, Jasin moved to the side to speak quietly with Gregil. Reven crossed his arms and pretended not to care, but I sensed a tension in him, as if he could snap into action at a moment's notice. Auric looked worried, and I wondered if he was scared they might find his journal. Slade, on the other hand, seemed far too calm considering the situation.

"You sure have a lot of weapons for ordinary travelers," a female soldier said, giving us a suspicious look.

"Can't be too careful these days," Slade said casually. "There are bandits everywhere. Especially in the Earth Realm."

She sniffed. "Maybe so. In the Fire Realm we take care of threats like that so our roads are safe."

Slade smiled at her like they were good friends. "So I've heard. Hence why I'm moving here."

The soldier nodded at that as if it made perfect sense and continued her search, but her suspicions seemed to have eased thanks to Slade. But as we waited, I heard someone shout behind us, and a man yell, "No, please!"

I turned toward the sound, where a young man was being dragged off a horse by another soldier. The man cried out again, but the sound cut short when the soldier thrust a sword into his throat. My eyes bulged and my own hand went to my neck in response. I'd heard the Onyx Army was especially brutal in the Fire Realm, like the Dragon they served, but it was different witnessing it in person.

"A thief," the female soldier said. "Got what he deserved."

"Naturally," Slade said, though his voice had shifted, becoming harder.

As the man's blood stained the road beneath us, I forced myself to turn away. There was nothing we could do for him. Even if we'd tried to help, that would only have gotten us killed too. But knowing that was little comfort.

When they finally let us go, we mounted our horses again and were allowed to move through the gates. On the other side I saw all the preparations to defend against elementals, but also spotted more dried blood and smelled a whiff of death. I could only relax again once the gate was far behind us.

The land here was flat, with great plains that spread as far as the eye could see and an endless sky full of large, fluffy clouds. Far in the distance I could barely make out the mountains where we were headed. The Fire Temple was located at a large volcano on the other side of those tall peaks, and Auric estimated we should be there in two more days.

None of us knew what to expect when we reached the temples. Though the Gods were still worshipped in theory, most people had forgotten about them over the years, and instead had begun to worship and fear the Dragons. We knew the Dragons got their powers from the Gods, but the Gods were distant and immaterial, while the Dragons were things we could see, hear, and fear. Few people made the pilgrimage to the five temples anymore, though Auric said that there were still priests tending to each one. Hopefully they would be able to give us a little more guidance or offer some much-needed answers.

As we approached the mountains, the plains turned rockier and the sky turned dark with thick, black clouds. I pulled my hood over my head just as rain began to fall. The spring shower was cool and refreshing after a long day of travel, until it turned into a heavy downpour that soaked us all through.

"I thought the Fire Realm would be warmer," Slade muttered, from where he sat in front of me.

"We need to get out of this," Auric said. "We should make for the town at the base of the mountains."

Jasin frowned as he glanced in the direction of the town. "That's Ashbury. Not a good idea. Someone might recognize me there. Plus, it's a pretty large city, second only to the capital of the Fire Realm, Flamedale."

Auric spread his hands. "We can't exactly camp out in this."

Jasin snorted. "Sure we can. What, not good enough for a prince?"

Auric glared at Jasin, while the rain continued to pummel us. The only one who didn't seem to mind it was Reven, who somehow remained dry through it all, like the water simply flowed around him. Having his powers would definitely come in handy right now.

"It wouldn't hurt to get supplies and a decent night's sleep before we set off for the Fire Temple," I said.

"More supplies?" Reven asked skeptically.

"Food, specifically. You guys eat as much as a small village. We're going to need a lot of it since Jasin says the land around the volcano is basically inhospitable."

Slade dismounted and placed his hand flat on the ground. When he straightened up, he shook his head. "There's no other shelter around here."

"To Ashbury it is," I said.

We ducked our heads and headed deeper into the storm with the promise of a hot meal and a warm bed urging us on. None of us spoke as our horses plowed through the storm, as eager to get out of it as we were.

By the time we got to Ashbury my clothes were completely soaked through. This city was one of the larger ones I'd seen and had a massive stone wall around it, along with a wide moat and fiery brazier burning bright every few feet, even in this downpour. Not to mention, a whole lot of soldiers.

By some luck, the guards—who looked as miserable as we were to be out in the rain—waved us through the gate without even inspecting us. I tensed as we passed through the metal entry, worried we'd encounter some trouble, but we made it into Ashbury without incident. The city was full of great stone structures with pointed, sharp architecture, but the streets were nearly empty at the moment.

As soon as we made it fully inside the town's walls, the rain fizzled out.

"Figures," Jasin said. "Should we keep going or stop here?"

"I'm not sure," Auric said.

"It could start up again at any moment," Reven said, gazing at the sky.

"Not sure about you, but I trust the water guy," Slade said.

"Let's stop," I said. It was still early and we were making today's progress even slower, but if it started pouring again we would be caught in it. Besides, we really did need more food—I couldn't believe how much these four men ate.

We found a quiet inn that wasn't on a main road where we could stop for the night and not draw too much attention. We left our horses there, but it was too early to eat or sleep, so we decided to do our shopping now while the sun was returning to the sky and the city was slowly drying off.

We headed for the market, but were slowed by a large crowd forming around a raised platform in what appeared to be the town square. Soldiers in black scaled armor stood watch around the fringes of the crowd, while more walked out onto the stage. Jasin pulled his hood low over his head as we moved between the people looking at whatever was about to happen.

"What's going on?" I asked, straining to see over the crowd around us.

Reven met my eyes, his face grim. "An execution is about to begin."

29

KIRA

My stomach dropped out from under me at Reven's words. As I stared at the platform, I noticed something I'd first missed—a large pyre. They were going to burn someone alive. But who were they executing and why?

Jasin's eyes darted around, his hand resting on his sword. "We should get out of here."

"I agree," Slade said. "Kira shouldn't be here for this."

A huge man stepped onto the platform and loomed over the crowd in his shining armor, the large dragon wings on his helmet flashing under the sun. Unlike the other soldiers, his armor and helmet were blood red.

Jasin swore under his breath. "That's General Voor."

"You know him?" I asked.

"I served under him for two years." He gripped my arm. "We really need to go. Now."

Auric glanced at the soldiers around the edges of the crowd. "It's too late. If we run out of here now it will be suspicious."

On the platform soldiers began dragging out a row of people who were all tied together in a line. They stumbled forward, at least ten of them, both men and women, young and old. One of them couldn't be more than twelve or thirteen, while another looked closer to her sixties.

"These people have all been found guilty of being part of the Resistance," General Voor called out, his voice oddly metallic from behind his helmet. "By order of the Black Dragon they will pay for their crimes. With fire."

I watched in horror as each prisoner was moved toward the pyre and tied to stakes rising out of it. The young boy stumbled and fell, and a woman I assumed was his mother jerked toward him to help. A soldier pushed her back hard, while another one roughly shoved the child toward the fire pit. The crowd remained hushed the entire time, although I caught a few people silently crying into their hands, while others nodded in support at the General. The soldiers glared at us from the sidelines the entire time, ready to step in if anyone got out of line.

"We have to help them," I blurted out, surprising even myself.

"We can't," Jasin set, his jaw clenched. "I don't like this any more than you do, but if we get involved we'll only put ourselves in danger."

"But we have to do something!"

"We can't. We'll expose who we are and likely get ourselves killed in the process."

"I'm with Jasin," Reven said. "We need to stay out of this and lay low. Besides, it's not our fight."

"Of course it is!" I turned to Slade and Auric. "Surely you don't also think we should just stand here and watch these people die?"

Slade stroked his beard slowly as he considered. "I agree we should help them, but only if we can get you out safely first."

I huffed. "I'm not going anywhere."

His green eyes met mine. "Kira, I don't like this any more than you do, but my responsibility is to protect you first."

"I'm going to help them whether you join me or not. So if you want to protect me, I suggest you stick by my side."

Auric eyed the platform as if it were a puzzle to solve. "Is there a way to rescue them while making sure we all get out alive and don't reveal our powers?"

"I don't know," I said. "But this is why we were given these powers. To stop the Black Dragon and her followers."

Jasin ran a ragged hand through his short, damp hair. "Maybe so, but we're not strong enough yet, and there are too many soldiers. And trust me, we do not want to get General Voor's attention. "

"We need to create a diversion," Auric said. "Jasin can set something on fire to distract the soldiers, and then we'll go in."

"This is a really bad idea," Reven muttered.

I gave him a sharp look. "Then come up with a better one, because we're doing this with or without your help."

"Fine." Jasin glanced around, as if checking where we were. "This city has underground tunnels that the Resistance use to get around. There's an entrance behind that shop over there."

"Where do the tunnels go?" Reven asked.

"To different parts of the city, but also beyond the walls."

"How do you know all this?" Auric asked.

Jasin hesitated. "That doesn't matter right now."

Determination crackled within me as the plan came together in my head. "So we distract the guards, free the prisoners, and get them to the tunnels, where we should be able to escape?"

"Exactly," Jasin said.

"Oh, is that all?" Reven asked sardonically, shaking his head.

"Are you sure you want to do this?" Slade asked me.

I swallowed and glanced at the prisoners on the platform, who were now all tied to the stakes and awaiting their fate. All my life I'd stayed out of trouble and kept my head down in order to survive. I'd never wanted to fight for a cause or overthrow an empire, I'd just wanted to survive another day. But if I was supposed to save the world from the Black Dragon, I couldn't hide in the shadows forever. Not if I wanted to fight for what was right.

My back straightened with resolve. "Yes, I'm sure. The Gods chose us so we could bring balance back to the world. It's time we started doing that."

"If we're going to do this, we need to hurry," Slade said, his face grim. "They're lighting the pyres now."

"Cover your faces and get to the prisoners. I'll cause a distraction." Jasin ripped some fabric off his shirt sleeve and tied it around his face to cover everything below his nose. Then he raised his hood again, so that all I could see were his eyes.

I wrapped my arms around him and gave him a quick squeeze. "Be careful."

He rested his forehead against mine briefly. "You too."

"We'll keep her safe," Slade said, resting a hand on my back.

Jasin gave him a nod, before slipping into the crowd. We covered our faces like he'd done and started toward the stage, weaving around the people in front of us.

Someone shouted as an empty cart in the middle of the crowd went up in flames. Panic spiked in my chest, even though I knew it was Jasin's distraction, and I forced myself to stay calm. People around us began screaming and pushing to get away from the fire, while soldiers rushed forward to investigate. I prayed Jasin could get away safely.

Unfortunately, the soldiers on the platform barely paused. General Voor instructed a few soldiers to deal with the blaze, but that still left half a dozen more, including the one setting fire to the pyre where the prisoners stood. With the twitch of his hand, Auric created a heavy gust around the pyre which repeatedly put the fire out, while we continued forcing our way through the crowd. But the soldiers were relentless, and eventually they got a true blaze going.

We were still too far from the platform and I worried we'd be too late, but then Reven raised his hand and water suddenly began to fall from the sky over the prisoners. If I didn't know better I'd think rain was pouring down, even if it was isolated to one location.

As the pyre's flames were doused, the General scowled. "Curse this weather," he said, as he drew his sword. "We'll have to deal with these traitors another way."

As the other guards readied their weapons, Slade let out a low growl, and then the ground beneath the platform began to shake. I held onto his arm to remain steady, while people around us screamed and tried to flee from the sudden earthquake.

The soldiers and the prisoners both crumpled to their feet as the wooden platform broke apart with a huge crack and collapsed to the ground. The four of us rushed into the broken wood, trying not to injure ourselves on the splintered pieces. The prisoners were all still tied to their stakes and had landed at awkward angles, but a quick glance showed they were still alive.

Auric and I began freeing the prisoners, using our swords to cut through their bindings, while Slade and Reven guarded our backs as the soldiers got to their feet. The General tried to stand as well, but Auric knocked him back with a strong blast of air.

"Come with us!" I shouted to the prisoners, once they were free. I counted twelve of them total, some a little scorched and others bruised or cut, but alive. They stumbled after me off the ruined platform, looking dazed and scared, but at least they kept moving. Auric, Reven, and Slade formed a circle around us, fighting off the soldiers who tried to attack us.

The crowd had thinned between the fire and the earthquake, and those few people who were left didn't stop us as we pushed through them. I led the prisoners toward the shop Jasin had pointed out, hoping we were going in the right direction, especially since more soldiers were starting to rush after us.

I spotted Jasin on the corner of the street ahead of us and nearly cried out with relief that he was safe. He waved us forward and called out, "Hurry!"

Jasin led our ragged group into an alley in the back of the shops, where he shoved a large flower pot aside to reveal a metal grate in the ground. He yanked the grate open, and I gestured for the prisoners to go in first, while my other mates moved to fight off the approaching soldiers.

"Get inside, quickly!" Jasin said, as he helped the prisoners down into the hole. "Kira, you too."

I started toward him, but then I saw Reven cornered against the wall, fighting five soldiers at once, including General Voor. My assassin moved like a dancer, a swirl of black clothing and blades, but even with all of his deadly skill there were too many of them, and their armor was hard to penetrate. The General's sword slashed Reven's thigh, making him fall back against the wall, and terror gripped my throat.

I drew my sword and plunged it into the back of the soldier closest to me, desperate to save Reven before it was too late. I fought off the next soldier and threw myself in front of Reven before the General could run him through with his sword. My blade met the General's and I stared into his rage-filled eyes under that red winged helmet, before he knocked the sword from my hand with his massive strength.

Reven suddenly grabbed me and shoved me behind him, as he brought up his twin blades to fight General Voor again. He managed to force the man back, and then a huge rumble sounded above us. A gust of wind knocked me and Reven back, as part of the shop beside us split apart and crumbled, forming a wall of rubble between us and General Voor. Slade and Auric stood behind us, and had likely just saved our lives.

"Come on!" Jasin grabbed my arm and dragged me toward the tunnels, with the others right behind us. Auric helped Reven, who was limping, but then an arrow fired from somewhere and struck my prince in the shoulder, making him cry out. My heart twisted at the sound, but he didn't slow.

One by one we dropped into the tunnels, where the prisoners were waiting for us in the darkness. Slade was last, and once we were all safe he caused the ground to close up above us, preventing the soldiers from following—and trapping us inside.

30
SLADE

J asin lit a torch, illuminating a lot of scared faces. "Is everyone all right?"

"I think so," the older woman said. Everyone hovered behind her, and I got the sense she was their leader.

Kira inspected the gash on Reven's leg with a frown, but he brushed her away. "I'm okay," he said.

She rested her hands on his thigh, near the wound, likely healing him as best she could. "You're not. We need to patch you up as soon as we get somewhere safe." She turned to Auric next to inspect the arrow in his shoulder.

"Thank you for saving us. My name is Daka." The older woman tilted her head as she watched us. "Are you part of the Resistance also?"

Kira hesitantly glanced at the four of us. "I suppose we are."

Daka nodded slowly. "The Gods must be on our side. They helped us escape with the wind and the rain and that earthquake."

"Plus the cart on fire," Jasin added, with a grin.

"Yes, of course. We must not forget the Fire God for watching over us in our time of need."

The other prisoners nodded, and while they'd previously looked defeated, now hope shone in their eyes. None of them knew we had caused all of those things, which was a good sign that the soldiers didn't either. And I supposed in a way we were there on behalf of the Gods.

"But where will we go?" a man asked. He had his arm around a woman who leaned against him. "Nowhere in Ashbury will be safe for us now."

"We'll have to leave the city," the woman at his side said.

"There's a Resistance hideout about a day's ride north from here," I said. I never thought I'd get involved with the Resistance again, but it seemed my life was inevitably tied to them. "I can draw you a map."

Kira's eyebrows shot up and I knew she had questions for me, but they would have to wait. Auric pulled out his map and some paper from his journal, and while Jasin hovered over me with his torch for light, I sketched out what I remembered. What the woman I'd loved once had shown me on her own map, all those nights ago.

I handed Daka the map. "I hope this helps."

She examined it under the light. "Thank you. I think we'll be able to find this. We truly owe all of you our lives and so much more."

Jasin removed the fabric from around his mouth and used it to wipe his face. "Come on. They'll find another way in to these tunnels soon, so we need to keep moving."

A young woman suddenly gasped and stepped back. "You. You're the soldier who killed my brother!" She pressed her back against the stone wall of the tunnel, her face pale. "He's one of them! The Onyx Army. He's going to turn us in!"

Kira stared at Jasin, who was grimacing, but then spoke quietly to the hysterical woman. "Yes, he was once part of the Onyx Army, but he's one of us now. I swear we're only trying to help you. And we need to get going."

"Come," Daka said, taking the other woman's hand. "What's past is past. Let's find our way to safety now so we have a future."

The younger woman stared at Jasin with terror in her eyes, but with some reluctance she nodded. Jasin's shoulders slumped when she finally turned away.

Our group walked slowly down the narrow tunnels after Jasin, who seemed to know where he was going. Reven's limp slowed him down, and when I moved to help him, I knew it must be pretty bad when he didn't protest my aid. Kira looked over with concerned eyes as the assassin leaned against me. She would be able to heal him, but we needed to make sure the soldiers didn't find us first.

When we reached the first junction, Jasin stopped to consider our location, before leading us down one of the diverging paths.

"Do you know where you're going?" Kira asked.

"Sort of," he said.

"More like getting us more and more lost," Reven muttered.

We walked for what seemed like hours, though it was hard to tell since there was nothing down here but the stone and the darkness. Others might feel claustrophobic in such a place, but not me. I would have been a good miner, but being a blacksmith had always felt like my true calling. Bending metal to my will was my strength even before I'd been given powers. Had I been shaped for this destiny my entire life, or was I chosen because of my affinity for metal and stone? I supposed I would have to ask the Earth God once I met him again.

Jasin stopped again, this time at a place where the tunnel diverged in three separate paths. He frowned, glancing around like he was looking for some clue. "I know it's not the left one, but I can't remember if the middle or the right leads outside the city."

Reven was right, Jasin was going to get us lost, and we didn't have time to waste. I rested my hand against one of the walls and closed my eyes. My senses expanded out and out, along the stone and rock, until a vague map of the tunnels formed in my mind. When I removed my hand and opened my eyes, I began walking down the middle path. "This way."

I guided us through the tunnels, brushing my fingers against the rough stone every now and then to make sure I was on the right path. As the walls grew closer and the air smelled fresher, I knew we were almost there.

At the last junction, I stopped and turned to the Resistance members. "If you follow this tunnel it will take you into the mountains where you should be able to get away."

"Thank you," Daka said, before turning to the rest of my companions. "Thank you all."

She shuffled down the tunnel and into the darkness, with the rest of the Resistance members following her. Once they were gone and I was sure they would make it out okay, I turned to the others. "Should we follow them?"

"We need to get back into the city and get our horses and supplies," Auric said, his voice weak. He was probably in a lot of pain from the arrow in his back.

"That might be dangerous," Jasin said. "Plus, we're on the opposite side of the city now."

"We need to stop somewhere soon," Kira said. "Both Reven and Auric need healing immediately or they won't be able to walk much longer."

"I'm fine," Reven muttered, but he was slumped against me and his face was pale.

Jasin ran a hand across his jaw as he considered. "There might be somewhere we can go near here."

"Somewhere safe?" Kira asked.

"Probably." He started back the way we came.
"Do you know how to get there from here?" I asked.
"Yeah, I know exactly where we are now."
"And where are we going?" Reven asked.
Jasin glanced at him. "Home."

31

KIRA

We emerged from the tunnels into what seemed to be the storeroom for a bakery. The air smelled of fresh bread and something sweet, making my stomach growl, but we didn't have time to delay. Reven and Auric were fading with every second, and while I'd done my best to stop their bleeding and take away the pain, I needed some quiet time with them in a safe place to heal them fully. Assuming I could, of course. My healing powers were still mostly untested and untrained. But I'd do whatever it took to keep them both alive.

As we walked out of the storeroom, the baker gave us a discreet nod, but didn't say a word. Was he with the Resistance too? I'd never thought much about their group when I lived in Stoneham and had always assumed they were somewhere far away, but maybe they'd been around me all along and I never knew it. Including Slade, it seemed. When we had a moment alone, I'd have to ask him how he'd known about the Resistance hideout.

We stepped out of the bakery and into the pouring rain, where night had fallen. As I pulled my hood over my head, Auric slipped and nearly fell, but Jasin caught him and helped him go on. Slade was already supporting most of Reven's weight at this point too. I wished I could do more than simply worrying about them. The streets were empty thanks to the downpour at least.

"Down here," Jasin said, as he turned down a street with a row of houses.

We stopped at the fourth house, which was done in the same sharp style as the others with a pointed roof and red trim. A pink flowering tree stood in front of it, the one cheerful thing in this entire miserable day. Was this Jasin's home? Was I about to meet his parents? Another thing to add to my list of worries.

Jasin paused at the front door as if hesitant, but then knocked on it. A beautiful woman in her forties with long, wavy auburn hair and Jasin's cheekbones opened the door and gasped. "Jasin! What are you doing here?"

"Can we come in?" he asked.

Her dark eyes swept over the rest of us and she opened the door wider. "Of course. Come inside and get dry."

We stepped into the house, which was warm and smelled faintly of a cozy fire. The furniture was dark and utilitarian with few trinkets, except for a sword hanging on one wall and a painting on the other. A chill ran through me when I got a closer look at the painting, which was beautiful even though it depicted the Black Dragon and her four mates sitting on top of a mountain, looking regal as they gazed out at the clouds with sunset hues behind them. It was both stunning to look at and terrifying to see it there.

"This is such a surprise," Jasin's mother said. "We thought you were stationed farther south."

"Jasin? I thought I heard your voice." A man with dark hair streaked with a touch of gray walked into the room. He paused when he saw the rest of us, no doubt an unexpected sight. Four strangers, completely soaked, and two of them injured. I didn't blame him for hesitating.

"Everyone, this is my mother, Ilya, and my father, Ozan. Mom, dad, these are...some friends of mine." Jasin glanced at the rest of us, before turning back to his parents with a grim face. "We're in a bit of trouble and need somewhere to lay low for the evening. Is it okay if we stay here?"

"What kind of trouble?" Ozan asked, his eyes narrowing.

Ilya waved him away. "Of course you can stay. Are you all in the Onyx Army with Jasin?"

"Not exactly," Slade said.

"I'll explain everything, but right now these two are injured and we need to treat their wounds," Jasin said.

"They can use Berin's bedroom," Ilya said.

She led us down a hallway with dark stone floors and opened the first door. We stepped inside a sparse room with a bed big enough for two people and little else. It looked like it hadn't been used in some time, but Ilya pulled out some blankets and pillows and got the bed ready for us.

"Thanks, Mom," Jasin said. "Let's leave them to it and I'll tell you what I've been up to."

With a nod to me and Slade, Jasin escorted his mother out of the room and shut the door behind them. Slade helped me ease Reven and Auric onto the bed, while they both groaned at the movement. It wasn't easy because they were both large, strong men, and their weapons and boots only made it harder.

Auric still had an arrow sticking out of his back, so he had to lie on his stomach. "Heal Reven first," he said, but his voice was weak.

"I'm fine," Reven said, his teeth gritted.

"Hold Auric down," I told Slade. "I'll get the arrow out."

Slade nodded and braced his weight on Auric's shoulders, keeping him in place. I wasn't sure what I was doing, although I'd removed arrows from lots of animals while hunting before, and this couldn't be all that different. I hoped.

I inhaled sharply, then pulled the arrow out with a quick, straight tug. Auric jerked and moaned and blood gushed from the wound. I rested my hand over it quickly to stop the bleeding, but his shirt was in the way. Although the bleeding slowed, I could sense that I needed more skin to skin contact if I was going to heal him fully.

"We need to get this off him," I told Slade, as I tugged at Auric's shirt.

Beside us, Reven had his eyes closed and I hoped he was okay, but I had to help Auric first. With much groaning from Auric, Slade helped me remove his cloak and shirt, along with his weapons, boots, and everything else except his trousers. But Reven was looking really pale too, and I worried he'd lost too much blood already.

"Reven too," I said, and Slade nodded.

We removed most of Reven's clothes as well, and had to slash open his trousers due to the gash on his thigh. I tried not to get distracted by all the muscular, naked flesh in front of me, and instead focused on what I could do to make them both better.

"Get in the bed with them," Slade suggested. "Your touch is what heals them."

Of course. I removed most of my own gear until I was in only my thin chemise, which was better since my clothes were soaked through with blood and water anyway. At first, I felt a touch of shyness at wearing so little around them, although they'd already seen me in my chemise over the last few nights. But then I pushed that feeling aside. These were my mates and they were all going to be seeing a lot of me soon, but more importantly, I didn't care how little I wore because all that mattered was healing Reven and Auric.

I crawled onto the bed between Reven and Auric, while Slade watched. His green eyes seemed to turn almost black as I slid between their bodies, and then he quickly looked away.

"I'll see about getting our horses," he said, his voice husky. He left the room before I could answer.

Was he jealous? Or aroused? I wasn't sure, but I couldn't think about that right now. Both Reven and Auric lay quietly with closed eyes and I couldn't tell if they were awake or not.

I took both of their hands first, working my fingers over their skin. Reven's hand was calloused, Auric's was smooth, and both of them dwarfed mine. I wasn't sure how to make my healing work, so I simply thought about how I wanted them to be healthy again. My feelings burned bright in my chest, surprising me with their intensity. I'd only known the men for a few days, but I already cared for them a great deal.

I wasn't sure if the healing was working and decided I needed to do more. I turned toward Reven, whose face was paler than normal. It was a miracle he'd been able to make it this far, although maybe my healing in the tunnels helped. I examined the wound and hesitated, then placed my hands on his thigh. The remains of his shredded black trousers hid the large bulge between his legs, but only barely. I tried not to stare at it, but my eyes kept finding their way back to that spot.

I pushed everything I felt into my touch as I ran my hands along his naked skin, feeling the hard muscles underneath my fingertips. After a few moments I began to see the wound close up. It was working!

He groaned and turned his head toward me, his eyes focusing on mine. He didn't say a word as I continued stroking his thigh, nor did he stop me when my other hand rested on his neck and moved up into his silky black hair.

"What are you doing to me?" he finally asked.

"Healing you." I trailed my fingers down his cheek and lightly touched his lips. Gods, he was beautiful. I so rarely got to be this close to him, or to stare into his eyes without him turning away. But for once he didn't move.

"Is that all?" he asked.

My breath caught. If I brought my lips to his and kissed him, would he stop me? Or would he kiss me back? If I shifted my hand slightly to brush against that bulge, would he pull away, or touch me in return?

Before I could gather my courage enough to try, he caught my hand in his and his eyes narrowed. "You protected me today and nearly got killed in the process. Don't ever do that again."

I yanked my hand away. "I couldn't let you die."

"I would have been fine. Just as I'm fine now." He rolled onto his side, facing away from me. "Don't trouble yourself further."

I stared at his back, wondering what that was about and trying not to feel rejected. But I didn't have the energy to worry about his behavior, not when Auric needed me too.

I turned to Auric next. His breathing was shallow and the arrow wound on his back—his very well-defined back—was deep. I rested my hands on his shoulder, sighing as our skin touched. As warmth spread from my fingertips, I slowly rubbed his shoulder and ran my hands down his back, spreading my healing to his entire body. Or that's what I told myself anyway. Maybe I just wanted to touch him some more.

His eyes fluttered open and he turned his head to smile at me. "Mm, that's nice."

I removed my hand and looked down at his shoulder, which was now healed up as if it had never been injured at all. "How are you feeling?"

"Like a horse ran over me," he said, with a low chuckle.

"That sounds about right," Reven grumbled.

I settled myself between the two of them, their bodies pressed close against mine. "You both need rest and more healing, so we're going to lie here for a while, since skin to skin contact seems to be what works best."

"I'm not complaining," Auric said, as he rolled on his side and curled up against me. He kissed me, while one of my hands found his naked chest again, savoring the feel of his coiled muscle underneath his smooth skin.

Reven didn't say a word, but he turned onto his other side and stared at me with his dark, dangerous blue eyes. I was so tempted to kiss him, but I wasn't sure he wanted that from me. Instead I rested my hand on his strong chest too, and he reluctantly draped one arm around my waist.

With both men wrapped around me, I closed my eyes and felt a strange sort of contentment settle over me. The overwhelming desire for both of them was there too, but this was more than lust. This felt right, as if they both belonged by my side. The only way it could be better would be if Jasin and Slade were here too.

3 2

KIRA

After both Auric and Reven fell into a deep sleep, I slipped out of bed, donned my clothes again, and quietly left the bedroom. Voices drifted toward me from the front room, along with the smell of something delicious. I looked forward to getting to know Jasin's family, even if I wished it had been under better circumstances. Plus, I was curious about where he had grown up and excited about getting a glimpse into his past.

I stepped into the main room and the conversation died off as everyone turned to look at me. Jasin sat at a dining table made of shiny black stone with his parents across from him, though he jumped to his feet when he saw me. Slade was nowhere in sight, so he must still be getting the horses. I hoped he was safe.

Jasin moved to my side and took my hand to lead me to the table. "Mom, Dad, this is Kira. My...betrothed." He glanced at me with his eyebrows raised, as if asking if that was all right.

I smiled at him and inclined my head. Betrothed was probably the closest thing to the truth, since we couldn't exactly tell them what was really happening between us. "It's very nice to meet you both."

"Please join us," Ilya said. "We're about to have dinner and we're so happy you could be here with us."

"Thank you," I said.

Jasin pulled out a chair for me and I sat down, unable to keep a small smile off my face. These past few weeks had been difficult and at times unbelievable, and hours ago we'd been running for our lives, but this moment felt refreshingly normal. It was nice to pretend the only worry on my mind was getting his parents to like me. If I closed my eyes I could even imagine this was real, and that Jasin was my betrothed and soon we'd be married and settle down somewhere. Except that wasn't right, because I was missing the other men who shared my heart—but still, it was a nice fantasy to escape into for the time being.

Ilya began serving pasta with tomato sauce and tiny slivers of beef, a specialty of the Fire Realm that I hadn't eaten in years. A loaf of bread coated in garlic and butter was also passed around, and I felt bad that the others weren't there to share this feast with us. Hopefully there would be enough leftovers for the three of them.

I took a bite and it was the best thing I'd tasted in weeks. "This is delicious. I can see where Jasin gets his cooking skills from."

"Thank you," Ilya said. "Although I'm not sure I can take much credit for those."

"True, he's never made me anything this good," I said with a playful smile.

Jasin huffed. "Only because we've been traveling. A meal like this needs a proper kitchen and fresh ingredients and—"

I rested my hand over his. "I know, I was only teasing."

"Were you in the Onyx Army also?" Ozan asked in a blunt tone. Unlike Ilya, he didn't smile at us, but stared at me with dark, unwavering eyes.

"No, I wasn't," I said, glancing over at Jasin with uncertainty.

"Where did you two meet?" Ilya asked.

"I met her in a small village in the Earth Realm," Jasin said. "I showed up in her town and there was just this immediate connection between us."

He met my eyes with a grin and I smiled back at him as that connection he spoke of flared bright. It was true, even when I'd been scared of him or uncertain of our destiny, I'd always been drawn to him.

Ilya gave Ozan a knowing smile, but he continued to watch us with a surly expression. "Ozan and I were both in the army, stationed in Emberton," she said. "That's how we met. Of course, I retired from service when I had my boys, and Ozan took a permanent post in this city to stay close to us."

"Our entire family has always served in the Onyx Army," Ozan said. "My father. His father." He looked pointedly at Jasin. "And my sons."

"I served for many years," Jasin muttered. "I did my duty."

"I can't believe you left," Ozan, his tone almost angry. "What were you thinking?"

"I was thinking that it was time for me to make a change," Jasin said. "The army wasn't for me, in the end."

"Not for you?" Ozan nearly yelled. "How can you say that after what happened to your brother?"

"Ozan…" Ilya said, resting a hand on his arm.

He shook it off and glared at Jasin. "And what about this trouble you're in now?"

"I already told you, I can't talk about that," Jasin said. He was normally so bold, but when facing his father, he'd shrunk back.

"Of course you can't. Don't tell me the army is after you?"

Jasin stared at his plate with his lips pressed into a thin line. When he didn't answer, that only made Ozan's face even angrier.

Ilya reached toward him again. "Ozan, please. Let's just enjoy our meal."

"No, I can't sit here and listen to this." Ozan shot to his feet. "One son dead and the other a deserter." He gave Jasin one last harsh look. "You bring shame to our family."

Without another word, he left the room.

Stunned silence descended over the table, until Ilya said, "I'm sorry about that. He simply needs some time to calm down."

"It's our fault for showing up here unexpectedly," I said, glancing at Jasin, who stared down at his food with a pained expression. "We'll be gone first thing in the morning."

She waved a hand. "It's no trouble, really."

The front door open and I tensed, until I saw Slade's large figure filling up the doorway. He shut the door behind him and was drenched from the rain still pouring outside. "I moved the horses nearby and got our things."

"Thank you." I wanted to rush to him and give him a hug, so relieved to see him back safely, but I couldn't do that in front of Ilya without raising even more questions.

Slade joined us for the rest of the meal, although we spoke little after that. Jasin's normal vibrant self had dimmed thanks to his father's words, and I longed to get him alone so I could try to cheer him up.

When our meal was finished, I helped Ilya clean up in the kitchen, while Jasin and Slade spoke together in low voices about where he'd put the horses and the plan for tomorrow.

"I'm sorry again about my husband," Ilya said, as she set the plates aside. "Sometimes his temper gets the better of him. I wish our first dinner with you had gone better."

I nodded. "Can I ask what happened to your other son?"

"He was killed while fighting the Resistance outside Flamedale. It was supposed to be an easy raid, but it was a trap. His entire squad was slaughtered by those traitors." Her voice turned venomous, until she glanced over at her painting of the Dragons. "Thank the Gods that Sark came and took vengeance for us with his fire."

"I'm so sorry," I said, though my throat was tight. Jasin's family was completely loyal to the Black Dragon and supported her rule. No wonder Jasin had joined the Onyx Army when he was younger. How could he not, in this household? But if they found out what we truly were, I wasn't sure how they would react.

33

KIRA

W hile Slade slept in the front of the house, I checked on Reven and
Auric, who were still passed out but seemed stable. Once I was
sure they were fine, I joined Jasin in his old bedroom.

Like Berin's, this room was sparse, although it had more paintings
done in the style of the one in the front room, plus a blank canvas in the
corner. The first painting was of a man who looked a lot like Jasin
swinging a sword while wearing the black scaled armor of the Onyx Army.
The other painting was of the Crimson Dragon in flight, his wings spread
while he blasted fire down at something below him.

"Did you do these?" I asked.

"I did, yeah," Jasin said, with some hesitation in his voice. Like he was
worried what I would think about them.

"They're beautiful." I studied them closer, noticing the skill of the
design and the blend of colors. I didn't know much about art, but I could
tell Jasin was good, even if the subject matter was rather disturbing for me.
"You're very talented."

He sat on the edge of the bed and began removing his boots. "Thanks.
I once wanted to be an artist, but of course my parents didn't think that
was a suitable career. My future was in the army and nothing else or they'd
disown me."

"I got that feeling. It's a shame, because these are gorgeous." I tore my
gaze from the dragon painting and examined the other one. "Is this your
brother?"

"Yes. Berin was about my age there."

I took in the warrior's handsome, determined face. "You look like him."

"Do I? He was five years older than me and I always looked up to him. I thought he was perfect. My parents did too. When he died...it was a mess."

I turned back to Jasin. "Your mother said he died fighting the Resistance."

"He did, yeah." He looked away, his face pained. "And when I heard that, I volunteered to fight them too."

"That's how you knew about the tunnels."

"Actually, Berin and I found them when we were kids and used to play in them. But once I began hunting the Resistance, I realized their people were using the tunnels to hide and escape too. That's how I tracked them down. And I was damn good at it."

I swallowed, remembering the woman tonight who'd recognized Jasin. "The past is the past. Isn't that what you said?"

"Maybe, or maybe the past never leaves us," he said, his voice turning ragged. "You have no idea how many terrible things I've done. How many people I killed. Like that woman's brother. I don't remember her, but I probably did end his life."

I moved close to where he sat on the bed and placed my hands on his shoulders. "You're not that person anymore. Even before the Fire God came to you, you wanted to leave the Onyx Army."

His throat bobbed as he swallowed. "I couldn't stay. There was something I did that I couldn't forget. Something I'll never be able to forgive myself for."

"What happened?" I asked.

He didn't speak for some time, and when he did, he wouldn't meet my eyes. "General Voor found a town near the Air Realm border that he claimed was made up entirely of Resistance members. He sent my squad to kill them all. Men. Women. Children. Even their pets. Every living thing went up in flames. We didn't even need Sark for it." A shudder ran through his entire body. "I swore I would leave the army after that, but I was too much of a coward. I could only work up the nerve after the Fire God visited me."

I tilted his head up, forcing him to meet my eyes. "Maybe that's why he chose you. To give you this second chance."

He let out a bitter laugh. "Or maybe he chose me because I'm just like Sark."

"You're nothing like Sark." I pressed a kiss to his forehead. "Tonight you helped save those people from execution. Sark would never do that."

"I'm not sure that saving a few people tonight will ever make up for my past sins." He rested his head against my stomach and I gently stroked his hair.

"This was only the start of something bigger. And once we bond together, you'll be a much better Crimson Dragon than Sark ever was."

Jasin pulled back and gave me a smile with a hint of his usual flirtiness in it. "I'm looking forward to that."

"Being a dragon or bonding with me?"

"Both." His hands rested on my waist, his thumbs brushing against the fabric of my dress, and I felt a flicker of desire at his touch.

"Me too," I said, before bending down and finding his lips with mine. I kissed him softly, trying to show him I forgave his past and wanted a future with him, but it soon turned into more. Passion took over, making our kiss deeper, as if we couldn't get enough of each other.

We kissed with an almost desperate need as heat flared between our bodies. He dragged me onto his lap, making my dress bunch up around my waist as I straddled him. I gasped as his hard length pressed against my core, while his hands found my bare legs. His fingers smoothed along my skin ever so slowly, inching higher and higher, until they rested on my thighs, so close to where I ached for him.

Together we removed my dress and tossed it aside, leaving me in only my nearly see-through chemise. His large hands rested on my waist and our mouths found each other again, but then I tugged on his shirt, wanting it off. He lifted it over his head in one smooth motion, revealing that tanned, muscular chest I'd glimpsed before, not to mention his equally well-developed arms. I splayed my hands across his stomach, feeling the strength rippling beneath my fingertips, then began exploring up to his shoulders and down his arms. With each touch I wanted more of him.

I reached for his trousers but he caught my hand and stopped me.

"I'm ready," I told him.

"I'm not," he said.

I blinked at him. "You...don't want me?"

"Oh no, I do." He rolled his hips slightly, rubbing his hard length between my legs. "Trust me, I really do. But not tonight."

"I don't understand."

He stroked my face as he gazed into my eyes. "We should wait until we reach the Fire Temple."

"Why? I thought you wanted to get some practice in first."

"Not anymore." He pulled me down to the bed and drew the covers over us, then wrapped me in his arms. "When we bond together, I want you to know it's not just sex for me. With you, it's going to be a lot more."

I snuggled up against him. "I know, Jasin. I'm sorry I doubted you before, or worried about your past."

He touched my lips with his fingers. "You were right to doubt me. Before I met you, I was lost. I'd been told my life should be one thing, even though it never felt right. I let others mold me into what they wanted instead of standing up for what I believed in. I did things I wasn't proud of. I never let myself get attached to anything or anyone. But all of that changed once I was sent to find you. The Fire God might have given me these powers, but you gave me purpose. You gave me something to fight for. And I care about you more than you know."

My heart warmed from his words. "I care about you too, Jasin."

"Now sleep," Jasin said, pressing a kiss to my forehead. "Because once we reach the Fire Temple, I promise you won't be getting much sleep at all with all the naughty things I'll be doing to you."

"I like the sound of that." I shifted my leg so it draped over him, wanting our bodies pressed as close together as possible. Though I still burned with desire for him, it was just as good being held in his arms and knowing he cared for me the way I cared for him. Whatever doubts I'd once had about him were gone. I was ready for whatever we would face at the Fire Temple.

34

JASIN

"Get up!" someone whispered.

My eyes opened with a jolt. I was instantly alert, reaching for my sword and ready to fight. Someone moved in my bedroom, a dark figure in the meager light of dawn. I prepared to attack until I realized who it was. My mother.

I relaxed slightly, until I remembered Kira was in bed beside me wearing nothing but her little chemise. My mother knew we were sharing a room, and she definitely knew about my reputation with the ladies, but it was an entirely different thing to have your mother walk in on you in bed with a woman.

"Hurry," Mom said, before tossing my shirt in my face.

I threw it over my head. "What is it?"

Kira stirred beside me, but then let out a yelp and drew the blanket up to cover herself when she saw who was in the room with us.

Mom peered through the curtains at the street outside. "Your father has done something terrible. You need to leave right away."

"Tell me." I grabbed my boots and began putting them on, while Kira quickly pulled on her dress.

Mom turned around with a frown. "He's gone to tell General Voor about you. They'll be here any minute now to arrest you as a deserter."

I swore under my breath as I jumped to my feet and strapped on my weapons. The sting of my father's betrayal cut deep, but I couldn't think about that yet. I had to focus. Remember my training. Get everyone out. Stay alive.

When Kira and I were dressed, we moved to the front of the house and found the others readying their things too. Everyone looked dazed and exhausted, but strong and alert. Slade was ready to go, and Auric and Reven both seemed to be completely healed, thanks to Kira's magic.

"It's best if you go out the back," Mom said, gesturing for us to follow her.

"How could he do this?" I finally asked, once we reached the back door.

"He's not thinking straight. I tried to talk some sense into him but he wouldn't listen." She shook her head. "I'm so sorry, Jasin."

I pulled my mother into a tight hug, while my heart hammered in my chest. When I pulled away, she turned to Kira to embrace her as well.

"I'm so happy I got to meet you," Mom said, before pressing a package into Kira's hands. "I wrapped up some food for all of you. Please take care of Jasin for me."

"I will," Kira said. "I promise."

We rushed through the door and out into the early morning light. Our horses were already waiting outside, tied to the fence with our things already packed on them. Slade had retrieved them last night and knew we might need to leave at a moment's notice.

I lifted Kira onto my horse, then climbed on behind her, securing my arm tight around her waist. For a second, I simply held her close, breathing her in while I tried not to think about how my father could turn me in as a deserter. Kira rested her hand over mine and gave it a squeeze.

"The north gate is nearby," I said, as I gathered my horse's reins.

"Let's go," Auric said.

We kicked our horses forward, but we didn't get far. At the end of the road, a row of mounted soldiers was already waiting for us. My father was in front of them—with General Voor at his side. The sight was like a dagger in my chest, though it didn't surprise me that he'd turned against me. I'd always been the disappointing son.

"There they are," my father said. "I knew they'd come this way."

"Halt," the General bellowed, sending a chill down my spine. How many times had I heard him shout out orders? How many times had he made me do things I'd later regret?

We were forced to stop and draw our weapons. My sword was too large to wield while riding with Kira, but I pulled out my knife while my horse stomped his feet. Auric, Reven, and Slade also prepared to fight at our side.

"Get out of our way, and none of you will be hurt," I called out. "We don't want to fight you."

"Surrender, Jasin," Voor called out. "Turn yourself in and face the penalty for being a deserter, and we'll let your woman live."

A flash of anger made me see red and I nearly charged him for even mentioning Kira. "Never."

"You can't win this fight," General Voor said, shaking his great helmeted head.

"Want to bet?" Reven asked, his voice cold and deadly.

General Voor stared at Reven, before his gaze swept over the others. "You...you were there yesterday at the execution. You helped those Resistance traitors escape." He let out a harsh laugh. "Ozan, it seems your son is not only a deserter, but a traitor as well."

"Is this true?" my father asked me. "The Resistance killed your brother. How could you help them?"

With his confidence, passion, and anger, my father had always commanded my respect, along with my fear. General Voor was the same way. I'd admired them, followed them, and obeyed them. For years I went along with what they wanted because I thought I had no other choice, or I thought they knew better than I did. Now I realized I'd traded one overbearing, controlling, tyrant of a father for another. But I was no longer a coward, and I was no longer under their oppressive thumbs. Kira and the others had showed me that it was time to stand up for what I believed in.

I stared my father and General Voor down. "I left the army because I could no longer follow orders when I knew they were wrong. And I helped those people because it was the right thing to do."

"You really are a traitor," my father said, then spat on the ground. "May Sark's flames turn your bones to ash."

"Get them," General Voor said.

At his command the soldiers charged toward us on their horses. Rage burned hot inside me, and I no longer cared if anyone knew about my magic. If my father wanted flames, I'd show him some damn flames.

I spread my hand and fire leaped up from the ground in front of us, creating a blazing wall between us and the soldiers. Once it was as high as my house, I yanked on the reins to turn my horse around. "This way!"

While the soldiers shouted and fell back from the flames, I led the others down the empty early morning streets toward the north gate. There would be soldiers there too, but it was the closest escape and we had to get out of this city fast.

Our horses galloped through the stone streets toward our destination. I gripped Kira tightly as I led the charge, praying I remembered the quickest route. Her other mates rode right at our heels.

Just when I thought we'd gotten away, General Voor appeared before us with two other soldiers. Slade flicked his hand and a stone wall crumpled down on top of the soldiers, sending them to the ground. I gave him a short nod as we continued racing through the streets.

I spotted the heavy stone gate up ahead and was relieved to see it was already open. Merchants and other travelers were already moving through it with their carts, forcing us to slow as we maneuvered around them.

"Stop them!" a soldier called out behind us.

The guards at the gate jumped to attention, grabbing their swords and bows. Two of them charged at us, but Auric blasted them both back against the wall. With a shout, we urged our horses forward and made it through the gate, but we weren't safe yet—not from the archers on top of the wall, who prepared to fire at us.

"I've got this," Reven said.

As the arrows flew, he pulled all the water out of the moat and sent it flying straight up, where it froze mid-air and formed a tall wall of ice between the archers and us. Impressive.

"Into the mountains!" I called out.

Our horses clambered up the rough, rocky slope, where the trees and brush soon blocked view of us, though I had no doubt the soldiers would be chasing after us soon. I kept looking behind us, expecting to see the General or my father, but the way behind us remained clear.

We pushed our horses hard until the sun was high in the sky, and Kira held my hand the entire time. Although it burned me up inside knowing my father had betrayed me and that I would never be able to go home again, it was all worth it—for her.

35
KIRA

After a long, exhausting day of riding up and down mountains on the way to the volcano, Slade found us a cave to hide in for the night. We'd seen no sign of the Onyx Army behind us so far, but that didn't mean they weren't following. Our only hope was to get to the Fire Temple and hope we would be safe there—or that we'd unlock Jasin's dragon form and be able to blast our way out.

We ate the leftover pasta Ilya had packed for us, but instead of sitting around a campfire and chatting, all the men retreated to different corners of the cave or slipped outside to be alone with their thoughts. I was surprised to find that I wanted the opposite of solitude and missed their company. After nearly two weeks with these men, I'd started to grow accustomed to having them by my side at all times.

"Can I sit here?" I asked Slade, who was sharpening his axe.

"Of course." He set down his axe and patted the spot on the blanket beside him.

I sank down beside him with a weary sigh. "Thanks. It's been a long day."

"Been a long week."

"True. But between fighting off soldiers, helping prisoners escape, and running up and down mountains, I'm feeling especially weary." I leaned back on my hands, stretching my legs out. "Do you think the Resistance members got away safely?"

"I hope so. Our escape this morning might have helped distract the soldiers who would have followed them."

I hadn't thought of that, but I nodded. "How did you know about that Resistance hideout?"

He ran a hand along his dark beard. "I used to be part of the Resistance."

"You were?" I blinked at him. "Did you fight against the Onyx Army with them?"

"No, nothing like that. I made weapons and hid some of them when they were in trouble. That was all."

"How did you get involved with them?"

"A friend convinced me to help them, but I tried to keep my involvement as minimal as possible. I didn't want to bring trouble to my town or to my family and friends." He frowned as he glanced at his axe. "Trouble found me anyway though."

"I know what you mean," I said with a sigh. "At some point we might want to find the Resistance and convince them to help us. It could be good to have some allies."

"We can try, although the Resistance survives by staying hidden. They might not be interested in helping us."

I thought of my parents, wondering again if they were also members of the Resistance, or if they were truly killed because of me. Or both.

"I suppose we'll worry about that later." I rested my hand on his arm. "But thank you for everything you did in Ashbury."

"It was nothing." He met my eyes and something stirred inside me as I admired his rugged, handsome face. I wanted to run my fingers through that beard and see if it was as soft as it looked. I wanted to kiss those sensual dark lips. As he looked back at me, I thought I sensed a similar desire smoldering inside him, but then he turned away and went back to sharpening his axe.

Sensing that our moment was over, I got up and walked over to Auric, who was studying a map he'd laid flat on a wide rock.

"How are you feeling?" I asked him. "Any problems with your shoulder?"

"None." He stretched his back and arms. "If I didn't know better, I'd think I'd never been injured."

"Good." I leaned against his side and peered at the map. "How close are we?"

"I think we're about here," he said, pointing to a spot in the mountain range cutting through the Fire Realm. He traced his finger across to a large black peak. "The Fire God's temple is here, near the Valefire volcano, on the edge of the Eastern Sea. I estimate we should reach it by tomorrow afternoon."

I nodded and wrapped my arms around myself. A confusing mix of emotions swirled inside me at the thought of reaching the end of this journey tomorrow. I was torn between feeling nervous, anxious, excited, and worried. I had no idea what to expect at the Temple, and I wasn't sure I was ready for what we would face there.

Auric must have sensed my unease, because he gave me a warm smile. "Don't worry. There should be priests at the Temple to guide you through what you need to do. Hopefully they can give us more information too."

"That would be good," I said, although I wasn't very enthusiastic.

"Are you hesitant about sleeping with Jasin?"

"A little." I glanced over at Jasin, who sat alone, staring into the fire he'd made. "Not because I don't want to do it. But it's my first time, and there's a lot of pressure riding on this."

"I understand." He took my hands in his. "For what it's worth, I think Jasin will take good care of you."

"Does it bother you, knowing you have to share me with him?"

"No, but it's common for people in the Air Realm to have multiple partners." He shrugged. "Obviously I would have liked to be first, and Jasin wouldn't be my choice to share you with, but he's loyal. Whatever he might have done in his past, he cares about you a lot. Everyone can see it."

"Thanks. I should probably go talk to him."

"Yes, you should." He gave me a quick kiss, then released my hands and went back to studying his map.

I joined Jasin by the fire and sat beside him, trying not to let my fear of the flames show. "I'm so sorry about what happened this morning."

He nodded, his face solemn. "I never thought my father would do something like that. I can only hope that one day my parents will forgive me and understand why I chose this path. Seems unlikely though."

I leaned against him, resting my head on his shoulder. "You did what you thought was best. I'm proud of you, even if they're not."

He pressed a kiss to the top of my head. "That's all I need to hear."

We sat in companionable silence as the flames crackled and popped in front of us, until I said, "Auric told me we'll reach the temple tomorrow."

"Good. I'm ready." He pulled back to look into my eyes. "Are you?"

"I think so. I'm still nervous about a lot of things, but I want to do this."

He arched an eyebrow. "Nervous about being with me?"

"Yes, and about all the fire." I swallowed. "I couldn't handle that burning house. What am I going to do in the Fire Temple? Or once you're a Dragon or I have fire magic of my own?"

He wrapped an arm around me. "I won't let any harm come to you, I promise. And once you have this magic, I'll train you. Reven would never admit it, but I've gotten a lot better over the last few days thanks to our training."

"Yes, you have. I was suitably impressed by the wall of flame earlier."

His cocky smile returned, and some of the melancholy lifted from his eyes. "Were you scared?"

"No, I wasn't," I said, surprised by my answer.

He let out a long breath. "I know you haven't always trusted me—both with my fire and with your heart, so that means a lot to me."

"I do trust you," I said, and meant it. Although his past reputation with women had worried me at first, I sensed his passion for me more than from any of the other men. Jasin wasn't the type to hold back—he said what he felt, often without thinking first, and that was one of the things I loved about him. You never had to worry about where you stood with him.

He brushed his lips against mine. "I'm ready for tomorrow. I want to be yours, and I want you to be mine."

"Me too."

He pulled me close and kissed me with all that pent-up passion, until I had to pull away to stop from dragging him down to the blanket to continue what we started last night, even with the other guys watching. Although I wouldn't mind if the guys watched, actually. Or joined in. I glanced over at Auric and Slade at that thought, but they were both point-edly not looking at us, as if trying to give us some privacy. But the fourth member of our group was nowhere to be seen.

"Where's Reven?" I asked, as I pulled away from Jasin.

Jasin shrugged. "Outside maybe?"

I sighed. "I should go check on him."

I slipped through the low entrance of the cave and into the small valley outside. Under the tiny sliver of a moon, Reven stood beside his horse, unpacking something from one of his bags. No, not unpacking—he was putting something in them.

"What are you doing?" I asked.

He turned his black-haired head toward me. "I'm leaving."

My stomach fell out from under me so fast I was nearly dizzy. "What? Why?"

"I never planned to be part of this team. Last night reminded me of that."

"Last night you helped those people. You saved my life. And after that..." I took a step toward him. "I started to think you cared about me. About our mission. What changed?"

"What changed is that you risked your life for me."

"I don't understand...why is that bad?"

"You nearly got yourself killed in the process. And today General Voor recognized me because of it, putting the entire group at risk." He shook his head, his voice dripping with disgust. "Caring for people makes you weak. I should have left a long time ago."

My throat tightened and I found it hard to speak. He was really leaving, just when I'd thought he was starting to truly be part of the group—and had started to have feelings for me. "What about the Water God?"

He shrugged as he closed up his pack. "He can find someone else to be his Dragon. Maybe he'll let you choose someone better this time."

The thought of having anyone else as the Azure Dragon and the fourth member of my team was too horrible to even consider. My entire soul rejected the very idea. "What if I choose you?"

He gave me a sharp glance. "That isn't an option."

"But we need you." I stepped closer, placing a hand on his chest. "I need you."

He gazed into my eyes and I saw a hint of something like desire there, which made me think he might stay after all. That all of this was just his way of trying to protect his heart and he didn't mean any of it, not really. When he took my hand my hope grew, but all he did was drop it.

"You'll have to find someone who gives a damn," he growled. "I have no desire to be an enemy of the Onyx Army. I get a lot of business from them."

I stumbled back, shocked and hurt by his words. "Is that all you care about? Business?"

"I care about surviving. And I need to look out for myself and no one else. You should do the same."

"But you know what we're fighting for. How can you walk away?" I wanted to shout and cry and beg him to stay. "Whose side are you even on?"

He pulled the hood over his head. "I'm on no one's side but my own. Thought you'd realized that by now."

"Reven, this isn't you. You're a good man. I know you are."

"That's where you're wrong." He swung up onto his black horse and look down at me. "You keep trying to make me into a hero, but you need to get this through your pretty head: there are no heroes in this world, and if there were, I wouldn't be one of them."

"Then go," I said, practically shaking with anger and disbelief. "If that's how you feel, then I don't want you here anyway."

"Trust me, you're better off without me."

And with that, he rode into the darkness, while I stared after him too shocked and heartbroken to even say goodbye.

36

AURIC

I folded up the map and put it away, then pulled out my journal to record my daily log of our journey. The others thought it was a waste of time, but someday my notes might be useful to someone else, perhaps the next people to follow in our footsteps.

I moved closer to the fire for more light, where Jasin was staring into it with a brooding expression. He wasn't normally a brooder—that was more Reven's style—but he had good reason after today's events.

I debated a moment before sitting near him. Jasin and I didn't get along on the best of days, but I wanted to change that. "Jasin, I'm sorry about what happened with your parents."

He inclined his head slightly. "Thanks."

"For what it's worth, I know what it's like to be the youngest brother and the disappointing son."

"Oh yeah?" He chuckled softly. "I bet your father would never betray you like that though."

"I'm not sure. I suppose we'll find out once we reach the Air Realm." Unease settled over me as I considered our next step after the Fire Temple. "I doubt I can hide from them once I return. Either way, it's a shame you had to experience such a thing."

Before he could respond, Kira burst into the cave, her face flushed and her eyes watering. Each one of us jumped to our feet.

"Are you all right?" Slade asked.

"Reven's gone," she said.

"What do you mean, gone?" Jasin asked.

She wrapped her arms around herself. "He left. He doesn't want to be one of my mates."

The others looked as shocked as I felt. Leave Kira? That was impossible. Even though we hadn't officially bonded yet, I couldn't imagine being anywhere except by her side, supporting her however I could. How could Reven not feel the same?

I took her into my arms and held her close. "I'm sorry."

As she rested her head on my shoulder, Jasin joined us and embraced her from behind. "He's an idiot," he said.

"I knew he wanted to leave, but I never thought he'd actually do it," Slade said. He remained back, but looked hesitant, as if he wanted to join but wasn't sure he should.

Kira pulled back and wiped at her damp eyes. "What do we do now?"

"The only thing we can do," I said. "Keep going."

37

KIRA

I glanced behind us for the hundredth time, hoping to see Reven's dark profile or his black horse, but he was never there.

"He's not coming back," Auric said. "I'm sorry, Kira."

With a sigh, I tightened my arms around Auric and rested my head on his shoulder. "Maybe, but it's hard to accept he's truly gone."

He guided the horse around a large boulder. "I know. But now you can find someone who really wants to be here."

I tried to think of it that way, but I couldn't shake the feeling that Reven's departure had left a huge hole in my heart. I'd thought we'd begun to develop something real, but clearly, I was wrong. Even though he'd kept his distance from me, I'd still felt the same connection with him that I did the other men. At first, we could pretend it was simply the magic drawing us together, but not anymore. The fact that Reven could leave proved there was no magic forcing him or the other men to stay with me.

As we approached Valefire, the volcano where the Fire Temple was located, the landscape became stark and ominous. The dense shrubs and scraggly trees began to thin out and the land became black from lava that had once spilled. Steam and boiling water kept bursting from holes in the ground, and we had to go around numerous deep craters the closer we got to the slope of the volcano.

I'd expected Valefire to look like a tall mountain, but instead it was more of a mound with a flat top, where a large plume of white smoke billowed into the bright blue sky. The ocean could be spotted behind it, along with more thick smoke.

Jasin stopped his horse suddenly, staring at the sky. "The volcano…it's erupting."

"That can't be right," Auric said. "The volcano is supposed to be dormant."

"It was. People used to walk right up to the crater and drop offerings in for the Fire God."

"Are we in any danger?" I asked.

"I doubt the Fire God would try to stop us now," Slade said.

Auric peered at the volcano. "We should be safe, since it doesn't appear to be too violent of an eruption."

"Where is the Temple?" I asked.

"It's at the top," Jasin said, his face grim.

I nodded. "Then we keep going."

The terrain became even rougher as we reached the base of the volcano. There was nothing living in sight, not even a weed. The blackened ground had strange rope-like patterns in it, which I realized were from a previous eruption where the flow of lava had hardened and solidified. The volcano rose high above us, under its swirling cloud of white smoke.

With great reluctance, we left our horses behind and took only what we needed for the climb. The slope up was full of black volcanic formations, mounds, and ridges, and we stumbled up it. More steam shot out in various places from vents in the earth, and the air grew heavy with heat and a smell like rotten eggs. I coughed and covered my mouth and nose with a cloth, while my eyes began to burn and sweat dripped down my forehead.

The climb was brutal, and at times I thought I might give up, but I kept going with encouragement from my three mates. We stopped for short water breaks and nothing more, even when our muscles began to ache and the sun slowly set behind us. *Only a few more steps*, I told myself over and over, until we finally reached the summit.

The ground was flat and smooth, before dropping suddenly into a crater in the center. An eerie orange glow rose up from the crater, illuminating an impressive building made of black glassy stone with tall, pointed towers.

A beautiful woman I guessed to be in her forties stood in front, wearing a red silk robe with black trim. She had pale blond hair and bowed low when we approached. "Greetings, ascendants."

I glanced at the others warily. "Were you expecting us?"

"Yes. Ever since Valefire erupted a little over a month ago, we knew the Fire God was stirring and new Dragons were rising." She swept her gaze across the men. "Which one of you has been chosen by the Fire God?"

"I was," Jasin said, stepping forward.

"Show me his gift."

Jasin spread his palm and summoned a ball of fire in the middle of it. The woman smiled and watched the flames flicker, then produced a matching one in her hand, making us gasp.

"How…?" he asked.

"My name is Calla, and I am the High Priestess of the Fire God." She closed her hand and the flame vanished. "Like you, I've been gifted a touch of his power in order to serve him."

"Does that mean you're a Dragon also?" Auric asked.

"No, that is your destiny and not mine." She frowned as she glanced between us again. "I expected four men, though."

My throat clenched up at the reminder. "One of them didn't want to be here."

"No matter. You only need the Crimson Dragon's ascendant today." She gestured toward the tall door of the temple, her long sleeves flowing around her. "Please come inside."

We followed her into a huge entry room with a large domed ceiling and dozens of torches, which seemed to flare brighter as we approached. I tried to ignore the flicker of fear inside me at the sight and kept walking toward a tall dragon statue made of the same smooth black stone as the rest of the Temple. Four older, handsome male priests waited for us in front of it, wearing similar robes to Calla's. They all bowed low as we drew near.

"These are the Fire God's priests," Calla said, as she smiled at the four men. "And my mates."

I'd heard that the High Priestesses followed the ways of the Spirit Goddess and the Black Dragon and took four mates in the same tradition, but I was never sure if it was true or simply rumors. Perhaps she'd be able to give me advice on managing four men with strong personalities.

We all exchanged names, while the priests stared at me and Jasin with both awe and curiosity.

"It is an honor to meet you," Blane, the first priest said.

"We've been waiting for you for a very long time," another priest named Derel said.

"You were?" I asked. "How?"

"It's time you learned the truth about the Dragons," Calla said. "But first, you're probably in need of some refreshments."

She led us into another large room with a long black table that was already prepared for a feast. Our exhaustion took over as we sank into the stone chairs, and two of the priests began pouring us red wine and cool water, while the others served us glazed beef with vegetables and pasta shells. I eagerly downed an entire glass of water before diving into my meal.

"What can you tell us about the Dragons?" I asked, once my weariness began to fade thanks to their delicious food.

Calla was sitting across from me and took a sip of wine. "The Black Dragon and her mates have ruled the world for the last six hundred and thirty years—but it was not always that way."

Auric leaned forward, hungry for her knowledge. "What do you mean?"

"Thousands of years ago, the Gods created elementals and humans. They believed we could exist in harmony. They were wrong. When humans began expanding into elemental lands the elementals fought back and we were no match for their magic. The Gods created the five Dragons to be their representatives, blessing those chosen humans with the powers of the elementals in order to protect the world and keep the balance. The Dragons acted as intermediaries between the two groups, and for many years there was peace."

Jasin paused between bites. "I thought the Dragons were supposed to rule us."

"Not originally," Blane said, as he refilled my water. "They were peace-keepers and protectors, not rulers. Instead, each Realm governed itself. Until Nysa."

"The Black Dragon," Slade said quietly, while a shiver ran down my spine at her name.

"What changed with her?" Auric asked.

Calla folded her hands in front of her. "Before Nysa, a new set of Dragons was chosen every fifty years. That way, none of the Dragons could gain too much power. But Nysa found a way to become immortal and stop new Dragons from being chosen."

"How?" Slade asked.

"No one knows. At first, the priests thought the Gods had gifted her with a longer reign because they were pleased with her work. But then the Gods stopped speaking to their priests and seemed to vanish from the world completely. Some believed they'd forsaken us or passed control to the Dragons. Others thought they were sleeping or dead. But I was visited by the Fire God twenty years ago, and he told me to prepare for your arrival. He began stirring again forty days ago."

"That was my birthday," I said. "When all of this began."

She nodded. "New Dragons were always chosen on the Black Dragon's twentieth birthday. For whatever reason, the Gods have woken again and they have selected all of you."

Jasin nodded slowly. "The Fire God came to me and told me to find Kira and bring her to this temple. Now what?"

Calla gave us both a knowing smile. "You and Kira must go into the altar room and bond, while the others wait here. Are you ready to begin?"

"I suppose so," I said, suddenly nervous as I glanced over at Auric and Slade.

"Your other mates will be well attended to, so you do not need to worry," Derel said.

"Thank you," Auric said. "I'm wondering if you have any old texts about the Gods or the Dragons I could look at."

"Certainly," Blane replied.

I rose to my feet and my three mates immediately stood in response. I glanced over at Jasin, my heart pounding. It was time.

Auric wrapped his arms around me, before turning to Jasin and giving him a nod. "Good luck."

"Treat her well," Slade grumbled at Jasin, before giving me a short nod. The four priests led them into another room, leaving me and Jasin alone with Calla.

"Follow me," Calla said, as she led us out of the dining hall and back to the main room. She took us to a tall black door with two dragons carved into it. "No one has used this room for about six hundred years, but we've prepared everything for you." She stopped in front of it and smiled at both of us. "Take as much time as you need. Once you've bonded, go through the other door."

Jasin reached out and took my hand. I held it tight and swallowed the lump in my throat as the door opened for us.

38

REVEN

My horse moved slowly over the rocky, hostile terrain while my thoughts churned. I'd followed behind the others at a distance to make sure they made it to the Fire Temple unharmed, but now my duty was over. I could leave.

I *should* leave.

So why didn't I?

I would love to blame it on magic, but I'd ridden far enough away last night to confirm there was nothing forcing me to be with Kira. The Gods had made me find her, but that was all. There was nothing tying us together now.

I drew in a long breath and turned my horse away from the volcano, urging her west. Kira didn't need me anymore. She was no doubt inside the Fire Temple already getting nice and cozy with Jasin. Once she was done, she could find another man to be her Azure Dragon.

It couldn't be me. The incident in Ashbury had made that all too clear.

If I closed my eyes I could still clearly picture Kira throwing herself in front of me, trying to protect me from those soldiers, and nearly getting herself killed in the process. A sharp spike of panic had struck me then, as it did now at the thought of her dying because of me. Like the last woman I'd loved.

Mara had been killed because of me, and I swore I'd never let that happen again. Years ago, I'd been unable to save her, and now I'd nearly failed Kira too. Which is why I had to leave. Caring for someone made you weak and only put them in danger. The sooner Kira stopped caring for me, the better.

My brooding thoughts were disturbed when I spotted some dark figures riding toward the volcano. Soldiers. They must have tracked us here from Ashbury.

Not my problem, I told myself. *Not my fight.*

I urged my horse forward, planning to keep my distance from the armored men. Kira and her remaining mates would be able to fight them off, especially once Jasin became a Dragon. They didn't need me. And I certainly didn't need or want them.

So why did I feel like I was making the biggest mistake of my life?

39

KIRA

Jasin and I stepped into another domed room made of that same black stone, with torches lit around a raised platform. In the center of it was a large bed decorated with red and black silk sheets and lots of soft-looking pillows. If I had any doubt before about what we were meant to do, it vanished now.

I ran my hand along the smooth wall as I slowly made my way toward the platform. "This stone is beautiful."

Jasin climbed the steps to the bed without hesitation and began removing his weapons and armor. "It's obsidian. Volcanic glass. Lots of jewelry in the Fire Realm is made from it. I've never seen an entire building though."

I followed him onto the altar and wrung my hands, feeling awkward. "Now what?"

He raised an eyebrow. "Do I need to explain to you how this works?"

"No," I said, my cheeks flushing. "It's just all so…forced."

A frown crossed his mouth. "If you don't want to do this…"

"I do," I said quickly, taking his hands. "Sorry, forced was the wrong word. It's just hard to get in the mood knowing seven people are out there waiting for us to get on with it. And what will happen once we do? Reven left. Fire still scares me. The Onyx Army is following us." I shook my head. "I don't feel ready to become the Black Dragon. Maybe I never will."

He drew me into his arms. "Do you doubt me?"

"No." I let out a nervous laugh. "This situation is just not very romantic."

"Maybe I can help with that."

He took my chin and captured my mouth in a smoldering kiss. Passion ignited instantly at his touch, as if it had been building inside me and could now finally be freed. As he kissed me harder, I wrapped my arms around him, desperate for more.

His mouth trailed down my neck, sending delicious tingles through my body. "Forget about everyone else. Tonight is about you and me. And I've been wanting to do this for a very long time."

"You have?" I asked, breathless.

"Since the first time I fell on top of you in the woods." His lips brushed against my collarbone. "Don't tell me you didn't feel the spark between us too."

"I did. I do."

He stepped back and reached down to grip the edge of his shirt, his eyes never leaving mine. As he lifted the fabric up, I let my gaze fall to his chest, watching the way his muscles rippled with the movement. He tossed the shirt aside, before his hands moved to the front of his trousers. He paused and one of his eyebrows arched, as if he was waiting for me to stop him. When I didn't move, he eased them off and kicked them aside, making me suck in a breath.

He wore nothing underneath.

"Like what you see?" he asked, with that cocky grin I loved.

I could only nod and stare, my throat dry. I'd seen a naked man or two before, and had nearly slept with one once, but Jasin was truly blessed by the Gods in every way. I took him all in, my eyes following the V of his hips to the large cock jutting from between his muscular thighs. Maybe *I* was the one who was blessed.

Hoping to show him I was just as eager for this as he was, I removed my dress, leaving me in only my chemise. He'd seen me in it before, but his eyes tracked my movements with hunger anyway. I slowly lifted the chemise over my head, making me as naked as he was.

"Gods, you're beautiful," Jasin said. "I could look at you for hours."

"Are you only going to look?" I asked, with a teasing smile.

"Oh no. I'm going to do a lot more than that." He set his hands on my hips, his fingers warm on my bare skin. "I'm going to touch. I'm going to taste. And then I'm going to make you mine."

He took me in his strong arms and lifted me up, then smoothly put me down on the bed with him on top of me. Our bodies were lined up, skin to skin, and I felt his hard shaft nudge between my thighs. A rush of need made me arch up against him, my breath quickening.

"I'm ready," I said, as I looked up at his handsome face.

He chuckled softly as he nuzzled my neck. "Oh, now you're impatient?" His lips danced across my skin like a tease. "We're just getting started."

His mouth moved down until he found my breasts, where my nipples were already hard for him. A soft moan escaped me as his tongue lazily slid over one taut bud, while his fingertips circled the other. When he sucked that nipple into his mouth, it sent heat straight to my core. My head fell back and my fingers tangled in his thick hair as he took his time with each breast, slowly driving me mad for him.

"Jasin," I gasped. "Please."

I wasn't sure what I was begging for, but Jasin moved lower at my words. His lips traced the underside of my breasts, trailed down my stomach, and brushed along my hips. With each touch my desire flared higher and higher, until my entire body clenched with need. Only then did he spread my legs wide and dip his head between my thighs.

At the first touch of his mouth, I gasped and nearly jolted off the bed. His hands gripped my hips, holding me steady as his tongue slowly swept along my folds. Pleasure simmered inside me with his warm breath on my skin, his rough stubble between my thighs, and his fingers moving to my bottom, lifting me up to his lips like an offering.

When his mouth found my most sensitive spot, I grasped the sheets and cried out. When one of his fingers slipped inside me, I thought I might surely die. It was too much, and yet I didn't want him to stop. He was the one worshipping me, but I was the one whimpering and begging for release. When he slid a second finger into me, my climax burst like a bonfire on a dark night, and I could do nothing but succumb to it.

As my body trembled, Jasin slowly moved up it, covering my skin with his own. "*Now* you're ready."

He nudged my thighs wider and moved between them, then took himself in hand and slowly rubbed between my folds, getting nice and slick. I was nearly dizzy with anticipation and almost started begging him again, when he guided himself inside.

Gods, he was big. And delightfully warm too, like sinking into a hot bath after a long, hard day. I felt every inch as he pushed deeper, and he watched my face the entire time, checking if I was in any pain. But nothing hurt, except this burning need within me that needed to be sated.

"More," I managed to say.

He gave me a self-satisfied smirk, then buried himself in me with one easy thrust. I cried out, not in pain, but from the sudden pleasure from being stretched and filled so completely. Our eyes met and the connection between us, the one I'd felt ever since we'd first met, burned hotter.

Jasin kept his eyes on mine as he began moving inside me with slow, smooth strokes. At first the pressure was intense and almost uncomfortable as my body adjusted to his size, but then it quickly gave way to the most amazing sensations. My hips began to buck in time to his thrusts as the delicious tension grew between my legs.

As if sensing my need, he pinned me down and took my mouth, while my hands found the hard planes of his back. He rocked deep inside me, our bodies moving together in a smooth rhythm that made my heart nearly burst because everything about this moment was so *right*. I was meant to be with Jasin, just as he was meant to be with me. And soon I'd be sharing this moment with my other men too.

But then Jasin sat back on his heels and dragged my hips up, making my back arch as he moved deeper inside me, hitting me at an angle that made me see stars. He reached a hand between us and began rubbing me at the same time. With each thrust he stroked the flame higher and higher until I thought I would truly combust.

"Come for me, Kira. Show me you're mine."

With his other hand on my bottom to guide my hips, Jasin coaxed an explosive orgasm out of me that had me moaning and writhing underneath him like some kind of wild beast. I clenched around him, squeezing him tight as he pounded me faster and gave himself over to the pleasure too.

Flames suddenly burst over Jasin's skin and I cried out at the sight, but we were both too far gone to do anything to stop it. He groaned and bent over me, pressing our bodies close as we both found our release together. His mouth claimed mine while the fire engulfed us, so bright it lit up the entire chamber. But it didn't burn my skin.

Intense flame roared through me, so strong I lost all trace of myself, and simply became fire and light and heat. But then came an overwhelming sense of Jasin, as if we were truly one, like two halves of a whole that had finally been put back together after far too long. I *knew* him, just as he knew me. And he was *mine*.

When I came back to myself, Jasin held me in his arms, while the last shudders of pleasure faded from our bodies. The fire was gone, as if it had never been there at all.

"What was that?" I asked.

Jasin pressed a soft kiss to my lips. "I think we're bonded now."

40

SLADE

I stared at the stark black stone walls, as if admiring the architecture of the temple could actually distract me from my thoughts. Auric leaned over a book and chatted with one of the priests about it like it was the most fascinating thing in the world. I supposed that was his way of dealing with the fact that Kira was on the other side of that wall sleeping with Jasin right now.

I crossed my arms. Why did it bother me so much? It's not like I wanted to be in there with her instead. Okay, maybe I did, but I *shouldn't* want that. Auric and Jasin were both in love with her, that was obvious. Reven was gone, after fleeing in the night like a villain. And then there was me. I cared for Kira a lot, but I wasn't sure I could ever give her my heart completely. Or get used to the idea of sharing her with three other men.

I'd heard that taking multiple partners was common in the Air and Water Realms, but after what I'd been through with Faya, the thought made my chest ache. This would be different, of course—Kira's mates were open about all of us sharing her, and it was part of our divine duty— but I worried it would still lead to heartbreak and trouble.

Even so, I would never leave like Reven. I would stay and do my duty, to fulfill the destiny the Gods had bestowed upon me, and to protect Kira however I could. I'd just have to protect my heart at the same time somehow.

The sound of footsteps and a door slamming caught all of our attention. Auric slammed the book shut and gave me a wary glance. I grabbed my axe, then led the charge back into the main hall. Soldiers poured into the room, led by the man in red armor with a winged helmet.

The Onyx Army had come for us.

41

JASIN

Kira ran her hand down the dark stubble on my neck as she gazed at me with a satisfied smile. "We should have done that a long time ago."

"I'm glad we waited. I wanted our first time together to be meaningful."

"It was perfect."

I pressed a kiss to Kira's neck as I held her close. Perfect wasn't enough to describe what we'd just shared. I'd been with plenty of women before, but sex had never been as good with anyone else. Then again, I'd never felt this way about anyone before either.

I loved Kira. I'd known for a while now, maybe since our first kiss, maybe even before that. I could tell she cared for me too, but I wasn't sure she was ready to hear those words yet or speak them back to me. It didn't matter though, because I felt the love between us every time we touched, like an everlasting flame that flickered but would never die. Now that we'd officially bonded, it was even stronger.

At that thought, I remembered the entire reason we were here, which had been easy to forget in the heat of the moment. "While I'd love to keep you here all night and make love to you again and again, the others are waiting."

She sighed and snuggled in closer against me. "You're probably right, but let's wait a few more minutes."

"My pleasure." I ran a hand down her back. "Are you sore at all? Do you need anything?"

"No, I'm fine. I just feel warm all over." She paused and a strange look came over her face. "Do you think I have fire magic now?"

"I don't know. Maybe. Do you feel any different?"

"Not really."

"I didn't either, at first." I paused, remembering the flames that had swept over us. "I wonder if I can turn into a Dragon now. I guess I thought the Fire God would appear to us or something."

"Me too. Maybe he was giving us some privacy." She lifted herself up to a sitting position, drawing my eyes to her full breasts. "Calla said we should go through those doors when we were done."

While the temptation to toss her back on the bed and cover those breasts with kisses was strong, there would be plenty of time for that later. "Let's go."

We reluctantly left the bed and donned our clothing again, then headed for the double doors at the back of the room. They were thicker than the one we'd entered through, and as we approached they opened with a blast of heat.

The doors led outside near the volcano's crater, which made the night glow orange in front of us. I slowly approached the huge circular pit, where the intense heat was coming from, while Kira hung back. I didn't blame her for being wary, but curiosity drew me forward and kept the fear at bay. Fire couldn't harm me anymore, and the chance to peer inside an active volcano was something I couldn't miss.

I got to the edge of the crater, where a stone ring had formed around it almost like a wall to hold the lava in. The crater went deep into the earth, where dark magma oozed and bubbled and flared up. I could only stare at it in awe, captivated by its beauty and power.

Suddenly a huge blast of lava shot up into the air and I fell back. The heat became so intense I wasn't sure I could bear it. I scrambled back to Kira, who stared up at it in awe. As I followed her gaze, I saw why.

From the crater rose a colossal dragon made of shifting, sliding lava, with bright bursts of fire for eyes. Most of his body remained inside the volcano, but his head and long neck towered over us, while his talons grasped the edge of the crater with an impact that shook the ground under us.

When his massive wings spread out behind him, sending lava flying into the air, I dropped to my knees in awe. The Fire God looked different from when he'd visited me before, but he was even more impressive and terrifying in his true form. Like the other Gods, no one knew his name. It was said the Gods' names were in a language that couldn't be understood by humans, and when I looked upon him now, I believed it. He was alien and incomprehensible and yet familiar at the same time, like this magic inside me recognized that it had once belonged to him.

"You have done well, my children," a huge voice boomed from his molten mouth, which was covered in large, sharp fangs dripping with lava. "But your journey is far from over."

No one would ever call me a humble man, but for the first time in my life I felt it, along with a sense of pride at being called his child. I bowed my head. "What do you wish of us?"

His fiery eyes burned into mine. "You are the new Crimson Dragon, my representative in this world. Serve me well and prove I have chosen wisely."

I swallowed and nodded slowly, feeling the huge weight of responsibility on my shoulders. "What must I do?"

"The others will look to you for leadership and guidance, and you must help them find balance. None of the elements exist alone. Even now, I am surrounded by my brothers. The air above me. The earth below me. The water beside me. Remember that."

That wouldn't be easy, especially when I was the one getting into fights half the time. Not to mention, we still didn't know where Reven had run off to, or if he would ever return. "I will try. But I have to ask, why did you choose me?"

His great wings fluttered, sending sparks flying into the air. "Each of the Gods values different attributes. I look for bravery, passion, and energy."

"There must be dozens of men who represent those qualities much better than I do."

"You misunderstand." His long, reptilian head lowered as his eyes focused on Kira. "We find the mate who will best bring out those qualities in *her*."

Kira's face paled as the God's talons inched toward her. "Did you choose me too?" she asked, though I heard fear in her voice. I was impressed she'd made it this close with her fear of fire, but she was handling it well, all things considered.

"No." His head tilted as he studied her. "Do not be frightened."

She bowed her head, as sweat ran down her temple. "I'm sorry. I've been afraid of fire ever since my parents were killed by the Crimson Dragon."

"In a way they were, and in a way, they were not."

Kira cast me a confused look. "They weren't killed by him?"

"The people who raised you were killed. The people who created you still live."

Kira's hand went to her throat. "They're alive?" she whispered. "Who are they?"

"This journey will lead you to them, but you may not like what you find." He suddenly reared up, his great flaming wings spreading wide. "Only together can you stop the Black Dragon and her mates. Now go. Your companions need you."

Before we could react, the Fire God descended into the lava again and vanished. The sky immediately darkened and the heat returned to a more bearable level. I wiped sweat off my forehead and shakily rose to my feet, then turned toward Kira. She looked like she was about to ask me something, but then a distant scream and a huge rumble drew our attention. The Fire God's words rang in my mind as we burst into a run back toward the temple's doors.

In the front hall, a battle had clearly been fought and lost. Numerous Onyx Army soldiers filled the room, and the dragon statue—which I now realized represented the Fire God and not Sark—had toppled over. Auric and Slade had been captured by soldiers and were on their knees with their hands bound behind them and swords at their throats. Calla lay on the ground bleeding from a gash on her chest, while her four priests hovered over her glaring at the man who pointed his large sword at them. General Voor.

As we entered, every single person in the room turned toward us. "There they are," the General said. "Surrender, and we'll let the priests live."

Rage exploded in me at the sight of Calla's blood, the toppled statue, and my friends being held captive. How dare they come into this sacred place and attack the priests here. These soldiers had once been men I'd fought beside, but now I only saw them as the enemy. The Fire God wanted passion and bravery? I'd give him that.

The heat flared inside me and I embraced it, letting it wash over me until I was burning alive. Blood red scales rippled over my skin as my entire body expanded and shifted and became *more*. My fingers turned to talons. My teeth became fangs. Fire burned in my throat as my long tail flickered. With a great roar, I spread my large wings.

I was a Dragon.

4 2
KIRA

Every soldier in the room fell to their knees except for the General, all of them gasping and crying out. "The Crimson Dragon!" some of them shouted, while others asked, "How?"

Jasin's new form was terrifying and awe-inspiring, and I felt a flicker of fear until he looked at me and his eyes were the same warm brown as when he was a human. And though he looked a lot like Sark, who had haunted my nightmares for so long, he was still Jasin, the man I had given my heart and body to only minutes earlier.

I rested my hand on his side, feeling the smooth, warm scales under my fingers, before turning to the General. "The Fire God has chosen a new Crimson Dragon. Leave now or feel his wrath."

"That's impossible," General Voor said. "Sark is the Crimson Dragon."

"Not for much longer," Jasin growled, with a voice I barely recognized. "Let them go."

The soldiers seemed hesitant, glancing between Jasin and the General, unsure of who to follow. The General pointed his sword at us. "We serve the true Dragons, not these imposters. Kill them. Kill them all!"

Two soldiers charged at Jasin, but he swiped them away with his massive talons. Others raised their swords to Auric and Slade and panic swelled inside my heart. Without thinking I reached out toward them and flames shot from my palms, setting both soldiers on fire. The men screamed, while I stared at my hands in wonder. I'd done it. I'd used fire. And I wasn't scared at all.

Jasin had given me both his magic and his courage.

Slade and Auric jumped to their feet and moved to protect the priests, though their hands were still bound. I prepared to launch more fire at the other soldiers, but then felt a blade bite into my neck and a large presence behind me.

General Voor gripped my arm tight, holding me against his chest with his sword at my throat. Blood dripped down my neck, and he was strong enough that I didn't dare move. Everyone in the room froze, with my three mates staring at me and the General. Auric looked worried, Slade had a stony expression, and Jasin, well it was hard to tell with his new reptilian face, but I knew he was furious from the bond shining bright between us.

"Surrender, or I kill her," the General called out.

"Get your hands off her," a cool voice said behind us.

General Voor cried out as a spurt of blood washed over me. It took me a second to realize it wasn't my own. He let me go and stumbled back, while my heart pounded in my chest as I spun away to face the man I so desperately hoped was my savior.

Reven held one of his swords in his hand and had murder in his icy blue eyes. He stabbed Voor a second time in the chest, then watched him fall to the ground. As soon as the General hit the ground, I rushed toward Reven and threw my arms around him, burying my face in his chest.

"You returned," I said, while my heart nearly burst with relief and happiness.

With his free hand he clutched me tight against him and gazed down at me. "I did."

"Why?"

He shrugged. "I knew you would need my help. Looks like I was right."

"Is that the only reason?" I whispered.

He took my chin in his hand and brushed his lips across mine ever so softly. "There may have been other reasons too."

With their General dead and a large dragon glaring at them, the soldiers all surrendered. Jasin shifted back into human form with a great slithering of scales and a rush of heat. He strode toward me and Reven. "Are you okay?" he asked me.

"I'm fine," I said, touching my neck. It didn't hurt anymore, and I had a feeling the wound was already healing itself.

He gave Reven a sharp look and I expected him to say something rude or angry, but instead he said, "Glad you're back. Don't do anything like that again." Reven only nodded in return.

The three of us rushed over to Auric and Slade, who had already removed the ties around their hands. Auric pulled me close for a kiss, whispering, "I'm so relieved you're safe." I turned to Slade, who wrapped his muscular arms around me in a protective, close embrace. He pressed a soft kiss to the top of my head, before releasing me.

Calla moaned, and I dropped to her side, my panic returning. She was covered in blood, as were the priests who were trying to tend to her wounds with worried looks on their faces. They were her mates, just like my men were mine.

I took Calla's hand in mine. "You're going to be okay."

She coughed and clutched her bloody chest. "No, I won't. But it doesn't matter. I fulfilled my purpose. Twenty years ago the Fire God chose me to be his High Priestess, just like he chose you, Jasin." Her eyes shifted to him, before going back to mine. "He told me I must come to the Fire Temple to prepare for the next Dragons. I've waited for this day for most of my life, and it is an honor to know I could help you both."

Jasin kneeled beside her and took her other hand. "You've served the Fire God well."

Her eyes fluttered shut. "Thank you."

As she faded away, my heart clenched and something burned in me like an ember. Through our touch I felt a kinship with her, like a twin fire flaring bright inside of both of us. I took Jasin's other hand in mine, forming a circle between us, and felt it within him too.

The gift of the Fire God was inside all of us.

While drawing strength from Jasin, I willed it into Calla, praying for the Fire God to help us heal his chosen priestess. Our hands began to glow with the same unearthly orange light from the volcano, as if lava flowed underneath our skin, and the heat became so intense I nearly let go. But I held on, and a second later Calla gasped and opened her eyes. The four priests around us cried out and rushed to her side.

"You healed her," Blane said, while the others praised both me and the Fire God.

"With Jasin's help," I said.

"The Fire God has truly blessed us all," Derel said.

"Thank you," another one said, whose name I had forgotten.

"It seems the Fire God still has more work for you," Jasin said to Calla.

"Thank you both," Calla said, as she sat up with a smile. She cupped my cheek and then did the same to Jasin. "I will cherish your gift and do whatever I can to help you."

"If everyone's good now, we need to get out of here," Reven said, with his lazy drawl. "The Crimson Dragon—the other one—is heading this way."

Fear gripped my throat, but Jasin wrapped an arm around me. "We can fight him," he said. "I can face him as a Dragon now too."

"No, we can't," Auric said. "He's immune to fire, just like you are. We don't stand a chance until more of us can shift too."

"He's right, we need to run," Slade said.

Calla got to her feet, with the help of two of her men. "You must hurry. Go out the back by the crater, then head down that side of the volcano. It leads to the ocean, to a dock where a ship is waiting for you. You can take that to the Air Realm and the next Temple."

She truly had prepared for our arrival, anticipating everything we might need. "Thank you," I said, hugging her quickly. "I hope we meet again."

"We will."

"What about our horses?" Auric asked. "And everything with them?"

"We'll bring them here and take care of them for you," the fourth priest said. "When it's safe, we'll make sure they are brought to you."

"Now go, quickly," Calla said. "There's no time."

43

KIRA

We grabbed our few belongings and rushed through the temple, past the bed where Jasin and I had made love, and out through the doors to the volcano's summit. It still glowed from the lava deep in its pit, but the Fire God was nowhere to be seen this time. We rounded the large crater and battled through the heat that threatened to suffocate us, but I wasn't afraid of it. Not anymore.

That was, until I saw the lava flowing down the side of the mountain. It bubbled and churned and slowly slid toward the base of the volcano, where it met the ocean with a burst of smoke and slowly hardened into new land. *A mix of all the elements*, I thought, remembering what the Fire God had told us.

"This is where Calla told us to go," I said. "But how do we get down?"

"I might be able to fly us down," Jasin said. "Although I don't really know how yet."

"That sounds like a good way to get us all killed," Reven said.

Auric's brows furrowed. "There must be a way down."

Slade ran a hand over his beard as he considered. "Maybe I can shift the rock…"

"That's it," Jasin said. "The Fire God said we had to work together if we wanted to succeed. Slade and Reven will form a path for us, Kira and I will keep the fire and heat away, and Auric will protect us from the fumes."

All the men nodded and pride swelled inside me as they made a plan to work together. We moved to the edge of the lava, where Reven sprayed water in a stream, which Slade used to solidify a path of earth. Jasin kept the rest of the flames away and we rushed along the new stretch of land, sweat dripping down all of our faces, and began to descend.

As Slade and Reven continued to create the path going down the mountain, Auric kept a bubble of clean, cool air around us. I did my best to keep the lava and flames back, but I wasn't sure how to use my new powers yet, and I suspected Jasin was doing most of the work.

The dock at the base of the volcano was made of the same obsidian as the Temple and somehow remained completely untouched by the lava, which flowed away from it. By the time we reached it we were all exhausted, sweating profusely, and covered in soot, even despite our best efforts. We stumbled forward toward the boat anchored at the end, its black sails already raised, like it had been waiting for us all this time.

"Anyone know how to sail?" Jasin asked, as we stepped onto the wooden deck of the ship.

"I know a little," Reven said, glancing up at the sails.

Auric looked up at the sails as he wiped sweat off his brow. "I've never been on a boat, but I think Reven and I can use our magic to steer it."

"Then let's get out of here," Slade said, as he cut through the ties holding the boat to the dock and used his magic to lift the anchor out of the water.

Reven shifted the current around us and Auric filled the sails with wind, pointing us north. To the Air Realm.

The boat began moving away from the dock thanks to their magic, and in a few minutes, we were out on the cool water under the endless night sky, leaving the volcano behind. I glanced behind us at the glowing summit and spotted a large dragon flying over it, his blood-red wings flapping once as he descended to the Temple. *Sark*.

This time I was certain he was looking for me. For us.

And soon we'd be ready to face him.

KISS THE SKY

HER ELEMENTAL DRAGONS BOOK TWO

1

KIRA

Fire burst into life inside my open palm, and with it came the fear. I forced myself to keep the flame going and to stare at the ball of light and heat in my hand, even as cold terror washed over me and sent shivers down my spine. For much of my life fire had been my torment and my terror, a reminder of my past and a deadly threat to my future, but not anymore. Now I was going to learn to control it—and my fear with it.

"Are you trying to kill us all?" a cold voice asked behind me.

I turned toward Reven, squinting against the bright sun behind him. "I need to practice if I ever want to get better with fire."

"Not on this boat." My black-haired assassin gestured around us. "This entire thing is made of wood. One stray spark and we'll all go up in flames."

He did have a point. I closed my hand over the ball of fire, immediately dousing it. "It's a good thing we have you then, isn't it?"

He scowled, but it didn't make him any less handsome. If anything, quite the opposite. "Nice to know my role in this group is to keep you and Jasin from burning the world down."

He shot a glare at Jasin, who stood on the other side of the boat talking with Auric while making flying gestures with his hands. Auric's golden hair caught the sunlight while he crossed his arms and furrowed his brow at whatever Jasin was saying. My fourth mate, Slade, sat nearby, ignoring the two of them as he sharpened his axe. He had the rich, dark skin common in the Earth Realm, along with a short beard and a large, impressive body that was all muscle.

167

"Your role in this group can be whatever you wish," I said. "Assuming you actually want to be one of us, that is."

"I'm here, aren't I?" Reven snapped, before spinning on his heel and stalking off, his black cloak trailing behind him. I sighed as I watched his brooding form disappear below deck. He was here, yes. But would he stay this time?

I leaned on the wooden railing and gazed across the waves. An unnatural wind—created by Auric—tousled my hair and filled the sail, guiding our boat northeast toward the Air Realm. In every direction all I saw was water and sky, a never-ending field of varying shades of blue that reminded me of my childhood spent in the Water Realm. After years living in the other kingdoms I only now realized how much I'd missed being surrounded by the ocean. I wondered if Reven felt the same, since he'd also grown up in the Water Realm, but I doubted he would admit it to me if he did.

I rarely thought about my childhood since it only brought pain, but now I closed my eyes and breathed in the salty air and let my mind travel back. Back to growing up on the shoreline under the shade of palm trees. Back to the smell of fresh fish off the boat. Back to my mother, with her hazel eyes and sandy hair, and my father, with his scratchy beard and sun-kissed skin. The Fire God had told me they weren't my birth parents, but to me they always would be my real family. Besides, I looked nearly identical to my mother, except I had red hair instead of blond. How could she not be my real mother? And if they weren't my birth parents, then who was?

Perhaps the Air God could tell me once we made it to his temple. This was only our first full day on this boat—we'd spend last night either trying to figure out how to sail, or passed out from exhaustion after our encounter at the Fire Temple—but we had many more days ahead of us before we would reach the Air Realm and the temple there. And after that our journey would continue across the other Realms, growing more impossible with each day.

For hundreds of years our world had been ruled by the five Dragons, the divine representatives of the Gods of earth, air, fire, water, and spirit. But in recent years the Gods had grown weary of the Dragons' oppressive control and recently chose new Dragons to take their place: me and my four mates. Only problem? The current Dragons had no interest in stepping down.

For most of my life I'd rarely spared a moment to think on the Gods, absent as they were, and when I thought of the Dragons it was with fear and anger. All of that changed on my twentieth birthday when I was struck by lightning and began having visions of the four men who would become my mates. A month later they each arrived in my village and I was forced to face the truth: that I was the next Black Dragon, who represented the Spirit Goddess and could control all five elements. The other men—Jasin, Slade, Auric, and Reven—each represented one of the other elements. And to unlock our powers and our Dragon forms, I had to bond with all of them.

Yesterday I'd bonded with Jasin, my confident, flirtatious soldier, who'd been chosen by the Fire God to be the next Crimson Dragon. Jasin had once served the current Dragons in the Onyx Army, but he'd had a change of heart after he was forced to do things he didn't agree with, including wiping out entire villages thought to be harboring members of the Resistance. At first I'd been hesitant to give my heart or my body to Jasin since he was a complete stranger to me, although not to other ladies it seemed. But after ten days of traveling to the Fire Temple together he'd won me over and I'd eagerly taken him as my mate.

The memory of it sent a rush of warmth through me now. His hands on my skin. His mouth between my thighs. The fire that had swept over us as the bond had completed. And when it was done, I'd been able to summon fire and Jasin could turn into a dragon.

Next I was meant to bond with Auric, my thoughtful, clever prince, who would represent the Air God as the Golden Dragon. He'd left behind his life as a royal and a scholar to be at my side, and I'd already come to value his kindness and intelligence. We were traveling toward the Air Realm now, where his parents ruled, though I wasn't sure what we would encounter there. Auric had sneaked away to be with me, and I had a feeling his family wouldn't be pleased with him. After Jasin's family betrayed us to the Onyx Army, it didn't seem wise to tell anyone else who or what we were. Either way, I was looking forward to bonding with Auric at the Air Temple, especially when I remembered his kisses, which had left me wanting even more.

Slade would be my next mate after Auric, though he didn't seem happy about that fact. He'd once been a humble blacksmith—although one who had connections with the Resistance, it seemed—before the Earth God had selected him to become the Jade Dragon. Slade hadn't wanted to leave his old life behind, and I got the feeling there was a woman in his past that was part of that, but I'd never once questioned his loyalty. I just wasn't sure if we'd ever have the kind of relationship I had with Jasin and Auric. Sometimes Slade looked at me in a way that made me think he desired me as much as I did him, but then he would turn away and the moment would be lost. I could only hope he would open up to me by the time we reached the Earth Temple.

Reven, on the other hand, had made it clear from the start he didn't want to be the next Azure Dragon, and didn't care one bit that the Water God had chosen him. Despite the undeniable chemistry between us, he'd resisted me and pushed me away at every turn. In the Fire Realm he'd eventually left us all behind, saying he wanted no part of our journey anymore and that caring for people made one weak. He'd returned a day later and saved my life, but I wasn't sure I could ever trust him again after he'd left us when we needed him most. But I'd have to find a way, because eventually we'd have to bond in the Water Temple too.

No matter what challenges we faced, I needed to take all four men as my mates to gain all of their elemental powers and become the next Black Dragon. Only then could we stop the current Dragons—and take their place as the protectors of the world.

"All right, I'm going to try it," Jasin said, his voice carrying over on the wind and interrupting my thoughts.

"Are you sure this is wise?" Auric asked, his brow furrowing.

Slade shook his head. "You're going to get yourself killed."

Jasin waved their concerns away. "I've got it handled."

"What are you doing?" I asked, as he tugged off his shirt and tossed it aside, revealing a chest rippling with muscles that were impossible not to stare at.

"Just watch and see." With those words Jasin walked confidently across the deck and gave me a wink, his auburn hair shining under the sun. He grabbed onto the ship's rigging and hauled himself up it with his strong arms, making my heart jump into my throat. With a mixture of fear and curiosity I watched his powerful body climb the ropes, going higher and higher, until he reached the top of the mast.

He spread his arms wide to the sun—and then he jumped.

I let out a cry as he fell toward the water, but then his body began to shift and grow. Blood red scales slithered across his skin, forming large wings and a long, snaking tail. Talons sprouted from his hands and fangs appeared from his mouth, and soon there was nothing left of my infuriatingly brave soldier except a formidable dragon in his place.

He flapped his great wings to keep from hitting the water, casting a gust of wind at the ship that sent us reeling. I gripped the railing tight as I watched him fly for the first time, while the other guys moved beside me, their eyes wide. Even Reven, though he crossed his arms like he wasn't impressed.

Jasin flew higher and unleashed a loud roar as he faced us, no doubt showing off because he knew he had an audience. Then he let out a strange sound that I thought might be a laugh before doing a flip in the air, clearly reveling in his new form. Under the sun his crimson scales gleamed, and my fear gave way to amazement. One day we would all be able to change forms like that and fly across the sky—including me. And once we mastered our powers and our new Dragon forms, maybe we'd be able to save the world. Assuming we could learn to work together first.

"He's going to be more insufferable than ever now," Reven said.

"No doubt," Slade agreed.

"I can fix that." With a wave of his hand, Auric sent a strong gust of wind flying toward Jasin, right as he did another flip. I arched an eyebrow at Auric, but he just shrugged.

Jasin awkwardly flapped his leathery wings to steady himself, but he couldn't regain his balance and began spiraling out of control. His scales rippled and shifted as if he was becoming human again while he plummeted from the sky. I gasped as his large reptilian body hit the water with a loud smack, sending waves across the deck and drenching the four of us. He sank below the water and I nearly reached for Reven to beg him to save Jasin, but then an auburn head surfaced in front of us.

Jasin tossed his wet hair back and grinned. "Is that the best you've got?"

Yeah, we had a lot of work ahead of us.

171

2

KIRA

Jasin practiced flying for another few hours while Reven and Auric guided our boat with waves and wind. Slade disappeared below deck, claiming all that open sky bothered him. He'd always been distant, but I sensed after my night with Jasin it had only gotten worse. He'd also been hit with a bad case of seasickness, which probably wasn't helping matters.

The area below deck was cramped and dark, almost like a cave, which was probably why Slade preferred it. This ship had been given to us by Calla, the High Priestess of the Fire God, and her four mates. It wasn't very large, just big enough for a small crew to maneuver, and I imagined it had once been used by them for fishing or for travel when needed.

I hoped Calla and her men were still safe. After we'd fought off the Onyx Army soldiers and escaped the Fire Temple, we'd spotted Sark, the Crimson Dragon, flying over it. Would he hurt Calla or her priests to get information out of us, even though they all served the Fire God too? I wasn't sure, but from here on out we had to assume that the Dragons knew about us. We could no longer hide in the shadows and hope that would protect us. Soon we would have to face them.

As night fell, my mates and I converged on the deck to eat supper together. We'd left most of our gear and supplies behind with our horses in the Fire Realm, which would soon prove to be a problem. Calla and her men had been thoughtful enough to stock the ship with food and other necessities, but that would only last us a short time. Once we reached the Air Realm we'd have to get more supplies and find another way to travel.

I broke off a piece of bread and passed it to Jasin, who did the same before passing it to Slade. "How many days will it take us to reach the Air Realm?" I asked.

"It depends where we're planning to dock," Auric said, as he took the bread from Slade. "We're making good time though."

"What are the options?" Slade asked.

Auric cocked his head as he considered. "There's the capital city, Stormhaven. It's the closest to the Air Temple, although we'll still have to travel on land for another week to get there. From a logistics perspective it's the clear choice, since we can reach it in three days and will be able to obtain new horses and supplies there." He drew in a long breath, his face grim. "The problem is that my family's palace is in Stormhaven."

"And the other option?" Reven asked.

"We continue past Stormhaven and around the bend for another five days to Galeport, then backtrack on land to the Air Temple."

"How much longer will that add?" Slade asked.

"Almost three weeks."

"Three weeks?" I asked, with a sigh. "I don't think we can spare that long. Not when the Dragons might already be hunting for us."

"If so, they'll eventually head to the temples to try to stop us," Jasin said. "The faster we get to them, the better."

"No, the less time we're on this ship the better," Slade grumbled, pushing his food away while clutching his stomach.

"We could disguise Auric and slip him into the city unnoticed," Reven suggested. I suspected he had plenty of experience doing that sort of thing from his former career as an assassin.

"Stormhaven it is," I said. "We'll sneak into the city, get what we need, and leave as soon as we can for the Air Temple."

Auric nodded. "I'll make the adjustments to our course with Reven."

It was the right decision, but I was disappointed I wouldn't be meeting Auric's family, even if that was probably for the best. Auric was a prince who had grown up in a life of luxury. I was a commoner who'd once made a living as a huntress, a bandit, and a traveling merchant. We weren't exactly suitable for each other, and even though Auric claimed he didn't care about our difference in status, his family certainly would. And then there was the whole Dragon thing we had to keep a secret too.

"Now that that's settled, tell us what happened the other night," Auric said. "You told us about the Fire God and what he said, but you didn't talk much about the actual bonding."

Jasin arched an eyebrow. "What, you want all the naughty details?"

"No, of course not," Auric replied quickly. "I simply want to know what to expect. Did anything…unusual happen?"

I glanced over at Jasin. "You *did* set me on fire."

"What?" Reven asked, his head snapping up.

Jasin grinned. "Yes, when we uh…completed. I assume that was the bond taking hold and passing my powers to her."

"Kira," Slade said, in that low, rumbling voice I would never grow tired of hearing. "Are you in any pain?"

"No, why?"

Slade rubbed the back of his neck without meeting my eyes. "A woman's first time can be…difficult."

"Oh." My cheeks flushed. "I'm all right. And if there was any pain, my healing powers must have taken care of it." Another benefit of being the representative of the Spirit Goddess.

Slade nodded and blew out a breath. "Good."

"You know I would never hurt Kira," Jasin said, looking offended at even the suggestion. "Trust me, I took good care of her. *Multiple* times."

Reven rolled his eyes. "Yes, we've heard all about your sexual prowess."

Gods, could this moment be any more awkward? My skin felt like it was on fire all over again. I coughed. "Jasin made the experience very…pleasant."

Jasin leaned back against the railing with a cocky grin. "I tried. Everyone should have a good first time, don't you all think?"

Slade let out a soft grunt. "Good? Mine was fast and awkward."

"Oh yeah?" Jasin asked. "Tell us about it. Who was the lucky lady?"

Slade's frown deepened as he glanced at me. "I'm not sure this is an appropriate conversation for us to have."

"It's fine," I said, waving it away. "I know you all had other women before you met me. I'm interested in learning everything about your pasts. Or whatever you're willing to share with me, anyway."

The men all hesitated and remained silent, but then Jasin spoke up. "Fine, I'll start. My first time was with one of my brother's friends. She was older than me and taught me how to please a woman."

"How much older?" Slade asked, arching an eyebrow.

"Only a few years. I think she was secretly interested in my brother, but he preferred men and I was the closest she could get." Jasin shrugged. "Both of us knew it wasn't anything serious, and we made each other happy for a while before she married someone else." He took a sip of water and gestured at Slade with the jug. "But if you're so righteous, tell us your story."

Slade stared down at the untouched food in front of him. "My first time was with a girl in my village. We grew up together and it seemed natural we would be married one day. Neither one of us knew what we were doing during that first time. But we figured it out together eventually over the years."

"What happened to her?" I asked, unable to stop myself.

His green eyes focused on me. "We never got married, if that's what you're asking."

I had a dozen more questions, but Slade's tone implied he had nothing more to say on the matter. I sighed and turned to Reven. "And you?"

"You don't want to hear my story."

"Well, now we definitely do," Jasin said.

Reven glared at him. "Fine, but it's not all fond memories like your stories." He ripped off chunks of his bread and threw them into the ocean without care. "I had to get by on the streets somehow after my parents were killed, and I discovered people will pay to have sex with young men. Quite handsomely."

Stunned silence met his words. I had no idea his parents had been killed, only that he'd told me he'd gotten his swords from his father, and I never would have guessed he'd spent part of his life doing something like that. There was so much more about his past—and everyone else's—that I wanted to uncover. But I had a feeling Reven's would be the darkest...and the hardest to crack.

"I'm sorry," I said, brushing my hand against his, where it rested on the deck.

He yanked his hand away. "Don't be. I'll do whatever it takes to survive. You should know that by now."

"On that cheerful note, what about you, Auric?" Jasin asked.

Auric had been silent the entire conversation, and now he brushed crumbs off his lap. "That's not something I wish to discuss with the group."

Reven arched an eyebrow. "It can't be any worse than my story."

"Maybe he's still waiting for his first time," Jasin teased, and Reven snickered in response.

Slade shook his head. "Leave him alone."

"I'm only trying to get to know my companions better," Jasin said, spreading his hands wide. "If we're going to be stuck together for the rest of our lives and sharing the same woman, we need to be able to talk about these things."

Auric stood and cast a sharp glance at Jasin. "You may be comfortable discussing these matters with everyone, but I am not. And I'd prefer if you respected my privacy in this matter."

He walked away and slipped below deck, while Jasin called out, "Auric, wait! I didn't mean anything by it!"

I shot Jasin a harsh look before going after Auric, while Slade just shook his head again. Every time I thought the five of us might be getting closer, something like this happened. I was beginning to think sharing four strong-willed men was never going to work out.

3

AURIC

I raked a hand through my blond hair, which had grown longer than I preferred over the last few days, while emotion churned inside me. I shouldn't have reacted that way—now they'd all suspect there was a reason for my vehement response. Perhaps I should have made up a story to placate them, but I couldn't lie to Kira. And she'd have to learn the truth eventually.

Kira came through the hatch and joined me below deck, her lovely face showing concern and her red hair a little wild from the wind. "I'm sorry about all that. Please ignore Jasin. He's simply trying to get a rise out of you. You know how he is."

I turned toward her and frowned at the worry in her eyes. Perhaps the time for truth was now. "I know. The problem is…he's right."

"What do you mean?"

I drew in a deep breath. "I've never been with a woman before."

She blinked. "You haven't?"

I rested my hands on her upper arms and gazed into her entrancing hazel eyes. "I'm sorry I didn't tell you sooner. I was waiting for the right moment, but it's hard for me to admit that I am lacking the knowledge or skills I require. Especially in something I wish to become an expert at."

"You don't need to be ashamed. Until the other night, I was inexperienced as well."

"Yes, it's probably fortunate that Jasin was the first one and not me, even if it made me jealous knowing he was claiming you."

She slid her arms around my neck and pressed a soft kiss to my jaw.

"Don't be jealous. Soon we'll reach the Air Temple and then we will be bonded too. We can become experienced together."

"It's not as simple as that," I said, shaking my head. "A man is easy to please, but a woman…a woman takes skill and practice to satisfy. At least, that's what I've learned from the books I've read on the subject."

Her lips quirked up in an amused smile. "Books?"

"The library in Stormhaven has a selection of books dedicated to bedroom skills. I've studied them all, so I know the theories and such, but I suspect it will be a different matter entirely to put what I read about into practice."

"Oh, Auric." She laughed softly and then pulled my mouth down to hers. Her lips were sweet, but as her tongue slid against mine I took control of the kiss, taking it deeper. I may have been inexperienced in bed, but kissing? *That* I was an expert on.

Kira's hands slipped under my shirt as I tugged at her lower lip with my teeth. While her palms smoothed across my chest, I trailed kisses down her neck, finding the spots that made her sigh. If nothing else, I was a fast learner—and I was going to make Kira my new object of study. I would explore her own body until I knew it better than my own. I would uncover every way to make her cry out my name in pleasure.

But there was more I had to tell her first.

I caught her face in my hands and met her eyes. "Kira, there's something else too."

"What is it?" she asked.

Before I could speak, Jasin dropped down into the cabin, interrupting me. I didn't pull away from Kira. Let him see that she was mine too. Though if he was bothered by it, he didn't show it.

"Sorry about all of that earlier," Jasin said, surprising me with his sincerity. Jasin and I had never gotten along, but perhaps he was making an effort now that it was clear we were both going to be a part of each other's lives for good, especially since we both loved Kira. Which gave me an idea.

"I didn't mean anything by what I said, and I should have let it go," Jasin continued. "You don't owe the rest of us anything, especially me. If you want to keep part of your past a secret, that's none of my business."

"Thank you for the apology." I hesitated, considering my next move. "But perhaps you can help me with something."

His eyebrows darted up. "Help you? How?"

"I need you to teach me the art of pleasing a woman."

Jasin burst into laughter. "Oh Gods, that's hilarious." He laughed again, but then noticed Kira and I were not in on the joke. His smile dropped into a frown. "Wait, you're serious. Oh. Wow. So you truly are inexperienced. Damn."

"I am, yes. You were correct. I've never had a first time." I gave Kira a heated glance. "Not yet."

"But...how?" Jasin asked. "You're a good-looking guy and a prince too. I can't imagine you couldn't find a woman or three to take to bed."

"It's tradition in the Air Realm for the nobility to remain virgins until marriage, both men and women. I've had plenty of opportunities, but I wanted to wait until I found my forever mate."

"I'm honored," Kira said, giving me a warm smile.

Jasin raked a hand through his already messy hair. "But why me? You and I barely get along as it is. I doubt getting naked together will help."

"It has to be you," I said. "You're the most experienced of us all and you've already bonded with Kira. Besides, we both know Slade and Reven would never agree."

"True." His gaze shifted to Kira. "Are you okay with this?"

She considered us both, her eyes dancing with interest. "The Fire God did say you needed to learn to work together..."

"Somehow I doubt this is what he meant," Jasin muttered.

"Jasin, despite our differences, we both want Kira to be happy," I said. "Though I realize this will be awkward at first, eventually all four of us are going to be sharing her. Maybe at the same time, if that's something she wants."

"Is it?" Jasin asked her.

Her cheeks flushed with obvious desire. "I think so."

Oh yes, she definitely liked the idea of us sharing her at once. The thought aroused me as well, but such a thing was fairly common in the Air Realm. My older sister had two husbands, and both my parents openly shared their beds with others on the side. I was more surprised that Jasin, from the uptight Fire Realm, was even considering this plan.

But he seemed satisfied by Kira's answer. "All right, I'll do it."

I gave him a respectful nod. "Thank you. I promise I'm a quick study."

"Then let's get started." He grabbed his shirt and yanked it off, then tossed it aside.

"Now?" I asked, shocked by his boldness.

Jasin shrugged with a wry grin. "Why wait?"

"Are you sure we're all ready for this?" Kira asked, even though her eyes were roaming all over Jasin's naked chest like she'd never seen anything better in her life.

Jasin stepped close to her. "We won't do anything you don't want to do."

Following his lead, I tugged my shirt over my head and was satisfied by the way Kira's gaze began to devour me too. She ran her tongue along her lower lip in the most alluring way, and there was no mistaking her arousal.

Jasin snaked an arm around Kira's waist and yanked her against him, then captured her mouth in a hot, passionate kiss. I watched them intently, studying the way she melted against him and how his fingers dug into her hips possessively.

But then she broke away and reached for me, pulling me close. Her lips found mine again and I skimmed my fingers across her nipples, feeling how hard they were through the fabric of her dress. Jasin kissed her neck at the same time, trapping Kira between the two of us.

I began to think this plan to involve Jasin might be one of my best yet.

4

KIRA

Last night I'd been a virgin. Now I was pressed between two gorgeous men, their hands and lips lavishing attention on my body. Jasin kissed my neck, while Auric claimed my mouth. Two hands stroked my breasts, and two others cupped my behind and gave it a quick squeeze. All I could do was relax into their touch and succumb to the overwhelming lust they stirred inside me.

I reached for them too, sliding my hands across their hard chests. Jasin was more muscular, a fighter through and through, while Auric was taller and leaner, but still strong. Both of them were perfect for me in different ways.

Jasin dragged my dress up over my head, revealing my naked flesh to Auric for the first time. Auric gazed down at me with a mix of reverence and hunger, taking me all in like he was memorizing every inch.

"Turn around," he said. "I want to see all of you."

I slowly spun, trying not to feel self-conscious under the gaze of both men. My natural inclination was to cover my breasts or my mound, but I kept my arms at my side, channeling a little of the bravery Jasin had taught me. These were my mates, and if I couldn't be naked with them, then who?

"Beautiful," Auric said, his voice rough. "The Gods could not have made you any better."

I flushed as I turned back to him, warm from his compliments. "I want to see you too."

"Whatever you desire." He reached for his trousers and my pulse quickened, but then we heard a sound above us that made us freeze.

Slade dropped below deck, his movements rushed. "We have a—"

He stopped when he saw I was standing completely naked before the other two men. The urge to cover myself or turn away became almost unbearable, but he was going to see me naked eventually—and I wanted to see his reaction.

He quickly looked away, as if shielding his eyes from the sight of my bare skin. "I'm sorry. I didn't know the three of you were...together like this."

"It's all right," I said, trying to hide my disappointment at his response. "Is something wrong?"

"Water elementals are surrounding the ship. Reven tried to speed us past them, but they're turning the sea to ice around us."

Jasin swore under his breath as he charged forward, still wearing nothing but his trousers. "I can fix that."

"Be careful," I said, as I quickly grabbed my dress and pulled it back on. "Remember, the ship is all wood."

We scrambled up the ladder and onto the deck, where Reven glowered at the sea. Our ship was marooned in a large patch of ice in the middle of the ocean, though I didn't see any elementals yet.

"About time," Reven snapped at us. "I've been turning the ice back to water, but there are too many of them down there."

"I've got this." Jasin leaped onto the railing and into the air, shifting into a dragon before he hit the ice. His change was faster this time, and he flapped his wings and blasted the ice with fire from his great fanged mouth.

"They won't last long against his fire magic," Auric said.

Slade watched Jasin fly higher with a frown. "No, but there are a lot more of them than him."

"And that's if he doesn't set the entire ship on fire and kill us for them," Reven muttered.

As Jasin took out the ice in front of us, the elementals burst onto the back of the ship with a crash of waves that sent cold seawater across our feet. At first I could only stare at the large, swirling masses of water with arms, glowing yellow eyes, and huge gaping mouths. But as Auric shot a gust of wind to knock the elementals back and Slade pulverized them with small pieces of metal, I shook myself out of the fear and shock.

I quickly formed a ball of flame in my hand, but then hesitated, worried I might miss and do damage to the ship. I hadn't had much chance to practice my magic yet, and we'd decided it was safer for Jasin to train me once we were on land again. But this was the only way I could stop the elementals—they were immune to normal weapons.

"I'll cover you," Reven said. "My magic doesn't work on them anyway."

I nodded. Auric and Slade had knocked two elementals back into the water, but I suspected that wouldn't stop them for long. Meanwhile, Jasin was fighting a large group at the front of the ship, his wings flapping as he did passes over them to rain down fire. I wasn't sure how long he could keep that up though, especially since his dragon form was still so new to him.

Three elementals glided across the deck toward us and began shooting strong bursts of icy water at us. Reven reached out and diverted the water back into the ocean before it could hit us, but the elementals kept getting closer.

"Dragons…must…die…" one of them said, surprising me. I'd never realized they could speak in our language.

"We're not like the other Dragons!" I called out, though it was clear there would be no reasoning with them.

The elementals suddenly charged us, their liquid bodies slicing through the wooden deck of the ship and sending splinters flying. One knocked Auric off the ship and into the water, while another began wrestling with Slade. The third came for me.

I threw my ball of flame, but only managed to graze the thing's shoulder, where the fire sizzled out. So much for that plan. Reven shot water at the elemental to protect me, but all it did was join the creature's body, making it stronger.

The elemental wrapped a cold, watery hand around my neck and lifted me up into the air. I forced fire to burst from my palms as I grabbed onto his head, which made the monster let out something like a scream. I kept up the pressure, making the flames hotter and stronger, and the elemental began to dissipate in front of my eyes. When it let me go I tumbled back into Reven, who steadied me while the elemental turned to steam and vanished.

I rubbed my aching throat, my heart racing, but there was no time to stop and recover. Slade was still grappling with the other elemental, using sharp pieces of the broken deck to attack it from all sides. I'd never seen him use wood before, only stone and metal, but there was little of that available on the ship and he must have had to improvise.

Auric burst out of the water, floating high into the air as if he was flying, and relief shot through me. He blasted an elemental across the deck and into the ocean, while Slade slammed the other one down against the deck. I rushed forward and used fire on it to take it out, while Jasin seared the ones in the sea. Slowly the elementals dipped back under the waves, retreating from the battle.

When they vanished, Jasin plummeted from the sky and collapsed on the deck in human form, the momentum ripping another hole into the wood as he rolled to a stop.

"Jasin!" I called out as I rushed over to him, worried he was injured from the fall or the battle. I reached his side and turned him over, but he only gave me a weary smile.

"It's nice to know I'm still your favorite."

"Hardly." I wasn't sure whether to smack him upside the head or kiss him senseless, which was pretty normal with Jasin. Instead I sat back on the deck beside him, exhausted after using my magic. No wonder the men trained every day to build their control and their fortitude. If I was ever going to get better with fire, I'd need a lot more practice.

Slade kneeled beside me and rested a hand on my shoulder. "Are you all right?"

I nodded and leaned into his strong touch while gazing across the ship. Our deck was a mess, the wood torn up and splintered, with a few gaping holes in it. There was so much water on the deck, and I couldn't tell if it was from the elementals or if the ship was taking it on. "I'm fine, but our ship isn't."

"I might be able to fix that," Slade said, his stony eyes surveying the deck.

"We have a bigger problem," Auric suddenly called out, drawing our attention.

Off the starboard side of the boat a massive wave was forming, created by the remaining water elementals. It was easily as tall as the ship. And it was coming right for us.

5

KIRA

I gaped at the giant wave speeding across the ocean, which would engulf
our ship in only minutes. "What do we do?"

Jasin hefted himself up to a sitting position with a groan. "I'll have to
face them again."

"You can't." I grabbed his arm to hold him back. If he couldn't even
stand, how was he supposed to deal with the elementals?

He shrugged me off. "What other option is there?"

"We run," Reven said.

Auric began filling the sails with air to speed us away, while Reven
controlled the water currents around the ship. Slade assisted by tying ropes
or adjusting the sails, while I tried to give Jasin some of my strength with
the touch of my hands. It didn't seem to do much, maybe because I'd
worn myself out already too.

And the giant wave kept coming closer.

"We can't outrun it," Auric called out after a few minutes, the wind
whipping at his golden hair. "We have to brace for impact!"

"Get below deck," Slade told me and Jasin in a firm tone.

"Not a chance." Jasin forced himself to his feet, leaning heavily against
the mast.

"Then protect Kira. She's the most important thing on this ship."

Slade's overprotectiveness sometimes got on my nerves, but I didn't
have time to argue that I could take care of myself. Not when the massive
wave would hit us in mere moments. "We need to work together," I said.
"That's the only way through this."

Reven faced the approaching water with his head high. "I'll hold back the water as best I can."

"I can try to put a bubble of air around us," Auric said.

Slade rubbed his beard as he considered. "I'll reinforce the ship. Make it stronger so it won't break apart under the wave."

"Kira and I will blast those elementals," Jasin said.

It wasn't a perfect plan and we'd likely all be sent to the bottom of the ocean, but it was something. It gave me strength knowing that even if my mates squabbled in their free time, they came together when it counted.

"Here it comes!" Reven yelled, as he braced himself against the railing. He cast a determined look at the wave and held it back as it came toward us, but all he could do was slow it down. If he'd had his dragon form maybe he could stop it, but there were too many elementals controlling this water.

The enormous wave crested over the ship, raining saltwater down on us and blocking out the sky. Fear gripped my throat as Auric raised his arms, causing the water to slam against an invisible wall around us. Slade bent down and rested his palms on the wood and metal of the deck, while the ship begin to creak and groan.

The wave drenched the entire ship with a great crash and sent it careening to the side, but Auric and Reven's magic kept us dry. Water buffeted their defenses relentlessly, and the two men were forced back while our small bubble of safety shrank.

From the view around us, we might as well have been completely underwater. Maybe we were, with the way the ship was lurching, making it hard for us to stand. I lost my footing and crashed into Slade, but he caught me and held me against him, as if he could protect me with his sheer size and willpower.

The wave didn't seem to end and I could tell my mates were losing the battle, as was the ship, which splintered apart under the pressure from the water. But then the elementals appeared through the wave, their glowing eyes giving them away.

I gripped Jasin's arm. "We have to stop them!"

He nodded, his face weary but his will unwavering. Together we stepped in front of the other men and sought out the elementals, but there were too many of them and my magic was still untrained. We couldn't afford for me to miss. No, we needed Jasin's magic.

I took Jasin's hand and felt the bond between us flare bright. I closed my eyes and willed my energy and healing magic from the Spirit Goddess to flow into him. As it did, a wave of exhaustion swept through me, even as Jasin's body began to glow faintly. I had no idea if this would work or how long I could do this, but we needed Jasin more than we needed me right now. He was the only one who could save us.

Jasin conjured fire in his other hand and it burned so hot it was almost blue. He cast it at the elemental nearest us and it went up in a wisp of steam immediately. He lobbed another ball of flame at the next one, and the next, clutching my other hand tight the entire time. The never-ending downpour buffeting the ship began to ease slightly. And as he worked I felt his resolve, his fear, his courage, and his exhilaration through the bond as if they were my own emotions.

The last elemental went up in a spray of mist, and the wave suddenly ceased its attack, dropping back into the ocean. The ship rolled violently and the deck was splintered and cracked in numerous places, but was otherwise intact. All four of my mates were alive, although exhausted and drenched with saltwater.

We did it.

That was my last thought before fatigue swept through me and I collapsed onto the deck, still clutching Jasin's hand.

6

SLADE

Kira's body hit the deck and I rushed toward her, even though Jasin was already kneeling over her. I knocked him out of the way and lifted Kira's small form into my arms. Her body was completely limp and her head rolled against my shoulder, her eyes closed, but she was alive at least. *Kira, what did he do to you?*

"I can take her," Jasin said, reaching for Kira again.

I pinned him with a stern gaze. "You've done enough."

"Is she all right?" Auric asked, his face lined with worry.

"She's still breathing," Reven said.

"She needs rest." I began to make my way toward the hatch leading below deck. The other guys followed right at my heels, while Kira's head rested snugly against my chest. I'd already been terrified for her during the elemental attack, but seeing her collapse had been too much and I'd been forced to jump into action. She seemed so small and fragile in my arms, even though I knew she was as fierce as any of us. If I could keep her cradled in my arms and safe forever, I would. She would hate it, but I wouldn't care if it meant no harm would ever befall her.

Gods, when had I begun to care so much for her? There was no denying it. I was fond of her, though I was hesitant to admit it even to myself. It had to be that damn mate bond between us making me want to protect her and be near her at all times. And it would only get worse once we were truly bonded at the Earth Temple.

As I jumped down into the lower quarters with Kira nestled in my arms, water splashed everywhere. It was up to my knees thanks to the wave that had attacked us, but otherwise the ship appeared intact down here. I'd have to do a more thorough appraisal soon, but first I had to get Kira settled.

Auric righted a hammock and I gently placed Kira into it, then brushed hair off her face with my knuckles. She didn't even stir, and I stared at her chest for some time to confirm she was truly breathing.

Then I turned toward Jasin and slammed him back against the nearest wall. "What did you do to her?"

His eyes widened. "Me? I did nothing!"

My grip tightened around his shirt. "Then what happened to her?"

"She took my hand and gave me her power. Our bond went berserk or something. I don't know!"

"That's why you were glowing," Auric said from behind me.

I released Jasin with a low growl, and he straightened up and glared at me in return. "I swear, I didn't do anything," he said. "I was completely wiped out, but then she touched me and I suddenly had a ton of energy again and I could summon more fire than ever." His face softened as he looked over at Kira. "I had no idea it would do this to her."

"She probably didn't know either," Auric said.

Reven shrugged. "She did this to herself. It's not Jasin's fault."

I swung my angry stare over to him. "No one asked for your opinion, deserter."

Reven's eyes narrowed at me and my fists clenched in return. Normally I was the calm, clear-headed one of the group who could ignore their constant bickering, but not when Kira was suffering like this. Jasin was the cause this time, but Reven had abandoned Kira before when she needed him most. She'd forgiven him somehow, but if it were up to me we'd be looking for a new man to represent water.

Auric touched Kira's forehead with the back of his hand. "She's going to be okay. She just needs rest."

I stiffened. "We don't know that. She's never been like this before."

"I'm worried too," Jasin said. "But I can feel her through our bond and she's still there. I think she'll be fine after she gets some sleep. The best thing we can do for her is to get this ship moving again."

I drew in a long breath and allowed my muscles to relax. "All right, but one of us needs to keep watch over her at all times in case something changes. And I'm taking first watch."

"No, we need you to fix the ship," Jasin said, which made me only want to slam him against the wall again. If he thought he was going to step up and be the leader of this group he was going to be met with some resistance, even if he'd bonded with Kira first.

"He's right," Auric said. "Reven and I can't get the ship moving again without your repairs in place, and Jasin's magic can't do much in that regard."

Jasin nodded. "I'll take first watch."

"I'll get the next one," Reven said, crossing his arms. "Once I get the water off this ship, you won't need me for a while."

I pressed my palm to my forehead, fighting off a rising headache, no doubt from dealing with Kira's annoying mates. "Fine."

I climbed up the ladder with heavy steps, my own exhaustion taking hold of me now that the thrill of the battle and the fear over Kira's collapse was behind me. I'd continue to worry about her until she was awake and could tell me herself she was okay, but there were other ways to protect her too. Like repairing this ship.

As the ship swelled and rolled, another wave of seasickness reminded me I should have stayed on land from the beginning. Without firm ground under my feet I was mostly useless in a battle, although I'd discovered I could control wood as long as all the life had left it. Living things were the domain of the Spirit Goddess, but old, hard wood was as lifeless as stone and seemed to fall under my control.

I used that power now to mend the splintered mast so that Auric could get the ship sailing again soon and allow us to continue on to the Air Temple. And after that...the Earth Temple, where I would fully bond with Kira. At first, I'd resisted the idea. Then I'd come to terms with it and considered it my duty. Now I was anxious to get there sooner than later. Once I was a Dragon I would be able to defend Kira and the others better. Gods knew Jasin needed all the help he could get in that area.

But the act of bonding would be a problem. Even if I desired Kira physically, things between us could never go beyond friendship and duty. I would never love a woman again without reservation, and even if I could, I wasn't comfortable with the idea of sharing her with other men. There was no way Kira could love all of us equally in the end, and I wasn't willing to be someone's second—or third or fourth—choice. I'd already been left for another man once. I was never opening myself up to that kind of pain again.

7

KIRA

W hen I opened my eyes I found Reven in the hammock beside me,
wearing nothing but his trousers. His cool skin pressed against
mine, and I discovered I wore only my threadbare chemise as well. One of
my mates must have changed me out of my soaked dress at some point.

With Reven's eyes closed he looked peaceful for once, especially with
his black hair messy. Younger, too. Or perhaps he appeared his true age for
once. How he would look if he didn't have his dark past weighing on him
all the time.

The second I moved, his eyes snapped open and fixed on me. They
were the color of the waves around the ship and just as cold.

"What are you doing here?" I asked, as I slowly rolled toward him, the
hammock drawing us close together. "And without a shirt on?"

"We thought touching you might heal you faster. Like when you heal
us." His jaw clenched, but he didn't move away. "It was Auric's idea."

"Of course it was." I rested my hands on the muscular ridges of his
chest. For healing, naturally. "How long have I been out?"

"Almost two days."

"Two *days*?" I pushed on his chest to rise to a sitting position. "What
happened to me?"

He sat up next to me and shrugged. "You collapsed after we fought off
the water elementals. We brought you in here to rest."

I scrubbed a hand over my face as the memories came back. "I gave
Jasin my energy and strength so he could fight the elementals off, but I
must have drained myself in the process."

"Seems that way."

I'd have to be more careful in the future, especially if it knocked me out for so long. I practically fell out of the hammock and righted myself on shaky legs, while my stomach ached with a hollow feeling and my vision blurred. "Oh Gods, I'm starving."

"I'm sure we can find you something." Reven got to his feet in one smooth motion that made me look like a graceless animal. He grabbed his shirt and tossed it on, the muscles in his back flexing and commanding my attention. It was truly unfair for someone so difficult to be so irresistible.

With Reven right behind me, I slowly climbed up the ladder and moved through the hatch onto the main deck, squinting against the bright sun. Where I'd expected disaster and wreckage, all I saw was the ship looking almost as good as new. Gods, I really had been out a long time.

"Kira!" Jasin called out from above me. "You're awake!"

He slid down a rope from the main mast and landed at my feet, while Auric floated down until his boots lightly touched the deck. Slade hopped down from the upper deck as he approached us. Yes, everyone on this ship was more graceful than me today.

Auric touched my face softly. "It's good to see you up again."

"You've learned a new trick," I said, leaning into his palm.

"Yes, and it's definitely coming in handy. Not all of us are eager to climb the ropes like Jasin here."

Slade gripped my shoulders and spun me around to take me in. "Kira, are you well?"

"I'm okay, thanks. Just hungry." I tried to pat down my hair, which was more unruly than ever, not helped by the warm breeze out here. "I can't believe I slept so long."

"Let me get you something to eat," Jasin said, before darting off.

"He feels responsible for what happened to you," Auric said quietly.

"He *is* responsible," Slade growled.

I reached for the railing to steady myself, feeling a bit lightheaded. "No, it was all my own doing. Don't blame Jasin for this."

"Why don't you sit down?" Auric said, taking my elbow and leading me along the ship. He helped me onto a nearby barrel, while the other men hovered around me. They'd already been over-protective of me, and now that I'd passed out in front of them I'd never get a moment to myself again.

"I'm fine, really," I said, though I did feel better now that I was sitting.

Reven handed me a flask, scowling the entire time. "Drink this."

I sighed at him, but then took a long sip of cool, deliciously fresh water. Before I knew it the flask was empty and my head had stopped spinning quite so much. With a flick of his fingers, Reven summoned more water into the flask, while Jasin returned with a spread of food—bread, cheese, and some fried fish. Enough to feed all of us, but he set it in front of me alone.

"Thank you, this is perfect," I said, as I popped a piece of cheese into my mouth.

"Reven caught us all some fish earlier, and I fried them up while Auric and Slade fixed the ship," Jasin said with a grin. Through our bond I felt him near me and sensed his emotions—mainly relief, with a touch of guilt and worry.

I managed a small smile at the group of men. "It's nice to see you all working together."

"Don't get used to it." Reven crossed his arms, but that only made me smile wider.

"Can you tell us what happened the other day?" Auric asked.

I took another sip of water before continuing. "I could tell Jasin was exhausted and I still don't know how to control fire very well, so I tried to lend him my energy and strength."

"It definitely worked. I'd never felt so powerful before." Jasin stroked my hair tenderly while I ate. "I only wish it hadn't drained you in the process."

"I'll have to be careful in the future. I'm still learning how to use all this magic and I haven't even begun my fire training." The thought of everything I had ahead of me was daunting. I'd have to master all five elements, and quickly. Along with everything else that came with being the Black Dragon.

"You just need to practice," Slade said. "It's the same as learning any new skill. The more you do it the better you'll get at it, and the longer you'll be able to keep it going."

I nodded. Archery had been the same way at first. When I'd first joined the bandits I had never held a bow before and thought I would never be good at it. Now the only one who could rival me with a bow was Jasin.

"We're growing stronger every day," Auric said. "Imagine how powerful we'll be once we're all bonded to you."

"Imagine how powerful the other Dragons are now," Reven countered. "They've had centuries to practice their magic."

"Let's hope we won't encounter one anytime soon." I couldn't help but glance back the way we'd come, wondering if Sark's blood-red wings were trailing behind us. Sooner or later we would have to face the Dragons—and we definitely weren't ready for them yet.

8

JASIN

That night I sought out Kira below deck after giving her a bit more time to recover. As I stepped down the ladder, she was staring at Auric's map of the four Realms, her finger resting near the Air Temple and her brow creased in thought. Her red hair hung loose around her shoulders, framing her graceful neck and that beautiful face I could stare at forever. *Mine*, something inside me whispered with satisfaction.

Though I knew she'd bond with the other men soon, I took great pride in being her first mate. She'd been hesitant to trust me at first, between my past as a ladies' man and a soldier in the Onyx Army, but eventually I'd won her over and proven my devotion to her. And a good thing too, because I'd realized before we even reached the Fire Temple that I was in love with her. I'd never felt so strongly about any woman before, and now I couldn't imagine a life without Kira in it.

"How are you feeling?" I asked, when she glanced up at me.

"Better, thanks." She pushed the map aside as I moved behind her and began massaging her shoulders. With a soft sigh she tilted her head back, relaxing under my firm hands. "That feels nice."

"Good." I brushed aside her hair and slid her dress down her shoulders so I could better knead her soft skin. "When you collapsed in front of us I was so worried. The other guys were too. Don't do that again, okay?"

"I'll try not to, but I can't make any guarantees. I'm still testing the limits of these new powers and I have a lot to learn. "

"Just be careful. I've never seen Slade so upset before."

She turned her head toward me. "Slade was upset?"

194

"Very. All of us were. Even Reven." I pressed my thumbs into the spot between her shoulder blades where I could tell she was extra tense. "At least I could still sense you through our bond so I knew you would be okay. The others could only trust my word on that."

"I understand. I can feel you through the bond too." She leaned back into my touch. "I can sense where you are and sometimes feel your emotions."

I chuckled softly. "Not sure I'm thrilled with *that* aspect of the bond."

"Why, are you hiding something from me?" she asked in a teasing voice.

"Not at all. Just as long as you can't read my thoughts. Although if you could, you'd see all the things I'd like to do to you now that we're finally alone."

"No mind reading, I promise." She stood and turned toward me with a seductive grin. "But maybe you can show me some of these things…"

"Are you sure? You're still recovering."

"I'm all right. Besides, we can test out the theory that touching gives me energy in return." But as soon as she stepped into my eager arms, she swayed a little and I found myself supporting her weight. She pressed a hand to her forehead. "Sorry, I got a little lightheaded there."

I held her tight against me as concern overcame my desire. "How about we just relax together instead?"

She nodded. "Probably a good idea. I'm sorry though."

I pressed a kiss to her lips. "Don't be sorry. All I want is to be by your side."

"Thanks. I wish I had the strength to do more. I'd like to continue what we started in the Fire Temple."

"Soon. Once we're on dry land again maybe."

Together we climbed into the hammock and she curled up in my arms. A sense of satisfaction and peace settled over me as she tucked her head against my neck. Before I met Kira I'd been the type of man who had a new woman in every city I visited, and I'd only spent a single night with each of them. Cuddling with a woman was out of the question—that was how people got attached, and that was the last thing I'd wanted. Until Kira.

"Auric will want to join us too," she mused, as she played with the collar of my shirt idly. "Are you sure you're all right with that?"

"I don't mind. I've shared women with other soldiers before, and if it makes you happy then I'm all for it. Even if Auric isn't my favorite person." I wrapped a strand of her red hair around my finger. "Although he's not my least favorite person anymore either."

"No? Who is?"

"Reven."

She snorted. "I think the other guys would probably agree with you."

"He left us when we needed him most. I'm not sure I'll ever trust him again."

"He came back at least," Kira pointed out.

"He should never have left in the first place." Why was Reven even here, when he didn't seemed to care about Kira at all? He wasn't good enough for her. At least Auric—annoying though he may be—was a prince, and he obviously loved Kira as much as I did. Even Slade, who avoided Kira as much as possible, obviously had feelings for her he wasn't ready to admit yet. But Reven? I couldn't tell what he wanted, and I worried he would only hurt her in the end.

"I have to believe the Gods chose all of you for a reason," Kira said.

As I held her close I stared up at the ceiling, the hammock creaking under us, matching the roll of the ship on the waves. "The Fire God said they chose us to help bring out certain aspects in you." For me it was bravery and passion, but I wasn't sure what the others were supposed to be helping Kira with. All Reven brought out in Kira was frustration, and Slade wasn't much better. It would be up to me and Auric to keep her happy during what came ahead, which was why I'd agreed to share her with the prince more than any other reason.

Kira was going to face a number of obstacles in the future and she needed people by her side she could trust, who would support her and help keep her strong no matter what she faced. I'd already pledged my heart, mind, and soul to that task. I had no doubt Auric would too. But would the other two, when the time came?

9

KIRA

As we approached Stormhaven, Auric's wind buffeted our sails and the ship sliced through the waves at an unnatural speed. I stood on the prow and gazed at the capital of the Air Realm in the distance, a barely visible assortment of tall buildings shining bright under the midday sun. With each passing moment it grew in size, and in only a few more hours we'd be stepping onto shore again.

The Air Realm was known as the center of culture in the four Realms, prized for its fine art, music, and literature. Thanks to a rich trade of dyes, spices, and oils, the Air Realm was also the wealthiest kingdom in the world. I'd never been to Stormhaven before in all of my travels, and I couldn't help but feel excited at seeing the City of a Thousand Spires, as it was called.

I wished Tash could be with me, especially since she'd always wanted to visit the Air Realm for the shopping and fine cuisine. She'd been my best friend in Stoneham, where I'd lived the last few years in the Earth Realm, and I missed her greatly. While I enjoyed the presence of my four mates, I missed speaking to a fellow woman now and then. Especially Tash, with her cheerful demeanor and easygoing attitude. Even after I'd killed her abusive father—in self-defense, of course—she'd remained strong and didn't seem to harbor any resentment toward me. I closed my eyes and imagined her now, likely running her family's inn, her dark hair braided as she worked. I prayed to the Gods she was okay and that I would see her again soon.

Auric moved to stand by my side, resting his hands lightly on the railing as he stared across the waves toward the city where he'd been raised. "We'll be there soon."

I turned toward him, examining his handsome, regal face. "Are you nervous?"

"A little. Reven assures me the plan will work, but I can't help but worry I'll be recognized, as it would be difficult to find anyone in Stormhaven who doesn't know my face. If my family finds out I've returned, I'm not sure what will happen. I can't imagine they'll be happy with me after I disappeared without a word when I went to find you."

"They must be worried about you."

"Probably," he said with a sigh. "It would be nice to see them briefly and let them know I'm safe, but that isn't a good idea."

I hesitated, but then asked the question lingering on my tongue. "Are they loyal to the Black Dragon, like Jasin's family?"

"I'm not sure how to answer that. My parents are good people who want what is best for their kingdom. That means serving the Dragons and bowing to their wishes, but I've also seen my parents stand up to them too. They'll protect the Air Realm however they can."

"I wish some of the other Realms had kings and queens who would think of their people's best interests and stand up to the Dragons sometimes."

"It's not easy. The last ruler who truly stood against the Dragons was the Earth King, and his entire family was slaughtered for it. Except for his youngest daughter, who was only four at the time. The Black Dragon raised the girl as her own daughter to ensure her loyalty, and now the Earth Queen is basically a puppet."

I'd heard that story about the Earth Queen as well. I shuddered. "I can see why no one wants to appear disloyal."

"Exactly. My parents must walk a fine line. So yes, they're loyal to the Dragons. But they're also not." He shrugged. "Politics."

"I don't think I could live that kind of life."

"No, me neither. I was never good at the political maneuverings and courtly intrigue. That life never felt like it was meant for me. I'm much happier now as one of your mates."

"We're lucky to have you. Without your wealth of knowledge, we would be lost. Literally."

"Glad I can be of use." His head tilted as he examined the city again. "I have to admit I'm eager to return to Stormhaven, even if only for a short while. I've traveled to many places now, but this will always be my home."

"I'm excited to see it. I've heard so much about Stormhaven. The markets. The cafes. The spires."

"Stormhaven gets terrible lightning storms, hence its name," Auric said, as he caught me gazing out at the city with awe. "The spires were originally built to protect the city from lightning strikes, but then it became a trend to build high into the sky to honor the Air God."

"The city is beautiful."

"You have to see it at sunset. There's nothing more stunning than the sun turning the clouds pink and the spires reflecting the light back." He turned toward me and lightly rested his hands on my waist. "I only wish the circumstances of our arrival were different and I could show you around the city and the palace. Maybe even meet my parents."

I swallowed my longing for those very things. "I would like that very much. Someday..."

"Yes, someday." He pressed a quick kiss to my lips before releasing me. "I should probably ease off on the wind and ask Reven to slow the currents as well so that those ships up ahead don't notice we're moving a bit too quickly."

I nodded. "I'll make sure everything is packed up and ready to go."

I headed below deck and found Slade putting the last few things in our bags, including some of the supplies Calla and her priests had provided for us. "Can I do anything to help?"

"No, I think we're ready." He tied off one of the bags and set it with the others.

I moved to the area where I'd kept my things and checked that my bow and sword were ready, along with the small bag I'd brought. "I bet you're excited to be back on land again."

"You have no idea. I can only pray I never have to be out at sea again. I need to be able to see the land at least. If this is my last time on a boat, even better."

I bit my lip and decided not to tell him that much of the Water Realm was made up of tiny islands and the Water Temple was only accessible by boat. By then he would be able to fly at least, although if he hated the ocean I couldn't imagine he'd like the sky much better.

"Did you do much traveling before we met?" I asked.

"No, not at all. I'd only left my village a few times. I never would have imagined I'd get to visit each Realm." Slade rubbed his beard, which had grown longer while we were on the boat. "Then again, I never would have imagined any of this."

"Me neither."

"You've been to the Air Realm before though, haven't you?"

"Yes, a few years ago." I debated revealing more, but that was a story better suited for another day. "Although this is my first visit to Stormhaven."

Reven dropped down onto the lower deck. "Watch your coins. Stormhaven is known for its thieves. All the Air Realm is full of bandits, actually."

I knew that all too well. With any luck, we would never come across the Thunder Chasers, the bandit group I'd once been a part of. At some point I would have to tell my mates about that part of my past, though I worried what they would think of me. Reven probably wouldn't care, but the others? A soldier, a prince, and a blacksmith would not look fondly on the things I'd once done.

"I thought the Air Realm was the wealthiest kingdom," Slade said.

Reven put on his twin swords. "It is. But it also has the weakest guard and the smallest division of the Onyx Army. The people here are peaceful, fat, and happy, with no desire to fight. Which is why thieves run wild here, and why getting in and out of Stormhaven will be easy."

"I hope you're right," I said. "Have you done…jobs here?"

"Two," Reven said. "I poisoned a man who was beating his mistress, on behalf of her sister. I also strangled a woman who was smuggling children on the black market."

A part of me wished I had never asked, and a part of me was fascinated by Reven's cold brutality and how he spoke so matter-of-factly about murder, even if the targets seemed like people who'd deserved it. I'd killed before, numerous times, but only in self-defense. I didn't think I could ever be as casual about taking a life as Reven was. Perhaps that was why the Water God had chosen him—to teach me to do what needed to be done without letting my emotions get in the way.

If so, I had a lot to learn.

10

KIRA

Without magic guiding our ship we seemed to creep into the busy harbor, passing boats both bigger and smaller than ours as we approached the dock. Reven shouted out orders to the other men to hoist the sails while he steered the wheel, his dark hair flowing in the wind. With his black clothing and his twin swords at his waist he looked like a pirate captain from the Water Realm. He'd originally claimed to know only a little about sailing, but luckily he'd remembered more than he'd let on. Without his expertise we would have no idea what to do, especially as we brought the ship up to the dock, but he'd clearly spent some time handling a ship before.

Maneuvering a ship like this with five inexperienced people was a challenge, even if the boat wasn't that big. As we neared the dock we came disturbingly close to another larger ship, and it was only with a touch of Reven's magic washing us to the side that we avoided colliding with it.

"Careful!" Jasin called out as he hauled on a rope.

Reven only glared at him as he turned the wheel and eased us up to the dock. Slade dropped the anchor and Jasin leaped out to tie the boat off, while Auric remained below deck, much to his dismay. He was the opposite of Slade and hated being in confined spaces, preferring the open air and the sky around him.

When the ship was secure I took in a breath of fresh air tinged with the smell of fish and something else like faint perfume. We'd made it to Stormhaven, and all around us the port was bustling with activity. Sailors hauled goods on and off boats, men and women in colorful clothing strolled along the marina with umbrellas to block the hot sun, and people at nearby stalls called out to offer food and more. Behind it all, the great city rose up with its many silvery spires glittering under the sun as they reached toward the sky. In the distance, the palace stood on a hill with the tallest spires of all, which disappeared into the clouds.

Jasin drew me in for a hug. "Stay safe."

Our lips brushed and I nodded at him. "We'll be fine."

The plan was for Slade, Reven, and I to go through the city and look for supplies and some new horses, while Jasin and Auric waited on the ship. Jasin had argued he should go with us too, but Reven was the only one beside Auric who had been to the city before, and Slade said he wasn't spending a second longer on the boat. I'd insisted on going too, which meant Jasin had to stay behind to protect the ship with Auric, who needed to stay out of sight until we returned. After night fell we would sneak him out of the city with our new supplies and horses.

"Are we ready?" I asked Slade and Reven.

Reven nodded and hopped off the ship. But as Slade and I followed him onto the dock, a number of soldiers suddenly approached us. They weren't wearing the black scaled armor of the Onyx Army, and instead had smooth metal armor that gleamed gold, with the symbol of the House of Killian etched on their chests. Royal guards.

"Halt," called out the one in the front. He was the only one with a white feathered plume on his helmet, which I assumed meant he was their Captain.

Reven rested a hand on the hilt of his sword, his muscles tense as though he was ready to start slaughtering them all, but I shook my head at him.

I stepped forward with a smile. "Is there a problem, good sirs?"

"All ships that are not registered with the Harbor Master must be searched by order of the King," the Captain said.

I tried to keep my face calm, though my heart was pounding. "Is that truly necessary? As you can see, our ship is small. We don't have anything of interest here. We're simply weary travelers looking for a better life in the Air Realm."

"That may be so, but I have my orders." The Captain glanced between me and the other men, his eyes lingering on Slade's large form for an extra second. "Have you traveled from the Earth Realm?"

He must think that because of Slade's dark skin, which was more common in the Earth Realm. Slade nodded. "Yes, from Mudport."

Jasin drew a bag of coins. "Listen, how about you say you searched the ship and go on your way. We can make it very worth your while."

"Is that so?" the Captain asked, and I held my breath, hoping he'd let us go. Instead he drew his sword and shouted, "Detain these people and search the ship!"

Reven reached for his sword again, but I grabbed his arm to still him. Violence might be his natural instinct for dealing with problems, but these men were only doing their job in service of Auric's family. Perhaps if we used our magic we might be able to escape, but not without drawing a lot of attention from the other people on the docks. Auric would never be able to remain anonymous that way, and word of us might even reach the Dragons. Right now our only advantage was that the Dragons might not know where we were.

"We don't want any trouble." I stepped forward and offered my arms in surrender. My mates grumbled, but they stood down. The Royal Guard dragged us each away from the ship and bound our hands, while their Captain watched. Soon they would begin searching the ship and would find Auric below deck. As rope was tied around my wrists, I tried to think of a way we could cause a distraction to allow Auric to get away unnoticed.

But then Auric emerged and stood above us on the ship's deck. "Let them go," he said. "They're with me."

"Prince Auric?" the Captain asked, before dropping into a hasty bow.

"Yes, it's me. Release my friends." My heart sank as Auric stepped forward, though he didn't look anything like a prince with his longer hair and his worn commoner's clothes. There would be no hiding him now. His family would soon learn he was here, and we would never be able to escape Stormhaven unnoticed.

"I'm sorry, your highness, but I can't do that. In fact, I need you to come with me." The Captain lowered his voice. "Your father has been searching for you and he's ordered us to detain anyone you are found with."

"That's not necessary," Auric said.

The Captain crossed the deck to Auric and spoke quietly. "I know it must have been difficult being kidnapped and held captive all this time, but you don't need to keep up the ruse. You're safe now."

Auric's eyes widened "I'm not being held captive!"

The Captain ignored him and turned toward the rest of his guard, who were also bowing at the prince. "Get those people to the prison! I'll inform the King immediately that his son has been rescued. Now, Prince Auric, if you'll just come with me."

He led Auric to a carriage, and though Auric protested and tried to explain that this was all a misunderstanding, no one seemed to listen. We were hauled into a different carriage forcefully and the door was locked shut, trapping us inside a small, windowless space. I sank back against the threadbare cushions with my hands bound behind my back as our carriage rolled away, leaving Auric behind.

So much for our inconspicuous arrival.

11

REVEN

Two guards shoved me and Kira into a small prison room, before the heavy door closed and locked behind us with a loud slam. I did a quick survey of the room: dark stone walls, a small window with bars, a meager cot with no blankets, one chamber pot in the corner, and rat droppings on the ground. Not the worst prison I'd been thrown into, but not the best either.

After I cut our wrist bindings with a sharp shard of ice, Kira sat on the edge of the cot and buried her face in her hands. "That did not go as planned."

"These things never do, although I wasn't expecting a search of the ship. The Royal Guard has definitely stepped it up since I was last in Stormhaven."

"I hope the others are okay." She ran her fingers through her hair to calm the tangles, her face lined with worry. "Where are Jasin and Slade?"

I inspected the bars on the window, but they were secure. "Being kept in another prison, I assume. Or being questioned."

She sighed heavily. "At least Auric should be safe. They wouldn't hurt him."

"No, but I can't say the same for us."

She glanced at the door, her brow furrowed. "What do we do?"

"We wait and plan our escape."

"Escape? Is that possible?"

I leaned against the heavy door and shrugged. "Wouldn't be the first time I've broken out of a prison like this."

"How?"

"When they come to feed us, we'll fight our way out. They took our weapons, but we still have our magic. Then we'll find Jasin and Slade and get out of here." Along with my swords. I wasn't leaving without them.

She shook her head. "Auric will get us out. We shouldn't use our powers unless we have no other choice."

"We'll see."

We lapsed into silence as I studied the room for any potential weaknesses. I stared out the tiny window, trying to get a sense of where we were, but all I saw were overgrown weeds.

"You did a good job handling the ship today," she said. "Where did you learn to sail?"

There she went again, trying to pry into my past. Why did she care so much? "Most people in the Water Realm know how to sail a boat. I'm surprised you don't."

"I learned how to paddle small boats, but not a ship of that size, though I did leave the Water Realm at thirteen." She tilted her head with that inquisitive look in her eyes I was starting to know all too well. "Did your parents teach you? Did they have a ship?"

I turned away from her to study the door, looking for any cracks, nails, or broken hinges. "Something like that."

She paused so long I thought perhaps she'd given up, but then she asked, "Was that true, what you said the other night about your parents? And your first time?"

I looked her in the eye. "Everything I've told you is true. I may keep secrets, but I've never lied."

"I'm sorry you had to go through all that." She looked at me with the pity I'd been trying to avoid. That was why I didn't tell people this stuff. I didn't need anyone's pity, and certainly not hers.

I lifted one shoulder casually. "It was a long time ago."

"Can I ask what happened to your family?"

My lips pressed into a tight line briefly. "They were killed by the Crimson Dragon, like yours were."

Her face paled. "Why didn't you tell me?"

I looked away with a scowl. "Because I didn't want you to think this makes us connected in some way. Sark is the Black Dragon's enforcer. He's killed a lot of families. It doesn't mean anything."

"But we *are* connected, and now I understand you a little more. Or better than I did, anyway." She rose to her feet and moved toward me with sympathy on her face. "The Dragons both took away our families. Did they think your parents were part of the Resistance too?"

"They *were* in the Resistance," I snapped. "They got themselves killed, along with everyone they cared about, all for their stupid cause."

"How is that stupid? They died for their ideals. We're fighting for the same thing now—to stop the Dragons."

I crossed my arms. "Trust me, that's not my idea. If it were up to me, we'd find a nice island to hide out on until this all blew over."

She stared at me with fire in her eyes. "You think we should run away?"

"If it saves our lives, then yes. If my family was smart, they would never have gotten involved with the Resistance—and they'd still be alive today."

She gestured wildly. "And what about all the people who will suffer if we don't stop the Dragons?"

"How is the suffering of the entire world our problem?"

"Because the Gods chose us!"

"And like I said, the Water God chose wrong."

With those words I would normally have stormed off, but all I could do was walk to the other side of our cell and face away from her. Gods, what was I even doing? And why had I come back to Kira? I had no desire to stop the Dragons or represent a God. I didn't want to be involved in this impossible fight. We were only going to get ourselves killed—including Kira.

Her small hand rested on my back and I stiffened up. "I don't think he did," she said.

I spun to face her. "You're wrong. I'm no hero. I don't care about saving the world. I don't even know why I'm still here."

Her fingers brushed against my jaw as she looked up at me in a way that made my chest clench. "I know why. Deep down you have a good heart, even if you won't admit it."

I took her beautiful face in my hands. "I've been many things in this life. A thief. A whore. A killer. But I have never once been a good man."

"It's not too late to start."

My thumb ran across her lower lip and I was seconds away from kissing her hard and showing her that I wasn't good at all, when the door opened. Kira and I jumped back as Slade was thrown into the prison with us. The door was locked again before I could even summon a shard of ice. Dammit, there went my plan of escape. If I hadn't been distracted by Kira, I'd have been ready.

"Slade!" Kira threw her arms around him. I tried to ignore that touch of jealousy twisting in my gut, along with the realization that I would have kissed her if he hadn't interrupted us.

I turned away and crossed my arms. It was better that we'd been interrupted anyway. Everyone I'd ever loved was dead, and I refused to love Kira and have her meet the same fate. But for some reason I wasn't able to walk away from her either. Gods knew I'd tried, yet here I was. Drawn by this invisible string to her side, no matter how much I wanted to fight it or escape it.

And in the end, it would probably get us both killed.

12

KIRA

I pulled back from my tight hug to examine Slade for any injuries. "Are you all right?"

He nodded as he leaned against me, his hands still bound behind his back. "They asked me some questions and roughed me up a bit, but nothing I couldn't handle. The biggest problem was that they think we kidnapped Auric."

"Of course they did," Reven muttered, as he bent down to cut the bindings on Slade's wrist.

I gestured for Slade to get on the cot and then pulled up his shirt, revealing his hard muscles and smooth dark skin. As I pressed a hand to his ribs, he inhaled sharply. He'd definitely taken a beating and would likely be black and blue soon, not to mention whatever was going on inside of him. A broken rib maybe. I closed my eyes and willed his body to heal, causing his cool skin to warm under my touch.

"What did they ask you?" Reven asked him.

Slade's eyes were closed and when he spoke it sounded pained. "They wanted to know what we were doing with Auric, how we had captured him, and why we had returned. I didn't tell them anything. I wasn't sure they'd even believe me if I did."

"Probably not," I said.

After I finished healing Slade, the door was thrown open and Jasin was pushed into the room by a guard. He stumbled forward and hit the ground on his knees, with a trail of blood trailing from his lip and his left eye puffy and swollen. Gods, what had they done to him? And why was he so much worse than Slade? Had he given them a hard time?

I rushed to Jasin's side and took his face in my hands, eager to heal him, but a gloved hand gripped my arm. I looked up at the plumed helmet of the Captain.

"Come with us," he said to me.

Two other guards stood behind him, pointing their swords at my chest. At the sight, Reven let out a low growl and summoned small blades of ice in his hands. Slade pushed himself to his feet and clenched his fists, while Jasin threw himself in front of me and growled, "Don't touch her."

A fight seemed inevitable even if I went willingly, and maybe fighting was the only way we would be able to escape and find Auric. I wished we could do it without shedding blood or revealing the secret of our magic, although I was less concerned about shedding blood after I'd seen what the guards had done to my men.

"Stop!" Auric yelled. My breath caught and relief rushed through me at the sight of him pushing through the wall of guards. As they parted, he stood tall before me, looking every inch the regal prince even in his common traveling clothes. "Let her go."

The Captain released me. "Yes, your highness."

Auric gestured at my other mates. "Release these people at once. As I told you earlier, there was no kidnapping. I left the Air Realm willingly, and these are my hired guards."

The Captain hesitated, but then nodded and stepped back so we could leave the prison cell. All of the guards sheathed their weapons, while Slade helped Jasin stand. Reven glared at the Captain as he sauntered by, making his way to my side.

We were given back our things, including all our weapons, and then escorted out of the prison into the bright afternoon sunlight. Another group of guards awaited us there, along with a gilded carriage emblazoned with the royal crest.

And just like that, we were released.

I wrapped my arms around Auric and gave him a quick kiss. "I knew you would get us out of there."

He kissed me back, but then grimaced. "Yes, I did. Unfortunately everyone knows I'm here now. Including my entire family."

"Can we get some horses and leave the city tonight?" Slade asked.

"No, I've been ordered to return to the palace, and the Royal Guard will make sure I comply." Auric glanced back at the prison, where the Captain and the other guards were watching us intently. "We have to meet with my parents before we can head for the Air Temple."

A servant opened the carriage for us, which was quite different from the one we'd traveled in earlier with no windows. This one had lush purple interior trimmed with yellow accents, all made of the finest velvet and trimmed with real gold. I sank into the cushion with Jasin and Reven at my side, with Auric and Slade across from us. Everyone except Auric was disgusting and bloody after being in the prison, not to mention hungry and tired from our ordeal.

Auric leaned back into the seat, his finely sculpted, perfectly clean face the only one who looked like it belonged here. "I'm sorry for all of that. Did they hurt you?"

"Nothing a little of Kira's touch won't fix," Jasin said, though he shifted uncomfortably in his seat. I took his hand to heal him and give him strength while the carriage began to roll forward.

"That should never have happened," Auric said. "Again, I'm sorry. Please let me know if there is anything I can do to help."

Slade grunted. "We'll be fine."

Auric sighed, leaning his head back. "Gods, this is a disaster. How am I going to explain this to my parents? I can't exactly tell them the truth, but I don't want to lie to them either."

"Keep it vague," Reven said.

"I shall. I told the guards you were mercenaries I'd hired to protect me during my travels. We'll stick to that for now, I suppose. But my family is going to have a lot of questions for me."

"Who else will we meet at the palace?" I asked. Although this wasn't how we'd hoped to spend our time in Stormhaven, I couldn't help but be curious about Auric's family and his home. I only hoped it went better for us than our meeting with Jasin's parents did.

"My mother and father. My siblings, if any of them are staying at the castle, though my oldest brother Niyal is probably at the palace in Mistvale and my sister Fema is likely on her estate with her husbands. My other brother Garet should be there though." He hesitated and opened his mouth like he wanted to say more, but then thought better of it.

While Jasin and Slade dozed off, the rest of us stared through the windows at the city as we moved through it. Everywhere I looked people were walking by in brightly colored clothing that flowed loosely and revealed plenty of skin. They stopped at little shops and adorable cafes, while above us the tall spires reached high into the sky.

The carriage climbed a hill as we approached the palace, which shined under the sun like a beacon. Auric's body was tense as we passed through a huge gate before traveling along a stone path lined with perfectly trimmed trees with tiny yellow and white flowers. I pressed my face close to the tiny window to see everything I could, filled with awe at the sight of the majestic white castle in front of us.

The carriage came to a halt in a courtyard in front of the palace. Auric stepped out first and glanced around with a tense expression, then turned to offer me a hand to help me out.

I stepped out of the carriage and gaped at the beautiful palace and all the guards and servants waiting for us, wishing that my hair was brushed, or that I wasn't covered in dirt and blood, or that I wore finer clothes. I'd never had anything very nice to begin with and I'd left most of my clothes with our horses at the Fire Temple. I supposed my dirty hunting leathers fit Auric's story that we were mercenaries, but I couldn't help but feel like an imposter standing there among such finery.

As the other men stepped out of the carriage, a beautiful woman with long black hair and smooth golden skin rode up on a glorious white horse. "Auric! You've returned!"

She dropped off her horse and smoothed her peach silk riding habit, then throw her arms around Auric. She pressed a kiss to his cheek, which gave me an uncomfortable feeling in my stomach that I tried to ignore. She could be related to Auric, perhaps a cousin or other relative, but there was something about the way she touched him that seemed familiar in a different way.

Auric has never been with a woman, I reminded myself. Though he'd certainly kissed at least one before me.

"Brin, what are you doing here at the palace?" Auric asked, sounding alarmed.

"I've been staying here for the last month, ever since you vanished. I'm so relieved you're all right." She brushed a piece of dirt off Auric's chest in a way that made me squirm. "I was so worried when you ran off like that without a word. Made me think you might want out of our arrangement."

"Yes, about that…" He glanced over at me and cleared his throat. Brin turned toward us like she hadn't even noticed us before. Her gaze swept over us with confusion on her lovely features.

"Auric, who is this?" I asked through gritted teeth.

"This is Lady Brin of House Pashona." His face turned grim. "My betrothed."

13

KIRA

At first I thought I must have heard Auric wrong. He couldn't be engaged to another woman...could he? But then I saw the way Brin smiled as she took Auric's arm, like they had known each other for years, and my doubts vanished. It was true. They were betrothed.

I wanted to turn and run away, to escape the heartache crushing my chest and making it hard to breathe, but there was nowhere to go. Guards surrounded us, the carriage had already rolled away, and there was no place to hide out here in the sunny courtyard. My next instinct was to yell at Auric and demand answers, but that would probably get me arrested again. All I could do was stare at this perfect, regal couple in front of me while my anguish and jealousy burned so hot I was surprised the ground didn't catch fire beneath me.

"How could you keep this from me?" I asked, my voice shaking with each word.

Auric stepped toward me, breaking free of Brin's grasp. "Kira, I can explain everything."

I shook my head and turned away, swallowing hard. Slade crossed his arms and gave Auric a stony look, while Reven leaned against a pillar and watched the scene unfold with a bored expression. Jasin rested his hand on my lower back and glared at Auric. "Is that the best you can say?"

Brin eyed us all with interest, then clasped her hands together. "I can see there's a story here, and I'm guessing it's one you don't want the entire palace staff to know about." She gave me a warm smile, then swept her gaze across my mates. "Why don't you all join me in my suite, where we can talk about this in private?"

All I wanted was to return to the boat and get away from this situation, but there was no escaping this. Auric was my future mate, and no matter how upset I was with him, I had to hear him out at least.

"All right," I said reluctantly. "Let's talk."

Brin led us inside the palace into a huge entry that was all velvet and silk, purple and gold, elegant and opulent. The front room alone practically dripped with wealth and sophistication, and I immediately felt even more out of place. Especially beside Brin, who wore clothing suitable for a princess and clearly knew the palace as if it were her own home.

How could Auric have kept something this big from me? He'd already done something like this once when he'd hid that he was a prince from me, but I'd forgiven him for that and even understood why he did it. Now I wondered how I could ever trust him again. He should have at least mentioned his betrothal to me at some point. Did he love this other woman? Was that why he'd kept it a secret?

Brin led us up a glorious white spiral staircase with a gilded handrail, then down a hallway with a soft carpeted floor that felt like I was walking on clouds. She spoke to a servant briefly to order up some tea, then swept us into a room done in pale yellow and soft pink.

Once we were all inside, Brin gestured for each of us to sit on the plush chairs and loveseats. I hesitated, worried I would dirty the elegant fabric with my clothes that had touched a prison floor not long ago, until she patted the cushion. I reluctantly sat across from her and opened my mouth to speak, but then a servant wheeled a cart into the room and we were forced to sit in awkward, tense silence while she poured us all a cup of tea. It seemed to take forever, yet at the same time I was afraid of what would happen once she finished and the truth came out.

As soon as we were alone again, Brin took a sip of tea and smiled at us. "Now we can talk."

Auric glanced between us with solemn eyes. "Kira, Brin, I owe you both apologies and explanations."

"And us," Jasin added, before he grabbed one of the small pastries off the tray and shoved it in his mouth.

"Yes, we're supposed to be a team," Slade said.

"Is it true?" I asked Auric, still hoping this was all a misunderstanding. "Is she your betrothed?"

"Yes, but it isn't what you think," Auric said quickly. "Our parents arranged our marriage when we were children, but we're not in love."

Brin laughed. "Gods, no. Auric is like a brother to me." She leaned close, like she was telling me a secret. "Besides, I prefer women."

Auric nodded. "Brin is my closest friend, and we agreed to marry since it seemed the best option to appease our parents. They expect us to marry within the noble families, and Brin is the only noble I can tolerate."

Brin playfully touched Auric's arm. "Aw, that's so sweet. You're the only man I could even imagine spending my entire life with." She turned her dazzling smile on me next. "Auric and I never planned to be exclusive with each other, and we never expected a grand romance or love of that sort. Truth be told, I only agreed to marry a man to continue the family lineage, but I fully expected to take a woman or two on the side." She glanced at my mates with amusement. "Or four."

"But why didn't you tell me?" I asked Auric.

He raked a hand through his golden hair. "I was planning to tell you, I truly was. I almost did when we were on the ship, but then we were attacked by elementals, and after that things were so chaotic... But I should have found the time. I'm truly sorry."

Brin touched my knee lightly. "If he was with you, I doubt he was thinking about me at all."

"Maybe, but it doesn't change the fact that your families expect you to marry." I gave Auric a pointed look. "And we have...other duties."

"Is that so?" Brin asked, arching one of her perfect eyebrows at Auric. "Does this have to do with why you disappeared for a month?"

"Yes, but I can't tell you more than that," he said. "I'm sorry, Brin, but I can't marry you. My path is with Kira, as is my heart."

She let out a dramatic sigh. "It's quite all right. Mom and Dad will be furious, but I'm happy you found someone you love."

Auric took my hand in his. "Kira, I'm so sorry I never told you about Brin. There were so many other more pressing things to deal with on our journey so far, and I rarely thought about my previous life here at all. But I should have told you about this and found a better way to handle all it in advance."

"Yes, you should have." I pulled my hand away, unable to hide the bitterness in my voice, and Jasin rubbed my back in support. Auric might be sorry, but would he have ever told me about Brin if we hadn't been forced to come to the palace? Was he hiding anything else? How would I ever know?

"This is why you didn't want to return to Stormhaven," Slade said. He'd remained standing along with Reven, and they both watched Auric with stony expressions.

"One of the reasons, yes." Auric stared at his hands, his face pained. "My parents won't be pleased with me ending the engagement, but there's no other option. In fact, I should probably meet with them now and tell them the news. They've no doubt heard that I'm in the palace and will be expecting me."

"They've been looking for you all over the kingdom and have been worried sick," Brin said. "Your brother Garet has been in Thundercrest all this time looking for you. I hope you have a good explanation."

He swallowed. "Not exactly."

"Better come up with one quickly then." Brin studied the five of us and tapped her red lips. "For now, we need to get you all some new clothes. We can't have you meeting the royal family looking like you just rolled out of the sewer."

"I can get some clothes for me and the other men from my quarters," Auric said, rising to his feet.

"And I should have something that should fit Kira," Brin said.

My mates grumbled, but they followed Auric out of the suite, leaving me alone with Brin. She took my arm and led me into another room. "Come now, let's get you ready to meet with the King and Queen."

I reluctantly followed her and watched while she began going through her wardrobe. "You don't need to do this…"

"Nonsense. It's my honor to help the woman who's captured Auric's heart." She pulled out a pale green gown that was finer than anything I'd ever owned and held it up to me. "Oh yes, this will be perfect on you with your beautiful red hair."

"Brin, I—"

"I insist you take this dress as a small gift from me to apologize for any pain I've brought you." She thrust the gown at me. "Besides, the King and Queen are waiting and you must look your best."

I hesitated, then took the luxurious silken dress from her. It was thin, like most of the clothes the people wore in the Air Realm, and would cling to my body. It was beautiful, and I couldn't exactly meet the royal family dressed as I was in my dirty, worn hunting leathers, but I was reluctant to accept it. Even when Brin beamed and began searching for shoes to go with the gown.

I didn't want anything to do with Brin. I didn't want to accept her gifts or spend a single second longer in her presence. I wanted to hate her for having a claim on Auric, but that was hard when she was being so friendly and kind. It wasn't her fault that Auric had kept their betrothal from me, and she was trying to help me.

So I swallowed my pain, clutched the dress close to my aching heart, and simply said, "Thank you."

14
AURIC

G ods, I was an idiot. I should have told Kira about Brin back when we were on the boat. Or when she'd found out I was a prince. Or from the very beginning. Now I wasn't sure I would ever be able to regain Kira's trust, even though Brin had never been anything more than a friend. We would have had a marriage of convenience and nothing more, and after meeting Kira I'd already planned on ending the betrothal as soon as I could. I only wished I'd handled the situation better. I'd thought I would have more time, and never expected Brin would be staying here at the palace. Now I realized I'd just been trying to put off the inevitable as long as possible, like a fool. And I might have lost Kira because of it.

Would she even want to bond with me once we reached the Air Temple? Or would she want someone else to be the Golden Dragon now? Somehow I would have to win her over again. And I would do it, no matter how long it took or what I had to do. But right now we had more immediate problems—like my parents.

After I'd found proper attire for myself and Kira's other mates, we met up with her at the top of the grand staircase. Kira wore a pale green silk gown that accentuated her strong, feminine body, and it was hard to tear my eyes away. She nodded at me, and the five of us descended the staircase and continued toward the back of the palace.

Although this was my home and everything about it was familiar, walking through these halls was strange now. Even my clothing felt stiff and awkward compared to the clothes I'd worn while traveling. I supposed it was because I was different—no longer a prince who spent his time in the library and avoiding balls, but a warrior who had traveled three of the Realms, could control air itself, and would soon become a Dragon…if Kira still wanted me.

A servant informed me that my parents weren't in their main receiving room, but in the private garden where my father often met with close friends and family when the weather was nice. Stepping outside and breathing in the scent of the flowers and the sea air filled me with nostalgia for when I'd played in these gardens as a child with my siblings. The palace might be known for its impossibly-tall shining spires, but the lush gardens had always been one of my favorite places as a child, including the one surrounded by a hedge where my family now waited.

As we approached, I heard raised voices and spotted someone standing with my parents through the hedge: a man with pale skin and black hair tied back in a severe ponytail, who instantly sent terror down my spine. I'd met him officially only once, but I'd seen him in the palace a handful of other times. I'd always been afraid of him, but that was nothing compared to the panic I felt now.

At first I worried he was there for us, but then Isen, the Golden Dragon, stared down my father with a sneer on his lips. "Are you telling me no?"

My father's face was stoic. "Of course not. I'm telling you it will take time."

"Time is the only luxury we do not have right now," Isen snapped.

The King spread his hands. "We're doing the best we can."

"Somehow I doubt that. Meet these demands, or you won't like the consequences." Isen's eyes shifted to my mother almost threateningly. "And neither will your people."

His form shimmered and then grew, quickly becoming a large reptilian beast with a long tail, large wings, and sharp talons and fangs. He darted into the air with barely a flap of his wings, his golden scales flashing bright under the sun.

"What's he doing here?" Jasin asked, his voice barely above a whisper.

Kira's eyes widened. "Is he looking for us?"

"I don't think so," I said. "It seems he's visiting the King for other reasons."

"Does he visit often?" Slade asked.

"Not often, but I've seen him many times over the years," I said. "Think of it this way. If Sark is the Black Dragon's enforcer, then Isen is her ambassador. He deals with the nobility, which mostly means keeping us in line and making sure we are loyal. Sometimes the Black Dragon decrees new laws and regulations, and he's the one who makes sure the rulers carry them out."

"You've met him before?" Kira asked.

"Yes, once. He's never very friendly." I drew in a breath and glanced back at my parents, who had sat at the table under a flowering olive tree and were speaking quietly to each other. "Are you ready to speak with my parents?"

Kira wouldn't meet my eyes. "No, but what choice do we have?"

I nodded, sharing her sentiment, and steeled myself before stepping forward into the patio where my parents were sitting. Both of them had the lush golden hair so prized in the Air Realm, and I'd gotten my gray eyes from my mother and my height from my father. At the sight of me, both of them jumped to their feet.

"Auric!" my mother cried out. She crossed the distance between us and threw her arms around me. "Where have you been all this time?"

"Son," my father said, resting a heavy hand on my shoulder. His disapproving eyes seemed to pierce right to my soul, seeing all my secrets, judging my actions, and finding me wanting. It was like being a kid all over again and realizing I was in deep trouble. "We're so glad you've returned. But we have a lot of questions."

"I'm sure you do," I said. "I've been traveling across the Realms, but I'm back now, at least for a short while."

"I'm so relieved you're safe, but who are these people with you?" the Queen asked, looking past me.

"These are my…friends and traveling companions. May I introduce Kira, Reven, Jasin, and Slade. And these are my parents, King Terel and Queen Hala."

Kira dropped to a curtsy, while the men beside her bowed. "Your majesties."

My parents looked suitably confused at being introduced to commoners, but managed to nod at them in return, though my father couldn't hide the pinch of his forehead. "I think it's time you told us where you've been all this time," he said.

Under his stony eyes I found I couldn't lie, and I couldn't come up with a good excuse. "I'm sorry, but I can't tell you."

"What do you mean, can't?" the King said.

My mother's eyes widened. "Were you captured? Held against your will? Truly, you can tell us anything. We'll love you no matter what."

"No, I left the Air Realm of my own free will." Gods, this was harder than I'd expected. I wracked my brain for a way to explain without telling them the whole truth. "I needed to get away from the palace and find my place in the world."

"But why didn't you tell us?" the Queen asked. "We were so worried."

"Because you would have tried to stop me, or would have sent guards with me. This was something I needed to do alone, but I'm sorry I made you worry. As you can see, I'm perfectly fine."

My father's frown deepened. "Does this have anything to do with your engagement to Brin?"

I cleared my throat. "Yes, in a way. I'm sorry, but I can't marry Brin anymore."

"Why ever not?" my mother asked.

I took Kira's hand in mine. "Because I've given my heart to another, and my future is with her."

Now I'd truly shocked them. For a moment they were both speechless, and then my mother pressed a hand to her chest and asked the others, "Would you mind giving us a moment to speak to our son alone?"

"Yes, of course," Kira said, as she met my eyes with a frown. I doubted she wanted to be here anyway after everything that had happened in the last few hours. I couldn't count on the other men to back me up either. I had to face my parents alone.

A servant whisked Kira and her other mates away, and as soon as they were gone my mother asked, "You wish to marry that…commoner?"

I bowed my head. "I do."

"No," my father said. "I forbid it."

My heart sank, but my resolve strengthened. "I'm sorry, but I'm going to be with Kira whether you like it or not."

He shook his head. "Son, you barely know this woman. Where is she even from? And who were those other three men?"

"It's complicated—"

"How do you know she doesn't only want you because you're a prince?" the Queen asked.

I raked a hand through my hair, frustrated with this questioning. Couldn't they trust that I wouldn't be with someone like that? "She didn't know I was a prince at first. She doesn't care about my money or status at all."

"I find that hard to believe," the King said. He sat in one of the patio chairs and gestured for me to do the same. "Tell us everything about her, along with a detailed account of your travels over the last few weeks."

I sank into the chair with a sigh. I could already tell was going to be a long night.

15
KIRA

W hile Auric spoke in private with his parents, we were taken to another small sitting room where supper was brought to us. I tried not to devour all of it within seconds, and I noticed my mates were eating just as quickly. None of us had eaten since we'd been on the boat in the morning, and for days we'd been living off of old bread and fish, plus whatever else Calla and her mates had left for us on the boat. It was a nice change to have someone else cook for us, and the food was exquisite— chicken roasted in a crisp lemon sauce with peppers and onions in oil and garlic, plus fresh bread, soft cheese, and olives. It was said the cuisine in the Air Realm was the best in the world, and tonight I thought that might be true.

The men kept stealing glances at me as we ate and asked numerous times if I was okay, but all I could do was nod. I simply couldn't find the energy to speak about what had happened in the last few hours with Auric. I needed some time alone to go over my thoughts and emotions before making a decision about what we would do next.

After we finished eating I was shown to my room, and I was so physically and emotionally exhausted I wanted nothing more than to collapse onto the bed and pass out. But when I stepped inside, the room was so beautiful it made me hesitate to touch anything. The room was done in sky blue and soft cream, making me feel like I was outside under an endless sky. In the center stood a huge four-poster bed, much larger and fancier than anything I'd slept in before, with more pillows than I'd seen in my life.

Truly, how could anyone need that many pillows? I could construct an entire new bed out of them.

Large windows on either side of the bed looked out at the ocean from behind some soft curtains, and there was also a small sitting area, dresser, and wardrobe. All of it was so beautiful and luxurious that it only served as a reminder that I didn't belong here...or with Auric. Meeting his parents and Brin had made that clear. I'd immediately seen the disdain in his parents' eyes when Auric announced he wanted to be with me, and after meeting Brin, I understood why—she was what they wanted for their son, and I had to admit it made more sense for them to be together.

How could I have thought his being a prince didn't matter? We'd lived completely different lives. He'd grown up in a castle with servants waiting on him hand and foot. I'd been on the run for years, taking whatever jobs I could to earn money. Auric should be with someone who understood this life, not me.

Besides, I was still mad at him. I wasn't sure I would ever be able to trust him again after he'd kept so many things from me. Maybe it would be best for all of us if we parted ways now and he went back to his old life. But then who would be my Golden Dragon?

The Golden Dragon... I'd seen the current one tonight for the first time and he'd instantly set me on edge. He'd been right there—if he had turned around, would he have realized who we were? And what did he want from Auric's parents?

As my thoughts churned, I allowed myself to sink onto the edge of the bed and drop my head in my hands. We'd come so close to ruin today in so many ways, it was no wonder I was exhausted. Maybe I'd be able to sort through all my tangled thoughts after I'd had a bit of sleep.

Someone knocked on my door. I slowly moved to open it and was surprised to find Slade standing on the other side. "My room is right next to yours in case you need anything," he said. "Are you all right?"

"Not really. I'm tired, overwhelmed, upset..." I shrugged helplessly. "But I'll be fine in the morning."

He rested his hands on my upper arms. "You don't have to be strong all the time, Kira. It's okay to cry or yell or break down. That's why you have us. We're here for you to lean on."

Tears filled my eyes at his words, which touched me deep to my core. "Thank you. For so many years I relied on no one but myself. I'm not used to having other people I can turn to for help or support. Except Tash, I suppose."

His thumbs slowly rubbed my arms. "You miss her?"

"Very much. I wish she were here. I'd love to have another girl to talk to about all this."

"Brin seemed nice enough."

My nose scrunched up. "Yes, but that only makes it harder. It would be so much easier if I could hate her. Besides, she's the one I want to talk about!"

He let out a low chuckle. "Maybe you can send a letter to Tash to let her know you're safe. It might make you feel better."

A smile touched my lips for the first time in hours. "That's a great idea. I'll write it in the morning and tell Auric to make sure it gets delivered to her. He owes me that, at least."

He nodded. "I know we're your mates and that makes things complicated. But don't forget, we're your friends too."

"And I'm lucky to have you." I sighed and leaned against the doorway. "Well, some of you. I'm not feeling very lucky to have Auric right now."

Slade ran a hand over his dark beard as he chose his next words. "Auric made a mistake, it's true. But we're all doing the best we can with this situation we've been put in. We each have pasts we'd like to forget, or things we're trying to run from. At least he is facing it now."

"That doesn't excuse him keeping this from me."

"No, it doesn't." His large, dark hand cupped my cheek and I thought he might kiss me for the first time, but then he turned away. "Get some rest, Kira."

I stared after Slade as he slipped into his room, then closed my own door. Would he ever see me as more than a friend? I was grateful for his friendship, I truly was, but I wanted more too. Someday. I wouldn't rush him, even if I couldn't stop thinking about how much I wanted him to kiss me. Did he feel that invisible tug between us too, trying to bring our bodies together? Or was I the only one?

16
KIRA

In the morning I found myself restless and unsure of what to do or where to go in the palace. What was my role here? And how long would we stay before continuing on to the Air Temple? While it was nice to have some time to rest and recover from our travels, every second we delayed increased the likelihood of the Dragons uncovering who we were or reaching the temple before us.

Jasin suggested we take this time to train, and while the idea of using fire would have previously terrified me, today I really needed to burn some of my anxious energy off.

The palace was nestled on a tall hill overlooking the city on one side and the ocean on the other, and Jasin and I trekked out to the end of the bluff overlooking the water, where the blue sky seemed endless. The bright sun warmed us as we stared down the edge of the steep, rocky cliff that disappeared into the ocean below us.

"This will do," Jasin said, glancing around at the sparse trees and rocks.

I inched away from the drop. "Isn't it a bit close to the edge?"

Jasin shrugged. "If you fall, I'll catch you. Don't forget I can turn into a dragon now."

"Sorry, but I'm not that confident in your flying skills yet."

"All right, we can move back a bit. I suppose it would be hard to explain why an unknown Dragon was flying near the palace." He moved to a safer location and spread his arms. "Let's see what you can do."

I summoned a small ball of fire and threw it at Jasin, who swept it away with an easy gesture. "How is that?"

"Not bad at all. You're a natural. Which is surprising since you were scared of fire only days ago."

"I learned by watching you, I suppose." Truth be told, I was still scared of fire and what it could do, but I had to get over it. And I could only do that with practice and training.

"Then you know that fire is the hardest element to keep control of. Summoning it is easy. But making it do what you want...that's the real challenge. I'm still learning that part myself." He pointed at a nearby shrubby bush and it instantly caught fire, but the blaze didn't spread to anything else. Jasin's face pinched as he concentrated, and I could tell it took a lot of effort to keep it contained. Then the fire vanished in a blast of smoke. "For now, let's just have you concentrate on throwing the fire and making sure it goes where you want it to go."

Jasin hurled a ball of fire at a nearby boulder, where it flashed and then disappeared with nothing to keep it burning. I nodded and summoned my own flames, then tossed them at the stone. As I did, the events of yesterday came back to me, including everything I'd been trying very hard not to think about, like Auric and how he'd kept the truth about Brin from me. I still cared for him, but how was I supposed to trust him now? Or bond with him in only a few days?

I tossed a huge ball of fire, enjoying the sizzle and the flash of heat. "This is exactly what I needed."

"Of course it is. Fire is all about passion. Anger, desire, excitement... When you channel these emotions, you'll find it easier to conjure fire." He tilted his head. "I get the sense you're definitely feeling some passion today."

I wiped the sweat off my forehead. "Anger, mostly. I trusted Auric and he kept a huge secret from me for the second time. How am I supposed to just accept that and move on now?"

"That's understandable. But we're all keeping things from each other. I didn't tell you about my brother's death, or that my parents were staunch supporters of the Dragons, Sark in particular. In fact, I purposefully kept that to myself because I couldn't stand to talk about it and I worried what you would think. Maybe Auric felt the same way about his engagement?"

I stared at Jasin. "Are you defending him?"

He held up his hands. "No, definitely not."

"Good, because his secret is different. I can't be with a man who is engaged to another."

Jasin shrugged. "It sounds like their betrothal was more for show or convenience than love, and he told his parents he wanted to be with you instead."

I summoned another ball of flame and rolled it around in my palms. "Maybe so, but it was still there all this time. I wish he would have told me from the beginning."

"For what it's worth, I think Auric loves you and you alone. You have every right to be mad at him, but I don't think Brin is a threat. Their engagement will end, and soon we'll be on our way to the Air Temple."

I glanced away, annoyed at how reasonable Jasin was being. Wasn't he normally the hotheaded one of the group? And why was he defending Auric when only days ago they'd hated each other? I knew I would have to forgive Auric and move past this somehow, but at the moment all I wanted was to let out my anger and smash things—or burn them.

I launched my next fireball, but it was bigger than I expected and went wide, hitting a large bush, which instantly went up in flames. The fire quickly leaped to a tree beside it and spread faster than I could have imagined, sending cold panic down my spine. Flashbacks of the fire that had taken my parents' lives flickered in my head as my heart pounded and my breathing grew ragged. I couldn't think, couldn't move, couldn't stop it.

"Get back!" Jasin stepped forward and gestured at the fire. His face was tight with concentration as he soothed the flames and contained them, then slowly made them smaller and smaller.

After a few minutes there was nothing but ash and smoke where the tree had been. I'd completely destroyed it, and I'd lost all control of the fire. I sank to the grass and stared at the charred ground, feeling empty and hollow. What if I'd lost control during battle? Or in a crowded area with people and houses? I could have killed someone. I could have destroyed innocent lives. How could I use fire when it had so much potential for destruction and pain?

Jasin sat beside me on the grass and began slowly rubbing my back. "It's over. You're fine."

"It's not fine. I lost control." I covered my face with my hands, which were still trembling.

"I did too, at first. Remember when Reven had to put out all my fires?" He pulled me close. "You just need more practice, that's all."

I nodded and buried my face against his shoulder, but if I was honest, I didn't want to practice my magic ever again. I didn't want that kind of power or responsibility. Even now, I couldn't help but think this was all a mistake and someone else should be the Black Dragon. How was I supposed to master all four elements when I couldn't even handle one?

REVEN

I n the morning I slipped out of the palace, unnoticed by any guards or servants, and headed back into the city. Stormhaven was already waking up even as dawn crested over the ocean waves to the east, a sight that always seemed wrong to me. The sun should be setting *into* the water, as it did in the Water Realm, not rising from it.

I moved through the brightening streets with my hood up, a shadow among the bustling crowds headed for the markets and shops. As the day heated up, I made my way to the docks, where the air smelled of salt and fish, while sailors hauled crates onto the ships. Our boat waited at the northern end, and though Auric had said he'd sorted everything out with the guard, I wanted to confirm it with my own eyes to make sure we had a quick exit strategy, especially since we didn't have our horses with us. All good assassins had at least three exits planned out in case something went wrong...and something always went wrong.

A royal guard was perched in front of our boat, but I had no interest in giving her an explanation to as to why I was there. When no one was looking, I dropped off the dock and slipped into the water, feeling the instant relief as the chill surrounded me. As the Azure Dragon's ascendant I could breathe underwater, and I easily swam over to the other side of the boat. I climbed up the outside of it while using my magic to remove the water from my clothes and send it back into the ocean. By the time I vaulted up onto the wooden deck I was completely dry and the royal guard didn't have a clue I was there.

From up here, everything seemed to be in order. I dropped down into the hatch leading below deck, and found evidence that the guards had tossed the place, probably looking for something incriminating so they could pin Auric's supposed kidnapping on us, or perhaps find an explanation as to where he'd been all this time. Our things had been taken during the search and had been delivered last night to us in the palace, but I checked a few nooks and crannies to make sure nothing had been left behind, then removed the spare knife I'd hidden under one of the wooden planks. Finally, I rearranged the hammock and cleaned up some of the other mess, before climbing back up.

As I walked off the ship, I gave the confused guard a nod. She called out some questions, but didn't follow me more than a few feet. Probably on orders to stay with the ship at all times. I turned a corner and left her behind.

It had been a year since I'd been in Stormhaven, but it hadn't changed much. People wore colorful, loose clothing, and the bustling crowd was ripe for pickpocketing. Cafes and little shops sold everything from clothes to art to pastries. For a split second I considered buying something for Kira to cheer her up after what Auric had done, but then dismissed the idea entirely. I wasn't trying to woo her. We weren't a couple. If I was smart, I'd just keep walking and never return to the castle at all.

Maybe that was why I ended up in a seedy neighborhood where the crowd didn't dare wander. A dark, unmarked building was tucked at the end of an alley, and I slipped inside. The tavern was otherwise empty this early in the day, and the bartender gave me a nod as I sat at the end of the bar. She had short, white hair and a tattoo of a dagger on her wrinkled neck, and though she didn't look like much of a threat, I knew better.

Zara poured me some ale. "Surprised to see you, Reven. Last I heard you weren't taking on any jobs at the moment."

I pushed my hood back. "I took some time off."

She nodded. "Always a good idea now and then. Don't want to get burned out. This is a tough profession."

My eyes narrowed. Me, burn out? Was that what others in the Guild thought? I took a long sip of the cold ale and then said, "I'm here now."

"That so?" She wiped down the counter as she eyed me with scrutiny. "As it turns out, a job came in last night that requires a special touch."

"My specialty."

"This one is high profile, with the biggest reward I've seen in all my days. Won't be easy though. Might be too much for even you."

"I doubt that." I gestured for her to get on with it. "What's the job?"

She leaned over the counter and dropped her voice. "The target is the King."

"The King," I said, my voice flat. "Why would someone want him dead?"

"I don't know. The order came from above." Her eyes flicked to the ceiling. "Way above."

"A Dragon?"

"I can't say any more." She refilled my drink and sighed. "The King is well loved here in Stormhaven and his reign has been a good one. It's a damn shame. But we can't exactly say no to the Dragons."

I tightened my grip on the glass. "No, we can't."

"Are you interested?" Zara asked. "Or should I find someone else?"

I chugged my ale as I considered, realizing this moment would define my path for the rest of my life. Zara was giving me the chance to return to my old life and prove to the Guild I was still the best. It would require killing Auric's father and serving the Dragons, but wasn't that who I was— an assassin for hire? I'd already walked away from Kira once. I could do it again, and this time it would be permanent. Or I could walk away from my past and accept my fate with Kira as the next Azure Dragon.

I set down my ale and met Zara's eyes. "I'll take the job."

18

KIRA

After my training with Jasin I returned to my room to take my midday meal alone with my thoughts. As I picked at the cod cooked with tomatoes and onions, I composed a letter to Tash telling her everything we had experienced so far, while trying to keep my wording vague enough that no one would know what our plans were if the letter got into the wrong hands.

The letter ended up being two pages front and back because once I started talking to Tash in my head I couldn't stop. I told her about Jasin's family and about Auric's fiancé. I told her about how Slade was distant and Reven had left for a short time. I told her about the weight of the responsibility that had been pressed upon me and my fears I would never become the leader I was supposed to be. And even though Tash wouldn't read my letter for some time, a great weight was lifted off me simply by writing it.

A knock sounded on my door and I called out for them to enter. As I folded up the letter and put it in an envelope, Auric stepped inside. My stomach twisted at the sight of him lingering in the doorway as if he wasn't sure he was truly welcome. He'd returned to his fine nobleman's clothing, his face had been shaved, and his golden hair had been cut short again. He looked every inch the handsome prince that he was, even though I'd liked his rougher traveling look too. I suspected the true Auric was somewhere between the two extremes.

"Can we talk, Kira?" he asked.

"Yes, I'm just finishing up a letter to my friend Tash back in Stoneham. Would it be possible to have it delivered to her?"

"Of course." He held out his palm and I set the letter in it. "I'll send a messenger right away."

"Thank you." I couldn't help but notice how stiff we were around each other and didn't like this new tension between us, even though I was still upset with him. "What did you want to talk about?"

His storm gray eyes stared into mine. "My engagement with Brin is over. We met with her parents this morning to make it official."

I let out a long breath. "That's a relief."

"Yes. Everyone is quite upset with me, but I've never been a very dutiful son or prince, so it's to be expected I guess. And soon we'll be gone anyway."

"When can we leave for the Air Temple?"

"Soon, but I need another day or two to appease my parents. My mother insists on throwing us a ball before we go."

My eyebrows darted up and anxiety fluttered in my stomach. "A ball?"

"Yes, to celebrate my safe return, however short it may be, but you don't need to worry. It will be drinking, dancing, and lots of food, and then we can leave for the Air Temple the next day." He cleared his throat. "That is, if you still want me to go to the Air Temple with you."

"I do," I said without hesitation. Though I was upset with Auric, he was still the one I wanted as my mate. The second he'd walked into my room I'd known that for sure.

"Thank the Gods." A smile lit up his face and he offered me his hand. "There's somewhere I'd like to show you. Will you come with me?"

I took his hand and he led me out of my room, down the great staircase, and along a hallway, where we reached two double doors. As he threw one open, I gasped. Inside was the giant library I'd glimpsed in my dreams when I'd first seen Auric. Every wall was covered in shelves that were packed tight with books of all shapes and colors. I'd never seen so many books before in my life, as they were rare treasures in most of the places I'd lived before.

One wall held gigantic windows that looked out at the ocean in the distance, and Auric led me to a small sitting area in front of them.

"This room is gorgeous," I said, as I sat on one of the plush couches.

Auric sat beside me on the same couch, our knees touching as he turned toward me. "It's my favorite place in the palace, and where I usually spend most of my days."

"I know. This is where I saw you in my dreams, though I only caught a few glimpses." I gazed in awe at all the tall shelves. "I'm glad I got to see it in person."

"Me too. I was nervous about coming to the palace, but I'm actually happy you met my family and saw my home, even if the circumstances could have been better. That's my fault, I know."

"I'm pleased I got to meet them too, although I doubt they will ever like me or accept me. And I'm still upset with you."

"I know, and I'm sorry. I should have told you long ago so that you knew what awaited us when we arrived in Stormhaven, and so you knew that the betrothal was not important to me." He took my hands in his and gazed into my eyes. "You're the one I love, Kira. From the moment we met I knew there would never be anyone else. I only hope you can forgive me for my mistakes. I never meant to lie to you or hurt you."

My heart thumped faster in my chest at his words. "I know you didn't, but it will still take some time for me to trust you again."

"I can live with that, as long as you still want me to be your Golden Dragon?"

"I do, although I can't help but question why you want the role. We come from such different lives. I'd managed to forget that while we were traveling, but being at the palace and meeting your family and Brin only showed me that maybe we don't belong together."

His brow furrowed. "Kira, you know I don't care about any of that."

I remembered the way the King and Queen had looked at me when Auric had said he wanted to be with me instead of Brin, and a hard pit formed in my stomach. "I'm a commoner. I've been poor and on the run most of my life. You're a *prince*. Your family will never accept me."

He squeezed my hands. "You may have started life as a commoner, but you're going to be the Black Dragon. Someday you'll be more powerful than any King or Queen."

I yanked my hands away, my stomach twisting. "Is that why you want to be the Golden Dragon? For the power?"

"No, not at all." He raked a hand through his shining blond hair. "Gods, I'm really messing up this apology. I want to be the Golden Dragon because I love you and can't imagine not being by your side. But also because I've seen what the Dragons have done to the world, especially these past few weeks we've been traveling. I've watched my parents try to subtly resist them for years, but they're unable to do much to defy the Dragons. For years I was the odd prince who had no real importance or role in the kingdom, and for the first time ever I have a purpose. With you, I can do my part to make the world better. That's what I want."

"But you could stay here as a prince, living a safe, calm life as a scholar and a husband to your friend. If you go with us, you'll be in danger every day."

He touched my cheek lightly. "I would rather be in danger and be by your side, trying to make the world better, than stay here in safety. All I want is to be your Golden Dragon, if you'll still have me."

I couldn't help but lean into his touch. "You're still one of my mates, Auric. And though I forgive you, I need some time before I trust you again."

"I understand, and I swear I'm not hiding anything else. This is it." He spread his arms wide. "And for what it's worth, I think you'll like Brin too, if you give her a chance."

"Maybe. If I can get over the urge to stake my claim on you every time she's around."

"Well, I won't argue if you want to do that." He leaned close, his eyes turning stormy. "In fact, maybe you should do that now, in case she's watching."

The hint of a smile touched my lips, and I couldn't deny the desire that flickered inside me when he was this close. "You're impossible."

"Jasin might be rubbing off on me."

"He told me to forgive you earlier, when we were training."

"Did he? Maybe I'm rubbing off on *him*." Auric brushed his thumb along my lips, his eyes searching mine. I parted my lips for him, taking his thumb into my mouth, and sucked gently. He let out a groan and then cupped my face in his hands and pressed his mouth to mine. I kissed him back roughly, our tongues dancing together, my hands sliding around his neck to pull him closer. I poured all my anger, doubts, and fears into this kiss, and he held me tight, like he was scared to let go.

"I worried I'd never kiss you again," he said, pressing his forehead against mine.

The doors flew open, making us both jump and pull apart. Reven stormed inside, his black hooded cloak trailing behind him. "I had a feeling you'd be in here. We need to talk."

I smoothed my dress, my cheeks warm. "Is something wrong?"

"Yes. The Golden Dragon has ordered the assassination of the King and Queen."

Auric's eyes widened. "How do you know?"

"Because I just took the job." Reven held up a hand. "Don't worry, I'm not going to do it."

"Then why did you take it?" I asked.

Reven crossed his arms. "Because if I didn't, someone else would."

"But what will happen if you don't do it?"

"They'll probably send someone to kill me too. Either way, I'll never be able to find work with the Assassin's Guild again." He gave a casual shrug. "I was ready to get out of the business anyway."

"Thank you," Auric said. "I appreciate you doing this for us."

Reven's face darkened. "The Dragons destroyed my family. They murdered Kira's family too. I can't let them do this anymore. Not to you. Not to anyone."

I jumped up and threw my arms around Reven. "I knew you were one of us."

"I wouldn't go that far," Reven muttered, though he reluctantly draped his arms around me.

"We need to speak with my parents immediately," Auric said.

I nodded, but then I had an idea. It was risky, but if the current Dragons wanted Auric's parents dead, perhaps they could be allies to us. Besides, I was tired of all the secrets and lies. "I think it's time we told them the truth about why you left."

19

KIRA

We summoned Jasin and Slade, while Auric asked for a meeting with his parents. A short time later we were led to a small parlor decorated in purple and gold, with small flaky pastries and tea already waiting for us.

"This is a bad idea," Jasin muttered, as we sat down.

"My gut tells me this is the right thing to do," I said. One thing I'd learned from a life on the run was to trust my gut, even when it was full of nervous energy, like now.

"I agree with Kira," Slade said. "No more secrets."

Reven leaned against the wall instead of joining us on the sofas. "There are always more secrets."

The King stormed into the room with his tall, commanding presence, followed by his wife and Auric. King Terel swept his gaze across the room and asked, "What is this about? My son says you have something to tell me?"

Reven stepped forward and swept into a low, graceful bow. "Your majesty, I'm a member of the Assassin's Guild. Today I met with a local contact to gather news and check in, but once there, I was offered a job: to end your life."

King Terel's eyes narrowed at Reven. "Why are you telling me this?"

"Because the one who ordered the assassination was none other than the Golden Dragon."

The King's hands clenched into fists. "That snake."

"Would Isen really do such a thing?" Queen Hala asked.

"It seems so," Reven said.

"Why would the Dragons want you dead?" Auric asked.

"Isen has been pushing me to conduct regular raids and public executions on the Resistance members, but I refuse," King Terel said. "I won't have my people living in fear all the time, or turn death into a spectacle."

"That's what they do in the Fire Realm," Jasin said.

The King nodded. "So I've heard. But here in the Air Realm we value freedom and peace."

"Do you support the Resistance?" I asked.

The King turned his intimidating gaze on me. "No, but we have ordered our guards and the Onyx Army here to look the other way on their activities sometimes. Still, I can't imagine the Dragons wanting me dead over that. What will my death accomplish?"

"The Dragons probably believe your heir would be easier to manipulate," Slade said.

King Terel rubbed his chin. "If so, they're right. Niyal's wife is pregnant with their first child. He'd do anything to protect them."

"What are we going to do?" Queen Hala asked with a sigh. "We can't give in to Isen's demands."

"Once the Assassin's Guild realizes I've failed in my assignment, they'll send someone else," Reven said. "You might want to leave the city and go somewhere safer for now."

King Terel snorted. "I won't hide. This is my kingdom and my home. Let them try to take me down."

"And I'm staying with you," Queen Hala said, as she took his hand.

He looked into her eyes and his face softened. "My love, it isn't safe. You should join Niyal at the palace in Mistvale."

She shook her head. "You're the one they want dead. I'm not leaving your side. But how can we end this? We can't openly defy the Dragons."

"Not yet, but that might change soon," Auric said.

King Terel turned toward him. "How so?"

Auric drew in a breath and straightened up. "Mother, father, there is no easy way to say this, but new Dragons have been chosen by the Gods. The five of us."

"New Dragons?" King Terel asked with a frown. "Is that possible?"

"It was surprising to us too, but it's true," Auric continued. "That's why I had to leave suddenly, to find Kira, who will one day be the Black Dragon. And it's why we must leave again in a few days to head to the Air Temple so that I can become the Golden Dragon."

Queen Hala blinked at her son. "I'm sorry, I don't quite understand. How can you be a Dragon?"

"I'm not a Dragon yet," Auric explained patiently. "That's why I need to head to the Air Temple."

"But how did this happen?" she asked, sounding completely baffled.

"The Air God came to me and chose me. I don't really know why."

King Terel crossed his arms. "Son, this all sounds very far-fetched. I'm not sure what game you're playing at, but I don't think it's helping the situation."

"We need to show them," Jasin said.

"Here?" I asked. "Now?"

"When else?" He opened his hand and a bright flame flickered into life, making the royals gasp.

Slade lifted a wooden table three feet in the air, while Reven grumbled but conjured water in front of us. Finally, Auric created a strong wind that lifted all the papers off the table and made them fly around the room before landing again in a pile in front of the King, whose mouth hung open.

"I know this is hard to believe, but it's the truth," Auric said. "We're going to be the next Dragons, and Kira here is the future Black Dragon."

"This is incredible," King Terel said. "I didn't realize the Dragons could be replaced. I thought they were eternal."

"Everyone does," I said. "But we recently learned that the Dragons were only supposed to rule for a short while before being replaced, to make sure they never became too powerful. The current Dragons somehow found a way around that and have wiped out any trace of the previous Dragons' existence."

"You said the Air God came to you?" Queen Hala asked her son. "And gave you these powers?"

Auric nodded. "Yes, outside in the courtyard one morning. He chose me, though I'm still not sure why."

She rested her hand on his shoulder. "You should have told us this from the beginning instead of running off without a word. We were all so worried about you."

"The Air God instructed me not to tell anyone. Besides, would you have believed me?"

She sighed. "No. I hardly believe it now."

He patted his mother's hand. "And now you see why I had to end my engagement with Brin. My destiny is with Kira and her other mates. We need to visit each of the temples to unlock our powers, and then we'll be able to challenge the Dragons. Do we have your support?"

"I'll do whatever I can to help," King Terel said.

"But what will we do about this assassination?" the Queen asked.

"Spread word that an attack was made but the assassin was defeated," Reven said. "That will buy you some time, at least."

"You may have to pretend to go along with the Golden Dragon's demands for a while," Auric said. "Until we can be sure the family is safe."

The King nodded. "It pains me to do such a thing, but I suppose I can have my guards do a few harmless searches for Resistance members. I'm putting my foot down on public executions though."

"When do you need to leave for the Air Temple?" Queen Hala asked.

"As soon as possible," I said.

She nodded. "We'll begin preparations immediately for your departure, but you must stay for the ball. I insist."

Auric bowed his head. "We'll attend the ball, but then we're leaving the next morning."

"It's settled then," the King said, rising to his full height. "Thank you for informing us of the assassination plot, and for telling us the truth about why you left. Now if you'll excuse us, we have some plans to set in motion." He moved toward the door with his wife at his side, but then he paused. "Auric, would you join us?"

Auric nodded and left the room with one glance back at me. I swallowed the anxiety brimming inside me, hoping we'd done the right thing by telling his parents who we truly were.

20

JASIN

As we returned to our rooms that night, Kira touched my arm. "Jasin, are you all right?"

I glanced away. "Yes, why?"

"You were quiet during dinner. I don't think I've ever seen you get through a meal without making a joke or saying something a little inappropriate."

I lifted a shoulder. "Wasn't in the mood."

She took my hand and pulled me into her room, then shut the door. "Tell me the truth. What's bothering you?"

I sighed and sank onto the edge of her bed. "Auric's parents."

"What about them? You don't trust them?"

"No, nothing like that." I dropped my head, feeling foolish. "They're being so supportive and understanding even after Auric ran away, broke his engagement, and told them what he truly is."

She sat on the bed beside me and rubbed my back. "And you're remembering how your father turned us in to the Onyx Army."

"Something like that," I muttered. "Trust me, it would have been even worse if they'd known our goal was to overthrow the Dragons."

"I'm sorry. This must be difficult for you."

"I'm happy for Auric, but it's a bitter reminder that I'll never have a family like that. My parents always tried to mold me into something I'm not. They never supported what I wanted, and then they betrayed me. Now I'm not sure I'll ever see my parents again. If I'm honest, I'm not sure I want to either."

She wrapped her arms around me and rested her head on my shoulder. "You're right. Auric is a lucky man. My parents are gone, as are Reven's. Yours turned against you. And Slade's…" She paused. "I have no idea about his parents. But either way, you're wrong about the rest of it. You *do* have a family. You, me, and the other men—we're in this together for the rest of our lives."

I snorted. "The other guys? We barely get along."

"Isn't that common in all families?" She pressed her lips to my cheek. "One day maybe your parents will come around. But if not, please know that you'll always have us."

"All I need is you," I said, sliding my hand into her hair. I lowered my head and covered her mouth with mine, tasting her sweet, soft lips. My tongue slid across hers as her breasts pressed against my chest, her fingers digging into my arms. Through our bond I felt her desire flare bright, and I wondered if she sensed how much I wanted her too. No, not wanted. *Needed.* Ever since being chosen by the Fire God I'd been burning up inside, and Kira's touch was the one thing that sated me.

I tilted her head back and left a trail of kisses from her jaw to her neck to her collar. She wore that tempting green gown she'd gotten from Brin, and I slid the straps off her shoulder one at a time. The silken fabric slipped down her skin and pooled at her waist, revealing full breasts and nipples already hard for me. I cupped them in my hand while kissing along her shoulder, enjoying the way they filled up my palm, her skin cool against mine.

A knock sounded on the door and Kira lazily lifted her head. "Who is it?"

"It's me," Auric said.

"Come in," she called out.

Auric strode into the room. "Kira, I—Oh! Jasin… I'm sorry. I'll just go."

"It's okay," she said, beckoning him over. "What is it?"

As he walked inside, I continued trailing kisses down Kira's chest, then took a plump breast in my mouth. Auric cleared his throat as he moved close to the bed.

"I… I wanted to thank you for agreeing to tell my parents. It's good to have everything out in the open now." His voice sounded strained, and I imagined he was getting hard watching everything I was doing to Kira and the way she responded to me.

"I'm glad it all worked out," she said, before I flicked my tongue over her nipple and she let out a groan.

"Is it okay if I…watch?" Auric asked. "I'd like to see what Jasin does to please you as part of my training. But if that isn't okay anymore, I understand..."

"Stay," Kira said, her voice breathy and sensual.

Auric moved to the edge of the bed and watched as I continued worshipping her breasts with my mouth, while she buried her fingers in my hair. She reached for Auric and he knelt on the bed beside her, then she pulled his lips to hers. It seemed she wanted him to do more than just watch.

But then he broke off the kiss and sat back to watch again. I gestured for him to join me, and then circled one of Kira's hard nipples with the tip of my tongue. She let out a breathy moan that only grew louder when Auric copied me on her other breast. When I sucked her nipple, he did the same. Together we had her moaning our names as we lavished attention on her breasts until I sensed it was time to continue Auric's education in other ways.

"Lie back," I told Kira. As she followed my order, I dragged her gown down her body and off of her, admiring her shapely hips and legs while pressing a few light kisses to them. Auric stared at her naked flesh like he had never seen anything more beautiful, and I couldn't disagree.

I ran my hands along Kira's thighs as I spread her legs wide for me and kneeled between them. She was so responsive and so trusting, I had no doubt she'd let me do anything to her. The thought made me even harder than I already was, and I couldn't wait to be inside her, but I couldn't forget I'd agreed to teach Auric too.

As he moved to stand at my shoulder to get a better look, I slid a finger between her folds. "Look how wet she is," I said.

"So beautiful," he whispered.

Kira moved her hands to cover herself, her cheeks pink. "You're making me blush."

I brushed her hands away. "Don't be embarrassed. We both think you're gorgeous. Now lie back and relax while I show Auric how to please you."

She rested her hands on either side of her and stared at the ceiling, while I took Auric's hand and brought it between her thighs. She let out a little gasp at the first touch of his fingers.

"Oh, Gods," he said, as I slid them slightly inside her, coating them in her wetness.

I released his hand. "Taste it."

Auric slowly licked the moisture off his fingers, while Kira and I watched. I didn't know why this turned me on so much, but it did. And I was pretty sure Kira felt the same.

"Like that?" I asked.

"Very much," he said.

"Good, because you're going to be tasting her a lot tonight." I took his hand again and dragged his fingers above her folds. As I found the right spot and had him start rubbing it, Kira began to moan again. "Feel that?" I asked, and Auric nodded. "That's the spot on a woman that brings them the most pleasure. If you forget everything else I'll teach you, remember that and you'll be fine."

Auric continued rubbing Kira there with a sly grin. "Ah yes, I've read about the clitoris in books."

I rolled my eyes. "Forget your books. Now watch and learn."

I shoved his hand aside and lowered my head between her thighs to finally taste her. I'd gone down on her once before at the Fire Temple, but I'd never get enough of her sweetness or the sounds she made when my tongue flicked along her sensitive skin.

I showed Auric what I was doing with my mouth, and then grabbed his hand once more and slid his fingers inside of her. He got the hint and began pumping in and out in time to my tongue's movements on her clit, while he watched me intently. I had no doubt he was taking mental notes of everything I did along with Kira's response to it, even while he brought her pleasure at the same time.

It wasn't long before Kira was tightening her fingers on my hair and gripping Auric's arm while she came with a shout. I felt her tremble underneath me and had no doubt she was clenching up around Auric's fingers as well.

I sat back and grinned at him. "Nice work."

"That was incredible," he said. "I could feel her orgasm."

"Just wait 'til you're inside her at the time." I quickly removed my clothing, then moved up Kira's body and pressed my lips to hers, my cock nudging between her thighs. She kissed me back eagerly, wrapping one arm around my neck while reaching for Auric with the other.

"Did you like that?" I asked, as I dragged myself between her folds. "Both of us touching you at once?"

"Gods, yes." She whimpered a little as she lifted her hips. "Please, Jasin."

How could I deny her? I couldn't, and with a slight nudge I pushed inside her tight entrance. She moaned, but it was clear she wanted Auric involved too, even if they weren't ready for sex yet. With one smooth movement I rolled us over on the bed, so that she was on top of me. "Sit up."

She rose up on my lap, taking me even deeper while giving me a view of her breasts dangling in front of me. "Ohh," she said, as she closed her eyes and began to rock back and forth on me.

"That's it, ride me," I said, as I gripped her hips. "Auric, move behind her and touch her breasts."

He followed my command, and I had to admit I liked being the leader here in the bedroom. Kira leaned back into his touch as his hands covered her breasts and his mouth pressed against her neck. I rocked my hips up at her, slamming my cock deeper inside her, increasing our pace.

"Now touch her in that spot I showed you," I told Auric.

He reached down and slipped a hand between us to begin rubbing her clit. Kira threw her head back as she rode me faster, and I knew she was unable to stop as the pleasure built inside her. Auric still had one hand on Kira's breast, and I reached up to stroke the other one, while lifting my hips in time to her movements.

"That's it," I said. "Find your release."

She pressed her hands against my chest as she let out a loud moan and began to shudder, her body tightening up around me. Watching her face as she came was the most beautiful sight I'd ever seen, and I couldn't help but follow her over the edge as the pleasure crested inside me. But I kept lifting my hips and Auric kept rubbing her until every last bit of pleasure was teased from her body, when she finally collapsed against my chest.

Auric moved beside me and wrapped his arm around Kira, as she pressed a kiss to his lips and then mine. "Well, I'd say that first lesson was a success."

21

KIRA

When I'd imagined stopping in Stormhaven on our way to the Air Temple, I'd never pictured myself stepping into one of the finest dress shops in the city. Nor that Auric's fiancé would be the one who'd convinced me to come here.

"Lady Brin," the clothier said cheerfully as he made his way over to us and dropped into a bow. "It's wonderful to see you again."

Brin took his hands with a sweet smile. "Thank you, Dumond. How are your husbands?"

The elderly clothier's face crinkled as he beamed at her. "Quite well, thank you. What brings you to my shop today? Is there something I can get you?"

"You may have heard that Prince Auric has returned to the palace and a ball is being thrown in his honor tomorrow night. I plan to wear the lovely lavender gown you made me the other week, but my friend Kira needs something to wear too. I'm hoping you have something that would work for her."

"I see." His eyes flicked up and down me, like he was taking measurements. I wore another borrowed dress from Brin today, this one in a pale yellow. "I do believe I might have a few gowns that would do."

"Thank you," Brin said. "I'm sorry for the short notice."

He waved it away. "It's no trouble. That's why I always have a few gowns in stock at all times."

"And that's why you're the best."

"Let me see what I can find," he said, before slipping into the back room.

Brin and I casually admired the samples on the floor and touched the fabrics on display. Every gown in here was worth more than all of my life's possessions combined. I was keenly aware that I didn't belong in this fine shop full of brocades, silks, velvets, and jewels.

"I'm so glad you agreed to come with me," Brin said, as she idly examined a pair of soft deerskin gloves. "I realize we were both put in an awkward position due to the way we met, but I do hope we can become friends nevertheless."

"Friends?" I asked, startled.

"Yes. I have so few real friends. Auric is the only person I'm close to. The other nobles are always playing games with each other or are far too stuffy. And the rest...well, I tend to break their hearts." She winked at me. "Luckily that isn't an issue with you, since you already have four suitors."

I wasn't sure how I felt about being friends with my mate's former fiancé, but I had to admit I found myself liking Brin despite myself. Instead of answering her, I asked, "Is there anyone you want to be with now that your betrothal with Auric has ended?"

"No one in particular. My family is trying to set up another marriage as soon as possible though." She sighed as she admired a deep green traveling cloak I'd been looking at earlier. "This would be lovely on you. I'll tell Dumond to add it to the order."

The cloak cost more money than I'd ever had in my life. "But I can't—"

She held up a graceful dark hand. "No arguments, please. I have no sisters either, you know. It's nice to shop for someone other than myself. And Auric told me to get you whatever you wanted."

I wanted to protest some more, but the truth was I did need some new clothes, especially if we were going to be in Stormhaven for a few more days. I bowed my head. "That's kind of you both. Thank you."

"As the Prince's new betrothed, you'll have to start looking the part." When I made a face, she laughed. "Is that not so?"

"I suppose I am, though we've never talked about marriage. Our relationship is...complicated. And I'm still upset with him for not telling me about his betrothal to you."

"I saw him slip into your room last night, so you can't be that upset with him," she said, with a knowing gleam in her eyes.

My cheeks flushed at the memory of being touched by Jasin and Auric together. "I've forgiven him somewhat, but not completely."

"You must understand that Auric has always been the odd one out among his family. They all love him, of course, but he's always kept to himself and been very independent. When he didn't, he was often teased by his siblings or ridiculed for being different by other nobles." She laid a hand on my arm. "When Auric neglects to tell you something, it isn't because he is trying to keep secrets, but because he has a hard time sharing parts of himself he knows others might disapprove of or dislike."

I sighed. "That doesn't excuse what he did."

"No, it doesn't, but I hope it explains it better." Her red lips quirked up. "But if you'd like, we can be mad at him together. I'm still upset he disappeared from the Air Realm without a word to me."

"He had a good reason, I promise."

She arched a perfect dark eyebrow. "Yes, though he still won't tell me what that is."

I was saved from having to answer when Dumond returned with two women who carried a gown each. "I believe either of these should fit with minimal alterations," he said. "Shall we try them on?"

I stepped behind a changing screen and donned the first dress, which was pale blue and made of the softest, lightest silk. It hugged my body when I put it on, accentuating my curves, and dipped scandalously low in the back. In the Air Realm people tended to show a lot more skin than I was used to, although I had to admit it did look nice.

I stepped out from behind the screen and Brin clasped her hands together. "Gorgeous," she said. "It fits you like a glove. Dumond, you are a genius."

He smiled at us both. "It helps when I have such beautiful women to work with."

I tried on the other gown next, which was pure white and covered in tiny clear crystals all over, with a low neckline and a skirt that slightly flared around my feet. I could only stare at myself in the mirror as I spun, the crystals shifting in color as they caught the light. My red hair hanging around my shoulders only added to the drama, as if the color had been heightened by the dress. My hazel eyes stood out too, like they were reflecting all the colors the dress caught.

Brin gasped when she saw me. "Oh, it's incredible. You must wear this to the ball."

I smoothed my hands down the skirts. "I've never worn something so fine in my life."

"Do you like it?"

In this gown I looked like a princess, like the kind of girl who belonged with Auric in the palace. "Yes, I love it. I'm just not sure I should be the one wearing it."

"Nonsense. We'll take both gowns," Brin told Dumond. "Although she'll wear this one to the ball."

He nodded. "Perfect. Let me make a few slight alterations and then we'll send them to the palace."

As he began sticking the dress with pins, I said, "Everyone is going to notice me in this dress."

"Good," Brin said. "You have the love of a prince. Why hide it?"

I couldn't help but smile. "I suppose."

While Dumond continued tacking the dress, Brin began picking out other things for me, such as shoes, jewelry, and accessories, plus that green cloak I'd liked. I decided to leave her to it, since I had no idea what would be proper for the ball and I could tell she loved doing this sort of thing.

Once I'd returned to my borrowed yellow gown and thanked Dumond for everything, Brin didn't stop there. She dragged me down the boisterous, colorful street to another shop, where I found fine traveling clothes that were more my style. The shopkeeper here knew Brin as well, and together they began picking out things for me.

By the time we were finished, I'd somehow ended up with an entire new wardrobe, courtesy of Brin's help and Auric's money. Every time I'd protested it was too much, Brin had ignored me. Now I had new boots, gloves, and riding clothes, along with my two gowns, two pairs of dress slippers, and much more. She even got me a few new chemises made of lace and silk, which I knew the men would love.

Hours later we climbed back into our carriage and relaxed against the seats. Who knew shopping could be exhausting? Or so time consuming? And the oddest thing was, I'd had fun, mainly because of Brin.

As the carriage began to climb the hill to the palace we both fell into tired, companionable silence while staring out the window. I'd been so hurt by Auric that I'd only thought of myself, but now I tried to imagine this situation from Brin's perspective. Her friend and betrothed had suddenly disappeared without a word and then returned over a month later with a new woman he loved and no explanation for where he'd been. Even if she didn't love Auric in that way it had to be difficult for her, especially with her family's pressure on her to marry. Yet she'd been nothing but kind to me.

"You should tell your parents you don't want them to arrange another marriage for you," I blurted out.

She blinked at my sudden words. "Why is that?"

"You deserve to be with someone you love. A marriage you don't want will never make you happy."

"You're probably right. At least if I married Auric I would be spending my life with a dear friend, but now my parents will likely try to marry me to someone I can barely tolerate. I do want children to further the family

247

line someday, but I don't care for men in that way. But what choice do I have?"

It was hard to believe the confident Brin would balk at sticking up for herself, but things were always harder with one's own family. "What would you tell someone else who was in your position?"

She tilted her head slightly as she considered. "To be honest with their parents and be firm about what they want."

"Then that's what you should do."

A faint smile crept over her red lips. "It's much easier to give someone advice than to take it. Especially when it comes to standing up to your parents. But I'll try." She leaned forward and took my hands in hers. "Thank you, Kira. I can see why Auric loves you."

"And I can see why you're his best friend."

I hated to admit it, but we might be in danger of becoming friends too.

22

KIRA

W hen we returned from shopping, Brin slipped back to her rooms, but I stopped when I saw some familiar horses outside the palace —along with some familiar faces as well. Calla, the High Priestess of the Fire Temple, was dismounting, along with her four handsome mates. I rushed toward them and called out, "You're here!"

Calla smiled at me as she tucked back her pale blond hair. "Hello, Kira. I'm glad to see you're doing well."

"I'm so relieved you're all safe," I said. "Thank you for bringing the horses. How did you know we'd be here?"

"We knew you were heading to the Air Temple and assumed you would stop here first. Word spread that the King's youngest son had returned to the palace, so I thought I would leave the horses here for safe keeping. Although I presumed you would already be on your way to the Temple by now."

"We're leaving in two days." I sighed at the reminder. "I wanted to leave sooner, but there have been some…complications."

Calla nodded. "When you get to the Air Temple, please say hello to the High Priestess Nabi for me. She and I have corresponded many times, though we've never met in person."

"I will. But what are you all doing here and not at your own Temple?" I remembered Sark flying over the Fire Temple as we left. "Are you fleeing Sark?"

"Not exactly. He questioned us extensively for information on who you are and where you're going next, but I refused to tell him anything. We decided it wasn't safe at the Temple anymore after that."

I shuddered at the thought of facing Sark. "I'm so glad he didn't hurt you."

"Oh, he wouldn't dare. You see, Sark is my grandfather."

"Your *what?*" I tried not to cringe back in horror.

She chuckled softly. "That was my reaction too when I found out."

"I'm sorry," I said, my head spinning from the news. "I'm just surprised Sark let your relation stop him. He's always seemed so heartless and cruel."

"Yes, he is. But he's never hurt me or my mates, despite his threats over the years. He's never let the other Dragons harm us either. Perhaps it's a sign there's still some humanity left in him after all."

"I doubt that," I muttered. "I didn't even know the Dragons could have children."

"It seems they can, though I've never heard of any others like me, and I don't believe the Black Dragon can have any herself."

I'd never even considered children, though I should have when I'd slept with Jasin. The Black Dragon had ruled for hundreds of years with no children born to her, so in the back of my mind I must have known I could not become pregnant. Now that it was confirmed, a heavy sadness settled over me. Having a child wasn't something I'd thought about much growing up and living on the run, but after meeting my four mates, I couldn't help but wonder what it would be like to have children with each of them. Not anytime soon, but after we'd completed the momentous tasks ahead of us and our lives had calmed down. Would we never get that chance?

It mattered little, since I had more immediate problems to focus on. Sark knew about our existence, and even if he didn't know who we were or where we were going, it was only a matter of time before he was able to track us down.

After I bid Calla farewell and told her where she could find their boat, I sought out Auric, who was in the library with his head in a large, ancient-looking book, while a map was spread out beside him.

"Calla has arrived with our horses," I said.

He let out a relieved sigh. "Thank the Gods she is safe."

"She didn't tell Sark anything about us, but it won't be long before he realizes where we are. Are we still planning to leave for the Air Temple the morning after the ball?"

He tapped his fingers on the book idly. "Yes. I've been making preparations, but I think we should ask Brin if she will go with us."

"Brin?" I shook my head. "I'm not sure that's such a good idea."

"We can trust her with the truth and we could use her help. No one knows the route to the Air Temple better than Brin."

"We agreed not to tell anyone after what happened with Jasin's family."

"Yes, but then we told my parents."

"That was different."

He gestured to the map. "The Air Temple is in the middle of the desert and it's easy to get lost out there without a guide, even with the best maps. I've only been once, but Brin's family goes every year. If we want to get there as quickly as possible, we need her guidance."

I stared at the map, then sighed. "All right, but we can't tell her what we are or why we're going to the Air Temple."

We called for Brin to join us, while a servant brought us all some tea and pastries. A few minutes later Brin sauntered into the library like it was her second home and smiled at us as she took a seat. "Hello again, lovelies. I was told you wanted to see me?"

Auric nodded. "We have something we'd like to talk to you about."

Brin's eyes sparkled as she leaned forward. "Are you finally going to tell me where you've been the last few weeks?"

"Not exactly." Auric cleared his throat and glanced at me. "I'm sorry. I wish I didn't have to keep it a secret from you."

"It's all right," she said with a sigh. "What did you want to talk about?"

"We need to go to the Air Temple," I said. "And get there as quickly as possible."

Her eyebrows shot up and I could see her trying to put the pieces together. "Is that so? In that case, you'll need a lot of supplies, along with camels."

"Camels?" I asked.

"Of course. The Air Temple is surrounded by harsh desert with nothing around it for miles. Horses would have a difficult time there." She reached for a quill and some paper and began jotting things down. "You'll need lots of water, for sure, along with shelter capable of surviving the heat and sandstorms…"

"How do you know so much about this?" I asked.

"My family's ancestral home is on the edge of the desert, so I'm quite familiar with what it's like traveling there. I've also been to the Air Temple once a year for my entire life. My parents are quite devout." She scribbled across the paper, biting her lip. "Don't worry. I'll make sure you have everything you need."

"Thank you, Brin," Auric said. "I knew we could count on you."

"Of course, it's the least I can do for my dear friends."

"Would you possibly be interested in coming with us as our guide?" I asked.

She pressed a hand to her chest. "Oh, I would love to, and I'm honored you've asked, but I can't. My parents want me to stay in Stormhaven to meet with potential suitors in the next few weeks. But don't worry, I'll make you an excellent map with the quickest route. I've done the trip in four days once, though much depends on the weather."

"That would be most appreciated," Auric said. "Thank you."

They began going over everything we would need, while I sat back and listened. In two days' time we'd be leaving Stormhaven behind and venturing into the desert. But could we make it to the Air Temple before the Dragons found us?

23

SLADE

On the day of the ball the palace descended into chaos. I managed to stay in my room for most of it, even though I found myself antsy and itching to be outdoors. I'd spent the past few days walking the palace grounds, trying to find some solitude with the earth and visiting the palace's blacksmiths to remind myself of who I was. Not a prince. Not an assassin. And not a soldier either. I was an ordinary man, and all I'd wanted was a simple life in my village. Now my life was anything but simple or ordinary.

I left to head out for a short walk outside to ground myself before the ball, but nearly ran into Kira in the hallway. She looked frazzled, wearing a white sparkling gown that was impossible to take my eyes off of, especially as it showed off every beautiful curve.

"Kira, what's wrong?" I asked.

She pressed a hand to her head and groaned. "My maid has disappeared and I need to finish getting ready for the ball and my hair is a mess and I have no idea what I'm doing. What will Auric's parents think of me when I show up like this?"

"You look beautiful." I took her arm and led her back to her room. "But let's see what we can do about your hair."

She followed me with a confused expression, but I sensed she was too frustrated at this point to argue with me. I knew she didn't feel like she belonged here, which was understandable. None of us did, not even Auric. But she wanted his parents to like her too, which I could also understand.

"Sit," I said, lightly pushing her into the chair at the dresser.

She sank down and stared at me in the mirror. "What are you going to do?"

I stood behind her and examined her for a moment, before picking up a brush. "I'm not sure yet."

I began to slowly run the brush through her glorious red locks, which shined with every stroke. Kira's hair was thick and had a tendency to get tangled, but I was gentle with it as I eased out the knots and pulled the brush through. She let out a soft sigh and her entire body relaxed under my care, though I suspected I might be enjoying it as much as she was.

I set down the brush and considered for a moment, then took small pieces of her hair in the front and began to braid it. She watched as I did this to both sides of her head before asking, "Where did you learn to do this?"

"From my sisters."

"You have sisters?"

I grunted. "Two of them. Both younger than me."

She smiled as I piled the rest of her hair atop her head and pinned it in an elaborate up-do with a few tendrils hanging down. "What are they like?"

"The younger one is a troublemaker. She's about your age and always finding ways to drive our mother mad, but she can put a smile on everyone's face she meets." I couldn't help but smile myself as I said it. "The other one is the quieter, more serious one. She married a few years ago and has a son."

"And your parents?"

"My father passed away some time ago from illness. My mother still lives, but hasn't remarried."

"I'm sorry."

I shrugged as I wrapped the braids around the bun I'd created. "It happened many years ago. I took over as village blacksmith, as was customary. Although now that I'm gone my cousin is running the shop."

"Do you miss your home?"

"Every day."

"I'd like to see it someday and meet your family too. Maybe on the way to the Earth Temple?"

"Maybe." I wasn't sure I wanted Kira to meet my family. That felt too…serious. I cleared my throat. "There. Finished."

"It's lovely. You're very talented at this." She admired her hair in the mirror with a smile. "Thank you."

"You're welcome."

She stood up and turned around, then wrapped me in a close embrace.

"I know you didn't choose this and don't really want to be here, but I'm so happy you're one of my mates."

I couldn't help but hold her against me, drawn to her soft curves and feminine body despite myself, even as her words warmed me from the inside out. "No, I didn't choose this life, and I'm still not sure I'm the right man for the role, but I do want to be here."

She looked up at me with hope shining in her eyes. "You do?"

"Yes. I'm honored to be your Jade Dragon." I pressed a kiss to her forehead before releasing her. "And I think you'll be an excellent Black Dragon."

She sighed as she turned to admire her hair in the mirror again, touching it lightly. "I'm not sure I agree. The other day I was training with Jasin and couldn't control my magic." A small shudder passed through her. "What if I can never master it? What if I hurt someone by accident?"

I rubbed her shoulders as I met her eyes in the mirror. "You will master it, in time. The four of us had a month to train before we met you, and we're still learning. You only need more practice with fire."

"But soon I'll have air to learn too, and then earth and water." She covered her face with her hands. "It just seems so overwhelming and impossible sometimes."

I sensed she meant more than just learning the magic, but everything else that came with being the Black Dragon. When we'd started our journey together we'd all still been in disbelief, but now the implications of our new roles were starting to set in. "You have a lot resting on your shoulders, it's true. But I have no doubt you'll rise to whatever challenge you'll face in the future."

"That's nice of you to say. I wish I could believe it."

"Believe it," I said. "You're smart, capable, kind, and strong. The world could not ask for a better woman as the Black Dragon."

Her eyes softened and she turned toward me. "Thank you."

I looked away, unnerved by the warmth in her gaze. "I'm only speaking the truth."

She rested her hand on my cheek and turned my face back to her, then pressed her lips to mine. Something rumbled inside me as her soft mouth opened for me, and emotions I'd tried to keep buried deep now burst to the surface. I found myself gripping her arms as I began to slowly kiss her back, unable to stop myself. It had been a long time since I'd kissed anyone and I wanted to take my time with it. I needed to savor every taste of her sweet lips and every touch of her soft tongue.

But then I realized what I was doing and abruptly pulled away, as every reason I'd had for keeping my distance from her came rushing back. I couldn't lose my heart again, not to Kira, not to anyone.

I stepped back, while her face filled with confusion. "No, I can't do this. I'm sorry."

"Slade—" she started to say, but I was already dashing out the door, wiping my mouth to try to remove the taste of her from my lips. Except I had a feeling I would never be able to forget that kiss...or stop wanting another one.

24
KIRA

I stepped into the ballroom and was immediately enchanted by the sights and sounds inside. Spinning gold and silver decorations hung from the ceiling and caught the candlelight from around the room, making the room seem magical. A group of musicians played in a corner, while guests in exquisite clothes danced across the floor. An entire wall had been reserved for food and drinks, the likes of which I'd never seen before. I headed there first to sample the tiny dishes laid out, although the massive dessert table was hard to ignore. I'd never seen such extravagance before in my life, and while I'd expected to hate the ball, I wasn't going to complain. Especially as I popped a meat pastry puff in my mouth and nearly died at the flavors exploding across my tongue. I followed it with some sort of brie and raspberry tart, which was equally amazing.

"Enjoying yourself?" Reven asked from the shadows, as I filled my plate with every single dish on the table. He wore all black, as usual, but tonight his clothes were finer than normal and he'd ditched the hooded cloak.

"Yes. Have you tried these?" I asked, before biting into a tiny sausage wrapped in more pastry.

He eyed my full plate. "I had one or two."

"Don't judge me. After being on the road for so long it's a nice change to eat like this, and it's not like I had the best meals before I met you either." Food in some parts of the world was hard to come by, especially when the Dragons demanded so much from their people. Back in Stoneham I'd usually eaten a little of whatever I'd caught in the forest after

ELIZABETH BRIGGS

Tash had fixed it up for me. I'd certainly never had anything like the food in the Air Realm before.

Reven took a sip of his red wine. "Don't get too comfortable. We're leaving in the morning."

"I won't, but even you can admit it's nice to be able to relax and enjoy ourselves for one night at least."

He lifted a shoulder in a casual shrug. "I suppose."

Jasin strolled over with a grin, wearing a fine navy blue coat that accentuated his broad shoulders and muscular frame. He offered his hand and asked, "Care to dance?"

"I'd like to, but I don't know any of the fancy dances these nobles are doing," I said.

"Me neither." He winked at me as he took my arm in his. "But we'll manage."

I shoved my plate at Reven, who grumbled as Jasin swept me onto the dance floor and into the crowd. The crystal-covered gown I'd bought with Brin shimmered around me, and many people stopped to look at the way it caught the light. Or maybe they were looking at me because they'd heard rumors the prince had broken his engagement because of me.

As Jasin took me in his arms, he said, "You look lovely."

"Thank you." I smiled up at him, admiring how the red highlights in his auburn haired seemed to dance under the torchlight. "You cleaned up nicely yourself."

He swept me across the floor and we managed to move together in time to the music. "It's strange to not wear my uniform at things like this, but I suppose that part of my life is over."

"Do you miss being in the army?"

"Not at all." He brushed his lips across my cheek. "I'm exactly where I'm meant to be."

"You seem so certain." I longed for that certainty. Lately all I had were doubts, it seemed. Take earlier, for example. Slade had finally let me get close to him, but after I'd kissed him, he'd ran away. Now I didn't even see him in the ballroom. Was he avoiding me again?

"Meeting the Fire God will do that to a man, I guess." He touched my chin lightly. "Don't forget, he gave you his blessing as well."

"True. Sometimes I still can't believe it happened."

"Believe it. And you have three more Gods to meet soon."

I nodded. Maybe once we reached the Air Temple I'd find some more clarity. There was still so much I didn't know, like who my true parents were and why I was the Black Dragon. I prayed the Air God would tell me something useful.

When the song ended, Auric appeared at my side wearing white and

258

gold, with his blond hair slicked back and his gray eyes shining bright. "May I steal her away?"

"I suppose it's your party," Jasin said with a smile, as he stepped back.

Auric clasped my hand in his, then settled his other one on my waist. "I've never seen a woman more beautiful than you tonight."

My face flushed and I looked down. "That's very kind of you to say."

"It's the truth. Every other woman in his is jealous. Look how they stare at you."

"Only because I'm dancing with you. Do you think they know...?"

"Know what?" he asked, as he led me across the dance floor with surer steps than Jasin. He was obviously quite experienced with this kind of dancing.

"That you ended your betrothal because of me?"

"Definitely. Gossip travels fast. But don't worry, I care not what anyone thinks, and Brin is doing fine too." He nodded in the direction of the drink table. I followed his gaze to find Brin standing there with wine in hand, speaking to three women who hung onto her every word. "She'll take at least one of them to her room tonight, I'm sure. Maybe all three."

I arched an eyebrow. "I thought you were supposed to stay virgins until marriage, as was custom for nobility?"

"She's never been with a man before. I suppose she considers that good enough for tradition."

"Would her parents ever let her marry a woman?"

"Perhaps, but they'd want her to marry a man too. They want an heir."

I sighed. "I like Brin. I didn't want to, but I do."

He grinned as he spun me around. "She has a way of sneaking up on you like that. At first you think she's another spoiled noblewoman, but then you discover she's so much more. And you haven't even seen her fight yet."

"She can fight?"

"All nobles can, to some degree. We're taught to defend ourselves from a young age. But I daresay she might be even better than me."

"It's kind of her to help us prepare for the journey to the Air Temple."

Auric nodded, but whatever he might have said next was cut off when a hush went over the crowd. People around us stopped dancing and turned toward the front of the room, then unexpectedly dropped into low bows. Auric's grip on my arm tightened.

As the wave of bowing reached us, I was able to see over the crowd at last. Two men gazed across the room with haughty, cruel expressions. One of them was Isen, the Golden Dragon, wearing black and gold silk. He had some nerve showing up here after he'd just ordered an assassination on the King.

But then I noticed the other man standing beside him. Tall, broad shouldered, with short blond hair so pale it was nearly white, he was the man who'd haunted my nightmares for years. The last few times I'd seen him were in his dragon form and from a distance, but now he was only a few feet away as a man. A mix of terror and rage battled for dominance inside me. I knew I'd have to face him at some point, but I hadn't expected it to be anytime soon. But here he was, towering over this ball as though he ruled here instead of the King.

Sark, the Dragon who had killed my parents.

25

REVEN

The key to being a good assassin was to remain calm at all times—and I was the best in the four Realms. I'd faced impossible odds and dodged certain death without breaking a sweat. I'd escaped prisons and survived torture. I'd stolen from the best thieves and murdered the most vile men and women. And never once had I lost my calm.

Until tonight.

The sight of Sark sent instant, poisonous hatred through my veins and I reached for my hidden weapons without thinking. With a small dagger in each hand, I charged forward—but was held back by a large hand on my shoulder.

"You don't want to do that," Slade said.

"Trust me, I do." I pulled away from him with some effort. Damn, the man was strong. It was like fighting against a boulder.

"Someday, yes. But not here. Not now. Not yet."

I gripped my daggers tighter, the rage boiling me from the inside out at the sight of the man standing there while people bowed before him. I wanted nothing more in the world than to stab my blade through his heart. Or better yet, make him suffer the way he'd made me suffer. The way he'd made Kira suffer.

But Slade had a point, though I was reluctant to admit it. If I stabbed Sark, would he even die? We knew so little about the Dragons since no one had dared oppose them. For all we knew they were immortal. The only way to defeat them was to become Dragons ourselves.

I sheathed my daggers and muttered, "Fine."

ELIZABETH BRIGGS

That didn't mean I would stand by doing nothing. I slipped back into the shadows, while Auric's parents made their way over to the uninvited guests with fake smiles plastered on their faces. I ducked behind statues and tables to get closer, but I wasn't planning on attacking, only listening. Although if the moment presented itself, I wouldn't mind attacking either.

"Sark, Isen, what an unexpected appearance," the King said.

"Are we not welcome?" Isen asked, arching a black eyebrow.

"Of course you are. We're delighted to have such esteemed guests. I'm simply surprised since you do not often grace our balls with your presence."

"Sark and I have business in the city and thought we might stop by." Isen cast a dismissive gaze across the crowd, which had reluctantly started dancing again, though the mood in the room had changed and become tense. "I heard there'd been an assassination attempt on your life. Is that so?"

"Yes, there was, but we dealt with it. The assassin is dead." The King paused. "You wouldn't know anything about that, would you?"

"You dare question us?" Sark asked, his voice more like a growl.

King Terel smiled at them like they were old friends. "Not at all. Simply hoping for some answers. But we'll uncover who was behind it, I'm certain."

Isen sniffed. "And that matter we discussed the other day? Have you had time to think on it?"

The King hesitated, then bowed his head. "Yes, I have, and I concede to your wishes. Tomorrow we'll begin searches throughout the city for Resistance members."

"See that you do," Isen said, his voice carrying a subtle threat. "Otherwise I can't promise there won't be more trouble in the Air Realm."

"We have reason to believe five people in particular are hiding in Stormhaven," Sark said. "One woman and four men. They might claim to have special powers, but they are tricksters and con artists. If you hear word of them, inform us immediately."

"I shall," King Terel said.

"Enjoy your party," Isen said, as he turned away and plucked a tiny pastry off the dessert table and popped it in his mouth. He gestured at Sark, but the Crimson Dragon stared at something behind the King, his brow furrowed.

I followed his gaze and saw Kira's pale face looking back at him. Auric held her in his arms, and I couldn't be sure if he was keeping her from running to attack Sark, like Slade had done with me, or if he was holding her up so her knees wouldn't give out on her. That burning hatred seethed inside me again as Sark took Kira in, and I reached for my daggers in case

262

he recognized her somehow. But then Sark spun on his heel and followed Isen outside onto the patio, where it had begun raining. They both shifted into their dragon forms and took off, while lightning flashed in the sky and thunder rumbled behind it.

As soon as they were gone a collective sigh of relief went up around the entire room and the dancing picked up. Even the music seemed livelier and the candles brighter. The Dragons had a tendency to suck the air out of any room they were in. Was it any wonder I had no desire to become one of them?

But that was before. Now, as I caught sight of Kira's pained expression and trembling hands, a new purpose and resolve filled me. Sark had taken everything from Kira, just as he'd done to me. Even so, I hadn't wanted revenge, not at first. I'd made my own way in the world and found a way to survive. After I'd been appointed the next Azure Dragon I'd tried to run from my destiny, but I'd been unable to stay away.

Everyone I'd ever loved was dead. I refused to love Kira and have her meet the same fate, but for some reason I wasn't able to walk away from her either. Gods knew I'd tried, yet here I was, drawn by this invisible string to her side no matter how much I tried to fight it or escape it. Maybe, deep down, I'd known this was the only way to avenge my family and take down the beast responsible for their deaths. The best way to fight fire was with water, after all.

To defeat Sark, I had to become a Dragon myself. And this time, I wouldn't run or hide from my fate. I would be the next Azure Dragon, no matter what it took.

I just had to make sure I didn't lose my heart to Kira in the process.

26

KIRA

After Sark's arrival at the ball and the way he'd looked at me, like he'd recognized me somehow, I hadn't wanted to dance any longer. Fear and anger had taken hold of my heart, and all I could do was return to my room and take deep breaths to calm myself. I reminded myself if Sark truly had recognized me or realized what I was, I'd be dead now. We were still safe and our identities were unknown, though I knew that wouldn't last much longer.

The Dragons were looking for us, that was for sure. Thanks to Calla, they didn't know who we were or even what we looked like, but it was only a matter of time before we were uncovered. Good thing we were leaving for the Air Temple in the morning.

A massive storm had begun raging as soon as the Dragons had left, and I stared out my window as dozens of lightning bolts hit the spires across the city, filling the sky with dazzling light. Thunder rumbled all around us, as if the Air God himself was displeased.

Heavy footsteps sounded outside my door, which was then thrown open. All four of my mates stood in the doorway looking as if they were going to charge in here with their weapons drawn to defend my honor.

Jasin stood at the front of the group, his dark eyes blazing. "Kira, are you all right?"

"You disappeared from the ball without a word," Auric said.

I gave them a faint smile. "Yes, I'm fine. I was just a bit shaken from seeing Sark and needed to get away from the crowd."

"Everyone in the entire room was shaken," Reven said. "The Dragons do that to people."

Auric's hands clenched into fists. "They had some nerve coming to the ball uninvited and threatening my father in front of everyone."

"Your father handled it well," I said. "Better than I would have."

"He's had many years of practice. And you did well too."

"I didn't. If not for you, I would have done something embarrassing." I shuddered when I remembered Sark's terrible gaze. "I thought for sure he recognized me at the end."

"He didn't," Slade said. "Or we'd all be dead."

"I thought the same thing." I sighed as I sank down onto the bed. "I wish I'd been able to face him without fear, but I was terrified. How am I supposed to actually fight the Dragons someday?"

Auric sat beside me and wrapped an arm around my shoulders. "You'll get there. No one expects you to fight them now. Or any of us for that matter. We have to unlock all of our powers first."

I leaned against him. "What if the Dragons stop us from getting to the temples?"

"We'll find a way somehow."

I nodded, but I wasn't convinced, and I couldn't get Sark's harsh voice out of my head. Nor Isen's cruel one, for that matter. At least the King had gone along with the plan to accede to some of their wishes to keep his family safe. I hoped we could count on his help someday too—we might need it.

"We have an early start ahead of us," Slade said. "Best we all get some rest."

The men agreed, but the thought of being alone in my room left a hollow pit in my stomach. I looked up at the four of them and asked, "Will you all stay with me tonight?" When they stared at me, I added, "Just sleep, nothing more. I just don't want to be alone, and I think I'll feel better if you're all by my side. But if you don't want to, that's fine also. I understand."

"You know I'm always happy to share your bed," Jasin said.

"Me too," Auric added.

Slade frowned and glanced at the bed. "Not sure it's big enough for all of us."

"Sure it is," Jasin said, as he flopped onto the bed. He patted the spot next to him. "We just have to get nice and cozy."

I laughed despite my dark mood and slid onto the bed beside him. He immediately wrapped me in his strong arms and pulled me close, pressing a kiss to my temple. Auric climbed onto the bed on the other side of me and draped his arm over my waist, caging me between the two of them, which was becoming one of my new favorite places to be. Slade reluctantly got onto the bed too beside Jasin, his body stiff as he kept his distance from us as much as possible. He'd likely get a sore neck and I wished he was touching me too, but at least he was here with me instead of pushing me away.

"I'll sleep in the chair, thanks," Reven said.

I reached for him, my heart aching with longing. "Reven…"

"That bed is plenty crowded without me joining in. Besides, someone should keep watch." He settled into a chair and propped his feet up on the table, crossing his arms behind his head.

I sighed, but I couldn't force him to want to be with me. He was in the room watching over me and that was enough, especially when he'd left me behind only a few days ago. The fact that he stayed now was a big step up.

"Thank you," I murmured, as I buried myself into Jasin and Auric's warm bodies. I reached over and ran a hand along Slade's muscular arm too, taking comfort from his nearby presence. I even felt Reven's closeness and support as I closed my eyes and drifted away.

When I woke, I found the three of us tangled together, limbs entwined, my hair draped across them, our heartbeats all in sync. Even Slade had come closer during the night as if he couldn't resist, and now his hand rested on my hip, while my foot rested on his calf. Jasin and Auric were wrapped around me too, and I was blissfully warm and calm for the first time in ages.

Except I really had to relieve myself.

I managed to untangle myself from the men without waking them, though Jasin reached for me and mumbled for me to come back. Reven's eyes popped open as I padded across the floor to the washroom.

"Sleep well?" he asked, showing no sign he'd been asleep at all.

"Very." I rested a hand on his shoulder. "Though I wish you would have joined us too."

"I don't think that's ever going to happen. Even if I wanted to, the other guys don't want me there with you. They don't trust me. For good reason, I admit."

"They will. Just give them time." I bent down and brushed my lips across his dark, stubbled jaw, making his shoulders tense up. I wanted to do more, so much more, but I had to be sure he wanted that too.

I slipped away to the washroom, and when I returned all the men were stretching and waking up, while morning light filtered through the curtains. Though I would have liked to return to bed with them, and possibly do more than sleep, it was time to get going. The Air Temple awaited us.

27
AURIC

We gathered outside the palace, where two carriages were waiting for us with our supplies already loaded onto them. The plan was to take the carriages out of the city and to Windholm, a town on the edge of Sandstorm Valley. There we would switch to camels for the rest of the journey into the barren desert where the Air Temple resided.

Brin and I had been overseeing preparations over the last two days, and I was grateful for her assistance since I hadn't been in the desert in many years and had never planned an excursion on my own. It was a shame she wouldn't be going with us, but it would be hard to hide what we were if she did come, so perhaps it was for the best.

My former fiancé stood with Kira by the carriages, while stroking the neck of a dappled gray horse. Kira laughed at something Brin said, and my heart warmed at the sight. Against all odds they'd managed to become friends, just as I'd hoped.

Kira wore her new riding clothes with a dark green cloak that brought out the color in her eyes and made her red hair pop. She had new boots too, and I was pleased to see that her shopping excursion with Brin had gone well and that she'd been able to obtain some suitable clothes, which she'd desperately needed.

Her mates had been more stubborn and wouldn't accept my offer to get them new clothing, although they'd allowed me to loan them things to wear while we were at the palace. I'd ceded defeat, but had made up for it by providing all of the supplies we'd need on this journey. It was the least I could do for the trouble I'd put us in by coming here, and for their understanding of my situation with Brin.

While Kira's other mates checked our supplies, I turned to the ladies and asked, "Are we all ready to go?"

"Just about," Brin said. "We just need to say goodbye to your parents."

I arched an eyebrow at her. "We?"

"I've decided to come with you after all." Brin flashed a dazzling smile at us. "You're going to need a guide. And thanks to Kira here, I'm a free woman."

"What do you mean?" I asked.

"Kira convinced me to stand up to my parents and tell them I wouldn't go through with an arranged marriage to a man. They weren't thrilled about it, but they said they understood."

"I'm so proud of you," Kira said.

I wrapped Brin in a quick hug. "That's wonderful. And they're allowing you to go on this journey?"

She tossed back her long black hair with a grin. "The King convinced them it would be good for you to have an escort, though I'm pretty sure they think we're just going to offer tribute at the Air Temple. Not that I know what we'll actually be doing, but I have a feeling it's more than that."

"Are you sure about this?" Kira asked. "It's going to be dangerous. The Dragons are searching for us, and we've also been attacked by bandits, elementals, and the Onyx Army."

"Sounds like you need someone to help watch your backs," Brin said with a wink. "Believe me, I'm ready to get out of this boring city and see some adventure. My blades haven't been put to good use in ages."

"All right, but if it gets too dangerous we're leaving you at the Air Temple," I said.

Brin waved her hand breezily. "I'll be fine. Besides, we all know you'll need my help so you don't end up wandering in circles out in the sand dunes."

"We appreciate you coming with us," Kira said. "I've never been to the desert before."

"It's beautiful in its own way, but deadly. Although with proper preparations we should be fine."

Our conversation died off when my parents walked out of the palace, their guards trailing behind them. The King loomed over everyone as he made his way down the steps while holding my mother's arm. Both of them wore royal purple and gold along with their crowns as they came to say goodbye to us.

I approached my parents with a hesitant smile, while Brin and Kira trailed behind me. "Mother, father."

The King stared at me for some time, then clasped me on the shoulder. "We're proud of you, son."

I'd never heard those words from my father before and my throat choked with emotion. "Thank you," I managed to get out.

"Please be safe," my mother said, as she squeezed me in a tight hug. "And come back whenever you can."

"I will, and I'll send updates if it's safe to do so."

She nodded and turned to Kira, then surprised me by embracing her too. "I'm sorry we didn't have more time to get to know you better, but I hope we can do so someday."

"I'd like that," Kira said. "Thank you for your hospitality."

The Queen turned to Brin next and gave her a warm smile. "Brin, please take care of these two."

"I will, your majesty," Brin said, as she dipped into a graceful curtsy.

My father nodded at the two ladies, and then focused his stormy gaze on me once more. "Before you go, there's something we'd like you to have." He gestured at a servant, who walked up holding a purple tasseled pillow. On top of it were two long, slightly curved daggers with golden sheaths and hilts inlaid with topaz.

The King lifted the daggers in his palms. "These are the blades of the first King of the Air Realm, who was said to be the brother of the Golden Dragon. I'd once thought that meant Isen, but now I'm not so sure. Either way, they've been passed down through generations to our family's greatest warrior. And now, Auric, we want you to have them."

I accepted the blades with awe in my voice. "I'm honored. Thank you. I'll do my best to restore honor to the position of Golden Dragon."

"We know you will," my mother said, as she patted my cheek.

I strapped the daggers around my waist, noticing how light they were despite their size and their golden sheaths. I'd seen the daggers hanging in the royal armory before and was shocked my parents were giving them to me and not to my brother Garet, who was the warrior in the family. All my life I'd been the odd one out and I'd believed I was a disappointment to my parents. This was finally my chance to make them proud and do my duty to protect the Air Realm—and the entire world.

I said one final goodbye to my parents, before turning away with my heart pounding loudly. Kira gave me a warm smile, while Brin's eyes shined bright. Together we approached the carriages, where the other men were waiting.

I nodded at them. "Let's get going."

28

KIRA

I watched through the carriage window as we left the city, but then my eyes grew heavy and I found myself dozing off. I suspected the others were doing the same. Leaving early after a long night at the ball was probably not the best idea, but none of us had wanted to delay any longer, not with the Dragons sniffing around for us.

According to Brin, it would take us five days to reach the Air Temple with her guidance. Two of those days would be spent in carriages, which wasn't the worst way we'd traveled so far. The men grumbled and complained, saying they wished they were back on their own horses and out in the open air, especially with the stuffy heat inside the carriage. For me this was a treat since I'd never had my own horse and had always had to ride behind one of them. The boat wasn't so bad either, except for the cramped quarters, but least Slade wasn't sick to his stomach in the carriage.

As night fell, we entered the town of Skydale and were taken by our guards and drivers to the finest inn, since nothing less would befit the prince. I didn't think Auric cared, but while we were traveling as part of a royal caravan we had to keep up appearances. Once we reached Windholm tomorrow we would discreetly leave behind our entourage and make our way into the desert alone. The carriages and royal guard would continue on to Thundercrest to make it seem as though the prince was visiting his brother Garet.

After using the washroom, I returned to my room and found Jasin and Auric already inside, talking low to each other with grins on both of their faces. They sat on the edge of the bed like they were waiting for me.

"What are you two gossiping about?" I teased, though it warmed my heart to see them both getting along.

"We were discussing Auric's lesson tonight," Jasin said.

"Is that so?" I asked.

Auric nodded. "We're only a few days away from the Air Temple and I want to be ready."

Jasin gave me a naughty grin. "Auric is going to pleasure you with his mouth tonight. How does that sound?"

The thought sent a rush of heat between my thighs, but I had an idea too. "I wouldn't complain, but I want to learn to do that too."

Jasin arched an eyebrow. "Is that so?"

I slid the straps off my gown and let the silken fabric shimmer down to the floor, revealing my naked skin underneath. Both men's eyes dropped to take in every inch of me. "I want to bring you pleasure with my mouth too, the way you do to me."

"Trust me, you already bring us pleasure," Jasin said. "But I'm always happy to teach you anything."

I moved close to him and he watched with hooded eyes as I opened his trousers slowly to reveal his large, hard shaft. I lifted his shirt up and off him next, then let my hands run along his muscular chest, enjoying the feel of him underneath my palms. He leaned back and let me touch him, and then I tugged his trousers off him, leaving him as naked as I was.

I wrapped my hand around Jasin's cock and he let out a groan. I'd had him inside me twice now, but had never touched him like this before. Now I wanted to get to know this part of him a lot better.

"Like this." Jasin wrapped his hand around mine and showed me how to stroke him the way he liked. I followed his movements until he released me and threw his head back, his eyes closed as he enjoyed my touch.

Auric watched with keen eyes the entire time from beside us, but he didn't join in. Last time he hadn't even removed his clothes, but tonight I wanted him to be more than just an observer. With one hand holding Jasin's cock, I reached for Auric and tried to tug off his shirt. He helped me get it off and then I ran my fingers along his hard nipples and down his long, muscular torso. When my hand reaches his trousers and began fumbling there, his eyes widened.

"Kira, are you sure?" he asked.

"Yes, I want you to join us tonight."

He kissed me hard in response, and I could taste the desire on his lips. My fingers yanked open his trousers, and I was greeted with his hard manhood. He was longer than Jasin, but not as thick. I wondered what it would be like to have him inside me, and if it would feel different than Jasin, as I wrapped my other hand around his cock.

Jasin and Auric both began touching me too, smoothing their hands across my skin as I stroked them together. They cupped my breasts and brought my nipples to their lips. They gripped my behind and yanked me closer against them. They let their fingers dip between my thighs to touch me in places that made me moan too.

But then Jasin pulled away. "Auric, lie back on the bed. It's time to start the next lesson."

Desire stirred inside me at his commanding tone. I had to admit I liked it when Jasin became dominant in bed. I think he enjoyed being the teacher more than he'd expected too.

When Auric was in position, I stared at his body with hunger, until Jasin said, "Kira, you're going to straddle his face. Don't worry, you won't hurt him."

I climbed up onto the bed and moved into position, while Auric's hands came up and began stroking my thighs and my bottom. With my legs spread wide and his face beneath me, I felt more exposed than ever, especially with Jasin watching intently from the side.

Auric gripped my thighs and lowered me to his mouth, and I let out a sigh as his tongue slid against me. He worked slowly, exploring and tasting every inch of me, until I was completely relaxed. Only then did Jasin move in front of me and kneel on the bed, his cock standing proudly at attention and making my mouth water.

Jasin slid his fingers into my hair as he kissed me roughly, then broke away and pushed my head down. I understood immediately and lowered my mouth to his shaft. At first I ran my tongue along it, tasting him and seeing what it did to him. But then his fingers gripped my hair tighter, and I opened my mouth to wrap around the tip of his cock.

"Yes, just like that," he said, as he slowly pushed deeper into my mouth. He took my hand and wrapped it around the base of his cock, while my other hand gripped his bottom for support.

Auric took this moment to slide two fingers inside me, while sucking and licking on me in that spot Jasin had showed him before. Pleasure unfurled inside me and I moaned around Jasin, who sank deeper between my lips in response. I stroked him and sucked on him, my hands and my mouth working in time, and his hips thrust against me in response. Even though his fingers in my hair kept me down I felt so powerful knowing I could bring him pleasure like this.

With Auric's mouth bringing me higher and higher and his fingers pumping inside me, I matched his movements around Jasin's cock. Suddenly it became too much and my thighs began to tremble. Jasin held me steady as pleasure consumed me and I moaned around him, while Auric kept licking and thrusting into me.

As the spasms faded, Jasin pulled out of my mouth and gathered me in his arms to help me off of Auric, who sat up and wiped his mouth with a grin. "Gods, you taste good. I could do that forever."

"You've had your turn," Jasin said. "Now I need her."

He spun me around and gripped my hips, pulling my bottom up. Now on my hands and knees, he loomed behind me, his hands on my behind.

"Mm, you have a lovely ass." His fingers dipped between my thighs, getting nice and wet, but then he moved them back between my cheeks. "I wonder if you'd ever let one of us enter you here."

The thought had never occurred to me before, and my eyes widened as he slid a finger along my back entrance. I gasped as he pushed slightly inside and a new wave of pleasure moved through me.

"I think she likes the idea of that," Auric said.

"Yes, she does." Jasin lowered his voice as he moved his finger slowly in and out of my tight hole. "She wants both of us inside her at once. Not tonight. But soon."

I couldn't help but thrust my hips back against him at the delicious image of being filled by both men, and Jasin chuckled softly. "Please," I found myself begging.

Jasin gripped my hips, then suddenly entered me from behind in one smooth thrust that had me crying out. He felt huge from his angle, like every inch of him was filling up every inch of me. My fingers dug into the sheets as he began to move in and out of me, controlling my hips to get the best angle. All I could do was throw my head back and enjoy.

But I wanted to touch Auric too. He'd brought me pleasure both times, but had never asked for any in return. "Come here," I told him.

Auric kneeled in front of me, and I lowered my mouth to his long cock. "Oh, Gods," he groaned, as I circled his shaft with my tongue, before wrapping my lips around him. Unlike Jasin, who had guided my movements, Auric stroked my head lovingly while I sucked on him.

With both men inside me, they found a smooth rhythm that brought me nearly to the edge already. Jasin thrust forward, pushing me further onto Auric before retreating again. Between the heat and solidness of Jasin entering me from behind, and Auric's length and musty taste in my mouth, I knew I wouldn't last long.

Auric's fingers suddenly tightened in my hair, and his cock pulsed under my tongue. "Kira, I can't—Ohhh…"

I sucked him harder in response, growing more excited knowing I'd done this to him. Jasin slipped a hand between my thighs and began to rub me in time to our movements, and soon I was moaning too. That sent

Auric over the edge, and he released himself in my mouth with one last thrust, shouting my name.

"Swallow it," Jasin commanded, and I did my best to comply.

As I licked Auric clean, Jasin pumped into me faster and harder, his grip on my hips tightening while his finger continued rubbing me too. I threw my head back and cried out loudly as my second orgasm struck me like a lightning bolt, and I felt Jasin join me in bliss only moments later.

Jasin gathered me in his arms as we collapsed onto the bed together. Auric curled up behind me, and I snuggled back against him too.

Jasin slowly kissed me, then he reached over and gave Auric's arm a squeeze. "You were both amazing."

"We're fast learners," Auric said, grinning back at him. They were so comfortable with each other now, as if they had become bonded too in the process of sharing me.

I nuzzled closer against them both. "We had a good teacher."

29

SLADE

The walls of this inn were way too thin. Much worse than at the palace, where I'd only heard a few brief moans. Now I heard *everything*.

I tossed and turned, even put the pillow over my head, but nothing helped. In the other bed Reven seemed to be asleep, but who could tell with him. If he was awake he probably didn't care, since he seemed to have no feelings for Kira at all.

Eventually Kira and her two lovers quieted down, though it took forever. But even then, sleep was elusive. I couldn't stop picturing her with both Jasin and Auric, torn between wishing I was with her too and wanting her for myself alone. I replayed our kiss in my head a dozen times, but all it did was make me frustrated. With myself, with the situation, with the other guys for being with her tonight. Somehow I had to get a grip on myself and my emotions.

In the morning, we got back in the carriages and continued on through the Air Realm, where the landscape started to become sparse with trees and the ground became rockier. I hated being in the carriage almost as much as being in the boat, and it didn't help that I was stuck with Jasin and Kira either. Every time they touched or giggled like lovers my teeth clenched and I glared out the window.

"Are you all right?" Kira asked me. "You seem...tense."

"Didn't sleep well," I said.

"I know a good cure for that," Jasin said with a sly grin. "Maybe we should invite Slade to our next 'lesson.'"

ELIZABETH BRIGGS

I crossed my arms. "Not interested."

Except I was, just a tiny bit. It was curiosity and nothing more, I told myself. We didn't share lovers in the Earth Realm, and I couldn't imagine doing it now either, even if the thought did rouse some lust within me. Probably because it had been many years since I'd been with a woman. I tamped those feelings down since I would never act on them. The others could have their fun, but my plan was to bond with Kira at the Earth Temple and that was it.

When we stopped at midday to relieve ourselves and have a bite to eat, I practically launched myself out of the carriage and away from Jasin and Kira.

Kira started to follow me and called out my name, but I kept going until I'd found a bit of privacy behind some bushes and a group of olive trees. All I needed was to be alone with the ground under my feet and then I'd feel better.

Footsteps padding in the dirt told me my solitude wasn't going to last. Kira stepped into the shade under the trees with me. "There you are."

"Just needed some space after being in that carriage all day."

"I can understand that, but you've been distant for a while now." She reached out to brush her fingers against my hand. "Is something bothering you?"

"No, I..." I stared down at the spot where we were touching. "It's nothing."

"You can tell me anything, Slade."

I scowled and ran a hand along my beard, choosing my words carefully. "I know sharing partners is common in some parts of the world, and in our situation it's unavoidable, but it's hard for me to accept. When a woman is mine, I want her to be all mine."

She swallowed, her eyes widening with what I thought might be desire, though that made no sense. "I'm still getting used to the idea of having four lovers too. I'm sorry it bothers you though."

"Ignore me," I said, shaking my head. "I'll do my duty, just as you will."

Her face fell. "Is that all I am to you? A duty?"

"Not at all. I care for you a great deal, Kira. I will protect you until my dying breath. And when the time comes, I will bond with you. But please do not ask me for anything more than that."

"I don't understand. The other night we kissed and I thought..." She sighed. "I do want to be yours, Slade. And I want you to be mine too."

Longing stirred within me, along with the desire to haul her into my arms and kiss her again. I wanted nothing more than those soft, sweet lips on mine and her supple body pressed against me. But giving in to those

276

desires would only make this more complicated. I couldn't get hurt again the way I'd been hurt before. The best thing to do was to end any pretense that we would become romantically involved. She had the other men, and that would have to be enough.

I stepped back out of her reach. "I'm sorry, Kira. I'll give you my body and my soul, but I can never give you my heart."

As I headed back toward the carriage, I told myself it was for the best, even if I hated leaving her there like that. She deserved better, but I was the one the Earth God had chosen, and we'd both have to find a way to live with that.

30

KIRA

W hen we returned to the carriages Slade made sure to be in a different one than me, and my heart sank even further. Every time I saw him I wanted him to wrap me in his strong arms and hold me close —or push me down and have his way with me. After our kiss the other night those thoughts were stronger than ever, but he'd made it clear he didn't see me in that way.

My four mates had been chosen by the gods to be mine, and in the process they'd had to give up their former lives to go on this quest with me. Only Auric and Jasin had been happy about that so far, while Reven and Slade had fought against their new roles. Though they'd both accepted their position now, I wasn't sure if they would ever love me or truly want to be with me.

I had two incredible men who wanted me—wasn't that enough? Except when I thought of Slade or Reven my chest clenched and I knew it wasn't. How selfish was I that I wanted all of my mates to love me?

While the sun was setting we arrived in Windholm, a small, dusty town with tumbleweeds rolling through it. Here the pace was a lot slower than in Stormhaven, and the people wore cloaks and scarves to cover their faces to protect against the frequent sandstorms. We were taken to another inn and retreated to our rooms, while Brin sorted out the details in town. And then we waited.

I managed to sleep a little, but woke instantly when Auric touched my arm and said, "It's time."

Brin presented me with a stack of clothes. "Put these on."

I donned a large, sand-colored cloak over my clothes, then pulled the hood low while yanking the scarf up so that only my eyes were visible. The others in our group did the same, and then we slipped from the inn and out into the dark, empty streets. A raging wind was already rolling through the town, and I ducked my head and followed Brin around the side of the inn, where a few people were waiting with camels. None of them gave us a second glance and no one seemed to recognize Auric. Not only did the cloaks protect us from the winds, but they disguised us as well.

I'd never ridden a camel before, but nevertheless was pleased to have my own mount this time. All of the beasts were sitting on the ground, and a man instructed me to throw my leg over the middle of the humps to mount the camel nearest me. The beast began to stand immediately, back legs first, making me fall forward, but I managed to find my balance after a moment.

Our supplies were already tied onto the camels, and then Brin took the lead. "Don't bother trying to control your camel. Just relax, let your body follow its movements, and try not to upset them. They're not particularly friendly."

With that warning she set off, and my camel jerked forward after hers. I had to hold on tight to keep from falling off as the beast's body rolled with an odd, jerky walk, completely different from the measured gait of a horse. At first my body wanted to fight it, but then I tried to relax my shoulders and follow Brin's advice, and it became much easier as I swayed with the camel's movements.

Soon we were riding out of town and down the hard dirt road into the desert at the bottom of the hill. The contrast was sharp and came upon us quickly, and in no time our camels' hooves were dipping into the sand. The mountains rose up on either side of us, the wind howled loudly, and the barren desert of Sandstorm Valley stretched endlessly before us.

We rode in a line through the sand for hours while the sun rose in the sky and beat down on us. Sweat dripped down my forehead, and I quickly became disoriented as we passed over identical dune after dune. All I saw around us was sand, which the wind kicked up into our eyes.

Brin called for a halt when the sun had neared its peak in the sky. We set up camp with small tents that would protect us from the worst of the sun and heat, and the men subtly used their magic to help us without alerting Brin. Reven refilled all of our water jugs, Jasin roasted a lizard he'd caught and ate it off a stick, and Auric and Slade kept the wind and sand out of our camp.

I wandered down a dune to find some privacy to relieve myself and to have a moment alone with my thoughts. The closer we got to the Air Temple the more apprehensive I became. Was I ready to bond with Auric?

Would the Dragons be there waiting? And what was I going to do about Slade and Reven?

As I climbed down the dune, the sand slid under my feet, endlessly changing. Just when I'd think I'd found a firm bit to walk on it would shift and my foot would sink, making me stumble.

"Careful there," a familiar voice said.

I spun around and came face to face with Enva, the older woman I'd met twice before. She'd always appeared out of nowhere and would disappear just as quickly, leaving me with more questions than answers. I'd once wondered if she was the Spirit Goddess, but she'd claimed she wasn't. "Enva, what are you doing here?"

Unlike me, she wasn't dressed for the desert. In fact, she wore the same hooded robe she'd worn the last two times I'd seen her. "Keeping an eye on you. I thought you'd be at the Air Temple by now."

"Why do you care so much about my fate?" I asked.

She waved my question away. "I care about the fate of the world, as should everyone."

I plopped down onto the sand, exhausted after hours of riding under the hot sun. My tailbone winced in protest, sore from being on the camel for so long. "While you're here, maybe you can answer some questions for me."

She shrugged. "Maybe, maybe not."

"The Fire God told me the people who raised me weren't my parents. Do you know who my real mother and father are?"

She pursed her lips. "I do."

I sat up straighter, my heart beating fast. "Who are they?"

"You're not ready for that. Next question."

I sighed, but tried again. "What am I supposed to do about my two mates who aren't interested in bonding with me?"

"How should I know? I'm not here for relationship advice."

Gods, she was impossible. "Why *are* you here?"

"To warn you."

The wind whipped at my hair, and I tucked it behind my ear. "Warn me about what?"

She leveled her steely gaze at me. "You may have noticed that you can sense Jasin through your bond now, and he can sense you in return."

"Yes. I assume that will happen with Auric too once we finish at the Air Temple."

"Indeed. They'll be bound to you, and through them you'll receive their magic. But they'll also be tied to your life force."

"What do you mean?" I asked.

"After you're mated your connection with them becomes so strong that if one of them dies, you will lose their powers. But if you die, they will die as well."

Her words shocked me to my core. "All of them?"

"Every one that is bound to you, yes."

My throat tightened up. "What can I do?"

"Nothing, but it's not all bad. With each man you bond with you become harder to kill, especially since you take on their resistances. Right now you can't be harmed by fire, for example." She tilted her head. "Of course, that means the Black Dragon is nearly impossible to defeat without destroying her mates first. But I think I've said enough."

I jumped to my feet, my boots sliding in the sand. "Wait, I have so many more questions."

She pulled her hood low as she turned away. "You'll get your answers soon enough."

And just like that, she was gone.

31

KIRA

For the next three days our group continued through the endless desert, sleeping when the sun was high in the sky and continuing on through the evening when it was cooler. We had little time to talk at all with the sand whipping at us and the camels' movements making it hard to do anything but continue forward. By the time we camped we were all too exhausted and sore to do anything but pass out or grumble at one another. Brin was the only one who remained cheerful, and if it weren't for her guidance I knew we would have certainly gotten lost out there.

On the third day we finally spotted something in the distance: a tower that reached high into the sky and disappeared into the clouds hovering over it. Around it was a small lake surrounded by palm trees, a welcome oasis in the middle of the harsh desert sands. The setting sun behind the tower kissed the sky with gold, and I understood why the Air God's Dragon was that color now.

We rushed toward the tower with renewed vigor, bolstered by the thought that our journey was nearing its destination. Enva's words still worried at me, but there was nothing I could do except move forward.

As we neared the tower, Brin let out a startled cry. "The tower…it's been destroyed."

Huge chunks of the tower had fallen off and now surrounded the structure, which I was surprised was still standing with all the damage to it. Brin lowered her camel to the ground and then jumped off it and rushed inside a crumbling doorway, calling out for Nabi, the High Priestess we were supposed to meet.

My mates and I followed after her, and once we were inside the temple the destruction was worse. A large spiral staircase that must have led up the tower was now in ruins and impossible to climb. Everything inside had been smashed or turned to rubble, as though the place had been abandoned for years—except Brin had claimed to have visited only a year ago.

We found Brin kneeling in the corner of the rubble, holding her hands to her face as shudders wracked her body. I rested a hand on her shoulder, but then I caught sight of what she was crying over: a burnt, broken body that had a woman's shape, with four larger bodies beside her. My stomach twisted at the sight, and at the memories it brought back of my parents' deaths.

"Nabi," Brin cried. "Who did this to you?"

I had a feeling I knew.

A prickling on the back of my neck alerted me to something behind us. Two glowing yellow orbs moved through the dark corners of the rubble, and I grabbed Reven's arm to get his attention.

"We're not alone," he said, as he reached for his twin swords.

Darkness gathered and began to form a human-looking figure across the room, and I realized the glow came from its eyes. Thin shadowy arms that ended in sharp claws reached toward us as it began to glide across the floor.

"What is that thing?" I asked, backing away.

"It's a shade," Auric said. "Don't bother with your weapons. Like elementals, they can only be killed with fire, earth, air, or water."

A shade? I stared at the thing before us in disbelief. I'd heard stories about the ghosts trapped between this world and the next, but I never was sure they were real. Few people saw them in person and lived to tell the tale, especially since shades wanted nothing more than to consume your life force. And I had a feeling they'd want mine most of all.

Brin backed up behind us, holding her long, thin blade despite Auric's warning. "How can we stop it?"

"Stay back," Jasin told her. "We've got this covered."

He formed a ball of fire in his hand and Brin gasped, but I supposed there was no keeping the secret from her any longer. This was the only way to defeat the shade.

Jasin launched the fireball at the shade and burnt it up almost instantly, but many more glowing eyes began to emerge from the shadows and from higher in the tower. They moved through the rubble in front of them as though it was nothing but air, their dark forms tapering off near the floor. Shades could turn invisible and insubstantial, making them deadly to most people. But we weren't most people.

Reven summoned shards of ice at the nearest shades, Slade gathered stones from the rubble and coaxed them to attack, and Auric blasted the shades with a tornado-like gust of wind. Jasin kept throwing fireballs and I conjured my own as well, though I hesitated before releasing them. What if my fire got out of control again?

Despite the men's efforts the shades soon surrounded us, and I couldn't believe how many there were. Eerie yellow eyes glowed from every direction, all fixed on me. One lunged toward Brin and she swiped her sword at it, but it simply passed through the monster's shadowy form. I threw a ball of fire at the shade and it sizzled and disappeared into a cloud of smoke, but there were still more coming.

The men worked together to fight the shades back, and I conjured fire whenever one slipped through and got too close to me or Brin. It was a lot like fighting the water elementals, except the shades had a cold, cruel hunger unlike anything I'd ever seen before, which terrified me in a primal way. These were the things that came for you in your nightmares, except they were real.

Another shade got too close and nearly reached Brin, but I shoved her out of the way and took it out with a burst of fire. Something slashed into me from behind that was both freezing and burning at the same time. Pain consumed me and I stumbled forward as I let out a cry, but then turned to blast the shade behind me as it lunged for me again with its claws. My knees gave out, and Slade caught me in his arms.

"Kira's hurt!" he called out.

The men formed a tight circle around me while the burning freeze continued down my spine, along with something wet. I reached back and found blood coming from the gash running along my back, which must have been from the shade's claws. Oh Gods, a lot of blood. A wave of dizziness washed over me and I would have collapsed if it weren't for Slade holding me up.

"Hang on, Kira," Slade said in his low voice that rumbled through my body. I rested my head against his chest as he carried me out of the ruined tower and into the darkening night.

"I'm okay," I managed to get out.

"Put her down here and I'll clean the wound," Brin said, as she rushed around us.

Slade set me down on my stomach and I closed my eyes as my face pressed against the cooling sand. I soon felt something soft press against my back, while I heard movement nearby.

"They're gone," Jasin said. "We got them all."

The men kept talking, but their voices blended together and I began to drift away. My back throbbed relentlessly, and I could only hope that my gifts from the Spirit Goddess would be enough to heal me.

32
JASIN

When Kira woke, I breathed a huge sigh of relief. Even though I'd felt her through our bond and knew she would live, it was still a comfort to see it with my own eyes. Especially since I'd felt some of her pain when she'd been injured.

The gash on her back had completely closed, though the skin there was still red and swollen. Her other mates and I had taken turns resting our hands on it in case our energy would somehow help her, though we weren't sure if it did or not.

"Jasin," she said slowly as she tried to push herself up with a pained expression. "What happened?"

"One of the shades sliced through your back, but Slade managed to get you to safety while we defeated them. You're mostly healed now, but you shouldn't move too much yet."

She managed to sit up, though she leaned against me. The tent over us flapped against the wind, and Auric had warned us there would be a bad sandstorm tonight. The others were currently moving our things inside the temple ruins now that it was empty, where we would be safer.

"I could have died," Kira said, clearly shaken. "And you too."

"We all could have. But we didn't."

"No, you don't understand." Her fingers wrapped tight around my wrist. "Enva visited me again the other night."

"She did? Why didn't you tell us?"

"Because I knew it would only make you all worry, and we needed to focus on getting to the temple." She drew in a ragged breath. "But I should have told you what she said."

I drew her closer against me. "What is it?"

"Once we're bonded, our life forces are tied together."

"Yes, like when you gave me your energy on the boat."

"Exactly. It's how I can share your powers as well, but Enva told me it comes with great cost." She closed her eyes for a moment before continuing. "If I die, all of the men bound to me will die as well."

I nodded slowly. "That makes sense. It also explains why the Black Dragon is always surrounded by some of her mates. They know if they lose her, they'll lose their lives as well."

"Jasin, what if I had been killed today?" Her grip on my wrist tightened and she spoke frantically. "You would have died too. And if I bond with the others, they'll all be tied to my fate. I'm not sure I can do this anymore."

"Yes, you can. This is your destiny, and we all know there are risks." I touched her cheek softly. "Besides, even without the bond losing you would be the death of me. I wouldn't want to live in a world without you in it."

"Maybe so, but the other men don't feel that way."

"They do. Auric certainly does. Slade and Reven do too, they're just afraid to admit it. But trust me, they love you as much as I do. How could they not?"

She looked up at me. "What did you say?"

I stroked her face as I gazed into her hazel eyes. "I love you, Kira. I've loved you since that first tussle we had in the forest and every day since."

The hint of a smile lit up her face. "I love you too."

I pressed my lips to hers, relieved to finally tell her how I felt and to hear her say it in return. The bond flared between us, confirming everything we'd said with a calm warmth.

Auric slipped into the tent. "Good, you're awake. How are you feeling?"

"Better," Kira said.

He settled in beside her and wrapped an arm around her waist. "I just explained everything to Brin. She took it pretty well, all things considered."

Kira nodded. "Is everyone else all right?"

"Yes, we're okay," Auric said. "Shaken up, but mostly by seeing you get hurt."

"Hard to believe there were shades in the temple," I said. "I didn't think they were real."

"Me neither," Kira said.

Auric's brow furrowed. "I've read about them in books, but never imagined I'd see one in person. It has to be more than a coincidence they were waiting for us, especially after seeing what happened inside that temple."

"Do you think they're working for the Dragons?" Kira asked.

"Perhaps," Auric said with a sigh. "The Dragons must have destroyed the temple and killed the High Priestess and her mates, though I'm shocked they would go to such lengths to stop us. Especially since they're all supposed to serve the Gods."

"I'm not," Kira said. "The High Priestesses serve the Gods, who've chosen us as ascendants. That means the priests serve us now and not the current Dragons."

"Which means all the people at the other temples are in danger too," I said.

"More reason to finish up here and hurry to the Earth Temple," Kira said, as she struggled to stand.

Auric placed a hand on her shoulder to hold her down. "Not yet. You need to rest some more. In the morning we'll find a way to the top of the temple, but not now."

Kira looked like she might protest, but then she settled back down. "Fine, we'll wait until the morning."

I almost pointed out that no matter how fast we rushed, we'd be unable to make it to the other temples before the Dragons did anyway. They could fly, after all. The other High Priestesses would likely be dead within days, while we would still be out here in the desert. But I kept my mouth shut as I helped Kira up and into the temple, while the sandstorm began to pick up around us. Slade and Reven both watched with concerned eyes as I tucked Kira into the makeshift bed we'd made up, and then she was instantly asleep.

I turned to the other men and said, "There's something you should know."

33

KIRA

When I woke again, I was inside the temple and nestled against Jasin's naked chest with my other mates sleeping nearby. I managed to extricate myself without waking him, though he tried to pull me tighter against him.

I slipped outside to relieve myself, where I found Brin sitting on a piece of rubble while she watched the sunrise. She glanced up at me with a weary smile.

"You're up early," I said.

"I've always been an early riser. I also had a lot to think about." She glanced over at me. "How's your back?"

I stretched and twisted, but felt no pain. "Seems to be completely healed now."

"Incredible." She leaned back as she gazed across the desert. "I never would have believed any of it if I hadn't seen you all fighting the shades. Now I understand why Auric didn't tell me from the beginning."

"If you'd like to return to Stormhaven, we would all understand. As you can see, our journey is very dangerous."

She sat up straight and met my eyes with a defiant look. "Definitely not. I plan to help you take down the Dragons however I can. I'm not sure how exactly I can help, of course, but I'm pretty resourceful. I'll find a way."

I couldn't help but smile. "Good, because I'm tired of being the only woman here, and I could use a friend by my side."

She jumped to her feet and embraced me in her arms. "I'd be honored to serve the next Black Dragon."

We chatted for a few more minutes before I headed back inside the temple. As soon as I stepped inside the crumbling archway, big, burly arms gathered me up, and I found myself pressed against Slade's muscular chest. His mouth came down on mine, and he caught my surprise with his lips. As he swept his tongue inside my mouth and kissed me hard, I slid my arms around his neck to pull him closer. I'd worried he would never want to kiss me again, and that he cared for me as nothing more than a friend, but the way he kissed me now told me otherwise—even if he wouldn't admit it out loud.

When he pulled back, he took my face in his hands and gazed at me like I was truly treasured. "Don't scare me like that again."

"I'll try not to," I said, breathless from his kiss.

He drew me in for another passionate kiss, before releasing me. "Now go and do what you need to do."

He gave me a short nod before walking away. I pressed a hand against the nearby stone to steady me, still shocked that had happened at all.

A soft chuckle behind me made me turn. Reven leaned against the wall, and I wondered if he'd been watching all of that. His black hair was slightly mussed from sleep, but his blue eyes were sharp. "He pretends he doesn't care, but he would do anything to keep you safe."

I moved toward him until we were only a breath away. "I know another man like that."

His eyes narrowed. "Except the difference is, I *don't* care."

I rested my hands on his chest. After Slade's kiss I was feeling bold, and I was ready to start taking things into my own hands with Reven too. "Liar."

"I've never lied to you."

"You're not lying to me. You're lying to yourself." I moved my hands up to grip the collar of his shirt and pulled him closer. "But it's okay, because I know you care, even if you don't."

I dragged his mouth down to mine and slid my tongue across his sensual lips until he parted for me. I kissed him with all of the desire and longing I felt every time we were together, even when he tried to remain distant and cold.

For a second I worried the kiss would be one-sided, but then Reven let out a groan and took control of it. He spun me around and pushed me back against the wall, his hands pressing against the stone on either side of me as his mouth devoured mine. He put his whole body into his kiss, and all I could do was be swept away by it.

When we broke apart, he practically growled, "That didn't mean anything."

I patted his cheek with a smile. "Keep telling yourself that."

He slipped away, while I walked further inside the temple with a lightness I hadn't felt in ages. Maybe there was hope for me and my two brooding mates after all.

I found Jasin and Auric waiting for me at the bottom of the ruined steps, both of them looking so handsome it made my heart skip a beat. They'd once hated each other, but now they were united as my lovers… and as friends.

Auric offered me his hand. "Are you ready?"

"Yes, but how will we get to the top? The steps have been destroyed."

"I'll fly you up," Jasin said.

I arched an eyebrow. "Is that safe?"

"I practiced flying discreetly while we were at the palace. I'm pretty good at it now." He gave me a cocky grin. "Trust me."

"We don't have any other option," Auric said. "It would take too long for Slade to repair the steps."

I reluctantly agreed to the plan and we moved outside, where Brin waited with Slade and Reven. She gasped as Jasin's form began to change and he turned into a great, winged beast with crimson scales.

"It *is* true," she whispered.

Jasin lowered himself down to the ground and spread his wings so I could get on. I hesitated at first, since I'd never ridden a dragon before, but then I was able to scramble onto his back. Auric followed me a moment later, wrapping his arms around me from behind. I gripped one of Jasin's hard scales for support and swallowed hard.

"Ready," I said.

Jasin leaped into the air and my stomach bottomed out at the sudden ascent. A great flap of his leathery wings brought us higher, and I held on tighter while the ground below us got smaller. To his credit, Jasin managed to keep us fairly level as he flew higher, and he did circles around the tower as he gained altitude.

Behind me, Auric let out a great whoop and spread his arms wide. "This is amazing!"

I wasn't sure about that, but the view of the endless desert around us was pretty impressive. Jasin climbed higher and higher and the ground below us shrank to the point where I could barely see the people below, and I began to wonder how just high this tower reached.

We burst into the clouds, where everything around us was white, and discovered the top of the tower had an open-air platform that awaited us.

Jasin set down on the edge of it and lowered himself so that we could slide off his back.

Auric patted Jasin's side. "Nice flying. You truly have improved."

"Thanks," Jasin said, with a strange reptilian voice. "Remember what I taught you."

"Thank you, Jasin," I said, before pressing a kiss to the top of his snout.

"You're welcome," he said with a wink, before leaping off the side of the tower and vanishing into the clouds.

Auric took my hand and we slowly stepped across the cloudy, dream-like platform, until we came upon a bed that was ready for us. I'd encountered a similar thing in the Fire Temple, and knew the High Priestess here must have prepared it for us before the Dragons killed her. I said a small prayer of thanks to her, before turning to Auric. "It's time."

34

KIRA

I drew in a breath. "Before we do this, there's something I need to tell you. Enva came to me the other night and—"

Auric held up a hand to stop me. "It's okay, I already know. Jasin told us what she said while you were sleeping last night. I understand."

"Are you sure you wish to do this? You'll be bound to me forever. If I die…"

He took my hands in his and gazed into my eyes. "Kira, I've never been more sure about anything in my life. I love you."

His words swept away my worries and filled me with light. Even though I'd been upset with him and wasn't sure I'd be able to trust him again, I found that my heart had forgiven him and was ready to move forward. "I love you too, Auric."

"You do?" He let out a relieved laugh and then pressed a dozen small kisses to my lips while he talked. "I'm sorry for everything I did, and I promise you I have no more secrets. All I want is to be your Golden Dragon and to serve at your side."

I touched his face lovingly. "I want that too."

He swept me into his arms and claimed me with a passionate kiss. Together we moved toward the bed, slowly removing our clothing as we went, unable to get enough of each other. I'd been hesitant about bonding with Auric a few days ago, but now I wanted this more than anything.

"You're so beautiful," he said, as he lowered me onto the bed and began caressing my body. "And smart, and strong, and kind. You're every-thing I could have wanted in a woman."

My nipples hardened almost painfully at his touch. "Auric…"

"Shhh," he said, as he moved down my body, leaving a trail of kisses in his wake. His mouth touched me softly everywhere, all the places he'd learned made me gasp and sigh. In a few days he'd already become an expert at pleasing me.

But I'd waited too long for this moment already. Every time we'd shared a bed with Jasin I'd wanted Auric inside me too, and I was more than ready. I dragged him back up my body and found his lips, then wrapped my legs around him, showing him what I needed. He settled in between my thighs and I practically ached with want, desperate to feel him inside me. It was just the two of us this time, and everything was perfect.

As he slowly slid into me, his face looked almost pained. He filled me up inch by inch until he was seated fully within me, and then he pressed his forehead against mine and let out a ragged breath. "You feel incredible," he said, and then his mouth lifted into a smile. "Definitely worth the wait."

"I'm honored to be your first," I said. "But I'll go mad if you don't start moving."

He lightly stroked my cheek as he stared into my eyes. "Me too, but I want to savor this moment. We'll never have another first time together."

He lowered his mouth to mine and gave me a kiss that made my toes curl and my body tighten around him. With a soft groan, he began to slowly move in and out of me, and his long length seemed to completely fill me, touching me in places I never imagined. But then he rolled us over so that I was on top of him, making me gasp as the position pushed him even deeper.

"I want to see you ride me," he said.

I sat up and rested my hands on his chest, enjoying how full this position made me feel. His hands circled my waist as I began to move slowly, allowing my body to find a natural rhythm. He looked up at me with stormy eyes full of lust and love as his fingers tightened on my hips. All my hesitations and doubts vanished and were replaced by a deep sense of rightness, a feeling that Auric was mine just as much as I was his, from now until eternity.

Auric thrust up into me faster and harder, urging me on. I threw my head back and let passion take over as I rocked against him. His hands slid up my stomach to my breasts, which he cupped in his palms while slowly rubbing my nipples in time to my movements. Then he lifted himself up and took one breast in his mouth, making me moan as his tongue flicked across my hard bud. I slid my fingers into his thick golden hair as he sucked on the other breast next.

He fell back and I began to ride him faster, my movements becoming wild as I bucked on top of him, unable to control myself. The delicious friction was building between us, and I could tell by the way he groaned that he felt it too. He met my thrusts over and over, his fingers digging into my skin, and we moved together in exactly the right way to push me over the edge. My body clenched up around him as I gasped and cried out, pressing my hands against his chest while the orgasm rushed through me. Auric kept lifting his hips to mine and then he was gone too, calling out my name as he came apart beneath me.

A strong wind swept over us and whipped my hair across my face as we rode through our pleasure together. We began to lift up into the air and I let out a shriek as a tornado swirled around and below us, but Auric only laughed and pulled me down into his arms, kissing me with so much love that my fear drifted away while we flew higher into the sky.

Slowly the wind faded and we floated back down onto the bed. I ran a finger along Auric's neck and gazed into his eyes, while he smiled back at me and held me tight.

"We're bonded now," he said, his voice content.

"Yes, we are."

He drew in a deep, satisfied breath. "I've always felt out of place or unsure about my destiny. But not anymore. This…this feels right."

It felt right to me too. No matter what had happened in our pasts, we were moving forward together—with Auric as my Golden Dragon.

35
AURIC

After the most incredible experience of my life, Kira and I donned our clothes and made our way to the edge of the temple's roof while holding hands. Here a thin ledge jutted out into the sky, and if it weren't for my magic, I might have been terrified of falling to my death as we moved across it over the vast emptiness below.

Clouds swirled in front of us as we waited at the edge of the platform, and slowly they began to coalesce and form something solid. Within seconds the clouds became a vast body with a long neck and tail that filled up the entire sky. Great wings flared out above us, glowing golden under the filtered sunlight. Lightning flashed in the beast's eyes, while steam billowed from its fanged mouth. It was larger than the Dragons we'd seen before and more primal and cosmic, like something from a dream that you would barely remember when you woke in the morning. As if I blinked, the image might slip away from me completely.

This was the Air God's true form.

Kira and I fell to our knees while the Air God flapped his wings, sending clouds and wind swirling across the sky. Awe filled me, along with a strong sense of humbleness. I'd been chosen by the Air God and I hoped he would still see me as worthy of being his representative.

"Rise," he commanded, though his voice was like the wind whispering secrets in my ears. "You have served me well, while my other Dragon has turned against me. For that, I shall grant you three questions. Use them wisely."

Kira glanced at me with uncertainty, and I nodded at her. I knew what she wanted to ask, even if I had a dozen questions of my own.

"Can you tell me who my parents are?" she called out into the sky.

"You are descended from the Spirit Goddess herself," the Air God rasped. "She gave birth to the first Dragon using all of the Gods' seeds, and Black Dragon Nysa was born many generations later in that lineage. You are her daughter."

Kira's face paled. "I...I don't understand. She can't be my mother!"

"When the Spirit Goddess's descendant reaches fifty years of age she always bears a daughter, who will replace her when she turns twenty after the Gods choose four Dragons to be her mates. This is how it was done for centuries, but Black Dragon Nysa prevented this from happening, allowing her rule to continue. Until you were born."

Kira seemed at a loss for words, her mouth opening and closing, and I knew she must be in complete shock at learning our greatest enemy was her mother. But that was only half of what she'd wanted to know. I stepped forward and asked, "Do you know who her father is?"

"No, only that he is not my Dragon," the Air God said.

That ruled out Isen, but there were three other Dragons, and Kira could be descended from any one of them. Assuming her father was a Dragon at all, and not someone else. I'd always assumed the Dragons were infertile until I'd learned Calla was Sark's granddaughter. Perhaps they could only have children with normal humans?

Kira needed some time to recover, and though I had an entire journal full of questions for the Air God, we only had one question left—and there was one thing only he could answer. "Why did you choose me?" I asked.

"I chose you for your wisdom, independence, and discipline. I saw that you would be a good match for Kira and would strengthen those traits within her."

I bowed my head. "Thank you. I'll do my best to honor you."

"Your three questions have been answered," the God said, as he extended his wings. "Now prepare yourselves. Danger approaches, and I cannot get involved further."

With those words he dissipated into the air, becoming nothing more than a strong breeze and a wisp of cloud. I knew we should find a way down the temple to prepare for whatever this danger was, but Kira was so distraught I wasn't sure she could move yet.

"Are you all right?" I asked her.

She covered her face with her hands. "The Black Dragon...I can't believe it."

I gathered her into my arms and held her close as a memory resurfaced of the one time I had seen the Black Dragon. She'd been doing a rare tour of the four Realms and had shifted into her human form briefly to speak to my father. I'd only seen her from a distance, but her fiery red hair had been unmistakable. The same red hair that I ran my fingers through now as I comforted Kira.

Kira might not want to believe it, but I knew in my gut that it was true. The Black Dragon was her mother.

"What if Sark is my..." she started, her voice rough with emotion but unable to finish the question.

Before I could answer, a roar burst through the sky, and I spun away from Kira just in time to blast away a burst of fire that had been flying toward us. Red scales and sharp fangs emerged from the clouds above as Sark appeared over us.

"Get back," I told Kira, as I moved to protect her with my body and my magic.

But then something else moved out of the corner of my eye. I saw a flash of gold before something hit me hard in the chest and knocked me off the platform. As I fell to the ground everything went dark, and my last thought was that I'd failed Kira.

36
KIRA

"Auric!" I screamed, as he dropped out of sight and disappeared into the clouds. Though normally I knew Auric could use his magic to float, Isen had hit him with his tail so hard it seemed my mate had lost consciousness. I nearly dove off the tower and tried to save him, but the Golden Dragon hovered before me and snarled, with the Crimson Dragon at his side.

"You." Sark's eyes seemed to burn right into me. "I knew it was you all along. I recognized your stench." He closed in on me, his dragon form looming tall. "Grab her."

His gleaming red talons reached for me, but I blasted him with my new-found powers of air. He shook my magic off easily, though it distracted him enough that I managed to dart out of his reach and hide behind the bed. I shot a burst of fire at Isen next, but he flapped it off with his shining wings.

"There's no use running," Isen said, his voice slimy in his dragon form.

"Auric!" I yelled again, praying he was still alive. I couldn't feel him yet through my bond, but I reached out with my senses and found Jasin's presence. "Jasin!"

"Your mates can't help you now," Sark said. "It's time you came with us."

"Is it true?" I called out, choking back my fear and anger. "Is the Black Dragon my mother?"

"She is," Isen said. "And she'd very much like to meet you."

I shook my head, unable to accept it, or the thought that Sark might be my father. Was that why he had killed my parents and tried to hunt me down? Had those kind people stolen me away from the Dragons somehow?

The two Dragons surrounded me, using blasts of fire and air to keep me from being able to run, and even though I knew logically that I should be immune to both those elements I wasn't ready to test that theory yet. They got closer and closer, reaching for me with their deadly talons, and there was nowhere for me to go. They would capture me and take me back to the Black Dragon—my mother.

But then shards of ice flew at Sark's side and he reared back with a roar. Stones knocked into Isen at the same time, pushing him back. I spun around as another blood red Dragon burst through the clouds and soared toward us. This one had a familiar smirk on his fanged face, with Reven and Slade on his back. Jasin opened his mouth and let out a stream of fire, which blasted against Isen's chest, while my other two mates kept up their assault too.

And then another Dragon shot into the sky, faster than I'd ever seen one fly before. It burst up over us and gleamed bright gold under the sun, before swooping down and slamming into Sark, knocking him off the tower.

Auric had returned.

He flapped his shining wings and did a spin in the air, already flying as if he'd been born as a dragon and not a human, then dashed toward me. Sark had already recovered and began rushing toward me again. I swallowed my fear and ran at full speed for the edge of the tower and then leaped off it, using my new powers of air to help guide me onto Auric's back. I hit him with a hard thump and scrambled to grab onto his scales before I slid off his back, but then I was able to swing my leg around and sit like I'd done with Jasin.

"You're alive," I said, rubbing the scales on his neck. "Thank the Gods."

He let out a roar in response as he spun us around on shimmering wings. Now riding on my own Golden Dragon, I faced off against the two Dragons we were meant to usurp. Jasin hovered at my side with my other mates on his back, and together we launched a stream of magic toward Sark and Isen.

With the four of us working together it seemed as though our combined efforts might work to push the Dragons back, and we might even defeat one of them for good. But then lightning formed in the air around us, nearly striking down my two Dragons. Jasin dodged one lightning bolt but his wing was seared at the tip, and Slade had to grab Reven to keep him from tumbling off Jasin's back.

As the lightning kept reaching for us, Auric let out another roar and a tornado formed in the air around Sark, while Jasin opened his mouth and spewed fire at Isen. Reven and Slade assaulted the Dragons with ice and rock, and I added my own fire and air too. We faced the other Dragons without backing down, using our magic in concert to drive them away, until the lightning around us ceased. With shrill cries, Isen and Sark flapped their wings and retreated back into the clouds, disappearing as quickly as they'd appeared.

I sagged against Auric's back, exhausted even though we were victorious. He turned his head to meet my gaze, and I spotted his intelligence and kindness even in his new dragon form. He was Auric through and through, even as a dragon. Jasin swooped over to fly beside us, while Reven and Slade scanned the clouds for any sign of the other Dragons returning. Pride and love swelled inside me at the sight of my mates. Somehow we'd stood up to two of the mightiest Dragons in the world—and we'd won.

37
KIRA

W hen we were certain that the other Dragons were truly gone, Jasin and Auric circled the tower together as they flew down to the ground, where Brin waited for us with a nervous expression. As Auric's scaled feet hit the ground, she leaped on us to hug both of us at once, which was a bit awkward since he was still a dragon.

"Thank the Gods you're all right," she said. "What happened up there?"

"Sark and Isen wanted me to go with them, but we managed to fight them off," I said. I debated telling her what the Air God had told me about my parents, but now wasn't the time. Besides, I wasn't sure I could even speak the words out loud yet.

"Incredible." She patted Auric's scaled side. "You look great as a dragon, my friend."

"Thanks." Auric stretched his wings, admiring his new shining form.

"You should have seen him," I told Brin. "He flew like he'd been doing it his entire life."

"A benefit of being the Air God's chosen one," he said.

Jasin touched down, and Slade and Reven leaped off his back. My two Dragons shifted back into human form and then my four mates surrounded me and wrapped me in their arms, passing me from one to the other to hold me tight and cover my face with kisses. Love and relief filled my chest as I kissed and hugged them back. These were my Dragons, my warriors, and my mates. No matter what happened or what we uncovered, they would stand by my side.

"How did you know we were in trouble?" I asked Jasin.

"I felt your distress through the bond." He grinned at Reven and Slade. "The other two weren't excited about climbing onto my back, but they didn't need much convincing when I said you were in danger."

"Only because we knew you couldn't handle it on your own," Reven said, as he crossed his arms. He was back to his brooding self, though I knew he cared for me.

"We'll always protect you, Kira," Slade said, but then he made a face. "Even if it means flying again."

"Thank you," I said. "We couldn't have defeated the Dragons without all of us working together, but now we need to hurry to the Earth Temple. The Dragons know who we are, and they know we have two temples left to visit. They'll be trying to stop us any chance they can, and will no doubt be waiting for us to arrive."

"Good thing we can fly now," Auric said.

"Can you both fly all the way to the Earth Temple?" I asked, glancing between Auric and Jasin. "With all of us on your backs?"

"Do we have a choice?" Jasin asked. "We'll manage it somehow. Even with frequent stops to rest it will be faster than taking the camels back to Windholm and then getting horses."

Brin nodded. "I'll set the camels free. They'll be fine."

"Then let's gather our things and set off," I said, as I gazed across the desert in the direction of the Earth Realm. Another long journey was ahead of us, and at the end of it was my mother. I shuddered at the thought before I turned away.

Together we went through our supplies and bundled up everything we needed, then left the rest behind. Auric and Jasin became dragons again, while the four of us climbed onto their backs and loaded our things onto them. I wasn't sure how far they could fly with our weight on them, especially since they were both new to this, but we couldn't delay here either.

As we lifted into the air, I thought again of the Air God's words about how the Black Dragon was my mother. I hadn't wanted to believe it, but I felt the dark truth of it within me, no matter how much I hated the thought. I could only pray that I would never become like her...or like whoever my father was. And when the time came, I would defeat her and her Dragons, because though they may have birthed me, they were not my family. My first family was the one that Sark had destroyed, and my new family was the group that surrounded me now.

We began to fly north in the direction of the Earth Realm, where I hoped to see Tash again, meet Slade's family, and bond with him at the Earth Temple. Our path wouldn't be easy, and even though we'd been victorious today, I knew we'd gotten lucky. To defeat the five Dragons we needed more than luck, especially since they knew where we would be heading next. We were going to need more allies, and though the King of the Air Realm was a good start, he wouldn't be enough—not when the Dragons had the Onyx Army and could control shades as well. We needed the Resistance on our side, along with anyone else we could find. But to get help, I was going to have to reveal who I truly was to the world. There would be no more hiding, not anymore.

I'd thought I could live my life in the shadows, but it was time to step into the light.

SHAKE THE EARTH

HER ELEMENTAL DRAGONS BOOK THREE

1

KIRA

I'd traveled the four Realms on foot, on horse, and even on camel, but
nothing compared to riding a dragon. I gripped Jasin's blood red scales
to steady myself as he spread his wings and glided over the Air Realm,
lifting us higher and higher. Slade's arms tightened around me while the
wind whipped at my hair and exhilaration danced through my blood. I
grinned and glanced over at Auric, whose golden body glinted under the
sun as he flew alongside us. Reven sat on the other dragon's back, his pose
deceptively relaxed, though he was always ready to leap into action. A
sense of rightness filled me at being surrounded by my four mates as we
embarked on the next part of our journey.

"We're about to enter the Earth Realm," Slade's deep voice rumbled at
my ear. He was probably anxious to get back to the ground. Slade didn't
like heights or anything that prevented him from keeping two feet in
contact with the earth. He never complained, but I could tell he was
uncomfortable from the tension in his body every time Jasin ascended.

"We should find somewhere to stop for the night," I said.

Slade scanned the area around us. "If I remember correctly, there is a
small lake northwest of here."

"I'll find it," Jasin's dragon voice growled out.

Another benefit of traveling by dragon—it was fast. Over the last two
days I'd watched the desert fade away to grasslands and plains and now to
forests that grew denser with each passing minute. Below us I caught sight
of the border crossing between the Air and Earth Realms, where the
guards glanced up at the sight of us flying overhead, but didn't seem

concerned. Most of the world didn't know yet that new Dragons were rising to overthrow the old ones, but soon they would. The time for hiding was over.

Within a few days we'd reach the Earth Temple, where I would bond with Slade, allowing him to turn into my Jade Dragon while unlocking my own earth magic at the same time. I'd already bonded with Jasin and Auric at the Fire and Air Temples respectively, and later I would bond with Reven at the Water Temple too. While Jasin and Auric had been eager to become my mates, Slade and Reven had been hesitant until recently. In the last few weeks they'd committed themselves to our destiny and had finally begun opening up to me, but I wasn't sure they'd ever love me like Auric and Jasin did. Slade and Reven both had secrets from their pasts that held them back, and I was still trying to break through their barriers. If we had more time, I might be able to do it, but we didn't have that luxury anymore.

My mates had been chosen by the four elemental gods of Fire, Air, Earth, and Water to replace the current Dragons that ruled the world—and those Dragons were not happy about it. At the Air Temple we'd fought their Golden Dragon, Isen, and Crimson Dragon, Sark, and now they knew who we were. We had to hurry to the next two temples before the Dragons could stop us, and they wouldn't let us succeed without a fight. They would do anything to prevent me from becoming the next Black Dragon and overthrowing the current one—my mother.

I'd recently learned that the Black Dragons were descended from the Spirit Goddess and were meant to protect the world for a short time, before their own daughters would take their place. However, the current Black Dragon, Nysa, had found a way to remain in power and had ruled for a thousand years without having a daughter...until now. Until *me*.

I still couldn't believe she was my mother. I'd lived in fear of the Black Dragon and her four mates all my life, especially after Sark killed the people I'd thought were my parents. Their deaths had haunted me for years, and the sight of fire had sent terror through me ever since. Now I could summon fire myself, but I still worried about losing control of it and destroying innocent lives.

How could the woman who spread fear and death throughout the world be my mother? And if she was my mother, then who was my real father?

As we entered the Earth Realm the sun dipped lower into the clouds, casting the sky in purple and pink hues. My stomach rumbled, reminding me it had been many hours since we'd eaten. Jasin's clawed feet hit the ground smoothly, and his blood red tail swished back and forth as I slid off his back. I stretched my aching muscles, which had grown sore from sitting on his hard scales for hours. At least my magic would heal me quick enough—a useful gift from the Spirit Goddess.

Auric touched down seconds later, carrying both Reven and Brin, Auric's former fiancé and my newest friend. Despite the dangers we faced, she'd insisted on joining us on our quest, and I appreciated having another woman in our group. She was also an excellent fighter and had guided us through the desert of the Air Realm without any problems. I had no doubt she'd be a valuable member of the team, even if I did worry for her safety.

After we all dismounted and stretched, we began to unload the supplies and gear strapped to the two dragons' backs. Once we were done, Auric and Jasin shifted back to their human forms. They both staggered a little as their wings vanished and their scales were replaced by skin and hair. They were both doing really well considering they'd only just learned how to fly, but I felt their sudden exhaustion through the bond we shared. Jasin had a little more experience being a dragon, but he'd had to practice flying for hours to get it right. Auric, on the other hand, had taken to flight immediately, as if he'd been born in the sky. But I sensed they needed rest and food or they wouldn't be able to keep up this fast pace much longer.

We'd landed in a small clearing on the edge of a lake, which was otherwise surrounded by thick, dense trees. The six of us went to work setting up the camp, the routine familiar after many days on the road together, although it had become a lot faster once we didn't have to hide our magic from Brin anymore. She'd learned the truth about us at the Air Temple when we'd fought the shades that had waited for us there, and she'd taken the news pretty well, all things considered.

As Jasin moved to light a campfire for us, he stumbled over a small rock. I'd never seen him move with anything other than confident grace, a remnant of his many years as a soldier in the Onyx Army. His warm brown eyes lacked their usual hint of mischief, and his auburn hair was messier than normal. He was still ridiculously attractive, the kind of man who turned heads every time he walked into a room, but the hours of flying had clearly taken their toll.

I touched his arm lightly. "Let me do this. You're exhausted."

"I'm fine. I just need something to eat." He shot fire from his fingertips into the pile of wood, then gave me a weary grin. "See? Nothing I can't handle."

I shook my head at his display and went to check on Auric. He was using his magic to clear away debris from around the lake so we'd have a place to sleep that night, but his tall frame was slumped with fatigue. Like Jasin, his golden hair was tousled from the wind, and his gray eyes seemed more unfocused than normal. Where Jasin looked like the good kind of trouble, Auric had the face of an elegant, handsome prince—probably because he was one. His father was king of the Air Realm and Auric was fifth in line for the throne, although he'd given up that life entirely when he'd become my mate.

"Tired?" I asked.

"A little," Auric said, with a thoughtful expression. "Our endurance is greatly increased as dragons, but we definitely feel the effects of flying all day once we return to our human forms."

"Rest," I said, rubbing his back slowly. "You and Jasin have done all the hard work so far today. We'll finish setting up camp and prepare some supper for us."

Auric leaned close and brushed a kiss across my lips. "I'd appreciate that. Thank you."

"Hey, where's my kiss?" Jasin asked with a grin that was impossible to resist.

I leaned close to give him a quick kiss, while Slade pointedly looked away and Reven rolled his eyes. A stab of guilt tore at me for favoring Auric and Jasin over the others, even if it wasn't intentional. I was still figuring out how to handle all of my mates and keep them happy, though I wasn't sure I'd ever fully master that skill. With four men as my lovers there was bound to be some jealousy and awkwardness sometimes, no matter how hard I tried to prevent it. It didn't help that Slade and Reven kept pushing me away either. I had to find a way to get closer to them quickly—and I only had a few more days before we reached the temples.

2

KIRA

While Slade set up our tents, Reven moved to the edge of the lake and yanked fish out of the water with his magic. Brin and I unpacked some of the other food we still had, and I noticed we were running low on supplies. We'd have to stop at a village and restock in the next day or two. When Reven returned with some fish, I attempted to roast them over the fire, but Jasin huffed and insisted I was going to ruin supper and took over. It was hard to argue when his cooking was much better than mine, and everyone knew it.

We settled around the fire and began eating, all of us too hungry to do anything but shovel food in our mouths at first. I tried to savor this rare, calm moment among Brin and my mates, as I had a feeling they would become fewer and fewer as our journey continued.

"We should reach the Earth Temple in two more days," Auric said, when the eating slowed. The temple was inside a peak called Frostmount, high in the northern mountains, where it was so cold few dared to tread. Another reason we'd have to visit a village soon. We'd left Stormhaven, the capital of the Air Realm, with the gear to travel through the scorching hot desert, not the ice and snow.

"What's the chance that the other Dragons arrive there first?" Brin asked, as she set her bowl down in the grass. She was one of the most beautiful women I'd ever seen, with smooth golden skin, flowing black hair, and effortless grace. It would have been easy to hate her, especially since she'd once been Auric's fiancé, but she'd managed to win me over somehow.

"Pretty high," Reven said, from where he lazily leaned against a small tree. "They had a head start and can fly faster than Jasin and Auric can since they don't have any passengers."

Brin tilted her head to the side. "But they don't know which temple we're going to, do they?"

"No, they don't," Jasin said, as he wearily stretched his legs out in front of him. "My guess is that two Dragons will be waiting for us at each temple. They might have troops with them too. We'll have to be prepared for anything."

Slade scratched his beard with a frown. "We barely managed to escape two Dragons at the Air Temple. How will we make it into this temple if they're prepared to stop us?"

"Assuming the Earth Temple is still even there," Reven added, bringing back memories of the ruined Air Temple we'd visited.

"We need allies," I said. It was something I'd been thinking about over the last few days while we'd been traveling, and I'd come to believe it would be the only way for us to defeat the Dragons. They were more powerful and experienced than we were, plus they had the entire military at their disposal. We'd also learned recently that they could control shades, malevolent spirits trapped between life and death that wanted nothing more than to steal life from others. For all we knew, the Dragons controlled the elementals too, though we didn't know that for sure. The six of us didn't stand a chance against all of that.

"Allies?" Brin asked, her dark eyebrows shooting up.

I nodded. "Now that the Dragons know who we are and where we're going, there's no hiding from them anymore. They'll do everything in their power to stop us, and we can't defeat them alone. We need help."

"Who would help us?" Auric asked, as he ran a tired hand through his golden hair. "Even my father would be hesitant to stand openly against the Dragons, as much as he would like to aid us."

"The Resistance," Jasin said. "They're the only people who have dared to oppose the Dragons."

Reven crossed his arms. "Except they do it from the shadows. Would they be willing to actually help us?"

"It can't hurt to ask, but how do we find them?" I turned toward Slade. "You were once part of the Resistance, and you helped those prisoners in the Fire Realm find a Resistance base. Do you know of one here in the Earth Realm?"

He hesitated, but shook his head. "No, the one I knew of was only temporary, and that was many years ago. I doubt they would still be in the same place."

"That's too bad." I sighed. "Can you tell us anything that might help?"

"There's not much to tell. I made them weapons for some time, but I gave up that life. I thought I was done with fighting and revolution and impossible wars." He scowled. "It seems the Gods had other plans for me."

I rested my hand on his knee. "If we can find them, do you think they'll help us?"

Slade's eyes were so dark they were almost black, as if he was lost in memories he didn't want to revisit. "I doubt it. They don't trust easily and they don't like to take unnecessary risks or expose their people in any way."

"Maybe once we show them who we are, they'll change their minds," Jasin said.

"They will," I said.

They had to—they were our only hope.

Once we finished supper, Auric and Jasin retired to their tents while Reven took first watch. I went to the lake to clean our utensils and bowls and then left them out to dry on a piece of wood. By the time I got back the camp was quiet, filled with only the sounds of crickets and the wind in the trees, and everyone else had gone to bed too. Jasin and Auric weren't the only ones who were exhausted after our days of traveling.

I peeked inside their tent and found them both fast asleep only a few inches apart. The summer night was warm, and they both slept without their shirts, showing off their tanned, muscular chests. Desire rippled through me as I gazed at them, and I removed my traveling clothes and slipped into the gap between their bodies. Jasin's hand slid around me to cup my behind, while Auric's arm draped across my waist. I let out a soft, contented sigh as their warm skin pressed against mine, while my magic helped ease their fatigue to give them energy to fly again tomorrow.

When I awoke, it was still dark and the camp was quiet. I carefully extracted myself from my two mates, threw on a dress, and climbed out of the tent. I disappeared into the brush to relieve myself, and when I returned I saw Slade leaning against a tree, keeping watch over our camp. I'd originally planned to return to bed with Auric and Jasin, but after seeing Slade there I couldn't resist going to him. With the Earth Temple getting closer every day, I needed to spend as much time with him as I could.

I moved close and breathed in the fresh, clean scent of pine trees and moist soil. "It's good to be back in the Earth Realm, isn't it?"

"It is," Slade said, as he straightened up. He was the largest of my mates and his broad shoulders were as wide as the thick tree behind him. With his dark skin, trim beard, and strong frame he had a rugged attractiveness that always made me feel safe and protected. I longed to be wrapped up in those muscular arms again and to press my lips to his soft, full mouth. "It's only been a few months, but it seems like forever since I left my village."

"I know what you mean." The girl who had worked as a huntress in Stoneham seemed like a distant memory, even though I'd been her not long ago. I'd changed so much since leaving that small town, as had the rest of my mates. "I wish we had time to return to Stoneham and visit Tash. I wonder if she's gotten my letter by now?"

"Probably," Slade said.

Tash had been my best friend for the last three years while I lived in the Earth Realm, but I'd left her behind when I'd embarked on this journey with my mates. I'd promised to visit if I could, but with the Dragons on our tail it wasn't prudent or safe. I'd sent her a letter from Auric's palace and he'd promised to use his faster courier, but there was no way to tell if she'd received it by now.

I leaned against the tree beside Slade and gazed at his serious face. "I would like to visit your village and meet your family too. Maybe once this is all over…"

His shoulders tensed. "Maybe."

My heart sank at his reaction, and I began to turn away. "If you don't want me to meet them, I understand. I know you didn't want this life."

His large hands settled on my waist, pulling me back to him. "It's not that. I'd like you to meet them, but I worry they won't have an easy time accepting this situation."

"You mean with the other men?" Multiple partners were almost unheard of in the Earth Realm, even though the practice was common in the Air and Water Realms. Slade had already made it clear he wasn't interested in sharing me with the other men. Sometimes I thought he might be able to love me if it was just the two of us in a relationship, but that wasn't an option. I understood his hesitation and respected his feelings, especially since this was all unexpected and new for me too. I'd never imagined I'd end up with four men, nor that I'd be able to have strong feelings for each of them, but here we were.

I would do whatever I could to make this situation more bearable for Slade, and the fact that he was still here showed he was willing to try to make this work. He'd originally claimed he was only with me because of duty, but when he'd kissed me it had felt like a lot more. And oh, how I longed for another of those kisses now.

His hands lingered on my waist. "The people in my village are very religious, but also very traditional. I'm not sure how they'll react to our relationship. It's a great honor to be chosen by the Gods as one of your mates, but sharing a woman simply isn't done in the Earth Realm. I'm still trying to accept it myself."

I slid my fingers along his bearded jaw, unable to resist touching him when he was this close. "I know, and I appreciate it. I wish there was something I could do to make it easier on you."

He took my palm and kissed it softly, and his tenderness made my heart skip a beat. "It's not only because of the other guys. There's something I need to tell you about my past too."

"What is it?" I asked, leaning forward. I was greedy for any scrap of information about him. Anything to get closer to him.

He opened his mouth, but then froze as we both heard a rustle in the leaves near us. I reached for my bow instinctively, but I'd left it in Auric and Jasin's tent along with my sword. Slade unsheathed his axe and changed his stance, instantly ready to defend me from any threat. I moved into position beside Slade, summoning small balls of fire into my palms. I was unarmed, but I wasn't defenseless.

As we stood perfectly still, I caught the faint snap of a twig in the brush. We weren't alone.

3
KIRA

Men and women with scarves over their mouths and dark hoods over their faces slipped through the woods and surrounded us. I couldn't tell how many there were, but I estimated at least six from the quick glimpses between the leaves and the soft sounds of their movements through the brush. Bandits, most likely.

Slade let out a low warning growl, but the bandits didn't attack. That wasn't like them—from my time as a bandit, I knew they preferred to take people by surprise. What were they doing?

A hooded man emerged in front of me, and I prepared to strike him down with a lash of flame until I saw his sword was still sheathed. He reached up and slowly lowered his hood, and my eyes widened as I took in his familiar face.

"Cadock?" I asked, as the fire in my palms vanished.

"Kira," he said softly. "It really is you."

I nodded, speechless at the sight of someone from my past I thought I'd left behind forever. Cadock strode toward me with a smile, his blue eyes flashing under the moonlight. He was just as attractive as I remembered him, although his thick blond hair had grown longer since I'd seen him and now hung about his shoulders. His frame had filled out too, becoming a warrior's body instead of a lanky teenage boy's.

He threw his arms around me and drew me in for a hug. "Gods, it's good to see you. It's been far too long."

Cadock's embrace had once meant everything to me, along with his approval, but I was no longer that young girl on the run, looking for a new family, searching for someone to love me. I had my mates now and a new purpose.

I stepped back, but offered him a warm smile. "Four years."

"When one of my scouts said they'd spotted you by the lake, I didn't believe it, yet here you are." He brushed his thumb across my chin as he gazed into my eyes. "And somehow you've gotten even more beautiful."

Slade shoved Cadock's shoulder, pushing him back. "Get away from her."

"It's okay," I quickly told Slade. "He's a...friend."

Cadock arched an eyebrow. "We were definitely more than that once."

I gave him a sharp look. Did the man have a death wish? I needed to quickly change the subject before Slade ripped off his head. "What are you doing in the Earth Realm?"

Cadock gestured around us. "The Air Realm has stepped up its patrols. We moved here a year ago and now wait for travelers on this side of the border. This is a good spot since people always camp by the lake." He gave us a wry grin. "Easy pickings."

"And you planned to do the same to us," Reven's voice said from the shadows. I hadn't even realized he was there.

Cadock shrugged. "We do what we have to do to survive these hard times. Kira did the same once."

"What is he talking about?" Slade asked, his green eyes narrowing.

"Ah, did she not tell you about that?" Cadock chuckled softly. "Don't worry, she gave up this life to settle down in a quiet town somewhere. Or so she said."

"I did, but the quiet didn't last," I muttered.

His eyes danced with amusement. "Of course not. You're not meant for a quiet life."

Jasin and Auric suddenly emerged from the tent, gripping their weapons and wearing only their breeches. Jasin asked, "What's going on out here?" while Auric called out, "Is everything all right?"

"We're fine," I said, raising my hands in a calming gesture. "I know these people."

"They look like bandits," Auric said as he lowered his sword.

Cadock let out a hearty laugh. "That's because we *are* bandits."

"Kira, I think it's time you explained," Slade said.

I sighed. I'd hoped I could keep this dark part of my past a secret, but there was no hiding it now. I turned to face my men and met each of their eyes in turn while I spoke. "I was once part of Cadock's gang. I'll explain everything later, I promise. But right now I'd like to talk to Cadock alone. Please."

"Definitely not," Slade said, stepping closer until he was right against my back.

I pinched the bridge of my nose, then asked Cadock, "Would you give us a moment?"

He shrugged, with a hint of amusement on his lips. "Certainly. I'm curious to see how this plays out."

He and his bandits slipped back into the forest, and I gestured for my men to join me by the fire. Not a single one of them looked happy, though I wasn't sure if it was from the revelation that I used to be a bandit or because I wanted to speak to Cadock alone. They were overprotective at the best of times, even though I was supposed to be the most powerful of us all—or would be someday.

"Is it true?" Auric asked, once they were all crowding around me. "You were once a bandit?"

"Yes, I was." I drew in a deep breath to steady myself and continued. "I was fifteen when they saved my life from two men who tried to capture me, and I became one of them because I had nowhere else to go. That gang, the Thunder Chasers, was like my family for two years, and Cadock's father led us. Cadock became my closest friend, and he taught me how to use a bow and to live in the wild. But after his father was killed, things fell apart and the gang became desperate. I decided I wasn't comfortable with what they were doing, and I left." I paused, and then added, "I'm not proud of the things I did with them, but it's the only way I stayed alive when I was younger."

"Cadock implied the two of you were…together," Reven said, arching an eyebrow.

My cheeks heated. Of course they would focus on that part. "We were, yes, but we were both a lot younger then. Nothing happened except for a few kisses, and I no longer feel anything for him."

Jasin sheathed his sword but kept his hand on the hilt. "Good, but there's no way you're talking to him alone."

"Agreed," Slade said, crossing his arms. "I don't like this at all."

"Cadock would never hurt me, and even though he may look like an ordinary bandit, he's clever and has a lot of connections," I said. "If anyone can tell us where the Resistance is, it's him. But I doubt he will do that if I have all of you hovering around me and glaring at him. I simply need a few minutes alone, and we won't be far. Just trust me."

"I do trust you," Slade said. "I don't trust *him.*"

I sighed. "If he tries to harm me, you can toss a boulder on him."

"Believe me, I will."

Auric rubbed his chin as he considered. "If you think he might have some information that could help us, then you should speak with him. Just be careful."

"Thank you," I said, relieved that at least one of my mates was on my side.

"Fine, but one of us is coming with you," Jasin said. "You knew this Cadock guy years ago, but you don't know what he's like now."

Reven stepped forward. "I'll go. He'll never know I'm there."

"Fine." I wanted to argue, but knew it was useless. This was the best compromise I would get from my domineering mates.

I grabbed my sword and my bow, just in case, and then headed into the woods with Reven falling into step at my side. He moved with the easy, predatory grace that came from a life as an assassin, and I managed to get one last look at his dark, deadly beauty before he slipped into the shadows. With his raven black hair, ice blue eyes, and sculpted face, he was the most striking of my mates. Being near him always made my heart race, and while I should have been afraid of him, I'd always known he would never hurt me. Instead, a calm steadiness settled over me as I walked through the woods, knowing his keen eyes were watching over me.

I squared my shoulders and set off to meet the bandit I'd once loved.

4

KIRA

I found Cadock near the lake, waiting alone. His face split into an easy grin at the sight of me. "So glad you decided to join me for a chat. I thought your companions would never leave you alone."

I hoped I wasn't making a mistake by trusting Cadock. Though I didn't think he or his people would harm me, it had been a few years since I'd seen them and things had obviously changed quite a bit. My hand was ready near my sword, though I tried to look relaxed. "It wasn't easy to convince them you wouldn't escape with me in the night, but I managed."

Cadock laughed. "If you run off with me, it will be of your own free will, I promise."

I moved to the edge of the black water, which reflected the stars back up at the sky. "How have you been?"

"Busy," he said. "Things were hard after my father passed, and only got worse over the years as the Onyx Army increased its patrols and food became harder to come by in all the Realms. I realized to survive we had to change our ways and join together with other gangs to become more than simple bandits. I convinced others to merge with us and we formed a sort of tribe. We now have camps across the four Realms and more people joining us every month."

"Impressive," I said. Cadock had truly stepped up as a leader over the years. "Your father would be proud."

"I hope so. But what are you doing on the road? And who are your companions?" He stepped closer, lowering his voice. "Has one of them replaced me as your man?"

"It's…complicated." I avoided meeting his eyes and then added, "I'm actually in a relationship with all four of them."

Cadock let out a deep belly laugh. "All four? Gods, you really have changed. Who would have thought little prudish Kira would take four lovers?"

"Just because I wouldn't sleep with you didn't make me prudish." I'd cared a lot for Cadock and had been tempted many times by him. We'd gotten close, but I'd always held back. Maybe a part of me had always known, deep down, that he wasn't the one for me and that I should wait for the right man—or in my case, *men*—to come into my life. When I'd slept with Jasin and Auric I hadn't felt any of that hesitation, it had simply been right, as if we were destined to be together. I'd never had that with Cadock, no matter how fond I'd been of him, or how much I'd desired his body. He might have been my first love, but he'd never truly had my heart.

"I apologize," Cadock said, holding up his hands in surrender. "It's simply hard for me to believe."

I had to confess the rest if I wanted to ask for his help, but it never got easier to say the words out loud. Especially to someone like him. "There's a reason for it. I'm the next Black Dragon."

Cadock scratched his chin. "I'm afraid I don't follow."

"The Gods chose us to overthrow the current Dragons and take their place. That's why we're traveling across the Realms."

He crossed his arms and gave me a skeptical look. "If this is some sort of con, it's the strangest one I've heard."

"It's not a con," I said, trying not to let my exasperation show. This happened every time I told someone who I was. I knew the blame was with the current Black Dragon for hiding the truth and spreading misinformation, and I'd once been just as skeptical, but sometimes it felt tedious having to convince people again and again.

"Then it's a dangerous delusion." Cadock shook his head. "I don't know what you're thinking, but you're going to get yourself killed if you go around talking like that."

Enough of this. I conjured a large flame in my hand, and he let out a short gasp. "I know it's hard to believe, but I am the next Black Dragon, and the others are my mates."

Cadock took a step back at the sight of the fire. "I caught a glimpse of you holding fire earlier but I thought it was sleight of hand or a trick of the light. It can't be possible…"

"It's real." I let the flames burn brighter as they danced across my fingertips. "We're going to overthrow the Dragons or die trying, and we're on our way to the Earth Temple now. But we need allies."

His eyes widened. "Allies? To fight the Dragons? No one is that suicidal."

Frustration settled over me as I closed my hand around the flame and let it die out. "I suppose that means you won't be joining our cause."

He let out a sharp laugh. "We're bandits, not soldiers. We don't fight for causes. We fight for survival and for riches."

"But you just said you wanted to be more than bandits, and we could use strong fighters who know how to survive in the wild."

"Maybe what you're saying is true, but what's in it for us?"

"The chance to live free of tyranny and oppression. Is that not enough?"

Cadock shrugged. "So we exchange one ruler for another. What difference does that make? We live outside the law anyway."

"But what if you didn't have to?" I asked, taking a step toward him and softening my voice. "I know you, Cadock. You're a good man with honor. We could offer your people a life where they won't have to run or hide anymore."

He reached up to touch a piece of my red hair. "I'm sorry, Kira. I still care for you a lot, but I have to think about my people, and I can't lead them into an unbeatable war."

"I understand." I bowed my head. Getting Cadock's help had been unlikely all along, but I'd still hoped I could convince him, especially once I'd learned how he'd changed over the years. As disappointing as it was, I couldn't blame him for wanting to keep his people safe, even if the fate of the world was at stake. "Perhaps you could help me with some information instead."

"Now that I can probably do. What kind of information?"

"We're looking for the Resistance."

He smirked. "Of course. The only fools who might be willing to fight by your side. Lucky for you, I know where their main base is located. Bring me a map and I'll mark it for you."

"Thank you," I said. "I really appreciate it, and we can pay you for the information."

He waved his hand. "No need. Consider this a favor for an old…friend."

We walked back into camp, where the others waited with suspicious eyes and tense shoulders. Auric brought out our worn, crinkled map and Cadock marked a spot at the edge of the mountains in the north, not far from the Earth Temple, and told us to look for a boulder shaped like 'two perky tits'—his words, not mine. As I scanned the map I noticed my old village Stoneham was directly on the path to it. Perhaps we'd have time to stop there, at least for a short while. We did need supplies, after all.

When Cadock was finished, I walked him to the edge of our camp and prepared to say our goodbyes. His eyes lingered on me with something like longing or regret, and he reached out to touch me again before stopping himself. "Kira, if you ever feel like giving up this mad quest, you're always welcome by my side."

A month ago his offer might have tempted me, but now I could shake my head with certainty. "Thank you, but this is my path."

5
SLADE

While the others packed up their things I stood under the trees near the lake, needing some space. It was the morning after our encounter with the bandits, and we were about to head out. I checked the map again, noting the supposed location of the Resistance base, and frowned. I'd never heard of a base there, but it had been years since I'd been a part of that world. Still, I didn't like it. We were trusting a bandit who likely would have tried to slit our throats and steal our things if he hadn't recognized Kira. Who was to say he wasn't sending us to our deaths?

"Almost ready to go?" Kira asked, as she moved to my side. Being so near her instantly made my body awaken in a primal way, reminding me of all the ways that I was male and she was female. Her shining red hair was tied back today, and a memory of brushing those long strands came to me, along with a desire to see her hair down about her naked shoulders, preferably spread out on a pillow below me.

"Just about." I shook off the thought and folded up the map. Jasin and Auric had shifted into their dragon forms and were stretching their wings and preparing for a long flight, while Brin and Reven were loading our supplies onto their backs. I couldn't believe they were all going along with this madness too.

Kira gave me a smile that brought back indecent thoughts again. Gods, she was beautiful. "We're going to stop at my old village to get supplies and rest for the night. We should make it to the base tomorrow."

I scowled. "Assuming there really is a base there. For all we know your 'friend' is leading us into some kind of trap."

"Why would he lead us into a trap?"

"I don't know. But I don't have any reason to trust a bandit either." Maybe he'd do it to make it easier to kill us and rob our corpses. Or maybe he'd do it to steal Kira away from us. Or maybe he just wanted to mess with our heads. How should I know?

She rested her hand on my arm and some of my tension faded. "You trust me though."

"Of course I do. But were you ever going to tell us you were a bandit?"

Her face fell. "I was going to tell you eventually. It's not exactly something you bring up in everyday conversation, and I was worried what you all might think." She looked up at me with hazel eyes that were tinged with worry. "Do you judge me harshly for what I've done?"

I sighed and pulled her into my arms, holding her close to my chest. The revelation about her being a bandit had come as a shock, even though I understood why she'd done it. I just didn't like the thought that she was hiding things from us. "No, we've all done some things we regret. I simply would have liked to know about your past before it came back and surrounded us with weapons."

Her fingers gripped my shirt as she gazed up at me. "I understand, but I'm not the only one whose past is haunting us. You mentioned there was something you needed to tell me, and you haven't explained how you got involved with the Resistance, but I'm not going to push you. We all have things we'd rather not talk about."

She was right, it wasn't fair of me to judge her for keeping secrets when I'd kept a few of my own. Secrets that would soon be uncovered once we arrived at the Resistance base. Better to reveal them now, no matter how much I hated talking about this part of my past.

"I'm ready to tell you now." I took a deep breath, and then I released her and stepped back. "I mentioned before that when I was younger I was close to a girl in my village."

"Yes, I remember."

I swallowed hard. Once the past came out, it couldn't be ignored or forgotten or avoided any longer. I'd have to finally face it. "Her name was Faya and we grew up together. There weren't a lot of other people our age in the village and it seemed inevitable we'd be married. But that never happened."

"Thank the Gods," Kira said with a tight smile. "Otherwise you wouldn't be my mate."

"Indeed." I rubbed the back of my neck, trying to figure out the best way to tell this story. "Faya had a strong rebellious spirit and wanted change and progress. When she was a child her father was killed by the Crimson Dragon for speaking out against the tax hike, and that moment clouded everything she did, as I'm sure you can understand. She tried to fix all the problems in our village and as she grew older she wanted to fight against injustice. I was the one who balanced her out and steadied her, especially when her passion made her act without thinking. But eventually I wasn't enough."

"What happened?" Kira asked.

"Faya became involved with the Resistance, who had a small camp near our village, and it was like she'd finally found her true calling. She encouraged me to get involved too, but I was hesitant because of the danger involved. I agreed to make them weapons and armor, but no more, and only because I loved her and could tell this was important to her. We were engaged to be married by that time, and I suppose I thought she would settle down once we were wed." I shook my head, disgusted at my younger self. "I was a fool. She began to spend more and more time with the Resistance, and especially their leader, Parin. I grew jealous and worried about her safety, and we fought a lot. She planned to become more active in the fight against the Dragons, and I longed for a quiet life without trouble. I wanted to be a husband, a father, and a blacksmith. She wanted to be a revolutionary." I turned away from Kira, unable to look at the pity in her eyes as I got out this next part. "On the eve of our wedding, Faya confessed she'd been sleeping with Parin and had fallen in love with him. She wanted to join the Resistance permanently and she asked me to come too. She said she still loved me and wanted to be with both of us. Parin had already agreed to share her…but I couldn't do it."

"Oh, Slade, I'm so sorry." Kira slid her arms around me from behind, resting her head on my back.

"After that night, I cancelled our wedding and cut all ties with the Resistance. I never saw her again." I turned toward Kira and returned her embrace, cradling her in my arms. "But that was many years ago. I've moved on with my life, and I see now that it was all for the best. I wasn't blameless either—I never should have tried to tame her spirit or prevent her from doing what she felt was right. And if I had stayed with her, I wouldn't be with you now."

Her brow wrinkled. "Are you sure you're happy with that? We'll likely never have a quiet life. Being with me goes against everything you wanted before."

"What I want has changed over the last few weeks with you." I pressed a kiss to her forehead. "I simply wanted you to know about Faya before we arrived at the Resistance base, as there might be some…awkwardness if she and Parin are there."

"Thank you for telling me." She rested her head against my shoulder. "That must have been horrible for you. She cheated on you and betrayed your trust. No wonder you've been so resistant to this relationship."

I stroked her hair as I held her close. "This path the Gods have sent us on has been unexpected and difficult to accept sometimes, but I'm committed to you and to our duty. Never doubt that."

"I know." Her eyes fixed on the collar of my shirt, and her voice came out hesitant. "Although I hope you'll come to care for me as well."

"I already do." Now that I'd revealed my past, speaking the words came easier. I slid my hand along the soft skin of her face, before tangling my fingers in the hair at the base of her neck. "Kira, I've always cared for you."

Her eyes flickered back up to my face, searching for the truth in it. "Always? I find that hard to believe."

"Always." I drew her close and caught her mouth with mine, giving her a firm kiss. Her hands slid around my neck and her body pressed close, waking up parts of me that had been long neglected. I'd been celibate since Faya had left me eight years ago, but soon that would change. I couldn't deny I was looking forward to it, especially because it was Kira. She was the first woman I'd wanted after Faya broke my heart, and I wasn't going to let her go. Even if it meant sharing her with the other men. I'd find a way to accept it somehow...because I had to. Kira was my destiny, and that meant the other men were my destiny too.

And she was worth it.

327

6

KIRA

As we flew across the sky, I thought about what Slade had revealed this morning. I understood now why he had such a problem with the idea of sharing me with the other men. Not only had he grown up in the Earth Realm, but he'd been betrayed by the woman he'd loved. Faya had tried to cover up for her mistake by claiming she still loved Slade and wanted to be with both men, but if she'd known Slade for so many years then she must have known that would never work. Slade was the most loyal, dependable man I knew—and he expected the same from the ones he loved. When she'd cheated on him she'd broken his trust along with his heart, and there would be no return from that.

Our situation was completely different, and though he may understand that on an intellectual level, his heart was still wary. Underneath his tough exterior he worried he would be hurt again. I had to show him that would never happen with me. But even if I did somehow, could Slade ever really love someone again? Or had his past relationship with Faya robbed him of that forever?

We stopped for a quick lunch, where we ate most of our reserves of bread, cheese, dried fruit, and preserved meat. I sat apart from the men with Brin, who couldn't believe she'd slept through the entire bandit encounter and had me repeat the story for her three times, before asking a hundred questions about my past.

"They lived in the Air Realm back then," I said, before biting off a piece of beef jerky. "Cadock rescued me. That's how I met him."

"Rescued you from what?" she asked, as she brushed a bug off her trousers.

"I stopped in a small village looking for work. By then I'd been on the road for a year by myself and coin wasn't easy for me to come by. I didn't have a lot of useful skills, and I'd become pretty desperate for some food and shelter. Two men caught me and tried to kidnap me. I think they wanted to sell me." I shuddered at the memory. "Cadock killed the men and saved my life. His father's gang took me in and taught me much of what I know now. If it weren't for them, I'd probably be dead by now. Or worse."

"Lucky for us that he found you," Brin said. "But I'm surprised you left."

"It's hard to explain, but as I grew older I began to feel like my place was somewhere else. And though I cared about Cadock a lot, I knew it was time to move on." I shrugged. "Maybe the Gods were whispering in my ear that my destiny was with four other men."

Brin sighed. "I can't believe I slept through it all. I always miss the excitement."

I leaned back and gazed up at the cloudless blue sky. "Don't worry, I have a feeling there's a lot more ahead of us. Starting with this Resistance base."

"You think we'll find trouble there?"

"I hope not. I don't know much about them though, and Slade is worried."

"I know little about the Resistance beyond rumors and whispers. I can't imagine they'd be a problem though. After all, you want the same thing as them." She patted my hand. "You have nothing to worry about. And if it does turn out to be a trap, I've got your back."

"I hope you're right." I smiled at her. "I'm so grateful you came with us on this journey."

"I wouldn't miss it for anything. I only wish I could be of more help." She shrugged. "When surrounded by people who can use magic and turn into dragons, it's hard to be useful."

"You help me keep my sanity, give me a break from my overbearing men, and let me vent to you about whatever is bothering me. That's more important than anything else."

She let out a delightful little laugh. "Yes, that is what friends are for, and I can see how you might need an escape sometimes. Very well then, what's troubling you these days?"

I bit my lip, then made myself ask, "You've had multiple lovers at one time before, haven't you?"

"I have..." she said, her voice laced with interest.

"How do you make sure you're giving each one enough attention?"

"I had a very detailed calendar," she said with a wink. "But truly, it's all about balance and being in tune with their needs and feelings. I'm sure you'll figure it out in time."

I wasn't so sure about that. I glanced over at Slade, who was shaking his head at something Jasin was saying. "What do you do when one of them isn't happy with sharing you?"

A frown graced her red lips as she followed my gaze. "Sadly, I'm not sure there is anything to be done. It usually ends up with one of you ending the arrangement."

I sighed. "In our case that isn't an option."

"Then I suppose you both need to find a way to ensure you're all happy. Communication and honesty is the best bet. If you love each other, you'll make it work."

If only it were so easy. Slade said he cared about me, yes, but love was another thing entirely.

We rejoined the others and took off again on our dragon steeds, and soon the terrain became familiar. My excitement and anticipation grew with each farm and hill we went over, every one bringing us closer to Stoneham—and to Tash. Brin was a good friend, but I'd only recently met her and we came from completely opposite worlds. She'd grown up among the nobility and was practically a princess herself. Tash, on the other hand, had been like a sister to me for years. Her family had taken me in and given me a home and a job when I'd been desperate to settle down somewhere, and she'd mended my bruised soul with her kind smile and warm heart. She was the first person I'd told about being the Black Dragon, and I couldn't wait to catch up with her again soon. I wanted to know all about how she was doing after her father's death, and learn how the inn was faring now that she was running it.

As we approached Stoneham, I eagerly gazed across the forest where I used to hunt, until I saw something strange. Parts of the forest had turned black, the trees turned to cinder, the leaves now ash. It started with a few small patches, but then it spread as we grew closer to the village, until there was nothing left of the forest but death and decay.

My hands gripped Auric's scales harder and I yelled, "Hurry!"

Auric and Jasin pushed harder, their wings beating at the air, and the burnt remains of the forest gave way to a much worse scene. And no matter how fast we flew, it was already too late.

All that remained of Stoneham were ruins. Homes and shops had become crumbled, blackened husks, and there was not a single living person in sight. The ground had split open right through the middle of the village, tearing apart the lives of everyone in it, and fire had finished them off.

Emotion choked my throat as Auric landed and I jumped off his back. The heady smell of lingering smoke clogged my nose as I ran down the road, but it didn't stop me from yelling out, "Tash? Launa? Anyone?"

Brin called out my name, but I ignored it. The others hung back as they took in the destruction, but I had to get closer to be sure it was real. I stumbled through the ruins in a daze, calling out for the people I once knew. Charred wood scattered the ground, which had turned thick and black, similar to the area around the Fire Temple's volcano where lava had once flowed. A few scattered bones poked through the black debris, but that was all I could find of the town's inhabitants.

A picture began to form in my mind of what had happened. Sark hadn't been the only Dragon who'd done this—this time he'd had help. The Jade Dragon had torn apart the very ground under the town, causing many of the buildings to collapse before Sark had set fire to them. Lava had risen up out of the deep trench and spread to envelop much of the town, and Sark had made sure anything it didn't touch was turned to cinders. There was nothing left.

Had anyone made it out alive? Or had Sark chased them down and roasted them one by one? Was that what those patches of fire were in the forest? My stomach churned at the thought, and I swallowed down bile as I continued forward.

At the edge of the village I found the rubble that had once been the inn—my home for the last few years. Some other buildings had partially survived, though they'd never be able to be salvaged, but not this one. It had been so thoroughly destroyed it was impossible to tell it had once been a two-story inn teeming with life. Now all that remained was a black crater in the earth.

I moved forward anyway, my heart unwilling to accept what my eyes clearly saw or the acrid scent in my nose. My boot struck something hard in the ash, and I glanced down at it. Something white stood out from the debris. A bone.

I bent down and touched the pale white surface, and revulsion instantly spread through me. I felt the lack of life within the bone keenly, and it made me want to yank my hand away. Death was the opposite of my spirit magic, and being so close to it tore at my soul. And worst of all, I could sense who this bone had once belonged to.

"Tash!" I cried out, my throat burning. I sank to my knees, instantly coating them in thick black soot, as tears streamed down my face. She couldn't be gone. None of this was real. It was a bad dream, a nightmare my mind had conjured up using memories of my parents' deaths, when

Sark had burned our home alive with them trapped inside. Except every one of my senses told me this was real, from the air I choked on, to the ash on my skin, to the bitter taste in my mouth. The bone in front of me was undeniable proof. I just didn't want to believe it.

The people in Stoneham were innocent. Tash was the kindest girl I'd ever known. And now they were gone. Forever.

All because of me.

7

REVEN

I slid off of Jasin's scaled back while Kira dashed through the ruined town. Slade started after her, but I stopped him with an arm across his chest. "Give her a moment."

He scowled, but reluctantly nodded as Kira slipped away. I keenly remembered coming home to a scene like this, and the shock and horror that came with it. There was nothing we could do for her until she had a few minutes to process what she was seeing. She'd lived through this before too and she was strong. She simply needed time.

Jasin growled as he looked around. "How could they do this?"

"This is what they do," I said, willing my voice to be hard to keep it from wavering. "We've seen it before."

"Never on this scale," Auric said, turning to face me. "Doesn't it bother you?"

I crossed my arms and ignored his question. Of course it bothered me, more than they knew, but I couldn't show that side to them. If I let one crack break through my cool exterior, I'd fall apart completely. The memories would come rushing back and they would wear me down until I was nothing but a husk, like those buildings in front of us. I wasn't going to let that happen, not when Kira might need me.

"These poor people," Brin said, clutching her hands to her chest. "They never stood a chance."

"Someone might have escaped," Slade said.

Jasin nodded, standing taller now that he'd found a purpose. "We

333

should look for signs of survivors. Auric and I can scout the surrounding area from the sky, while the rest of you can search the town itself."

Fools. There were no survivors, that was obvious. They just needed something productive to focus on to make them feel less helpless at the sight of so much death and destruction. I knew what that was like, so I let them carry on without voicing what a waste of time it would be.

Auric and Jasin took off into the air while Brin and Slade carefully examined some of the rubble. Once they were gone I picked my way through the debris, following Kira's path to the end of the town. I spotted her kneeling in front of what was once the inn she'd worked at, and now was nothing more than ash and bone. I really should give her a few more minutes alone, but something tugged at me, urging me to join her. If anyone knew what she was going through, it was me.

Kira didn't stir when I approached, even when I rested a hand on her shoulder. She simply stared at the place that had once been her home, her arms hanging listless at her sides, her knees pressing into the blackened ground. Dirty tears stained her face, and I resisted the impulse to wipe them away.

"The others are searching for survivors," I said quietly.

She finally looked up at me with haunted eyes. "But not you."

"We both know the Dragons wouldn't leave anyone alive." Unlike the others, Kira and I had seen this before. We'd both lost our families to the Crimson Dragon's fire, and we knew how he worked. But her face crumpled in response to my words, and I wondered if she'd held onto some hope that her friend was still alive. I was a complete ass. "I'm sorry, Kira."

"This is my fault," she whispered. "This wasn't random. The people here weren't part of the Resistance. They're dead because of *me*."

"They're dead because the Dragons are cruel, heartless bastards who think nothing of destroying lives." Gods, how did I always end up as the one who comforted her? One of the other guys should be doing this. Even Slade would be better than me. I wracked my brain, trying to think of something I could say to make her feel better. "For all we know, the Dragons had problems with the town that had nothing to do with you."

She shook her head at my feeble attempt, and though we didn't share a bond yet, the guilt and heartbreak were clear on her face. "I led them here by sending Tash that letter. The Dragons must have intercepted it and guessed we'd stop here while we traveled through the Earth Realm. They did this to leave us a message that this is the price of opposing the Dragons. They won't simply destroy us—they'll destroy everyone we love."

I couldn't deny what she was saying since it was probably the truth, but if I let her sink into this kind of grief she might never come out of it. She blamed herself for what the Dragons had done, and that guilt would crush her spirit and make her want to give up entirely. I knew that all too well from experience.

Kira was the next Black Dragon and we needed her to be strong. She had to keep fighting. She had to rise above this and move forward. We needed her—and so did the world.

"And how are you going to respond?" I asked, making my tone hard.

Her head snapped up. "What?"

I narrowed my eyes at her. "You're the next Black Dragon, aren't you? Are you going to sit back and do nothing? Are you going to let them do this again to another town? Another family? Maybe Auric's, or Slade's?"

"No!" she cried, her hands clenching into fists.

"Then what are you going to do about it?"

She rose to her feet and wiped away the last of her tears. Resolve straightened her shoulders and made her stand taller. Determination tilted her chin up, and anger made her eyes turn to deadly slits. I watched the transformation take hold of her, turning her from victim to avenger in the space of seconds.

When she spoke, her voice was like ice and I heard the steel behind it. "I'm going to stop them."

"Yes, you are." I didn't doubt it for a second.

She stared into the ruins of her village one last time, before turning to me with an unforgiving look that made me wonder if I'd pushed her too far. "And then I'll make them pay for what they've done."

8

KIRA

W e buried what bones we could find, until all of us were covered in soot and the day grew late. I decorated Tash's grave with a few flowers Brin brought me and then stood over it for a long time, silently saying my goodbyes while the biting wind tore tears from my eyes. My mates stood behind me, giving me space, until it was time for us to go.

As we left Stoneham, the only thing that held me together was the thought of vengeance and retribution. The Dragons had taken so much from me over the course of my life, but no longer. I'd been on the run for so long, hiding from my destiny, but now I was ready to fight back. I was going to destroy them—or die trying.

We left the ruins of Stoneham behind and found another spot in the forest for us to camp for the night. A few of the others visited a nearby town for supplies and warmer clothes, but I didn't join them. I wouldn't put any more innocent people at risk with my presence.

As we set up camp, the others kept trying to comfort me or ask how I was doing, but I told them to leave me alone. Nothing they said or did could make this any easier or bring Tash back. The only thing that would ease the unrelenting ache in my chest was the death of all five Dragons before they could hurt anyone else.

I ate something—I had no idea what—and then visited the nearby river to clean myself off, although my movements were routine and my mind was barely there. The anger faded and I went completely numb for a while, until I remembered Tash again. The grief became so strong it made me double over. She was *gone*. I would never again see her smile, or hear her laugh, or eat her food. We'd never get to catch up on the last few months we'd been apart. The Dragons had taken her from me, and she was never coming back.

I'd lost so many people in my life that it should have gotten easier to lose another, but it never did. I doubted it ever would. I let the pain wrap around me and turn back into anger, filling me with red hot clarity. I had no one left except the people with me now, but none of my mates' families were safe while the Dragons were alive. We had no choice but to stop them.

Jasin stepped between the trees as he approached the river. "Kira?"

"Not now," I said. "I'd like to be alone."

"Are you sure?" he asked, his voice even closer.

"Just leave me be!" The words came out in a rush, and I immediately regretted my harsh tone. Jasin was only trying to help, but I couldn't deal with him right now, or anyone else for that matter. A tangled mix of emotions threatened to choke me—overwhelming grief, fiery anger, and crushing guilt for being the cause of all of this mess—and I rushed to my tent to get away.

But when I slipped inside, I found someone else waiting for me. An elderly woman with white hair, wrinkled skin, and eyes like steel. Enva. The strange woman who'd appeared to me ever since my twentieth birthday, when all of this had started. She always offered a few hints and tidbits of information, then vanished and left me with more questions than I'd had before.

"What are you doing here?" I asked. To say I wasn't in the mood to entertain her cryptic advice tonight was an understatement.

"I sensed that you had questions."

I cast her a sharp glare. "I always have questions, but I've had a rough day. This isn't a good time."

She studied me as I sat across from her. "Yes, I know. I'm sorry about your friend and your village. Being a Dragon can be a great burden sometimes."

"How would you know?" I snarled.

She gave me a sad smile. "I was one too, once. Many years ago."

My annoyance at her presence instantly vanished. "You were?"

"I suppose it's time you learned the truth." She folded her wrinkled hands in her lap. "Kira, I'm your grandmother."

I gaped at her. "My grandmother."

"Yes. Nysa, the Black Dragon, is my daughter."

"You mean..." I swallowed, trying to wrap my head around her words. "So it's true. The Black Dragon really is my mother?"

"She is."

337

I stared at the old woman before me, looking at her in a new light. My *grandmother*. A sense of rightness settled in my chest, and I knew it was true. "And you were the Black Dragon before her?"

"I was, although I was known as the White Dragon."

I blinked. "I didn't know we could be anything else."

She pursed her lips. "Yes, well, there's a lot you don't know. Much of that is Nysa's fault. She had all of our family's history destroyed, along with all information about previous Dragons. It's a miracle she let people remember the Gods, but even she can't wipe all traces of them from the world."

I had so many questions I didn't know where to start. I wanted to know about her time as the White Dragon, and how it had led to Nysa becoming the Black Dragon and ruling for so long. But instead I found myself asking, "How are you here? Aren't you over a thousand years old at this point?"

"I would be. Assuming I was still alive." She waved away my questioning look. "I died a long time ago, but I'm trapped between life and death. My connection to the Spirit Goddess and my magic lets me watch over you and sometimes manifest for a brief period, although it takes a lot out of me so I can't stay for long."

"Why are you trapped?"

She pursed her lips before responding. "That is a longer tale, which needs to wait for another visit. The short version is that the way to the afterlife has been closed for the last thousand years. Everyone who dies is trapped—not only me."

"Everyone?" Horror crept over me as I imagined how many people that would be after all this time. And now Tash was one of them, along with everyone else I'd known in the village. "So those souls that can't find peace…is there any way to save them?"

"There is. You must defeat Nysa."

Easier said than done. I'd been determined to stop the Dragons earlier, but now my task seemed even more challenging. "Does she control the shades?"

"Yes, she does."

As I suspected. I dragged a hand through my hair. "What about the elementals?"

"No. The elementals hate both the Dragons and the shades."

Finally, a small bit of good news. I rubbed my eyes, suddenly exhausted. "How am I supposed to defeat her and the other Dragons? They're so much more powerful than we are."

"I've noticed." She snorted. "You need to train more. Now that you have two bonded mates, practice combining their elements."

"Combining...how?"

She rolled her eyes up at the roof of the tent like I was a complete fool. "Fire and earth together make lava. Water and air make fog. It's all fairly obvious."

I nodded slowly. "And fire and air make lightning."

"Exactly. Your mates will be able to combine their magic through their connection with you. Then you'll all be able to summon the joint elements."

That explained how the Dragons had summoned lightning during our fight at the Air Temple, and how Stoneham had been covered in lava. If we could figure out how to combine our magic in such a way we might have a chance. Or at least more of a chance than we had now.

"I wish I could tell you more, but the other side pulls at me already." She pressed a wrinkled hand to my cheek and stared into my eyes. "Stay strong, Kira. The journey is long and fraught with danger, but you're on the right path. Keep going and you'll find your way."

I pressed my hand against hers, wishing she didn't have to leave. It wasn't fair that as soon as I'd found another member of my family, I was losing her again. "I will...grandmother."

She faded away before my eyes, until it was like she had never been in the tent at all. I rubbed my weary face and thought on her words. I'd tried to deny that the Black Dragon was my mother, hoping it hadn't been true, even when my gut had told me it was. There was no denying it any longer, but that didn't mean I had to become her either. Enva, the White Dragon, had proved that. She had been helping me all this time, so she must disapprove of her daughter's actions and wanted Nysa stopped too. That couldn't be easy for her, but perhaps she'd grown tired of watching the world tumble into chaos and had to do something to help stop it. I'd have to ask her at her next visit, whenever that would be. I shuddered at the thought of her trapped between life and death, along with all those other people. Nysa must be the cause of it somehow, if stopping her would put an end to it.

At least now I had an idea of what to focus on: figuring out how to combine the elements.

9

AURIC

Kira's eyes burned with determination as she stood before us. "We need to make lightning."

It was the morning after we'd discovered Stoneham had been destroyed, and she'd told all of us about her visit from Enva while we'd had some bread and cheese. Then she'd insisted Jasin and I train with her immediately while the others prepared for us to depart. The tone in her voice had left no room for argument, and now she stood before us with her hands clenched in fists, her shoulders stiff, and a fierce slant to her lips.

All night long I'd tossed and turned, worrying about how she was doing and wishing I could comfort her, but she'd made it clear she wanted to be alone. Any time one of us tried to talk to her—and we'd all tried—she'd sent us away. Now I wondered if I should have tried more. I wasn't sure I liked this new, rage-filled Kira that had emerged after she'd spoken with Reven. Gods only knew what he'd said to her to make her turn her grief into fury. I'd never seen her like this before and wasn't sure what to make of it...or how to undo it.

Jasin arched an eyebrow at her. "And how are we supposed to do that?"

My brow furrowed. "Yes, you said we needed to combine the elements, but it doesn't seem like Enva gave us any actual information on how to do that."

Kira crossed her arms. "It must not be that hard to figure out. We'll just have to try."

I sighed and looked over at Jasin, who shrugged. We stood near the river we'd camped beside, away from the others and within reach of water in case things went wrong during training. I summoned a ball of swirling air in my palm, while Jasin did the same with fire. We moved closer and raised our hands to combine the two elements together—but all it did was snuff them both out.

"Well, that didn't work," Jasin said. "Now what?"

"Maybe I need to do it," Kira said. She summoned both elements in her hands and tried to force them together, with the same result. We'd been practicing with air in the few moments we could find since we'd left the temple, and she'd picked up the basics of controlling it quickly. I sensed she found it easier—or less intimidating—than fire. Of course, it would take a lot more training before she was a master. After all, I was still learning new things every day, including lightning it seemed.

"Gods!" Kira yelled, as the elements disappeared from her hands. Her eyes filled with tears and she wiped them away with quick, angry strokes. She was trying to mask her grief by channeling it into fury and action, but it was still there under the surface. She would have to deal with it at some point, but not today I supposed.

"We'll get it eventually," I reassured her. "What else can we try?"

"I don't know." She turned away, her face twisted with frustration. I hated seeing her like this, but wasn't sure what to do.

"Remind us again what Enva told you," Jasin said, in a tone one usually reserved for trying to calm a wild animal. I could tell this was tearing him apart too.

Kira scowled. "She said you'll be able to combine your magic through your connection with me."

I nodded slowly as I considered her words. "Maybe she doesn't mean we should literally combine them, but somehow access the other's element through our bond."

"Is that possible?" Jasin asked.

I spread my hands. "Your guess is as good as mine."

"Can you feel each other through the bond like I feel the two of you?" Kira asked.

I shook my head. "Not that I've noticed, but my bond with you is still so new. I'm only beginning to feel your presence."

"It gets stronger when we're touching," Kira said. She reached for both our hands, linking the three of us together. From the corner of my eye I saw Slade, Reven, and Brin packing our things and giving us curious looks. They had to be worried about Kira too, but they knew better than to interrupt us during training.

My bond with Kira burst inside me at her touch, much stronger than it had ever been before. Waves of grief, anger, and guilt washed over me and it took me a moment to realize they were coming from her, along with a

341

sense of desperation and determination, plus a dash of frustration and impatience. I sucked in a sharp breath as I sorted through her emotions and found my way back to my own self again.

"I think I can feel Auric through the bond," Jasin said. "But it's very faint."

When I glanced over, his eyes were closed. I copied him and searched through that tangled web that was my sense of Kira and there, in the distance, was a small flickering flame that felt like Jasin.

"I sense you too, but only barely," I said.

"Try to access each other's magic," Kira said.

I reached through the bond for Jasin's flame, but it was faint and elusive. I felt a slight tug inside me and wondered if it was him doing the same. We faced the river and in front of us the air shimmered with a slight buzzing sound, like a spark being struck. Kira's face tightened and her hand gripped mine harder, but then the sound vanished. We'd lost it.

Sweat beaded on Jasin's forehead. "Almost got it, but the bond is still too weak."

"Maybe it will get stronger with time," I said. "The Dragons have been bonded for hundreds of years, after all."

"We don't have time!" Kira said, obviously exasperated. She dropped our hands and pinched the bridge of her nose. I longed to pull her into my arms and tell her everything would be all right, but I knew she would only push me away right now.

"We'll keep trying until we get it," Jasin said.

Slade trudged through the brush toward us and called out, "We're ready to leave when you are."

Kira sighed. "I suppose we should get going if we're going to reach the Resistance by nightfall."

I rested a hand on her back. "It was only our first attempt. We'll get there eventually."

We began to follow Slade back to the camp, when a loud splash caught our attention. We froze and turned toward the river, my magic rising as I prepared to defend against a potential threat, and I felt Jasin do the same. Reven and Brin rushed to our sides, both holding their swords and ready for battle. Kira stood in front of us, facing the river like a warrior queen as she slowly drew her sword.

If the Dragons had found us, we weren't going down without a fight.

10

KIRA

The river was wide and flowing fast, and farther down it something large flailed about in the water as if drowning. I couldn't make out what it was—an animal or a big man perhaps—but it seemed to be fighting against a rock, or perhaps holding onto it. No, I realized as it drew closer, the thing splashing about *was* the rock.

"It's an elemental!" Auric said with a gasp.

Jasin immediately summoned fire into his palms. The only way to stop elementals was with magic—we'd learned that when a group of water ones had attacked our boat while we were at sea. But this elemental didn't appear to be attacking us—it seemed to be in trouble.

"It's small for a rock elemental," Slade said.

As its stony head burst above the water and tried to drag in a breath, I realized why it was so small. I dashed toward the river, leaving the others no choice but to follow. "It's a child!"

"What are you doing?" Jasin asked, as he trampled through the brush behind me.

"We have to save it!" I called over my shoulder. The small elemental was clearly drowning, it's body too heavy and dense for it to stay afloat. It must have fallen in the river, and there didn't seem to be any other elementals around to rescue it. If we didn't help, it would die.

We reached the edge of the river where the elemental struggled against the current. My mates spread out around me, still wary, while I tried to figure out a rescue plan.

"This isn't safe," Slade muttered.

Auric nodded. "If there's one elemental here, there must be others nearby."

"For all we know this is a trap," Reven said, crossing his arms.

"I don't care. We have to help it." I knew I was taking a big risk, but I wasn't letting a child die on my watch, whether it was human, animal, or elemental. "Reven, use your magic to rescue it."

He scowled, but made a lazy gesture toward the river. The water changed from rushing past us to slowly creeping forward. While the current brought the elemental closer to us, Jasin and Auric watched the trees for an attack. I waded out into the river and tried to grab hold of the elemental's rocky body, but it let out a terrible sound, like steel scraping against stone.

"It's okay, we're trying to help," I told it. I had no idea if it could understand me, but hopefully the sound of my voice would show I wasn't a threat. The elemental's glowing eyes widened, but when I reached for it again it didn't fight back. But I couldn't move it on my own—the elemental was nearly as big as I was and a lot heavier than I expected, even though it was small for its kind. Slade jumped into the water next to me and grabbed the other side of the elemental, and together we heaved it out of the river and onto the grassy banks.

The elemental coughed and water ran out of its mouth, its eyes still huge and glowing bright gold. I tried to pat it on its back, but wasn't sure if it had lungs or not—it seemed to be made entirely of thick, gray stone. Now that it was out of the water I could see it had a large, rounded chest that made up most of its bulk, along with two thick arms and short, stumpy legs.

"You're all right now," I said to it, as I kept patting its hard back. The elemental was shaking, but it didn't try to escape, so it must have sensed we weren't going to harm it. The others kept their hands near their weapons, but they wouldn't attack unless they thought I was in danger.

Movement caught our attention, and four much larger rock elementals emerged from the trees down the river. They moved surprisingly fast considering their squat legs, and their glowing eyes fixed on us with obvious malice. Brin and my mates tensed beside me, sensing a looming fight, but Enva's words last night gave me the idea to approach this differently. If the elementals weren't working for the Black Dragon, that meant they didn't need to be our enemies...assuming I could reach them somehow.

"Don't attack," I said to my mates quietly. "I want to talk to them."

"Talk?" Jasin snorted. "Elementals don't talk. They attack."

"I want to try."

I helped the elemental child to its feet, making sure it could stand on its own. It suddenly spotted the other elementals and let out that strange sound again, then rushed toward them. The larger elementals quickly surrounded it, as if making sure it was all right. I walked toward them slowly, waving for my mates to stay back. This would have to be handled carefully, or it would all go wrong...and we would likely only have one chance.

One of the elementals broke apart and faced me. Its face was stony and incomprehensible, with a gaping mouth full of jagged rock and those eerie glowing eyes. We stared at each other without moving, and then it asked, "Why did you help him, Spirit Dragon?"

The voice that came from the elemental was like the deep rumble of an earthquake, and the words were spoken slowly, as if it wasn't used to our language—but it was speaking. My heart leaped at the knowledge we could communicate with them.

"I didn't want him to drown," I said. "We mean your kind no harm. We only want to talk."

"We are no friend to the Dragons," he grumbled.

"We're not like the other Dragons. We want to stop them and restore balance to the world. A world where both humans and elementals can live in peace together."

"Perhaps," the elemental said, obviously unconvinced.

The other elementals were now watching us, and the small one made a sound I didn't understand. One of the others replied, and they carried on for a few seconds in their gravelly language while I looked on. The leader rumbled something back at them, before turning to me again.

"We are in your debt, Spirit Dragon." The elemental did not sound pleased about that, but it was hard to tell with its strange voice. I was too surprised to respond immediately, and then it was too late, as they all stomped back into the forest.

"That was incredible," Auric said, moving to my side. "I had no idea the elementals could speak our language. I need to record this immediately."

Jasin put out the fire in his hands. "It was still risky helping them. They nearly attacked us even after we saved that little one."

"Yes, but it was worth it," I replied. "Now we know they can communicate with us, and if they hate the other Dragons as much as Enva said, we might be able to convince them to become our allies."

"That seems unlikely," Reven said.

Slade rubbed his beard. "It's worth trying."

"Kira will make it happen," Brin said. "Especially now that they owe her."

I stared after the elementals for another moment, then turned toward my team. "We'll worry about that another day. Right now we need to find the Resistance."

11
JASIN

Auric pointed one of his talons at a mountain in the distance and I nodded. We both tilted our wings slightly to adjust our course, and exhilaration took hold as the brisk wind rushed over my scales.

Being a dragon was incredible. I could fly for hours without growing tired, cross great distances faster than any horse, and was stronger than ever before. Even with Slade and Brin on my back, along with half of our supplies and equipment, I barely noticed the weight. And with fire burning in my lungs, along with my sharp talons and fangs, I could defend Kira better than I could before.

Auric and I flew closer to the snow-capped mountains, and the air around us grew colder. We knew from Cadock's mark on the map that the Resistance base was somewhere on the edge of these mountains in a cave, and he'd instructed us to look for a rock in the shape of two breasts, but so far we hadn't spotted them.

"There," Brin said, from my back. Her arm stretched over my right wing and I followed it's direction to the base of a mountain where two large, rounded boulders pointed at the sky. I didn't see an entrance, but assumed it would become more obvious once we got closer.

Auric and I swooped down into a nearby forest and found a good spot to land, since showing up as dragons probably wouldn't elicit a good reaction. Once on the ground, we hid anything we couldn't carry and then began the trek to the mountain. None of us felt like talking much with the memory of Kira's village still fresh in our minds, along with that dangerous encounter with the elementals. Kira thought she might be able

347

to convince them to help us, but I wasn't sure even she could reverse hundreds of years of conflict and turn it into an alliance.

When we reached the mountain range and stood beside the twin rocks, the way inside was no more clear. It wouldn't be a very good secret base if the entrance was obvious, but I'd hoped for something more than this. If that bandit had betrayed us or led us astray, I was going to track him down and make him pay.

"I didn't see an entrance while flying overhead," Auric said.

I glared up at the mountain. "Cadock probably lied to us. I bet he has no idea where the Resistance base is."

"He wouldn't do that," Kira said, as she pulled her cloak around her to fight off the chill. "It's here. We just need to look for it."

"I can find it." Slade took a few steps forward and pressed his palm against the slope of the mountain. He closed his eyes and his face became calm, while we stood back and waited. He'd done this before and he'd always been able to find a cave, a lake, or whatever we were looking for with his magic. A useful trick indeed.

When he opened his eyes, he removed his hand and turned to us. "Follow me."

We began to climb the steep side of the mountain, and I longed to have my wings so I could simply fly up it. It didn't help that my steps were dragging and hesitant either. I wasn't exactly thrilled to be going into the Resistance base, and had no desire to get there any faster, even if it was what Kira wanted.

When I'd been part of the Onyx Army I'd committed horrible acts against the Resistance in the name of duty. I'd helped slaughter entire villages thought to be harboring their members even though it had made me sick. Disobeying my orders had never been an option, no matter how much I'd secretly questioned my superiors. At the time, I'd tried to justify my actions because my brother had been killed by the Resistance, or by telling myself that the Dragons knew what had to be done to keep the world safe. Now I knew better. The guilt and regret tore at me with every step, and I'd do anything to go back and reverse the damage I'd caused and bring back the lives I'd cut short.

When we'd visited the Fire Realm we'd rescued a few prisoners from execution and escorted them to safety, but one of them had recognized me from my past crimes. She'd been terrified of me, and I couldn't blame her for her reaction, even if it had made me feel like the worst human being in all the four Realms.

Now I was about to face those people again, and would be forced to look into their eyes knowing I'd once been their enemy and their executioner. I liked to think that I'd changed and that I could atone for my sins

348

by stopping the other Dragons, but I wasn't sure I could ever make up for my mistakes. All I could do was stand by Kira's side and try to be a better man in the future.

Slade stopped about halfway up the mountainside and found a small crevice that was nearly impossible to see due to the shape of the rocks around it. "I think this is it."

He slipped through the crack, and the rest of us had to follow one by one. A very defensible entrance since you could easily pick off people as they entered. I rested my hand on my sword in case there was trouble.

Through the crevice, the stone opened up to a wider cave and we spread out inside it. A large metal door stood in front of us and Kira approached it, paused for a moment, and then banged on it sharply three times.

After a brief wait, two heavily armed guards stepped out of the door, before it slammed shut behind them again. They pointed swords at us as one said, "State your business here."

We all glanced at Kira, who stood at the front of our group. "We're here to speak with the leader of the Resistance," she said. "Parin."

"There's no Resistance here," the female guard said. "You should turn around and head back wherever you came from."

Kira stood tall and met the woman's gaze, her voice stern. "We know that isn't true, and we have information your people would definitely like to know about. We're here to help you fight the Dragons."

"And why should we believe you?" the male guard asked.

Kira's jaw clenched and she raised her hands, likely about to use her magic to prove who she was. But then the door opened behind the guards and a dark-skinned woman with hair cropped close to her head stepped out. She was lithe and beautiful, with a fierce intensity in her eyes that made me think she was not to be underestimated. A large sword hung from her hip, along with a dagger on the other.

"Slade?" she asked, her voice almost breathless as she stared at him. "Is that really you?"

Slade's jaw clenched and his brow furrowed. It was the most emotion I'd seen on his stony face in days. Maybe weeks. Whoever this woman was, he was not pleased to see her. "Hello, Faya."

"Gods, it is you." She pressed a hand to her chest, her brown eyes wide. "What are you doing here?"

"We need to speak with Parin," Kira said, her voice hard. She wasn't happy to see this woman either. Was this the girl Slade had loved and lost many years ago? That would explain a lot.

Faya blinked, and finally saw the rest of us standing there. "Of course.

Come inside. I'll take you to Parin." She flashed Slade another questioning look. "And then we can catch up."

The guards lowered their weapons and allowed us to pass. Faya led us through the metal door and we stepped into a massive, domed space that took my breath away. The cave stretched for such a great distance that I couldn't see the end of it, while the dark gray stone slanted into a perfectly smooth ceiling high above us. Wooden and stone buildings filled the giant cave, laid out in a way so there were small roads running between them. More armed guards awaited us inside, while people walked about and gave us curious looks before continuing on to their destinations. Many of them were armed, but some looked like civilians. I even saw a small child running after a woman. This wasn't just a base, this was an entire village. And none of them screamed or cried out at the sight of me—maybe my past would truly stay behind me this time.

12

KIRA

"Welcome to Slateden," Faya said. "Home of the Resistance."

"Impressive," I said. There was no hint from outside that any of this existed, but there must be hundreds of people living here.

"When did you do all this?" Slade asked.

"About five years ago. We realized we needed a more permanent base of operations, and one that was completely hidden from the world." She gave us all a sharp look. "It's a secret any one of us would die to protect."

I met her eyes with a hard look of my own. This was Slade's former fiancé, who had betrayed him with another man and abandoned him to join the Resistance. She'd hurt one of the men I cared about more than anything in the world, and even if we became allies I would never forgive her for that. And now she had the nerve to think we'd expose this place?

"We're honored to be welcomed inside," Auric said diplomatically.

"Your secret is safe with us," Jasin added.

Faya nodded and continued walking into the village, past small houses and shops. I fell into step behind her and sneaked a glance at Slade, whose face remained hard. It had to be uncomfortable for him to see Faya again, but he'd done a fine job of hiding it so far.

She led us to a wide, wooden building with a slanted roof and double doors. Guards were stationed outside of it, and they nodded at her as we stepped inside. The interior was sparse, as was the rest of Slateden from what I'd seen, favoring function over form. We walked up a narrow staircase, and then she knocked on a plain door.

"Come in," a voice called out from inside.

351

"Give me a moment," Faya told us, before slipping into the room and closing the door behind her. I exchanged awkward, anxious looks with my mates and Brin while we waited outside, but Faya emerged only a minute or two later and opened the door wide. "He'll see you now."

"I'll wait out here," Brin said, stepping back. It was part of our plan—she'd try to explore the base and learn what she could while the rest of us spoke with Parin.

We left her behind and stepped into the room, where a man sat behind a plain wooden desk with his hands folded upon it. His skin was dark like Slade's and Faya's, as was common in the Earth Realm, but his head was smooth and hairless, while his deep brown eyes took us in with a discerning look. He was probably in his mid-to-late thirties and attractive in a way that was both commanding and approachable. There was no doubt in my mind this was Parin, the Resistance leader.

"Slade, it's good to see you again," Parin said, although there was an edge to his voice that made me doubt his sincerity. Faya had moved to stand just behind his shoulder, and watched the exchange with interest.

"Parin," Slade replied, crossing his arms and setting his jaw.

"Who are your companions? I'm told they wish to speak with me?"

I stepped forward and introduced myself and the others before adding, "We've come to ask for your help."

Parin leaned back in his chair and his eyes took me in with curiosity. "And why should we help you?"

"We share a common goal—to overthrow the Dragons and free the people of their rule. We'd like to form an alliance with you."

He arched an eyebrow. "The five of you, and who else? Do you have an army? A spy network? What exactly can you offer?"

Anger threatened to rise up inside me, anger that had been all too close to the surface ever since I'd discovered Stoneham, but I clenched my fists and reminded myself that I had to be diplomatic if I wanted to win this man over. "No, we don't have any of those things. But we have something more powerful—the Gods' favor."

"The Gods?" Parin laughed. "The Gods sleep while the rest of the world spins into chaos."

"They sleep no longer," Slade said.

"How do you know that?" Faya asked.

"Because we've met them," Auric replied.

Both Faya and Parin appeared doubtful, and it was clear that words alone wouldn't convince them. "The Gods have chosen us as their new Dragons," I said, as I summoned balls of swirling fire and air into my palms. "I'm going to be the next Black Dragon, and these are my mates.

We're planning to defeat the current Dragons and bring balance to the world—but we could use your help."

I expected shock or disbelief, since those were the normal reactions when I told people who we were or showed them my magic, but Parin's expression didn't change. Faya didn't react either, for that matter. I let the magic in my palms sputter and die out.

"Yes, we've heard about you," Parin said.

"You knew about us already?" Reven asked.

Parin nodded. "I've heard reports of the Dragons searching for five people matching your description, along with rumors of people who rescued Resistance members using the elements and strange Dragons flying the skies. I had a feeling you'd come see me at some point."

"Then you'll help us?" I asked.

"That I haven't decided." He drummed his fingers on the table as he scrutinized us. "Yes, we both share a common goal—for now. But what happens if you do overthrow the Dragons and take their place? How do we know we aren't trading one dictatorship for another?"

"We have no interest in ruling," I said. "The Gods told us that the Dragons originally had another role—to keep the world in balance and to protect both humans and elementals. The individual Realms ruled themselves, and the Dragons traveled the world to assist where they could. Nysa and her Dragons took their role too far and somehow found a way to defy the Gods, attain immortality, and become rulers of this land. We plan to return the power to the leaders of the Realms and to the people, while we'll act only as peacekeepers and guardians. And when the time comes, we'll step down so other Dragons can take our place."

"A lofty plan, but forgive me if I find it hard to believe people could throw away all that power and control so easily. Especially the likes of you." His eyes swept over us, becoming hard. "Slade, who turned his back on the Resistance long ago. Jasin, a member of the Onyx Army who used to hunt down my own people. Auric, a prince whose father serves the Dragons. Reven, who was once the infamous assassin known as the Black Hood, if I'm not mistaken. And you, Kira. Once a bandit, and still little more than a child. And you truly think you can save us all?"

My back stiffened. Everything he'd said was true, and he'd mentioned things even I hadn't known, like Reven's assassin name...but he was wrong about us. "That's not who we are anymore. Where we began does not define what we will become. What matters now are the actions we take in the future."

"I've done terrible things in the past, as have many of us here," Jasin said, all the cockiness gone from his voice for once. "I can tell you that I've changed and that I wish to make things right now, but I understand if you don't believe me. I'm willing to take whatever justice you demand for my crimes, but please don't let my actions color your opinion of Kira, or stop you from helping her. My crimes are my own, as should be my punishment."

"None of us asked for this," Slade said, stepping forward until he stood at my side. "We all had lives we were forced to leave when the Gods chose us." He glanced at Faya. "But you know me. I wanted to spend the rest of my days as a simple blacksmith and had no plans to leave my village. But the Earth God sent me to find Kira, and we all became committed to her cause. None of us is doing this for the power or the glory."

"I believe you, Slade," Faya said, before turning to Parin. "And if Slade trusts these people, perhaps we should trust them as well."

"Perhaps." Parin studied me closer. "What exactly do you need help with?"

"We need to reach the Earth Temple and the Water Temple, but the Dragons know we'll be going to both," I said. "We assume they'll be waiting for us at each one, and we're not yet strong enough to defeat them. Any information or help you could provide would be greatly appreciated."

Parin and Faya exchanged a look that spoke volumes, though I wasn't sure what exactly passed between them. Eventually Parin stood and moved to the back wall, where he picked up a small green statue in the shape of a dragon. Made from jade, I assumed.

"My mother made this for me," Parin said, as he turned and offered it to me.

I took the tiny statue carefully and studied it. The craftsmanship was exquisite, from the talons and the fangs to the delicate scales. "She carved it?"

He smiled as I handed it back to him. "In a sense. She was the High Priestess of the Earth God."

"Did she make this cave too?" Auric asked.

"She did." He set the tiny dragon back down and faced us again. "Many years ago, when I was a young man of seventeen years, she met with the Fire God's High Priestess and was told that new Dragons would arise to defeat the current ones. My mother was skeptical, but she tasked me and my sister with the duty of preparing for an upcoming battle anyway. My sister trained to become the next High Priestess, while I joined the Resistance. Back then it was small and lacked firm leadership. I rose through the ranks and eventually was voted in as leader." He spread his hands. "And now here we are, at the moment I've spent my life preparing for, and I only wish my mother could have lived to see this moment herself."

"I'm sorry," I said, my stomach sinking. "Can I ask what happened to her?"

His hands slowly formed into fists. "The Dragons recently paid a visit to the Earth Temple and left no one alive."

I bowed my head and swallowed back my fury. "They did the same thing at the Air Temple. I'm so sorry. Is your sister…?"

He shook his head. "Thankfully my mother had already sent her away. She's in hiding now, but she's ready to take on the role of High Priestess when it's safe again."

"It won't be safe until the Dragons are gone," Jasin said. "They've become the enemies of the Gods and those who serve them."

"So it seems." Parin paused and then offered me his hand. "Yes, Kira, we will help you."

I clasped his hand briefly as relief flowed through me, taking away some of the tension in my limbs. "Thank you."

He gave a sharp nod. "I can get you inside the Temple without a problem—there are many secret tunnels, thanks to my mother, and even though it's been destroyed we should be able to gain access. But you're right that there are Dragons waiting for you. I received a report this morning that the Jade Dragon and the Crimson Dragon were both there and seemed to have no plans to leave. Even if we do get you inside, they'll never let you complete the bonding."

"We need a distraction," Reven said. "Can your people provide that?"

"They can, though it'll be dangerous. I hesitate to send my people into battle against an opponent they can't possibly win against."

"All we need is some time," I said. "And we can help. We have two Dragons of our own."

He nodded. "That does make the odds better. But we can discuss strategy in greater detail tomorrow. For now, you must be exhausted from your travels. My wife will show you to rooms where you can rest for the night, and I'll have some food sent up too."

"Thank you," I said, although I didn't miss the way he'd addressed Faya. Slade hadn't either, from the way his shoulders stiffened. This alliance could prove to be difficult for both of us, but it would be worth it if it meant defeating the Dragons. With the Resistance by our side, we might actually have a chance.

13

SLADE

An hour after we'd retreated to our guest rooms, a knock sounded on
my door. I'd been preparing for bed and wore only my trousers, but
I assumed it was Kira knocking and went to let her in. Instead I found
Faya at my door.

She wore a thin gray dress that hugged her curves, her sword was
gone, and her face was as lovely as I remembered, though her thick hair
had been cut short and she looked like a mature woman now, instead of
the fresh-faced girl I'd known. We'd both gained several years since we'd
last seen each other.

My jaw clenched and I checked the hallway behind her to make sure
we were alone. "You have some nerve coming here at this hour. And alone,
too."

"I simply came to talk, nothing more," Faya said.

"We have nothing to talk about."

"Maybe you don't, but I do." She stepped forward, her voice low but
genuine. "Slade, I'm sorry for what I did all those years ago. I know I hurt
you terribly, and that was never my intention. I made so many mistakes
back then."

I'd waited years to hear this apology, but now it was a little too late. I
crossed my arms and leaned against the doorway. "Yes, you did."

"I understand if you can never forgive me, but I wanted to apologize
anyway since we'll be working together. Parin said it was foolish, but I had
to try to make this situation less awkward. There are bigger things at stake
here than our feelings."

"That's the only reason I'm here," I said, my voice gruff. Everything about this encounter made me uncomfortable, but for Kira's sake I should try to get along with Faya and Parin. I forced myself to uncross my arms and loosen my shoulders. "When did you and Parin wed?"

"Six years ago."

"Are you happy?"

"I am. This is my place—at Parin's side." She gave me a slight smile. "And you? I can't imagine you were pleased about being chosen as one of Kira's mates."

"I wasn't at first, but I've come to accept my destiny."

Her smile widened as amusement danced in her eyes. "I always knew you were destined for greatness."

I snorted. "I never wanted greatness. I wanted a home, a family, and a warm meal on the table. Nothing more."

"So you say, but it was obvious to me that neither of us was meant for a quiet life in Clayridge. We weren't meant for each other either." She paused as she studied my face. "Are you fond of her, at least?

"I am."

"Good. I hope one day you get your home and family with her, even if you'll never have a simple life." She reached up and touched my cheek, her fingers soft. "I want you to be happy too, Slade. Even if it's not with me."

A sense of peace settled over me. I touched her hand gently as it pressed against my cheek. "Thank you. And I'm sorry for everything I did too. I wasn't the perfect fiancé either."

A soft noise in the hallway caught my attention. I pulled away from Faya and peered around her to see if someone was there, but didn't spot anyone lurking about. I shook my head and stepped back, meeting Faya's eyes. "I appreciate your apology. Working together won't be a problem."

She inclined her head. "I'm glad to hear it. Have a good night, Slade."

"And you, Faya."

I shut the door and retreated back inside my room. It was small, little more than a bed with a table beside it, and the walls were rough, unfinished wood. The entire building housed traveling Resistance members when they stopped into Slateden, so it made sense there was nothing fancy about it, although the state of the wood did irritate me. Based on the construction of the building and most of the rest of the town, I guessed it had all been erected quickly and with the least amount of work or supplies.

Back when I'd helped the Resistance they'd had small camps that moved constantly to avoid detection, with other members hiding in different towns. I'd housed a few of them myself many times due to Faya's involvement with them.

Looking back, I should have seen that Faya would leave me for this life, and knew I should have cut her loose long ago. She'd never wanted to stay in Clayridge and be the wife of a blacksmith—she'd always had a need to fight. She'd broken my heart, betrayed my trust, and made me question whether I could love again—but seeing her today only made me realize it had all been for the best. She'd been my first love and an important part of my past, but she wasn't my future. Kira was—and I knew what I felt for her surpassed anything I'd once felt for Faya.

14

KIRA

S he's touching his face.

Pain lanced through me at the sight, especially when he didn't pull away. They spoke in low voices in his doorway and then he laid his hand over hers on his cheek. He wore no shirt, she wore a dress that left little to the imagination, and it was far too late for a social call. He should have sent her away, but instead he looked at her tenderly—and my heart broke.

I quickly rushed away, unable to stand the sight of them together for another second. Faya must have gone to Slade's room to rekindle their old romance and he hadn't sent her away. If I stayed longer would I watch him invite her inside? I couldn't bear the thought.

I'd visited the washroom and had decided to check on Slade to see how he was doing after seeing Faya again, but then I'd caught the two of them together. The anguish was so strong it was hard to see straight, and I reached for anger to steady me, like I'd done after Tash's death. How could Slade do this to me? Did he feel nothing for me at all? I was his mate. He was mine. *Mine.*

I found myself stumbling through the hallway away from the scene, but I didn't stop at my room. Instead I sharply banged on the one next to it.

Jasin opened the door with a grin. Like Slade, he wore only his trousers, and the sight of his naked chest ignited a fire inside me. His grin faded when he saw my face. "Kira, are you all right?"

"I want...I need..." I shook my head, unable to find the words to describe the turmoil inside me. I wanted to tear something apart with my bare hands. I wanted to lose myself for the rest of the night. I wanted someone to desire me as much as I desired them.

Somehow Jasin knew exactly what I needed, because he dragged me against him and slanted his mouth across mine. He kicked the door shut and I heard it bang behind us as I met his kiss with equal force, sliding my tongue against his. His hands were rough and demanding as they moved down my body, following my curves. I clutched his bare shoulders and pressed against him, craving his passion, his strength, his fire.

Warmth poured through me at his touch and I forgot everything but the heat of his lips and the feel of him against me. I ran my hands down his sculpted chest as my entire body sang with need for him. Through our bond I felt his lust rising too, along with his desire to claim me, please me, love me.

He pushed me back against the hard wall and his dark eyes met mine. I stared back at him, licking my lips, and he let out a low groan before taking my mouth again in a searing kiss. His hands moved down to yank my dress up to my thighs, baring me to him. I reached for the fall of his trousers at the same time and yanked them open. I was desperate to feel every hard inch of him inside me. There was no holding back, not tonight.

His fingers slipped between my legs, where he found my pulsing hot core already wet for him. My nipples tightened as he dipped between my folds, and I took hold of his cock in response. It strained toward me, hard, hot, and throbbing. His fingers plunged deep inside me, but I needed more. I needed all of him.

"Jasin," I gasped, as I lifted a leg to wrap around his hips, trying to bring him closer.

In response, he lifted me up and pinned me against the wall, aligning our bodies together. My back arched as he filled me completely, all the way to the hilt. We both groaned and clung to one another as we were joined, and I realized it was just the two of us for the first time since the Fire Temple. No Auric tonight, just me and my Crimson Dragon becoming one.

He planted a hand on the wall by my head while the other curved around my bottom, holding me in place as he began to thrust into me. My legs tightened around him and I moaned as his mouth moved to my neck. He took me with pure, unleashed need, and I couldn't get enough.

"Mine," I whispered, as I dug my nails into his behind, pulling him deeper into me. Jasin had been my first mate and he'd never wavered in his devotion to me. He'd loved me from the beginning...and he knew exactly how to drive me wild.

"Always." He slammed into me, claiming me as his mate too.

We fell into a passionate rhythm of push and pull, give and take, in and out. Soon there was no more talking, only heavy breathing as the friction between us built. My body seemed to wind tighter and tighter with each slide of his cock, and when he lifted me up higher to get a deeper angle, I fell apart. I clenched around him as pleasure pulsed through me, and I felt his own release only moments later, not just in my body but through our bond. He called out my name and buried himself in me one last time as his hot seed filled me.

Jasin brought his lips to mine again for a slow, loving kiss while we clung to each other and the last flames of passion faded. My heart pounded and I couldn't quite catch my breath, but the earlier tension was gone thanks to Jasin. He carried me to his bed and set me down in it, then wrapped his body around mine. He was so warm it was almost too much, but I couldn't bear the thought of moving away.

"I love you," he said, brushing his lips against my shoulder.

I relaxed against him even more. "I love you too."

"When you arrived you seemed upset. Do you want to talk?"

"No." I'd have to deal with Slade eventually, but not tonight. All I wanted now was to sleep next to my mate.

Jasin nodded and let it go, and that was why I'd come to him and no other. I'd wanted his fiery passion and the release he could bring, not Auric with his probing questions and kind eyes, or Reven with his cold voice and icy distance. Jasin had given me exactly what I'd needed, and now his love wrapped around me like a comforting blanket. The bond between us flared brighter than ever before, causing my emotions and his to become one big jumble of satisfaction and love.

It gave me an idea.

I turned in his arms to face him. "I think I know how to increase the bond between you and Auric. We need to invite him to bed again."

Jasin flashed a naughty grin as he brushed a piece of hair off my cheek. "Whatever my lady desires."

15
KIRA

Over the next day, my mates and I met with Parin, Faya, and other members of the Resistance to discuss strategy and make plans. Though I was ostensibly in charge among our group of Dragons, I felt comfortable leaving most of the decisions in this matter to my mates. Jasin had served in the Onyx Army for many years, Reven was an expert at stealth and infiltration, Auric was a fountain of knowledge, and Slade knew both the layout of the Earth Realm and the Resistance's inner workings. It'd be stupid now to ignore their expertise, and I was quite content to sit back and let them work, although I chimed in whenever I had an idea.

By the end of the day, we'd worked out a plan. In a week's time many members of the Resistance, along with Jasin and Auric, would ambush a large Onyx Army fort known as Salt Creek Tower. We believed a direct attack against such an important location would force any Dragons at the Earth Temple to come out to defend it, especially once they realized two of my mates were there too. The fort was close enough to the Earth Temple that the Dragons could fly there quickly, but not too close that it would be an obvious distraction. Once they were gone, Slade, Reven, and I would sneak through a back tunnel into the Earth Temple so we could complete the bonding. If Slade still wanted that.

I'd avoided him all day, and every time Faya spoke my stomach clenched tight. My mind kept drifting back to that image of the two of them standing together, before wondering what had occurred afterward. I tortured myself with thoughts of the two of them in bed together, and they only made my anger and misery grow.

But I couldn't avoid Slade forever.

It was late by the time we went back to our rooms, but I never made it to mine. Slade stopped me with a large hand on my shoulder. He turned me back to face him and my chest hardened.

"Is something wrong?" he asked. "You've been unable to meet my eyes all day."

My fists clenched at my side. "I saw you last night...with her."

Understanding dawned across his face. "She came to apologize. Nothing more."

"It looked like a lot more than that," I said, remembering the way he'd covered her hand with his own.

He shook his head. "We talked, that was all. We both needed some closure so we could work together without any problems. But I swear, nothing happened."

My jaw clenched and I looked away. "How am I supposed to believe you?"

He took my chin and dragged my eyes back to his. Sometimes I forgot how unusually green they were, as if he'd been chosen by the Earth God from the moment he'd been conceived. "I haven't kissed a woman other than you in eight years. And that's the way I plan to keep it."

His lush mouth found mine and he gave me a kiss that left me with few doubts of his sincerity. Even when we'd first met I'd found myself staring at his full lips and wondered what it'd feel like with them against my own, and the reality was even better than I could have imagined. He coaxed my mouth open and worked magic with every stroke of his tongue, making me melt against him.

"I don't want Faya," he said against my lips. "Only you."

"Slade..." I pressed my forehead against his. I'd waited so long to hear those words from him and I wasn't prepared for the rush of emotions that swept through me when it finally happened.

He took my arm in his and moved us into my guest room, then softly shut the door. Once we were alone, he lovingly caressed my cheek as he gazed into my eyes. "Speaking with Faya only made me realize the depth of my feelings for you. I tried to deny them for so long, but I won't do it any longer. I can't."

"Finally," I said, as I pressed another kiss to his lips.

"Yes. I'm sorry it took me so long." He drew me into his arms and against his broad, muscular chest. I let my arms slide around his neck, clinging to him as the sensual kiss swept us both away. His long, hard length pressed against my stomach, and I groaned when I realized his desire mirrored my own.

His kisses made my knees weak, and I pulled us both down to sit on the bed. I needed to touch him, to taste him, to confirm he was mine. I gripped his shirt and dragged it up his chest, and our lips broke apart for only a few seconds as he helped me lift it off him. My hands splayed across his hard stomach, feeling the smooth ridges of his muscles and all the coiled power underneath. His skin was so dark against mine, and I loved the contrast between us. Hard and soft, dark and light, male and female—a perfect balance for each other.

He left a slow, delicious trail of kisses down my neck that had me aching for more. And when he pushed my dress off one shoulder and pressed his lips to my uncovered skin, I couldn't help but moan.

"I want you," I said, sliding my hands down to the hard bulge I'd felt earlier.

He caught my hand in his much larger one, stopping me from opening his trousers. "Not yet. Not until the Earth Temple."

An overwhelming need to be joined with Slade made it hard for me to think, to breathe, to live. "Please, I can't wait. Let me touch you at least."

He dragged my dress lower, until it freed one of my pale breasts. "When I finally take you, I want it to be in the Earth Temple before the Gods. I want everyone to know that I'm your mate for all eternity." His mouth continued lower, along the curve of my bosom. "But somehow I can't seem to stop myself."

"There are other things we can do," I said, as my hand moved to the back of his head, holding him against my chest.

He let out a low chuckle that vibrated against my skin. "Yes, there are."

He took the hard bud of my nipple between his lips then, making me gasp. His tongue slid along my sensitive skin, awakening every nerve in my body and sending a rush of heat between my thighs.

Just when it became almost too much, he tugged the other side of my dress down and began to lavish attention on that breast too. I threw my head back and succumbed to the pleasure of his mouth all over me, and the relief that came with knowing he wanted me as much as I wanted him. For so long I'd thought he wasn't interested in me romantically or sexually, that he was only with me out of duty and loyalty, but with every stroke of his tongue and sensual touch of his hands he showed me how wrong I'd been.

I dragged him back up to my lips, needing to kiss him again, and we fell back into the bed together. While our mouths collided, our hands slowly explored each other's bodies over our clothes. We touched each other like we had all the time in the world, so different from my encounter with Jasin last night, but just as satisfying.

While we kissed, my legs tangled with Slade's and my skirts inched their way up around my thighs. I felt one of his large hands settle on my bare skin just above my knees almost possessively, and I held my breath as he began to inch his way upward.

When his fingers drew close to my core, I draped my thigh over his hip, spreading wide for him. I stroked his bearded jaw and stared into his rich, emerald eyes. "Touch me," I whispered.

His thumb brushed that spot between my thighs, and I gasped. Yes, *that* was where I needed him. Ever so slowly he ran another finger along my wet folds, tracing my skin and learning me with exquisite patience. My hips strained toward him, craving more, and I was rewarded by the slow slide of one of his large fingers inside me.

I reached for his trousers again and this time he didn't stop me as I slipped inside and took hold of him. His cock was so thick it barely fit in my hand, and was the perfect mix of velvety soft and rock hard. I couldn't wait to feel it inside me, but for now I was content to wrap my fingers around its length. Slade groaned as I took him in hand and seemed to get even harder somehow. The sound, deep in his throat and all male, only made me desire him even more.

I began stroking his length the way Jasin had showed me, and was rewarded with another low rumbling from Slade. He slipped a second finger inside me, while his thumb began to rub that spot Auric had once called a clit.

Slade started up a slow rhythm that felt divine and fondled my breasts with his other hand as he claimed my mouth again. While we shared deep, passionate kisses, our fingers began to move faster, bringing us both closer to release. We moaned and sighed as we touched each other, our hips rocking together while my breasts crushed against his broad chest. His thumb pressed harder against my most sensitive spot, and I gasped into his mouth as sensations crashed over me. My body tightened up around his hand as pleasure took hold of me, and then I felt him surge in my palm as he joined me. He kissed me the entire time while the last tremors ran through us both and a sense of satisfaction settled over me.

As our heartbeats slowed to a normal pace, Slade wrapped me in his dark, muscular arms and pulled me against his chest. I snuggled up against him, savoring this closeness and how right it felt. I no longer had to wonder if Slade wanted me or cared for me—he'd showed me the depths of his feelings tonight.

"Thank you," he said, pressing a soft kiss to my forehead. "It's been a long time since I touched another woman that way. I was worried I'd forgotten how."

"You definitely don't need to worry about that," I said with a smile.

"I'm glad to hear it." He slipped his fingers through the long strands of my hair, idly playing with it. "We have a few days while the Resistance prepares and moves into position. I thought perhaps we might visit my village in that time to make sure my family is safe."

I sat up a little to look him in the eyes. "Truly? You're all right with me meeting them?"

"Yes. I think it's time." He cupped my cheek and brought his lips to mine again. "You're my future, Kira. I'm not going to deny that any longer. And it's time everyone knew it too."

16

REVEN

W hen I woke the next morning, I found the Resistance base a frenzy of activity. Soldiers were arming themselves and preparing for travel, while other people rushed around, delivering supplies and messages, or gathering their things. It would take a week for them to reach Salt Creek Tower since they didn't have dragons they could ride to get their people into position quickly. Those who wouldn't fight would remain here in relative safety, but were prepared to escape if things went badly and the Dragons tracked the Resistance back to Slateden.

I avoided the commotion and found a quiet room used for training that now sat empty, where I pulled out my twin swords. When something was bothering me I found physical exertion and the familiar slice of my blades helped clear my mind. Not that something was bothering me, not exactly. It just annoyed me that I hadn't seen Kira much in the last few days, except when we were in meetings with Parin. She spent all her free time with her other mates, the ones who followed her around like they couldn't stand to be apart from her for a single minute and proclaimed their love daily. I would never be one of those men, and I had no right to demand her time when I couldn't give her anything in return. I shouldn't be annoyed. I shouldn't want her attention all to myself. But I was a selfish bastard at the best of times.

"There you are," Kira said, from the doorway. "For a while there I'd worried you'd run off again."

"I haven't, but I can still change my mind." The reminder of how I'd left her once stung, but I ignored it as I lowered my blades. She wore her

367

hunting leathers today, and I admired the way they clung to her body and showed off her shapely hips and ample breasts. She'd come looking for me, and that was something at least.

"I came to tell you that we're leaving today to visit Slade's village and check that his family is safe. I'd like it if you would come with us, but it's your decision of course."

"I might." If she wanted me there I would go, but I didn't want to seem too eager either. I raised one of my swords. "Care to join me for a couple rounds?"

She stepped into the room, her eyes bright. "I think I can spare a few moments."

I passed her one of my swords, since hers was absent. "How generous of you."

She swung the blade, growing accustomed to its weight. "Don't tell me you missed me."

If only she knew. I gave her a wicked smile. "I'm sure you wish I did."

We each took position across from each other and got into fighting stances. I'd been training with Kira whenever we had a spare moment, usually when we camped for the night or before we took off in the morning, and her form had improved a lot over the last few weeks. She'd never be as good as me (then again, who was?), but I was satisfied she could defend herself better now.

Kira attacked first, but I easily parried her blow and countered with my own. She danced out of the way, and I admired how light on her feet she was. Her eyes took on that determined look I'd seen a lot lately, and she adjusted her stance and struck again.

"You're getting better," I said, as I sidestepped her strike.

"All thanks to you." She gave me a wry grin. "Or should I say thanks to the Black Hood?"

I shook my head at that ridiculous name. "No one calls me that anymore. And I'm happy to take the credit, but you're also more focused these days."

Her grin faded and she gripped the sword tighter. "If I'm going to stop the Dragons, I need to be focused." We traded blows again for some time, before she asked, "What do you think of the plan?"

"It's risky. It assumes the Dragons will leave the Earth Temple to defend against an attack, but there are a lot of things that could go wrong. And you'll be in the center of the danger if it does."

"Then it's a good thing I'll have you with me to watch my back."

That was something I'd insisted on before agreeing to this mad scheme. The plan had Kira and Slade sneaking into the Earth Temple, and there was nothing stealthy about Slade. They needed me to scout ahead and keep them safe. But even if we succeeded, that was only the beginning of our problems.

"And what will we do when it's time to visit the Water Temple?" I asked. "The Dragons won't fall for this trick twice."

Her brows pinched together. "I don't know, but we'll have to worry about that when the time comes."

She attacked me with renewed vigor that I sensed was born out of her own frustration and grief. I decided to let her gain the advantage to boost her confidence, but she struck harder than I expected. The blade flew out of my hand, and a victorious smile lit up her face.

She levelled her sword at my neck. "Surrender."

"Never." We were both breathing heavily from the exertion, and the air became thick with sexual tension. I darted forward and stole the sword from her hand, then pressed her back against the wall, the blade at her throat. "You still have a lot to learn."

She gazed into my eyes as I pinned her there, and I became aware of the rise and fall of her breasts and the feel of her soft body against me. "I'm eager to learn anything you want to teach me."

Her words brought all sorts of naughty things to mind, and I couldn't resist capturing her lips with mine. The sword fell from my hand and hit the ground with a sharp clang, but I was too wrapped up in kissing Kira to care. I caged her in, then dragged her arms up over her head, pinning them to the wall. With one hand I held her there, as I let my other hand skim down her side, finally allowing myself to touch her the way I wanted. Last time she'd initiated the kiss, but now it was my turn.

Her body melded against mine as the kiss grew deeper and more intense. When my thumb slid over her taut nipple it earned me a soft, delicious gasp. Her touch, her taste, her responsiveness…it all made me want to devour her.

"Kira, are you in here?" Brin's voice called. I jerked away from Kira and released her arms as the door to the room opened. Brin poked her head in, then flashed a knowing grin. "Sorry, didn't mean to interrupt."

I reached down and picked up both my swords, then sheathed them. "It's fine. We were done anyway."

Brin nodded. "We're almost ready to get going."

"I'll be right there," Kira said.

Brin shut the door and left us alone again. I turned back to Kira, who stared at me, her face flushed, her lips parted. I immediately wanted to haul her against me and take her mouth again, but that moment had passed.

"Will you join us?" Kira asked.

I had no interest in meeting Slade's family or visiting another small, boring village, but the thought of being apart from Kira suddenly seemed unbearable. If it were any other woman I would have walked away by now, but for some reason I couldn't stay away from her. "I will, but only because someone needs to be there to keep you all out of danger."

"Of course." She granted me another smile that tempted me to reach for her again, and I forced myself to turn away. Curse this stupid destiny that tied me to her. It would make fools of both of us before the end. Especially when she realized I would never be able to love her the way she wanted.

17

KIRA

Slade's village, Clayridge, was to the west of the Resistance hideout, and as we flew toward it, anxious butterflies flittered around my stomach at the thought of meeting his family. I'd already met both Jasin and Auric's parents, but for some reason this visit made me the most nervous. Maybe because I sensed how close Slade was with his family and I desperately wanted them to accept me. I worried too that the Dragons had found out who Slade was and done the same thing to Clayridge as they did to Stoneham. I could only pray that his family remained anonymous and safe.

Jasin and Auric flew high, their wings brushing the clouds, to avoid us being detected. Parin's words made us cautious, knowing that rumors were already beginning about us—rumors that could bring the Dragons after more innocent people if we weren't careful.

When we flew over Clayridge and saw it was still intact, I let out a sigh of relief. From where he sat behind me, Slade gave me a slight squeeze of his arms. His family was still safe from the Dragons—now I just needed to get them to like me.

My dragons discreetly set down in the nearby forest and returned to their human forms, and then we walked toward the town. Clayridge was about the same size as Stoneham, but it was set up on a hill with a river flowing down below. The terrain was especially rocky, but Slade led us along a well-trodden path up toward the village. Red clay roofs began to appear as we crested the hill, and soon I could see a cluster of stone buildings with a thick wall between them and us. A wall that was meant to protect against elemental attacks, dotted with braziers that could be lit at any moment and large buckets likely filled with water.

A lookout guard stood on top of the wall near the gate, and called out to us as we approached. "Slade, that you?"

Slade chuckled softly. "It's me, Lon. Let us in, will you?"

"Aye!" the young guard called out, then disappeared from view. The gate slowly creaked open moments later, and we were quickly surrounded by cheery dark-skinned men and women who all wanted to welcome Slade back to the village. He greeted each of them with a kind word, a pat on the back, or a warm nod as he led us inside. My nerves wound even tighter as I smiled at everyone, who would no doubt know who we all were by the end of the night. In a small town like this, nothing remained a secret for very long.

As we moved inside the village, more people came out of the houses and shops to give Slade a wave and a fond greeting. Everyone seemed to know him and love him here, and with each step some of his hard demeanor melted away. It made me wonder what he was like before he'd been sent to find me against his will. Or before Faya had broken his heart.

Ahead of us, an older, sturdy woman with warm brown eyes rushed out of a small house. "Slade! You've returned!"

"Mother," Slade said, as a smile lit up his face. An actual smile. Had I ever seen him truly smile before? Not like this, certainly.

The two of them collided in a tight embrace, and then she pulled back and took his face in her hands. "Oh, I'm so glad you're safe. Let me look at you." She patted his cheeks like he was a boy, even though he towered over her. "We were all so worried after you left. Are you all right?"

"I'm fine." He turned toward us as if to begin introductions, but was interrupted by another woman leaping out of the house and running toward him.

"Big brother!" the young woman cried out. She was about my age and strikingly beautiful, with smooth dark skin and braids piled atop her head. Like Slade, she was tall, but she had also the curves of her mother. I remembered Slade mentioning his younger sister was a troublemaker, and I suspected part of it was because of the way she looked—she would always turn heads.

"Leni!" Slade laughed as he swept his sister up in his arms and twirled her around.

More people streamed toward us, enveloping Slade and giving him warm hugs and kisses on his cheek. I sensed family resemblance in most of them, and a sense of longing spread through me as I watched awkwardly

from the sidelines with Brin and my other mates. We were outsiders, forced
to watch the celebration, and it was a keen reminder that I didn't have a
family anymore. And even when I had one, it had been nothing like this.

Jasin glanced at the others and cleared his throat, before speaking to
me. "I think we'll go find an inn and get some rooms while you meet the
family."

I started to protest, but then saw how tight Jasin's face was and remembered how he'd been upset around Auric's family too. His own parents had
betrayed us not long ago, and seeing this probably reminded him of what
he'd lost. Explaining the situation to Slade's family would be easier without
my other mates at my side too.

I gave Jasin's arm a quick squeeze. "All right. I'll find you later."

The four of them slipped away, leaving me alone to face the crowd. I
swallowed hard and plastered on a smile, unsure of what else I should do.

Eventually Slade was able to break apart from his family. He moved to
my side and took my hand in his, sending a signal to all of them that we
were close. Warm happiness filled me, even as color spread to my cheeks.
"Everyone, this is Kira. She's the one I was sent to find by the Earth God."

"Kira, welcome to Clayridge," Slade's mother said, as she moved
forward to embrace me in a warm hug. "I'm Yena, Slade's mother."

"It's so nice to meet you," I said.

Slade brought two women over to me—the curvy sister I'd seen before,
and another one who was a little more plain but had the same striking
green eyes as Slade. "These are my sisters, Leni and Wrin."

"Hello—" I started to reply, but Slade was already continuing his introductions.

"And this is Wrin's husband Merl, and their son Tam," he said, indi-
cating a lighter-skinned man and a boy I guessed to be about five. Slade
then pointed to more people surrounding us. "I'd also like you to meet my
aunt Edda, my uncle Heim, and their son Noren, who took over as the
town's blacksmith for me."

I quickly nodded at a woman who looked a lot like Yena but taller and
thinner, an older bearded man, and a young man who had Slade's muscles
and gave me a kind smile. Slade then went on to introduce me to a dozen
other cousins, distant relations, and friends of the family who had joined
us—so many I knew I would never remember anyone's names. They all
gave me hugs or shook my hands, and it was both overwhelming and
wonderful. With so much love it was no wonder Slade had never wanted to
leave this place.

"Get back, let the poor girl have some room to breathe," Yena said, as
she forced her way through the crowd to me. She interlocked our arms and

began to lead me toward the small house I assumed was her own. "Come now. We must have dinner, and then you can tell us everything about yourself."

Everything? I swallowed hard as the nervous butterflies returned to my stomach. Now the interrogation would begin.

18

KIRA

Yena led us inside her home, which was cozy and warm with a stone hearth already lit. Slade spoke a few more words to the people outside before following us, along with his sister Leni. We were immediately swept into the dining area, with a long wooden table and two benches. The air smelled of freshly baked treats.

"Sit down and relax," Yena said, as she nudged me to the bench. "You must be exhausted after all your travels. I'll get us some food and you can tell me all about your journeys."

"That's very kind of you." I slid onto the bench and Slade moved in beside me.

"Be careful, or mother will stuff you so full of food you'll never be able to walk again," Leni said, as she sat across from me. She gave me a warm, dazzling smile that reminded me so much of Tash it sent a pang of longing and grief through my heart.

The door banged open and Slade's other sister Wrin came inside too. "You better not start without me."

"Of course not, dear," Yena said. "We'd love for you to join us. Where are Merl and Tam?"

Wrin sat beside her sister. "I sent them home for the night. They weren't happy about it, but I'm not missing out on hearing what Slade's been doing all this time."

"I'm sure it will be all over town by the morning anyway," Leni said, rolling her eyes.

Wrin studied me with intelligent, serious eyes that looked so much like Slade's. "So you're the woman he left Clayridge to go find."

I ducked my head. "I am, yes. Although I didn't ask for any of this either."

Slade's mother began dropping wooden bowls of steaming hot stew in front of each of us. Wrin jumped up and brought over a loaf of bread, while Leni served everyone some ale. Everything about it reminded me of my time with Tash and her family in Stoneham, from the delicious smell of the stew to the slightly bitter taste of the ale. Grief tried to sink its claws in me again, but I forced it back down. Stoneham and Tash were gone, but Clayridge and Slade's family were alive, and I would do everything in my power to keep it that way.

When all the food was served, Yena plopped down across from us. "Eat! No need to wait for me."

Slade wasted no time digging in and then he closed his eyes as he savored the stew. "It's been far too long since I had good food like this."

Yena smiled and patted her son's hand. "There's nothing better than a home cooked meal. Now eat up, you're looking far too skinny after all that travel."

I held in a laugh. Slade looked anything but skinny. He was a mountain of a man made of pure muscle with arms the size of tree trunks, but I sensed this was just Yena's way.

She gave me a smile. "You too dear. You're very pretty, but you could use some more meat on those bones of yours."

I flushed and shoveled a spoonful of stew into my mouth. Warm flavors exploded on my lips, and I caught the taste of rabbit, carrots, and more. It was definitely better than the food we'd been eating while on the road. "Thank you. It's delicious."

"Glad you like it." She barely touched her own food and instead took in the both of us while we ate, like she couldn't drink in enough of us with her eyes to satisfy her.

Leni pointed her spoon at Slade. "You better start talking, or mother is going to burst with impatience."

"Let them swallow their food at least," Wrin said, shaking her head.

Slade slowed down, his bowl already half empty, and glanced at me. I had no idea how much these women knew already and I was completely overwhelmed by the situation, but I sensed he wanted me to speak. I set down my spoon and asked, "What did Slade tell you before he left?"

"We knew that the Earth God had chosen him for a great mission," Yena said, her voice bursting with pride. "He was given great powers, and then was sent to find and protect you...although he was unable to tell us why."

"None of us believed it at first, until he showed us his magic," Wrin said.

I arched an eyebrow at Slade. "I thought you weren't supposed to tell anyone about your encounter with the Earth God."

Slade shrugged. "You try keeping a secret from these three."

"He had to tell us something, or no one would have let him leave Clayridge," Leni said.

Wrin nodded. "It's true, my brother is a very important and respected member of this village. He could have been the next mayor, if he'd wanted."

Slade scowled and shook his head. "I was a simple blacksmith, nothing more."

"Nonsense, dear," Yena said, before turning to me. "Slade worked hard to keep this town running and make sure it was safe. Beyond what he did as blacksmith, he volunteered with the town guard and convinced everyone to build the outer wall after an elemental attack took two lives. We've been attacked three more times since then, but we've always held them off thanks to Slade."

"Three?" Slade asked, his spoon pausing halfway to his mouth. "There was another one while I was gone?"

"Yes, this time an air elemental, if you can believe that. Must have wandered far from the Air Realm to make it all the way out here." Yena shrugged. "We were able to keep it out without any issue."

"Good to hear," Slade said, though I could tell it bothered him that he hadn't been here to protect his town. He obviously cared a great deal for the people of Clayridge.

"Now hurry up and tell us where you've been all this time," Leni said.

The others gave Slade expectant looks, and he finally sighed and launched into the tale of how the Earth God had chosen him as the new Jade Dragon, how he'd found me along with my other mates, and how we were on a quest to overthrow the Black Dragon and had recently joined up with the Resistance to help us get into the Earth Temple. I stayed quiet as I ate my stew, worried about what his family would think of all this—especially Slade sharing me with three other men.

"That's quite a tale," Yena said, when Slade lapsed into silence. "And it all sounds quite dangerous, but I'm sure the Earth God chose you because he knew you could handle it all. I'm very proud of you, Slade."

"It sounds incredible," Leni said, her eyes dancing with excitement. "I wish I could have been there for all of it."

"You're not upset about me being only one of her mates?" Slade asked.

"It's not something I'm comfortable with myself," Yena said slowly, as she glanced at me. "But who are we to questions the Gods?"

Wrin nodded. "You can't turn your back on the Earth God's will. Do you think you'll get to speak to him at the temple?"

"I expect so," Slade said.

A knock sounded on the door and Yena got up to open it. Brin stood on the other side and was quickly ushered in. "You're one of Slade and Kira's companions aren't you?" Yena asked. "You must join us!"

"Thank you," Brin said with a smile as she stepped inside. Her eyes caught sight of Leni and her gaze seemed to linger there before she turned to me. "I simply wanted to let Kira know that we've booked rooms at the inn for the next few nights."

"Very good," Yena said. "I'd love to house you all, but as you can see my home is rather small. But please, sit with us and I'll get you some food. And tell us your name, child."

Brin hesitated, but then slid beside me. Across from Leni, who was definitely watching my friend with interest. "My name is Brin of House Pashona, and it's an honor to join you for a meal."

"House Pashona?" Leni asked, even more intrigued. She leaned forward, giving us a glimpse of her ample cleavage. "You're nobility?"

Brin offered her an alluring smile. "I am, yes. From the Air Realm. But please, don't let that change your opinion of me. As you can see, I'm simply one of Kira's traveling companions now."

"Brin is a good friend," I said. "I'm lucky she agreed to join us. Being with four men all the time can get rather...complicated. It's nice to have a woman I can talk with."

Leni let out a dramatic sigh and rested her chin on her hand. "You're all so lucky, traveling the world, fighting bandits and Dragons, helping the Resistance. I'd do anything to get out of this boring town."

"Why don't you?" Brin asked.

"Definitely not," Slade said. "She's too young."

"I'm twenty-one!" Leni said, then turned to me and Brin. "How old are you two?"

"Twenty," I replied, while Brin said, "Twenty-two."

"See, they're the same age as me," Leni said. "And Slade, you started helping the Resistance at my age. Why am I not allowed to do anything?"

Yena returned and set a bowl in front of Brin, then patted Leni's head like a child. "It's not safe for you. Slade had to leave to fulfill his destiny, but your place is here."

"My place is wherever I decide it is," Leni said, as she rose to her feet. "And I don't plan on staying in Clayridge for the rest of my life."

She walked out of the house, while her mother sighed. "I'm sorry for that. She's been like this ever since Slade left."

"I'll talk to her," Slade said.

"She'll get over it," Wrin said. "Just like she got over that traveling merchant who stopped by. And the soldier before that."

"Leni has always had her head full of big dreams. I'm not sure she'll ever be satisfied here." Yena waved it away with a sad smile. "But enough of that. Tell us more about you, Kira. Where are you from?"

I took a deep breath and settled in to tell them about my life. I could already tell this was going to be a long night.

19

AURIC

While Kira spent time with Slade's family, the rest of us took over most of the inn. Brin grew restless and went off to explore the town on her own, while Reven, Jasin, and I shared a meal together. Jasin and I both ate like we had the hunger of five men after flying for much of the day, while Reven watched with amusement. We'd been served some sort of questionable stew common in the Earth Realm, a far cry from the fine dining of the Air Realm, but I was so hungry I didn't care. And maybe I'd gotten used to such things after weeks of travel, because it actually tasted pretty good.

"Kira has an idea for how we can increase our bond," Jasin said, in between bites. "If she returns tonight, we should meet for more…training."

I arched an eyebrow. "Sounds promising."

"Is that what you two call it?" Reven asked. "Training?"

"Jasin has been very instructive," I said.

Reven snickered. "I'll bet he has."

"You're welcome to join us too," Jasin said. "I'm sure Kira would enjoy that."

Reven paused as he brought his tankard of ale to his lips. "Perhaps some other time."

We retreated to our rooms after our meal. I'd splurged and gotten everyone their own rooms since the inn was empty and my father had given us plenty of gold for our journey. But as soon as I was alone in mine, a creeping loneliness settled over me. I'd spent the last few weeks sharing a tent with Jasin, and I found myself missing his presence. Who would have thought the two of us would become so close, when we'd originally hated each other?

I debated going to his room, but dismissed the thought as too childish. What would we even talk about? Jasin was a former soldier, and I was a former prince. We had little in common besides Kira. It was incredible we managed to get along at all.

I decided to open my notebook and add some notes about our journey while I waited. I'd recorded everything we'd been through so far in the hopes it would be of use someday, perhaps to our daughter when it was her turn to become the next Black Dragon. Assuming we didn't fail—but I refused to entertain that thought.

When a knock sounded on my door an hour later, I rushed to open it. Jasin and Kira stood on the other side, and my heart pounded with anticipation.

"How was your evening with Slade's family?" I asked, as they stepped inside my dimly-lit room.

"Good." Kira sat on the edge of the bed. "Better than I expected, although it was a little overwhelming. I'm glad I got to meet his family though." She rubbed the spot on the bed next to her. "But I'm happy to have some time away from them too. Did Jasin explain the plan?"

I sank onto the bed beside her. "Not in any detail."

"She thinks the key to strengthening our bond is to share her body together," Jasin said with a grin. He took the spot on the other side of Kira and began slowly massaging her shoulders.

I grinned back at him. "I like the sound of that."

"We thought you might," Kira said, as she leaned into Jasin's touch. He slid his hands down her arms and began to kiss her neck, making her sigh. I watched them for a few moments, enjoying the sight of Jasin bringing my mate pleasure, but then I couldn't resist joining in.

I took her mouth in a hungry kiss and cupped her breasts in my palms, teasing her hard nipples through the fabric of her dress. It had been a week since we'd bonded at the Air Temple, and I was eager to be inside her again. But even once we'd done this a thousand times, I knew I'd never get enough of her. She was my one and only—my mate.

Jasin and I both gripped the fabric of Kira's dress and worked it up, pulling it above her head and tossing it aside. Once she was completely nude I let my eyes soak her in, devouring the sight of her bare skin and lush curves. Gods, I could stare at this woman forever.

The door creaked open behind me, and we all froze. I snapped out of it and quickly moved in front of Kira to block her from sight. The three of us turned as one to look at the door—and saw Reven standing there.

20

KIRA

Reven paused in the doorway, his eyes slowly taking in the scene. "Apologies. I thought this was my room."

From the tone of his voice, I didn't believe that for a second—but I didn't mind either. If anything, the thought that he'd come to join us only made my already racing heart pound even faster.

"Don't go," I said.

He lingered at the door, perhaps waiting for someone to protest or taking a moment to make up his mind. Or maybe he wanted even more of an invitation.

I reached toward him. "Join us."

That finally brought him forward. He shut the door, his eyes never leaving the scene before him of my naked body pressed between Jasin and Auric. "I'll stay…but just to watch."

Reven crossed the room and sank into an armchair in the corner, his pose deceptively casual, and laced his arms behind his head as if waiting for the show to begin. Desire flared between my thighs at the thought of his piercing blue gaze on me the entire time I was making love to the other men.

But I couldn't forget Auric and Jasin either. I wanted them to be comfortable with this. I touched both of their chests, glancing between them. "Are you all right with this?" I asked in a low voice.

Auric threaded his fingers through mine. "I want whatever makes you happy."

Jasin's lips touched my ear. "I invited him earlier. I didn't think he would actually come though."

"You did?" I asked.

A naughty grin touched his lips. "I thought you would like it."

"You know me so well," I said, before catching that grin in a passionate kiss. Not long ago I'd been a virgin. Now the thought of multiple men touching me at the same time seemed not only natural, but right. I blamed Jasin for corrupting me, although it was Auric who'd first initiated these training sessions. Maybe he was to blame too. Not that I minded one bit.

The two men surrounding me resumed their kissing and touching, as if we'd never been interrupted and didn't have another man watching our every move. I helped remove their clothes, sliding my hands along their smooth, hard bodies that I loved so much. They were both so perfect, sometimes it was hard to believe they were mine.

"Tonight we're going to try something new as part of your training," Jasin said, as his hand slipped between my thighs, finding me already wet. But then his fingers slid back, back, back, to my other, forbidden entrance. "I'm going to take you here tonight, while Auric takes you from the front."

My eyes widened. He'd talked about claiming me from behind before, and the idea had intrigued me—especially if it meant joining with both of them at the same time. "Will it hurt?"

"A little, but it will feel good too." He nibbled on my ear. "Trust me."

I closed my eyes and relaxed against him. "I do."

With his other hand, he reached for a vial of liquid from the night-stand. "I got this in the Air Realm. The oil will make it easier, and we'll go slow. If it's too much, we'll stop."

I nodded, eager to get started, even though I was nervous too. While Auric began slowly stroking me between my legs, Jasin coated his fingers in oil and began to work it into me from behind. I gasped at the sensation, though it didn't hurt, not at all. When Auric's fingers entered me in front too, I got a glimpse of what the rest of the night would be like... and I wanted more. I bore down against their hands, taking them deeper, and Auric's mouth found mine again. While the two of them stretched me out and moved inside me, my tongue slid against Auric's in a sensual dance. Jasin kissed the back of my neck, and everything felt so good I wasn't sure how it could ever get better...but knew this was just the beginning.

"Good," Jasin said. "You're ready. Now sit on Auric, but don't take him inside you yet."

Auric gathered me into his arms and I climbed onto his lap, straddling his hips, his cock brushing up against me. I took his length in hand and began to stroke it, while leaning forward to kiss him some more. His hands found my breasts and he began caressing my nipples, while I felt Jasin's cock brush against me from behind. I tensed up, but he kissed my shoulder and whispered, "Relax."

His warm voice calmed me, and my body became pliant at his touch. He began to push inside my back entrance, and at first the stretching was so intense it took my breath away. He already felt huge, and it seemed impossible he'd be able to fit completely inside, but he kept going. Gods, it was so tight, I wasn't sure I could stand it. My fingers dug into Auric's shoulders and Jasin paused.

"You're doing great," Jasin said, kissing my neck some more. "Almost there."

"Keep going," I said, as I willed my body to relax. "I want this."

Auric's fingers found my clit while I continued stroking him, and when he began to rub me there it all got so much easier. The sensations were so intense, and I found myself pushing back against Jasin, wanting more. The pain vanished, until only pleasure remained.

When he was fully sheathed, we both let out a delirious sigh. Jasin felt huge inside me, but still it wasn't enough. I needed Auric too.

Without words, Jasin and Auric shared a look that communicated everything that had to be done. Jasin's fingers dug into my hips as he lifted me slightly, while Auric guided himself into me. I sank down onto his hard cock, taking him deep inside, and if I'd thought it was a tight fit before, it was nothing compared to having both of them inside me. As my hips rested against Auric's, I closed my eyes and savored the exquisite fullness with both of them inside me, their bodies pressed tight against me on all sides.

"Still all right?" Jasin asked.

"It's amazing," I said, breathless. I turned my head and drew Jasin in for a kiss, then brought Auric close for one too. Their mouths both pressed against my lips, their tongues sliding into me, and I found myself kissing them both at the same time. The kiss deepened, the three of our lips and tongues tangling together in the most intimate way. Soon I had no idea where I ended or any of them began. We'd truly all become one.

Our kiss broke apart as we became overwhelmed with the need to move. Jasin began, slowly pulling out of me before sliding back in. The tightness back there made me gasp, but my body quickly grew used to it, and then Auric began lifting his hips to thrust into me too. I clung to his body, unable to do anything but take what they were giving me and enjoy every second of it.

I could tell they were overcome by it too, from the way they groaned against me and bucked harder. And when Jasin reached out and grasped Auric's muscular arm, it nearly became too much for me. Especially when I felt Auric's hand slide from my naked hip to Jasin's, urging him on. It wasn't just me with them, it was all three of us bonding together and sharing this moment.

I raised my head and my eyes locked with Reven, who stared at the scene with rapt attention. I wanted to give him a show. I wanted him to see what he could have too, someday. If only he would let me in.

But then he stood and came toward the bed, surprising me. He bent down, took my chin in his hand, and captured my lips in a kiss. I reached for him, my fingers sliding around his neck, but then he pulled back and straightened up. But I didn't want to let him go.

I gripped his shirt, then slid my hand down to his trousers, pressing against the hardness there. He'd definitely enjoyed watching, and that knowledge only made me more excited. I tore at his trousers, yanking them open, revealing his long length. He didn't stop me. Instead, he gazed down at me with his intense blue eyes as I took his cock in hand and brought it to my lips. My mouth slid over the head and he let out a soft groan, while tangling his fingers in my hair.

Auric and Jasin kept going through it all, rocking me between their bodies, their pace growing faster. I couldn't hold on much longer, not with the incredible feelings they sent through me. But I needed Reven too, that was clear to me now. It couldn't be just me with Auric and Jasin forever, I needed *all* of my mates equally.

I took Reven into my mouth as far as I could, while circling the base of his shaft with my hand. He gripped my hair tighter and his hips jerked, like he couldn't help himself. Like he didn't want to give himself to me, but was unable to resist.

I sucked on him hard, feeling my own release approach. I sensed through the bond that Auric and Jasin were close too, but they were holding out for me. Together the four of us moved in a sensual dance, back and forth, in and out, with my body taking everything they gave me and still wanting more. If only Slade were here too…

The instant Reven reached down to pinch my nipple, I was gone. His touch pushed me over the edge, and I cried out while tightening up around Auric and Jasin. Ripples of pleasure more intense than anything I'd ever felt before began to overwhelm me, and I was completely lost in the sensations. They were my mates, and in this moment I truly felt as though I belonged to all of them.

Each man released himself into me only seconds later, while I was still trembling. Jasin's head pressed against my neck as he came hard into my behind, while Auric thrust up into me faster until his seed filled me. Reven was last, gripping my hair tight while he finally let himself go into my mouth. I swallowed everything he gave me and our eyes remained locked on each other's, though his face was indecipherable.

When it was done, he slipped out of me, closed up his trousers, and then walked out of the room without a word. It was just like him, and all I could do was sigh and shake my head, while relaxing against my other two mates.

We fell onto the bed, the three of us a tangle of bodies without end. The kissing began again, hands sliding against each other's skin, this time to comfort and show affection rather than induce desire or pleasure. The bond between us felt stronger than ever, and I sensed their satisfaction and love through it. Not just for me, but for each other too. It amazed me how far they'd come from those first jealous fights and heated arguments to snuggling together on the bed, with me pressed between their naked bodies. I loved them both so much, and nothing made me happier than knowing they'd truly come to care about the other during the last few months. Well, except for the thought of my other two mates joining me in bed like this too.

Someday, maybe...I could hope.

21

KIRA

In the morning Slade showed me around the small village, pointing out the houses of friends and relatives, or showing me things he had helped repair. A lot of it reminded me of Stoneham, although Clayridge was better defended—not that it would have helped against the Dragons anyway.

The tour ended at a stone house near his mother's, with smoke coming out of the chimney. "This used to be my house and my shop," Slade said. "But now my cousin Noren lives here."

"You said he took over as the town's blacksmith?" I asked.

"Yes. Before that he was my apprentice. I would have liked to train him for a few more years, but the Gods had other plans."

He led me around the back of the house, where the shop was located. There was a gray horse tied to a post nearby, and a wave of heat struck me as we approached the open door. Inside, Noren stood over an anvil, where he was working on a horseshoe. A large stone forge took up one wall, and against the other was a table with a variety of metal tongs and hammers with a sketch of some armor. Over it was a shelf with some helmets and gauntlets, while a variety of weapons and shields hung from the walls.

Noren looked up and brushed sweat off his forehead. "Morning."

"I came to see how you're holding up," Slade said.

"Meaning you want to see if I'm keeping up the family legacy." Noren grinned. "It wasn't easy at first, but I managed without you. I've taken on my own apprentice now too."

Slade clasped him on the shoulder. "Good man."

They chatted a bit longer about blacksmith things I didn't understand, before we stepped outside again. I gave the horse a quick rub, and then Slade and I kept walking, taking a leisurely stroll down the hill to the river and the surrounding forest.

"Do you feel better now that you know the shop is in good hands?" I asked.

"A little," Slade said. "Although Noren seems so young to me. Too young to be running the shop. Then again, I was his age when I took over for my father too."

I guessed Noren was about my age, and it hit me how much older and more experienced Slade was. He'd talked about how he'd been settled in his life, and for the first time I truly understood what he'd meant. He'd spent years building his profession and helping his town, and then he'd been forced to give all of that up. For me.

"How old are you?" I asked Slade, realizing I didn't know the exact number.

"Thirty-two."

I missed a step in my surprise. Twelve years older than me. "Truly?"

He reached out to steady me with a hand on my elbow. "Too old for you?"

"No, not at all." I continued walking. "But it's no wonder you think the rest of us young and foolish."

"Young, yes," he said with a trace of amusement. "Foolish…sometimes."

"I can see now why you had a hard time giving up this life."

"It was difficult, but I don't regret it. After Faya left, this town was never the same for me. It wasn't until finding you that I began to feel whole again—like I'd discovered my true place in the world. This village will always be my home, but it's no longer where I belong."

"And where is that?" I asked, as I stopped beside the river.

"By your side." He cupped my cheek in his hand. "Wherever you go, I'll be there with you."

"My loyal protector," I murmured, as I leaned into his touch.

His head lowered and his mouth pressed against mine. He gripped my hip, digging his fingers into the fabric of my dress while he kissed me long and hard until I was practically moaning for more. I slid my hands down his chest and under his shirt, running my fingers across his bare stomach.

A sharp sound in the forest broke us apart, and I was reminded of when Cadock's bandits had interrupted us before. But as I peered through the trees it wasn't bandits I saw, but two young women raising swords at each other. Leni and Brin lunged and parried, laughing as they danced away from each other and then drew close again. There was something about the way they moved and looked at each other that made it clear this was more than just sword fighting practice.

"You're better than I expected," Brin said, her voice carrying through the leaves. "Where did you learn to fight?"

"Slade and Noren taught me," Leni said, as their swords clashed again. "I joined the town guard three years ago, and became its leader when Slade left to find Kira. What about you?"

"My parents had me trained in combat from the time I could hold a sword. They were terribly worried their precious only child would be kidnapped and held for ransom or some such. It's never happened, of course, but I can hardly complain."

"Impressive. I'll admit, you might be able to teach me a thing or two."

"Oh, I can teach you a great many things, my dear," Brin said, her voice sensual.

I covered my mouth to hide my amusement, especially since their conversation so closely mirrored the one I'd had with Reven the other day. I had a feeling theirs would end the same way too.

"One of them is going to get hurt," Slade said, shaking his head.

"Brin is an expert swordswoman, and your sister doesn't seem too bad either."

"Not what I meant." He scowled as he watched them tumble to the ground together, their laughter ringing out around us.

I took his hand and led him away from what was likely to become an intimate moment. "Let them have their few moments of happiness. They're fleeting enough at the moment."

He let me drag him away, and then entwined his fingers with mine. Just the simple act of holding hands with him was so much more than I ever thought I would get from him, and I took my own advice and allowed myself to feel content.

"You seem happier too," he said, studying my face. "After Stoneham we were all worried about you."

"I'm still upset about that, and I'll miss Tash forever, but coming here and meeting your family has eased some of the pain." I squeezed his hand. "Thank you for bringing us here. You seem like a weight has been lifted off your shoulders too."

Slade nodded. "Once my family knew the truth about our situation, it became easier for me to accept as well."

"That's a relief. I worried after what happened with Faya you would never be okay with it."

He spoke slowly as we continued back along the river toward the village. "It was different with Faya. I never believed she loved both me and Parin. As soon as she was forced to choose between us, she picked him and abandoned the life we'd created together without a second thought. That's why I couldn't understand how you would be able to love all of us equally, but now I know you're nothing like her. She went behind my back and cheated on me. You've been up front about this complicated relationship with me from the beginning, and you've never tried to hide anything about it. That honesty is important."

"Does that mean you're not upset about having to share me with the others anymore?"

"I don't mind it as much as I used to," Slade admitted. "Traveling the world with you and the others has opened my mind to a lot of things I never experienced while living in Clayridge. I suppose being one of your mates has changed me too. I only want you to be happy, whether it's because of me or the other men. Or all of us."

An image came to mind of Slade joining in while I was being shared between the other three men and I felt a flush of heat between my legs. I doubted Slade would ever want to do that, but I couldn't deny the idea excited me.

As if conjured by my thoughts, Jasin and Auric emerged from the village, heading for the river. We'd agreed to meet in the afternoon to continue our training, but I hadn't realized the day had gotten so late.

"Ready to get started?" Jasin asked, as they approached.

"If we're interrupting, we can come back later," Auric said.

"We're going to try to summon lightning again," I explained to Slade. "Do you mind?"

"No, it's fine. My mother has demanded my help with fixing her roof this afternoon anyway." He lowered his head and brushed a kiss across my lips. "I'll see you tonight for dinner."

"I wouldn't miss it."

He headed back toward the village, and I turned to my two mates with a smile I couldn't hide. They'd both noticed the kiss, judging by the smirks on their faces.

"Things with Slade are better then," Jasin said.

"They are. He's finally starting to open up to me, and he said he's getting used to the idea of sharing me with the rest of you."

"That's good to hear," Auric said. "For a while, I was worried he wouldn't be able to do his duty at the Earth Temple."

"I don't think that will be a problem anymore," I said, my face flushing for no good reason. I'd shared my body with both these men last night, so why did talking about being intimate with Slade feel so embarrassing? Maybe because our budding relationship was more private, and a part of me wanted to keep it that way.

Jasin took my hand in his. "I'm glad you're happy. Now let's get to work."

22

JASIN

As soon as I touched Kira our ever-present bond sparked bright, like a fire suddenly flaring to life. I always felt her in the background of my mind, but her presence became almost overwhelming when we touched.

She reached for Auric with her other hand, connecting the three of us. "Can you sense each other?"

"Yes," Auric said, his eyes closed. "Much stronger than before."

I closed my eyes and reached out, sorting through the tangled threads of identity and emotion to separate Kira, Auric, and myself. I focused on the feeling of Auric and followed the trail back, going deeper than ever before. He was a mix of excitement and nervousness, but I stretched beyond all that until I found his core self. His strength, his wisdom, his innate goodness. And there, wrapped up in all of that, was his air magic.

"I feel it too," I said.

"Now draw upon your magic while reaching for the other one's power," Kira said. "Try to combine the two elements of fire and air to create lightning."

As I seized the magic, I felt both Kira and Auric inside me, tugging and pulling, searching and finding. Fire came to me as if by instinct now, but drawing upon Auric's magic was a lot harder. Every time I tried to grasp it, it seemed to slip through my fingers.

I heard a low buzzing sound and opened my eyes to small sparks flashing in front of us. My hand tightened around Kira's as I tried to build up the magic, but then it fizzled out and was lost. The sparks vanished.

I ran a hand through my hair. "Damn. We almost had it."

"Maybe we just need more time for the bond to grow stronger," Auric suggested.

Kira sighed. "We don't have time. We face the Dragons in only a few days, and we have to be prepared."

"Then we keep trying." I reached out and grabbed Auric's hand too, forming a circle between the three of us. Instead of closing my eyes, I looked straight into Auric's gray ones. And then I reached for the magic again.

A bolt of bright white energy shot down from the sky and hit the tree beside us, making us all jump. The energy disappeared instantly, but left behind the impression of heat and power, along with the blackened remains of a tree trunk.

"We did it," Auric said, his voice impressed.

"Yeah, we did," I said, dropping their hands. "But I'm not sure what good it does us. We can't stand around in a circle holding hands every time we need to call lightning."

"Sark and Isen summoned it at the Air Temple without even touching," Kira said. "We simply need to practice more."

"At least we know it's possible now," Auric said.

Kira held out her hands as she glanced at both of us. "Let's try it again."

I groaned, but took hold of both of them and called forth the magic again. The lightning came easier this time, but it was erratic, hitting the surface of the water with a jagged strike. We were going to have to spend all our free time practicing this to be able to actually control the magic in a way that would be useful in battle. Right now we had just as much of a chance of hitting each other as the enemy.

"Good," Kira said, after the next three attempts. "Now do it again."

"Couldn't we go back to the other kind of training?" I asked, flashing her a naughty grin. "I liked that a lot better."

"We all did," Auric said.

Kira shook her head. "We will at night, and during the day we're going to do this. Every day until you're throwing lightning from your hands like you throw fire and air."

I groaned, but then turned to Auric. "Fine, but let's at least make this more fun. Ten coins says I can throw lightning before you can."

His eyes gleamed as he smirked at me, that old competition between us coming back to the surface, except this time in a friendly way. "You're on."

23

KIRA

Over the next few days we settled into a slower pace while staying in Clayridge that seemed to suit all of us. I practiced sword fighting with Reven, trained in magic with Auric and Jasin, and spent time with Slade and his family. After such a long time on the road, it was good for all of us to stop and breathe for a while. News had spread through the village about what we were, and people treated us with respect and awe, but otherwise little changed. Meanwhile, Brin and Leni got even closer—I caught sight of them kissing numerous times, and while their relationship seemed destined for heartbreak, none of us wanted to interfere with their happiness. But we all knew how hard it would be when it came time for us to leave.

We only had a few more days until we were supposed to meet the Resistance at the Earth Temple and I keenly felt our time running out with each minute. Once we left Clayridge we would have to face the Dragons again, and there was no guarantee any of us would survive the encounter. I pushed myself to train even harder, remembering Tash's blackened bones and the ruins of my village.

It was while training with Jasin and Auric by the river that we heard a panicked shout ring out in town. We immediately stopped what we were doing and rushed back into the village, searching for the source of the trouble.

Brin rushed over to us as soon as we stepped through the gate. "One of the Dragons has been spotted heading this way!"

Jasin let out a growl. "Auric and I can take him."

I shook my head, my heart clenching. "No, you'll put the people here in danger. The Dragons can't know we've been here."

"Do we have time to escape?" Auric asked.

"I don't think so," Brin said. "We have to find somewhere for you to hide."

"My old house," Slade said, from behind us. "I used to hide Resistance members in a panel in the floor."

Reven stepped out of the shadows. "How do you know the people in this village won't turn us in?"

Slade leveled a steely gaze at him. "They won't."

I had to trust that the people in the town cared for Slade enough to be willing to hide our secret. There was no time to do anything else. "Let's go."

Our group hurried to Slade's house, where a surprised Noren opened the door. Once Slade explained what was happening, Noren ushered us inside with a worried expression. As the door shut, I heard a deep screech outside along with the heavy flap of wings, and a chill went down my spine.

Slade took the lead as he rushed us through the house, and I barely had time to glimpse dark wood furnishings before we were taken into a back bedroom. Slade and Jasin shoved the bed aside, then threw open a panel in the floor. The space inside was small and dark, but I quickly hopped down into it, my feet landing on packed dirt. My mates followed me, but Auric and Slade both had to duck down since they were too tall to comfortably fit inside. It was a tight squeeze with the five of us and the air had an old, moldy smell, but I prayed we wouldn't be stuck inside too long.

Brin and Noren helped lower the panel over us, trapping us inside, and then they shoved the bed back into place to cover it up. The cramped space instantly felt tighter, darker, and more suffocating. Auric gripped my hand tightly—he didn't like being in enclosed places like this. Slade, on the other hand, probably felt right at home.

Footsteps sounded, and then Leni's voice whispered, "Are they safe?"

"Yes," Brin said.

"The Jade Dragon just landed," Leni said. "He's searching the village for five people—one woman and four men. What will we do when he comes here?"

"We'll convince him there's no one here but us."

The Jade Dragon—here? I'd never seen Heldor in person before, even while living in the Earth Realm. He rarely left the capital of Soulspire or the Black Dragon's side, and acted as both her guardian and her right hand man. The fact that he was here likely meant that all the Dragons were looking for us—and they were desperate to find us.

Slade took my elbow and moved me over by a few inches, placing me in front of a small crack that allowed me to see some of what was going on above us. Brin and Leni were embracing, while Noren had left the room at some point.

For some time we waited. My mates shifted around me, visibly uncomfortable and anxious, but remaining quiet as the heaviness of the situation pressed upon us. I strained to hear anything from outside the house, worried I would catch a scream or a shout, but if there were any they were muffled. I silently prayed to the Gods that the Jade Dragon wouldn't find any reason to hurt the people of this town, who had shown us nothing but kind hospitality since we'd arrived. But with every second that passed, I grew more and more apprehensive.

Then I heard a low voice say, "What's behind this door?"

"A bedroom," Noren said. "Like I told you, there's no one here."

"Then why do I not believe you?"

The door to the bedroom banged open, and I couldn't help but jump. Brin and Leni let out surprised gasps from the bed above us, where they must have been waiting. Heavy footsteps shook the floorboards above us as the Jade Dragon entered the room in his human form. I couldn't see much of him, but I could tell he was a large, broad man from the way he moved. For a second I got a glimpse of dark, muscular skin decorated with tattoos, along with a shaved head.

"No one here?" Heldor asked. "Then who are these two?"

"My cousin and her girlfriend," Noren said with a hint of annoyance. He moved to the bed and shooed them off it. "What have I told you before? I don't care if your families don't approve, you can't use my room for your illicit encounters. Get out of here!"

"Sorry," Leni and Brin muttered, and I caught a glimpse of their mostly naked bodies as they bent down and grabbed their clothes off the floor. They must have planned this with Noren as a distraction.

They hurried out of the room, and Noren sighed. "I apologize, my lord. They'll find anywhere to sneak off together."

Heldor let out a grunt, walked the length of the room, and then turned on his heel and stormed out without another word. I let out a relieved breath, and I sensed my mates calming too. Although none of us would be able to relax completely until the Jade Dragon had left the town and everyone was safe.

I wasn't sure how long we waited until the bed over us was moved and the panel opened. Bright light blinded me for a moment, and then a hand reached down to help me climb out. Noren, Brin, and Leni waited for us at the top, and Leni threw her arms around her brother as he emerged.

"He's gone," Brin said.

396

"Did he hurt anyone?" Slade asked.

"No, he made a lot of threats and scared people pretty good, but that's it," Leni said. "I'm so glad he didn't find you."

"No one told him about us?" Reven asked, as he climbed out.

Noren puffed up his chest. "Of course not. We protect our own."

"That's very noble, especially since we've put you all at risk," Auric said.

"I never should have brought us here," Slade mumbled.

Reven brushed dust off himself. "Perhaps it's time for us to leave."

I reluctantly nodded. "Yes, with each minute we stay we put these people in greater danger."

"But we don't want you to go!" Leni said. "Having you here has been the best thing to happen to this boring town in years."

"We don't want to leave either," I said with a sigh. "But it's best for everyone if we go now, no matter how much we'd like to stay."

"Come with us," Brin said, taking Leni's hand.

Her face fell. "Gods, I want to, but my mother would never let me leave. Let alone my overbearing brother."

"I let my parents dictate my life for far too long and almost married a man I didn't love because of it." Brin glanced over at Auric apologetically, but he just shrugged. "It was hard to break free and do what I knew I needed, but it was worth it."

"She is not coming with us," Slade said. "End of discussion."

"See?" Leni said, rolling her eyes. "I'll never get out of this town."

We left Noren's house and returned to the inn to pack up our things. When we emerged, a large group waited for us with Yena at the front of it. She threw her arms around Slade, her eyes wet.

"Please be careful," she said, as she pulled back to look at him. "Come back to us once this is all done."

"I will, mother," Slade said.

Yena turned to me next and enveloped me in a hug, her arms soft and comforting. For a few seconds it reminded me of what it was like to have a mother of my own. "You be safe as well. Slade needs you."

I nodded, my throat closing up with emotion. Wrin handed us some food she had packed for us to eat on the road, while the rest of Slade's family hugged him and said their goodbyes. Many of them wished me well too, and the tightening in my chest grew worse with each goodbye. I'd had no idea I would come to care for this village so much, or that I would have such a hard time leaving it.

Leni rushed down the road with a bag thrown over her shoulder and a sword at her waist. "Don't leave without me!"

"Leni!" Yena cried out. "What do you think you are doing?"

"I'm going with them." She moved to Brin's side and stood tall. "I know you don't approve, mother, but I have to do this. I feel it in my bones. This is my destiny."

Yena pursed her lips, but then slowly nodded. "I always knew you would leave us. I only hoped I would have more time before then. Please be safe."

"Thank you, mother," Leni said, throwing her arms around Yena. "I promise I'll be careful."

"You're letting her go?" Slade asked, his face incredulous.

"I am," Yena said. "Leni is a grown woman and must make her own decisions, even if I will always worry for her. Please promise to watch over your sister, will you?"

"I'll do my best," he said with reluctance.

"More like I'll be the one watching over him," Leni said, nudging him in the side.

"We're lucky to have you," I said. "Are we ready?"

Jasin nodded, and he stepped back as his body began to change. There was no more hiding anymore, and the crowd gasped as Jasin shifted into a large red-scaled dragon before them. Some people shied back, fearing his new form, but others moved closer like they wanted a better look. Auric shifted into his own dragon form next, his golden wings bright and regal under the sun, and the crowd let out more impressed sounds.

I turned toward the crowd and raised my voice. "Thank you all for your hospitality. These past few days in your village have been some of the best of my life, and I'll cherish them always. We apologize for any danger we may have put you in, but we're impressed by your bravery and loyalty in the face of threat. We truly appreciate all you have done for us and hope to see you again one day."

I gave a short bow and then climbed onto Auric's back, while the crowd cheered and murmured behind us. Slade got on behind me, while the others clambered onto Jasin's back. Leni grinned from ear to ear as she sat in front of Brin, and I hoped we were doing the right thing by taking her with us. I didn't want any more lives on my hands, although I knew that was becoming inevitable. As the future Black Dragon, people would always follow me...and so would death.

24

KIRA

We stopped beside a small lake to camp for the evening, and I immediately missed the comforts of Clayridge, including a hot meal and a real bed. On the other hand, it eased my mind to be on the road again, knowing we were less of a threat to the villagers' safety now that we were gone.

After eating some of the food Wrin had packed for us, I retreated to the edge of the lake by myself and sat on the banks. Although I told myself I wanted time alone, I secretly hoped Enva would appear to me again, as she often did when I was troubled. The old woman could be infuriating and confusing, but she was also my grandmother and I wanted to get to know her better. But after a few minutes of staring at the smooth water she never arrived, and I gave up on that hope.

This time, it didn't surprise me when Reven emerged and sat beside me. No matter how much he tried to keep his distance and pretend he didn't care, it hadn't escaped my notice that when I was upset and ran off to be alone with my thoughts, it was usually Reven who sought me out first to comfort me. His form of comfort might be more unconventional than the other men's, but I appreciated his presence nonetheless.

"Are you ready for tomorrow?" he asked, as he stretched out his long legs beside me.

"As ready as I can be," I replied. "I'm mostly worried about Jasin and Auric, along with the others fighting beside them at Salt Creek Tower. Our role seems easier in comparison."

"They'll be fine. They're both strong fighters and quick thinkers."

399

I nodded, but I wouldn't feel completely at ease until the battle was over and all the people I cared about were out of danger. Except as soon as this battle was over, we were sure to face another one soon.

"What of you?" I asked. "If we get through this, we'll be visiting the Water Temple next. Are you ready for that?"

"I'm not going to run away, if that's what you're asking." His hand rested on my knee, then slid upward in a tantalizing way that made me hold my breath.

I turned toward him, pressing softly against his hard chest. "Does that mean you've accepted your role as the next Azure Dragon?"

"I have." His strong hands wrapped around my waist, and he pulled me onto his lap and against his chest. "I want to defeat the Dragons as much as you do. And I'll admit, the perks of the position are pretty appealing."

"What perks would those be?" I asked, suddenly breathless now that we were so close and his hands were on me. I let my fingers slide up to his neck, thrilled at being able to touch him in return.

"You." He crushed his lips against mine, kissing me hard. Weeks of pent-up desire between us was suddenly unleashed, and I tangled my fingers in his thick black hair as I kissed him back with the same passion. His tongue danced with mine, and his teeth nibbled along my lower lip. We'd kissed before, and done a lot more that one night, but this was different—because now he'd agreed to be my mate.

He pressed me down onto the grass, his body hovering over mine, and took the kiss deeper. He kissed me with his entire body and I clung to him, worried he'd back away, but he didn't this time. His hands drifted up to cup my breasts through my dress, and I let out a low moan. My legs spread to let him position himself between them, and I felt his hard bulge nudge against me. Our hips grinded together, creating a delicious friction that made me crave more.

When his hands moved down to my knees and began to slide up my bare legs, I was practically begging for him to continue. He found the slick wetness between my thighs and I looked up at him with hunger, longing to become one with him, but a part of me was surprised he wasn't stopping either.

"You don't want to wait until the Water Temple?" I asked.

"Why wait?" His mouth descended on mine again while he continued the slow grind of his hips against mine, except now he slipped a finger inside me too. "We both want this right now. Or should I stop?"

Unease mixed with my desire at his words, even though his touch made it hard for me to think. "The others all wanted to wait to bond at the temples because it would be more special that way."

"I hate to break it to you, but if you're waiting for this to be special between us, you'll be waiting forever." He lowered his head to kiss my neck as his fingers continued their delicious torment inside me. "This is just sex, that's all. But trust me, you'll enjoy it."

"Just sex?" I lightly pushed him off me and sat up. "But I thought you wanted to be my mate."

He dragged a hand through his black hair. "I agreed to sleep with you and become one of your Dragons. I'm here, I'm not leaving, and I'm committed to our cause. Isn't that enough?"

"No, it's not." I yanked my dress down to cover my legs, even though my body silently pleaded for him to continue what he'd been doing. "I want more."

"I don't have anything more to give." His eyes darkened, his mouth turning into a scowl. "I'm not capable of love, not like you want."

"I don't believe that."

"Believe it," he growled. "Long ago I watched everyone I loved die, and I'll never let myself feel that way again. Like I told you before, love makes you weak, and I won't be weak ever again."

"You're wrong. I've lost everyone too, but I haven't closed myself off because of it. Loving the others has made me stronger—and not just with magic. The other men give me confidence and courage, wisdom and empathy, and the support I need to get through all of this. The only way we'll survive the upcoming battles is with love." I reached for him again. "I'd like to love you too, Reven. Just let me in."

"It's never going to happen. You need to get that into your head already." He got up and walked away, leaving me alone and cold beside the lake with only the stars overhead for company.

A deep sadness settled over me at the thought that Reven would never love me as much as I loved him, but there was nothing I could do about it. I couldn't force his heart to let me in, and I didn't want any other man as my mate. We were stuck together, and I'd have to accept that things between us would never be exactly as I wanted. Whatever Reven offered would have to be enough…even if I would want more for the rest of my days.

25

KIRA

The next day we flew north into the mountains toward the Earth Temple. It was located on top of Frostmount, the tallest point in the realm, although we weren't going there, not exactly. We were meeting Parin on another mountain in a cave that he said would lead us into the temple without anyone noticing. As his mother was once the High Priestess, I was inclined to believe him, even though it was hard to trust a relative stranger with something this important. But Slade seemed to trust Parin, even if he didn't like him, and I trusted Slade.

The air grew colder and colder as we approached the snow-covered mountains, and I pulled my fur-lined hood over my head. We'd bought cold weather clothing and supplies during our time in Clayridge, but I wasn't sure anything could fight off the chill here.

Auric and Jasin were careful to fly high in the clouds, and cautious when they came down to land beside the cave entrance, which was covered in frost. They shifted as soon as we were off their backs, and only then did Parin emerge from the shadows.

"I'm not sure it will ever get any less terrifying seeing two dragons flying toward me, even if I know they're my allies," Parin said, shaking his head. "But I'm glad you made it."

"Thank you for meeting us here," I said. Parin was putting his own life in danger by guiding us through these tunnels, but he'd insisted on coming with us, even though it meant leaving his people to fight without him. Faya would be leading the battle at Salt Creek Tower, and I knew he must be worried about her, just as I worried about my mates.

"Are your troops in position?" Jasin asked.

"They are," Parin said. "Everything is ready. They're simply waiting for you to join them."

"Then this is where we go our separate ways," Auric said, turning to me. He drew me in for a tight hug, then kissed me softly on the lips. "Be careful, Kira."

"You too." My heart clenched, knowing I was sending two of my mates into danger, and that I wouldn't be there to protect them. They probably felt the same about leaving me.

Jasin grabbed me in his warm embrace next, kissing me hard. "I'll look after Auric. Don't worry."

"Thank you. I know he'll look out for you too." I reached out and grabbed both their hands, connecting us again and feeling the bond surge between the three of us. "I love you both."

My two mates replied that they loved me too, and after more kisses they finally stepped back. I hugged Brin next, making her promise to stay safe, and overheard Slade talking to his sister in a low voice.

"You don't have to fight," he said. "It's not too late to back out."

"I want to fight," Leni said, standing taller.

He hugged her tight and seemed reluctant to let her go. Then he turned back to Jasin and Auric. "Take care of my sister for me."

"We will, I promise," Jasin said.

"As if she were our own blood," Auric promised.

As the goodbyes finished, I retreated to stand between Slade and Reven. Slade's hand rested on my lower back as worry made me bite my lower lip, and together we watched as Jasin and Auric returned to their glorious dragon forms. With a few flaps of their wings they were in the air again, and then they were gone.

"They'll be fine," Reven said. We'd avoided each other since last night, and I still felt a pang of sadness when I remembered what had happened, but I had to get past that now.

"I hope so." With a sigh, I turned toward the cave. According to Parin we had a long hike ahead of us through the icy tunnels, and standing here worrying about the others wouldn't accomplish anything.

"Follow me," Parin said, as he led us into the darkness.

26

AURIC

After hours of flying we reached the rendezvous point, a cave near Salt Creek Tower where the Resistance had gathered. Brin and Leni hopped off and removed the supplies from our backs, and then we shifted into our human forms again. I popped my shoulders, which were always a bit stiff after using my wings, while the others checked their weapons. Even though I was likely to remain a dragon for much of the battle, I strapped on my own long, curved daggers, a gift from my father that had been in our family for centuries, passed down from the brother of the first Golden Dragon.

A somber mood had settled over all of us, both from leaving Kira and the others behind, along with the upcoming battle we were about to face. Brin and Leni laced their hands together and spoke in quiet voices, though I had no doubt they'd be ready to fight. Brin was an excellent warrior, and I'd heard she'd been helping Leni train too. If Leni was half as dangerous as her brother, she'd be a formidable force.

"The Earth Realm sure likes its caves," Jasin muttered, as he strode toward the entrance. Brin and Leni followed a few steps behind him.

I kept pace with him. "Perhaps that's why the Resistance has the largest presence here. Easier to hide from the Dragons."

Jasin shrugged, and we stepped inside the damp, dark cave. As my eyes adjusted to the dim light, I took in the sight of dozens of warriors gathered, with more stretching back into tunnels and out of view. Parin had promised us a hundred men and women, armed with bows, axes, swords, and more.

Faya pushed her way to the front of the crowd. Last time I'd seen her she'd worn slim, simple dresses, but now she was geared for combat in silver armor with a large sword strapped to her back. After visiting the quiet town she'd grown up in, I could see why she had felt stifled there.

"We're ready to begin moving out," she said. "At your command, we'll begin the attack."

We quickly went over the plan again, clarifying a few things, while Jasin and I chugged water and shoved food into our mouths for energy. Once we were ready, we moved outside of the cave, while the fighters began to head toward the fort.

I turned toward Jasin and clasped his hand in my own. "Good luck today, my friend."

"You too." He drew me in for a quick embrace, and we gave each other a tight squeeze. "I've got your back out there."

"And I've got yours."

As we pulled apart, I keenly felt the connection between us, even without Kira here. And from the way he met my eyes, I knew he felt it too.

I turned to Brin next, then wrapped her in a close hug. My oldest friend, my former fiancé, and now my close companion on this strange journey. I had no idea if this thing with her and Leni would work out, but I was happy she'd found someone who made her smile. "Take care of yourself, okay?"

"I always do," she said with a wry grin. "Don't get yourself killed either."

I chuckled softly. "I'll do my best."

I gave Leni a nod, and then the two women joined the ranks of the other warriors. I'd be watching for them from above, trying to keep them safe, and I knew Jasin would be doing the same.

I became a dragon once more, feeling my body shift and grow, along with the rush of power that came from the transformation. My skin became scales, my hands became talons, and my teeth became fangs. Great, golden wings spread from my body, and with a mighty roar I launched into the air, with Jasin at my side.

Together we flew toward Salt Creek Tower to begin the assault, while the Resistance's fighters surged forward. According to Faya, she'd already sent a few men and women to sneak into the fort itself, and they would open the gate for us. If they failed, Jasin and I would have to get it down somehow.

The fort came into view, consisting of a few stone buildings with a large wall around it surrounded by a narrow moat. Onyx Army soldiers in their black armor lined the top of the wall, and they let out a shout when they saw us coming. Our fighters spread out in front of the wall, while the soldiers inside the fort prepared for battle.

Jasin gave me a nod, smoke already coming from his nostrils, and then flew forward. I hung back and circled low over the Resistance fighters. We'd decided Jasin would lead the offensive, focusing on taking out as many of the soldiers in the fort as possible, while I'd help defend our own people. Partly because his magic was better suited for an attack, and partly because I'd never been in a battle like this before, while Jasin had seen plenty of them. I was no stranger to combat, but warfare was an entirely new experience for me.

Jasin glided over the fort and let out a loud, terrifying roar that hit me all the way in my bones. I opened my mouth and released one of my own in response, signaling the attack was to begin—and hopefully sending fear into our enemies.

The heavy metal gate at the front of the fort opened, and our fighters surged forward into the keep with a loud cry. At the same time, Jasin unleashed a stream of red hot fire, taking out a line of soldiers on the wall. The ones he missed launched arrows at our people, but with a blast of air I sent them flying back to the archers.

Below us, people met in battle with a clash of swords and the spilling of blood. I caught sight of Brin and Leni fighting back to back, cutting down their opponents with ease. When a man leveled a spear at them, I dove down and caught it in my talons, then drove it through his chest. My tail whipped around, knocking two other soldiers down, and I began slashing with talons and teeth, while blasting out air strong enough to knock others back.

I don't know how long this continued, or how many we killed or lost in combat. My scales and claws grew slick with blood, but I kept fighting while Jasin continued to set the fort on fire all around us. And then I heard a terrible screech overhead that stopped me in my tracks.

I glanced up to see two dragons swooping down to oppose us, one with blood-red scales and the other's the deepest green. Just as I'd expected—Sark, the Crimson Dragon, and Heldor, the Jade Dragon. The ones who'd destroyed Kira's town with lava, earthquakes, and fire. And now we had to hold them off as long as possible so Kira and Slade could finish the bonding.

As I flew up to meet the other dragons in combat, I opened myself to my bond with Kira and sent her a single, frantic feeling: *Go!*

27

KIRA

I pulled my fur cloak tighter around myself, wishing I'd brought even warmer clothes. Only the flame rising from my palm emitted any warmth—or light—inside the dark, frosty cave.

We'd been going uphill in the tunnel for what seemed like hours, although it was impossible to tell. The walls were unnaturally smooth, like in the Resistance base, but there were few other signs that anyone had been this way before and no way to tell if we were going in the right direction. Parin led us forward and claimed to know where he was going, and Slade pressed his hand to the rock and then nodded, but it was still eerie facing step after step of nothing but cold, dark stone.

"We're almost there," Parin said, an eternity later. "We should stop here until we get the signal."

I sank against the wall, my body eager to take a break. There was nothing to do now but wait and pray our plan worked. I closed my eyes and reached for Jasin and Auric to reassure myself they were all right, but I found a wild mix of emotions that threatened to overwhelm me. They were still alive, and I had to accept that that was enough for now.

"How much farther to the temple?" Reven asked.

"Not far now." Parin leaned against the side of the tunnel opposite me, his face grim. "I forgot to mention…we received a report that the Water Temple has been destroyed by the Dragons too. There's nothing left. I'm sorry."

I drew in a deep breath and nodded. The news made my heart sink, but I couldn't focus on that now. I'd known getting to the Water Temple would be difficult and it had just become even more impossible, but we had to face one challenge at a time. Besides, I couldn't even think about bonding with Reven at the moment. I was still too bruised after last night. "Thanks for letting me know."

We sipped water and ate some of the food we'd brought with us while we waited. Slade paced back and forth, while Reven became so still I almost wondered if he was asleep. I tried not to fret over how the others were faring in their battle, but it was difficult.

Suddenly Auric's presence filled my mind and I felt him urging me to move, to go, to hurry. I scrambled to my feet. "I got the signal!"

We jumped back into action, our bodies recovered after the break, and continued forward with Parin at the lead. The plan had worked, but we had to hurry since we didn't know how long the Resistance could keep the Dragons away. Eventually they would realize this was a distraction and come back to stop us. We needed to be finished by then.

Parin stopped in front of a spot in the wall that looked like it had caved in at some point. Water flowed through the cracks in the rocks in a steady trickle, pooling around our feet. "The temple is through here, but I've never seen this water before."

"I can move the rocks," Slade said, stepping forward.

"Wait." Reven crouched down, dipped his finger into the water, and stared at the cracks where it was coming from. When he straightened up, he said, "The room on the other side has been flooded. When you open it up, I'll divert the water away."

"The Azure Dragon must have done this to keep us out," Parin mumbled.

"Most likely," Slade said.

Reven instructed us to stand to the side with our backs against the stone, and then nodded at Slade. The rocks began to slide away from the wall, slowly at first, allowing larger bursts of water to break through. Soon they began to tumble down much faster, and a huge wall of water rushed out. Reven raised his hands and stopped the water from hitting us, then sent it flowing through the tunnel where we'd already been. It filled the entire passage, a great torrent racing down the mountain like it was desperate to escape. Slade formed the rocks into a small dam, helping Reven block the water from hitting us as it roared by.

Eventually the flood slowed to a mere trickle, and it was safe enough through the gap Slade had made. It opened to a large cavern with shining wet stone and rocks that dripped cold water in a steady pattern. I raised the flames I'd summoned and gaped as the light caught on hundreds of sparkling crystals built into the walls, which shimmered all around us in every color of the rainbow. A large jade green dragon statue had toppled over in the middle of the room, it's head cracked and one of the wings shattered.

"This is the Earth Temple," Parin said, bowing his head. "Or it was."

"It's beautiful," I whispered, as I stepped forward and touched one of the glittering jewels. Even with evidence of the Dragons' destruction here and the missing priests, I could feel the magic of the temple all around me.

"This is where they killed my mother, along with her priests." Parin ran his hand along the wing of the dragon statue as we took it all in.

"Including your father?" I asked softly.

"No, he died a few years ago. Perhaps that is a blessing."

"We'll honor their sacrifice by completing our duty to the Earth God," Slade said.

Parin nodded and led us forward. Our boots squished and splashed in the leftover puddles as we walked around the rubble and debris. He took us through another tunnel, leading to a splintered, soaked door. "The bonding chamber is through here. I'm sorry it's not in better condition."

I peered through the crack in the door at the room inside. "It's not the most romantic place, but it'll do."

"We'll wait outside and stand guard," Reven said.

While they retreated back to the main part of the temple, Slade opened the broken door with a loud creak. My heart probably should have sank at the sight of the remains of the bed, which had been completely torn apart and turned to splinters, or the knowledge that we had to rush through this. But I was finally going to bond with Slade, and I couldn't help the small smile on my lips as I turned toward him. "Are you ready?"

He reached out and took my hand. "I am."

We stepped inside together and surveyed the destruction. It was hard to tell what furniture had once been in the room since all that remained was wreckage. The only thing that still stood was a gray marble table against one wall. Slade led me to it, while his magic slammed the door shut behind us.

Anticipation made my desire and excitement even stronger, and when he took me in his arms and kissed me, my heart leaped. He nudged me back until my behind hit the edge of the table, and then he eased me up onto the edge of the cool stone. The position lifted me up higher, allowing me to kiss him easier while my arms circled his neck. My knees spread wide and he moved between them, his hard, muscular length pressed against me.

"I wish we didn't have to rush," he said, as his hands slid down to my breasts, slowly rubbing my nipples through the fabric of my dress. "I wanted to go slow and take all night learning your body and what makes you sigh. This will be the first time I've made love to a woman in many years and I'd hoped to savor it, especially since it's you."

His words sent a rush of warmth to my core as I imagined all the things we would do together. "Next time we'll take as long as you want, I promise."

"Yes," he said, with hunger in his eyes. "Next time."

His mouth descended on mine again and I pressed against him, my body throbbing with desire. Soft lips trailed over my earlobe and down my neck to my collarbone, nuzzling and tasting, and I closed my eyes with a sigh. But then I felt Auric and Jasin reaching for each other's magic through the bond, their emotions a mix of frenzy, fear, and determination, and I knew we had to hurry. Slade's seductive touch made me want to take my time too, but we couldn't forget that others were fighting and dying for us to have this moment.

I reached for Slade's shirt and lifted it over his head, revealing his dark, muscular chest. I drank in the sight of the sculpted lines of his body, all the smooth planes and hard ridges just begging for my touch. When I reached out and lightly ran my hand along those muscles he let out a ragged breath, and then claimed my mouth again. While we kissed, his fingers caressed down my hips and gripped the fabric of my dress, then inched it up my legs. My breath hitched with excitement, but then he pulled back and met my eyes.

"There's something I need to say first." His hands slid along my bare thighs as he spoke, his deep, sensual voice wrapping around me like a blanket. "I gave away my heart once and had it broken. I never thought I would ever love again, and didn't want to even try. And then I met you…" He drew in a breath, his fingers tightening on my skin. "I didn't want to love you either. I tried to resist you for so long. But there was no use. I fell for you anyway." His head bent, his brow pressing against mine. "I love you, Kira."

I brushed my fingers against his jaw, while my heart felt like it would burst out of my chest. "I love you too, Slade."

"You somehow mended my heart and showed me it was possible to love again. Even if the Gods didn't demand I spend my life with you, I would do it anyway." He dropped to his knees in front of me. "I'm yours."

He was the biggest and strongest of my mates. He could crush me both with his magic or without it. And now he was kneeling in front of me. There was nothing sexier than seeing such a powerful man on his knees before me, and the space between my legs softly ached with need.

He coaxed my thighs to spread wider for him, his green eyes moving to gaze at the place that throbbed for his touch, and I knew what he planned to do.

Even as my body said *oh please yes*, I rested a hand on his shoulder to stop him. "We don't have time."

"I don't care. I'm going to taste you, even if only for a moment. I've been thinking of little else for days."

Stubborn man. I knew I should tell him no, that we needed to hurry, but I wanted his mouth on me, that lush, full mouth I'd been tempted by since we'd met. When his head dipped down and I felt the roughness of his beard against my inner thighs, all my protests were silenced. I forgot about everything except his mouth as it pressed against me and his tongue as it stroked me. I leaned back, my hands planted on the table, as he hooked my legs over his shoulders and began to feast upon me.

My eyes fluttered closed, my breathing grew rough, and every nerve in my body seemed to burst into song. With each firm stroke of his tongue and soft touch of his lips I lost myself even more. Slade loved me, he truly loved me, and he showed me over and over how devoted he was to me. *Me*, not his duty to the Earth God or as the next Jade Dragon, just me. And I could finally admit how much I loved him too.

I cried out, my legs trembling, as the orgasm shook through me like an earthquake. Slade held my hips in place as he wrung every last drop of pleasure out of me. Only then did he release me and straighten up again —and when our eyes met I knew it was time for him to truly claim me.

28

JASIN

All around us the battle raged, but Auric and I focused on the two Dragons in front of us. We'd been dodging blows and throwing magic for the last few minutes, keeping them distracted as best we could while our people fought below us. As long as we kept the Dragons busy, Kira and Slade would be able to bond. I just hoped they were quick about it.

Sark spat a ball of fire at Auric, and I pressed my wings close and dove to block it. The flames struck my scaled chest and I absorbed the magic into my own body, then let out a loud roar in response. I briefly felt Auric's gratitude through the bond, before Heldor collided with me. He was the largest dragon I'd ever seen, and he slammed us both to the ground with his massive strength. We slid through the dirt, knocking soldiers back with our wings and tails, before smashing into the stone wall surrounding the fort. I tore at him with my talons and fangs, then managed to roll out from under his grasp. I backed up and let out a stream of fire from my mouth, but he yanked rocks from the wall to block my magic.

The ground underneath me shook and tore open, and I leaped into the sky again, where Sark and Auric were battling. I expected the Jade Dragon to follow me, but instead he stomped his feet and released a deep roar that made the soldiers around him balk. Lava began to spew from the newly formed crack in the ground, spraying the men and women nearby—both our fighters and the enemy's. Heldor didn't seem to care who he hit, and lava began to flow in a massive wave, threatening to cut down every person in its path, regardless of who they fought for.

"You'll kill your own soldiers!" I called out.

Heldor ignored me and continued on, making the crack wider to take up the length of the entire courtyard. People screamed and ran, the battle momentarily forgotten as they tried to escape the red hot magma, but some of them were too slow in their armor and were pulled down and consumed. How could he do this to his own people, the ones he'd come out here to defend? Did he care nothing at all for their lives?

I fought back the lava and the flames as best I could, trying to give people time to escape, but it wasn't enough. We had to stop the Dragons.

I reached for Auric through the bond, while glancing up at his shining form. He darted above me, performing whip-fast acrobatics in the air to avoid Sark's flames. Through our many hours of training we'd gotten a lot better at this, and had learned that proximity was most important, but visual contact helped too. I felt Auric acknowledge me and mentally clasp my hands. His magic mingled with mine, and I focused on Heldor and released it.

A giant lightning bolt shot from the clouds and struck the Jade Dragon on his large scaled head, and he staggered back like he was dazed. Auric threw some lightning at Sark above me too, although the other dragon was able to dodge the blast. Without Isen nearby, Sark would be unable to create lightning of his own, and we kept up the assault, paying him back for the attack at the Air Temple.

I heard Faya's voice call out for a retreat, and caught sight of Brin staggering toward the gate with one arm around Leni. Lava blocked their path, and I used my magic to remove the heat from it, turning it to stone. They rushed over it and out of the fort, hopefully on their way to safety.

Heldor recovered from the lightning bolt and threw more rocks at me, which I dodged. Mostly. One huge boulder struck my left wing, clipping it and shooting pain through my shoulder. I swore under my breath and leaped into the air, but each beat of my wings was agony.

I crashed back down to the ground and Heldor let out a deep, throaty laugh as he approached. Auric dropped down in front of him, blocking my body with his own, and launched another bolt of lightning at Heldor. It struck him in the chest, knocking him back, and the huge green dragon slumped to the ground.

"Jasin, are you injured?" Auric asked.

I stood up and shook myself off, but pain shot through me. "I'll be all right. I'm not sure I can fly though. I'll need Kira to heal me later."

A harsh shriek filled the air, and Auric and I both looked up as Isen, the Golden Dragon, swooped down toward us. Where had he come from? And could we really defend against three dragons, especially now that I was injured? I bared my teeth and readied my wings. We didn't have a choice but to fight.

I sent fire up at Isen, but he dodged easily, his nimble form darting through the sky. A tornado formed over us, whipping up all the debris on the ground, and Auric flew up to stop it. I bit back the pain and dodged the swirling, rushing winds before they surrounded me, but my injured wing slowed me down and prevented me from taking off. I managed to knock a soldier in black armor out of the way with my tail before he was caught up in the tornado, just before it dissipated.

The air around us cleared—and that's when I realized Sark and Heldor were both gone.

29

KIRA

Slade quickly removed my clothes and tossed them aside, then gazed at me with hungry eyes. I sat on the edge of the table, completely bared to him, while the echoes of pleasure made my body loose and limp. Yet I still craved more.

"I've never wanted any woman the way I want you," he said, as he dropped his trousers to the floor. I got a glimpse of his huge, hard cock before he moved between my thighs and nudged it against my core. Later I would explore every inch of him in great detail with my hands and my mouth, but for now I needed him inside me. I wrapped my arms around his neck and pulled him closer, finding his mouth again while his long length entered me.

He was big, almost too big, but I didn't want him to stop. My hips strained toward him, begging for more, but once he was fully inside he paused. He was as hard as the marble under me, pulsing with strength and need, and I thought I would die if he didn't move soon.

I caressed the smooth slope of his back down to the rounded curve of his behind, then gripped him tight, pulling him deeper inside. "Slade, please."

At my words, he let out a ragged breath and unleashed the desire that he'd kept locked inside so long. He pushed me down so I lay flat against the cool stone table, his strong hands circling my waist, and then he began to pump into me with sure, steady strokes. I gasped and lifted my hips in time to his movements, while he gazed down at me with a look of pure, ravenous lust.

My legs wrapped around Slade's hips as he stood over me, my breasts rocking with each deep glide of his cock. He took me thoroughly, possessing me completely, making me his woman with every thrust.

When he arched over me to take one of my nipples in his mouth, I couldn't help but cry out. He thrust faster, deeper, his movements becoming frantic, and I tangled my fingers in his thick hair and gave myself up to him. Release found me first and I gasped as the sensations crashed over me, my body tightening around him. He let out a low groan as he pounded into me harder, and the room around us began to tremble. I clung to Slade's shoulders, but his skin had turned to stone, and I realized with a start that mine had too. But he didn't stop, and pleasure quaked through us both without end.

When he finally calmed, our skin returned to normal and the room stilled. Slade relaxed on top of me, and I enjoyed the feel of his strong body in my arms, pressing down on me. His lips melted against mine and love shimmered between us like one of the crystals on the walls.

"I wish I could hold you like this for hours and fall asleep with you in my arms," Slade said, as he reluctantly released me. "But we should probably leave the temple in case the Dragons return soon."

I sighed as reality came crashing back down, and all my worries about my other mates returned. "You're right, although the Earth God should come speak with us first. The other ones did, at least."

"Even more reason for us to dress then," he said, grabbing his trousers off the floor.

As soon as we'd donned our clothes, the temple began to rumble again, like it had when the bonding had completed. Only now it grew more intense, to the point where I had to hold onto the table to steady myself.

Suddenly the floor split open in front of us, and Slade rested a hand on my shoulder as if to protect me. A huge talon appeared at the edge of the crack, and then a giant dragon clawed his way out of the crevice. His body was made entirely of crystal, like the ones embedded in the walls, and when he moved his scales shifted colors like a rainbow shining across his skin. I'd never seen anything more beautiful before.

The Earth God was so large that Slade and I had to press against the wall behind us to have any space at all. His wings arched behind his back and we dropped to our knees before him as his sheer physical power and strength filled the room. I'd met two Gods before, but I'd never lost that sense of awe and wonder when confronting one.

He took us in with eyes that seemed to be made of the blackest opals, while his huge tail whipped about, tossing stones and splintered wood aside. "My avatar and my descendant. Your bonding pleases me."

Slade bowed his head. "We are your humble servants, my lord."

The crystal dragon's eyes lifted and took in the room, then seemed to see beyond it into the main temple. He let out a growl that made the mountain quake, and his tail smashed harder against the ground. "Those traitorous Dragons have destroyed my temple and murdered my priests. They must be overthrown." Those deep, black eyes focused on us again. "You must bring balance to the world."

"We're trying," I said. "But we don't know how to defeat the others. We're not strong enough yet."

"You will grow stronger the closer you become to your mates," the Earth God said. "But you already knew this."

I nodded, relieved to hear that my instinct in bringing both Auric and Jasin into my bed together was the right one. The two of them wouldn't be a problem, but the other two would be more of a challenge. I felt closer to Slade than ever before, but I wasn't sure if he would ever agree to truly share me with the others. And Reven had made it clear he only wanted a physical relationship, nothing more.

The Earth God lowered himself to the ground, stretching his silvery talons out before him like a lazy, fat cat. "The Black Dragon and her mates are no longer as close as they once were. They are fractured and splintered. Doubt and distance threaten to divide them. If you and your Dragons become a strong, cohesive group, you will become more powerful than they are."

Easier said than done, but I would do my best to bring them all together. Of course, that only solved one of our problems. "But the Black Dragon is immortal and has the power of the Spirit Goddess, plus the magic of all of her mates. How can we stop her?"

"You must defeat each of her mates first. Once you do, she will lose their powers and strengths. Only then will she be weak enough to overcome."

That meant we'd have to take them down one by one before facing her, in order to stand a chance. My stomach twisted at the idea, and it took me a second to realize it was because it meant killing both of my parents in the process. I despised them and everything they did, but they were still my blood. "My father...do you know who he is?"

"No, but I can tell you he is not my Dragon. It must be one of the others."

My heart sank. I'd been hoping the Earth God could tell me who he was, or at least confirm he wasn't the Crimson Dragon. Sark had killed the people who had raised me, and if he was my true father, I wasn't sure how I would ever be able to live with that.

"You must continue your voyage now," the Earth God said, as he rose to his feet and shook out his wings. "Remember that the fate of the world journeys with you, as do the Gods' blessings."

"Thank you for your wisdom," Slade said. "And for choosing me to be your Dragon."

The Earth God gave us a nod, and then his wings tucked tight and he dove straight into the crevice. It closed up behind him, leaving no trace he was ever there. Slade and I let out a collective held breath—and then we heard a shout from the other room.

Slade pressed his hand against the nearest wall and closed his eyes, and I knew he must be spreading his senses throughout the cave as he'd done before.

His eyes snapped open. "The Jade Dragon is here."

30

REVEN

I was leaning against the fallen statue of the Earth God and trying to ignore the way the mountain kept shaking, when something made me reach for my twin swords. A flicker of movement. A change in the air. A sense that danger was coming.

I'd stayed alive this long by trusting my instincts, and I wasn't about to stop now. I gestured at Parin, who crouched down in the debris while I moved into the shadow of the dragon statue.

Three men walked inside, and I sensed their power immediately. Sark, with hair so pale it was almost white, Heldor, as large and broad as Slade except covered in tattoos, and a third man I'd seen only once before in his human form—Doran, the Azure Dragon. He had blond hair hanging past his shoulders and a matching beard, with skin that spoke of many hours under the sun. All three of them were in their human forms, probably because the cave entrance was too small for them to get through as dragons. Each was dressed in black leather fit for fighting or traveling, but none carried weapons.

"We're too late," Doran said, his voice icy cold. "They've already left."

Heldor shook his head. "No, I sensed the earth moving. They must still be here."

"If they are, they won't be leaving," Sark growled.

My hands tightened on the hilt of my swords at his voice, but I couldn't let my rage or my need for vengeance consume me. I wasn't sure if Kira and Slade were finished or not, but I had to hold these three off as long as I could—and Parin would likely be no help. It was just me, a former assassin with a bit of magic, against three immortal Dragons. I didn't like these odds.

"Fine, let's look around," Doran said, sounding bored.

I waited until the three of them split apart, then I crept into position. As Doran passed by, I lunged out with my sword—but he quickly dodged it. He spun around, a blade made of ice forming in his hands, and blocked my next blow with it.

"Found one," he called out to the others.

We struck and parried, beginning a complicated dance of swords, while the others moved closer. Sark let loose a blast of fire at me, but I ducked under it, while Heldor grabbed rocks leftover from the temple's destruction and hurled them at me. I threw up a wall of ice to block them, then continued my assault on the man I would soon replace. Doran moved with the grace of a seasoned fighter and was as fast as I was, providing me a challenge. If it were just the two of us I thought I could probably best him, but all three of them? Even I wasn't that good.

I sensed Sark moving behind me, and realized I was surrounded. But then Parin let out a shout as he lunged from the corner and struck Sark with his sword from behind. Sark let out a roar and grabbed Parin by the neck, instantly lighting him on fire. The man's horrifying screams echoed throughout the cave, and I summoned water to douse him, but it only dulled Sark's flames for a moment before they sprang up again. With Doran and Heldor both attacking me, and Sark's hand around Parin's throat, the man didn't stand a chance.

But then Sark was knocked back by a strong blast of air, which also snuffed out the fire covering Parin's body. Kira and Slade stood at the side of the cave, and they didn't waste any time joining the fight. Slade grabbed some of the boulders around the room and sent them to knock Doran down, freeing me to throw knives of ice at Heldor. Three against three—I liked those odds a lot better.

Magic flew and swords flashed as the fight broke out across the ruined temple. Kira faced Sark down with a look of pure hatred in her eyes, throwing both air and rocks at him. At least the bonding was completed in time. Now all we had to do was escape.

A section of the cave suddenly broke apart and crashed down on top of me. Slade turned and caught it in time, stopping Heldor's magic with his own. Lava erupted in front of Sark at the same moment, making Kira step back with a gasp. Doran moved behind her, his movements swift and decisive, and caught her arm. He pressed something across her mouth and nose, a cloth of some sort. From my days as an assassin I knew it had to be some sort of poison or intoxicant. Probably nightwillow oil, which could knock a grown man out in seconds—I'd used it before to incapacitate people I had no interest in killing.

Kira tried to fight, but she was caught off guard and trapped between Sark and Doran. I called out and lunged toward her, but lava sprang up all around me and Slade, keeping us away. She struggled for a few seconds while Slade and I desperately tried to put out the molten lava flowing around us, and then her body went limp. She collapsed against Doran, and there was nothing we could do to stop it.

The Azure Dragon swooped Kira into his arms and began walking out of the cave with her. Sark and Heldor turned toward us to make sure we couldn't follow, and the lava suddenly leaped up—directly at Slade.

I knocked him out of the way, throwing up a wall of ice at the same time. Some of the lava still got through and splashed against my side, making me hiss from the burning pain. My magic put it out, but the damage was already done.

Sark turned and followed after Doran, leaving only Heldor behind. I clutched my burning side and turned to face the remaining Dragon, while calling out to Slade, who was getting to his feet.

"Go!" I said. "You're the only one who can save Kira now!"

Slade hesitated, glancing between me and Heldor, before nodding. His magic would be useless against Heldor anyway, and he could fly and I couldn't. We both knew this was what had to be done.

Slade created a bridge of rocks over the lava and dashed across them, while Heldor made the cave around me quake. Rocks and crystals fell as Slade ran, and I threw bolts of ice at Heldor to distract him. As Slade reached the cave's exit, he glanced back one more time at me. I could see from his eyes that the decision haunted him, but Kira was more important than any of us. He knew this as well as I did, and he finally turned and ran down the tunnel, leaving me to my fate.

It was just me and Heldor now, and if these were my last moments alive, I wasn't going out without a fight. I reached deep inside myself, finding that connection to the Water God I'd once tried so hard to escape from, and let it free. Cold water rained down from the roof of the cave, turning the lava to sizzling black stone. As Heldor tried to go after Slade, I closed up the cave entrance with a wall of thick, glimmering ice.

"Not so fast," I said.

The Jade Dragon turned back to me, his face hard. I limped forward, shooting shards of frost his way, but he knocked them all aside. He gestured and the ceiling above me ripped apart and came tumbling down. I threw up some ice to stop it, but knew it wouldn't be enough, not when the entire cave began to break apart over me.

The air grew thick with dirt and stone as it rained down on me, and even my strongest magic couldn't stop an entire mountain from collapsing on my head. No matter how I tried to hold up the stones above me, they soon surrounded me, striking me and rendering me immobile.

As the world around me went dark, my last thought was that I should have told Kira how I truly felt about her—and now I'd never have that chance.

31

SLADE

I rushed through the cave after Kira, my heart pounding and my chest tight. I couldn't lose her, not when I'd only just bonded with her. She was everything to me, even if it had taken me far too long to realize it, and I'd be damned if I was going to let the Dragons steal her away.

When I reached the cave's entrance, scalding hot air burned my skin. Steam, I realized, as I stumbled back. Created by Sark and Doran together, no doubt as a way to slow me down. Through the foggy haze I saw the two Dragons flying high, up into the clouds, already a good distance away—taking Kira with them.

I let out a guttural roar as my body began to shift and change, growing larger and forming scales, forming wings and a tail. Power and strength filled me like nothing before, and I felt as though I could take on anything and survive. Like two other Dragons.

I forced my way back out into the burning steam, my scales offering some protection from the scalding heat, and when I reached the edge I stretched out my wings. I pictured Jasin and Auric flying and tried to copy what they'd done, but couldn't lift off the ground. I drew in another boiling breath of hot, humid air, and tried again. Why wasn't this working? Auric had been able to fly immediately, and Jasin had picked it up almost as fast. I didn't understand what I was doing wrong. And with every second, Kira got farther away.

I tried everything I could think of to fly, moving my wings in all sorts of different ways, but the best I got was a foot or two up before my huge body dragged me back down. It was like my wings weren't strong enough to carry me. Frustration made me growl and roar, my tail slamming into the earth and sending rocks flying, but it was useless. I'd never catch her at this rate.

The mountain began to cave in behind me, the ground under me quaking, and then a hole burst open in the side of it. The Jade Dragon flew out of it, soaring over me, and then headed up into the clouds. I tried once more to follow him, with no success. And behind me, the mountain continued to collapse—with Reven still inside it.

I'd left him behind, knowing it might mean his doom, and I hadn't even been able to go after Kira. Indecision and frustration tore at me. I hated giving up on Kira, but I had no way of following after her. My wings were useless, and I knew this failure would haunt me forever, but there was still something I could do to save Kira's last mate.

I let out one final, angry roar and turned back toward the mountain to save Reven.

Auric and Jasin arrived while I was using my last reserves of magic to uncover the rubble that had crushed Reven. By now I didn't hold onto any hope that he was still alive, but I had to do something. Especially since Kira was gone, and my dragon form had failed me when I'd tried to go after her. Parin was dead too, his skin blackened and charred from Sark's flames. I'd held no love for the man, especially after he'd taken the first woman I'd loved, but I'd respected him and his cause. None of that mattered now though. I'd failed him too.

"What happened to you?" Jasin asked, noticing my burnt skin, a gift from the steam Sark and Doran had left behind. Jasin didn't look much better though—he clutched his arm and walked stiffly, as if he was injured. "And where's Kira?"

Auric was only a step behind Jasin. "Is she all right? Did you complete the bonding?"

I sat back on my heels and wiped dirty sweat off my brow. "She's gone. The Dragons took her."

Jasin's eyes practically bulged out of his head. "What do you mean, gone?"

I bowed my head, the shame and guilt overpowering me. "I couldn't stop them."

The others were silent as my words sank in. Jasin began to pace, tearing at his auburn hair like he was possessed, while Auric stared at the wall for so long it started to worry me.

"If they kidnapped her then they want her alive," Auric finally said. "We still have time to rescue her."

Jasin stopped pacing. "Right. We'll be able to find her through the bond. Although I don't feel anything right now."

I sat back on my heels. "They did something to Kira. Knocked her out with something. Maybe that's why."

"Maybe," Auric said, and then glanced around. "Where's Reven?"

I gestured to the rubble in front of me. "I've been trying to dig him out for the last few minutes."

Auric stared at the huge pile of rocks in horror. "He's under there?"

I nodded. Guilt tore me apart once again. "He saved my life, and then he told me to go, knowing it would likely mean his death. Why would he do that?"

"Because we're brothers," Jasin said, resting a hand on my shoulder. "Come on, we'll help you dig him out. And then we'll find Kira."

Auric offered me some water, which I gladly chugged, and then I returned to the task at hand. I used my magic to pull the rubble away, while Auric used air to help lift the smaller rocks. Jasin explained that he'd been injured during his battle with the Dragons and couldn't do much in the way of lifting, but he created a fire in the middle of the room, preventing us from freezing as the night grew colder.

I rolled away a large boulder, and spotted a strand of black hair. "He's here!"

The three of us worked together to carefully remove the rest of the rocks covering Reven's body, worried if we moved them too fast it would cause another collapse in the tunnel and possibly hurt him more. It took us a long time, and we worked solemnly, knowing we would likely find only a corpse.

When we dragged Reven's body out, it was rock hard and bitterly cold. His clothes were torn and his side was charred, his skin burnt off where he'd been hit by the lava. He'd given his life to protect me and Kira. Gods, how was I going to break it to her that one of her mates was dead and it was all my fault?

But as I sat back, I noticed something odd. Reven's body was encased in a layer of ice, which covered him like armor from head to toe, protecting him from the world around him. The others crouched beside us, staring at him.

Auric pressed his head to Reven's frosty chest and listened. "He's still alive. Barely."

Jasin rubbed his hands together and reached for Reven. "Perfect. I'll warm him up, while you see if you can get more air into his lungs."

"No!" Auric said, shoving Jasin's hands away. "The ice is the only thing keeping him alive. If we warm him up, he'll die."

"Are you sure?" I asked, frowning at the ice-covered body. Keeping him in such a state seemed unnatural, but what did I know?

Auric nodded. "He's too badly injured. I'm shocked he's still alive as it is, but he must have summoned the ice to protect himself as the cave collapsed. But now the only one who can heal him is Kira."

I clenched my fists. "We have to rescue her."

"Yes, you do," a male voice said from the shadows. "But you can't do it alone."

We turned toward the sound, reaching for our weapons and our magic, and saw a man standing in front of us, though he stayed out of the light. Something about the way he stood was familiar, but I couldn't see his face, only that he had longer hair.

"Stay back!" Jasin yelled, drawing his sword.

"Who are you?" Auric asked.

The man's deep voice echoed through the cave. "I'm the Azure Dragon, and I'm here to help you rescue Kira."

Anger leaped into my throat and the ground quaked under my feet in response. "You were the one who took her," I growled. "Why would you help us?"

The man stepped forward and the light from the fire illuminated his face, revealing hazel eyes. Kira's eyes. "Because I'm her father."

32
KIRA

I forced my eyes open, though my eyelids felt as if they were made of stone. My entire body ached, and when I moved I realized it was because I was crumpled on the ground on my side. My vision was blurred, but as I sat up and blinked, the world slowly came into focus again.

The first thing I noticed were the bones. They surrounded me, forming a cage around my body just large enough for me to stand inside, and I was pretty sure they were human. The gleaming white bones crisscrossed over and under me, although the sides of my new, morbid prison had large enough gaps for me to see through. Not that there was much to see—beyond the bones was an empty, dark room with a single torch to illuminate it.

I spun around, hesitant to touch the bones after the revulsion I'd felt before. Where was I? The last thing I remembered was fighting Sark and the others, and then Doran grabbing me and pressing something to my face. I'd been unable to stop him, and then I'd woken up here. Whatever he'd done must have knocked me unconscious for some time...which meant I was being held by the Dragons.

I reached out for my bond with my mates, but felt nothing from them. Something was blocking me, like a wall I couldn't find my way around. I had no way to tell if they were injured or even still alive. And worst of all, without the bond they'd never be able to find me.

Could it be the bones preventing me from reaching them? I hesitantly wrapped a hand around one of them, part of an arm from the looks of it, and felt that same horror and repulsion as before. I quickly let go and gasped, stepping back, except there was no escape from the cage that surrounded me.

Footsteps approached from across the room and I tensed. A woman with long, luxurious red hair moved toward the bone cage with confident, deliberate steps. She wasn't particularly tall, but she practically glowed with strength and power, and even though her skin was unwrinkled, her green eyes held the wisdom of more years than one person should ever live through. She was so beautiful it was hard to look away from her, even though I sensed a darkness within her I'd never felt before...except from the shades.

There was no doubt in my mind who this was—Nysa, the Black Dragon.

My mother.

She stopped in front of the cage and I fought the instinct to shrink back from her. The way she looked at me made my skin crawl, but I wouldn't cower in her presence. I was the next Black Dragon, and I would stand tall and face her, even if it was the hardest thing I'd done before.

She gave me a smile that was so lovely it made my chest hurt. "I've been looking for you for a long time, Kira." She reached for me through the cage, as if to stroke my hair. "You're more beautiful than I ever imagined."

I flinched back, my heart pounding. "Stay away from me."

Her hand fell and her smile vanished. "I'm sorry. You must think me a monster, don't you?"

I didn't answer, trying to gain control of my emotions. This woman was my enemy, and I was meant to destroy her and take her place, but she was also my mother. Some primal part of me longed to hear those kind words from her and wanted to lean into her touch. Yet I couldn't forget all the horrible things done in her name, or the misery she'd inflicted upon the world for hundreds of years.

She let out a soft sigh. "Yes, in some ways I am a monster, but there's a reason for everything I have done, and there's much you don't know." She paused and regarded me with those ancient eyes. "You see, sometimes you must become a monster to protect the world from something even worse."

I had no idea what she was talking about, and wasn't sure I could believe anything she said anyway. But she'd kept me alive for some reason, and that meant something.

"What do you want with me?" I asked.

"Right now, I only want you to rest." She gripped the bone cage in front of me and gazed into my eyes. "As much as it saddens me, your fight will soon be over."

With those words she turned and walked away, leaving me to wonder what she had in store for me. I desperately reached for my mates again through our bond, but couldn't find them. I was truly on my own here.

But I wouldn't give up. I would fight back. I would find a way to escape. I would be reunited with my mates again.

And then we would stop the Black Dragon and her men, once and for all.

RIDE THE WAVE

HER ELEMENTAL DRAGONS BOOK FOUR

1

JASIN

I glared at the man in front of me with his all-too-familiar hazel eyes. Doran, the Azure Dragon, was one of the men I'd spent months training to defeat. It was my destiny to help overthrow him and the rest of the Black Dragon's mates to restore balance to the world. They'd only brought chaos, misery, and death to the four Realms, and now they'd kidnapped the woman I loved. I wanted to rip his head off, set fire to his body, and watch his bones turn to ash, but I couldn't—because he'd just told us he was Kira's father.

Doran had the tanned, weathered skin of a man who spent his days in the sun, and his long sandy hair was wind-tossed and a little wild. While Isen, the Golden Dragon, had the bearing of a prince, and Sark and Heldor, the Crimson Dragon and the Jade Dragon, were obviously warriors, Doran looked more like a sailor or a pirate, especially with his scruffy beard, plain white shirt, black trousers and boots. I wasn't fooled by his appearance though. The man was dangerous, and he was our enemy.

"Why should we believe anything you say?" I asked, while my hand lingered on the hilt of my sword and fire burned inside me, begging to be released. Slade and Auric tensed beside me, ready to join me if things turned ugly. We stood in the ruins of the Earth Temple surrounded by shimmering crystals on the stone walls, a broken Dragon statue, and two bodies on the ground. One of them was Reven's.

Doran held up his hands as if in surrender. "I realize you have no reason to trust me, but Kira's life is in danger and we need to rescue her before it's too late."

"You knocked her out and carried her away, but now you want to rescue her?" Slade asked, his voice a low growl. His green eyes were hard as stone and a thin layer of sweat coated his dark skin despite the chill in the air. He'd been unable to stop Kira from being kidnapped, only minutes after he'd completed the bonding with her that allowed him to turn into a Dragon, and it obviously weighed heavily on him.

Auric's gray eyes flashed with anger. "If you're her father why would you kidnap her in the first place, knowing it would put her life in danger?"

"Kira was obviously going to be captured one way or another," Doran said. "I took matters into my own hands to make sure she wasn't injured in the process. The others would not be as careful with her life as I was."

"You could have helped us stop them," Slade said, crossing his thick, muscular arms.

"Perhaps, but I'm not ready for Nysa or the others to know my true loyalties yet. The Black Dragon still trusts me, which allows me a great advantage." Doran's eyes narrowed. "But I won't let my daughter be killed either. I've spent my entire life protecting her and making sure the other Dragons never found her. I'm not about to stop now."

My fingers still hovered near the hilt of my sword despite his words. I wanted to believe him, but we had no reason to trust anything he said. "I don't like this," I said to Slade and Auric. "For all we know he could be leading us into a trap."

"I could be," Doran agreed. "But you're never going to be able to rescue Kira without my help. Especially with one of your men down."

Reven's body was encased in a thin layer of ice, the only thing keeping him alive after the Dragon attack. Beneath the ice, his black hair was thick with dried blood, and his side was horribly burned. He'd sacrificed himself to protect Kira, and her magic was the only thing that could heal him. By saving her, we'd be saving him too.

Unfortunately, we couldn't save the life of the man lying beside Reven. Parin had been the leader of the Resistance and despite his uncomfortable past with Slade, he'd led Kira and the others to the Earth Temple. He'd died trying to protect Kira from the Dragons, and he'd be remembered as a hero once this was all over.

Auric ran a hand through his short blond hair, his face pinched. "I don't trust Doran either, but he has a point. Without our bond it could take us a long time to find Kira."

At his words, I searched for Kira again and found only emptiness. Ever since I'd bonded with Kira at the Fire Temple, I could feel her presence, but something was blocking me now. Somehow the Black Dragon was making sure we couldn't find her.

"Tell us where she's being held," Slade demanded, squaring his broad shoulders as he faced down the Azure Dragon. "Then we'll decide whether or not we need your help."

"She's in Soulspire," Doran said, naming the capital of the four Realms, where the Black Dragon ruled with her mates. "Inside a secret part of the palace."

Damn. He was right that rescuing Kira would be nearly impossible for us. I'd been to Soulspire once, back when I was a soldier in the Onyx Army, and the palace was heavily guarded. Not to mention, the other Dragons would be there, and we weren't yet a match for them. Having Doran on our side could tilt the balance toward us, but I still wasn't convinced this wasn't a trick. For all we knew he was luring us to our own deaths or to a prison cell beside Kira's.

"What's your plan exactly?" I asked. If he told us how to rescue her, perhaps we'd be able to accomplish it without his help. "Do you even have one?"

Doran gave me an amused look. "I'm not that much of a fool. If I tell you my plan now—and yes, I do have one—you'll rush ahead without me, and then you'll all be dead. Not that I care, but Kira needs you alive."

Well, it was worth a try.

He spread his hands. "Listen, I can't prove to you that I'm her father or that I'd do anything to protect her. All you have is my word, and my promise that if we do nothing, Kira will be dead within a few days."

Auric glanced between me and Slade. "As much as I hate to admit it, I don't think we have a choice. We need to work with him, even if it is a trap."

"If it's a trap, we'll be ready," I said, slamming my fist into my other palm. "But what are we going to do with Reven? We can't leave him here in the ruins of the Earth Temple."

"We could stop by the Resistance hideout on the way and leave Reven with them," Auric said. "He'd be safe there, and we can return Parin's body at the same time so they can bury him."

"No," Slade said immediately. "We can't lead Doran to the Resistance. I won't put all those lives in danger by revealing their location to a Dragon."

Doran chuckled. "No need to worry about that. I already know where it is. They're in the mountain by the two rocks that look like breasts."

"How do you know?" I asked.

"I'm the Black Dragon's...scout, you could say. It's my job to know these things and many more. But don't worry, I haven't shared this information with Nysa or the other Dragons yet. I have no interest in seeing the Resistance wiped out."

Slade scowled at him while Auric looked thoughtful. I tried to come up with another place where we could leave Reven, but all I could think of was Slade's village, except we'd put all those innocent people in danger too. I briefly considered leaving Reven with Auric's father, the King of the Air Realm, but Stormhaven was too far out of the way and time was of the essence. Taking Reven to the Resistance hideout was our best option.

Doran rolled his shoulders and turned toward the tunnel that led out of here. "Enough debating. I don't know how much longer the Black Dragon will keep Kira alive. Right now, Kira is an amusement, but she's a threat to Nysa's rule and will have to be eliminated soon. We need to get moving."

"There's one more problem," I said, rubbing the spot on my back that hurt even in my human form. "Auric is the only one of us who can fly at the moment. One of my wings is busted, and Slade just got his Dragon form a few hours ago."

Doran shrugged. "That's not an issue. Someone can ride with me."

Ride on the back of our enemy? As if this day couldn't get any worse.

2

KIRA

I woke to pain. The bone cage surrounded me, cutting off my bond with my mates and blocking my powers. Every time my bare skin touched one of the white bars, revulsion and horror filled me. I'd tried to stay awake, but after being left here for untold hours exhaustion had finally taken over. Except I could only sleep upright without bringing on waves of disgust, and my back and neck ached from the uncomfortable position. Even worse, every now and then my head would drop to the side, my cheek would brush against one of the dreaded bones, and I'd nearly empty my stomach.

A noise caught my attention and jerked me fully awake. A footstep on the stone floor. Heavy. Probably male. Not my mother then.

The Black Dragon had only come to visit me once, and since then I'd been left alone. I wasn't sure how long I'd been locked in this prison, or whether it was day or night. The room that held my bone cage was empty except for a single torch, with no windows and only one door. After my mother's cryptic words that I wouldn't be alive much longer, I'd tried to summon my powers of earth, air, and fire, but found I couldn't use them in here. Without my magic or my weapons, I wasn't sure how I'd ever escape, but I was determined to not let this be the end.

The door opened, and my worst nightmare stood in the doorway. Sark, the Crimson Dragon, who had once murdered the people I'd called my parents. I knew now that the Black Dragon was my true mother and one of her Dragons was my father. Probably Sark himself, although the thought made me feel sicker than touching the bones did.

But Sark's crimes didn't end there. He'd murdered Reven's family too, he'd helped destroy the town I'd lived in for the last few years, and he'd killed my best friend, Tash. He'd taken so much from me and from the people I cared for, and I wanted nothing more than to defeat him and stop him from hurting anyone else.

He strode into the room and the torch beside him flared brighter, illuminating his nearly white hair, which was cut in a short military style. He wore red and black armor, similar to what the Onyx Army wore, but even more ornate. Hatred filled me as he drew closer and his cruel brown eyes met mine. He carried a tray of food, which he thrust through the bone cage with a single command. "Eat."

My stomach twisted with hunger, even as I glared at him. The last time I'd eaten had been during the climb to the Earth Temple with Slade, Reven, and Parin. How long ago was that? It felt like an eternity, but for all I knew it had only been a few hours. Were my mates all right? Were they looking for me now?

The tray smelled heavenly and was piled high with roasted chicken, carrots, and potatoes, along with a pitcher of water. I considered whether the food and water might be poisoned, but quickly dismissed the idea. My gifts from the Spirit Goddess would probably heal me from any poison, and the Dragons could have killed me instead of locking me up. No, they wanted me alive…for now. They must have a plan if they were feeding me, but what?

"Take it," Sark said, thrusting the tray forward again.

My resolve failed, and I snatched the tray out of his hands, making sure not to touch him. I retreated to the back of my cage and began to pick at the food, while he crossed his arms and watched me the entire time I ate. Hunger quickly took over and I began to devour the food under his dreadful gaze like an animal trapped in a cage, waiting to be turned into a meal. All they had to do was fatten me up first.

When I finished, I threw the empty tray through the bars of my cage at him. He dodged it easily with a grunt, picked it up off the floor, and turned to walk away. Fury rose up in me and I called out, "Why are you keeping me here? What do you want?"

He left the room without answering me, the door slamming shut and locking behind him. With anger fueling me, I wrapped my hands around the bone cage and shook it hard. That heavy revulsion and nausea filled me, but I held on for as long as I could and used all my strength to try to pry a bone loose. Nothing budged. I was forced to let go, staggering back as sweat dripped down my forehead and bile clung to my throat.

There would be no breaking through this cage.

For a few minutes I had to focus on breathing in and out to make sure I didn't bring up the food I'd just eaten. When I no longer felt sick, I sighed and slowly sank to the floor. My head fell forward into my hands and I rubbed my temples, unsure if I wanted to scream or cry. I couldn't escape, I had no idea if my mates were alive or dead, and all I could do was wait and pray for a way out.

Where was Enva? She usually came to me when I was upset, and I could use my grandmother's advice now more than ever. Perhaps the bone cage was preventing her from manifesting too?

One thing was certain: I was truly all alone here.

3

SLADE

The journey to the Resistance hideout in the mountains was tense. None of us trusted Doran or wanted anything to do with him, but one of us had to ride on his back, so I'd volunteered. I considered it my penance for letting Kira be kidnapped. What good was being a Dragon now if I couldn't actually fly? Kira was captured, Reven was in a coma, and Parin was dead—all because of me. Nothing I did could ever make up for my failures, but the least I could do was return Parin's body to the Resistance and then prepare to rescue Kira.

As the Earth Realm soared below me, I tried to quench the fear and unease that came with being so far above the earth. Without my feet on solid ground I never felt comfortable, not since the Earth God had blessed me with his favor and his powers. That blessing now seemed to be holding me back. Would I ever be able to fly? Or would I be useless as a Dragon forever?

Doran set down in the forest while Auric—with Jasin and Reven on his back—landed at the Resistance base's secret entrance in the mountain. We'd decided it would be better for everyone if the Resistance didn't know we were working with Doran, for fear it would cause a panic or provoke an attack. We needed him, no matter how much we hated it.

A short while later, Auric returned and collected us, along with Parin's body. With Doran's commonplace clothes and his hooded cloak covering much of his face, no one recognized him when we entered the Resistance hideout. I wasn't surprised, since he was rarely seen in his human form, especially in the Earth Realm. Besides, no one expected a Dragon to look more like a carefree drifter than one of the men who ruled our world through fear and death.

As we stepped into the smooth caves of the hideout, we were greeted by an older woman named Daka who we'd met once before. We'd rescued her and a few other people from the Onyx Army in the Fire Realm before they could be executed for being members of the Resistance.

"It's a blessing to see you've returned," Daka said. Her brown hair was streaked with gray and her skin was tanned and wrinkled, but her eyes shone bright. "Please come in and we'll get you settled. You must be exhausted."

"It's good to see you made it to the Resistance base alive," I said.

"Yes, thanks to you." She smiled, but then her smile fell when she noticed our dwindled numbers and the two lifeless bodies we'd brought with us.

"I wish we were here under better circumstances," Auric said. "Unfortunately, Kira has been kidnapped, one of our men is in a coma, and Parin... He gave his life fighting the Dragons. I'm sorry."

Daka covered her mouth as she let out a soft cry, her eyes filling with tears. "Oh, Parin, no. What will we do without him leading us? And with Faya gone too…"

Her tears reminded me of my failure, and I looked away, focusing on the hidden town of Slateden behind her. The stone and wooden buildings stood below the high, domed ceiling of the cave, but the roads were nearly empty today. Most of the Resistance members had left to fight the battle at Salt Creek Tower and wouldn't return for another week, including my sister, Leni. Auric and Jasin had assured me she was alive when they last saw her, but I would continue to worry until I saw her with my own eyes.

Auric stood up straighter, though his voice was weary. "I'll bring Faya back. She's needed here now."

I rested a hand on Auric's shoulder. He'd already flown across the Earth Realm for hours with no break, and now he was preparing to set out again. The man had to be exhausted, and I respected him more than ever. "And my sister?"

He nodded. "Don't worry. I'll get her and Brin too."

I nearly hugged the man. "Thank you."

"I should be going with you," Jasin grumbled, the frustration clear in his brown eyes. "Stupid wing. Make sure you eat something before you go."

"I will," Auric said, as they clasped each other in a quick hug. The two of them were like brothers now, which was still hard to believe, considering they'd once hated each other.

As Daka took Auric away to find some food, Jasin sighed. "I wish I could do more."

I knew exactly how he felt.

Sleep proved elusive that night. I tossed and turned, worrying about Kira, praying my sister was unharmed, and hating myself for my failures. When the sun began to rise, I gave up, threw off my blankets, and went to find some food.

I nearly crashed into my youngest sister in the entrance to the guest house, along with her girlfriend, Brin. Relief flooded me as I swept Leni into my arms. She was the most headstrong, stubborn, and frustrating woman in our family, but she was alive and that was all that mattered. She and Brin had joined the Resistance in the battle at Salt Creek Tower, even though she was too young and inexperienced as a fighter, in my opinion. I wished she was back at home and safe with our mother and sister in Clayridge, but she was an adult and didn't listen to her overprotective brother anymore, much to my dismay.

"Slade!" she said as she embraced me back.

I pulled back to look her over, my grip tight on her arms. Her dark skin was smudged with dirt and some of her small braids were starting to come undone, but she appeared to be well otherwise. "Are you unharmed?"

"Yes, I'm fine. I twisted my ankle, but it's already better." She glanced over my shoulder with a smile. "Brin had my back."

I turned toward Brin and bowed my head. "Thank you."

With golden skin and silky black hair, Brin was beautiful and had the grace of a woman born to money and power, although she was an excellent fighter too. She was a noblewoman from the Air Realm and had once been Auric's fiancé, though they'd never been more than friends. I just hoped she wouldn't break my sister's heart.

She gave me a dazzling smile. "I would never allow any harm to come to Leni, and she protected me as well."

"I did what I could." Leni nudged me in the side with a grin. "So is it done? Did you and Kira get intimate? Are you a Dragon now?"

My shoulders tensed. It was bad enough talking to my sister about "getting intimate." It was worse being reminded of my failure. "Yes, we bonded and I'm a Dragon now, although I'm still not used to it. But we were attacked by the other Dragons, and Kira was taken. I... I couldn't stop them."

Leni squeezed my arm. "I'm sure you did the best you could."

"Tell us everything," Brin said.

I gave them the quick rundown of what happened, although I didn't mention that Doran was helping us. In return, they told me about the battle at Salt Creek Tower with the Dragons. By the end of their tale they were both yawning, and I guessed they had been up all night as they flew here on Auric's back.

I sent them both to get some rest, and then caught sight of a beautiful, dark-skinned woman with short hair on the street outside the guest house. Faya's head was bent and her eyes were red, but her back was straight as she walked alone. I headed outside to speak with the woman I once thought I'd marry.

"I'm sorry about Parin," I said. "He died a hero and fulfilled his duty to the Earth God. We would not have found the Earth Temple without him."

Faya nodded. "His mother would be proud. Thank you for bringing his body back to us so that we may bury him."

"It was the least we could do to honor his sacrifice." I touched her arm. "I truly am sorry, Faya. What will you do now?"

She gazed down the empty streets of Slateden, her face a mixture of grief and grim determination. "The Resistance still needs a leader. I will step up and do what I can until they can elect someone else. It's what Parin would have wanted."

"You'll make a good leader."

"I doubt I could ever be the leader Parin was, but I'll do my best." Her hand rested on her lower stomach. "Not only for his sake or the Resistance's, but for his child."

I stepped back, my eyes dropping to her waist. "You're pregnant?"

"Yes, I'm three months along. We tried for years without success and never thought it would happen. Now he won't get to see our child born." She sighed and her body sagged, all the energy leaving her small frame. "At least a part of him will live on."

I wrapped my arms around her and clasped her in a warm embrace. She buried her face in my chest for a few moments, allowing me to lend her my strength, before pulling away. Over the years, Faya had been my lover, my enemy, and now my ally. We'd been through a lot together and our shared history would always be a part of us. Until recently I'd wanted nothing to do with her, but now I only wished the best for her and her child.

"I heard you're leaving soon to rescue Kira," she said. "Take whatever supplies you need for your journey."

"Thank you. Please watch over Reven for us until we return."

"We will. No harm will come to him, I swear it."

We said our goodbyes and I returned to my room in the hopes of getting a few more hours of sleep before our journey. Gods knew I would need it to face what was ahead.

4

KIRA

I waited in my cage for an eternity with only a bucket in the corner, a torn and dirty blanket, and whatever food and water the Dragons brought me. The bucket was a gift from Heldor, who came to see me after Sark. His face was solemn as he gave it to me, and thankfully he didn't wait around to watch me use it to relieve myself. Isen brought me the blanket some time later, though he warned me not to get too comfortable because I wouldn't be there very long. I could only imagine what Doran would gift me with when he came to visit me next.

When the door opened again some time later it wasn't Doran who stepped inside, but Nysa. In an instant it became hard to breathe, my entire body tensing with anticipation and dread at the sight of her. My mother was incredibly beautiful, with an ageless quality I'd only seen before in the other Dragons. Her hair was the same red shade as mine and hung in luxurious waves to her shoulders, but her eyes were the color of emeralds. She had the kind of beauty that would turn every head in a crowd, even if she hadn't been the most feared woman in the world.

"Good morning, Kira," she said, as the door shut behind her and she approached the cage.

Was it morning? I couldn't tell. How many days had I been here now?

"How are you feeling?" she asked, her voice pleasant. She wore a long white and black gown that trailed along the floor behind her with each graceful step, and it was impossible not to stare at her.

I ignored her question. "What do you want with me?"

She stopped a few inches from the cage and clasped her hands in front of her. "I need to take your life. Believe me, it's not something I want to do, but it's what must be done."

"Then kill me already! Why wait?"

"It's not that simple." She tilted her head as she studied me from head to toe. "You must understand, I do not want you to die. If it were up to me, we would rule together as mother and daughter."

My fists clenched at my side. "I have no interest in ruling, and certainly not with you."

She waved her hand dismissively. "Your view of me is distorted by what others have told you. The truth is that everything I do is meant to protect this world. Including your sacrifice."

A hard lump formed in my throat. "Sacrifice?"

"Unfortunately, yes." She let out a long sigh. "I will drain your life force, and it will keep me and my mates young until my next daughter is born."

Horror and revulsion filled me, even stronger than when I'd touched the bone cage. "Your *next* one?"

"I do have to apologize," Nysa continued, as if she hadn't heard me. "This would be a lot easier for all of us if you were still a baby, like the others before you. Now you've bonded with some of your mates and I must take extra precautions since you won't be drained so easily. Of course, it also means your strength will become mine, making me even more powerful." She dipped her head. "I will do my best to honor your sacrifice."

All I could do was stare at her with my mouth hanging open as I absorbed everything she said, along with the implications. When the Gods created the five Dragons they were only supposed to be in power for a short time before being replaced by their daughter and her mates, beginning the cycle anew. All of that ended with Nysa, and I'd never known why. Until now. "That's how you've lived so long. You drain the life from your own children."

"I have no other choice."

I'd always thought she was a monster, but I'd had no idea how dark her soul truly was. How many of my sisters had died before me to keep her immortal? How many babies had she drained to keep herself young?

"Oh, Kira." She reached for me through the cage and I jerked back. She wrapped her hands around the bars instead, untouched by the revulsion that always struck me. "If I could save you, I would. But this is the only way to contain her."

"Who?"

My mother gave me a sad, lovely smile before stepping back. "The Spirit Goddess."

I could only stare at her as she left the room. Why would she want to contain the Spirit Goddess? We were descended from the Spirit Goddess and had been given her powers. The other Gods of Fire, Earth, Air, and Water were all her mates, and they'd tasked us with protecting the world. We'd been given our own mates to help us accomplish this task, and the Dragons were meant to serve the Gods and carry out their will—except Nysa and her Dragons seemed to be the enemies of the Gods instead. I'd assumed it was because Nysa had refused to give up her power, but maybe there was more to it?

It didn't matter. Nysa was evil, power hungry, and completely insane. She had to be in order to murder her own children to extend her life. She'd said she had a good reason and was trying to protect the world, but I didn't believe it. Nothing could make me do that to my own child. *Nothing.* Nysa was a monster, a mother who sucked the life from her own babies, and no matter how much she said she didn't want to kill me, no one was forcing her to do it. And she'd made the same decision many times before.

The horror over what Nysa had done—and wanted to do to me—suffocated me, and I became consumed with the need to get away. I grabbed the bucket off the floor and slammed it against the cage as hard as I could. I did it over and over, the metal hitting the bone loudly with each blow, hoping for something to give way. Just one little piece. *Please,* I prayed to the Gods, *give me a way to escape from here. Let me free, so I might find a way to stop her.*

The door flew open and Sark stomped inside the room. "What's going on in here?"

I dropped the bucket and glared at him, while my entire body shook with anger and disgust. "How could you let her do it? She's killing your own children, and you stood there and allowed it for all these years!"

His lips curled up in a sneer. "Stupid girl. You don't know anything."

"I know a real father would protect his daughter," I spat out.

"Sometimes sacrifices must be made for the greater good. Now quit your banging or I'll take that bucket away, along with everything else you've been allowed."

I gave him a look full of hatred and loathing as I picked up the bucket and banged it against the cage, making the bones rattle. Maybe if he tried to take the bucket, I'd be able to overpower him and escape. It wasn't a great plan, but it was better than nothing and I was desperate at this point.

But he didn't open the cage or come after me. Instead, the metal bucket suddenly grew so hot that I yelped and was forced to drop it. Sark had used his fire magic through the cage somehow, even though I couldn't use mine.

"Be quiet, or next time it won't only be the bucket getting burned," he growled.

After he left, I realized he hadn't confirmed or denied being my father. The bucket hadn't done a single thing to the bone cage, and I had nothing else to use to escape besides a ragged blanket. But I wouldn't give up. I couldn't. Somehow, I would get out of here—and then I would make sure that none of my sisters would ever be killed again.

5

AURIC

Our cart pulled up to the black gates of Soulspire and I shifted in my seat, tugging my wide-brimmed hat low over my face. We'd bought the cart at a farm a few hours away, along with clothes that would help us blend in and look like merchants, plus some apples and oranges to complete our disguise. The farmer had been delighted with our money and I was thankful my father had provided us so much gold for our journey before we'd left the Air Realm. It was almost all gone now, but it had served us well while it lasted.

We hadn't seen Doran since his large blue form had flown over us toward the palace. We could only pray he was getting Kira out and fulfilling his side of the bargain, instead of leading us into a trap. I had a feeling he would be true to his word, even if the others disagreed with me. Or maybe I just wanted to believe Doran was on our side because if he wasn't, we would have a much harder time rescuing Kira.

We'd spent the last few days flying toward Soulspire, which was located in the center of the continent where the four Realms met, and Doran had told us his plan when we'd stopped to rest last night.

"The Spirit Festival starts tomorrow, and it's the biggest celebration of the year in Soulspire," he'd said. "The Black Dragon herself always makes a speech in the afternoon and the revelers will fill the streets, wearing masks and celebrating being alive. It can get a bit wild, if you know what I mean. It's the perfect time to rescue Kira."

"And how exactly will we do that?" Slade asked. We all sat around a

ELIZABETH BRIGGS

clearing as we finished our meal, and despite having traveled with Doran for days, everyone kept an eye on him. None of us trusted him yet.

"You won't," Doran said. "I will."

"That doesn't work for us," Jasin growled. He disliked the man more than any of us, although I wasn't sure if it was a natural fire and water opposites thing or if it was related to his issues with his own parents. Jasin's father had betrayed us, and I didn't blame him for suspecting Kira's father would do the same.

Doran gave a casual shrug. "Too bad. I'm the only one who can walk into the palace where Kira is being held without a problem. Any one of you would be stopped by the hundreds of guards and killed or captured before you came anywhere near her. Assuming you could even find her once inside." He shook his head. "No, I will free Kira and lead her out of the palace through the sewers. You'll meet me there and escape with her."

"Why do you need us at all then?" Jasin asked.

"I can get Kira out of the palace while the other Dragons are busy with the Festival, but they'd notice if I flew off with her. I need it to look like she was rescued by her mates to maintain my cover."

Jasin's eyes narrowed, and I held out a hand to stop him from replying. I cleared my throat. "How will we get into the city undetected? You can fly into Soulspire, but we cannot."

Doran ran a hand over his beard. "Many people will be traveling to the city for the festival, especially merchants and performers. If you look convincing enough, they'll let you in without a problem. Trust me, no one will be looking for you. They'll be celebrating life in every way they can." Doran smirked. "Let's just say a lot of babies are born in Soulspire nine months from now."

We hammered out the rest of the details as we ate. None of us liked that Doran would be getting Kira out alone, but we couldn't think of a good way to get into the palace ourselves.

Sneaking into the capital proved to be easy though. It had been my idea to buy the cart and pretend to be farmers selling our wares, and as the gates opened and the guards gestured for us to enter, our disguise seemed to be working. Slade snapped the reins and our horses pulled us forward into the city.

I'd been to Soulspire twice before. Once as a young child, which I barely remembered, and a second time when I was older, perhaps about twelve. My father had taken me and my brother Garet with him while he attended to some business with Isen. All I remembered was the gleaming black palace looming over me and the claustrophobic feel of being surrounded by Onyx Army soldiers watching our every move.

Both of those things still existed today, except the city had been transformed from the somber, imposing one of my memories to a chaotic, festive, and colorful splendor. Banners and flags hung from every building, splashing the black architecture with a rainbow of colors. Every street was crowded with people in their finest clothes, wearing intricate masks that covered much of their faces, except their lips—which many used quite generously on each other. Most of the masks resembled animals, while others were decorated with flowers and leaves, all to honor the Spirit Goddess.

As we continued through the city, the crowd made it difficult to maneuver the cart toward the location of the sewer entrance. Alcohol and food flowed freely, music burst out of packed taverns and cafes, and people danced and threw confetti in the streets. Others were sharing kisses or locked in intimate embraces, their hands wandering under skirts and inside trousers, and I could see what Doran meant by it getting a little wild today.

A longing for Kira tugged at my soul, but when I reached for her through our bond, I still found nothing. I hadn't realized how vital feeling her in the back of my mind had become, but now it was as if a piece of myself was missing. I couldn't sense Jasin or Slade either, not without Kira acting as the bridge between us, but at least they were here beside me.

"I think this is it." Slade stopped the cart outside some stone steps that led down to an arched metal door. A guard stood in front of the sewer entrance, wearing the scaled black armor and winged helmet of the Onyx Army.

I nodded. "It matches the description Doran gave us."

Jasin quickly knocked out the guard and dragged him through the door, which Slade opened with his magic. Once the guard was tied up, we left him there and continued forward. Jasin created a ball of flame to illuminate the dark tunnel that surrounded us, made of black stone with low domed ceilings that our heads nearly reached. A terrible smell lingered in the air, and we walked through ankle-deep water and Gods only knew what else. The tunnels were old and in some sections the water was deeper, leaving us no choice but to wade through it. I cringed to think of what my clothes would smell like when we got out of the place.

"Where's Reven when we need him?" Jasin muttered, as we dipped into a waist-high patch of murky water.

Slade pressed his hand against a slimy wall and closed his eyes, using his magic to spread his senses through the earth. "This tunnel leads up to the palace. How far are we supposed to go to meet them?"

"I'm not sure," I said. "I suppose we should keep walking until we see them."

Jasin snorted. "If they're even coming."

I opened my mouth to reply when I spotted something up ahead. Tiny pinpricks of dim light that looked a lot like a pair of eyes. I immediately reached for my two long knives, which had been a gift from my father.

Jasin made his fire flare brighter, casting light across the tunnel and illuminating six shadowy figures with long claws. They seemed to be made of darkness itself, their bodies disappearing into the gloom where their feet should be, except for those sickly yellow glowing eyes.

"Shades!" I called out, as I reached for my magic and sheathed my blades. Shades were once thought to be myth, but we'd fought them before at the Air Temple and now knew they worked for the Black Dragon. Shades could drain the life of anyone they touched and were immune to most weapons, but magic could hurt them. The Black Dragon must have left them here to stop anyone from entering the palace this way, though it seemed dangerous to have so many in the middle of the capital. Maybe she kept them here in case she ever needed to unleash them across Soulspire.

We all stepped forward and prepared to attack, gathering our magic around us. I tapped into the unseen currents of air that floated around us at all times and sensed the quick breathing of my companions. The air here was damp and polluted with foul smells and toxins, but it still served me.

I slammed the shades with a huge blast of wind, knocking them all into the wall of the tunnel. Slade caused the stone there to grab hold of the shades, imprisoning them while they let out spine-tingling shrieks, and then Jasin incinerated them one by one.

"That was a lot easier than I remember it being at the Air Temple," Jasin said, as the shades turned to smoke.

I grinned. "We've had a lot more practice using our magic and working as a team."

"Wait," Slade said, holding out his arm to stop us from moving forward.

Dozens of glowing eyes lit up the tunnel ahead of us, blocking our path. I counted at least twenty pairs before giving up, and more seemed to fill the tunnel every second. I swallowed hard and prepared to fight them, while Slade and Jasin did the same. If we were going to get Kira out safely, we'd have to defeat them all.

6

KIRA

The door to my cell opened, jerking me awake. A tall man stood in the doorway, dimly lit by the dying embers of the torch outside my cage. I recognized his long blond hair and tanned skin—the Azure Dragon. I was wondering when he would show up. The others had been by at least twice now.

I'd seen Doran three times before. The first was a year after my parents were killed by Sark. I'd been traveling with some merchants and we'd stopped in a small town in the Air Realm. He'd shifted to his human form and spoke with one of the merchants, while his cold eyes searched around as if he was looking for someone. I left the merchants the next morning, worried I was putting their lives at risk. Much later, I saw Doran fly over the Earth Realm after I'd met my mates, and we'd hidden while his huge dragon form had circled over us before finally leaving.

The last time I saw him was when he'd kidnapped me a few days ago.

I saw a bundle in his hands and wondered what he'd brought to pacify me until my life was sucked away to keep him and the others alive. I still wasn't sure why they bothered, honestly. Maybe they really were fattening me up like a pig they prepared to slaughter.

"We don't have much time." Doran said, as he approached my cage. He offered me a bar of soap and a wet wash cloth in one hand, with a bundle of fabric in the other. "Get clean and change into these clothes as quickly as you can."

I frowned as I took the items from him and watched his back as he left the room. After untold days in the same clothes I'd worn in the Earth

Temple I was eager to change into something new and be moderately clean again, but the fact that Doran had brought me this now probably meant my time was up. They were getting me ready for my sacrifice, I was sure of it.

The dress he'd given me only reinforced that theory. It was a long gown made of the finest velvet in a deep green, trimmed in silver and adorned with intricate designs across the bodice. A long, hooded cloak in dark gray completed the ensemble, and he'd even brought me some clean undergarments too. I supposed they wanted me to look beautiful for them when they drained my life.

I sighed and washed myself as best I could before changing into the new clothes. Once I was done, some of the haze from the days spent in the cage seemed to lift. Being clean and wearing a fresh set of clothes made me feel like a human being again instead of an animal trapped in a cage. And if they thought I would go easily to my own sacrifice they were in for a surprise.

Doran entered the room again and his gaze quickly swept over me. "Good, you're ready." He unlocked the bone cage with a key I'd never seen before. "Now follow me and do everything I say. We'll need to hurry."

Why he thought I'd hurry to my own death was a mystery, but then again, the Dragons were all very odd. In the brief snippets of conversation I'd shared with the others they'd spoken as if I should be honored they were going to kill me.

The cage opened and I stumbled out of it. The second I was past the bones, energy rushed through me, as if I'd taken a breath after being underwater too long. My magic filled me with power and reconnected me to my mates. I sensed Jasin and Auric immediately, like bright sparks in my consciousness, and relief made me nearly laugh out loud. Slade was there too, a cool, reassuring presence in my mind, but our connection was still new and not as strong.

They were close. Were they coming to rescue me?

For the first time in days I had hope, and I channeled it as I reached for Auric and Jasin's magic, combining it and gathering it in my palms. I turned toward Doran and with a bellow of rage I launched a lightning bolt at him. It struck his chest and threw him back against the wall, knocking him out with a sizzling sound.

I'd never done that before. During training I'd been able to summon lightning for only a second and it had been little more than a spark, even though Jasin and Auric had been able to master it. But my determination to get out of here and find my mates again made me stronger, and nothing was getting in the way of my escape.

I threw open the cell door and started to rush out, but a strong hand grasped my shoulder and yanked me back.

"What do you think you're doing?" Doran asked, clutching his chest where I'd struck him.

I jerked away and gathered fire around me like a shield. "I won't let you take me!"

"Take you?" He stepped back from the flames and rolled his eyes. "I'm trying to help you escape!"

"You...what?"

"I'm here with your mates. They're waiting outside." He held out his hand and offered me a small black mask covered in twirling dark green vines. "Put this on and we'll go to them."

I plucked the mask from his hand and stared at it. "Why would you help me?"

"Kira, I'm your father."

The floor seemed to fall out from under me and I staggered back. My first thought was, *thank the Gods it isn't Sark*. The doubt came next, but as he held my eyes, I realized they were a mirror of my own. I took him in slowly and caught other similarities in our features too. He truly was my father.

And not a very good one.

Fire flared around me. "You knocked me out and kidnapped me!"

"To protect you!" He sighed and dragged a hand through his long sandy hair. "I'll explain everything later, I promise. Right now we really need to get out of here before anyone notices us. We have a small window while Nysa and the others are busy, but it will only last so long, and we don't have much time to meet your mates."

"Where are they? Are they all okay?"

"Put on your mask and follow me. I'll take you to them."

I donned the mask, snapping it over my head. "Why the mask?"

"Today is the Spirit Festival. The entire city is wearing masks. It's the perfect time to escape Soulspire." Doran put his own mask on, which featured tiny brightly colored fish, before stepping out of the room into a dark corridor. He scanned the length of it before setting off, clutching his side where I'd injured him. I wasn't sorry. He deserved it, even if he was helping me—which I wasn't positive he was.

I drew in a long breath, quickly weighed my options, and then followed him. If this was a trick, I'd fight back with everything I had, but I couldn't stay in that prison one more second.

The corridor was empty and had a musty smell with no windows, making me wonder if we were underground. I hadn't realized we were in Soulspire, although I'd suspected it. I'd never been to the capital before, and I was beginning to realize that without Doran's help I might never have made it out on my own. Assuming he was truly helping me now and not leading me to my death.

We walked with quick purposeful strides and I fell in step beside him, although my limbs were stiff from being in a cage for so long and my muscles were weak from inactivity. As we continued through the long stone halls, we passed a few guards, who stood up straight and nodded at Doran. They completely ignored my presence, and I had a feeling it was only because I was at his side.

"Where are we?" I asked in a low voice.

"The lower levels of the palace," Doran said. "Keep moving."

That burst of energy when I'd exited the cage had begun to fade, and now a bone-deep exhaustion was beginning to set in. I pushed past it and kept moving, fueled by the knowledge that I would see my mates again soon.

Doran stopped at an unmarked door and opened it, then gestured for me to enter. All I saw was darkness and a putrid smell hit my nose. I gagged and stepped back, but Doran shoved me forward through the door. He slammed it shut behind us and I quickly summoned a flame to fight back the darkness.

We were in a domed tunnel of some sort, with a thin trickle of water running down the center of it. Doran grabbed a torch off the wall and lit it with the fire in my palm, then gestured for me to follow him. "Your mates are waiting for us in these sewers. Once we find them, they'll get you out of the city."

"You're not coming?" I asked.

"No, I still have work to do here, but I promise I'll find you later. I've waited a long time to be reunited with you and we have a lot to talk about."

I gave him a skeptical look as we began walking down the dark tunnel. He'd had twenty years to find me, and Gods knew I could have used his advice and help during the last few months. Or after Sark killed my family. Or any of the other times I'd found myself on the run or in danger. It was difficult to believe he'd suddenly become a loving father now, when he'd been absent all these years. And why was I any different from my sisters, who he'd allowed to be murdered for centuries?

I didn't trust him one bit and I had a million questions for him, but I also recognized he was my only hope of getting out of here. I followed him down the tunnels despite my hesitations, but as soon as we had a chance to talk, I would need some answers.

The moment I saw a familiar broad-shouldered frame ahead of me, I let out a loud cry and stumbled forward. "Slade!"

He turned toward me, and his eyes widened. He crossed the distance between us with a few steps and swept me up into his arms. I laughed and sobbed at the same time, so relieved to be in his arms again.

"Kira!" Jasin called out, but he was busy holding off five shades with Auric at his side.

Doran gestured idly and each of the shades turned to ice, then broke apart into a million pieces. Gods, he was powerful. It was a grim reminder that we still had a lot to learn to match the other Dragons' strength.

As the shades vanished, my other mates rushed forward to wrap me in their arms and sprinkle my face with kisses. I was overjoyed to be united with them again and to see with my own eyes they were safe.

But then I realized one person was missing.

"Where's Reven?" I asked, suddenly worried.

Each of their faces darkened. "He's injured," Auric said. "But now that you're free, you can heal him."

"*What?*" My heart pounded and panic gripped my throat.

"There's no time to explain," Doran said. "Take Kira and get her out of the city. I'll meet you back at the Resistance base in a few days."

Wait, Doran knew about the Resistance base? My head spun as I tried to take everything in, realizing I'd missed a lot while I'd been captured. I was desperate to know what happened to Reven and how badly he was hurt, but I had to force my worries down., because we still weren't safe yet.

"Come on," Jasin said, taking my elbow.

"Thank you," I told Doran. I had so many mixed feelings about my father, but he'd kept his word and brought me to my mates.

I turned away to follow the others out of the tunnels, but then a cruel voice stopped me in my tracks.

"I should have known you'd betray us, Doran."

7
KIRA

S ark's broad frame filled the tunnel ahead of us, his black armor
gleaming under the firelight. His hateful eyes fell on me. "I remember
you now. Nysa sent me to find a girl in a small fishing village in the Water
Realm and told me to kill her family and bring her back alive. I took care
of the parents, but the girl wasn't there. When I went to look for her,
Doran stopped me." His cruel gaze snapped back to my father. "You told
me she was your daughter, a product of a fling with another woman."

Doran stared the other Dragon down. "Yes, and I said if you told Nysa
about her, I'd tell her about your own discretions, and if you touched one
hair on Kira's head, I'd kill your granddaughter too. The Fire God's priestess, isn't she?"

My mouth fell open as they argued. Doran had saved my life back then
and I'd never known it. Had he been looking out for me all this time
without me realizing it? No, I couldn't believe it.

"But you lied," Sark spat. "She's *Nysa's* daughter."

"Yes, but she's still mine." Doran stepped in front of me. "And I won't
let you hurt her."

"You fool! We need her. You know that."

"Maybe so, but I can't do this any longer."

"You think any of us want this?" Sark asked. "I've watched my own
daughters die too. None of us likes it, but it has to be done."

"Not anymore. It's time this ends. Let her go, and she'll break the cycle.
None of our children will have to die again."

Sark stepped forward, his voice menacing. "I can't do that."

Doran sighed. "I had a feeling you'd say that."

His body began to shift and grow, forming scales and wings. "Get Kira out of here," his dragon voice growled, while his large body filled the tunnel. "I'll hold him off and find you later."

Sark had begun to change too, becoming the blood red dragon of my nightmares, while Slade grasped my hand and began to drag me forward.

"No!" I struggled. I'd only just found my father and begun to realize he might not be the monster I'd thought he was. I had too many questions for him, and now they wanted me to leave him behind to fight the man who had haunted my memories for so long. "With all of us here we can take Sark down for good!"

"I know you want to fight him, but this isn't the time," Auric said. "Reven needs you."

I blinked at Auric as his words pierced my red veil of anger. Something about the way he said them made me realize things must be even worse than I'd imagined with Reven. And as much as I wanted to stop Sark, I was exhausted and could barely walk, let alone fight. The others looked weary too from fighting the shades. I sensed dull pain in Jasin as well, which meant he also needed healing. As Auric had said, this wasn't the time for this fight. I reluctantly nodded and began to move forward.

Sark's large red tail slapped down in front of us, blocking our exit and making us jump back. Doran's dragon form wasn't as large but was more agile, and he pounced on top of Sark, knocking him down.

"Go!" he roared, just before Sark rolled back on top and began to tear at my father with his claws.

We took off at a run just as fire began to spew from Sark's mouth and an icy chill permeated the air as Doran fought back. As much as I wanted to stay and help my father, I had a duty to my mates and everyone else. I only prayed I would get a chance to speak with Doran again later.

My mates led me through the dark, musty sewer tunnels, and by the time we emerged we were all drenched and smelling like rotten eggs...or worse. A cart with two horses waited outside, and we climbed into it.

I made sure my mask was securely fastened as Slade urged the horses forward and the cart began to move through the city. I glanced back and saw the tall spires and black arches of the palace, where I'd been held all this time without even knowing it. The main tower rose high in the center, giving Soulspire its name. That was where the Black Dragon was said to live, at the top of that tower. I shuddered at the memory of the last time she came to see me, when I'd learned her true plan.

Jasin wrapped an arm around me. "It's okay. You're free now."

Auric passed me a blanket, which Jasin helped wrap around me.

"The things I learned..." My voice trailed off, and all I could do was shake my head. I had to tell them everything Nysa had said, but the horror was still too great to speak it out loud. In time I would be able to tell them, once we were safe and everyone was healed. But not yet. I was still coming to terms with it myself.

Slade drove the cart through the streets of Soulspire and I gazed about in a daze, taking in the colorful decorations, lively music, and amorous couples. It was hard to believe I'd been trapped in a cage made of bones while all of this joy was going on outside the palace walls. Somewhere in the city Nysa and the other Dragons were making a speech. What would Nysa do when she learned I escaped? Would she hurt Doran?

I leaned my head on Jasin's shoulder, the weariness finally taking its toll. At first, I worried someone would recognize us, but no one cared about a few dirty looking people in a cart, not with the festival going on all around us. Auric grabbed us a few pieces of meat on a stick, which I greedily ate along with some of the apples and oranges in our cart, and then we pulled up at the gate to exit the city. The guards barely even glanced our way as they waved us through. Slade urge the horses forward, and then we were free. I let out a relieved sigh as we left the city behind.

8

KIRA

We traveled by cart for the rest of the day, worried we would be spotted if any of my mates shifted into their Dragon forms. Isen's golden body flew overhead at one point, but he passed us by without slowing. I watched the sky for the sight of dark blue wings, but never saw them. At least I never saw red ones either.

While we traveled into the Earth Realm, the others filled me in on everything I'd missed while I'd been held captive. I healed Jasin while snacking on the apples and oranges in the cart to keep my energy high, then took a long nap between him and Auric. I avoided questions about what happened to me during the days I'd been in the bone cage. I wasn't ready to talk about it yet and would rather wait until Reven could join us for that conversation anyway.

By the time we stopped to rest for the night, we were all exhausted. Slade found us a cave that would offer us shelter and protection from the Dragons' eyes, and we spread out inside it and prepared for bed. There was a smaller cave in the back of it, and I followed Slade there once Auric and Jasin had settled down to sleep. I'd noticed that Slade had seemed especially quiet and distant today, and I wanted to make sure he was all right.

I moved behind him and slid my arms around his strong chest, nuzzling my face against the back of his shoulders. "I missed you."

"I missed you too," he said, although his voice was gruffer than normal, and he pulled away from me.

"What's wrong?"

His jaw clenched. "It's my fault you were kidnapped, and my fault that Reven is injured."

"How could that be your fault? The Dragons attacked us, and you defended us the best you could."

He stared at the wall of the cave, which had a thin trickle of water running down it. "Reven stayed behind so I could go after you. He sacrificed himself for us, but I failed to save you. When I went after the Dragons, I couldn't fly. I had to watch them take you away while I stood there, completely useless."

I moved beside him and slowly rubbed his back. "We'd just completed the bond only moments before. No one would expect you to be able to fly so soon. It took Jasin some time before he could fly as well."

"Only a day. And Auric could do it immediately."

"Auric can control wind. He doesn't even need wings to fly. And Jasin was able to practice on our boat with the ocean around us in case he fell. You tried to fly off a mountain to rescue me the first time you shifted into your dragon form. That's bravery, not failure."

"I doubt Reven would see it that way."

I grasped his hands with mine. "Reven would understand. If your places were switched, I know you would."

Slade let out a long sigh. "What if I can never fly? I'll be useless to you as a Dragon."

"If Heldor can fly, then surely you can too." I squeezed his hands. "The Earth God picked you for a reason and he believes in you. I believe in you. The others believe in you. Maybe all you need is to believe in yourself." He scowled in response and I pressed a soft kiss to his cheek. "I promise once we heal Reven we'll do whatever it takes to help you fly. You will get there, I'm sure of it."

"I hope you're right." He slid his arms around me and dragged me against his chest, resting his head against mine. "I was so worried I might never see you again, that I'd finally bonded with you only to lose you forever."

"I'm here." I tilted my head to press soft kisses to his neck. "You rescued me. Nothing can keep us apart for long."

His large hands splayed across my back, holding me close. "I want to feel you in my mind the way the others do."

"You will," I promised, and then kissed my way up his neck to his jaw, my lips brushing against his dark beard. "And there is a way to speed it up."

"Is there?"

I slipped my fingers under his shirt, stroking his smooth, muscular stomach. "I've been able to increase the bond with Auric and Jasin by spending time in bed with them. We could get started on that now..."

"Hmm," he said, as his hands slid down to cup my bottom. "We *were* rushed last time, and I promised to make love to you all night long when I could."

"Yes, you did." I pressed against the hard bulge in his trousers and overwhelming need swept through me. I'd been separated from my mates for days, unsure if I would ever see them again, and the only thing I could think about was being close to them now. A primal urge took over, as if the only way to reassure myself Slade was really here with me was to feel him inside me. "And you can have me all night. Just take me now first."

"You're very demanding tonight." He gripped my dark green dress in his hands and dragged it up my legs.

I gave him a coy smile. "Aren't you meant to serve me?"

"And serve you I will." His lips moved to my ear and his deep voice whispered, "Many, many times."

My dress came off and hit the ground, and then Slade's lips were on me, coercing my mouth open. As we kissed, he trailed his fingertips along the underside of my breast, making me arch my back to get closer. His hands were large and rough, the hands of a man who'd spent his life working a forge and a hammer, and I trembled as they moved across my naked skin.

I gripped his shirt and tugged it over his head, desperate to touch him back. The sight of his dark, muscular chest sent a pulsing surge of desire between my thighs. I pressed my palms against his rippling stomach, feeling the coiled strength inside him, before sliding my hands down to undo his trousers. As they fell, he kicked them off of him and stepped back, allowing me to take in the glorious view.

He gestured at the cave wall and the stone moved, forming a short ledge that looked almost like a chair. He sat on it like a king on a throne and beckoned me forward. "Take what you need, my queen."

How could I refuse such an invitation? I climbed onto his lap to straddle him, feeling his rock-hard cock slide against me. My breasts pressed against his muscular chest, my nipples tight with lust, as I lined our bodies up. Slade's green eyes met mine as the anticipation made us both breathe faster, hearts pounding, and then I sank down with one hard push.

He groaned and threw his head back, exposing his thick, dark throat. I kissed the spot right where his beard met his neck and gripped his broad shoulders to steady myself. His hands gripped my waist, and together we began to move as one. I rocked my hips up and down, grinding against the spot where our bodies joined, and he met me with every thrust.

Each roll of my hips pushed his cock even deeper, and the friction of our bodies rubbed me in exactly the right spot to make the pressure build. Slade grabbed my chin and dragged my lips back to his, taking my mouth in a demanding kiss, as his other hand slid to my behind. He squeezed me there, encouraging me to move faster and harder, and I let instinct take over. The bond between us strengthened, allowing us to feel what the other was feeling, and it pushed us both over the edge.

We shattered at the same moment, our bodies so connected it was like one overwhelming orgasm that broke us both apart and then put us back together. Slade crushed me to his chest, claiming my mouth again, as the last tremors of pleasure rumbled through us.

We rocked together for a while, my arms around his neck, our lips dancing across each other's. He held me close in his strong embrace, and I was content to stay in his arms forever.

But after a few minutes Slade lifted me off him, spun me around, and planted me on the ledge—which had now grown into the size of a bed.

"Now it's my turn," Slade said, as he began to move down my body with determined eyes, his mouth finding every spot that made me moan.

I had a feeling neither of us was going to get much sleep that night.

9

REVEN

For a long time, there was nothing but cold, dark pain.
A burst of warmth broke through the chill. A tingling sensation spread through my limbs. Familiar voices echoed through the darkness.

"Not too fast, Jasin," Auric said. "We only want to melt his hands for now."

"Don't worry, I've got this."

That cocky bastard. My lips tried to twitch into a grin but didn't move. Neither did the rest of me. I couldn't speak. I couldn't breathe. I couldn't even open my eyes. What was wrong with me? Where was I?

Soft hands slid into mine, and they felt so hot I would have hissed if I could. "Come back to me, Reven," Kira said, her voice mournful. A wave of relief hit me at the sound, though I wasn't sure why.

"His fingers twitched," Slade said.

"It's working," Auric said. "Start on the rest of him, Jasin. Slowly."

Memories returned in fragments. Kira being kidnapped. Lava striking my side. Heldor bringing down the Earth Temple on my head. And after that only cold, black death.

Except I was still alive.

The chill began to fade and suddenly a burst of air filled my lungs. My heartbeat pounded in my ears. My skin burned and froze at the same time. Agony spread through my limbs and forced my mouth into a scream, though no sound came out. I was alive but starting to wish I wasn't.

Kira's voice was the only thing that held me together, telling me to stay with her over and over. *I'm trying*, I wanted to tell her. I struggled to open my eyes, to get one more glimpse of her, but the pain became too much. I couldn't hold on any longer.

The last thing I heard was the others raising their voices in panic as the darkness took me again.

My eyes snapped open and I jerked to a sitting position, reaching for weapons that weren't there, the memory of pain still fresh in my mind.

"It's okay," Kira said, her arms wrapping around me. "Just relax."

"Kira?" my voice croaked out. I barely recognized it.

"Shh." She stroked my hair with the gentlest touch. "You've been through a lot, but it's over now. I'm here."

My arms wrapped around her and I held her close as I breathed in and out. It took some time before my body stopped trembling and I could let her go. Only then did I realize we were both naked and in bed together. An unfamiliar bed, in an unfamiliar room, but none of that mattered. My gaze traveled down to take her in, and the sight of her lush curves woke me up more than anything. Not that I had the energy to do anything about it at the moment, but I still liked the view.

"How am I alive?" I asked, as I lowered myself back onto the bed. Sitting was too much effort. In fact, everything hurt.

Kira touched my face softly as she settled beside me. "You were badly injured during the fight at the Earth Temple, but you surrounded yourself with ice, which kept you alive in a sort of suspended state. Jasin melted the ice while I healed you."

"I remember." I touched my side and found it healed, though still tender. "How long was I out?"

"Over a week."

"A *week*?" I shook my head, trying to clear it. "The Dragons captured you. Slade stopped them?"

"Not exactly, but I'm safe now. We'll talk about it later. For now, you need to rest and recover. Then we can head to the Water Temple."

Right, the Water Temple. Where we'd be bonded together forever.

I turned on my side to face Kira, grunting with the effort. Emotions churned inside me. Big, scary ones. The kind that made a man want to profess his love for a woman and beg her to stay with him forever. Strong feelings like this made me uncomfortable. So I did the only thing I could. I took her lips in a deep kiss as my hand roamed across her body, cupping her breast and stroking her nipple to make it hard, before moving down her stomach and sliding between her legs. If I turned this to sex, maybe the feelings would release their grip on me.

She gently took my hand to stop me and wove her fingers with mine, then pressed a kiss to my forehead. "Not yet. You need to recover more first. Just let me hold you."

I squeezed my eyes shut, trying to contain the emotions threatening to burst out of me. "It's been a long time since I let anyone hold me."

She wrapped herself around me, her skin sliding against mine. "You can tell yourself it's for healing purposes, if that makes you feel better."

"Is it?" I'd done something similar once when she'd passed out from giving Jasin too much of her strength, and I'd probably used the same damn excuse then too.

"Yes, but it's not the only reason. The guys told me what happened, and then I saw you..." Her voice trembled as her arms squeezed tighter. "I realized how close I'd come to losing you. Now I don't ever want to let you go."

Dammit, those emotions were back and even stronger now. I couldn't keep them in any longer. "Kira, I..."

That was all I got out. I tried to say the words. I wanted to, dammit. But I hadn't said them in so long, and every person I'd said them to had died not long after. I couldn't lose Kira too.

She pressed a soft kiss to my lips. "I know."

I buried my face in her thick red hair, breathing in her scent, and just let her hold me. The turmoil inside me died down, and I relaxed against her. Our naked limbs tangled together, and even though we weren't having sex, it was the most intimate moment of my life. I closed my eyes, and let sleep claim me again.

1 0

KIRA

Doran arrived a day after Reven woke up. He strolled into the Resistance hideout as if he belonged there, and no one seemed to recognize him in his dusty traveling clothes and heavy cloak. I kept expecting someone to realize he was their enemy, but no one paid him any attention.

At the sight of him walking through Slateden, I was torn between relief and apprehension, unsure if I should run to hug him—or in the opposite direction. The only thing I could think to say was, "You're alive."

He smirked and tipped his head. "Sark and I can't kill each other, though Gods know we've tried many times over the years. The bond with Nysa prevents us from doing anything other than roughing each other up a bit. But don't worry, I made sure he couldn't follow me here."

"Thank you for helping us. I'm not sure I could have escaped without you."

"Of course. Unfortunately, Nysa and her mates all know I've betrayed them by now. I can't go back to Soulspire." He chuckled as he pushed back his hood. "Guess that means I'll be sticking with you for the rest of your journey. Now, where can I get some food around here? I'm starving."

Sticking with us? I wasn't sure how I felt about it, but I had more pressing things I wanted to talk about first. "I can have something brought up for us. I have a lot of questions for you."

"I'm sure you do, and I'll do my best to answer them all. While we eat."

I gathered all my mates and my father into a room that Parin had once used to meet with spies and soldiers. Now that he was gone and Faya was busy trying to keep the Resistance running, the room had sat unused. Food and drinks were placed along the long wooden table, and although I'd asked for something simple, the kitchen staff had outdone themselves. I suspected many people in Slateden were feeling aimless without their leader and needed something to channel their energy into.

My mates sat around the table and none of them looked happy to be there. Jasin glared at Doran while loading a plate with food. Slade leaned back and crossed his arms, his face stony. Auric spread his journal and quill out on the table and prepared to take notes. Reven sat beside me and watched Doran closely, but his face was paler than normal. This morning I'd told them all about my time being held captive by the Dragons, and about how Nysa had stayed alive so long, and they weren't particularly pleased with Doran right now.

Doran began shoveling food into his mouth, ignoring the suspicious looks the others gave him. I watched him for a long moment, studying his face, still shocked to be sitting across from my true father. My father, who had done nothing to stop Nysa for years.

"Is it true?" I asked, my throat tightening. "All those children before me?"

His face turned grim and he set down his fork. "It's true. Every thirty years Nysa bears a daughter, who should become the next Spirit Dragon if the cycle was allowed to continue. Except Nysa drains their life and their inherent magic to keep herself alive, along with the rest of us."

"And you just let that happen?" Jasin asked.

"For a long time, yes. It's not something I'm proud of, but for many years I thought it was necessary. It was only when Kira was born that I realized how corrupted Nysa had become, and how she'd tainted the rest of us through our bond with her."

"Why was I any different?" I asked. "And how did I survive?"

Doran's eyes met mine. "You survived because, for the first time in all our years, Nysa had twins."

His words slammed into my chest, knocking me off balance. At first I couldn't speak, too stunned, trying to make sense of what he'd said. Finally I whispered, "I have a sister?"

"You did," Doran said, his face darkening with pain. "It had been many years since I'd sired a child with Nysa. All of us traded off to ease the burden of watching our own children be sacrificed, but it was eventually my turn again. I wanted to stop Nysa, but the bond makes it difficult for us to act against her, and we'd all resigned ourselves to the fact that we could do nothing." He drew in a long breath before continuing. "When I learned Nysa was having twins, I realized I had a chance to save one of them. Your sister was born first, and Nysa drained her immediately. She never even got a name, as most of them didn't, but I called her Sora, after my mother. While Nysa was busy with her, I named you Kira, after my sister, and switched you with a baby who had died only hours before during childbirth. A servant rushed you out of the palace and to safety, while I informed Nysa that her second child hadn't made it."

Tears welled up in my eyes at the thought of the twin sister I'd never known, and anger filled me knowing Nysa had killed her and Doran had done nothing to stop her. "Why didn't you save both of us?"

"I wanted to, more than anything, but it wasn't possible. Nysa needed a sacrifice to keep herself alive. If I had taken both of you, Nysa would have scoured the earth until the two of you were found. She wouldn't have stopped until you were both drained, making her doubly powerful." He stared at the plate in front of him, his voice low. "Your sister's sacrifice allowed you to live. If I could have done it any other way I would have, and I've spent the last twenty years trying to make sure Nysa never found out you were alive, so that your sister's death wasn't in vain. But I still mourn Sora every day, along with all the other daughters I've lost over the centuries."

Slade reached over and took my hand under the table, and Auric did the same on the other side. I gripped their hands hard, fighting back tears as heaviness filled my chest. *Sora*, my soul called out, searching for this missing part of myself. I hadn't known she'd existed before this day, but there had always been an emptiness inside me I'd never understood. Maybe all those years I'd spent running, searching for a family, and longing for someone to love me was my way of trying to find my lost twin again. But I wasn't sure there was anything that could fill that void.

I pushed my plate away, my appetite gone. My mates stared at me, and I felt their sympathetic worry through the bond. There was nothing they could do to help with this though. It had been bad enough knowing Nysa had killed my sisters for hundreds of years, but learning she'd taken my twin too…

By the Gods, I was going to make her pay.

I wanted to rush back to Soulspire and take her out this instant, but I couldn't let anger drive me into doing something foolish. I had to learn more before I could do anything, and I still had a lot of questions for my father.

I drew in a deep breath to steady myself and focused on one of the other questions. "The people who raised me…who were they?"

"Your mother was my great-granddaughter, the result of an affair I had long ago. She was the last of my descendants, and she took you in and swore to protect you." Doran's fist clenched around a biscuit, turning it to crumbs. "I'll never forgive Sark for what he did to her."

That explained why we looked so similar, except for our hair color. My adopted mother's hair was long and blond, which I realized now was the same shade as Doran's hair.

Doran wiped his hands on a napkin. "I've watched you from the shadows your entire life, Kira. I've tried not to interfere too much, but I've always been there, working to keep you safe. Unfortunately, that often meant acting as Nysa's devoted servant for much of your life. It's freeing to know I don't have to continue that act any longer."

Auric paused from scribbling in his journal and looked up. "What about your bond with Nysa? Won't she be able to find you here?"

Doran shook his head. "Over the years I learned how to block Nysa through the bond. It helps that I haven't slept with her since before Kira was born either. The bond between us has naturally weakened over time." He ran a rough hand over his scraggly beard, his eyes distant. "It's hard because I still love her, despite everything she's done. I always will. But she's become…corrupted. And through the bond, the rest of us became corrupted too. I was able to find my way out of it, but the others are too far gone. Which is why they all need to be defeated."

"You want us to kill your mate," Reven said, his eyes narrowed.

"It's the only way to stop her and to save Kira." Doran pushed his seat back as if he was about to stand. "There's a lot more I need to tell you, which will help you understand Nysa better and how she became so corrupted, but we need to start heading toward the Water Temple as soon as possible. Only once you've bonded with all four of your mates can you hope to stand against her."

"But the Water Temple was destroyed," Slade said.

"And the Dragons know we'll be going there," Jasin added. "They'll be waiting for us."

"No, they won't," Doran said. "And it hasn't been destroyed, because I moved it years ago. None of the Dragons know where the real Water Temple is. I made sure of that."

"Where is it?" Auric asked, his quill clenched in his hand and his eyes bright with the promise of secret knowledge.

"In the far reaches of the Water Realm. It will take us a few days to get there, so I suggest we leave as soon as we're able to."

"It depends on Reven," I said, glancing at him. "He's still recovering and—"

"I'm fine," he said quickly. "I'm ready to go."

Doran stood and glanced around the table. "Then I guess it's time for us to head out."

11

KIRA

That evening there was a small funeral for Parin, now that most people had returned from the battle at Salt Creek Tower. As the ceremony began, Slade opened up a large hole in the side of the mountain with a mighty tremble that seemed to shake the entire world. Parin's body had been cleaned and prepared, and members of the Resistance lowered it into the hole while Faya watched with stoic eyes. Once Parin was placed inside, Faya dropped in the small jade carving of a dragon, meant to represent the Earth God, which Parin's mother had made. Slade then covered up the tomb with dirt and rocks, allowing Parin to become one with the mountain that housed the Resistance hideout. As the son of the Earth God's High Priestess, it seemed a fitting resting place for him.

When it was over, there was a somber celebration with food and soft music in Faya's house. I wanted to offer my condolences to her and to tell her that Parin was a hero, but she was surrounded at all times by other people. I even saw my father speak to her for a few minutes, and I wondered who Faya thought he was. A strange traveler come to join their cause? Just another member of the Resistance?

"Kira," Brin said, drawing my attention away from my father. She threw her arms around me and gave me a quick squeeze. "I'm so glad you're okay. When the others told me what happened I was worried, although I knew you'd find a way out."

"I only escaped thanks to my mates and..." My eyes found my father again.

She followed my gaze. "Who is that? I saw him with you earlier."

I wanted to tell her. In fact, I was desperate to talk to her and have some girl time, but not here. Too many people surrounded us, and I didn't want them to hear what I had to say. "Would Leni mind if I dragged you off to talk?"

Brin glanced over at her girlfriend, who was speaking with Slade. "I doubt it. Besides, a little jealousy now and then only spices things up, right?"

We walked out of the house, although not before Brin grabbed a bottle of wine and some tiny little cakes and pastries. Once back in my guest room we eagerly kicked off our shoes and climbed onto the bed, sitting across from each other. A pang of sadness shot through me at the memory of doing this with my best friend, Tash, and the reminder that I never would again. Sark had taken that from me, like he'd taken so many other things.

Brin poured us some wine before spreading the desserts out in front of us. She eyed them carefully, before plucking a flaky pastry from the plate. "All right, I'm ready."

I chugged a big gulp of wine. "The man you saw...he's my father."

Her eyes widened. "Really? Wait. Does that mean...?"

"Yes, he's a Dragon. The Azure one."

"Wow. I've never met him before, only Sark and Isen. What's he doing here?"

"He's left the Black Dragon and has joined our cause. He wants to protect me and help me defeat her. Or so he says."

She took a bite of her pastry as she considered this. "What's he like?"

I picked up my own pastry and eyed it. "I'm not sure yet. He helped me escape and he's given me some answers about my past, but it's hard to trust him, knowing what he is. Even if I do learn to trust him and get to know him, it's my destiny to overthrow him." My throat grew tight. "To defeat the Black Dragon, I have to kill all her mates first. That includes my father."

Her eyes turned sympathetic. "What are you going to do?"

"I don't know yet." I took a bite of my pastry, sending flaky bits all over the bed. "There's more too. When I was being held captive, I met my mother. She was beautiful, regal, and...she's a monster."

I quickly told Brin everything that had happened and what I'd learned about my sisters, including my twin. Brin let me get it all out, and it was so good to talk to someone who wasn't directly involved, like my mates were. They all wanted to leap over themselves to protect me, shelter me, and make me happy, but Brin could just listen and offer unbiased advice. Sometimes that's all I needed.

"This definitely calls for more wine." Brin poured more wine into my glass from the bottle she'd swiped. "Eat another dessert too, it'll make you feel better."

"What do you think I should do?" I asked, before shoving a bite-size raspberry cake into my mouth.

Brin tapped her nails against the glass while I chewed. "I think you should listen to Doran and ask him more questions. He obviously has a great deal of information, and he's probably your best bet for learning how to actually defeat the other Dragons, but keep your distance too. Even if everything he says is true, he's not innocent in all of this. He's part of the reason Nysa is in power and the world is in chaos."

I nodded. "We need him to get to the Water Temple. I'll try to learn more on our journey."

"And when the time comes to defeat the Dragons?"

I stared into my wine. "I'll do what I have to do, I suppose."

Brin leaned forward and gave me a squeeze. "You're strong. You can do this."

"Thanks. There are some days—okay, a lot of days lately—when it all seems overwhelming and impossible."

"Just take it day by day, step by step. Like crossing things off a list. Step one: get to the Water Temple and bond with that sexy assassin of yours." She nudged me with her elbow. "At least you'll get some action from Reven finally."

I couldn't help but smile at that. Trust Brin to find the bright side if it involved sex. "I am looking forward to that part."

"I don't blame you. If I liked men, I'd be drooling over him too."

"How are you and Leni doing, anyway?"

Her face lit up at the mention of her girlfriend. "We're good. Really good. From the moment we met I felt this spark, but sometimes that goes away quickly. The spark with Leni hasn't burnt out yet." She leaned back and smiled, her face relaxed. "Now that I don't have marriage to Auric hanging over my head, I'm truly free to be who I want to be, and I can be with the person I want to be with."

"I'm happy for you. I really like Leni." I swirled my wine in my glass. "What are you going to do now? Do you want to come with us to the Water Temple?"

"I do, but I think I should stay here. The Resistance lost a lot of people at the Salt Creek Tower battle and Parin is gone. Leni and I can do some good here if we stay. For once, I feel like I've found somewhere I can be more than just a rich noble, attending parties and flirting with dignitaries. I can do some good here. Make a difference." Her voice had turned serious and now she shook it off with a grin. "Besides, you don't really need me. You have your four muscular mates and the Azure Dragon too."

"I always need you as my friend, but the Resistance is lucky to have your help."

She sat up a bit. "I actually have a specific idea for something I wanted to run past you."

My eyebrows shot up. "What is it?"

"Rumors are beginning to spread about you and your mates. I'd like to encourage them."

"Why?"

"It gives people something to fight for, and it'll spread hope. The world is ready for a change in leadership, and people have been oppressed for too long. New Dragons rising up to challenge the old ones? The Resistance would be overflowing with new recruits."

I brushed crumbs off myself and the bed. "I see your point. Do whatever you think is best. We're not hiding anymore, and you're right that it's time the world knows about us."

"Exactly. Although we need to call you all something else. We can't have two Crimson Dragons, and so forth. That's just way too confusing for the general public."

I hadn't thought of that before, but Enva had mentioned she'd been called the White Dragon, so it seemed the names were changeable. "You can call us the ascendants. That's what the priests and Gods say."

"That works, but I think we need something more too." She tapped her lips in thought. "What if we use gemstones? We can call Jasin the Ruby Dragon, for example. It'll distance him from the Crimson Dragon's reputation, which would be a good thing. Crimson makes one think of all the blood Sark has spilled. Rubies are regal, beautiful, and passionate. Then we can use emerald, citrine, and sapphire for the other men."

"I like it, but not sure the men will. And what will they call me?"

"The White Dragon? It has a nice contrast to the Black Dragon."

"No, that's what my grandmother was called. How about the Silver Dragon?"

"Perfect." She clinked her glass against mine. "Trust me. This is what I'm good at, and with the support of the people, you'll have a much easier time rallying people to your cause, and maintaining order once you defeat the Dragons."

"I hope it goes that smoothly." Great, something else to worry about. I'd spent so much time trying to figure out how to defeat the Dragons I hadn't stopped to consider what would happen if we won. All I knew was that I didn't want to rule, not like my mother. I just wanted peace.

"It will all work out," Brin reassured me. "Just promise me you'll come back after the Water temple and fill me in on everything."

"I will. I'll probably need someone to talk to after dealing with my four mates plus my father." I groaned at the thought. "I think this is going to be a long journey."

12

KIRA

We left for the Water Realm in the morning, beginning a journey that would take many days and return me to the place where I'd grown up. I'd avoided going back ever since I'd left when I was thirteen, and I both longed to see the sparkling blue waters again and dreaded returning to the place where I'd lost my family. I wondered if Reven felt the same. Our childhoods had so many similarities, at least from the bits and pieces I'd learned from him, and I wished he would open up to me more, but it was something I couldn't force.

He was doing better physically, at least. Some color had returned to his face, and he no longer looked quite as frail and thin. I tried to touch him as much as possible, hoping my healing would help him recover faster, and to reassure myself he was truly all right.

We soared southwest across the Earth Realm, leaving behind the ice-covered mountain peaks and flying over forests and fields. There'd been some argument over which dragon I would ride, with everyone saying that Doran couldn't be trusted. Both Jasin and Auric wanted me to fly with them, but that meant Slade or Reven would have to ride with my father. In the end, I decided to have faith in Doran and told my mates I'd be riding with him—end of discussion. They didn't like it, but Doran had proven himself so far, and I wanted to show I trusted him, even if I was still hesitant about it. I hoped it might bring us closer, and as a result of that he might reveal more about the past.

And maybe I just wanted to be near my father too. I'd spent my entire life yearning and searching for a family. I'd moved from place to place, trying to find a replacement for the parents I'd lost and the twin sister I never knew I was missing. First I'd tried to find my family with merchants, then with bandits, before landing with Tash and her mother. Now my family consisted of my mates, but I loved them in a different way.

A part of me knew that my relationship with my father would be fleeting and short-lived. I wanted to soak up as much time with him as I could before it was over. Even if he was something of a monster, I was curious about him—and my mother too, if I was honest. They'd lived a long time, and I knew so little about them, beyond the myths and rumors.

"What did you do before you became Nysa's mate?" I asked, when we stopped to take a quick break. Talking while flying was difficult except for a few short words yelled into the wind, so this was our first moment to chat.

"I was a pirate," Doran said.

"Really?" I had to admit he did look the part.

He leaned against a tree and took a swig of water. "It's been a long time since I thought about those days. I grew up in the Water Realm, and your grandmother and her mates had brokered a truce with the elementals, so they didn't attack us as long as we stayed out of their way. That opened the seas to travel, and I joined a merchant's ship at thirteen. At sixteen, we got attacked by pirates. They told me I could join them or die. Seemed like an obvious choice." A slow grin spread over his face. "By the time I was twenty-five and the Water God came to visit me, I was captain of that ship."

"What happened then?"

His grin faded. "I gave it all up for Nysa."

Of course he did. Just like my mates gave up their previous lives for me. "Did you love her?"

"I did. I do. I always will." He met my eyes. "But I love my daughter more."

I stared at him and grasped for a way to respond. He turned away before I could find an answer, and then he shifted back into his dragon form to take off. All I could do was stand there, reeling in shock, while a warm feeling spread through my chest, followed by a deep, unbearable sadness. I'd waited so long to hear words like that...and now they were from my enemy.

Doran led the way, pushing us hard the entire time. When we finally stopped it was late in the evening, and we managed to find an abandoned farm to spend the night in. The roof was caving in on the farmhouse and everything had a layer of dust, but I supposed it was better than camping outside. Jasin lit a fire in the slightly moldy hearth, and we sat around it while we ate some of the food we'd packed.

Doran spread the map out in front of us. "We're going to take a slightly longer route to avoid the other Dragons, who will no doubt be looking for us around the old Water Temple."

"What can you tell us about the other Dragons?" Jasin asked.

He lifted one shoulder in a casual shrug. "What do you want to know? I've spent many lifetimes with the bastards. It's hard to narrow it down to a quick summary."

"Tell us about each one of them," Auric said. "What did they do before they were chosen by the Gods? What are they like now?"

Doran leaned back in a rickety wooden chair and folded his hands behind his head. "Isen was a nobleman, Sark was a soldier, Heldor was a carpenter, and, like I told Kira earlier, I was a pirate."

"That sounds oddly similar to our lives before all of this," Slade said.

"You're probably more like the Dragon you're replacing than you realize, and you'll probably take on similar roles once this is all over. Her protector, her enforcer, her scout, and her diplomat." He chuckled softly. "What can I say? Each of the Gods has a type."

"I'm nothing like Sark," Jasin said with a scowl.

"No? He's brave, passionate, and hot-tempered. He acts without thinking but can be strategic when it comes to battle. He'd fight and die for his beliefs and he's willing to stand up and be a leader when required. Sound like anyone we know?" He smirked, and Jasin's scowl only deepened. "But you're right—Sark is different from you in some ways. He will murder innocents, including children, and feels no guilt as long as he believes it will help the Black Dragon. Sark's the darker version of you, twisted and corrupted by years of serving Nysa."

"Does that make you the darker version of me?" Reven asked, arching an eyebrow.

"I suppose." Doran appraised Reven. "We both have a view of the world that's more gray than black and white. We're both willing to do whatever needs to be done, preferably from the shadows. We collect secrets to use as leverage. We guard our hearts and can come across as cold, but only to hide how much we feel. Am I right?"

Reven looked away sharply and didn't answer.

I leaned forward, curious. "What makes you darker than him?"

Doran's face turned serious. "I doubt Reven would have waited centuries to act when he believed something was wrong."

Awkward silence fell over the room. "And Heldor?" I finally asked.

"Heldor is fiercely loyal to the Black Dragon and rarely leaves her side unless she commands it. Most of us have had other lovers over the years, but Heldor has never once strayed. He's the strong and silent type, calm under pressure, and generally level-headed. But he has a low tolerance for nonsense, and he follows Nysa without question. He'll do anything for her."

"What about Isen?" Auric asked.

"Isen is smart, calculating, and likes to collect knowledge, although his motives are different from yours. For him, it's all about power. In the old days, he was often the mediator of our group, and trust me there were many times when none of us got along. He prefers not to fight unless he must, although he has no problem murdering people in cold blood either. His favorite method is to suffocate anyone who disagrees with him." Doran turned to Auric. "I can teach you how to do that, if you'd like."

"No, thank you." Auric's face paled. "That sounds horrible."

"Why hasn't Isen done that to us?" Jasin asked.

"Suffocating someone with magic requires a lot of concentration, and it takes longer than you think to choke someone to death. He prefers to use it to make sure he gets his way—anyone watching is usually too terrified to disagree with him after that."

"How do we defeat them?" Slade asked.

Doran let out a harsh laugh. "Right now? You can't. They're stronger than you, and they've been Dragons for centuries."

Reven sneered. "What are we supposed to do? Wait a hundred years before trying to take them down?"

"No, because I'm going to train you." My father leaned forward, the firelight dancing in his eyes. "I'll teach you how to use your powers and how to work together. In our time, the previous Dragons mentored us before they stepped down. You've been at a disadvantage because you've had to figure everything out on your own." He looked at each of us in turn. "With my help, you might actually stand a chance."

13

SLADE

In the morning, I woke early and took a walk through the abandoned farm, down a steep hill. When I was out of sight of the farmhouse, I shifted into my dragon form for the second time. The transformation was strange as my bones cracked, expanded, and changed. Wings formed on my back. My fingernails turned to talons. My teeth turned to fangs. And everything around me suddenly got a lot smaller.

Compared to the others, I was massive. In my human form I was broader than Kira's other mates, but I hadn't realized it would translate to this body as well.

I glanced behind me again to make sure no one had followed me, trying to get used to the way my long neck moved, almost like a snake's. With the sun cresting the horizon, my scales turned to green fire, and I had to admit they were beautiful.

I took a deep breath and raised my wings. The fear of failing a second time nearly held me back, but I had to try this again. For Kira.

I beat my wings as fast as I could and managed to lift up onto my claws, but that was as far as I got. It was like the ground itself was holding me down, preventing me from flying. I let out a frustrated roar before becoming a human again.

I knelt and picked up a handful of dirt, then let it run through my fingers. Would I ever be able to fly, or would I be condemned to the ground forever?

"Heldor had difficulty flying at first, too," Doran said, making me jump. He stood behind me, appearing out of nowhere like Reven did sometimes. Sneaky bastards. "It's not your fault. Your Earth magic makes it hard for you to fly. That connection with the ground is so strong you'll have to learn to overcome and let go of it before you can lift off. I can help you." He examined me. "It doesn't help you're such a large Dragon either, about the same size as Heldor when you shift. You'll need to build up your wing strength too."

I scowled at him, but his words felt right, and I had to admit I did need help. I had no idea what I was doing, and I didn't have time to figure it out on my own. He'd lived for hundreds of years and had seen Heldor go through the same thing once. I gritted my teeth and said, "I'd appreciate your help."

Doran chuckled. "I doubt that, but I'll give it to you anyway. There's no way you can defeat us if you can't fly."

"You *want* us to defeat you?"

"Of course." He said it casually, so casually I suspected he might be lying. Like Reven, he was hard to read, and secrets perpetually danced behind his eyes. Until recently, I wouldn't have trusted either of them. Then Reven went and saved my life and nearly died in the process. And Doran… Well, he'd helped Kira escape and had protected her. I wasn't ready to let down my guard completely with him, but I was willing to listen to his advice.

Doran waved a hand at me. "All right, turn back into a dragon."

"You want to do this now?"

"You have somewhere else you need to be?"

I scowled at him, then took a few steps back to give myself space, and returned to my dragon form. The others would be up soon, but for now we were alone out here.

He nodded as if confirming his suspicions. "Like I thought, your size is going to make it harder for you to fly. You'll need to practice with your wings every day to build up their strength."

I groaned, though it came out more like a growl. My voice was different as a dragon. Deeper. Louder. More gravely.

"But the real thing holding you back is your own magic," Doran continued. "Along with your own self-doubt."

Now I really did growl at him, though he ignored it and kept talking.

"What I want you to do is try to let go of your earth magic. I know it's a part of you but try to block it out however you can."

How did he expect me to do that? The moment the Earth God came to me, I became a different person. No longer a simple blacksmith living in a small town, but someone destined for bigger things. Even when I wondered if he should have chosen another, or missed my old life, or tried to guard my heart from Kira, I'd never wavered in my faith. The magic was a fundamental part of me and had become as natural as breathing.

I felt the earth through my clawed feet, which dug at the dirt. The only time I didn't feel the earth's presence was when I was flying on one of the other dragons' backs, or when we were on a wretched boat. Even on a boat I'd managed to connect with the wood and the metal, but soaring high in the sky—it was hard for me to feel comfortable with that. Like a part of me was cut off.

Maybe that was the problem. I tried to focus on that uncomfortable feeling now. I pictured riding on the back of Auric or Jasin as they soared across the sky, and how empty and adrift I felt. I hated it, but when I tried to take off this time, my feet left the ground.

I didn't get far. My wings flapped rapidly to hold me up, but I knew they wouldn't last long.

From below, Doran called out, "Nice work! Try to hold it as long as you can."

I hovered above him for a few more seconds, before hitting the ground in a thump, sending a cloud of dirt into the air around us.

Doran coughed and waved it away. "Good. Now I want you to do that every day. Preferably multiple times."

I groaned and set my head down, already tired from that short flight— and from dealing with Doran.

He walked away while I rested there, enjoying the sun on my back and the dirt under my scales. As the sky grew brighter, I heard footsteps approach. Kira. I raised my head and met her eyes before looking away quickly, ashamed she had to see me like this. I was a failed dragon who could hover for a few seconds at best. She deserved better.

"I never got the chance to see you as a dragon," she said, as she approached. Her arms wrapped around my head, embracing me. "You're beautiful."

I let out a grunt, but nudged my head up against her chest, enjoying her touch. The bond between us, which I hadn't noticed before except when we'd had sex, suddenly took over my mind. I sensed how happy she was to see me like this and felt her belief in me. My own doubts slowly fell away. I couldn't fly now, but I would keep practicing every spare moment I could—for Kira.

14

KIRA

We reached the coast that evening, just north of the border between the Earth Realm and the Water Realm. Doran showed Reven and Slade how to turn saltwater into water we could drink, while Auric and Jasin rested after flying the entire day with few breaks. I took a walk down the shore, my toes digging into the wet sand for the first time in years, while lazy waves stretched closer and closer to my feet. The moon was bright overhead, making the surface of the water shimmer, and I bent to pick up a shell that almost seemed to glow.

"Kira," a voice whispered across the salty breeze.

I jerked upright and spun around, the shell clutched in my palm. My grandmother Enva stood ankle-deep in the water, yet when the tide pulled back, she showed no signs it had ever touched her. She strode toward me, her gray skirts completely dry, her white hair shining under the moonlight like a pearl. She'd once been called the White Dragon, and though she'd been dead for centuries, she was trapped between this world and the next along with every other person who had passed. But unlike the others, her connection to the Spirit Goddess allowed her to hold onto enough life to manifest in front of me for a short time.

"I'm sorry I couldn't help while you were being held captive," she said, as she drew near. "The bone cage prevented me from visiting you."

"I assumed as much," I said, relieved to see her again. "Why does the bone block our powers?"

"Your magic stems from life, and bones are objects of death. They're abhorrent to us, completely opposite of our very nature."

I frowned as I examined the shell in my palm. "But I've killed many animals and even people before. I've been around many dead bodies. It wasn't until I touched Tash's bones that I encountered that horrible feeling."

"Ah, because there's a difference between killing to preserve life, and killing only to end it. When you hunt animals for food for yourself or others, you're sustaining life. When you've killed people, it was to defend yourself or protect other lives. All of those things are part of the natural cycle of survival. But when someone is murdered, their bones become tainted with darkness."

"Nysa could touch them. How?"

Enva's face darkened. "That is the ultimate question. I suggest you ask your father."

I stared at her, while wind tugged on my hair and completely ignored hers. "So Doran truly is my father."

"Of course. But you knew that already."

"I did, but I wanted to hear you confirm it. Why didn't you tell me?"

"It wasn't my place, and I knew you wouldn't take it well. Not at that time."

I sighed. She was probably right. "What of everything he told me about Nysa—is it all true?"

"Yes, he has been honest with you. He's just left out something very important. Something you should ask him about."

"What is that?"

Enva's eyes burned into mine. For the first time I realized they were the same green as my mother's. "Nysa told you she has to stay alive in order to keep the Spirit Goddess contained. Ask him why."

I nodded slowly. "I assumed it was so the Gods couldn't replace her."

"Not entirely. I would tell you myself, but it's a long tale and I expect you'll have many questions. I already feel the other side pulling me back now."

"I wish we had more time together. There's so much I want to know about your life. Like what was it like when you were a Dragon? Doran said you negotiated a treaty with the elementals and brought peace?"

"Every set of Dragons has one great challenge to face. Mine was the elementals. When I became the White Dragon, the elementals had ravaged the four Realms and humans were living in fear. The balance had tipped too far in one direction, and my mates and I did what we could to level the scales again." She gazed across the water with a distant look in her eyes. "For some time, we had peace. And then the shades came."

"Was that my mother's challenge?" I asked.

"It was the start of it." Enva sighed and stared at the sand at her feet.

"There's another reason Doran should tell you this tale. It hurts me too much to speak it aloud. I love my daughter, no matter how twisted she's become. I understand why she did what she did, even if I disagreed with it. I only wish I could have prevented all of this or found a way to save her from the darkness. I'm her mother, and I failed her...and now I must help you defeat her."

I took her hand, which felt solid even though she wasn't really there. "No one should have to make such a choice."

She squeezed my hand in return as she began to fade before my eyes. "Nysa and I both made mistakes, but I know you will be the one to right them. Stay strong, Kira..."

She disappeared from sight as her last words floated away on the wind. A sense of sadness filled me as I stood alone with the waves lapping at my bare feet while I clutched a shell in my hand. I released it into the water and turned to walk the distance back to my mates, while I mentally prepared myself for another conversation with my father. One that I wasn't sure I was ready to have.

I stepped through the camp the others had set up, past a bonfire Jasin had started, where fresh fish now roasted. My mates stirred as I strode past them but must have seen the serious expression on my face because none of them said a word. Doran was stretched out in front of the ocean, leaning back as he gazed up at the stars, his hands folded across his stomach. He looked up as I approached and his expression changed, as if he sensed that something had occurred, but he wasn't sure exactly what.

I stopped in front of him and met his eyes. "Tell me about the Spirit Goddess."

15

KIRA

My father ran a hand over his beard, which was looking more rugged with each day that went by. "I'd planned to tell you about this once we reached the Water Temple, but I suppose now is as good a time as any. Sit down. This might take a while. And someone get me some ale."

I sank onto the ground across from him, pulling my knees to my chest, while my mates gathered around. "Nysa told me she had to drain my life in order to contain the Spirit Goddess. What does that mean? Why would she need to contain her?"

Doran scrounged up a bottle of something dark from his pack and popped off the top of it. "I'll get to that, but I need to start at the beginning. The first thing you need to know is that the Spirit Goddess is really two entities: Life and Death. Twin sisters, two sides of the same coin, bound together as one."

Auric grabbed his notebook and began furiously scribbling in it. "Why have we never heard of this before?"

"All records of this are long gone. Nysa made sure of that." My father took a long swig of his alcohol before continuing. "Long before any of us were on this earth, the Spirit Goddess ruled with her four mates, the other Gods of Fire, Earth, Air, and Water. They created the elementals to represent each God and humans to represent the Goddess. But over the years the Death side of her became too strong and corrupted the Spirit Goddess. The balance of life and death shifted too far to one side. To stop the world from falling into darkness, the Gods broke up the two aspects of Life and

Death, creating two separate Goddesses instead of one. The Death Goddess was banished to the Realm of the Dead, where she became its ruler, while the Life Goddess stayed here with her four mates. They created the Dragons to act as their representatives in the world, and to make sure that the Death Goddess could never return."

"I thought the Dragons were created to keep the balance between elementals and humans," Jasin said.

"That is one of their duties, yes. But they were also created to ensure that the Life Goddess had assistance in protecting the world from the Death Goddess. Kira you are actually a descendant of the Life Goddess, as were all the other female Dragons before you."

That would explain why the bone cage harmed me the way it did, but not why my mother was immune to it. "What about Nysa?"

"I'm getting to that." Doran scowled and stared at his bottle. "When Nysa turned twenty, she became a Dragon, like her mother. Back then she wasn't dark or evil, not like you know her now."

"What happened?" Slade asked.

He took another chug of his drink as he gazed into the fire. "Shortly after she became a Dragon, shades began appearing in our world in vast numbers, sucking the life from both elementals and humans alike. We learned later that they were the creation of the Death Goddess. She'd grown tired of living in the Realm of the Dead and jealous of her twin for having all four mates to herself. She sent the shades to attack us, and they fed her power with each life they took. Soon, she had enough power to leave the afterlife and return to our world. When she did, she brought death and darkness everywhere she went, and every time she took a life, she grew stronger. And with the Death Goddess gone, the way to the Realm of the Dead closed, trapping all fallen souls between the two worlds. No one has been able to find peace since then."

"Enva mentioned that," I said, nodding.

Doran arched an eyebrow. "How do you know of her?"

"She comes to visit me sometimes."

"Does she? Interesting." His eyes turned haunted, the firelight flickering in his eyes. "Yes, the Death Goddess's arrival changed everything. The Life Goddess fought her twin sister, but their battle nearly tore the entire world apart. The Death Goddess had become too powerful from all the lives she had stolen. As a last resort, we worked with the Gods to bind the two Goddesses together again, but all it did was create a dark, twisted Spirit Goddess who began to devour all life with an insatiable hunger. We realized we'd made a terrible mistake, but the other Gods refused to help us separate them again. The Spirit Goddess was their mate, their queen, their leader, and they had to obey her. So we decided all the Gods had to be stopped, for the sake of the world."

"How do you stop a God?" Reven asked.

"It's not easy." Doran drained the last of his bottle and tossed it aside. "We imprisoned all the Gods in their temples, one by one, using the element that is their opposite. Fire versus water, earth versus air, you get the idea. Once they were gone the Spirit Goddess was weakened and we tried to imprison her in the Spirit Temple, but we failed. She was too strong, even then. But Nysa found a way to cage the Spirit Goddess...by trapping her within her own body."

I gasped. "The Spirit Goddess is *inside* Nysa?"

"She is. It was the only way to stop her, although we didn't realize the consequences of doing such a thing." His jaw clenched. "Nysa fought against the Death Goddess's darkness for years, but eventually she succumbed to it and became the Black Dragon. She still maintains some control, which is how she keeps the Spirit Goddess contained, but she's become twisted...and incredibly powerful. She controls both life and death magic, along with all the elements, making her nearly unstoppable. With a single touch, she can drain a person's life, and her body heals itself immediately. That's on the rare occasions she is injured at all, since she's immune to all five elements."

I dug my toes into the sand, taking in everything he'd said. It was a lot to absorb, and it made our task seem even more daunting. "Is it even possible to defeat Nysa? And if we do, what will happen?"

"It's possible but won't be easy. And if Nysa dies, the Spirit Goddess will be unleashed upon the world again. This is why she started sacrificing her own children...and why we reluctantly went along with it."

"I don't see how any of you could agree to that," Slade said with disgust, echoing my own thoughts.

"No, because you didn't see how bad it was when the Spirit Goddess was free. She would have wiped out all life on this world within months. If we let her continue, this would be a second Realm of the Dead under her rule." Doran pinched the bridge of his nose. "Nysa was desperate to keep the Spirit Goddess contained, and she tried draining humans, elementals, and shades, but none of it extended her life. But then she had a daughter, continuing the Dragon cycle. The magic within the child was strong enough to keep Nysa—and by extension the rest of us—alive for another thirty years, when she could have another child." He shuddered a little. "It was horrible, but we told ourselves it was one life taken in exchange for millions saved. We didn't realize what the toll would be on our own souls."

"And yet you kept doing it," Jasin growled. "For hundreds of years."

My father dropped his head. "We had no other choice. Until Kira and her twin sister were born."

"Why were we different?" I asked.

Doran's eyes rested on me again. "All of our daughters were born with both life and death magic inside them, except for the two of you. Your magic was split, with Kira having life magic, and Sora having death magic. I thought it was a sign that the Spirit Goddess could be divided again, and our mistakes could finally be undone." He clenched his fists in the sand. "After I got Kira to safety, I released the Fire God from his prison. I was the only one who could do it, since I'd been the one who put him there. Once the Fire God was freed, he helped me release the other Gods one by one in secret, so that they could choose Dragons for Kira's mates when her twentieth birthday arrived."

Silence settled over the group as we took in everything he'd said. His story explained so much about my past and about why Nysa did so many horrible things, but I didn't feel any relief now that I knew the truth.

Finally, I asked, "How are we supposed to stop the Spirit Goddess?"

"That I don't know," Doran said. "All I know is that this horrible cycle can't continue. We thought we were saving the world, and maybe we did for a short time, but now I fear we've made it even worse."

"Would the Gods be able to divide the Spirit Goddess into two halves again?" Auric asked.

Doran shrugged. "They have the ability, and that was the deal when I freed them. Will they hold up their end of the bargain? Who knows."

"Then we can't trust them either," Reven said.

"I agree," Doran said. "But right now, we need to focus on defeating Nysa. Otherwise, we won't have to worry about any of that."

Everyone's faces were grim as we prepared for bed. My mates asked me if I was all right, but I didn't know what to say. Doran's words had shaken all of us, making us realize the task ahead of us was much more daunting than we'd realized, and the price of our failure was even higher than we'd imagined.

As I pulled my blanket around me, my eyes stared at the moonlit waves and tried to make sense of it all. We'd reach the Water Realm the next afternoon, thanks to Doran's relentless pace. I was torn between wanting to hurry as much as he did, and wondering if we should stay away, after what we'd learned. The longer we waited, the more chances the Dragons would find us or the new Water Temple first. The sooner we got to the Temple, the sooner I would have to face my mother. The Gods had told me it was my destiny to defeat her, but they hadn't told me everything. By defeating my mother, I would be unleashing something much worse on the world. How could I do that, without some plan to stop the Spirit Goddess?

I'd have to ask the Water God for advice when we spoke to him, except now I wondered if the Gods had been honest with us all along. They could be as twisted as the Goddess, manipulating us to do what they wanted— freeing her.

Things had once been so clear. The Gods were good. The Dragons were evil. Now I realized nothing was as simple as black and white. My mother had a reason for what she'd done, something she and the other Dragons had believed was right. The Gods had their own plans and their own reasons. Even Doran and Enva had motives that might be contrary to what I wanted. The only people I could trust were my mates. I knew in my core they would never betray me, and they would always steer me true. Everyone else wanted something from me. My life. My service. My power.

But I wasn't sure what I wanted anymore, or what the best action was for the entire world. For the first time since this all began, I wasn't certain of my path anymore.

16

AURIC

The Water Realm was connected to the Earth Realm by a bit of land that jutted out in a peninsula, before splitting into hundreds of islands that made up of most of its territory. Doran was taking us on a long route to avoid running into the other Dragons, flying us over turquoise waters and islands with white sands and tall palm trees stretching into the sky.

We took a break at midday after hours of travel. Still in my dragon form, I stretched my wings and devoured some food to combat the aches and exhaustion of flying for days with people and supplies on my back, though I could tell I was getting stronger. Every day my endurance as a Dragon was building, as was my skill at flying. Now if only we could get Slade to fly too. He practiced every morning before we set off and could hover in the air for a few minutes, but anything more than that was still a problem. I wished I could help him in some way, but this was something he had to do on his own.

I spotted Kira standing by herself across the small island, gazing out at the clear blue water with troubled eyes. I trudged over to her and curled up around her with my large scaled body, giving us a hint of privacy from the others. "Are you all right?"

"I'm okay," she said with a smile that looked forced. "Just thinking about what we learned last night."

"It was a lot to take in. So much of what we thought we knew about the Gods was a lie." I'd recorded everything Doran had told us in my journal, which was running out of pages at this point. Every time we spoke with him we learned something new, something which had been lost over time or removed from history purposefully. The other Dragons had kept people living in ignorance and fear, with knowledge restricted to the few. That would not be our legacy.

Kira sighed. "I'm not sure we can trust anything the Gods tell us, and I have no idea what to do about Nysa now. We have to defeat her, but I worry that doing so will only make things worse. And although I still hate her, I understand why she became the person she is now. She thought she was doing what was best for the world but made some bad choices that led her down a dark path. Who's to say we won't do the same?"

I wrapped a golden wing around her. "We'll figure it out. I have faith in you, and we'll be with you through all of it."

She ran her hand along my scales slowly. "Thanks. I couldn't do this without the four of you at my side."

"Once we reach the Water Temple, I'll talk to the priests and see if they have any old texts about the Gods. Perhaps we'll find something useful."

"Perhaps," she replied, although she sounded doubtful. I didn't have much hope either, but I had to try.

She leaned against my large side, gazing out at the water again. I wished I could shift back into my human form and hold her, but I still had all the supplies strapped to my back, and we would be leaving soon. Doran would grumble at us if we held the group up by even a minute.

"We'll be at the Water Temple soon at this pace," I said, trying to distract her from her dark thoughts. "Is Reven going to be ready?"

We'd all heard them arguing the night before we went to the Earth Temple, and Reven had never been very amenable to the idea of becoming a Dragon. But he'd also sacrificed himself to save Kira, so we knew he cared for her—even if he didn't want to admit it to himself.

"I think so. Things with him have been...difficult." Her eyes darted to Reven, who stood apart from everyone else, leaning against the palm trees with his arms crossed. As usual, his brooding face made him look like he would rather be anywhere else, unless you noticed that he was turned toward Kira. He always kept an eye on her, even though he tried to make it seem like he didn't care.

I rubbed my head against her side. "I think he'll come around when it's time."

"I wish I had your optimism."

"It's not optimism. I believe in you, and in your other mates." I grinned, giving her a glimpse of my fangs. "And I don't see how Reven could possibly resist you."

She took my large, scaled head in her hands, then pressed a kiss to my forehead. "Thank you. I always feel better after we talk."

Through our bond I did sense that her troubles had lifted slightly. They'd always be there, at least until all of this was over, but they no longer weighed her down quite so much. Good. If I could ease Kira's burden or make her smile, I'd done my duty as her mate.

"Enough standing around," Doran roared, as he flexed his wings. "Do you want to make it to the Water Temple before the Dragons find us? Then let's get moving."

The others grumbled at the shortness of our break while Kira rolled her eyes. I nudged her with my tail. "Come on, let's join the others before your father yells at us again."

"He can be quite annoying, can't he?"

"Sometimes, but he's just looking out for you."

"Is he?" She cast a skeptical eye at him. "You're the only one who seems to trust him."

"I'm trying to give him the benefit of the doubt. I truly think he wants to help us." I flexed my talons and bared my fangs. "But if he turns against us, I'll be ready."

17
KIRA

W e stopped that night at a small fishing village where everyone knew
Doran and greeted him warmly—a reaction I'd never seen before.
Most people cowered in fear from the Dragons, but he'd flown right into
the village and had shifted in front of them. Instead of hiding, people had
run out to say hello with smiles on their faces.

"I saved them from a group of elementals a few years ago," Doran
explained, as he led us to the small building that served as a tavern and inn
for sailors.

"I thought we were supposed to be traveling in secret," I said.

"Trust me, no one from this town will go running to the other Dragons, and it's such a small, inconsequential village none of them will bother
coming here."

I glanced across the town, with its wind-battered and sun-bleached
buildings, some of which had straw roofs. Palm trees blew lazily overhead,
and the air smelled of saltwater and fresh fish from the nearby harbor.
Memories of my childhood, living in a place just like this, came rushing
back. "This town reminds me of Tidefirth."

"Does it?" Doran asked. "I suppose it is similar."

"Is it possible to go back there?"

"No. Sark burned it down after you left, probably to punish me for
making him spare your life. The entire village is little more than ash, along
with all the people who once lived there." He rested a hand on my
shoulder briefly. "I'm sorry."

Pain gripped my heart. Sark took all those innocent lives...and for what? Some petty rivalry between the two of them? Maybe he and Nysa had started out with good intentions, but they'd done many terrible things over the years too, which couldn't be forgiven. They had to be stopped.

As night fell across the quiet town, I wandered through the small harbor, eyeing the various boats docked there. I spotted Reven sitting on the end of the pier, his legs hanging over the water, the breeze teasing at his black hair. He was so handsome it took my breath away, even after all this time, and I couldn't help but be drawn to him.

He didn't look up as I sat beside him. We sat in silence for a few minutes, simply enjoying the sound of the waves, the feel of the wind, and the way the stars appeared as night crept over the ocean.

His voice finally broke the silence. "The Water Realm brings back old memories."

"Good or bad?" I asked.

"Both."

I nodded, understanding what he meant. "This village reminds me of the place where I grew up. A tiny fishing village like this one. Until Sark came and destroyed it all." I turned toward him, watching the profile of his face. "Where did you grow up in the Water Realm? A town like this?"

He shrugged. "All over."

"You moved around a lot?"

He fell silent, and I worried he wouldn't answer. Reven hated talking about his past. I knew almost nothing about it, and every time I'd tried to ask him, he'd ended the conversation and made it clear he wouldn't say anything more. When he did give me some tidbit about his past, I hoarded it like treasure and pored over it for days. He'd gotten his twin swords from his father. He knew how to sail a boat. His parents were members of the Resistance and had been killed by Sark. But the rest? It was still a mystery.

"I grew up on a ship," Reven said, surprising me.

"Were you a pirate like Doran?" I asked. It would explain the swords and how his father had trained him to use them so expertly.

An amused smirk made Reven even more gorgeous. "No. I was in a traveling carnival, actually."

I blinked at him. Of all the things I'd expected to learn about Reven's past, that was not one of them. "You what?"

"My family's ship was part of a performing troupe that sailed from one island to another, putting on a show in each one."

I had a hard time imagining Reven growing up in such a life. "What kind of performers?"

He shrugged. "Jugglers, acrobats, magicians, animal tamers... We had it all."

"Your family did all that?"

"My parents were known as the Twirling Blades, and they had an act where they danced with their swords, threw knives, and performed other stunts that few could believe." He ran a hand over one of his swords at the memory. "They raised me to be one of them. I never knew any other life. Until Sark took it all away."

"I thought your family was killed because they were in the Resistance."

"They were. Our role as traveling performers made it easy for us to carry messages and to transport or hide people. The carnival was the perfect front for what they were truly doing. I had no idea at the time." His face turned grim. "One day I got into a fight with my parents over something stupid and ran off. I left the boat and went into the city to try to get into trouble. When I got back, all our ships were destroyed. Every single one of them. My parents. My sister. My aunts, uncles, cousins... In one blow, Sark had taken everything I had ever known."

I took his hand and gave it a squeeze. "I'm so sorry."

He kept going, as if he hadn't heard me. "I didn't know what to do. I blamed myself. I told myself if I'd stayed behind, I could have stopped him, or helped some of them escape, or something."

"How old were you?"

"Ten."

"Oh, Reven. There was nothing you could have done. If you were there, Sark would have killed you too."

His hand tightened around mine. "Yes, I know. But the guilt of surviving is hard to get rid of, even if logic tells me there was nothing I could do to save them."

"I understand. I have the same guilt." I leaned my head against his shoulder. "What did you do after that?"

"I fled back into the city, but I knew no one there and had nothing but the clothes on my back and my father's swords, which I'd managed to save from the wreckage. I ended up living on the streets, trying to use my skills to make money, but no one wanted to pay a kid to play with swords. I became a thief in order to survive." He tilted his head back and stared up at the stars. "Turns out those same skills that made my family a good group of performers also made me a good criminal."

"Is that when you become an assassin?"

"No." He scowled and pushed himself to his feet. I could tell by the shuttered look on his face that he was done talking, and probably regretted revealing so much to me. "I think that's enough reminiscing for one night. We have another long day ahead of us tomorrow."

He began to turn away, but I was tired of him always pushing me away. We would be at the Water Temple soon. Something had to change.

I jumped up and caught his arm. "It's fine if you don't want to talk about your past. I know it can be painful. But don't shut me out, please. In a few days we'll be pledging our lives to each other and I have to know that you're serious about this."

"I told you I was." His eyes narrowed and he jerked his arm away. "You want to know how I became an assassin? Fine. I thought I'd spare you the dark details tonight, but since you insist…"

I sighed. "Reven—"

"A man named Harman found me and convinced me to work for him," Reven said, his voice menacing as he spat out the words. "He had a whole gang of street kids and he made us do terrible things. Stealing was the least of it. He sold our bodies to monsters who liked children. He murdered anyone who disobeyed or questioned him. But at least we were fed, and we had each other. I found a new family. A girl."

I wanted to take Reven into my arms and hold him as he spoke about what was obviously a painful tale, but I kept my distance. I worried if I made even the slightest movement, he'd get spooked and run away again.

He stared across the dark waters as he continued. "Her name was Mira. I was fourteen by then, and she was a year younger than me. It was innocent, or as innocent as it could be for two kids who had been forced to grow up way too fast. She was beautiful and kind, and I told her I'd do anything to protect her. When Harman decided he'd sell her off to a man five times her age, we made a plan to run away…but we didn't get far. Harman's men caught her, and she was killed while trying to escape them." His hands clenched at his side. "At the sight of her blood, I lost it and murdered them all with my father's swords. They were the first lives I took. And then I went back and killed Harman too, along with everyone else I could find. I hunted down every single man and woman he had ever worked with and made sure they'd never prey on children again. That's when the Assassin's Guild invited me to join them." He met my eyes again and spread his arms wide. "And now you know everything. I've been a thief, a whore, and a killer. There's only darkness and death in my past. Forgive me if I don't like talking about it."

Reven's voice was cold and his face was hard, but I could sense the pain inside him. I wrapped my arms around him and held him silently, until some of the tension in his body relaxed and he reluctantly embraced me in return.

"Thank you for telling me," I said. "I'm sorry you went through all that, and I know it must have been difficult to talk about. But your past shaped you into the man you are today. A man I love."

"Don't say that." He took my face in his hands and stared into my eyes. "Don't say those words."

I gazed back at him defiantly. "I'll say them if I want. I don't care if you don't say them in return. But I love you, and I know you care for me too."

"Dammit, woman." He covered my mouth with his and kissed me hard. I melted against him, my curves molding against his strong body, trying to get closer. His tongue glided across my lips, parting them, as his hand gripped the back of my hair to hold me tight. He claimed me with this kiss, branding me as his, showing me how much he cared, even if he couldn't speak it out loud.

When he released my mouth, his voice was rough. "I've lost everyone I've ever loved. I told myself that love made me weak and swore to never do it again. But when you were kidnapped and that cave fell on me, the only thing that kept me alive was the thought of you. I might not be able to say those words, but I feel it too."

"I know," I said, kissing him over and over. "I know."

Reven may not be able to tell me he loved me, but I knew his heart belonged to me. His face was tormented as he stared down at me, and I ran my thumb across his lips, wishing I could get him to smile. Enough with the bad memories. Maybe I could remind him of some of the good ones now.

"I see now why you're such a good assassin and fighter," I said. "Did you learn anything else while working as a performer? Something fun?"

He looked confused for a second, but then he smirked. "I'm a damn good juggler, actually."

I laughed. "I don't believe it."

He pinned me with a dark look, then retrieved six throwing knives from his belt. With a grace I could never possess he launched them into the air, juggling them back and forth with movements almost too fast to see. If I didn't know better, I'd think he was using air magic as he made the blades fly high, catching them mid-air and throwing them again with the flick of his wrist, before finally collecting them all in one hand and performing an elaborate bow.

I clapped with a big, silly grin on my face. "I have to admit, I'm impressed. And surprised. I never expected that."

He gave me a wink. "What can I say? I'm good with my hands."

"Are you?" I pulled him close, my fingers gripping his black shirt. "I'm going to need a demonstration once we get to the Water Temple."

"I think we can arrange that," he said, before capturing my mouth again, making desire race through me.

Only a few more days, and then Reven would truly be mine.

18

KIRA

Doran's talons hit the sand. "We're here."

I glanced around from where I sat on his back. We'd landed on a small island, barely big enough for the three dragons to stand on together. There were two large rocks, a lone palm tree, and a cluster of seaweed that was being washed on shore. Water surrounded us in every direction, stretching as far as the eye could see.

"What do you mean, we're here?" Jasin asked, his voice gravelly in his dragon form.

"I hate to agree with Jasin, but this doesn't look like a temple," Reven said, from Jasin's back.

Still a dragon, Doran strode to the edge of the island, where the waves met the land. "The Water Temple is below us. We'll have to swim to get there."

I peered down into the crystal blue water but saw nothing. "How do the priests survive living underwater?"

"The Water God protects them," Doran said, as if it was obvious.

"Here's a better question, how are we supposed to get down there?" Jasin asked, shying back from the water before it could touch his claws.

"We'll manage," Doran said. "Auric can shield himself with a bubble of air, while Reven can keep the water away from Jasin. I'll protect Kira. Now, follow me."

He trudged into the water, his wings folding at his side, his tail swishing at the waves. I clutched onto his dark blue scales while Auric and Jasin trailed behind us. Auric didn't seem troubled at all, but Jasin hesitated before entering the ocean. Reven muttered something to him, and the red dragon grumbled and stepped forward into the water.

As soon as Doran slipped below the waves, I held my breath—but found it wasn't necessary. He created a bubble around me by pushing the water back, forming a circle of air that allowed me to breathe. Even though the ocean surrounded us, I remained dry. Doran, on the other hand, didn't seem to need air to breathe underwater. Reven copied him and shielded Jasin as they braved the ocean, while Auric created a similar bubble of air around himself and Slade.

The three dragons walked across the bottom of the ocean, until it sloped down suddenly. The deep water below us was dark, and I couldn't see anything down there. A trickle of fear ran down my spine as I gazed at the vast, deep darkness, filled with the unknown. What if our bubbles gave out? What if something horrible was lurking there?

All I could do was trust my father as he launched himself into the dark depths of the ocean. He sped along the invisible water currents faster than I could have imagined, using his wings to propel him forward. The other two dragons followed, although they were not as fast or as sleek. Doran was in his element, swimming forward into the darkness with no light to guide him. Me, on the other hand, I couldn't see a thing, except for the quick movement of a fish now and then as it darted out of our path. I summoned a bright flame in my palm, but it barely illuminated everything. After a few seconds, I gave up.

Something appeared in the dark depths. A pale glow below us, which Doran led us toward. I caught sight of hundreds of silvery fish dashing back and forth in a cluster stretching far and wide, that almost looked like a busy road. Below them I glimpsed something that looked like the top of a tower, where the glowing light was coming from.

A large, pale structure with towers and turrets slowly revealed itself as we moved deeper. The architecture was intricate, a beautiful thing of swirls and arches that flowed like water itself, somehow looking completely natural rising from the ocean floor. It was impossible to tell how old the building was, but I sensed it had been there a long time.

Doran landed on the bottom of the ocean in front of a giant statue of a dragon at the entrance. As he stepped forward, we passed through a shimmery veil that rippled across my skin. He dropped the water bubble around us, which was no longer needed.

A large dome of air surrounded the Water Temple, allowing us to breathe safely while we were visiting. Fish swam on the other side and high above us, coming right to the edge of the dome but not entering it. I stared up at it in awe, marveling at the Water God's power.

The other two dragons emerged behind us. Auric created a warm gust of wind that had him dry within seconds, while Jasin shook off the water like a dog as soon as Slade slid off his back. My father didn't seem bothered by the water dripping off him at all.

"This structure looks like it's been here for hundreds of years," Auric said, after returning to his human form. "I thought you said this wasn't the original Water Temple?"

"It's not," Doran said. "Long ago, when I first became a Dragon, there were many temples to the Gods across the four Realms. After Nysa came to power, we imprisoned the Gods in their largest temple, and then had some of the others destroyed. Others naturally became abandoned over the years as people lost faith in their absent Gods. This was one of those temples. The priests have been slowly restoring and preparing it ever since the Water God was freed. When it became clear that Nysa wanted all the temples destroyed, the High Priestess and her mates moved here for safety."

The tall stone door at the front of the temple opened with a loud rumble. A small woman with curly black hair and olive skin stepped through the door. She looked to be a few years older than I was and wore a shimmering blue robe with a necklace made of seashells. With her short height, round face, and warm smile, she was more cute than beautiful, and I instantly felt comfortable around her.

"Kira, this is Opea, the High Priestess of the Water God," Doran said.

Opea bowed low before me. "It is an honor to meet you, and all of the ascendants. We've waited so long for this day."

"The honor is ours," I said.

She turned to my father. "It's good to see you again, Doran."

"You too. How's little Wella?"

"Walking now and a real nuisance," Opea said with a laugh. "Please, come inside. We have food and refreshments and have prepared some rooms for you."

We stepped into a large entry room with walls the color of pale sand and shiny sea green tiles on the floor. Four handsome men waited for us, and Opea introduced us to her priests. One of them held a squirming toddler with the same round face as Opea but lighter hair, who I guessed was Wella.

Opea escorted me to a bedroom, while the priests took the men in a different direction. As soon as the door to the room opened, I gasped. Inside was a bed larger than any I had seen before, easily wide enough for me and all my mates.

"Does this meet your needs?" Opea asked.

"It does. I've never seen such a grand bed before. How long have you been waiting for us?"

"We've been ready for months now, ever since Doran informed us it was time to abandon the old temple. We weren't sure how soon you would visit us, but we've been prepared." She gave me a calm, pleasant smile. "Now please, rest and relax as much as you need. There's a washroom attached to this room for your convenience, and I'll have food sent up for you. Your mates are staying in rooms down the hall. The bonding room is ready for you, but there's no rush. You're welcome to take a few days to recover first, if you'd like. We're quite safe down here."

"Thank you," I said. Rest sounded nice. I felt like I could sleep for days, but then I remember Reven's heated kiss. "I'd prefer to do the bonding sooner than later."

"Of course," she said, with a knowing wink. "When you're ready, you can proceed to the bonding room from the door in the back of the great hall."

She bowed once and then left me alone in the large, elegant room. The same curved lines from the temple were reflected here in the furniture, and the fabrics were soft and luxurious in colors of white, gray, and aqua blue. Glittering seashells and dried starfish served as decorations, along with a fern that looked like it should be growing off the ocean floor.

I moved to the washroom, where I found a large round pool with clear blue water, which I realized was a natural spring that fed in from outside the temple. The water was cooler than I liked, but I used my fire magic to warm it up, and then stripped off my clothes and settled inside. The pool was big enough that my mates and I could all sit in it, and I allowed myself to stretch out and float on my back as the warm water melted away all the dirt and tension from traveling over the last few days.

For the first time in ages, I felt safe. No one could find us here, deep beneath the waves. I didn't have to constantly look over my shoulder and prepare for a possible attack. The temple wasn't in ruins or filled with death, and we didn't have to hurry.

I only wished this peace could last.

19

REVEN

After washing up and changing into fresh clothes, I sought out Kira's bedroom. I knocked sharply and she called for me to enter. When I stepped inside, I caught a glimpse of her pulling a light green robe around her body. Memories of the last time I'd seen her naked came rushing back. Her skin glistening with sweat as she was pressed between Jasin and Auric. Her soft curves as they ran their hands over her. Her full lips as they opened for me...

"Are you ready?" she asked. Her hair was still damp, making it a darker red than normal, and her face was flushed with life. She looked too damn beautiful to be real.

I'd been resistant to this bonding thing from the beginning. I hadn't wanted to be one of Kira's mates, or the next Azure Dragon, or the Water's God's chosen one. Even once I'd accepted my fate and grown to care for Kira, the idea of having sex with her in some ritual felt so... forced. Everyone in the temple would be waiting for us to get on with it, knowing exactly what we were doing the entire time. We might as well be on display. But now that she was standing in front of me, her eyes full of hope and desire, her body naked under that robe?

I was ready.

I yanked her toward me and took her mouth, hard. She let out a little noise of surprise as my lips moved across hers and my tongue slipped inside. She melted against me immediately as we kissed, the perfect size and shape to fit against me, and my hands couldn't help but seek out her bare skin. I tugged open her robe and gripped her hip, holding her in place as I angled her head to kiss her deeper. Gods, she tasted good. Before Kira, kissing had never been something I cared about. Now I could do it for hours and never grow tired of feeling her lips against mine.

She drew back slightly and met my eyes. "We're supposed to do this in the bonding room."

"I've never been good at following rules."

I dragged her mouth back to mine, pulling her tight against me, so that her hard nipples brushed against the fabric of my shirt and the bulge of my cock pressed between her thighs. She let out a throaty hum of desire, and I ground myself against her, driving us both a little mad with need.

My hand slid down her hip and dipped between her thighs, finding her wet and pulsing for me. I stroked her once and she widened her legs in response, while her fingers curled into my shirt like she was trying to stop me from pulling away. I wanted to tell her there was no chance of that, but my mouth was devouring hers and my fingers were exploring the silky, swollen folds she'd offered to me.

When I glided into that tight wet heat, she let out a moan against my lips. Her thighs tightened, trapping my hand between them, while I slid in and out of her slowly. With my other hand I held her up, knowing her knees would be weak when I was through with her. I slipped another finger inside and rubbed her clit at the same time, feeling her tense around me. Knowing how close she was already encouraged me to move faster and deeper, forcing her to rock her hips in time with my movements, her arms tightening around my neck for support. She cried out my name into my mouth as the climax swept over her, her body turning to liquid against me.

I slowly removed my fingers and held her until she could stand on her own again. "Told you I was good with my hands."

"You weren't kidding." Her eyes were dazed as she closed her robe and tied it.

I took her hand in mine. "Let's find this bonding room."

The hallway and the great room were both empty, much to my relief. The hour must be late, though it was hard to tell deep below the ocean, where sunlight couldn't reach. I certainly wasn't tired—no, my body was full of energy, the same rush I got when I was about to slit someone's throat from the shadows or leap into a fight. The anticipation only made what was coming even sweeter.

The door to the bonding room opened easily at my touch. The first thing I saw was the floor-to-ceiling opening to the ocean on one side. The dome must end right there because fish swam just outside, and we could almost reach out and touch them. Coral and seaweed lined the ocean floor, and I caught a glimpse of an eel poking its head out of some rocks.

A raised path led from the door to a large bed, and around this platform was a shallow pool of water, only knee-high. The pool's floor was covered in shining seashells that caught the flickering candlelight around the room.

"It's beautiful," Kira whispered.

One of the other guys would have told her she was even more beautiful or something, but I wasn't good at this romance crap. I'd never had a real relationship. I hated talking about my feelings. And sex? Sex was always for a purpose. Making money. Getting information. Relieving stress. Never for love.

Until now.

I grabbed Kira around the waist, feeling her curves under that thin robe, and picked her up, wrapping her legs around me. She let out an excited laugh, then settled into my arms as I carried her to the bed. I set her down on her back and grabbed her wrists, pinning them to the bed. I loomed over her body, caging her in, giving her no way to escape.

"Now you're mine," I said.

She looked up at me with open desire and complete trust. "What are you going to do with me?"

Her robe had fallen open and I raked my eyes down her body. "Everything."

My gaze lingered on her full breasts and narrow hips, before dipping down to that triangle between her legs, already wet from my touch. Damn, she was stunning. Why had I resisted her so long?

That was over now. She was impossible to resist, and I was done trying to fight it.

Still holding her wrists, I bent my head to those perfect round breasts and flicked my tongue across her hard nipple. She arched her back in response, begging for more, and I sucked one of those dark buds into my mouth. The soft moan from her lips turned me on even more, as did the taste of her. I'd never considered myself a lucky man, but I was starting to change my mind about that.

I worshipped each breast until she was begging and writhing under me, desperate for more. An overwhelming need to be inside her took over, and I released her wrists so I could tear off my clothes. Her eager fingers reached up to help me, her eyes hungry as I removed my shirt and tossed it aside. The rest of my clothes hit the floor, and then I moved over her again.

"I never thought this moment would come," she said, as she gazed up at me.

The intensity of her eyes was too much. She wrecked me, and I was going to fall apart if she kept that up. The urge to claim her as my own grew too strong to ignore, and I couldn't wait a second longer. I grabbed her waist and flipped her over onto her stomach, making her gasp. I yanked her hips up so they were level with mine, and then I rammed myself deep inside.

She let out the most beautiful scream I'd ever heard as I filled her from behind, the sound echoing throughout the room. I grit my teeth at the feel of her tight, damp heat. My hand wrapped around her thick red hair, tugging her head back, forcing me deeper inside. I arched over her to press my lips to her neck, and she trembled under my touch.

"I have a secret," I said into her ear, as I held her there. Not moving yet, just enjoying the feel of her body squeezed tight around my cock.

"Only one?"

I nipped at her shoulder. "I think you know all the rest by now."

"Tell me," she said, her voice husky.

"I've never done this before with anyone I actually cared about."

With that, I began to move. I rocked into her with hard, rough thrusts, and she pushed her hips back at me, taking me deeper. With one hand gripping her hair and the other on her hip, I completely controlled her body, forcing her to accept whatever I gave her.

I took her hard and rough, slamming into her again and again, and her moans of pleasure only grew louder. I reached between her thighs to find her clit, and each time I pushed forward, my fingers rubbed against her there. She tightened around me, her body close to the edge, and I was right there with her. I'd thought I was claiming her, but she was the one taking everything from me and still demanding more—and I wanted to give it to her. Not just tonight or in the bedroom, but for the rest of our lives.

I felt it when she came apart. Every wet inch of her clenched around me, and it felt so good I couldn't stop the pleasure from cresting over me too. Water shot into the air around us, while ice spread across our skin, locking us together. I buried my face in her neck, inhaling her, while our bodies rocked together through it all.

The ice melted away and the water sank back into the pool around us. I kissed the back of her neck, as I pulsed inside her, before gathering her in my arms and lowering us to the bed. How had I ever lived without Kira? She made me feel so damn alive.

"I love you," I said, the words slipping out of me. I couldn't stop them anymore. I didn't want to.

She touched my face and smiled. "I know."

20

KIRA

I must have dozed off in Reven's arms, because at the sound of rushing water my eyes snapped open. I yanked my robe up around me, covering my naked skin. Reven sat up and shoved me behind him, protecting me with his body. Water poured into the dome in front of us, and I worried that the entire thing would crash down and crush us under the weight.

The water rushing in began to take shape, forming a large body with four legs, a long tail, a head with a pointed snout, and great wings that rose upon its back. A huge dragon arose in front of us, a creature of pure swirling water with glowing white eyes and fangs made of ice shards.

"The final binding is complete at last," the Water God said.

I reached for my magic, finding the fluid grace of water deep inside me alongside the other three elements, and summoned a snowball in my palm. A large smile spread across my face as it slowly melted against my fingertips. We'd done it. I was bound to each of my mates now, able to use all four elements, along with my own life magic.

"Can I turn into a dragon now?" I asked aloud.

"Not yet," the Water God said. "Not until the Spirit Goddess gives you her blessing."

"The Spirit Goddess is trapped inside Nysa," Reven said dryly. "Something the other Gods failed to mention."

The great dragon flexed his watery wings. "When you defeat Nysa, our Goddess will be freed. Only then will you be able to unlock your true powers."

"But if we free her, the Death Goddess will turn this world into another realm of the dead," I said.

The glowing eyes narrowed. "Doran told you this, but he is also the one who imprisoned us for nearly a thousand years. Nysa and her mates wanted unending power and immortal life. Now they lie to spread doubt through your hearts."

I glanced at Reven warily. "Is it true that the Spirit Goddess is actually the twin Goddesses of Life and Death, bound together?"

"That is true. One cannot exist without the other. Life and death. Dark and light. There must be balance."

"If we free her and the balance shifts too much to one side, can the Gods help us split the Spirit Goddess apart and banish the Death Goddess from this world?"

"We can. If it comes to that, we will."

I nodded. It was the most we could ask for.

The dragon's tail swished back and forth in the low pool. "Do not forget that to defeat Nysa, Doran must be destroyed first. He will tell you anything to protect himself and his mate. You cannot trust him."

That was true, but could we trust the Gods either? I wasn't sure. "I understand."

"The time of the Black Dragon is over, and now the ascendants must rise. Do not fail us."

The Water God began to flow back into the dome, losing shape, but Reven called out, "Wait!"

The huge dragon paused, reforming instantly, and asked, "Yes?"

Reven's brow furrowed. "Why me? I'm not a hero. I didn't want this. I rejected my fate at every turn. You must have known I would, but you picked me anyway."

"The Fire God looks for courage. The Air God chooses one with wisdom. The Earth God seeks out stability. I value change."

"Change?" Reven asked.

"Adaptability. Resourcefulness. A certain fluidity in morals. The world is never as simple as black and white or right and wrong. It is always shifting, and my Dragon shifts with it. I did not want a hero. I wanted someone who would survive, and change, and grow, and show the ascendant how to do the same."

"I see…" Reven said, although he sounded more confused than ever. I reached for his hand and gave it a squeeze. I was certain he was the perfect person to be the next Azure Dragon and my mate, even if he wasn't. He'd made me wait and doubt and nearly tear my hair out plenty of times, but that had only made it even better when he'd finally admitted his feelings for me. Jasin and Auric had loved me from the start, but Slade and Reven had made me work for it—and I'd learned something from each of them. I couldn't have gotten to this point with Reven if not for the other men, and I saw now how each one complemented me and made me become a better person. Including Reven.

"Trust in the Gods," the dragon said. "We created you. We chose you. And we have reasons for everything we do."

With that, he collapsed with a huge splash, and was gone. I had to give the Gods credit, they were good at dramatic entrances and exits.

Reven turned toward me and slid his hand around my waist, bringing me back to him. "Now that that's done, it's time for round two."

I couldn't help but laugh as he pulled open my robe and eased me back onto the bed. "Is that so?"

"I've waited a long time for this night. The other men have been with you multiple times, but we have some catching up to do. I'm not letting you go until I've explored every inch of you. Multiple times."

His head bent to my chest and he ran his tongue in the valley between my breasts, making me gasp. For once, I didn't have to rush off after speaking with a God. No one was waiting for us or coming to attack us. We could spend the entire night in the bonding room if he wanted.

And as Reven kissed his way down my body, I had a feeling he wasn't in any rush to leave either.

2 1

KIRA

In the morning we met for breakfast with the others in a dining room with windows that looked out to the ocean. Opea and her priests served us fruit and pastries, which they said they traded for when they visited a nearby island once a week. I didn't question it too much. Despite the remote locations of the temples, the Gods always found a way to provide for their priests somehow.

As Opea and her priests left so that we could have privacy, I thought of Calla, the High Priestess of the Fire God, and wondered how she and her mates were doing. The last time I'd seen her had been in the capital of the Air Realm, but I wasn't sure if she planned to stay in Stormhaven until it was safe for her to return to her temple. Sark was her grandfather and he'd kept my presence a secret in exchange for Doran keeping quiet about her. Did that mean Sark actually cared about Calla in some way? I'd always assumed he was heartless, but maybe even the worst Dragons had something or someone they cared about.

I gazed across the table at my father. Was I his weakness too? Or was he playing me this entire time?

Reven must have seen my troubled look because he reached under the table and gave my thigh a squeeze, reminding me of our night together. My worries melted away, and I gave him a grateful smile.

"I'm guessing the bonding went well," Jasin said with a smirk as he took his seat across from me.

"How can you tell?" I asked.

Slade began to load up his plate with food. "You look content. Less troubled."

I smiled and looked down at the plate in front of me as color flooded my cheeks. "I suppose I am. Everything feels like it's as it should be."

"Now that you've bonded with all of us, what is the next step?" Auric asked, as he folded a napkin across his lap.

I sighed. "I can access all of your powers now, but the Water God told me I can't become a dragon myself until the Spirit Goddess blesses me. Which could prove difficult."

"You need to confront Nysa," Doran said, before popping a piece of melon into his mouth. "I suggest we do it at the Spirit Temple near Soulspire, since that's where the blessing needs to take place."

"Somehow I doubt the other Dragons will let us just walk in there," Reven said.

Doran nodded. "Once they learn you've obtained all four elemental powers, they'll know you're heading for the Spirit Temple next. I would expect it to be heavily defended with both shades and soldiers from the Onyx Army, along with the Dragons themselves."

"We'll never get in there," Jasin muttered.

"Not alone, no," Doran said.

I picked at the food in front of me as I considered. "We need to call upon our allies."

"What allies?" Reven said. "We have the Resistance, who just lost their leader and… Oh wait, that's it."

"I can speak with my father," Auric said. "He has no love for the Dragons but was scared to turn against them. I might be able to convince him to change his mind, if I explain how close we are to defeating them. Perhaps he could lend us some of his soldiers."

Jasin arched an eyebrow at me. "What about that bandit gang you were once a member of, Kira? Would they help us?"

I took a long sip of orange juice. "Cadock's men? I asked before and he said no, but it couldn't hurt to try again. We are desperate, after all."

Reven rolled his eyes. "They'll never say yes. I'd have better luck convincing the Assassin's Guild to join us."

"Do you think you could?" I asked.

He opened and closed his mouth, then scowled. "Maybe. They might do it if we paid them well."

Jasin dragged a hand through his auburn hair. "Even if they all said yes, which is unlikely, it still won't be enough."

I glanced between my father and my mates, then spoke the idea that had been brewing in my head for some time. "We need to ask the elementals to help us."

"The elementals?" Doran asked with a sharp laugh. "Why would they ever agree to that?"

"The elementals hate the Dragons and the shades, according to Enva," I said. "They might be willing to side with us if we explain that we're planning to defeat them."

Jasin shook his head. "Just because you saved one elemental doesn't mean they'll fight beside us."

I shrugged. "It can't hurt to ask."

"It can if they attack us."

"He's right, it's a big risk," Slade said. "Even asking them to help could be dangerous."

"We have to try," I said. "Humans think the elementals are our enemies. Elementals think the same of us. But it doesn't have to be that way. There were times when our two kinds were at peace."

"You think you can unite elementals and humans and erase hundreds of years of hatred and fear?" Reven asked.

"Not overnight, no. But this would be a good first step. I just want to talk to them. I know it's dangerous, but we need them. I don't think we can do this without their help."

Auric drummed his fingers on the table with a thoughtful expression. "How would you even contact the elementals? There are different types of them spread across the world."

"They have a capital, of sorts, past the Fire Realm," Doran said. "There's a council of leaders, one from each type of elemental. I could take you there."

"Won't they be suspicious if we show up with one of the Dragons we're planning to replace?" I asked.

"So I'll keep out of sight," he said with a shrug.

"There's another problem with this plan," Auric said. "It'll take a long time to visit all these different groups and try to convince them to help us."

I glanced between everyone at the table, weighing the options, before saying, "We'll have to split up. Slade will go to the Resistance, Auric will speak with his father, Reven will ask the Assassin's Guild, and Jasin will try to convince the bandits. Doran and I will find the elementals."

Jasin shook his head with a frown. "I don't like the idea of splitting up."

"Especially if it means none of us will be with you to protect you," Slade said.

"I'll keep her safe," Doran said. "You have my word."

"But can we trust your word?" Reven asked.

Doran's eyes narrowed. "I would never do anything to harm my daughter. Surely you know that by now. Have I not done everything I said I would?"

"Forgive us for being cautious," Auric said. "We're just trying to make sure Kira stays safe."

I pinched the bridge of my nose, fighting off an oncoming headache, probably from the stress of this combined with the lack of sleep. "I know this plan isn't ideal, but this is the only way. The longer we take, the longer the Dragons can prepare to stand against us. We have to recruit allies, and we have to do it quickly. We must split up, even if it puts all of us in danger." My voice softened as I looked at each of them. "I'll have Doran, and I can control all four elements now. You don't need to worry about me."

Slade reached for my hand. "We always will worry."

"It's settled then." Doran pressed his palms on the table and stood. "But before we rush off to the four corners of the world, you each need more training first. Meet me in the courtyard in an hour."

After he was gone, Reven fixed me with a dark look. "You know you can't trust him."

"I don't trust him," I said, remembering the Water God's comments last night. "But he has kept his word so far, and he's helped us a lot. We would never have found this temple without him. He might betray us in the end, but we'll be prepared if he does."

Slade rubbed his beard. "I have another idea. I've been wondering if it's possible to imbue a weapon with all of our magic."

"How would that work?" Jasin asked.

"I'm not sure, but it might be effective against Nysa once we've defeated her mates, or perhaps even against the Spirit Goddess." Slade shrugged. "I'd like to try, but I'd need my forge."

"We could plan to reconvene in your village," Auric said.

The plan was set. Now we just had to find a way to pull it off.

22

JASIN

Doran waited for us in front of the temple, where he leaned against the large dragon statue. He stared at the fish swimming outside the dome and something in his expression reminded me of Kira. She often got lost in her thoughts too, especially when something was weighing heavily on her mind, which was often lately. Although after her night with Reven she was smiling a little easier, at least. A few days of peace and rest at the Water Temple would be good for her too, even if I was itching to get moving and take action.

Doran heard us approach and turned toward us. "Good, you're all here." He moved to stand before us and scrutinized us in turn. "If you're going to fight the Dragons in a few weeks, you'll need to be better prepared. Right now, you're not even close to being ready. I'm amazed you've survived this long, honestly."

"Great speech," I mumbled. "I feel so inspired now."

Reven smirked beside me, while Doran shot me a sharp look before continuing. "Today we're going to focus on opposing elements. Each element has a direct opposite—fire and water, earth and air, life and death. As I mentioned before, this is how we imprisoned the Gods, using the element they were weakest against. You'll be strongest when fighting someone with opposing magic, whether it's a Dragon or an elemental, but you'll also be at your weakest. I want you to pair up—Reven with Jasin, Auric with Slade—and practice blocking each other's magical attacks."

"And me?" Kira asked.

"You and I will start your water magic training today."

Reven and I moved to the other side of the courtyard, both of us wearing matching scowls. Maybe we were supposed to be opposites, but sometimes I thought I had more in common with him than I did with the others. I hadn't liked the guy at first, but now we had an unspoken understanding. And we both seemed to feel the same way about Doran.

"I should be the one training her in water," Reven growled, once we were out of earshot.

I snorted. "Now that her perfect father is here, she doesn't need us for that anymore."

We took up positions facing each other and summoned our magic. I threw a ball of fire at Reven, but he met it with a blast of water and they both sizzled out.

"She's going to be heartbroken when his true colors emerge," I said, as Reven threw shards of ice my way. I put up a wall of fire to block them, melting them before they could hit me.

"And we'll be there to comfort her."

"Unless we're all split up." My jaw clenched as I formed a sword made entirely of fire and lunged at him. I hated this plan we'd come up with. Leaving her alone with Doran was a bad idea, but she wouldn't listen to reason about it.

Reven formed a shield of water and blocked me, then let the water reform into two daggers, which he threw at me. I knocked one away, but the other grazed my arm, making me flinch.

I rubbed the small cut, which burned with cold. "Nice one."

Reven nodded at my compliment. "The Assassin's Guild headquarters are on the way to the Fire Realm and not far from here. I can take care of business there quickly and then follow Kira and Doran from a distance. If I feel anything through the bond, I'll be able to get to Kira fast."

"That would make me feel a lot better about this plan. Do you think he'll try something?"

"No, but I like to be prepared for anything."

"Me too. And even if he isn't a threat to her, the elementals could be."

"Exactly."

Doran walked over to us while we shot more fire and water at each other. "How are you both doing with this?"

"Fine," Reven said.

"I will say, I'm impressed," Doran said. "The two of you haven't known each other long, but you don't seem to hate each other. Sark and I…" His face twisted. "Let's just say it took a long time before we could work together."

"That isn't a problem for us," Reven said.

"No, and not for Slade and Auric either it seems."

"We're a team," I said, puffing up my chest a little. "Brothers united with a shared cause—protecting and loving Kira. Whatever personal issues we had with each other, we've managed to get past them."

"So I've seen." Doran rubbed his chin, his eyes thoughtful. "Nysa's mates and I can barely stand to be in the same room as each other. We've never been very good at working as a team, and the bond chafes at us after all these years. Blocking the other Dragons out was the only way I could stay sane. But things are different with all of you—and that's how you'll defeat the other Dragons."

I couldn't imagine hating Kira's other mates like that. Sure, we'd had our differences at first. We'd gotten into fights. We'd questioned each other's loyalties. But in the end, we'd united under our shared love of Kira and our common purpose of defeating the Dragons. All I had to do was reach for the bond with Kira and I felt her mates there too. Auric was the strongest, like a sunny breeze brushing against my mind, and I'd started to feel Slade's cool, stony presence recently. Now that Reven had bonded with Kira there was a new awareness too, a tiny cool flicker that I knew would quickly grow into more.

Doran spent a few minutes showing us how to imprison the other person with our element, and then Reven practiced encasing me in ice, sometimes just my feet so I couldn't dodge his attacks, and sometimes my entire body. I did the same with Reven, surrounding him with flames, and at one point making him yelp. Across the courtyard, Slade and Auric were practicing similar tactics with their own magic. I had a feeling we'd need some healing from Kira after this was all over.

"I think that's enough for now," Doran called out, sometime later. "We're going to practice again over the next few days, using different combinations, until you're used to fighting every kind of magic. Slade, I want you to also spend some time practicing your flying. You're almost there, and we need you to be ready before we depart. Reven, you should do that too. And all of you should work on building your bonds with Kira and each other. That will be the key to winning against the other Dragons."

With that, he dismissed us and went back into the Temple. A grin spread across my face, despite my weariness and pain in all the places Reven had hit me. I knew exactly how I wanted to work on strengthening our bonds. And I had a feeling the other guys wouldn't mind either.

23
KIRA

As I prepared for bed after a long day of training with Doran, I heard a knock. I opened my door and found Jasin, Auric, and Reven standing outside, each one so handsome it made my pulse race.

Jasin leaned against the doorway and gave me a sinful smile. "I thought you could use some company tonight, so I invited the others. Doran did tell us to work on building our bond, after all."

"Yes, he did." Excitement fluttered inside my stomach as I gestured for them to come inside. Memories of the last time the four of us shared an evening together came rushing back, and I could only hope for another night like that. "I was about to take a bath. You should all join me."

"I invited Slade too," Jasin said, as they stepped inside.

My eyebrows darted up. "Did you? That was kind, but I doubt he'll join us."

He shrugged. "You never know. I think he'll surprise you."

"This bed is enormous," Auric said, pushing his hand on it. "We'll definitely have to take advantage of this later."

"This bath is too," Reven said from the other room.

"A suite built for a Dragon and her mates," I said, as I followed Reven's voice.

Jasin dipped his hand in the bath. "Oh yes, this is definitely my favorite temple."

My men quickly removed their clothes and I took in Auric's tall frame, Jasin's abundance of muscles, and Reven's toned physique. Each one of them was already hard and ready for me, and at that moment I knew I was the luckiest woman in the world.

They stepped into the pool, which Jasin had heated to the perfect temperature to soothe away any aches and pains from today's lessons. I dropped my robe, baring myself before them, and they gazed up at me as I slipped into the bath beside them. My men wasted no time in circling me, their eyes hungry, their intentions clear. Jasin's mouth found mine first, his lips warm against mine, before Reven dragged my face toward him to kiss me next. Auric's arms circled me from behind, and I turned my head to taste his lips too. Their naked, wet bodies surrounded me, sliding against my bare skin, and desire raced through my veins.

The three of us had done this before, but now it was different because I could sense Reven through the bond. With every touch and kiss, his presence in my mind grew stronger. I no longer had to wonder if he loved me or if he would ever open up—he had given himself to me completely last night, and all my doubts about him had vanished.

I heard footsteps and looked up to see Slade standing on the edge of the bath. "You're here," I whispered.

Slade shrugged. "Jasin invited me."

"Told you," Jasin said with a wink.

"And you're okay with this?" I asked.

"The idea of sharing you doesn't bother me anymore, not like it did." Slade tugged off his shirt and tossed it aside, revealing that dark, muscular chest that just begged to be touched. "I'd like to try."

"Really?" I asked, my heart skipping a beat in anticipation.

He slid down his trousers and stepped into the bath. He was already hard as steel, which made me think he might be telling the truth. "I want to do whatever makes you happy, and I can tell this does. I admit, I'm a little curious too."

I wrapped my arms around his neck and kissed him to show how much this meant to me. "We'll go slow and you don't have to do anything you don't want."

He chuckled softly, his voice low and delicious. "I can handle it."

He leaned back against the edge of the bath, spreading his arms wide. I nestled up against him, kissing his bearded neck, running my hands along his shoulders and his strong chest, down to his hard cock. I took it in hand, enjoying the way it filled up my palm, as I kissed him again.

But I couldn't neglect my other mates either. I turned and faced them, but Slade's arms wrapped around me, pulling my behind up against his hips. He held me against him, his cock nestled between my cheeks, his hands on my breasts. I leaned back on his chest and turned my head to kiss him, while the other men watched us with rapt expressions.

They moved forward through the water, drawing closer to me as if they couldn't resist. Jasin and Auric took up position on either side of me, kissing my shoulders, my neck, and the curves of my breasts, while I rested against Slade's chest. Reven claimed the middle, and he dipped under the water with a filthy expression that made my breath catch. He spread my legs wide, and then his mouth moved between my thighs, his tongue darting out to flick against me. I cried out and wove my fingers in his black hair under the water. He stayed down there, licking and sucking on me without coming up for air, using the fact that he could breathe underwater to my advantage. With each touch of his mouth and stroke of his tongue I came apart more and more, while Jasin and Auric took turns claiming my lips and Slade's strong body held me in place.

But it wasn't enough. I dragged Reven up out of the water and captured his mouth with mine, greedy for more of him. His hard body pressed against me, pinning me between him and Slade. I wrapped my hand around his behind and pulled his hips against me. His cock slid easily inside me, exactly where it belonged, and he let out a low, sensual groan.

Auric and Jasin moved to the sides of the bath to watch, while Reven began to pump into me. He grabbed onto my hips to get better leverage, while Slade's hands cupped my breasts and pinched my nipples. Every time Reven thrust into me he pushed me back against Slade, who grunted as his cock rubbed between my cheeks. I wanted him inside me too, but wasn't sure Slade was ready for that level of sharing yet. He was already doing so much more than I ever thought he would. I turned my head and studied his face, observing the hunger in his eyes, before his lush lips came down on mine again.

Slade dipped a hand between me and Reven, finding my clit and stroking it. The water surged around us and I clutched Reven's shoulders with one hand and touched Slade's face with the other, letting them control my body completely. I never felt more cherished than when I was squeezed between two of my mates, and I sensed their passion and love through the bond like a warm glow in my chest. The orgasm crested over me like a wave and swept Reven along with it, making him groan and push deeper inside me with his release. He rested his head against my shoulder, his arms wrapped around me, while Slade held both of us steady.

I kissed Reven slowly, then turned my head to kiss Slade next. "Was that all right?"

"More than all right," Slade said. "I want to watch you with all of them."

"I think they'll be happy to oblige," Reven said with a grin, as he moved to the other side of the tub to watch the next round.

Jasin took Reven's place immediately and gripped my chin in his hand before kissing me hard. He spun me around so I straddled Slade, while he shoved my wet hair aside and kissed the back of my neck. I wrapped my arms around Slade and my lips found his, while Jasin cupped my breasts and squeezed them roughly.

I felt Jasin's cock against my thighs, and then he slid into me from behind with one deep thrust, making me gasp into Slade's mouth. Jasin began to rock into me, sliding me against Slade with each movement. Slade's hard length pressed between us, pulsing with need, but it wasn't his turn yet. He took it in his hand and began rubbing it against my clit, sending sparks throughout my entire core.

I threw my head back and held onto Slade tightly as the two of them stroked me from different angles, making my desire rise higher and higher. I was caged between my two strongest mates, trapped between their muscular bodies, and I gave myself up to them completely. My climax hit me hard and fast, like flint striking steel and sparking a bonfire. Jasin rode me harder and deeper, his movements rough and fast as he pounded into me, and then he exploded too.

He leaned against my back and kissed my neck, while Slade claimed my mouth again. I knew Slade had to be close from the way his cock pulsed against me, but he didn't seem to be in any hurry. He actually seemed to be enjoying this, which still surprised me.

After Jasin moved away, Auric took my hand. "Come. Let's try out that giant bed of yours."

He helped me out of the water, dried me off with a quick gust of warm air, and led me into the bedroom. My other mates followed as Auric and I sank onto the massive bed, and they spread out around us. Auric and I kissed and stroked each other, but then I moved over to Slade's body, needing to touch his hard length after being teased by it for so long. Auric grabbed my behind as I crawled across the bed, lifting it up as he got in position behind me.

Slade watched everything that was happening intently with his hands folded behind his head, his dark cock standing straight up at attention. I brought my head down and kissed the tip of it, while Auric lined himself up. Slade groaned, and I swirled my tongue around the head of his cock, as Auric gripped my hips and began to push inside slowly. I took Slade into my mouth inch by inch and let out a low hum of approval as both men entered me at the same time.

I looked up to see Jasin and Reven watching us, which only excited me more. One of Slade's hands came down to grip my hair, his hips arching up slightly off the bed, making me take more of him. At the same time, Auric slid deeper into me from behind, filling me up and stretching me wide, before he finally bottomed out inside.

Auric began to move, pulling out slowly before thrusting deep again, and I pushed back against him to take even more. He felt so deep and big back there it was almost too much, yet I still wanted more. Slade filled my mouth completely, and I used my hands to work his shaft as I sucked on him. He'd given me so much tonight by joining us, and I wanted to give him something in return.

The three of us found a rhythm, with Auric rocking me forward and making me take Slade deeper between my lips. Jasin and Reven moved in on either side of me and began kissing and stroking my breasts, my stomach, and that spot between my legs that begged for attention.

The touch of all four of my mates at once was the most incredible feeling, and another orgasm shuddered through me, this one stronger than all the others. It seemed to go on for an eternity, filling my entire body with pleasure. Slade's fingers tightened in my hair and he groaned, his hips thrusting up at me faster as his seed spilled into my mouth. That sent Auric over the edge too, and he slid deep inside me one last time as his own release came.

I fell onto the bed between Slade and Auric, while Jasin and Reven moved over me. I kissed each of them one by one, feeling their love through the bond, which had grown stronger in the last few minutes. If we kept this up, we would be unstoppable.

24

KIRA

W e spent a week at the Water Temple, which was good for everyone. We hadn't had a chance to rest since we'd visited Slade's village, and while there we were constantly worried the Dragons would show up and attack. Down here we could truly relax, although we did miss sunshine and fresh air and were all starting to get a little sick of eating fish at every meal.

My mates and I spent our days training with Doran and discussing strategies for the battle at the Spirit Temple. And our nights...we spent those strengthening our bonds together, both as a group and one on one. Sometimes I would share a bed with only one of my mates, since I sensed that they needed their alone time with me. On other nights, two of them would join me in bed. And on our last night together, they all did, taking turns to please me over and over.

And then it was time to leave.

We stood outside the temple, with all of our supplies packed and ready to go. Opea moved forward and embraced me. "Good luck on your journey. We shall be praying for your success."

"Thank you for everything," I said.

Opea's handsome priests bowed before us, while her daughter clung to her skirts and peered out at me. I'd considered asking for their help at the Spirit Temple, since Opea had been blessed with magic from her God like the other High Priestesses, but I was too worried about her young daughter growing up without a mother.

I turned toward my mates and was immediately swept up into Jasin's arms. He gave me a kiss so full of passion that my cheeks grew red at the thought of my father watching us. I laughed and pushed him back. "I'll miss you too, Jasin."

"Be careful," he said, before stepping away.

Auric embraced me next, before giving me a warm kiss that was a lot less embarrassing but still wonderful. He'd spent much of his free time scouring the temple's library, but he hadn't been able to find any real information about the Spirit Goddess. "I'll be counting down the days until we meet again."

"Me too."

Slade gave me a strong hug next, his muscular arms squeezing me hard. I was so proud of him—Slade had worked day and night to practice flying alongside Reven, and Doran had decided they were both ready to travel. I pressed a soft kiss to his lips, and then he rested his forehead against mine as he simply held me close.

"Come back to us," he said.

"I will."

Reven was last and he stepped forward slowly, then took my face in his hands and kissed me hard. "I'll see you soon. Watch your back."

His words were casual, but I knew what he meant. "I love you too," I whispered to him.

He gave me a wry smirk, before stepping back. My chest tightened as I stared at the four of them, wishing we didn't have to be apart for so long. But my bond with each of them was stronger than ever, and even though we'd be far away, we'd still be together.

My mates said goodbye to each other next, while I turned toward my father. He was already in his dragon form, and one of Opea's priests had fastened some of our supplies to his back. He swung his head toward me. "Are you finally done with your tearful goodbyes?"

"There were no tears," I said, as I climbed onto his back. He snorted, and then we watched as my mates transformed too. As they stood before me, four glorious dragons with a rainbow of shimmering scales, pride and love filled my chest. Saying goodbye to them and sending them into possible danger was tougher than I expected. Okay, now the tears might come.

My father dashed into the water before I could start crying, preventing me from saying any more sentimental words to my mates. He was probably worried if I stood there any longer, I'd call this whole thing off. I wouldn't, even though the idea was appealing.

The bubble of water surrounded me as Doran swam up toward the light. My mates followed, with Reven and Auric shielding Slade and Jasin. We breached the surface with a huge spray of saltwater, with Doran leaping straight from the ocean to the sky. I heard the others emerge and climb onto the small island, and soon we were all flying high.

At the sight of so many wings catching the wind currents, I longed for my own dragon form too. Soon, I hoped.

We circled each other in one last goodbye, and then everyone took off in separate directions. I watched my mates as their shining bodies got farther and farther away, until I could no longer see them at all.

Doran and I headed south toward the Fire Realm, where he said the elementals had their capital city. I wasn't thrilled to go back to the Fire Realm, which held some bad memories from our encounters with the Onyx Army, but Doran had assured me we wouldn't run into any trouble there.

Over the next few days, Doran soared high in the clouds to avoid anyone catching a glimpse of us and reporting back to the other Dragons. They were still out there somewhere looking for us, and I could only pray that my mates were staying out of sight as well.

When we weren't flying, Doran spent a lot of time training me to use my magic, especially water and earth since I'd had little chance to use them yet. I had the easiest time learning water, which Doran said was due to his blood running through my veins. I wasn't sure if that was true, or if I'd just gotten better at magic overall after using three other elements already.

While we ate, Doran told me stories about his childhood and his life as a pirate, alternating between making me hang onto his every word as he spun a thrilling tale and laughing as he recounted some trouble he'd gotten himself into. I especially liked his stories of his sister Kira, and I could tell they'd been very close all those years ago. But he hardly spoke of anything after he'd been chosen by the Water God and said little about his time with Nysa and the other Dragons. I couldn't tell if the memories were too painful, or if he was purposefully hiding things from me about them.

He asked me a lot of questions about my own past too, although he already knew a lot about it. He'd watched my entire life from the shadows, including during my childhood in the Water Realm, my time with the merchants and the bandits, and when I'd lived in Stoneham for the last few years.

"I saw you once," I said, one night over supper. "When I was fourteen."

"Ah, yes. I was making sure those merchants were looking after you."

"And if they weren't?"

He shrugged. "I would have found a new place for you."

"When I saw you, I was terrified. The only Dragon I'd seen until then had been Sark, and I worried you were looking for me so you could finish his job. I ran away the next morning."

"Yes, I remember. It took me some time to track you down again." He sounded almost...proud. But his response only made me angry.

"For the next few years I was on the run, all alone and living in fear, struggling to find my next meal. Why didn't you help me at any time?"

"I wanted to, many times. All parents want easy lives for their children. If things were different, I'd have made sure you were raised in a palace, with everything you could have ever desired, but I knew that would harm you in the end. An easy life wouldn't have prepared you for what you're going through now. You had to learn to be a survivor and a fighter on your own. So I stayed back and let you find your own way, even though it was torture for me."

I sighed. "I understand, but I can't help but wish I'd known you all my life. Even if I didn't know you were my father, it would have been nice to know someone was on my side."

"It was too dangerous. I couldn't risk Nysa or the other Dragons finding you." He reached over and patted my hand. "I wish things could have been different, but I'm happy I get to spend this time with you now."

He didn't say it, but I knew underneath those words was the sentiment that our time together would be short. My throat closed up and I had to look away before I started crying. I was starting to wish he would betray us —otherwise there was no way I'd be able to defeat him when the time came.

And if I didn't? Then Nysa would win.

25
KIRA

When I spotted Valefire, the volcano where the Fire Temple was located, Doran said we were getting close. He continued past it, out over the ocean, toward an island he'd claimed few knew about. Except him, of course.

Hours later, a wide expanse of bright green land came into view in front of us. Mountains stretched high into the sky and smoke rose from one of them. But as we approached, we heard something behind us. The snap of wings.

Doran spun around, his fangs bared, preparing to fight—except when the sunlight caught the other dragon's scales, we saw they were nearly the same shade as Doran's.

"Reven!" I called out, both excited and relieved to see him.

"What's he doing here?" Doran growled, though I couldn't tell if he was annoyed or not due to his dragon voice.

Reven hovered beside us, looking glorious as a dragon. "I finished my discussions with the Assassin's Guild early and decided to join you here. They said yes, by the way. For a price."

"That's good," I said. "We'll find a way to pay their fee, somehow."

"You didn't trust me with Kira, did you?" Doran asked Reven, his eyes narrowed.

"Of course not," Reven said. "And this way, I can take her into the elemental city instead of you."

He huffed. "You think you can do a better job convincing them than I can?"

Reven stared him down. "Neither one of us is doing that, but Kira will be a lot more convincing if she isn't seen working with the enemy."

"He's right," I said. "Arriving with you was always going to be a problem. It would be better if you waited back by Valefire while Reven and I spoke to the elementals alone."

Doran bared his fangs and I could tell he didn't like this idea, but finally he relented. "Fine. But if you're not back within a day, I'm coming to get you."

"That's acceptable," I said.

The two dark blue dragons landed on the water, folding their legs under them and bobbing up and down on the waves. I carefully switched from Doran's back to Reven's, and then reached out to touch my father's snout.

"We'll meet up with you soon," I said.

Doran grumbled, but then wished me luck before taking off. I leaned forward and wrapped my arms around Reven, pressing my face against his sun-warmed scales.

"I'm so happy to see you again," I said.

"I love you too," he replied. I laughed as he launched into the air.

The island where the elementals lived was huge, but Doran had already told me where we needed to go, and I directed Reven toward the northern end. Crystal clear waters surrounded the island, which was covered in thick green plants everywhere except at the center, where a volcano that rivaled Valefire spewed heat and ash into the sky. We passed it by, flying high overhead, and spotted various structures made of stone dotted across the land.

As we approached the northern end of the island, we spotted more structures below us, forming a large city. Reven swept down toward it, and we began to make out elementals of every kind moving about the streets. Heavy rock elementals trudged alongside floating air elementals, while scorching hot fire elementals spoke with ones made of ice. I'd never seen so many in one place before and had never seen the different types interacting together. I'd always thought elementals stuck to their own kind, and that was that. Clearly I had a lot to learn about them.

Reven swept down and landed at the edge of the city to not cause a panic, but we drew attention anyway. Dozens of elementals surrounded us, their glowing eyes menacing, and I held up my hands in surrender.

"Please don't attack," I called out. "We come in peace and only wish to talk."

"Dragons," a water elemental hissed. "You are not welcome here."

I climbed off of Reven's back and he shifted into his human form. "I know the other Dragons are your enemies, but we are not them. We are the ascendants, and we want to stop the Black Dragon and bring an end to her reign."

"Impossible," an earth elemental grumbled.

"All we ask is that we have a few minutes to speak to your leaders."

The elementals began to speak in their own language of sounds I didn't understand. I heard a crackling, a splash, a gust, and the scraping of stone, and though it seemed they were arguing with each other, it was hard to tell for sure.

"Come with us," a fire elemental finally said, allowing me to breathe again.

A few of the elementals began to lead us inside the city, toward a tall pyramid that reflected sunlight. Made of glass, I realized, as we drew closer. The stone buildings around us were not especially intricate, but they were sturdy and functional. Humans thought elementals were little more than animals, living in caves and attacking cities for resources, but this confirmed my belief they were more like us than people knew.

We were brought inside the pyramid into a large room where four statues of the Gods in their dragon forms stood over their elements. I spotted a fire slowly burning in a pit of coals, a serene pool of water, a garden with fresh dirt, and an altar with incense and wind chimes that released a light tinkling sound. A large chair sat in front of each statue, facing toward the center of the room.

"Wait here," a fire elemental said.

Everyone else left the room then, taking much of the light with them as heavy doors closed and trapped us inside. One beam of light stretched down the top of the pyramid from high above us, dimly illuminating the room from the center.

Another door opened and four elementals entered, each with a small silver circlet on their heads. They took the chairs in front of their God's statues, while Reven and I stood in the center, under the beam of light. Each elemental's glowing eyes pinned us with a stare, though it was difficult to read the emotions on their faces. I tried not to squirm under their gaze, standing tall and facing them with as much confidence as I could muster.

"Spirit Dragon and Water Dragon," the air elemental said. It looked like a barely-contained whirling tornado with arms. "Why are you here?"

"We've come to discuss an alliance," I said.

The fire elemental leaned back in its chair, its body made entirely of flames and radiating heat. "Why would we want such a thing?"

"Because you want the same things we do—to rid of the world of the current Dragons and restore peace between humans and elementals."

"We tried peace before," the water elemental said, with the body of an upside-down tear that shifted like waves. "In your grandmother's time. It didn't work."

"That was a long time ago, and it might have worked if not for the shades and the Black Dragon. I think it's time we tried again. Or at the very least, let us unite against our common enemies for a short time." I stepped forward and glanced between each of them, putting my heart into my words and hoping they heard my sincerity. "Humans and elementals do not have to be enemies. We're more alike than anyone realizes, and we can learn so much from each other. When I become the next Spirit Dragon, I will be an advocate for both humans *and* elementals. I only want peace and balance—that's the task the Gods have given me."

"We've heard a tale of how you saved one of my kind," the rock elemental spoke up. Like the one I'd rescued, it resembled a giant boulder more than anything, except it had arms and legs. "We owe you a debt, which is why you were allowed to arrive in Divine Isle unharmed. No other human has been so honored in hundreds of years. But that does not mean we trust you."

"I'd like to hear her proposal," the air elemental said.

"A battle will be held at the Spirit Temple on the day of the Fall Equinox. The goal is for my mates and I to get inside the temple, defeat the current Dragons, and take their place. We're looking for allies to fight with us, as we know the other Dragons will have the support of the shades and much of the Onyx Army."

"An impossible battle," the fire elemental said. "You will all be destroyed."

The water elemental waved a fluid hand at the fire elemental, as if trying to shush it, before turning back to me. "Who will fight by your side?"

"The Resistance," I said. "And soldiers from the Air Realm." Probably.

"The Assassin's Guild has agreed to join us as well," Reven added.

"We're also contacting others who might be willing to assist us." I decided it was better not to mention they were bandits. "But we fear it won't be enough, especially against the shades. Not without the aid of the elementals."

The rock elemental crossed its arms. "What you ask is too much. Many of our kind would perish."

"And how many more will perish if things continue as they are?" Reven asked. "The humans, shades, and Dragons all see your kind as an enemy, something that should be wiped out from the world. By helping us, you will begin to change the minds of humans, and remove the Dragons and the shades from power."

"I don't want to put anyone in danger," I said. "But this is the only way to stop the Dragons for good. The Gods chose me and my mates to do this, but we need your help." I swallowed, then added, "Please. For the good of the world."

The elementals began speaking to each other in their strange language, while Reven and I waited. It was clear they were arguing by the raised voices and frantic gestures, but we didn't understand any of it. The earth elemental's grumble made the floors vibrate like an earthquake, while the fire elemental flared so hot it made us step back. The water elemental whipped its arms about, sending cold droplets across the room, while the air elemental's passionate words made our hair and clothes fly back.

When the elementals calmed, they all fixed their glowing eyes on us again. "We cannot help you," the rock elemental said, its voice low and final.

My heart sank. I'd really thought they would agree to help us. After all, we wanted the same things, or so I'd thought. Without the elementals, I wasn't sure if we would stand a chance.

"We cannot get involved in the affairs of humans," the fire elemental said. "Especially when there is no obvious benefit to our kind."

The water elemental nodded. "If you succeed, we will speak to you of a potential alliance then. If not, then none of this will matter anyway."

"But the outcome of this battle affects all of your kind too!" I said. "You can't stand by and do nothing while the world slips further and further into darkness. This is your chance to help bring back balance and peace, for both humans and elementals alike."

"We have given you our answer," the air elemental said. "It's time for you to leave our lands."

"But—"

Reven took my arm. "Come on, Kira. They've made their decision."

I drew in a shaky breath, trying to accept that I had failed. I wanted to yell at them, beg them to help us, plead with them to reconsider, or whatever it would take, but I knew they wouldn't change their minds. The division between humans and elementals was too strong and too old. I'd been a fool to think I could end hundreds of years of conflict so quickly. I'd hoped they would see that we could change, and that I was different from my mother, but they couldn't.

But I *was* different from her. Even if the elementals wouldn't help us, I wouldn't stop fighting for peace. As long as I survived what was to come.

26

SLADE

Kira should have been back by now.

I stared at the horizon in the direction I imagined she would arrive from on the back of a dark blue dragon. Sometimes I thought I saw something, but it was just a bird. It was always a bird.

Auric clasped a hand over my shoulder. "She'll be okay. Reven is with her."

"We don't know that."

I'd been the first to arrive in Clayridge after we'd all set out on our different tasks. Jasin had arrived a day later, with Auric showing up two days after that. And then…we'd waited.

"I can sense them both through the bond," Auric said. "If they were in danger, we'd know it."

"They should have been here by now." I couldn't keep the scowl off my face. I didn't like being separated from Kira and not being able to see for myself she was safe.

"Come, the hour grows late, and your mother has prepared another feast for us. Staring at the sky isn't going to bring Kira back any faster." He gestured toward the house behind us, where I'd grown up. Warm, hearty smells drifted out of the open windows, beckoning us inside.

"Fine," I grumbled, as I started to turn away. Except from the corner of my eye I spotted something, which made me pause. Another bird, most likely.

Except it was too big for a bird.

"Wait," I said. "What is that?"

We both watched the black speck in the sky as it grew closer. Definitely not a bird.

"It's Reven!" Auric said.

"How can you tell it's him and not Doran?"

"Reven's scales are a darker blue."

I grunted in response as we watched the dragon fly closer, growing larger with each second. When I saw the two people on his back, I could finally breathe easier. As soon as Reven landed, Kira leaped off his back and rushed toward us. I caught her in my arms and squeezed her close, while Auric hugged her from behind.

"I'm so happy to see you both," she said, as we held her between us.

Auric stroked her hair. "It's been far too long."

"We were getting worried about you," I said, pressing my forehead against hers.

"Sorry, it took us longer than expected due to some bad weather, plus we had to go around Soulspire…"

Jasin ran out of the inn and swept Kira up in his arms and spun her around, while she laughed. They shared a few words, while Doran hopped off Reven's back. The older man gave us all a nod, but his face was tight.

"I'll be at the inn," Doran said. "Meet me there tomorrow for breakfast so we can go over everything and begin your next round of training." He strode off into the dark town after that, without bothering to ask where the inn was.

"What's his problem?" Jasin asked.

Reven changed into his human form and walked toward us. "He's been like that ever since we got to Divine Isle, where the elementals live."

"What happened?" Auric asked.

"It's a long story," Kira said. "Is that food I smell? I'm starving."

I took her arm in mine. "Come inside. My mother has cooked way more food than any of us can eat and would be happy to see you."

As soon as we stepped inside, Brin and Leni jumped to their feet. "Kira!" Brin said. The three women exchanged hugs, and then Brin patted the seat next to her. "Sit down and eat. We must hear about where you've been."

"Not before saying hello to me." My mother rushed forward and grabbed Kira in a tight squeeze. "It's so good to see you again, dear."

"And you, Yena," Kira said, placing a kiss on my mother's cheek. "The food smells wonderful, as usual."

"Now you can sit," my mother said, with a laugh. "Leni, help me bring everything out for our guests."

Leni jumped up and ran to the kitchen, then returned with a giant roasted turkey that Jasin had caught us earlier. I began carving it, while they brought out more food—potatoes, onions, peas, and bread—along with tankards of ale.

While we all dug in, Kira told us about her encounter with the elementals, including the beauty of the island, the grandness of their capital, and the disappointment of their refusal to help.

Jasin clenched his fist tightly around his tankard. "I can't believe they said no. Don't they realize that we want to help them too?"

"They want to stay neutral and see what happens," Auric said. "They probably consider it the safest thing to do for their people."

"Cowards," Jasin muttered.

"It's frustrating, but there's nothing we can do about it," I said. "We'll do the best we can without them."

We took a few minutes to load our plates and eat, before Jasin asked, "What's going on with Doran?"

Kira sighed. "He's been distant and grumpy ever since Reven found us. He's upset we don't trust him and thinks he could have done a better job convincing the elementals to join us. Maybe he's right, I don't know."

"He's not," Reven said. "The elementals hate the other Dragons. If he'd been with you, they wouldn't have spoken to you at all."

"Perhaps." She drew in a long breath and gazed across the table at me and Auric. "Please tell me the rest of you had better luck."

"We did," Auric said. "My father agreed to send troops from the Air Realm's division of the Onyx Army, along with plenty of supplies. My brother Garet will be leading them."

"Thank the Gods," Kira said, closing her eyes briefly. "And what of the others?"

Jasin took a sip of his ale. "Cadock took a lot of convincing, but he finally agreed in exchange for his people being pardoned of all their crimes and given positions in your new government or military."

Kira raised her eyebrows. "I'm surprised he agreed at all. I'm sure we can figure something out for them."

"The Assassin's Guild has agreed to fight with us as well," Reven told us. "For a fee, naturally."

"That's good news," Auric said.

"The Resistance is willing to help, of course," I said. "Although they have fewer people than they did before due to the fight at Salt Creek Tower. However, they're sending messages to their other bases and expect a lot more people to join. Especially now that rumors have become widespread about a second group of Dragons."

"Is that so?" Kira asked.

"The Resistance have been spreading them," Leni said. "All thanks to Brin."

Brin nodded, a slight smile on her lips. "People need something to fight for, a cause to rally behind. Tales of how you've fought the Dragons are spreading like wildfire. You're already becoming legendary. I expect more people are joining the fight against the Dragons every day."

"Yes, but did you have to go with those names?" Jasin asked, arching a brow. "Ruby Dragon, really?"

Brin laughed. "Trust me, people love them. It sounds regal, like you were meant to rule."

"It could be worse," Leni said. "They could call you the Pink Dragon."

"My scales are not even close to pink!" Jasin said.

"What are they calling me?" Reven asked, as he tore off a piece of bread.

"The Sapphire Dragon," Auric said. "I'm Citrine, and Slade is Emerald."

Reven made a face. "I don't remember agreeing to that."

Leni grinned, clearly enjoying every second of this. "Too bad. The names have spread now, and you're stuck with them."

I began ticking off a list on my fingers. "So we'll have people from the Resistance, the Air Realm's army, the bandits, and the Assassin's Guild. Will it be enough?"

"Oh, and Calla and her priests," Auric added. "They're still in Stormhaven under the protection of my father, but they wanted to help us."

"Good," Kira said. "It will be useful to have another magic user there. Especially against the shades. I don't know if it will be enough, not without the elementals, but it will have to do."

"There's one thing that might help," I said. "While we waited for you, we've been working on imbuing our weapons with magic. I think we've mastered it now, and we can do your sword tomorrow."

"Yes, look at this." Jasin stood up, moved back from the table, and pulled out his sword. The blade lit up on fire, making Kira gasp.

"We did it to all our weapons," Auric explained.

Reven leaned forward, his eyes intrigued. "Can you do my swords too?"

"Yes, I can," I said. "And now that you're here, we can enchant Kira's sword too, with all four elements. We'll get started tomorrow."

"How long do you think you'll be in town?" my mother asked.

"About a week," Kira said.

My mother sighed, but nodded. "Well, I wish it were longer, but I know you have important things to do. It's just so good having all my children back in Clayridge." She wrapped her arm around Leni and gave her a squeeze, before turning back to us with a smile. "And you too, Kira. All of you, really. It's been a delight getting to know Auric and Jasin the last few days, and I'm sure you're just as lovely, Reven. You're all family now."

Reven shifted in his seat, looking uncomfortable, while Kira's cheeks flushed. I reached over to take her hand and gave it a squeeze. I'd once worried my family would never accept our relationship or this situation, but my mother had treated Kira like my betrothed and the other men as if they were my brothers. I knew she worried about us and the upcoming battle, but she believed in us and in our destiny. I couldn't ask for anything more…except that we make it through the battle alive.

27
KIRA

We met with my father in the morning to go over everything the others had learned on their journey and to discuss strategy. After that, my mates and I went to Slade's old forge, which was now run by his cousin, Noren.

The blacksmith's shop was open on one side, allowing smoke to billow out. I leaned against a tree as I watched my men work. Slade enchanted Reven's twin swords first, until they gleamed with a thin coat of sharp, deadly ice.

Slade walked over to me. "We're ready for your sword now."

I pulled my blade out of its sheath. Auric had bought it for me early in our adventures, and it was still the nicest thing I owned. It also fit my hand perfectly, the weight and balance exactly suited for my size.

I chewed on my lip as I handed it to him. "You're sure this will work?"

He nodded. "Trust me. I've done this to all of our weapons now."

"Yes, but you only did one element then."

"I'm confident it will work. If not, I'll make you a new sword. I promise."

He returned to the forge, where he heated up the metal in my blade. I squirmed as it turned red-hot, and that's when he placed it on a slab between my four mates. They stood in a circle around it, holding hands with each other, their eyes closed. Nothing happened at first, and I worried all of this was for nothing, but then I felt the magic growing. Fire danced across the sword before sinking into it. A gust of air swirled around it, and the blade absorbed that too, followed by a ripple of water that turned to ice, cooling the sword down. The metal hardened and shifted color, becoming lighter and stronger.

When the men stepped back and opened their eyes, my sword emitted a faint silver glow. Slade picked it up and presented it to me.

"A sword fit for the Silver Dragon," he said.

I wrapped my hand around the hilt and was struck by the powerful magic running through it. All four elements were in there, acting as one. I held the blade up to the sunlight and it flashed bright silver.

Yes, this was a sword that could take down Dragons.

While the men practiced using their enchanted weapons against each other, I sat on an old tree trunk and ate some dried fruit. My sword lay across my lap, but I was hesitant to use it against my mates now for fear of truly hurting them.

Doran leaned against a tree beside me, making me jump. I hadn't heard him approach. Sometimes he was a little too much like Reven, sneaking about like that.

"Nice sword," he said. "Can I see it?"

"Of course." I handed it to him before popping a dried apricot in my mouth.

He held it up, testing the weight, catching the light. When he held it, the silvery glow dimmed, as if it only reacted strongly to my magic. He gave a few practice swipes at the air, and then he grunted. "Not bad. Now the real test."

He sliced the blade across his forearm, opening a thick cut. Fire danced across his skin, and the edges of the wound blackened. He let out a sharp hiss and staggered back.

I jumped to my feet and ran to him. "What are you doing?"

"Testing it out, since you won't do it yourself."

"I didn't want to hurt anyone!"

He gave me a sharp look as he pressed a hand over his wound. "I hope that mercy won't hold you back when the time comes."

I rolled my eyes. "Let me see your wound. Maybe I can do something for it."

"I doubt it."

I clasped my hands over the wound, feeling how hot his skin was, while blood slipped through my fingers. "I was able to heal the Fire Priestess."

"Were you?" His eyebrow arched. "Guess it can't hurt to try."

I focused on his wound, trying to stop the bleeding, reaching for the life magic always lingering inside me. It was much harder to send it into my father than it was to heal my mates. He and I didn't have the bond entwining our lives together, but there was something else instead. A recognition that a part of us was the same.

Slowly the bleeding stopped, and the cut sealed itself up. The burn took the longest to heal, as if the fire magic that caused it was fighting me still. But in the end, I won the battle, and his skin was smooth again.

Doran held up his arm and inspected it. "Impressive. I'm not sure even Nysa could heal someone who wasn't one of her mates."

"It only worked because you're my father. The magic sensed that we were connected." I took the sword from him and sheathed it. "Well, did it meet your expectations?"

"It did. I wanted to make sure my water magic wouldn't block it, but that wasn't a problem. Instead it burned me with fire, while air and earth helped make it stronger. Quite painful and potent. It will be able to take down any of the Dragons, including Nysa once she's weakened."

I sank back onto my tree stump, suddenly exhausted from the healing. "Why have you been so distant for the last few days? Ever since we met with the elementals you've been acting oddly."

"I'm sorry. I guess I got upset when Reven arrived and I realized none of you trust me still. I don't care about what the others think, but I thought you and I had become close." He ran a hand through his long, sandy hair. "Or as close as we could be, considering the circumstances."

"I do trust you, but I also knew that Reven was right and we had a better chance of getting the elementals to help us without you there." I sighed. "Not that it made much difference in the end."

His hand rested on my shoulder. "You did the best you could. The elementals were never going to help us."

"I realize that now. I just don't know how to defeat the Dragons without them."

"Hmm." He glanced up at the sky. "It won't be easy. Especially since the Dragons know we're here now and have probably guessed our plans."

I sat up straight, my muscles tensing. "They do?"

"I've felt both Sark and Heldor's presence nearby."

"Will they attack Clayridge?"

"No, they'd have to be stupid to do that. We outnumber them, and you can control all the elements now. They're just watching and waiting to see what we do next."

I chewed on my lower lip, worrying about the innocent lives in this village. Doran couldn't know for sure that the Dragons wouldn't attack. "Maybe we should leave soon."

"Wherever we go, we'll put people at risk. That's why we have to face them soon. Only problem is, they know we're coming. They'll be preparing too."

My fists clenched. "So be it. As you said, this has to end soon. One way or another."

Doran's eyes caught mine, mirroring my own. "Just remember, you're my daughter. Whatever happens, I'm on your side. Always."

I swallowed the unexpected emotions rising inside me. "I know, father."

28

AURIC

"Today we're going to work on combining the elements," Doran said. It was time for yet another training session, and we all stood beside the river and faced him, with the afternoon sun bright in the sky. "I already know you can do lightning, thanks to Kira hitting me with a bolt when I was rescuing her."

Kira shrugged. "I thought you were taking me to my death."

Doran snorted. "How did you learn to do that one anyway?"

"Enva told us it was possible and then it was a lot of trial and error," I said.

"And frustration," Jasin added. "Mostly frustration."

Doran scratched at his scraggly beard. "You've done well, considering you had no one to train you. What other combinations can you do?"

"That's it so far," Kira said. "The bond with Slade and Reven was too new to do any others yet."

Doran nodded. "Hopefully it's grown enough by now. The benefit of combining elements is that there's no immunity to them. Both Sark and Isen can be hurt by lightning, for example."

"What will we do about Nysa?" Reven asked. "She's immune to every element."

"You let me worry about her," Doran said. "After the other dragons are defeated, she'll be vulnerable to attack."

I thought about asking whether that included him, but the troubled look on Kira's face made me hold my tongue.

"The hardest elements to combine are the two opposite ones," Doran continued. "Fire and water make steam, while earth and air create sand-storms. We'll work our way up to those. You can already do lightning, so we'll skip that."

"We want to learn to make lava," Slade said. "Or at least be able to stop it."

"A good choice. Probably the most deadly and destructive of the combined elements. Fine, you two can work together today, while Auric and Reven will make fog."

"Fog?" Jasin asked. "How will that be useful?"

Doran crossed his arms. "Not everything is about striking your enemies down. Sometimes there are better ways of handling things. Fog can conceal and confuse. It can hide a huge group of soldiers on the battle-field. It can make it easier to escape from a bad situation. And when you get good enough, you can make clouds and cover the sky with them too."

"It sounds perfect," I said, thinking of all the possibilities. With both Reven and Jasin's magic flowing through me, I could create entire storms on my own.

Reven and I moved closer to the forest, while Jasin and Slade headed for the edge of the river in case they had problems. But as I faced Reven, I began to have doubts this would work. I didn't know him all that well yet, and his bond with Kira was new. Jasin and I had become close, despite our differences, and Slade and I had an easy understanding and friendship. But Reven? He was hard for all of us to get to know. Kira had often commented on how Reven pushed her away or locked her out, but it wasn't only her that he kept at a distance. Combining our magic took a connection, and the man was a wall of ice that was nearly impossible to cross. Luckily, I knew how to fly.

"Fog would have been useful in your previous profession, I imagine," I said.

Reven let out a soft grunt in response. "Those days are over."

"Yes. I wanted to thank you again for what you did for my father. You didn't have to do that." Reven had taken the contract on my father's life to make sure no one else did, even though it ended his career with the Assas-sin's Guild forever.

"I wasn't going to kill him," Reven said, sending me a sharp look.

"No, of course not." Damn, I was really bungling this one up. "I simply meant that I appreciated how you handled it, and the sacrifice it required of you."

"It was time to move on from that life anyway."

"And yet you went back to them to ask for their help. Was it a problem, since you failed to complete your last mission?"

He smirked. "It was, until I turned into a dragon in front of them and made it rain in the middle of the room."

I grinned back at him. "I would have loved to have seen their faces."

"All right," Doran called out, interrupting us. "Try to reach for your partner's magic through the bond. It might be difficult to find at first, but it's there. Once you've found it, grab tight and let it loose with your own magic."

I stared into Reven's cold blue eyes, searching for him within the bond. Jasin was easy to find, like a bright spark jumping behind my eyes that grew stronger with my attention on him. Slade was harder to find, but when I focused on him, his steady, strong presence filled my mind. Creating a storm of sand or dust with him wouldn't be too difficult, I imagined. But when I searched for Reven, I felt nothing.

"This isn't working," Reven said.

"It will. It took a long time for me and Jasin to figure it out, but we did eventually."

"The two of you are close," Reven said, his lip curling as if the idea bothered him. "But you and me? We have nothing in common."

"I don't think that's true." I tilted my head, studying him. "Jasin and Slade both let their emotions dominate them. With Jasin it's obvious, but Slade is just as guilty of it, he just doesn't react as passionately or as hastily. His emotions build up under the surface, until they can't be contained anymore. But you and I—we think things through. We take our time. We research different options before we come to a decision. We both value knowledge above most other things. Our lives have been completely different, but we're more alike than you think."

"I suppose," Reven said. "Although you value knowledge for the sake of having it. I value what it can do for me. It's a means to an end, not an end in and of itself."

"True, but we still prefer to trust our minds more than our hearts, which can make it difficult for us to open up to people or can lead us to make bad decisions. I made mistakes with Kira that I now regret. I kept secrets from her about who I was, because my mind told me it was the best thing to do at the time. Maybe if I'd listened to my heart, things would have been easier."

Reven was silent, staring at the river's flowing water. Behind us, Jasin let out a shout as he and Slade made the ground rip apart and lava shoot from the cracks, while Kira and Doran applauded.

"Maybe you're right," Reven finally said. "I locked away my heart for so many years I'd convinced myself I didn't have one anymore. Kira forced me to realize I was wrong about that."

I chuckled softly. "She has a way of making us confront the things about ourselves we would like to ignore. Annoying, isn't it?"

"Very." Reven let out a long breath. He glanced over at Jasin and Slade, the star pupils of today's training session, as they made lava spurt into the air. "We can't let them show us up. How do we do this?"

"Jasin and I found it easier if we were holding hands and staring into each other's eyes. Maybe that would help?" I stretched out my hands toward him, palms up.

Reven rolled his eyes and grabbed my hands. "Fine."

His skin was cool against mine, and his eyes were the pale blue of the early morning sky. When I searched for him through the bond this time, I found a small, cold ripple. I grasped onto it, pulling it toward me, unwilling to let go, and the ripple became a wave, growing stronger the more I tugged at it. Now that I knew what he felt like in my mind, I was certain I could find him again, and it would be easier next time.

When Reven's breathing suddenly changed and his eyes widened, I knew he'd found me through the bond too. His fingers tightened around mine and something passed between us. The air around us began to grow murky. Fog rolled off the water, creeping around the forest, becoming thicker with each passing second. Soon, I couldn't see anything except Reven. The rest of the world had been cut off, hidden away by the magic we'd created. I saw the wonder in his eyes as he took it in, and then we grinned at each other. Somehow, I didn't think we'd have a problem connecting anymore.

29

KIRA

Over the next week we trained harder than we ever had before. We faced each other in teams and one on one. We fought with our weapons, with our magic alone, or—for the men—in their dragon forms. Doran barked out orders the entire time, pushing us to fight harder, to keep going, to never back down. He gave us tips on the other Dragons' weaknesses and showed us how to use our powers together to defeat them. We learned more from him than we had in the entire few months we'd known each other.

And I worried it still wouldn't be enough.

Every night, we returned to our rooms in the inn, exhausted, beaten, bloody, and burnt. My men and I had no energy for lovemaking—we simply curled up in bed together, all five of us holding each other tenderly, and my touch healed my mates while we slept. Our bonds grew stronger, and with it, our magic.

The other Dragons had hundreds of years on us. We would never be as strong or as experienced as them. But we had something they'd lost over the years—love.

The days rushed by, and soon it was time for another bittersweet goodbye as we said farewell to Slade's family and the town that had sheltered us not once, but twice. We packed our things, hugged everyone tightly, and then prepared to take off—and that's when I noticed we were one person short.

"Where's Doran?" I asked, as I glanced about.

Slade frowned. "It's not like him to run late."

"I saw him fly away last night," Leni said. "I assumed you knew, so I didn't mention it."

I took a step back as my knees nearly gave out on me. The world spun around me, and I felt like I might actually throw up. "He left?"

"Oh Gods," Auric said, his eyes wide. "Doran had the map with all the battle plans. If he took that with him…"

Jasin swore under his breath. "That bastard. I knew he'd betray us!"

"We don't know that for certain," Brin said, though her voice wasn't very convincing. She rested a sympathetic hand on my back. "There must be some explanation."

"Yes, exactly." I clung to her words, desperate to hold onto hope. I refused to believe my father would betray us, after everything he'd done. "He told me to remember he's on my side. Maybe he's not really betraying us but trying to help us in some way."

Slade wrapped a strong arm around me. "I know you want to believe that, but it doesn't seem likely. If he was helping us, he would have told us his plan, not sneak off in the middle off the night."

"The Water God warned us about this," Reven said. "He said Doran would turn against us because he would never be willing to give up the power and his own life."

"But why would he help us all this time only to betray us?" I asked.

"Because he wanted us to trust him!" Jasin growled. "Now he's run back to Nysa and he knows all our weaknesses and our plans."

"We'll have to completely redo our strategy," Auric said, his brow furrowed. "If that is even possible."

Jasin's eyes flashed with anger. "We can adjust some things, but he'll be able to anticipate which ones. We're doomed. We might as well call this all off now."

"We can't call it off," Brin said. "We'll just have to do the best we can."

I stared at my mates, feeling their rage and frustration through the bond, and knew they were right. My father really had betrayed us. Everything he'd told me was a lie. All this time he'd been working for Nysa, acting as her scout and her spy, like he always did. And we'd played right into his hand, doing everything he asked, falling for all of his lies. In the end, he was as corrupted as she was, and there was no redemption for him.

I clenched my hand around my sword, feeling the magic within it. "We're going to continue with our plans. And when we come face to face with the Dragons, we'll destroy them." My voice hardened into steel. "All of them."

We set off for the Spirit Temple, which was in the middle of a large plain just south of Soulspire. We'd advised all our allies to meet us in a valley east of there on the day of the Fall Equinox. It would take us a few days to get there, and it never escaped my mind that Doran was hours ahead of us with all of our plans. My mates pushed themselves hard, flying as fast and as long as they could, and every night they were completely exhausted.

On the last night before we expected to arrive, I tossed and turned beside my men, unable to sleep. All I could think about was facing my father, and what I would have to do to stop him. Eventually I stood and walked away, hoping the quiet forest would bring me some peace.

I found Enva sitting on a large rock nearby, like she'd been waiting for me for hours.

"Hello, Kira. Come sit beside me."

I leaned against the stone, gazing across the dark forest and listening to the quiet sounds of night. "Did Doran really betray us?"

"It seems that way. He's heading to Soulspire now with your battle plans. I'm sorry."

I covered my face with my hands as I tried to gain control over my emotions. "I can't trust my mother. I can't trust my father. I'm not even sure I can trust you. The only people I can count on are my mates."

"Yes, as it should be." She patted my arm softly. "Doran had to return to Nysa. He is bound by magic to be loyal to her. He might have been able to resist it for some time, but when she calls him through the bond, it's difficult to ignore."

"Does he even care for me at all?"

"Yes, I'm sure he does. He did save your life as a baby, and he has watched over you your whole life, much as I have. But he has been bound to Nysa for nearly a thousand years. Their lives are entwined. It's difficult for him to fight against her, even for you."

"I feel so stupid. Everyone warned me not to trust him, but I wanted to believe in him."

"You're not stupid. You wanted a father. There is nothing wrong with that."

"There is when he now has all of your secrets and can turn them against you."

"Don't give up hope." She smoothed my head softly, the touch so nurturing it surprised me. "You and your mates were chosen by the Gods to protect this world. I have faith that you'll succeed."

I leaned against her body, which looked frail but was surprisingly sturdy, especially considering she was a ghost. "I wish I didn't have to kill my parents," I whispered, giving voice to the thing I'd kept inside so long and was afraid to admit.

"I know. I wish the same thing." She sighed and continued stroking my hair. "It's a terrible situation the Gods have placed us in, but there's no other way. If it makes you feel better, I believe by ending my daughter's life, you will be freeing her. She wasn't always like this. She was brave, and kind, and passionate. Sometimes a little too confident, arrogant, and reckless, but she took after her father, my Fire Dragon. Like him, she would do anything to protect other people, which is why she imprisoned the Spirit Goddess inside herself. Now she's become corrupted and I don't recognize her anymore, but I know my daughter is in there somewhere, screaming for all of this to end." She took my face in her hands gently. "Deep down, Nysa wants you to win too. I truly believe this."

I nodded slowly and she wiped away a stray tear I couldn't hold back. "I'll do my best to free her."

She wrapped her arms around me. "I know you will. You're the only one who can."

With those words, she vanished.

I sat there for some time, listening to the sounds of forest, thinking about Enva's words. I didn't know if she was right about my parents or not. The more I learned about myself and the world, the less I truly knew for certain. All I could do was listen to my gut and hope it led me down the right path in the days to come.

A branch snapped behind me, and I sensed Jasin approaching. His strong arms slid around me, and I relaxed against him. He said nothing, simply held me close, letting me draw upon his strength until I was ready to talk.

"Now I know how you felt when your father betrayed us," I said.

"It's a terrible feeling, isn't it?" He pressed a kiss to the top of my head. "It's horrible enough when your parents believe in something you know is wrong, and no matter how much you try to convince them otherwise, they won't be persuaded to see your side. When they turn against you for those same beliefs, it's like a dagger in the heart."

I leaned my head against his shoulder. "You were right about Doran all along. I should have listened to you."

"I wish I'd been wrong. Gods know I'd do anything to save you from going through this and from suffering the same hurt that I did." He smoothed my hair away from my face and gazed into my eyes. "But we're not defined by what our parents do. We make our own choices, and we can choose to make better decisions than them. Or we can try, at least."

I turned in his arms and pressed a kiss to his lips. "When did you become so wise?"

"I'm spending too much time with Auric obviously."

I snuggled up against him. "I like that the two of you are close."

"We're a family, all five of us—thanks to you. You brought us together, and you made us work out our differences and fight for a common goal. You made each of us want to be better people. And no matter what happens, none of us will ever betray each other. Or you."

The truth of his words flowed through our bond. My adopted parents were long gone, my birth parents were my enemies, but my mates...they were forever.

30

KIRA

As my dragons soared over the peaks of the mountains, the valley beyond it came into view, and with it, our army. It was the day of the Fall Equinox, and hundreds of men and women had come to fight for our cause. I was honored by their bravery and their belief in us, but also felt the heavy weight of their lives hanging over my head. I was responsible for all of them and would mourn every life lost in my name.

On the eastern side, Onyx Army soldiers were assembled, their scaled black armor decorated with the yellow markings on their shoulders that meant they were from the Air Realm. Mixed in with them were others in golden armor with the symbol of House Killian on their chest, representing the royal guard. The King had truly come through for us, and by sending his troops he was showing the world he stood with us against the Dragons. If we failed today, it would likely mean the end of his reign.

To the west, a more ragtag group of men and women had gathered, which I assumed was a combination of the Resistance, the Assassin's Guild, and Cadock's people. They wore common clothes and whatever armor and weapons they possessed. Some were bandits. Some were farmers. Some were assassins. Many were seasoned fighters, but many more were not. Yet they were all here, willing to fight for what they believed in. I prayed we weren't sending them all to their deaths.

In the center, large tents had been set up, and that's where we headed. Faces looked up at us and cheered or simply stared in awe as my four dragons flew overhead. As we descended, I heard shouts about the ascendants and cheers for the Ruby, Sapphire, Emerald, and Citrine Dragons.

The men might not love the names, but as Brin had said, they'd already stuck.

People backed away as my dragons landed, giving us space. I slid off Slade's back and nodded at everyone. I wasn't used to so much attention and didn't particularly like it, but I had to get used to this sort of reception. I'd spent so much of my life hiding and running, sticking to the shadows and avoiding being noticed, but those days were over. Everything had changed now, and soon the entire world would know who I was, no matter the outcome of this battle.

While Brin and Leni dismounted, a man in gold armor stalked toward us. I immediately recognized him as one of Auric's brothers, even though we'd never met before. He was ridiculously tall, even taller than Auric, and wasn't lacking in muscles either, judging by the way he filled out his armor. But where Auric's face was chiseled perfection, this man was plain, with blond hair cropped short, pale gray eyes, and a square jaw.

My dragons shifted to their human forms, sending a ripple of awe through the crowd, and Auric stepped forward. The two blond men clasped each other in a hug.

"Thanks for coming." He turned toward me with a smile. "Kira, this is my brother, Garet. He leads the King's Guard."

"A pleasure, my lady," Garet said, with an elegant bow.

"It's nice to meet you," I said.

"Garet will be leading my father's troops," Auric said.

His brother nodded. "Yes, we have men and women from both the King's Guard and the Air Realm's Onyx Army division. We're ready to serve however we can."

"We appreciate your help," I said.

Brin moved to our side with a smile. "It's good to see you again, Garet."

The three nobles continued chatting, but my attention was drawn to another man approaching us. I walked toward him with a smile I couldn't hide. "Cadock!"

The man I'd once considered my first love grasped me in a friendly hug before stepping back. He looked down at me with his bright blue eyes, while his tousled blond hair blew in the breeze. "You're looking as beautiful as ever."

I smiled but ignored the compliment. "I'm so happy you changed your mind about helping us."

"I didn't want to, but your man here is pretty persuasive," Cadock said, nodding at Jasin, who'd come to stand beside us.

Jasin shook Cadock's hand with a wry grin. "I did what I had to do."

"How did you convince him in the end?" I asked. "I never got the whole story."

Cadock smirked. "Jasin challenged me to a fight. If he won, I had to agree to support your cause."

"And if you won?" I asked.

"He'd have to clean our outhouse for a week."

"Don't worry, there was no chance I was going to lose," Jasin said.

Cadock chuckled. "So you say, but as I recall it came pretty close there at the end."

I shook my head as they continued to joke around, and spotted Faya speaking to some people, including Slade's sister, at the edge of the crowd. I made my way over to her with a frown. "You shouldn't be here."

"Hello, Kira," Faya said. "Of course I should be here. I'm the leader of the Resistance now."

"You're also pregnant," I said.

"Only a few months," Faya said, waving it away. "I'll stay back during the fight, but I'm not going to send my people into battle without me. What kind of leader would I be?"

"And if the fighting reaches you?" I asked.

"I'll be fine." Faya touched the hilt of her sword. "I can still fight. And now I have another thing worth dying for—my child."

Leni moved to Faya's side. "Don't worry. Brin and I will protect her with our lives."

"I appreciate that," I said.

"I don't need protection," Faya snapped, but then she sighed. "But I wouldn't mind having two friends fight beside me."

Cadock and Jasin strolled over. The bandit leader bowed before Faya, then took her hand and placed a kiss over her knuckles. "Why hello there. I'm Cadock, leader of the Thunder Chasers. You must be Faya. I've heard a great deal about you, but no one ever mentioned your beauty."

Faya rolled her eyes. "Probably because they knew I'd cut them in half for speaking about me that way."

A charming smile spread across Cadock's face. "Beautiful and fierce. I love it."

Reven caught my attention, bringing over an older woman with short, white hair and a tattoo of a dagger on her neck. She was dressed in all black, with a hooded cloak that didn't conceal the numerous throwing knives at her waist. "Kira, this is Zara. She'll be speaking for the Assassin's Guild. She also helped train me when I first joined."

"Is that so?" My eyebrows shot up. This was the first person I'd ever met from Reven's past. "What was he like back then?"

Zara grinned. "Just as surly and brooding as he is now. A fine fighter though. I knew the moment we met that he was meant for something big. I had no idea it would be this though."

"None of us expected anything like this," I said. "We appreciate the help of the Assassin's Guild."

She shrugged. "We go where the coin is. And we've been promised a lot of it."

"You'll definitely be compensated," I said. Assuming we made it through this alive.

Zara slapped Reven on the back. "We protect our own too. Reven is one of us, and now he's a Dragon. We'll do whatever we can to assist him."

Reven looked surprised by this. "Thank you, Zara."

"Don't get too soppy on me," Zara said with a grin. "We're mostly here for the coin."

"Of course," I said.

Another familiar face emerged from the crowd. Calla, the High Priestess of the Fire God. She was a beautiful woman in her forties, with hair the color of straw, and she wore the red silk robe of her station. She started to bow before me, but I grabbed her in a hug instead.

"I'm so happy you're okay," I said. "Many of the other priests have been killed by the Dragons."

"So I've heard," Calla said, as she stepped back. "The Air Realm has been kind to us, although I do miss our home at the volcano. I pray we'll be able to return to the Fire Temple once this is all over."

"I hope so." I chewed on my lower lip. "Although we've discovered everything is more complicated than we expected."

I quickly told her about the Spirit Goddess and Nysa, hoping she had some advice for how to stop her.

"I've never heard of such a thing," Calla said. "But if anyone can stop her, it is you."

"Do you think the Gods will truly help us?"

"I cannot say. Sometimes the things they do seem confusing to us, but later on they make sense. They see a much larger picture than we do." She touched my cheek. "Have faith, Kira. You were destined for this, and you will succeed."

Jasin raised his voice, drawing our attention. "If you'd all head inside the tent, we can get started working on our strategy for tomorrow's battle."

I drew in a steady breath as the gathered people stepped into the large command tent to begin preparations. Jasin and Auric had made some changes to our plan after Doran left, but they wanted to get the input of the other leaders too. I watched them all filter in through the tent flaps, and then I followed them inside.

31
KIRA

We spent hours going over every single detail of tomorrow's battle, hammering out the plans until everyone was satisfied with them. Or as satisfied as we could be, considering tomorrow we'd be going up against a far more powerful opponent and many people would die in the battle. Worry gnawed at me, not just for the people I loved, but for everyone who would be fighting for us tomorrow. I wished there was some way to spare them all from this, but to save the world we had to go to war.

The hour was late and the camp was quiet by the time we retreated to the tent that had been set up for us. Originally, we'd been given five tents, but I'd asked for one large tent instead. This might be our last night in this world, and I was going to spend it with my mates at my side.

Five cots had been set up around the room, but we shoved them to the side and then covered the floor with blankets and pillows. We spread out on the makeshift bed, facing each other like we'd done beside so many campfires during our travels. Now our journey was almost at an end, and the feeling was bittersweet. Especially since we had no idea what the outcome would be tomorrow.

Slade's large hands settled on my shoulders and he began massaging them slowly. "You seem tense."

I leaned back into his touch. "Just worried about tomorrow."

"We all are," Auric said. "But we've done everything we can to make sure the battle goes our way. Now we just need to get some rest."

Jasin rested his hand on my thigh. "We will, but not yet."

"What are you planning?" I asked.

He brushed his lips against my neck. "We're going to take your mind off tomorrow."

I relaxed a little more and tilted my head to give him better access. "All I want is to spend the evening in the arms of my mates…in case it's our last time together."

"Don't talk like that," Slade said, his fingers tightening on my shoulders.

Reven took my face in his hands. "Tomorrow is not going to be the end, I promise."

Jasin nodded. "Our close bond gives us an advantage. The other Dragons don't stand a chance."

Through the bond I knew they were worried too, but they were also confident we'd succeed. I focused on that certainty and nodded.

Auric began removing my boots. "You definitely need to release some tension. Otherwise you'll never get to sleep."

Jasin's lips traced patterns on my neck. "I know the best way to do that."

While Auric began rubbing my feet, the other three men slowly removed my clothes, lightly kissing every spot of skin they revealed. I melted into their gentle, comforting touches, and by the time I was undressed, I was little more than a puddle in their arms.

"We're going to take care of you," Slade said, as he lowered me down onto my back. "Just relax and enjoy it."

From the pile of blankets and pillows I stared up at the tent while the four men surrounded me. Auric kissed his way up from my ankles to my knees to my thighs, while the others kissed the sensitive skin at the inside of my arms, the curve of my breasts, and the slope of my stomach. Their love wrapped around me like a warm blanket, easing all of my troubles.

Auric spread my legs wider and dipped his head between them, kissing me there. As his mouth moved over me and his tongue began to explore, the others continued their slow worship of the rest of my body. I reached for them, grabbing onto their shirts and trousers, wishing I could touch them too. My fingers brushed against the hard bulge in Reven's trousers and the rough beard coating Slade's jaw, while Jasin's lips found mine.

As Auric wound me tighter and tighter with the stroke of his tongue between my legs, my other mates removed their clothing. The sight of their strong bodies being slowly revealed made me almost dizzy with desire, and I tangled my hands in Auric's golden hair as the tension built inside me. He increased the pressure of his tongue and it became too much, making me gasp and moan as the orgasm gripped me.

Auric sat back and removed his clothing next, while I floated down from the place he'd taken me. My four mates gazed at me with lust-filled eyes and I couldn't decide which one I wanted first.

"I need you," I told them. "All of you. Don't hold back."

Jasin removed a small bottle of oil from one of his bags. "We won't. We're all going to be yours tonight."

My pulse sped up at his words and at what the oil meant. We'd used it once before, and I was excited to try it again with all my men. "Two at a time?" I asked, my voice practically begging.

"If that's what you want," Reven said.

"I do. Auric and Slade. Reven and Jasin. The opposite elements inside me at the same time."

"That can be arranged," Slade said.

I'd been worried he wouldn't be interested in sharing me like that, but he didn't even hesitate as he pulled me toward him and began kissing me, his hard, naked body pressing against my soft curves. Auric's hands fell on my behind, giving it a squeeze.

"I've always wanted to take you here," Auric said, sliding his finger between my cheeks. "Ever since I saw Jasin do it."

"Please," I said, before Slade's mouth claimed mine again.

Jasin poured some oil on his hand and began to rub it against my tight entrance, while Auric laid back on the blankets and coated his cock, getting it nice and slippery. Jasin's fingers slid into me easily, stretching me and preparing me for Auric, and then he moved aside.

Slade's hands circled my waist, and he guided me backwards onto Auric, so I straddled him in reverse. Auric gripped my hips, and together the two of them guided me down. I felt Auric's hard length at my back entrance and tensed for a moment, but then my body relaxed as I slowly sank down onto him. I groaned as my tight hole stretched against his large size, and Slade wrapped his arms around me to hold me in place.

"Are you okay?" he asked.

I nodded and lowered myself even more, taking Auric inside me inch by inch. With every second that passed the uncomfortable stretching gave way to pleasure as he filled me up, until my behind rested against his hips and he was completely inside me.

"Gods, you're so tight, Kira," Auric said from behind me, his voice strained almost like he was in pain. "It's incredible."

"You feel so big," I said, rocking a little against him.

"Ready for me too?" Slade asked, his brow furrowed like he worried he might hurt me.

I slid a hand around his neck and drew him toward me to kiss him, my need for him growing with every second. "Very ready."

Auric held my hips while Slade got in position in front of me. His large cock edged into me, and it seemed impossible they would both fit, but somehow Slade pushed all the way inside. I wrapped my arms around his neck as my body grew weak, already overcome with pleasure from being taken by both of them at once.

Slade held me tight, steadying me, as he started to slide in and out. With every thrust he pushed me back onto Auric, and every time he retreated, Auric lifted his hips to follow. I threw my head back and let their rhythmic glide rock me between them, their movements almost leisurely, like they could do this all night. Their long, deep thrusts touched me everywhere, filling me completely. I found myself matching their speed and then increasing it, demanding more from them as I spiraled higher and higher, chasing the release only they could bring. We reached it together, shaking and moaning as the bond snapped tight between us.

I slowly came back down to earth while Slade kissed me and Auric's hands caressed my back and hips. On either side of us, Reven and Jasin watched, stroking themselves as they waited for their turn with me.

Slade kissed me one last time, before he stood and helped lift me off Auric. My knees were so weak I could barely stand, but Jasin was immediately there, sweeping me into his arms. He wrapped my legs around his waist, and I clung to his neck as our lips found each other's. He devoured my mouth as his cock plunged inside me, making me cry out.

Reven moved to stand behind us and his hands cupped my bottom. He'd already oiled himself, and he pushed into my back entrance, pinning me between him and Jasin. I was stretched wide thanks to Auric and Slade, and both Reven and Jasin filled me easily.

Together they held me up as they caged me between their hard bodies and began to thrust into me. Unlike the other two men, Jasin and Reven had no intentions of going slow. They both liked it fast and hard and a little rough, and my nails dug into Jasin's arms as they pounded me together. They rocked me back and forth, giving and taking, sliding in and out in a rhythm that got faster and faster. They were fire and ice, cool and hot, and I burned and melted all at once between them.

Jasin claimed my mouth while Reven buried his face against my shoulder, and all I could do was cling to them as I came so hard I was sure my cries could be heard by everyone in the nearby tents. The two men let go at the same time, losing control for that brief instant, giving everything to me.

At first, all we could do was hold onto each other and try to breathe, sweat dripping down our bodies, which were still joined together. Slade and Auric grinned at us from the makeshift bed on the floor and patted it in an invitation to join them.

Jasin and Reven carefully lowered me down into the arms of the other men, who helped me get comfortable in my slightly dazed state. All four of them wrapped themselves around me, a combination of coolness and warmth, and I kissed each of them slowly.

"I love you all," I said, as the bond flared bright, so strong I could almost see it filling the room. Each one of my mates told me they loved me too, and I knew that whatever happened tomorrow, they were with me until the end.

32
JASIN

The sun breaching the horizon made the clouds above us look as red as blood. An ominous sign, if one believed in such things. I didn't, of course, but it certainly set the mood as I gazed across the sea of troops lined up in front of me. Soon the field before the Spirit Temple would be covered in their blood, all so we would have a chance to defeat the Dragons.

The plan relied on the soldiers buying us time so we could get inside the Spirit Temple and defeat the Black Dragon as quickly as possible. None of us had any idea what would happen after that, especially once the Spirit Goddess was freed. The Water God had made it sound like the Gods would help us split the Goddess's essences, but nothing was certain.

The Spirit Temple rose before us at the end of the plain on a hill, nestled up against the mountains beside a waterfall that fed into a clear lake. The temple shimmered where sunlight touched it, due to the walls made from a pale marble that looked like pearl or shell...or maybe bone. Great columns held it up on every corner with ivy and roses twining around them. Above the grand entrance a relief depicted animals, plants, elementals, and dragons, though it was hard to make out the details from a distance. A beautiful garden surrounded the temple, filled with fruit trees, vegetables, and flowers, while the waterfall splashed beside it into a stream that fed down into the valley.

The plains in front of the temple were flat and rich with good soil and thick vegetation. I'd been told that they'd been covered with herds of wild animals until the soldiers arrived. Now the animals had scattered, and the two armies faced each other across their former home.

The Black Dragon's army stretched far and wide, blocking entrance to the Spirit Temple. Onyx Army soldiers in their gleaming black armor waited for the command to attack, lined up in columns that were all too familiar to me. Red, blue, and green markings flashed on their shoulders, along with a few sporting yellow. If the Fire God had chosen another as his Dragon, I'd probably be with them now, wishing I were anywhere else.

On either side of them, dark shadowy figures hovered off the ground, their eerily glowing eyes staring across the field. There were hundreds of shades, more than I'd ever seen before, and the sight of them sent a chill down my spine. Their deadly hunger was palpable even from a distance, and they wanted nothing more than to drain the life from every person who stood behind me.

Today I wore the Onyx Army armor again, except instead of the red markings for the Fire Realm, mine were bright silver—the color we were using to represent Kira. Across the field, dozens of black banners were raised with a silvery dragon in the center and red, blue, green, and yellow corners. The banner of the Silver Dragon and her mates.

Our army was made up of many different people from all over the four Realms. Men and women with armor and weapons stood side by side with people in regular clothes holding torches, buckets of water, or piles of rocks. Everyone had a task, a way they could help to fight the soldiers or the shades, but there was no question that we were outnumbered and outmatched. If the elementals were fighting beside us, we'd stand a better chance—but they were not. We'd have to do the best we could with what we had.

Garet signaled that they were ready, and I moved to stand in the middle of the field, facing our army. Once there, I shifted into my dragon form, while Kira's other mates stretched out beside me and did the same. Kira walked over wearing her fighting gear with a flowing silver cloak, her glowing sword on her hip. When my red scales flashed under the sunlight she climbed onto my back. I spread my wings and took to the sky, hovering over our soldiers.

"The Black Dragon and her men have ruled over this world for too long," I called out, my dragon voice louder than mine could ever be. "They were meant to protect us, and instead they oppressed us. They were meant to bring peace and order, and instead they brought death and chaos. They were meant to serve the Gods, and instead they imprisoned them. It's time for new Dragons to rise."

Auric, Reven, and Slade flew into the air beside me at those words and let out ear-splitting roars that echoed across the land. The soldiers below us raised their weapons and shouted and cheered, their energy growing with their fervor. Kira had asked me to give this speech, to become the leader the Fire God had told me to be, and though I'd been reluctant at first, I was ready to embrace my destiny as Kira's General. Kira was their symbol, the thing they fought behind, but I would be the one leading them into battle.

"Today we fight for the Silver Dragon," I roared. "We fight for freedom, justice, and equality. We fight for the four Realms. We fight for the Gods. And most of all, we fight for the future of our people." I spread my wings wide. "Today the Black Dragon will be defeated, and the Silver Dragon will ascend!"

The cheers and shouts grew louder, and the army started forward across the field into the fog Auric and Reven had summoned, hiding their numbers. Ahead of them, pools of lava waited for the other army, courtesy of me and Slade. Below us, I spotted Calla and her priests, ready to fight the shades. Garet led the soldiers, directing them to march ahead. The Resistance, the bandits, and the assassins filled in the gaps, while Faya stood in the back with Brin and Leni at her side, all of them looking fierce. As I gazed down at them, I truly believed we could win this battle.

Until the Black Dragon emerged from the Spirit Temple.

33

KIRA

A massive dragon with scales the color of midnight filled the sky, blocking out the sun. Storm clouds surrounded her, lightning flashed behind her, hail fell around her, and the ground beneath her rumbled. The sky turned dark and ominous, and the other four Dragons flew to her side. My heart clenched at the sight of my father with them.

I'd never seen the Black Dragon as anything other than human before, and she was truly terrifying like this. Her claws and talons were razor sharp, and dark, deadly power emanated from her, much like it did from the shades. I found myself gripping Jasin's scales tighter as fear spread through me.

When she spoke, her voice echoed across the plains. "Surrender now and your deaths will be quick and painless. Fight, and my shades will feast on your souls while my Dragons rip you to shreds."

Her words were probably supposed to make me want to run away, and though I was terrified, all they did was make me angry—and even more determined. I raised my sword into the air and reached for the power inside me. A bright silver light appeared and stretched high into the sky, casting a glow over my assembled army and breaking through the darkness. "We will never surrender! Your time is at an end!"

Her green eyes narrowed. "Then you shall meet your doom."

As soon as she spoke the words she dipped down, plummeting toward the ground so fast it only took her seconds to reach it. She stretched her talons wide and scooped up a handful of our soldiers in each fist, then reared back into the sky. I thought she would let the men fall to their deaths, but as they screamed and struggled, she opened her mouth and a stream of darkness began to flow from their mouths into hers. One by one the soldiers' heads drooped, their bodies becoming lifeless, while my mother's scales seemed to become blacker and blacker.

"She's draining them," I whispered, horrified at what I was seeing.

"And taking their life to fuel her own power," Jasin said, as Nysa opened her claws and let the bodies drop to the ground, one by one.

How were we supposed to stop her? She had no weaknesses. She could control all the elements, and thus was immune to them. She could drain the life of anyone she touched and it only made her stronger. We had no way to defeat her. And even if we did, we'd have to face the Spirit Goddess next.

Her soldiers and shades lurched forward, clashing with our army. The sounds of battle began to ring out, while the storm raged on around us, casting lightning and hail at our soldiers. I spread my arms and reached for it with my magic, calming the raging elements until the clouds began to dissipate, and the sun shined through again.

But the storm was only the beginning of our problems. While the soldiers and shades fought, Sark spewed flame, Heldor ripped open huge trenches in the ground, and Isen created a tornado to tear through our ranks. My own mates dashed forward to combat them, finding the other Dragon they were strongest—and weakest—against, the way Doran had taught them.

Doran…my eyes searched the battle for him, but he wasn't attacking our army. Where did he go?

As Nysa swooped down again to reach for more lives to drain, another dragon slammed into her, knocking her back. They hit the ground in a tangle of black and blue scales, claws and fangs flashing.

My heart leapt into my throat. "Father!" I screamed.

He was actually fighting her, even with the bond between them. His words came back to me. *You're my daughter. Whatever happens, I'm on your side. Always.*

He hadn't betrayed us. He'd been doing everything he could to get close to Nysa again, to win back her trust, so that he could surprise her in this moment. Nysa did have one weakness—her own mates. She wouldn't kill one of her own, not without making herself vulnerable. Doran couldn't kill her either, not without killing himself in the process, but he could distract her for a while to give us a chance.

"Doran is buying us time!" I called out to Jasin. "We have to take out the other Dragons."

"We should get to the Spirit Temple," he said. "The Dragons will follow us and that will give our soldiers a better chance."

"Let's go. Hurry!"

He took off, darting toward the Spirit Temple. Lightning streaked toward us, but I directed it away before it could hit Jasin's wings. He spun and dove, avoiding the numerous elemental attacks flying through the air, and I held on tight. In the chaos I lost track of my other mates, though I knew they were out there, fighting the other Dragons.

Below us, Calla threw fire at the shades around her, while her priests and other people fought with torches, water, and rocks—but it wasn't enough. The dark, ghostly figures swarmed over them, draining their lives, and I knew it wouldn't be long before Calla and her priests succumbed too. And once they were gone, there was little to stop the shades from devouring the rest of our people.

"Wait," I called out to Jasin. "We have to help them fight the shades or they'll never make it."

"We don't have time!"

"We can't let them all die!"

Jasin let out a frustrated roar, but then he changed direction, darting down. As we flew over the shades, he let out a stream of fire while I blasted them with lightning and ice. They let out horrifying shrieks as they disappeared, but more filled their place almost instantly.

We fought and we fought, but as I took in the battle around us, my hope of victory quickly diminished. We were stretched too thin and the other Dragons were too strong. There were too many shades, too many soldiers, and not enough people on our side to fight them back. Getting to the Spirit Temple would be impossible without sacrificing the lives of everyone fighting for us on the battlefield. Was that what it would take?

I couldn't do it. Which meant we were going to fail.

I prepared myself to make a tough decision, though I wasn't sure if it would be to retreat or to push forward. But then a bright flare shot up from the crest of the southern mountain, drawing my attention. A fire burned, spreading wider and wider across the rocky slopes.

No, not a fire, I realized, my breath catching in my throat. Fire elementals.

They were moving fast, gliding over the land as they approached, and there were hundreds of them. Not just fire, but earth, air, and water elementals, all heading toward us at speeds that only a dragon could match.

"They came." Tears filled my eyes and I let out a soft laugh, the relief making me almost giddy. Somehow I had gotten through to them, and they'd changed their minds and decided to fight. And with their help, we might actually stand a chance.

34
KIRA

A surge of hope renewed my energy and Jasin and I fought back the shades until the elementals joined the fray. Our new allies struck down the shades with ease, along with many of the Black Dragon's soldiers who weren't prepared to battle such things. Our soldiers shied away at first, hesitant about the elementals, but then rallied when they realized they were on our side.

Once I was sure the elementals had it under control, I touched Jasin's neck to get his attention. "To the Spirit Temple!"

He let out a roar in response and spread his wings, lifting us over the battlefield to fly toward the shimmering building ahead of us. The other Dragons were still fighting, and elemental attacks flashed through the air, but we rushed past all of them. As we approached the temple, I saw the entrance was sealed with stone, and there seemed no other way inside. With my earth magic I blasted the barrier apart, sending rocks flying, and Jasin dove for the hole I'd made.

Another dragon let out a shriek and a tornado suddenly slammed into Jasin, knocking me off his back. I flew through the air in a daze, trying to breathe, scrambling to grab hold of something. Then my training kicked in and I gathered the air around me, stopping my fall and lifting me higher into the sky.

As I hovered there, a dark green dragon flew toward me. I leaped onto Slade's back, and he sped toward the temple. With his great size he was slower than Jasin, but we managed to fly through the entrance and come to a halt inside.

Jasin and Isen were right at our heels, both of them crashing into the floor with heavy thuds that sent cracks through the marble. Isen was up first, his lithe golden body twisting to attack Jasin with his claws, but Slade blocked him with his own larger frame. My Emerald Dragon let out a deep roar that made the entire temple tremble, and the marble below us split open down a line from him to Isen. The other dragon leaped into the air to avoid the attack, before throwing a lightning bolt at Slade.

Slade shifted back into a human, decreasing his size instantly, and rolled out of the way—a trick we'd learned from Doran. He yanked his axe off his back and charged forward with a shout, his eyes wild. Isen knocked Slade back with his tail, but then Jasin tackled him, tearing into his side with his claws. I trapped Isen's front and back legs with earth magic, forming stone around them so that he was unable to move. He struggled against me and I added ice, making it creep up his body, but he was so strong I knew I couldn't hold him for long.

"Now, Slade!" I yelled.

Slade's axe flashed with a glow the color of fresh leaves before he swung it at Isen's chest. The Golden Dragon let out a piercing shriek as the blade cut through his scales, fueled by Slade's own magic. Isen thrashed and fought with everything he had, blasting us with lightning and wind that sent us flying back, but we didn't stop.

Where the axe touched Isen, stone began to form. Dark gray slate quickly spread across his body, covering the golden scales, while his ear-piercing howls continued. When the stone covered his face, the Golden Dragon finally went silent.

Slade yanked his axe from Isen's chest. As soon as it was removed the dragon's body broke apart, crumbling into hundreds of pieces of rubble at our feet.

A soul-rending scream filled our ears from outside the Spirit Temple, so loud and horrifying it could only be from the Black Dragon herself. She'd sensed her mate had died, and although I empathized with how much pain and suffering she must be going through, I didn't feel bad for what we'd done.

As if responding to her screams, the temple walls on every side of us suddenly burst apart in a spray of stone and dust. It covered us, blinded us, and filled our lungs. When I could see again, I realized she'd torn open the temple's walls, leaving only the roof and the columns holding it up. What had once been a beautiful building was now little more than ruins, which looked as though they might collapse at any moment. Gods, the Black Dragon was powerful. Too powerful, even now with one of her mates gone.

Now that the temple was open to the world on every side, I could see the other Dragons fighting under the hazy sky. Sark and Reven shot fire and ice at each other, both moving so quickly they were little more than a blur. The Black Dragon tossed my father aside, causing him to hit the rocky mountain behind the temple, where he fell and crashed into the stream below. She then soared back into the thick of the battle, grabbing more of our soldiers in her talons to drain their lives. We had to stop her quickly.

A huge green dragon slammed against the floor of the temple in front of me, his wings spread so wide it blocked out everything else. "You'll pay for what you've done," Heldor growled.

He snapped at me with his fangs, but then Auric was there, yanking me out of the way with his air magic. He blocked me with his golden body and faced Heldor down, while Jasin and Slade moved in from either side. Four huge dragons ready to fight, and me standing in the middle of them.

"Go," Auric told me. "Help Reven. We've got this one."

I sheathed my sword and ran out of the temple, or what was left of it anyway. As the plains below me came into a view, I stared at the destruction before me, the revulsion from so much death nearly overpowering my senses. It was against everything my life magic stood for, and it took all my power not to run away. The Black Dragon fed on death and misery, eating the darkness and becoming stronger. It was time to take away more of her powers and end this nightmare forever.

35
REVEN

I felt a tug through the bond, urging me to go to Kira, and I changed
course immediately to swoop down toward her. She stood in front of
the crumbling temple, covered in pale dust, making her red hair appear
almost white. As I drew near, she leaped onto my back, her eyes blazing
with determination.

"Let's stop Sark, once and for all," she said.

A grin spread across my face, making my fangs emerge. Sark had taken
everything from us—and now he was going to pay. "I was thinking the
exact same thing."

I launched us into the air, the wind whipping at my wings. Sark rose
before us, his blood red body shining under the sun. Hatred filled my
chest, along with my need for vengeance, but I didn't let it consume me.
This wasn't only about revenge or justice. This was about stopping him
from hurting anyone else.

My body was already burnt in three places, and my ice had torn
through the scales on Sark's back. We'd already been fighting for what felt
like hours, but neither of us could best the other. With Kira by my side,
that might change.

The Crimson Dragon opened his mouth and scorching hot fire flew
toward us. I let out a stream of water from my own mouth to combat it,
while Kira threw bolts of lightning and blades of ice at Sark. He managed
to dodge them all, moving unnaturally fast despite his size. In both forms
he was an expert of combat, and he'd had many years to hone his skills.

568

He was the one fighter I was willing to admit might be even better than me.

Across the field, the Black Dragon suddenly let out another of her terrible screams, which tore through my ears, struck me in the heart, and ripped through my bones. Balls of fire suddenly rained down from the sky, as if the sun itself was attacking us, and soldiers below us screamed in agony as they hit the fields and consumed them. Kira did her best to stop more flames from falling or the fires from spreading, while I blasted what I could with water, but it was too much for us to handle. The Black Dragon's magic was too strong, fueled by her pain over her mates' deaths and the lives she'd been stealing.

She fixed her beady black eyes on the temple and suddenly rushed toward it, flying so fast she was little more than a dark blur. A spike of panic shot through me. Auric, Jasin, and Slade were in there, and they were no match for her. Doran flew after Nysa only seconds later, but one of his wings appeared to be injured, slowing him down. They might be able to distract her for a short time, but that was all.

"Heldor must have fallen," Kira said.

"We need to take out Sark now!" I called to her.

"Get me close to him!"

Sark was momentarily stunned by the death of Heldor, but he quickly recovered and let out a roar of his own. He blasted us with unending fire, but I wove through his attacks, while Kira deflected them away from us. But every time I tried to get close to him, he darted away.

I reached for Auric's magic through the bond and summoned thick clouds around us, hiding us from Sark's gaze. He tried to burn them up with streams of fire, searching for us in the haze, and I flew past him, then swept back around. I approached him from behind as quietly as possible and drew up alongside him.

Kira launched herself off my back, using her air magic to guide her onto Sark's crimson body. As she landed, he spun around and let out a harsh shriek, while she held on tight so she wouldn't fall. He swiped for her with his claws, but she drew her sword and stabbed it into his back, forcing him to release another pained roar. Ice began to form around the wound, but then his entire body erupted into flames and melted the ice.

The bastard wouldn't die, and I worried he would hurt Kira if this continued. She was immune to his fire, but not his fangs or claws. She yanked at her sword, unable to budge it from his scales, as he tried to knock her off him and slashed at her.

I flew up high then dove down toward him, pressing my wings close to my side. When I was seconds away from slamming into him, I shifted into human form, my black cloak flying behind me as I drew my swords.

Flames scorched me and I covered myself with a layer of ice, but it quickly melted away. I had no air magic to guide me, but I landed on his back beside Kira, and stabbed both my swords into his thick neck.

Sark let out an unholy scream and the flames shot higher, burning me despite my own magic's protection, but I refused to let go.

"This is for my family," I said, as I dug my father's twin blades deeper into Sark's neck. Ice spread from the dual blades and across his body, consuming the flames. As his body froze, he tried to knock us off him, his wings beating at the sky and his talons reaching for us, fighting until the very end.

The last bit of life left Sark as the tips of his wings froze, and we began to plummet to the ground. Another mournful, horrible scream came from the Spirit Temple as the world rushed up at us. We were too low for me to safely turn to a dragon—we'd hit the ground before I could raise my wings.

Kira grabbed me around the waist, and I felt her magic wrap around us. We jumped off Sark's back just before he struck the earth with a heavy thud. His body cracked into a million pieces of ice at the impact, and they all exploded outward with dirt and grass from the garden where he'd crashed. Kira and I leaped wide, her air magic guiding our landing, taking us away from the danger and safely planting us on a patch of grass nearby.

I straightened up and brushed myself off, while eyeing Kira to make sure she was all right. My clothes and magic had melted into my skin from the knee down, and now that the fight was over the pain from my burned and blackened skin became agony. None of that mattered though, because Sark was gone. The millions of pieces of ice that had once been his body melted away under the dim sunlight and sank into the earth, and the weight of my families' deaths lifted off me. They were avenged, along with Kira's family and friends, and everyone else who had lost their loved ones to the Black Dragon's enforcer.

"Three Dragons defeated," Kira said, with something like awe or disbelief in her voice as she stared at the Spirit Temple's remains.

"The Black Dragon must be weakened now," I said.

She took my hand and clenched it tight. "Time to face her."

36

KIRA

The second I touched Reven I realized how badly he'd been hurt by Sark's fires. He stumbled forward anyway, but his feet and legs were so burned it must have been excruciating. Still, he shifted into his dragon form, his scales blackened in many places, and lowered himself so I could climb onto his back.

"You're hurt," I said, as I got on.

"We'll worry about that later," he said through gritted teeth.

As he took off, I placed my hands on his scales, knowing I wouldn't be able to do enough to heal him, but hoping it would ease the pain. He flew into the open space between the columns of the Spirit Temple, where dragons fought, and magic flew.

Doran, Auric, and Slade all surrounded Nysa, who bared her fangs and hissed at them, before lashing out with ice and a swipe of her claws. If she touched them, she'd be able to use her death magic against them and drain their lives. Jasin was crumpled against a pillar, unconscious, injured, and in his human form.

Every time one of my mates got a blow in with their air or earth magic, I felt a sense of hope—before watching Nysa's scales heal themselves almost immediately. She wasn't immune to fire, earth, or air anymore, but the Spirit Goddess inside her made her powerful anyway. And with Doran's water magic too, she was nearly unstoppable.

"Protect Jasin!" I told Reven, as I hopped off his back. I knew he would never listen if I told him to stand back and rest, but he might do this for me. "She still has water magic, and Jasin is weak against it!"

Reven hesitated, clearly itching to fight, but then let out a snarl and stomped over to stand guard over Jasin's unconscious body. As he did, Slade was thrown back against one of the huge columns, bolts of ice piercing his wings. He hit the ground with a heavy thud that shook the foundation of the temple, sending debris falling from the cracked and broken ceiling.

I rushed into the battle just as Auric was tackled by my mother, her talons tearing into his scaled back, making him cry out. Ice formed around his body, holding him in place, and she opened her mouth to drain his life. I drew my sword and rushed her with a yell, desperate to save my mate, but she slapped me with her tail and sent me flying, along with my sword.

As I hit the ground, Doran slammed into Nysa's body, knocking her into a pillar. It snapped under her weight and part of the roof caved in on her. But I knew she'd be back up soon.

All of my dragons were injured. I felt their pain through the bond, and there was nothing I could do about it. The Black Dragon was too strong for us to defeat—but I had to try anyway.

Doran flowed into his human form and bent down to pick up my sword. His hazel eyes met mine as he gripped it tight. "There's only one of her mates left now."

I realized at that instant what he was about to do and panic gripped my throat. "Don't do this! There has to be another way!"

"We both know there isn't. I love you, Kira."

"Father, no!" I yelled as he stabbed the sword into his chest. Fire spread across his body instantly, engulfing him completely. I rushed toward him and made it to my father's side seconds after he hit the ground, but by then it was already too late.

Through the fire I cradled Doran's head in my hands, tears leaking down my face, as the light left his eyes. I'd once hated and feared him, and then I'd doubted him, and then I'd grown to love him. He knew I would never be able to kill him, even after he seemingly betrayed us, and he'd given his own life so we would have a chance.

As the fire vanished, I buried my head in my father's chest, letting myself sob, my hands covered in his blood. Nysa screamed behind me, her voice filled with pain as she reared up out of the debris. I could only imagine how bad it must hurt to feel every single one of your mates' deaths. I wished with every breath that it hadn't come to this—or that I didn't have to defeat my own mother now.

Enva's words came back to me and I wondered if it was true that Nysa, deep down, didn't want to fight me and just wanted this all to end. She hadn't attacked me so far, and she hadn't killed my mates. Maybe it was true. Maybe I could find a way to break through to her and convince her to stop.

I pressed a kiss to my father's burnt forehead and whispered, "I love you too." Then I pulled my sword from his chest and turned to face my mother.

Nysa stomped out of the rubble and shook it off, her tail whipping about her and her wings raised. Shadows clung to her black scales and her eyes glowed like the shades outside. She looked like she was about to tear the entire world down.

I moved in front of her, my sword at my side, and yelled, "Mother!"

She gazed down at me like I was an insignificant bug in her path, one that she could stomp at any moment. "You," she said, putting so much venom in the word it burned me.

"I don't want to fight you, mother, and I don't think you want to fight me either. Neither one of us has to die today."

"You're wrong," she said, yet she didn't move to attack me.

Hope surged inside me and I stepped forward. "Free the Spirit Goddess and we can work together to defeat her. With the Gods' help, we can split her into Life and Death, and send Death back to the Realm of the Dead."

She dipped her head low, her sharp fangs glistening as they drew near. "You killed my mates," she hissed. "And now I shall do the same to yours."

She brought one of her huge clawed feet down on me, pinning me to the ground with her talons. As she loomed over me, she opened her mouth wide and began to drain my life—along with my mates' through our bond. Inky blackness squirmed up from my throat and into her, making me weak. With my life being sucked out of me I couldn't move, couldn't breathe, couldn't fight—I was going to die at the hands of my own mother.

Suddenly a wave as tall as the temple crashed into her, knocking her off me. Reven stumbled toward her in his dragon form, assaulting her with non-stop water, giving me a chance to recover. I drew in a deep breath as I got to my feet and reached for my life magic, letting it restore me.

There was no reasoning with Nysa. Whatever goodness that had once been inside of her was gone, lost to the corruption that had taken hold of her. It was time to save her from what she'd become.

I summoned all of the elements at once, causing my body to rise up into the air while fire and water swirled around me and huge chunks of the temple's marble lifted to my side. Lightning danced in my hair. Lava gathered at my fingertips. Fog spread through the temple.

My mates moved behind me, facing Nysa down, each one battered and broken but still fighting. They gathered their magic and reached through the bond that linked us all to fortify it.

My connection with my mates gave me strength. The blessings of the Gods gave me power. Love and compassion gave me purpose. I collected all of that inside me, and then I released it at her, hitting her with every element. My mates joined in, blasting her from every side, making her arch her wings and scream. Fire and ice, earth and wind, lightning and lava, steam and storm—it all converged on her in one final push.

I reached out with my air magic and grabbed hold of my sword while Nysa's body tried to heal the damage we inflicted on her. All four elements inside my blade leaped to my command and the sword flew through the air, hitting Nysa in the heart. It buried deep into her chest, and every element spread out from it, washing over her one by one.

She reared up and I prepared to strike again, worried it wouldn't be enough—but then her body changed. She resumed her human form, so small and unassuming compared to the dragon she'd once been, and then collapsed.

My magic vanished and I hit the floor, then took off running toward her. The hilt of my sword protruded from her chest, but she still managed to cling to life, even as black blood seeped onto the cracked marble. I kneeled over her, and her eyes met mine.

"You don't know what you've done." Her voice was a gravely whisper laced with pain.

"I'm sorry," I said, my throat closing with emotion. "I wish it didn't have to end like this."

"When I die, she'll be released." My mother coughed up blood, turned to the side, and spat it on the floor. "I'm the only thing holding her back, even now. When I let go, there will be no stopping her."

I couldn't help but rest my hand upon her head, touching the hair that looked so much like my own. "Rest now. You've held her long enough. The Gods will help us."

"The Gods." She let out a bitter laugh. "The Gods lie."

I didn't know what to say to that, so I simply stroked her head as the life drained out of her. I sensed my mates moving behind me, but they gave us space.

"Forgive me, Kira," my mother said, her voice weakening. "It was the only way."

Her eyes fluttered shut, and with one last gasp, she was gone.

37
KIRA

The black blood pooling on the ground beneath Nysa began to move. At first it was only a few drops darting across the floor, small enough to make me think it was a trick of the light. But then more blood joined it in a flowing line, before converging in the center of the temple. I backed away from Nysa's body slowly as it was drained, and the puddle before me grew and grew. It lifted up and began to take form, becoming a massive dragon that filled the temple with inky darkness.

"Get ready," I told my mates, who were all in their human forms now.

They spread out around the Spirit Goddess as her body dripped black blood. She raised her head and let out a terrifying roar that shook the world.

One by one the Gods appeared. The volcanic Fire God, made of lava and ash. The stormy Air God. The sparkling, crystalized Earth God. And finally, the fluid Water God.

The Spirit Goddess swung her head around, taking in the temple and her Gods. "After centuries of imprisonment I am finally free."

Power seeped from her body with every bit of dark blood that dripped down her limbs. Revulsion, dread, and a sense of wrongness made me bend over and gag. It was like touching the bone cage, but a thousand times worse. My instincts screamed at me that this was unnatural, that I needed to get away from it as quickly as possible, but I couldn't run from this. I had to face her.

"You must split the two halves of the Spirit Goddess," I told the Gods, trying not to gag again. "Hurry!"

"No," the Fire God said, with a finality in his voice that made me tremble.

"No?" Reven asked.

"We have no wish for her to be separated again," the Fire God said. "Like this, she is whole."

"She's been corrupted," Auric said. "There's barely any life left in her, only death."

"She is our mate," the Earth God said, his voice a deep rumble.

"But you said you would help us separate the Life and Death sides of her," Jasin said.

"We needed you to defeat the Dragons so that our Goddess would be freed," the Water God said.

"You lied to us," Slade said.

"We are the Gods, and you are meant to serve us," the Air God said. "This is why we chose you."

The Spirit Goddess loomed over us, making me feel small and insignificant. "It's time for the Gods to return to power. We've been forgotten for too long, but we shall be worshipped again." She snarled at us. "Now kneel."

Nysa was right—the Gods had lied to us. We'd made a mistake by trusting them. They were just as corrupted as the Spirit Goddess was, just as Nysa's mates had been corrupted too. But unlike Nysa and her Dragons, there was no way to kill a God. They'd created us and gave us a small fraction of their powers. We didn't stand a chance against them.

There was only one thing for me to do.

"We will never kneel," I said.

"Then you will die." The Spirit Goddess wrapped one of her claws around me and lifted me into the air. "We no longer need the Dragons."

At the Spirit Goddess's touch, the revulsion became so strong I thought I might pass out, but I pushed through it. "Do it now!" I yelled at my Dragons.

My mates each formed a ring around the Gods using their elements. Doran had given them a quick lesson in how to imprison the Gods, and though it would be more effective in the temples, this would hold them temporarily. As the fire danced around Jasin, he yelled, "Water God, I bind you in fire!" Auric imprisoned the Earth God at the same moment, the wind whipping his hair around, while Slade and Reven did the same to the Air and Fire Gods.

With the Gods imprisoned, the Spirit Goddess was weakened. But instead of fighting her, I drew her into me. It was like the opposite of healing my mates. For them, I gave up some of my life magic and my energy. Now I grabbed hold of the life and death magic that surrounded me and sucked it in. I drained the Spirit Goddess, like the Black Dragon had drained the lives of my soldiers.

Her body broke apart into black blood, which streamed into my mouth, my eyes, my nose, my ears. Her essence blasted me so strong my arms flew to my sides, my body buffeted by the nonstop stream of magic that coursed through me. I hovered in the air as every last drop of that disgusting blood filled me.

In the distance I heard yelling and saw magic flying, but nothing could hurt me now. Anything that dared to injure me I healed instantly. Not even the other Gods could stand against me now.

"Stop, Kira!" Jasin yelled.

"Don't do this!" Slade called out.

"This is the only way," I told them, my voice booming around us. "She must be contained."

They didn't understand. They couldn't feel her like I could. If she was allowed to remain free, she would destroy the world. The second she entered my body I'd known it. And if the Gods wouldn't help us divide her, imprisonment was the only way.

When the last drop of black blood entered me, power unlike anything I'd ever known spread through my consciousness. All I knew was darkness, death, and a hunger that could never be satisfied. But deep inside that thick shroud was a small light, a spark of life, a fluttering of hope. I tried to reach for it, but was quickly overwhelmed by death again.

I gazed across my ruined temple, seeing beyond it, feeling the dead soldiers outside, the ones that were injured, and the ones still fighting and full of life. They were all mine. I was more powerful than any other being in this world. Stronger than the Dragons or the other Gods. I was the beginning and the end, life and death, darkness and light. I controlled shades and elementals, plants and animals, the living and the dead, and soon they would all bow to me. I would use this power to reshape the world. A dark queen, ruling all five Realms with my mates at my side.

I heard people yelling my name over and over, their voices frantic. I focused on them again, the four handsome men I'd taken as my lovers, and recognition slowly dawned. Something of myself fought for control again.

"Kira, you have to let her go!" Jasin yelled.

I shook my head. "I can't. She'll destroy everyone if she's free. She hungers for death and will never be sated until this world is in ruins."

"Don't make the same mistakes your mother made," Auric said.

"I won't. I can contain the Spirit Goddess without becoming corrupted, and then we can use her power to change the world."

"You might be able to fight her for a few years," Slade said. "But she'll corrupt all of us eventually."

"No!" I roared, both at them and at the Spirit Goddess inside me who fought for control. I couldn't let her win. I wouldn't!

"Kira, you have to fight her!" Reven yelled.

I screamed and covered my head with my hands, the power threatening to tear me apart. Clarity dawned and for an instant I was Kira again. "I can't—she's too strong!"

"Yes, you can," Reven said, staring into my eyes. "Otherwise you'll have to live countless lives with the Spirit Goddess inside you. Killing your own children to keep her contained. Are you willing to do that?"

"No—never!"

"Then fight!"

I reached again for that tiny flicker of life inside me, and this time I found it. I grabbed hold and yanked, dragging it through the darkness, fighting with every ounce of my being against the black death trying to consume me.

Enva's voice suddenly drifted to me, like a whisper on the wind. "Don't give up, Kira."

"Enva!" I cried, begging for her to help me, though I knew she couldn't.

She appeared before me, her form translucent and glowing with a faint silver light. "I'm here."

Other people began to appear alongside her, with the same silvery bodies and pale glowing eyes, like the opposite of the shades outside. Nysa appeared first, looking young, bright, and brave. Doran stood at her side, his eyes proud as he smiled at me. Sark, Heldor, and Isen stood behind them, their features lacking the cruelty I'd seen before. This must have been how they'd looked before they were corrupted.

But then more luminous figures appeared beside me, standing close, forming a tight circle around me. Young women I felt a strong connection to, though I'd never seen them before. *Sisters*, a voice deep in my soul whispered in recognition. Nysa's other daughters, stretching back centuries, freed now that she was dead. They gave me their strength and their unconditional love, and their silent encouragement and support gave me hope.

In front of them stood a woman with long red hair, hazel eyes, and features identical to my own. I faced a mirror image of myself.

Sora, my twin sister.

"Kira," she said. "We're here to help you."

"How?"

"Together we can divide the Spirit Goddess into her two halves. I am death, while you are life." She smiled at me as she took my hands. "From the beginning, it was always meant to be this way."

I swallowed, my fingers tightening around hers. "I'm not strong enough."

"You are. Focus on the life inside you, and I'll draw out the death. We can do this together."

"You're not alone," Enva called out.

"We'll give you our power," Nysa said.

"You can do this, Kira," my father added.

Their magic suddenly filled me, until I was overflowing with life and light and love. They sent me so much power it began to balance out the darkness inside me and let the buried life magic grow. I sensed the two halves of the Spirit Goddess within me and held tight to the side of life. My twin tightened her grip on my hands and opened her mouth, drawing out the darkness from within me. It flowed out of me and filled her up, but where it had corrupted me, she was able to stay in control of herself. She'd been born with the power of death from the beginning, and now she fed upon it,

The Spirit Goddess fought inside me, trying to stay whole, while her Gods yelled and fought my mates keeping them prisoner. Sora and I managed to hold on, backed by the magic of our sisters and our parents, and I felt lighter and lighter with each second. When the last bit of death's essence had left me, my sister released my hands. The connection was broken. The Spirit Goddess was split in two, each part of her trapped within my sister and me.

"Now it's time to open the gates to the Realm of the Dead and send everyone home," my sister said, her voice thick with dark power. "Including the Death Goddess."

A blast of dark magic erupted from her, and one by one our sisters took on a look of relief before vanishing. Sora had opened the gates to the Realm of the Dead, allowing all the departed souls to finally pass through and find peace.

"I don't want you to go," I said. "I only just found you."

"I am with you always, Kira. Life and death will eternally be joined together. But now I must take the Death Goddess back to where she belongs."

I nodded, a tear slipping down my cheek. Sora gave me a warm smile, and then she disappeared.

Enva wrapped her arms around me next. "I knew you could save us all. Goodbye, granddaughter."

Before I could reply she faded away, her face looking truly peaceful for the first time. Tears streamed down my face, my heart torn between happiness and sadness. I'd never see them again, but their suffering was finally at an end.

ELIZABETH BRIGGS

Sark, Isen, and Heldor bowed their heads low to me in a sign of respect, before they disappeared, leaving Doran behind.

My father placed a hand on my shoulder. "I'm proud of you, Kira."

I turned to hug him, choking back a sob. "I couldn't have done it without you."

He patted my back once before drifting away. There was only one ghost left.

"You're going to make a fine Dragon," Nysa said, her translucent hand reaching toward me to curl around my cheek. I placed my hand over hers for just an instant, before she left me with the words, "Thank you for freeing me. I love you, Kira."

After she vanished, the temple was empty except for my mates and the Gods they held prisoner. Inside me, all I felt was the Life Goddess, who was relieved to finally be herself again, untainted by corruption. I searched deep inside and found nothing left of the darkness.

I took a deep breath…and I released her.

38
KIRA

Light flowed out of me and formed a beautiful, shining dragon, so bright it nearly hurt to look at her. Flowers bloomed at her feet, and she gazed down at me with a motherly smile.

"Is it over?" I asked.

"It's never over," the Life Goddess said, her voice warm and comforting. "Life and death fight an eternal battle, and one cannot exist without the other. My sister and I will always be connected. But if you mean is she safely trapped in the Realm of the Dead? Then yes."

"Thank Gods," I said, with a sigh of relief.

She let out a laugh that wrapped around me like a warm hug. "No, thank you for freeing me. And now I shall purge my mates of their corruption."

She turned to look at the imprisoned gods and then sent a burst of light out from her. It flowed into them, filling them up, and when it was over they each glowed a little brighter.

"What do we do now?" I asked her. The Gods had said before they wanted to rule without us. Did they still want that?

"You shall continue your duty of bringing balance to the world, while we watch over you from afar. There is much to be done, but we have faith that you are up to the task." She lowered her head and pressed a soft kiss to my forehead that filled me with love and hope. "I give you my blessing."

As she pulled away, my body began to change. I grew larger and stronger, while my hands became claws, my skin became scales, and my teeth became fangs. Glowing silver wings sprouted from my back, and a long tail whipped behind me.

The Life Goddess gave me a nod, her eyes kind, before she disappeared in a flash so bright I had to look away. When the light dimmed, the other Gods were gone too.

"Kira…" Slade placed a large, dark hand on my silver scales. "You did it."

Reven smirked. "I knew you could defeat her."

"I couldn't have done it without all of you." My voice sounded deeper and stronger as a dragon.

Auric stroked my snout. "You're magnificent."

"Let's go end this battle," Jasin said.

The others turned into dragons and we flew out of the ruins of the Spirit Temple, over the battlefield. The shades were gone, taken back to the Realm of the Dead with the Death Goddess, and the Black Dragon's soldiers had already surrendered. I stretched out my senses with my enhanced life magic, which I could access now that the Goddess was freed. There were so many dead, far too many, and many more injured. Zara and Garet had both fallen, much to my dismay. I ached at the thought of telling Auric that his brother was gone, and Zara's death meant the Assassin's Guild was leaderless. Leni was badly wounded, one of her arms severed from her shoulder, and I wasn't sure if she would survive. Slade would be devastated if his little sister passed, and I prayed that she would make it.

There were more casualties that tugged on my heart. Enva was gone, along with the sisters I'd barely gotten to glimpse, including Sora. And of course, the Dragons. Doran had sacrificed himself to give us a chance, proving he was truly a father to me. And Nysa… Well, I understood Nysa a lot better now after encountering the Spirit Goddess. The things she had done could never be truly forgiven, but she was my mother, and she'd tried to protect the world as best she could.

Even with all these losses, there was still so much life—and hope. Elementals and humans had fought side by side, fighting back the darkness that had overtaken our land, and I felt confident this was the beginning of a fresh start for our two races. Other friends were still alive—Brin, who had fought valiantly to protect Faya and her unborn child; Calla and her priests, who had kept the shades at bay for so long; and Cadock, who had led the bandits in a noble fight despite his earlier misgivings. Not to mention hundreds of lives I didn't know but could feel before me, their souls bright lights on the bloody fields.

As the sun sank to the horizon, my Dragons and I flew high and drew the attention of everyone still standing. Faces turned up at us, filled with awe and relief.

"The era of the Black Dragon is over," Jasin called out. "All hail the Silver Dragon!"

The soldiers and elementals below us let out a loud cheer that seemed to echo throughout the entire world. This battle was truly over, but now the work of rebuilding the four Realms would begin.

I turned to my mates, my forever family, who had stood by my side through it all. This wouldn't have been possible without them. The love we had for each other was what brought us our victory today. And whatever happened next? We would be together for it, preparing for the day when our own daughter would take my place.

39

JASIN

ONE YEAR LATER

The sounds of combat rang out all around me. Swords clashing together. Fists hitting flesh. Shouts and muttered curses. I couldn't help but smile as I gazed across the courtyard. Dozens of men and women fought in pairs, practicing and sparring while sweating under the hot sun. Once they had been bandits, Resistance fighters, assassins, or Onyx Army soldiers. Now they were mine.

The Silver Guard, I'd called them. The most loyal and dedicated soldiers, sworn to serve the Silver Dragon as her soldiers now that the Onyx Army had disbanded. Each Realm was transitioning to governing itself with its own military, since Kira had no interest in ruling. Our plan was to work as mediators and guardians of the world, and as part of that I would lead this elite fighting force, which suited me well. As for Kira's other mates, Auric was handling diplomacy with the leaders of the four Realms, Reven was working with the elementals while also managing a team of spies and scouts, while Slade was acting as Kira's right hand man and personal guard. In the end, they weren't that different from the roles Nysa's men held, except our goals were a lot different. We didn't want power or domination, we wanted harmony and peace. Gods knew the world needed it right now.

Other sounds caught my attention, drawing my gaze up toward the hammering, pounding, and yelling. Renovations on Soulspire palace had recently begun to transform it from the run-down, dark, imposing fortress it had been under the Black Dragon's rule to the new home of the Silver Dragon. We'd all been surprised when Kira said she wanted to live here after being imprisoned inside it, but she'd argued that the central location between the four Realms and the long history of housing the Dragons made it the perfect place for us to reside. It just needed some work to make it home.

Cadock walked past the sparring soldiers and made his way toward me. His knee had been injured during the battle at the Spirit Temple and he'd walked with a slight limp ever since, although it hadn't slowed him down much. He wore the bright armor of the Silver Guard and acted as my second in command.

"Training is coming along nicely," I said to him.

"Yes, I think the new recruits will be ready soon."

"How are things with Faya?" I asked. Cadock had become smitten with the former Resistance leader, but after she'd lost her husband to the Dragons she'd been hesitant to start a relationship again, especially while taking care of a baby boy.

He rubbed the back of his neck. "One step forward, two steps back. I love her, and little Parin too. I asked her to marry me and she said maybe someday."

I clasped his shoulder. "You're a good man. She sees that. She just needs time."

"I know. I told her I'd wait as long as it takes. I'm not going anywhere." He drew in a breath. "That's not why I'm here though. There are some people asking to see you."

"Who?"

"They say they're your parents."

My spine stiffened. I hadn't seen or heard from my parents since my father had betrayed me by turning us in to the Onyx Army for helping the Resistance. I'd tried to block them from my memory ever since, too hurt by the knowledge that he was more loyal to the Black Dragon than his own son. What were they doing here now?

I considered sending them away, but I did miss my mother, and I had nothing to fear from my father anymore. The least I could do was see why they had traveled all the way from their home in the Fire Realm to visit me.

"Send them to my office," I said.

Cadock nodded and walked away, while I watched my recruits a little longer, letting their rhythmic fighting movements calm me. I'd never wanted to be a soldier in the Onyx Army, but my parents had made it clear that was my one path, and I'd been damn good at it even though I'd hated it. When I'd met Kira, I'd been ashamed of my past and the things I'd been forced to do, but at her side I was finally able to accept my destiny.

I was a protector, and when I fought for something I believed in, I was proud of this work.

I reluctantly turned away from my soldiers and headed for the nearby barracks, where I'd claimed a large room for my office. I'd chosen it because it had windows that looked out at the training grounds and the palace, allowing me to keep an eye on everything. I also liked the lighting in the room—it was good for painting.

My parents were already waiting inside when I arrived. They sat in the two chairs across from my desk but jumped to their feet when I shut the door behind me.

"Mom, Dad," I said. "What are you doing here?"

"Oh, Jasin," my mother said, clasping her hands to her chest. "It's so good to see you."

"Your mother has been worried about you," my father said.

I took her hands in mine and gave them a squeeze. My mother was the only reason I'd escaped when my father had betrayed me, and I'd missed her also. "Please sit down."

I walked around the table as they sat down again. I noticed their eyes drifting to the painting behind me, which depicted the Silver Dragon flying in front of the ruined Spirit Temple, with her other Dragons flanking her. A memory of the day we'd won.

"That's beautiful," Mom said, as I sat across from her. "Did you paint it?"

"I did." Although we'd had a lot to do after the battle at the Spirit Temple, Kira had insisted we take some time for ourselves too. Once the world had settled down a bit, we'd spent two weeks in the middle of nowhere, relaxing and recovering from our ordeals. I'd done that painting then, along with many others, including some I definitely wouldn't want my parents to see.

"It's beautiful," my mother said. "I'm so happy you're painting again."

"Why are you here?" I asked again, pinning my father with a steely gaze.

He shifted in his seat uncomfortably. He looked a lot older than I remembered. "I've come to tell you I deeply regret what I did that day, and I'm sorry. I thought I was helping you."

My eyes narrowed at him. "You turned me in to the Onyx Army. You effectively sealed my death sentence. How is that helping me?"

"General Voor promised you wouldn't be killed, only brought back into the Onyx Army and punished. I hoped you would realize the error of your ways." He shook his head, staring down at his hands. "I see now that I was wrong. About a lot of things. I only hope that one day you'll be able to forgive me."

"We're moving to Soulspire," Mom said, surprising me. "The Fire Realm has nothing left for us except bad memories. We'd like a fresh start somewhere near you."

I crossed my arms, leaning back in my chair. "You think that by moving closer and saying you're sorry I'll forgive your betrayal?"

"No," Dad said. "I only hope that you'll give me a chance to try to mend things between us. I love you, son, and I'm proud of you. Really damn proud."

I sighed and pinched the bridge of my nose. I disliked my father, but I loved him too, and I missed my mother. In the past, I would have gone into an angry rage and told them to get out of my office, but I'd changed since meeting Kira and the others. Maybe my father could change too.

"I'm not sure forgiveness is possible, but it would be good to see you more often," I said.

My mother's smile made it worthwhile, while my father nodded eagerly. Our relationship might never be what it was, but this was a start in the right direction at least.

After they left, I felt Kira's presence draw near. I stood and walked to the door to greet her with a kiss. She had a blank canvas under her arm.

"Everything all right?" she asked.

"It is now," I said. "What did you bring me?"

She held out the canvas. "I thought a few hours of painting might do you good. You seemed stressed, and that guest room in the west wing of the palace needs an artist's touch."

I chuckled softly as I set the canvas aside and drew her close. "That's very thoughtful of you. But I think I need some inspiration from my muse first."

I pulled her into the room and shut the door with a wry grin. As my lips found her neck and my hands slid down her body, she let out a husky laugh filled with desire. I would never grow tired of that sound—or of loving Kira.

AURIC

FIVE YEARS LATER

Ｔhe gardens outside Soulspire palace were full of people in their finest clothes, all of them chatting with excitement and anticipation as they waited for the wedding to begin. When the music ended a hush went through the crowd and the two brides stepped forward, wearing matching gowns in different colors. Brin's gown was pale yellow and decorated with citrines to represent the Air Realm, while Leni's was the color of fresh new leaves with emeralds for the Earth Realm. The gown was cut so that it didn't hide Leni's missing arm but celebrated it, a reminder of our triumph at the Spirit Temple and everything we'd sacrificed for peace.

With their hands clasped, Brin and Leni moved to stand in front of the altar, which was decorated with crystals, incense, candles, and bowls of water, representing the four elements. Calla, the High Priestess of the Fire God, greeted them both with a smile and began the ceremony.

I watched my best friend as she spoke the words binding her life to Leni's, and I couldn't help but smile. Brin had become one of my advisers in the last few years, helping me with diplomatic relations between the four Realms. After Kira released all the Realms to rule themselves independently, the Air and Water Realms had adapted easily and were eager for this change, but the Earth and Fire Realms had a harder time with it. They'd relied so much on the Black Dragon's control and guidance that they'd struggled without it, but things were getting better now. Brin had been a big part of that.

Leni, on the other hand, worked for Reven. She'd proved to be a good scout and spy, plus she wasn't afraid of the elementals…or anything else, really. And she never let her injury hold her back.

As the ceremony wrapped up, Kira took my hand with a bright smile. I caught Slade's eye and he gave me a warm nod. His large family stood around him, his mother crying happy tears into a handkerchief and his other sister beaming with happiness. Brin's parents were there too looking much more stoic, although they were smiling, and their eyes were bright. They'd accepted their daughter and the woman she loved, even if they'd once wanted me to marry her instead.

When the two women kissed and were proclaimed a married couple, the entire audience cheered. Kira raised a hand and petals of all different colors rained down on the garden like snow, and everyone turned their heads up toward the blessing.

"We never had a wedding," I said to her. "Does that bother you?"

"Not at all," Kira said. "We don't need one. Our souls are bound together for all eternity. That's stronger than any wedding ceremony." She nudged me with her hip. "Besides, we get enough attention as it is. It's nice to have a day honoring our friends instead."

"Yes, it is." I glanced around the garden, which Kira had put in last year to honor the Life Goddess. Hundreds of people now celebrated on its lawn, dancing to the music and congratulating the happy couple. There were elementals among us too, the ambassadors who had been staying in the palace the past few years while the negotiations with their people progressed. Reven had been a big part of that, and though relations with the elementals weren't perfect, they were getting better. He spoke with one of them now while sipping a glass of wine, with Jasin beside him nodding at something he said.

Behind them, I caught sight of Cadock and Faya dancing with her son Parin, now about five years old. They'd gotten married two years ago, and Faya was pregnant with her second child now. She was another of my advisers, helping me with the Earth Realm in particular. As Cadock picked up Parin I noticed his slight limp, another reminder of our victory and everything we'd lost to achieve it. A touch of old sadness struck me as I remembered my brother Garet, who'd also fallen that day. I knew he would be proud of what we'd accomplished since then.

Kira and I made our way through the crowd, speaking to a few people along the way, before finally reaching Brin and Leni. They were still holding hands, their cheeks flushed, their eyes dancing with joy.

"Congratulations," I said, giving them each a kiss on the cheek.

"Thank you," Brin said, flashing a dazzling smile at Leni.

Kira gave each of them a hug. "I'm so happy for you both."

"I couldn't imagine two people more perfect for each other," I said. "It's about time you two got married."

Leni laughed. "Brin was resistant for a long time, but I finally convinced her to marry me."

Brin waved her comment away. "I wasn't resistant, we were just busy!"

"Sure, that's what it was." Leni rolled her eyes with a smile.

"Excuse me if I was hesitant to get married after being forced to be betrothed to this man for so long," Brin said, nudging me with her elbow.

I laughed. "Oh, so now it's my fault?"

"Ignore her," Leni said. "We wouldn't have met at all if not for you."

Slade rested a hand on his younger sister's shoulder. "We're all very happy that it worked out this way."

We chatted for another few minutes before Brin and Leni were called over to talk to someone else, leaving the three of us alone in our corner of the garden.

"You and I are officially family now," I said to Slade.

He wrapped one of his thick arms around my shoulder. "We've been family since Kira first brought us together."

Kira leaned against me with a smile. "And this is why we don't need a wedding."

"As usual, you're right," I said, kissing her on the cheek.

No, we didn't need a wedding. As Slade said, we were a family, bound to each other, heart and soul, our destinies entwined from our first breaths to the day we would leave this world. And in a few years, we'd have one more addition to that family. I, for one, couldn't wait.

41

SLADE

TEN YEARS LATER

I stared down at the bundle in my arms, taking in her perfection. Her skin was smooth, soft, and dark—not quite as dark as mine, but close. She had my dark hair too, although not very much of it yet. Her eyes were hazel though, like her mother's.

Kira watched me rocking little Sora from the doorway for a moment. "Well, there's no doubt she's your blood. She looks just like you."

I grinned as my daughter stared up at me with her big eyes. Before little Sora was born, we'd had no idea who had sired her. I had to admit I'd been thrilled seeing that she was mine, since I'd always wanted children. "She has my skin and hair, yes, but her beauty is all yours."

"Let's hope she has your calm temperament too."

Sora opened her mouth and let out a piercing wail in response, making both of us laugh. Even when she was crying, she was cute somehow.

"It's probably time to feed her again," Kira said.

She settled in the rocking chair in one corner of the nursery and got all her pillows and blankets together, while I pressed a kiss to Sora's forehead. When Kira was ready, I handed her our daughter so she could begin nursing.

"Do you need anything?" I asked as they settled in.

"I don't think so, but thank you."

I nodded and relaxed in one of the other chairs with a sense of quiet contentment. I'd once wanted a simple life as a blacksmith in a small town with a wife and children. My life had ended up anything but simple, but somehow it turned out even better than I'd expected. I had a woman I

591

loved more than I could ever imagine, three men who were like brothers to me, and a purpose that fulfilled me—and now my life was truly complete with the birth of our daughter.

Auric popped his head in the room. "The delegation from the Fire Realm has arrived."

"Thanks for letting me know," Kira said. The Fire Realm was in a dispute with the Water Realm over trade rights, and they wanted Kira to mediate. "Please tell them I'll be down in a few minutes."

He nodded. "Can I get you anything?"

Kira smiled at him. "No, thank you."

All of Kira's mates were eager to help out. With four fathers, Sora would never be short on love or attention, that was certain. Each man had already shown that they loved her as their own, and I didn't mind them sharing in the fatherly duties. Someday Sora would be the next ascendant with her own set of mates, and we would be there to train and guide her.

When Sora was finished, I took her from Kira again. "I'll put her to bed."

"Are you sure?" Kira asked.

I patted Sora on her back and got a good burp in response. "Yes. Go meet with the ambassadors and nobles. You know I hate that stuff anyway."

"Trust me, it's not my favorite either, but unfortunately it's necessary." She touched Sora's tiny nose, then gave me a kiss. "Thank you."

"It's my pleasure."

Kira straightened her clothes, drew herself up, and prepared to be a leader again. She worked hard, and our advisers had suggested that Kira get other women to nurse the baby and watch over her, but she'd refused. She wanted to raise Sora herself, and I sensed it was especially important to her after what happened with her own parents. The other men and I supported her as much as possible in both of her roles as the Silver Dragon and a mother. I knew there were times when it would be rough, but I was confident she could balance both, and we'd help her however we could.

After Kira left the room I changed Sora, then hummed a nursery rhyme my mother had sung to me and my sisters when we were little. When Sora's eyes drooped, I set her down in her bassinet. The future leader of the Dragons let out a big yawn and farted at the same time, making me laugh.

Yes, this life could be messy, complicated, and dangerous, but it was perfect.

42

REVEN

TWENTY YEARS LATER

While I leaned against the tree, Sora picked up the five small knives and tested their weight. Her little brow furrowed, while her dark hair blew in the breeze, and I waited in case she had any questions. When she was satisfied with the blades, she spun toward the target and threw them one by one. Each one hit the bullseye, her aim perfect, her throw confident.

I couldn't help but grin, my chest bursting with pride. "Nice job."

"Thanks, Dad." She did a little bounce and ran over to the target to yank the knives out.

Sora might not be my child by blood, but there was no doubt she was my daughter. I'd never wanted kids or imagined I would have them, but now I couldn't picture my life without her in it. Naturally I was her favorite dad because I'd taught her all the fun stuff. How to throw knives. How to sneak about without being heard. How to pick locks. Kira joked that I was a bad influence, but I argued these were all things our daughter would need one day. No matter how safe we tried to make the world, there would always be problems the Dragons had to handle, and I wanted Sora to be prepared for anything.

"Take five steps back and try it again," I told her.

She nodded and did what I asked, with all the seriousness of a very determined ten-year-old. These training sessions were my favorite time of the day. I rotated with the others, each one of us claiming a few hours with the ascendant. Jasin taught her combat and war strategy, Auric taught her diplomacy and history, and Slade taught her how to build things. The rest of the time she spent with her tutors, playing with other kids living at the palace, or with Kira to learn about her future role as a Dragon.

Silver wings spread overhead, drawing our attention to the sky. "Mom's back!" Sora squealed.

The Silver Dragon circled down and landed beside us, and Sora ran over and wrapped her arms around Kira's neck. Kira nuzzled her scaled head against her daughter, before transforming into a human again. She'd been visiting the Earth Realm with Slade and Jasin after reports of shades in the area. I looked her over quickly, checking for signs she'd been in combat, but saw none.

"How did it go?" I asked.

She stretched her neck and shoulders. "We didn't see any shades, but Jasin and Slade are patrolling the area for another few days to make sure. What have you two been doing?"

"Training," I said.

"Look what Dad taught me," Sora said. She grabbed the five knives and launched them into the air, juggling them with skill.

Kira arched an eyebrow at me. "Wow. That looks…dangerous."

"Oh, Mom," Sora said, rolling her eyes as she caught all five knives. "It's fine."

"She's a natural," I said. "And besides, if she gets hurt, she'll heal it quick enough."

Sora had already come into her healing powers thanks to the Life Goddess, who'd blessed Sora early as a gift for us freeing her. It already looked like Sora would surpass her mother in magic, as she could heal anyone she touched and cause plants to grow. Animals loved her too, naturally. I could only imagine how powerful she would be once she received the magic of her future mates too—although the thought of her with mates was too terrifying to think about just yet.

"Just be careful," Kira said, while stroking Sora's hair.

"We always are. Don't worry." I wrapped my arms around Kira and kissed her, while Sora squirmed away and said, "ew." She danced off across the courtyard, finding something else to entertain herself with, while I held her mother in my arms. "I missed you."

"I missed you too," she said, leaning against me. "Come to my room tonight, after she's asleep."

"I was already planning on it," I said, kissing her again.

43

KIRA

THIRTY YEARS LATER

Storm clouds rolled over the garden, crackling with the promise of what was to come. Any moment now the rain would begin, lightning would strike, and my daughter would be blessed by the Gods.

"Will it hurt?" Sora asked me, as she had done many times while she was growing up.

"Only for a moment," I said.

It was her twentieth birthday, and today her mates would be chosen. It had been over thirty years since that day for me, but I still remembered it well. Enva had appeared to me for the first time and then I'd been struck by lightning, doused in rain, whipped by wind, and had fallen in the mud. Now I knew it had been the four Gods blessing me with their elements, but back then I'd been confused, especially when I wasn't injured afterward. Sora, at least, was a lot better prepared.

"Don't worry. You can handle it." I smoothed her dark hair and gazed into her hazel eyes. She was so beautiful, a young woman with so much strength and such a good heart, embodying all the best things of each of my mates. "I'm so proud of you. I know you're going to do great things."

She drew in a breath and stood a little taller. "Thanks, Mom. I have a big legacy to live up to, but I'll do my best."

"I know you will." I pressed a kiss to her forehead, and then I moved back to where my mates were waiting off to the side, giving Sora some space. Though we'd all aged by thirty years since we'd first met, they were still just as handsome, and our love had only grown stronger over the years.

Slade paced back and forth relentlessly. "How are we supposed to just stand here and do nothing while our daughter is hit by lightning?"

"The better question is, how are we supposed to stand here and do nothing, knowing her mates are going to be chosen today?" Jasin asked.

"She'll be fine," Reven said, though I noticed his face was looking a bit pale and his brows were furrowed.

"Yes, she will," Auric said, as he nervously ran a hand through his golden hair. "She's prepared for this her whole life."

"I'm not worried," I said. "Most women only have one overprotective father. She has four to watch over her."

"We're not overprotective," Slade said, even though he was the worst of them.

Jasin scowled. "All I know is that these mates of hers had better treat her right, or they're going to have to deal with me."

"The Gods did a good job of choosing all of you," I said. "We have to trust they'll find the perfect men for Sora too."

Auric tilted his head with a thoughtful look on his face. "If I recall correctly, none of us were perfect when we first met you, but we grew into the roles. We'll have to allow her mates to do the same."

"And if they don't, I'll take them out and dispose of the bodies where no one can find them," Reven said with a dark grin.

I shook my head. "No one is taking them out. Besides, Sora can handle herself. You've all made sure of that."

Sora crossed her arms and called out, "How long am I supposed to wait?"

"I'm sure it will be soon," I yelled back.

She huffed and gazed up at the sky as rain began to pelt down on her face. It was hard to believe she was all grown up now and ready to become the next Silver Dragon, or whatever color she ended up as. We'd spent the last thirty years trying to bring peace to the four Realms so her transition would be as easy as possible, and I hoped Enva, Doran, and Nysa would be proud of all we'd accomplished. The four Realms governed themselves independently, and we'd prevented many wars from starting between them over the years. The elementals and humans lived in relative harmony, and when shades crept out of the Realm of the Dead, we swiftly dealt with them. The world had changed dramatically, and I had no idea what challenges Sora would face as she took over as its guardian, but I was confident she could handle them.

As for us? My mates and I were ready to step back and begin our retirement. We'd help train Sora and her mates, of course, but our time as peacekeepers, mediators, and warriors was at an end. I had to admit, I was excited for a long, well-deserved break.

Lightning streaked down from the sky and struck Sora, making her entire body go rigid, her arms spread wide as if she was embracing it. Wind wrapped around her, lifting her into the air, while rain soaked through her clothes and mud splashed against her skin. My mates tensed beside me and I felt their anxiety and worry through the bond as we all watched. I'd never admit it out loud to them, but I was worried too. How could I not be? Sora's life was about to change forever. But I also had faith in our daughter and knew she would find her way, just like we did.

It was time for a new set of Dragons to rise.

EMBRACE THE DARK

HER ELEMENTAL DRAGONS BOOK FIVE

CHAPTER ONE

S ome people had no idea they were destined for greatness. I'd spent my entire life preparing for it—and today my destiny was supposed to begin.

Nervous, excited energy woke me before the sun. After tossing and turning for an hour, I accepted that falling back asleep was futile, so I rose with the dawn and dressed in my combat leathers. My Ascension wouldn't happen until this afternoon, which meant I had many hours to fill until then. Burning off some energy was the only way I'd get through the longest day of my life.

My steps echoed along the white marble halls of Soulspire Palace, and I nodded to the few guards I passed. The morning's silence melted away as I neared the kitchen, which was already bustling with activity as the staff prepared for the banquet tonight in my honor.

The head chef gave me a bright smile and offered me a warm blueberry muffin. "Happy birthday, Sora," she said, and a chorus of echoes went up around the room from the other cooks and servers.

"Thank you," I told everyone, before shoving half the muffin in my mouth. Fresh out of the oven and delicious. Another young woman offered me a glass of milk, which I chugged down.

"Would you like us to make you some breakfast? An omelet, perhaps?" Hada asked.

"No, but thank you." I grabbed an apple off a nearby tray on my way out the door. My stomach was too twisted to eat much of anything, and I doubted I'd be able to sit still long enough for a full meal anyway.

I crunched down on the apple as I headed outside into the fresh, cool air. Clouds gathered overhead, but otherwise it was a beautiful morning, the kind that made you feel like the day could only bring good things. I headed past the garden my mother created to the training grounds, where dozens of soldiers were already sparring with each other. I scanned the area for one of my fathers, Jasin, who led the Silver Guard, the elite fighting force dedicated to serving the Dragons. I didn't spot him there, but I did see someone else who made me smile.

Erroh caught my eye and grinned before jogging over to me. I tried not to admire the way his muscular body looked in his soldier's uniform and dragged my gaze back to his face instead. Not that it helped, since his face was just as appealing. His dark hair was cut military-style, showing off his chiseled cheekbones, golden-brown skin, and warm eyes. He was the spitting image of his father, Cadock, except with the coloring of his mother, Faya. Both Cadock and Faya worked for my parents, with Cadock acting as Jasin's second in command, and Faya handling diplomacy with my other father, Auric. Erroh was only a few months older than me, and since he'd also grown up in the palace—along with his older siblings Daka and Parin—he'd been my best friend for as long as I could remember.

"Happy birthday," he said as his arms circled me. I leaned into his embrace for probably a little too long. As we pulled back, our faces turned toward each other and our lips were close, way too close. For a second we paused, tempted to close the gap, but then we broke apart and looked away quickly. We both knew the Gods would choose my four mates later today. Erroh and I could never be together. Not as anything more than friends, at least.

He cleared his throat and rubbed the back of his neck. "I can't believe it's finally here."

"Me neither." I couldn't meet his eyes. The moment had grown awkward, as it always did whenever we spoke of such things. If I were any other girl, without a Gods-ordained destiny, we'd probably already be married.

"I'm guessing you couldn't sleep and that's why you're out here so early," he said. He knew me so well.

I nodded. "I thought I might have a run through the Gauntlet to burn off some energy. Care to join me?"

Erroh glanced behind him at the other soldiers, but his sparring partner had moved on to someone else. He turned back and grinned at me. "You know I never miss a chance to be humiliated by the Ascendant."

I nudged him in the arm. "You might beat me this time."

"On your big birthday? I wouldn't dare."

We passed the soldiers' training area and headed around the buildings toward an elaborate training course where I often practiced running, jumping, and climbing. The Silver Guard used it also, but it had originally been designed for me by my four fathers. The soldiers called it the Gauntlet, and running it successfully was one of their major tests. I'd been doing it since I was seven.

We climbed up the ladder to the first platform, where we had a perfect view of the rising sun making the sky the color of pink roses. The Gauntlet spread before us, with different platforms and various challenges all designed to test my skills. I tied my wild, curly brown hair back in a tight bun and shook out my limbs. "Ready?"

Erroh finished stretching out his arms and nodded. "First one to the finish line has to get the loser a present."

I cocked my head at him. "I'm not sure that's how winning is supposed to work."

He shrugged and then took off, leaping from the platform to grab onto the zipline overhead. He zoomed down it, and I cursed him under my breath and hopped onto the zipline right after him. He hit the ground on the next platform with me only seconds behind him, and then we both ducked down under the first obstacle and scrambled over the next one.

My focus narrowed to my own movements as I jumped across small steps over a pool of water, before climbing up to another platform. From here I carefully crossed the rope walkway suspended over the same pool of water, belly crawled through a dark moss-covered tunnel, and then wove my way through thick forest and large rocks until I reached the next platform. We kept going, racing through the course and overcoming other obstacles, including huge swinging stones I had to dodge between, holes in the ground that randomly shot bursts of fire or water, and an area with heavy wind that could knock you over if you weren't careful.

Finally we reached the last platform, this one a steep rock hill with only a few handholds, made by my other father Slade with his earth magic. I climbed it while breathing heavily. Only then did I notice Erroh again beside me, and we pulled onto the platform at the same time. We both leaped across and grabbed onto the rope hanging before us, then swung to the next one and grasped it, and kept going like this until we reached the other side. I got there only seconds before him and sprinted over the random obstacles in the way, until I reached the end. I grabbed the white flag and raised it triumphantly, while Erroh came to a halt beside me. We both bent over and tried to catch our breath, sweat dripping from our brows.

"I let you win," he said.

"Sure you did." I threw the balled-up flag at his chest. "If you're expecting a present for losing, forget it."

He grinned and hung the flag back in its spot. "Ah well, it was worth a try."

We climbed down the platform and sat on the grass to stretch our legs and calm our racing hearts. I wiped sweat off my forehead and leaned back, gazing at the clouds gathering overhead. For those few minutes on the Gauntlet my mind had been blissfully clear, but now the thoughts slowly crept back in. Today I was twenty years old. Today I would be blessed by the Gods so I could take my mother's place as the Silver Dragon. Today my life would change forever.

"What distraction do you need now?" Erroh asked, breaking me out of my fog. "Shall we get our swords? Throw some knives? Head into town and drink some ale at a seedy tavern?" He waggled his eyebrows at this.

I laughed. "You should probably get back to your own training. I might run the Gauntlet a few more times though."

"Whatever you want," Erroh said with a grin. "I'll just have to get you drunk at the banquet instead."

"That sounds good. I'll need to be drunk to deal with all the stuffy noblemen and diplomats. Speaking of, is your brother going to be there?"

"No, Parin is still on assignment in the Earth Realm. I'm sure he sends his best wishes and all that." Erroh stood up and brushed the grass off his uniform. "Daka isn't coming either, unfortunately. The baby is still too young for them to travel. But I'll be there representing the family, don't you fret."

"Thank goodness for that." I stood up and almost reached for him, but then stopped myself. "Thanks for the distraction today, and for being so understanding about…everything. I know it hasn't always been easy, but I'm glad you're my best friend."

His jaw clenched a little, but he smiled. "I'll always be there for you, Sora. You know that." He leaned forward and pressed a kiss to my fore-head. "Good luck today."

He walked away and I allowed myself to check out his behind one last time. In a few hours the Gods would choose my mates, and then I'd only have eyes for them. But for now I could at least admire my first love a little longer.

After running the Gauntlet until my muscles twitched and sweat ran down my body, I finally returned to the palace. I stopped in the kitchen to grab a drink and some food, but paused when two familiar faces rounded the corner ahead of me. They abruptly halted when they saw me, and one of them gave me a charming smile, while the other had on a permanent frown. Carth and Zain, total opposites, and yet somehow best friends. They were also two of the most handsome men I'd ever seen.

Carth was dressed in fine silks that brushed across his tan skin, the soft yellow and pale blue marking him as a nobleman from the Air Realm. His sandy hair always looked windswept, and his sea green eyes and muscular swimmer's body hinted at his origins in the Water Realm. When he was four years old, his family was on a boat that was lost in a storm. Water elementals rescued him and brought him to Soulspire, where he was adopted by Brin, a friend of my parents, and Leni, my aunt. That made Carth my adopted cousin, which made my desire for him rather awkward. It didn't help that Carth was an incessant flirt either.

Zain wore the black and red armor of a guard of the Fire Temple, and his eyes were the blue of the hottest part of a flame. His grandmother was the former High Priestess Calla, who helped my mother during her time as Ascendant. Calla was like a grandmother to me too, and that made Zain sort of like an older, protective brother to me. He was always serious and somewhat aloof when I was younger, though his eyes were always on me. As I grew older, the looks he gave me changed and became something different, something that made my heart race. Last time I saw him was a year ago, when we shared a secret, passionate kiss against the outside wall of the Fire Temple, his fingers skimming across my breast. After that, we never spoke again. The whole encounter confused and excited me, even though I'd tried my best to put it out of my mind.

"Hey there, birthday girl," Carth said, before wrapping a tan, muscular arm around my shoulders. "How are you feeling? Excited? Nervous?"

"Both those things, and many more as well," I admitted.

"But mostly excited to meet your mates, I imagine." Carth pressed a hand to his chest dramatically. "Oh, that I could be one of them."

Did he? Or was he being dramatic? I could never tell with Carth. I'd secretly longed for the same thing for years, but my mother's mates were all strangers, so I'd never held out much hope it would happen.

Zain lifted his chin. "The Gods know what they are doing, and will pick the best men for the role."

Carth nudged his friend. "Sure, but wouldn't it be nice if she got to pick? Or at least could tell them her preferences?"

"We do not question the will of the Gods," Zain said sternly. Then he rested a warm hand on my elbow. "Just know that whatever happens, we will always watch out for you."

"I'm sure I'll be happy with their selection," I managed to say, as heat crept up my neck from the two men's touches. Both of them had always been there for me my entire life, but I was sure things would change between us after today.

"If not, you can always come to me on the side. I'll make sure you're well taken care of." Carth gave me a wink, while Zain rolled his eyes. "See you at the banquet tonight."

They continued on their path, and I let out a sigh while I watched them go, admiring their muscular physiques and the way they moved. Two more men who were completely off-limits because of who I was. Carth had asked the same questions I'd had my entire life, but I'd always been afraid to admit them out loud. How did I know the Gods would really choose my best mates? They'd done a good job with my mother, but what if things were different for me?

Why didn't I get any say in my own future?

CHAPTER TWO

Finally, it was time.

I made my way to my mother's garden, which she'd created before I was born in honor of the Life Goddess. As I walked along the path, I noticed a white rose had been trampled into the stone, and bent down beside it. I brushed my fingers across the wilted petals and gave a little push, and the flower lifted up and healed thanks to the energy I gave it. Once the rose was as good as new, I continued into the garden.

My parents were all waiting there among the verdant leaves and colorful flowers, but otherwise we were alone. I stepped toward them as storm clouds gathered overhead, threatening rain at any moment. One by one my fathers gave me a hug and wished me a happy birthday. Slade, my father by blood, came to me first, his dark eyes proud as he gave me a big bear hug. He was a very large man, and as a kid there was nowhere safer than on his lap, especially when he'd read me a book in his deep voice. Jasin was next, and he lifted me up and spun me around like I was still his little girl. He'd always been the fun dad who used to make messy art with me out in the courtyard with paint and pastels, although he'd been serious about my combat and military training. Then came Auric, who rested his hands on my shoulders and gave me a kiss on the cheeks, before wiping a tear from the corner of his wise gray eyes. Auric always encouraged my imagination with dolls and miniature horses and dress-up parties, and at night he would read me stories until his voice was hoarse. Finally came Reven, whose face showed no emotion until he pulled me against him and whispered in my ear, "Good luck, kid." The sentiment in his voice made my chest tighten as I hugged him back. Sometimes I felt I was more like Reven than anyone else, even though we shared no common blood. He'd taught me all my favorite things, from lock picking to throwing knives to parkour, and he always gave me space to be myself.

My four fathers stepped back, and my mother, Kira, moved closer and embraced me. She smelled like fresh jasmine and her hug was warm and comforting as I buried my face in her red hair. As I pulled back, the sky darkened, the clouds blocking the sun.

"Your twentieth year is finally here." Mom smiled wistfully and glanced at her mates. "I don't think any of us are ready."

"I am." I straightened my shoulders. As of today I was an adult, and soon I would be mated with four men so I could begin to take my mother's place as guardian of the world. I'd prepared for this moment my entire life and I was ready for it...wasn't I? A flicker of doubt made my stomach churn. "Will it hurt?"

"Only a little," Mom said.

I nodded. Kira had gone through this without any training. She'd had no idea she was the Ascendant, and had been shocked and confused by what had happened to her—what was about to happen to me. Unlike her, I'd had five people prepare me for this moment, and I was going to face it bravely.

"Don't worry. You can handle it." Mom smoothed back my wild curls as she gazed into my hazel eyes, which mirrored her own. "I'm so proud of you. I know you're going to do great things."

I drew in a breath and stood a little taller. "Thanks, Mom. I have a big legacy to live up to, but I'll do my best."

"I know you will." She kissed my forehead, and then returned to stand with my fathers a short distance away. There was nothing more they could do for me now. I was on my own.

Slade began pacing back and forth, and I heard my parents start to murmur quietly to each other, no doubt fussing over me in their own way. I could only make out a few words, but it sounded like they were plotting to deal with my mates if they ever hurt me. I pitied my future mates a little— they had no idea what was about to happen to them, or that they'd have to live with my four overprotective fathers. At least Mom never had to deal with that.

As I waited and nothing happened, I started to wonder if we'd gotten the time wrong. Auric had unearthed an old book in the palace from back before the Black Dragon—my grandmother—had ruled, and it had laid out the basics for the Ascension. It would occur exactly twenty years after the moment of the Ascendant's birth, which should be right now. And yet...nothing.

Hurry up already, I told the Gods.

I crossed my arms and called out, "How long am I supposed to wait?"

"I'm sure it will be soon," Mom said.

I huffed and raised my eyes to the sky, just as rain began to pour down on me, as if the Gods had heard my plea. Within seconds, I was soaked. I started to call out again, and that's when the lightning bolt shot down from the clouds and hit me.

The words in my throat turned to a silent scream as my whole body stiffened. Energy coursed through me, crackling with power, and I spread my arms wide as if it might shoot out of me and relieve the pressure—but that didn't help. Wind swirled around me and lifted me into the air, embracing me with its magic, and then I dropped down hard into the mud. I was covered from head to toe in it, and all I could do was kneel as the magic overwhelmed me. Slowly it receded and the rain slowed to a light drizzle.

I lifted my head. As I did, I felt a strange unease in my stomach, and darkness spread out from me in a circle, turning the grass and plants brown. Leaves and petals fell and shriveled up into dust, leaving only hard branches behind. The circle of death stopped just before it hit my parents, and then the magic disappeared and the sun peeked through the clouds again.

"What was that?" I asked, as I rose to my feet. My limbs felt weak, like I'd just run for miles, and something wasn't right. Mom had never mentioned a ring of death when she told me the story of her own Ascension.

"I don't know," Kira said, her face troubled. "Auric?"

He shook his head. "I've never read about anything like that happening before."

Reven's fists clenched. "It has to be the Death Goddess."

"You think she's making her presence known?" Jasin asked.

Slade growled. "Is she tries to harm Sora, we will defeat her again."

Mom bent down and touched the ground, and the grass and plants all returned to life, as if it had never happened. "It's probably nothing," she said, as she brushed dirt off her hands. "However, we will send out extra patrols tonight in case more shades return, to be safe."

I nodded, though I had a feeling she was only saying that to keep me calm. Something wasn't right and we all knew it, but we weren't sure exactly how bad it was yet. All I knew was that my family would be with me to face whatever the problem was...along with my new mates, who I should be meeting soon.

That night there was a banquet in my honor celebrating my twentieth birthday and my Ascension. The day marked the beginning of my parents' retirement, and the start of the next dragon cycle. Important people from all four Realms, plus the elementals' home Divine Isle, all came to give me gifts and wish me a happy birthday, either to size me up or try to earn my favor. It should have been a joyous occasion for me, but I found myself distracted all evening as I thought about what happened during my Ascension.

It didn't help that Erroh was missing from the banquet either, along with Carth and Zain. I knew things would change between us after this day, but I still hoped we could all be friends. Perhaps knowing my mates had been chosen for me was too hard for them. I understood that, but I still felt like a part of me was missing all evening, and every time I glanced at their empty seats my chest ached. Whatever happened to Erroh getting me drunk tonight?

I made an excuse to head to bed as soon as I could without being rude. Mom gave me a knowing smile. "Ready to dream of your mates?" she asked, as she kissed me on the cheek.

I nodded. It was time to move on to the men who *would* be there for me. "I'm anxious to meet them."

She smoothed a wayward piece of curly hair on my head. "Me too. I'm sure the Gods have chosen well."

I could only hope she was right, even as I wondered what the Death Goddess could be planning. Whatever it was, it couldn't be good.

It took me forever to fall asleep, but once I did, the dream came, just as Mom told me it would. She'd seen Jasin first, and since he was the first of her mates to arrive and the first she bonded with, I had to assume the man I dreamed of would be my first as well.

The man in my dream had straight black hair that hung past his shoulders and shone like ink, and a face that looked familiar, though I couldn't place it. He wore no shirt, and I admired his impressive broad shoulders and muscular chest. Tattoos ran down both his arms, and though I couldn't make them out too well in the dream, I spotted one with a skull.

A wicked grin spread across his handsome face, and I only saw cruelty in his pale eyes. He looked down at a man kneeling before him, and then grabbed him by the neck and lifted him up in the air. The poor man flailed and kicked, while my future mate laughed and held him with one hand— an impressive show of strength. All the life drained out of the man, and the black-haired fiend dropped the body to the floor with a smirk. He brushed off his hands, as if wiping off a bit of dust on them, and then turned away.

I woke with a start and a lump of dread in my stomach. How could that man—that *murderer*—be one of my mates?

Who had the Gods chosen for me?

CHAPTER THREE

The next morning, I woke late. I'd tossed and turned so much that once sleep finally took me, it didn't want to let me go. I slowly bathed and dressed, remembering the strange, deadly man in my dream, and wondering about the other men I might dream of next. As I pulled on a casual green gown and tied back my wild hair, I stared at myself in the mirror, at my light brown skin and hazel eyes.

Today I was a new person—the Ascendant. Yet I didn't feel any different. I was still just Sora. Daughter of heroes. Child to four fathers. Girl with an inescapable destiny.

I headed to the small dining room where my family often shared an informal meal together, wondering if I would find any traces of breakfast. A few pieces of fruit and bread remained, and I put together a small plate. A servant rushed in and offered to make me something, but I declined. She returned anyway with some juice and scrambled eggs, because the staff always took good care of me. I thanked her profusely and then sat down to eat in the quiet room.

As soon as I took the first bite, the door burst open and Erroh rushed inside. "There you are!" he said, as he came toward me. "I've been looking for you."

He seemed excited to see me for some reason, but all I could think of was how he'd skipped my birthday banquet. "Is that so?"

He slid into the chair beside me. "I have something to tell you."

I raised an eyebrow as I stabbed my fork into my eggs. "Is it an explanation for where you were last night?"

"Yes, actually. I'm very sorry about that, but something happened. Something incredible." He drew in a deep breath. "The Air God came to me."

I dropped my fork. "What?"

His eyes danced with barely-contained excitement. "Sora, I'm one of your mates. Can you believe it?"

"No, I can't." I stared at him, and he gazed back with sincerity. Was it possible? All of my mother's mates had been strangers, so I assumed mine would be as well. "Is this a joke of some kind?"

"Definitely not. Watch." He waved his hand, and a huge gust of wind hit the flower vase on the table and knocked it over, spilling water everywhere. He jumped up and righted it immediately. "Oops, I did not mean to do that. I have a lot to learn, obviously."

I let out a surprised laugh. Erroh was one of my mates! My first one, at that. Tears of joy hit my eyes and I jumped up to throw my arms around him. He hugged me back hard, and then our lips met without any hesitation. He kissed me with so much passion it made my heart race, and relief swept through my entire body. Kissing Erroh felt natural and so right, and now I could do it for the rest of my life without guilt or worry. I didn't have to give him up after all.

"You have no idea how much I prayed for this," Erroh said, as he pressed his forehead against mine. "I've loved you my entire life, and I couldn't stand the thought of not being with you. I begged the Gods to choose me, and the Air God listened."

"I always loved you too, but I didn't think it was possible for you to be my mate, so I never let myself hope." I let out a long breath and laughed softly. "Oh, this makes me feel a lot better."

He pulled back and studied me. "What do you mean? Is something wrong?"

I hesitated, but there was no hiding anything from Erroh, my best friend for my entire life. And now my mate. "My dream last night... I'm sure it's nothing."

His brow furrowed. "You didn't dream of me?"

"No. I should have, but it was someone else."

"Perhaps everyone's Ascension is different. So much was lost during your grandmother's rule. For all we know, it happened much differently for her than for your mother."

His calm voice always settled my nerves. I smiled. "Yes, I'm sure you're right. If the Gods chose you, they must know what they're doing."

The door opened again, and Carth strolled inside with a big cocky grin, followed by a more serious Zain, with eyes that smoldered as they landed on me. The instant they arrived, my knees grew weak, and I grabbed onto the nearby table to steady myself. I suddenly knew why they'd also missed my banquet—they'd been chosen too.

"Let me guess, Water and Fire?" I managed to ask, though I was suddenly breathless.

"How did you know?" Carth asked.

I pressed a hand to my spinning head. "All three of you missed my banquet last night. Erroh was chosen by the Air God. It only makes sense you were chosen by Water and Fire. I just can't believe it's possible."

"It's a great honor to be chosen by one of the Gods," Zain said. "And now we can continue protecting you, as we've always done."

Carth nodded. "It makes sense. The three of us have always looked after you your entire life. We've always been your closest friends. Who else would the Gods choose but us?"

When he put it like that, perhaps it did make sense. They said the Gods always chose the best mates for the Ascendant, and maybe they looked into my heart and saw how much I cared for these three men, even though I'd tried to deny my feelings my entire life. Now I didn't have to do that anymore, and it was a huge relief. My last and final mate, my future Earth Dragon, would no doubt be a stranger, but that would be all right. I'd have my three oldest friends by my side through whatever came next.

I gave Carth a hug and kissed his cheek, and then did the same for Zane. Both of them let their hands linger on me, igniting heat between my thighs. "I'm so happy you were both chosen. Truly."

"Now we just need to wait for your final mate and then we can start visiting the temples," Erroh said, with a wide grin.

"I'm sure we're all looking forward to that," Carth said, his smile turning naughty.

I glanced between the three of them. "Are you all okay with this—with sharing me?"

"I always knew it was your destiny," Erroh said. "I'm just glad I get to be one of your mates."

Carth shrugged. "Doesn't bother me. The more the merrier."

"I was raised by four fathers," Zain said. "I understand the dynamics of it."

I let out a relieved sigh. "Good. All I can hope now is that they've chosen well for my fourth mate."

I thought back to my dream. That black-haired man must be the one chosen by the Earth God. Perhaps I didn't have dreams of these three because I already knew them?

My mother walked in, along with my father Slade. "We heard you were having a late breakfast," Mom said. "Did you have a restless night dreaming of your mates?"

I glanced quickly at the three men. "Something like that."

"I'm sure they'll be arriving soon," Slade said, as he grabbed a piece of bread.

"Actually, three of them already have." I gestured to Erroh, Carth, and Zain. "The Gods have chosen them for Air, Water, and Fire."

Mom blinked at the men, her face showing obvious surprise. "Oh! How…unexpected."

Slade's brow furrowed as he studied the three men, in particular, Carth. "These are the men the Gods chose?"

Mom elbowed him in the side and smiled at me. "How nice that you already know each other. That will save you a lot of trouble."

Slade grunted and grudgingly said, "I suppose the Gods know what is best for Sora."

I knew things would be awkward between my mates and my fathers, but this was worse than I'd expected. These men had known my parents all their lives. My parents had watched them grow up beside me, from the time we were children. Now they would have to train them and watch them become my mates. We all knew what *that* involved.

Zain cleared his throat. "We're all very honored and excited to begin training with you."

"Don't expect us to go easy on you because you're Sora's friends," my other father Reven said from behind me. He was so stealthy I hadn't even heard him come in, and now he eyed Carth with disdain. "If you hurt her or break her heart, we will end your life. Painfully. And no one will find the bodies."

Mom held up a hand. "That's enough of that, Reven."

"He's right though," Slade grumbled.

"Don't worry Uncle Slade, we'll take good care of her," Carth said, then gave Slade a friendly punch in the arm. Slade growled at him in response.

"No one is going to hurt Sora," Erroh said. "We all care about her very much."

"I hope that's true…for your sakes," Reven said.

I covered my face with my hands. This was going to be a disaster.

My parents always knew this day would come, so two years ago they moved me into a separate wing of the palace in preparation. My suite had a huge living space plus an equally large bedroom, and was surrounded by four other smaller suites prepared for my mates. Each of those rooms sat empty for years…until today.

Over the course of a few hours, my three mates moved into their new suites. Each one was decorated for their element—Carth's was done in deep blue and sea green hues, Zain's in fiery red and black, and Erroh's in pale yellow and sky blue. The last room was hunter green and warm brown, still sitting empty, but not for long.

Once the three men were all moved in, we had supper sent up so we could share a meal together in our new dining area. I gazed across the stone table at my three friends, now my three mates, marveling over how things could change so quickly for us overnight. And yet, everything about it felt *right*. These men had always been destined to be mine.

Things were already different though. Zain and Erroh were both in plain clothes, no longer wearing the uniforms of their previous stations. They were both giving up their careers to become my mates.

"I'm sorry you had to say goodbye to your previous lives," I told them, as we began to eat. "I'm sure this is a big change for all of you."

Erroh shrugged. "I only joined the Silver Guard so I could protect you and be near you. This is even better."

"I did always wonder why you joined," I said with a smile. Growing up, Erroh had always had his nose in a book, until I dragged him off on some adventure and got us both into trouble. When he'd joined the Silver Guard at eighteen it had been a total shock. Now it made a lot more sense. My heart warmed knowing he'd done it to be near me, even though he thought he could never have me. "What about you, Zain? Are you sad you had to leave the Fire Temple for Soulspire?"

Zain shook his head. "I served the Fire God at the temple, and now I serve him here. I'll miss my family, but I'm confident this is the best place for me."

"And you, Carth?" I asked. He still wore his nobleman's finery, with his silk shirt open just enough to give me a peek of his tan, sculpted chest.

Carth let out a short laugh as he grabbed his wine. "My sister is set to inherit mother's estates, so I've always been the spare and able to do whatever I please." A sensual grin spread across his face. "And right now, that's you."

Heat spread to my cheeks and to other places in my body, reminding me of what I would soon be doing with these three men. In order to gain my elemental powers, I would have to bond with each of them at the different temples across the four Realms. Mom had told me what would happen during the bonding, but not in too many details, of course. Still, I had an idea of what to expect.

Erroh rolled his eyes. "The texts all say she has to bond with her mates in the order of their arrival, so you'll have to wait your turn. The Air Temple is first."

"Sounds like someone is eager to get started," Carth said with a smirk.

Erroh rested his hand over mine. "I've been waiting to be with Sora for a long time. I'm ready whenever she is."

Carth trailed his fingers down my forearm. "You know, I was the first one in the room after Erroh. Therefore we should head to the Water Temple after Air, isn't that right?"

Zain scowled. "You most certainly were not. I entered the room first. I knew about the order rule, and I made sure to be the first in."

Carth shook his head. "I think if you search your memory, you'll find I'm correct."

Erroh winked at me as they argued. He didn't care who went next. He would be my first.

I couldn't help but be happy it would be him. I'd been attracted to Carth and Zain for years, but Erroh I'd loved since we were kids. Now that I could allow myself to be free and honest with how I felt, I was sure of it.

As his thumb stroked my knuckles and the gazes of the men all rested on me, desire made my heart race. I was ready. Wasn't I?

CHAPTER FOUR

My mates' training began the next day, bright and early. Each of the men lined up outside in the courtyard facing their new teachers: my fathers. Zain bowed low to Jasin, who snickered in response. Carth made a joke to Reven, but his hard expression never changed. Auric clasped Erroh on the shoulder and gave him a few kind words with a smile. At least the two of them got along.

Mom was busy meeting with some elementals and had to skip this session, but promised she would try to make future ones. Slade stood beside me with his arms crossed while they began. Everyone spread out a bit for safety purposes, and then my three fathers showed off an easy move using their element. Jasin created a small flame in his hand and moved it from one palm to the other. Auric made leaves swirl around his head. Reven blasted Carth in the chest with water, making the poor guy stumble back. I pinched the bridge of my nose and hoped this wouldn't be a total disaster.

"I'm curious to see who the Earth God chose for you," Slade said.

I remembered the dark man in my dream. Last night I'd had another vision of him, this time drinking beer while he cheered someone on with a cruel smile. "Me too."

Slade must have heard something uncertain in my voice because he wrapped an arm around my shoulders. "Have faith, daughter. Everything will make sense in time."

I leaned against him, taking comfort in his warm strength. I was truly the luckiest woman in the world to have four wonderful fathers, even if it was sometimes annoying or frustrating. Or awkward, like during this training.

As we watched, Zain set fire to a small patch of grass, Carth flooded the area around his expensive shoes, and Erroh had a hard time producing another gust of wind at all. I sighed. "Were the four of you ever this bad?"

"Unfortunately yes," Slade admitted. "We didn't have anyone to teach us how to use magic either. Don't worry. They will learn quickly with our help. You will too."

I couldn't wait to have all that power under my control. As soon as I bonded with each man, I would be able to use their element. Once I had the power of all four, I could become the next great dragon leader—like my mother.

But first, I needed my final mate to arrive.

Over the next few days my mates' training continued, while I spent my time impatiently waiting for the Earth God's chosen one to arrive—and dreading the moment too. Every night I dreamed of the same black-haired man, and every night he scared me more and more.

In the evenings, my mates and I shared more meals together and tried to move from childhood friends to something more. It wasn't as easy as I'd expected. It didn't help that the men were so exhausted after training they didn't have much energy for socializing. I started to wonder if that was my fathers' plan all along.

I was practicing sword fighting with Zain and Carth to hone my skills in defending against two attackers, when Erroh rushed past. He called out, "It's Parin! He's returned from the Earth Realm!"

Zain tilted his head as he sheathed his sword. "I thought he wasn't supposed to return for another month."

Carth shrugged. "Negotiations must have gone well."

"Or very poorly," I muttered.

Parin was Erroh's older brother, and he took his name from his father, who'd died while leading the Resistance against my grandmother, the Black Dragon. Parin's mother Faya later married former bandit turned soldier Cadock, and together they had two more children, Daka and Erroh. Parin worked as a diplomat to the Earth Realm, and often traveled back and forth between there and Soulspire.

We headed over to the courtyard in front of the palace, where Parin's contingent had arrived. He'd already exited his carriage and was speaking with his brother in hushed tones. As he lifted his head, his dark eyes met mine and lingered there. I sensed something in them, something I'd never seen before.

Parin was ten years older than me, and he'd always treated me like a little sister. He'd been my first crush growing up—the incredibly handsome older brother of my best friend with rich, dark skin, even darker coarse hair, and warm eyes that missed nothing.

"Welcome back," I said.

"Thank you." He glanced at his brother with something like worry on his face, then turned back to me. "I need to speak with you. Alone."

My eyebrows darted up. "Is something wrong?"

"Not exactly."

"What's this about?" Erroh asked.

"It's not something I care to discuss in front of you. I'm sorry, brother."

"It's fine." I didn't want the two of them to fight, but I was very curious as to what this was about. "Let's go inside so we can speak privately."

Parin and I went into the palace and to one of the receiving rooms, this one decorated in soft gold tones, while Erroh waited outside.

"What did you want to speak with me about?" I asked, once we were alone. I looked up at his handsome face and swallowed. I'd rarely been alone with him before and he made me nervous in a way no one else did. All of a sudden I felt like a little kid again, with a big, embarrassing crush on an older man I could never have.

"Sora, I must tell you something." He reached out and took my hand, but with hesitation. "I am one of your mates."

My jaw fell open and I yanked my hand back, more in shock than anything else. "That's not possible."

"I assure you, it is. The Earth God came to me a few nights ago and gave me my new purpose." He paused, searching my eyes. "I do apologize for missing your birthday festivities."

"But...but..." I had so many questions and suddenly my mouth didn't seem to work right. How could all four of my mates be men I already knew? Why would they choose Erroh's brother—wouldn't that complicate things? And who was the man haunting me at night if not my fourth mate? "But my dream…"

"Your dream?" Parin asked, his brow pinching together in concern.

I shook my head, trying to clear my thoughts. "Are you sure you're my mate? I don't mean to be rude, but I'm having a hard time believing this is possible."

"I can prove it, of course." He raised a hand and the stone table beside us lifted off the ground. His control was already good, much better than the others had been at first.

It was true, then. Parin was my fourth mate.

I took a few steps backward, completely overwhelmed, and the back of my knees hit a gilded red armchair. I collapsed into it and pressed a hand to my forehead. Parin was my fourth mate. I could barely wrap my head around that as it was, but it also meant my dreams weren't leading me to him. Did this mean I had a fifth mate? No, that couldn't be possible. None of the archives had spoken of more than four mates. The dreams had to be related to something else. Something from the Death Goddess.

Something bad.

"Are you all right?" Parin asked.

I looked up at him with a weak smile. "Yes. Sorry. Just feeling a bit overwhelmed by all this."

He offered me his hand. "Understandable."

I slide my hand into his and felt a little tremor of desire as we touched. "Are you comfortable with this new role? With…being my mate?"

He shifted on his feet and looked away. "It will take some adjustment, but yes. Though I will no longer be a diplomat in the usual sense, being a Dragon will allow me to do much of my previous duties but with even more authority."

"I see…." It sounded like he was more excited about his new job than being my mate. Would he ever see me as more than a little girl?

"We must speak of Erroh." Parin's face became pained. "I realize this will be difficult for him. You may not know this, but he's always loved you. I'm not sure how to break this to him, although he must have met your other mates by now."

"He *is* one of my mates. They chose both of you. And Zain and Carth too."

He blinked in surprise. "How is that possible?"

I spread my hands, still finding it hard to believe myself. "No one knows. It seems the Gods have decided the four of you are the best mates for me."

He stroked his chin. "I suppose having Erroh as one of your mates makes this easier in some ways, and harder in others."

Definitely harder now that Parin was one of my mates too. How would I handle having two brothers as my lovers? Oddly, the idea didn't bother me, but only excited me more. I took a deep breath. "I understand things might be confusing and strange at first, but the Gods must have done this for a reason."

"Indeed." He gave a firm nod. "I suppose we must inform the others."

I swallowed. "I suppose we must."

Parin opened the door for me, but as soon as he did, we spotted Erroh right on the other side, staring at us with his face ashen.

"You heard?" I asked.

"Auric taught me how to carry sound on the wind," Erroh said absently while staring at his brother. "How could you?"

Parin held up his hands. "I did not ask for this. I'm sorry, brother."

Erroh's gaze swung to me. "Are you all right with this?"

Two gorgeous brothers I'd secretly wanted all my life were now mine. It was hard to complain, but I could tell he felt betrayed. "The Gods have chosen, and we have to trust they know what's best for us."

Parin clasped a hand on his little brother's shoulder. "I'm relieved you were chosen too. I know you've always cared for Sora."

Erroh shrugged off his touch. "I have, yes. As have Carth and Zain. But what about you?"

Parin stiffened. "I cared for her too, of course."

"Not in the same way!"

This was getting very uncomfortable. Mostly for me. I stepped between them. "Enough. You're both my mates, and you'll both have to accept that."

Erroh grumbled something, but reluctantly nodded. Parin just sighed. I could tell this was going to be a problem. What were the Gods even thinking?

CHAPTER FIVE

W hile servants moved Parin's belongings into his room, Erroh stood to the side with his arms crossed and watched with a scowl. I was on my way to see my mother, but stopped to nudge him in the side.

"I thought you'd be more excited to have your brother return home safely," I said.

Erroh dropped his arms and sighed. "You're right. I should be happy to see him. I'm just not sure about sharing you with him. The others, fine. But my own brother?"

"I know what you mean." I swallowed, but for me it was because the thought made my heart race. "The gods must know it'll work out."

Erroh gave me a flat stare. "You can't tell me you're excited about this. We've always avoided Parin. He's such a bore!"

I had to bite back a laugh. Was that what Erroh thought? The truth was that I'd avoided Parin because I hadn't wanted anyone to know about my silly crush. But there was no hiding such things from the Gods, it seemed.

I gave Erroh a kiss on the cheek. "Be kind to your brother. He's just as shocked by this as you are."

He huffed. "I'll try."

My mother came down the hallway on the heels of a man carrying a big box. "You wanted to see me?"

I nodded. We stepped into my private quarters, and I shut the door behind us. "I was just about to come to your study. I thought you were in a meeting."

"I decided to come to you instead." She pushed back a strand of red hair with a smile. "Truthfully, I couldn't wait to get out of there. As soon as I got your note, I used it as an excuse to cut the meeting short."

I laughed as we headed over to the siting area beside an enormous window looking out over my mother's garden. "Was it that bad?"

Kira sank into one of the chairs and poured herself a cup of tea. "Just wait 'til you're the one who has to listen to noblemen whine about their problems all day long. Now, what did you want to talk about? Is it your mates? It's certainly odd that they're all men you already knew, but it must be nice for you too. Or at least a lot easier than mating with four strangers."

"That's not it. Not exactly." I sat across from her and twisted my hands nervously in my lap. "Did you ever dream about any men that weren't your mates?"

"No, never. Why?" She furrowed her brow and gave me her full attention.

"I've been having dreams like you did, but only of one man, and he's... He's terrifying." It was hard to say the word out loud. I wasn't scared of anything. Few people could best me at combat, and soon I would have the powers of the elements and a dragon form of my own, and then I'd be unstoppable. Possibly stronger than my mother, thanks to my lifetime of training. Yet somehow the man in my dreams unnerved me. He made me feel…vulnerable.

Mom leaned forward and studied me. "A man who isn't one of your mates?"

I nodded. "I thought he would be my fourth one, but then Parin arrived. Now I'm more confused than ever."

"You're sure he's not one of your mates? Perhaps it's a dream from the future and he has a different appearance?"

"No. I'm absolutely sure he's a different man." His appearance haunted me even while awake. Not just his appearance. His ruthlessness. His cruelty. His darkness.

I described the things he'd done in my dreams to her in a halting voice, and when I was done, Mom sat back and sighed.

"This is very unusual. I'll have your fathers look into it. I would help too, but there have been reports of missing elementals in the area and I want to investigate them immediately. I'm sure Auric or Reven will find something about your dreams though." She reached across and took my hand. "Don't worry. We'll figure this out."

"I can't help but be worried. The Death Goddess must be involved somehow."

"If she is, we'll confront her together. I defeated her once before, after all. She has no chance against the two of us and all our mates."

I let out a long breath, hoping she was right. "They're not my true mates yet. Not until we go to the temples and bond. I'd like to get started on that right away, especially if we'll need to face the Death Goddess. We can head to the Air Temple tomorrow even."

Mom frowned and studied my face. "You don't need to rush into this. Focus on your mates. Get to know them."

"I already know them. I grew up with them, after all."

"It's different now that they're your mates, and not just your childhood friends. Your relationship with them needs time to flourish and grow."

"We might not have time," I grumbled.

"You have plenty of time. Your fathers and I are in no hurry to step down. We'll only do so when we're sure you and your mates are ready for the responsibility." She ruffled my curls a little. "Patience, my love."

I sighed. Patience never was one of my strong suits.

At dinner that night, I tried to follow my mother's advice.

"Let's all try to get to know each other better," I said, once we were eating. The chefs had made one of my favorite dishes from the Air Realm, with chicken, bell pepper, lemon, and cheese, layered on thin pasta. "Which meal is your favorite: breakfast, lunch, or supper?"

"Dessert," Carth said, with a lazy grin. "I like to get right to the good stuff."

"Breakfast." Erroh tilted his head. "No, lunch. No, breakfast. I can't decide."

"How is this supposed to help us get to know each other better?" Zain asked.

"Just answer the question," I said.

He shrugged. "I don't really have a favorite."

I sighed and turned to Parin, who had been especially quiet ever since he arrived. "And you?"

He gave me a warm smile. "Supper. I like salty foods, and the more pepper the better."

Erroh made a gagging sound. "Parin is obsessed with pepper. He puts it on everything. I'll never forget when Daka and I were sick and Mom and Dad were out, so Parin made us some soup. He put so much pepper in it we nearly gagged."

"Pepper soup!" I laughed. "I remember that."

"Oh," Erroh said, his face falling. "Of course you do."

"My favorite is supper too," I said quickly. "Followed by dessert." Silence hit the table as we all continued eating. I wracked my brain for another question. "Favorite animal?"

"Owl," Erroh said.

"I've always been partial to dolphins," Carth said.

Zain waved a hand. "These questions are silly. We already know everything about each other."

"Not everything," I muttered, but I had to admit it did feel silly asking these questions.

"No? What's the next one—favorite childhood memory?" Zain snorted. "Most of our memories feature each other, I bet."

I leaned forward. "Well, what is your favorite childhood memory?"

Zain looked at me with his intense blue eyes. "The four of us—you, me, Carth, and Erroh—sneaked away one afternoon and headed into the woods. I'm sure it was your idea, Sora."

"It always was," Erroh muttered.

"Shush." I threw a bread roll at him.

"We found that one large, gnarled tree, and Carth challenged us to get to the top first. I was determined to win, but I fell and broke my ankle." Zain paused and something smoldered in his eyes. "You climbed down and healed it."

I remembered the moment. We were young then, but I was right at the age when I was beginning to realize they were boys and I was a girl and that meant something. I turned to Parin, who had gone quiet again. "And then Parin came and found us."

Carth chuckled. "Yes, if I remember correctly, he made us all go back inside."

Parin ducked his head. "I was simply trying to keep you out of trouble."

"That's your favorite memory?" Erroh asked. "Getting injured?"

"I think he probably enjoyed the healing part the most," Carth said with a wry grin.

"I enjoyed being with my friends," Zain snapped.

"I love that memory too," I said. "The best times were when we were all together." Zain has grown up in the Fire Temple or the nearby town of Sparkport, while Carth spent much of his time at his parents' estates in the Air Realm. All my favorite memories were when they came to visit Soulspire with their families.

"Exactly my point," Zain said. "You already know us, better than anyone."

It was hard to argue with that. I did know them, through and through, and there was no way to force the change in mindset from friends to lovers. Only time and togetherness would do that.

I knew Mom said not to rush, but frankly I was already tired of being patient. I wanted to bond with my mates and to gain my elemental powers and my dragon form. Especially if the Death Goddess was rising again.

I set down my fork and looked at the men one by one, even Parin, though the fact that he was one of my mates still hadn't fully sunk in. "We should leave for the Air Temple tomorrow morning."

"I agree," Erroh quickly said.

"Of course you agree," Carth said with a snicker. "But the sooner we head to the Air Temple, the sooner we can go to the others too."

Zain looked as though he was about to speak, when we heard shouting outside and the sound of running footsteps. We all exchanged a worried glance and shot to our feet, then headed out the door to see what the commotion was about.

The guards were all heading outside toward the front gates, where a large number of soldiers crowded together. Erroh pulled a female guard aside at the door, and asked, "What is this about?"

"They caught the criminal Varek trying to enter the palace!" she said.

My stomach dropped. Varek was the most notorious criminal in Soulspire, leader of a gang called the Quickblades. He was incredibly mysterious, and although the guard in Soulspire had been trying to capture him for years, he'd always eluded them. I'd never seen him before, only vague sketches from the few witnesses of his criminal activities. Witnesses who usually went missing later. Why was he here?

My mates and I pushed through the crowd to where the soldiers surrounded a tall man with long, black hair and muscular arms covered in tattoos. As soon as I laid eyes on him I jerked to a halt, my heart lurching.

He was the man in my dreams.

Jasin moved forward and leveled a sword at Varek's throat. "Explain your presence here quickly, before we slap you in chains and drag you to our prison."

Varek appeared unphased by this, and way too calm considering dozens of soldiers surrounded him. "I'm here to speak with *her*."

His head turned and when his eyes landed on me I sucked in a sharp breath. As our gazes met, I felt that spark, that connection, that *something* I had with the other men too.

There was no denying it. Varek was my fifth mate.

CHAPTER SIX

I pushed my way through the crowd toward Varek, vaguely aware of my other mates following behind me. Everyone's eyes were on me, until large silvery dragon wings blocked out the moonlight. People scrambled out of the way as my mother landed with a heavy thud, then bared her fangs at Varek.

"What business do you have with my daughter?" Kira roared.

Varek stared back at the dragon without fear, and then bowed, but not out of respect. He made it seem flippant or cocky somehow. "The Death Goddess sends her regards."

Mom let out a roar that would have most men quaking in their boots, but Varek just crossed his arms. Unbelievable.

As I moved beside my mother, my other fathers showed up too. They weren't in their dragon forms, but they were just as intimidating. "Explain yourself," Slade demanded.

Varek's eyes landed on me again. "The Dragon Goddess has named me her champion, and she demands Sora take me as her fifth mate."

A chorus of gasps went up from the soldiers and other onlookers, making me wish we'd gone somewhere private for this conversation.

"Impossible!" Auric said. "The Ascendant has only ever had four mates."

Varek lifted his shoulder in a casual shrug. "Not anymore."

"This is preposterous," Parin said behind me. "Send the man away."

"No," I finally said, my voice ringing out through the courtyard. "He speaks the truth. I've had dreams of him."

"What?" Erroh asked.

Mom shifted and shimmered back into her human form, her brow furrowed. "He is the one from your dreams?"

I nodded, swallowing hard. This dark, deadly, dangerous man was one of my mates. There was no escaping it, no matter how much I wanted to resist the idea. Yet as much as it horrified me, I was drawn to him too. I couldn't look away from his skull tattoos, or the wicked gleam in his eye, or the sensual curl of his lips.

"Prove it," Zain said, and Carth nodded in agreement.

"I don't think you'd like to see my powers in action," Varek said, his voice dripping with threat. "But perhaps a small demonstration is in order."

He bent down and ran his fingers through the grass, and a wave of death and decay spread out around him, instantly turning it brown and dry. The entire crowd gasped, and the hollowness inside me grew. There was no denying it now. The Death Goddess had given him her magic.

"You don't need him to gain your elemental powers or your dragon form," Reven told me. "You could refuse him."

Varek let out a cruel laugh. "If you refuse, the Death Goddess is prepared to unleash the Realm of the Dead upon the living."

"She wouldn't dare," Mom said.

"She would. She has been denied respect for far too long. Every other God has a Dragon, and she demands one as well."

Hushed mutters and whispers rippled among the crowd, until Jasin called out, "Silence!"

I stepped closer to Varek and faced him, keenly aware of the eyes upon us. "Do you even want to be my mate?"

"I'll serve the Goddess however she requires." His dark gaze turned hungry as it slowly roamed down my body. "Though I can't say it will be a hardship to mate with a princess."

"I'm not a princess," I snapped.

His only response was a harsh laugh. I hated him already, even as the look he gave me sent desire racing through my veins. It wasn't fair—the mating bond made me want him, no matter how awful he was.

"You have a week to accept this, or there will be a war between the living and the dead," Varek said. "Find me at the Lone Wolf Pub in the north end of Soulspire with your answer."

He turned on his heels and began to walk out the gate, but Jasin and Reven raised their swords. "Halt!" Jasin shouted.

Varek laughed. "What are you going to arrest me for? Coming to see my mate? I think not."

No one made a move against him, because he was right. No one would defy the Gods like that. As we all watched, he strolled out of the gate and disappeared into the night.

"I'll follow him," Reven said, before he slipped into the shadows. Having a former assassin as your father had its perks. Or it was going to make everything worse. I couldn't be sure yet.

"Leave us," Jasin commanded, and the guards departed and the crowd reluctantly dispersed.

As soon as they were gone, Mother rushed toward me and pulled me into her arms. I was too horrified and shocked to do anything but let her hold me.

"You're certain he's the one from your dreams?" Mom whispered with her head against mine.

I lifted my head away and nodded. "Yes. I'm sure of it."

"That doesn't mean you have to accept him," Kira said. "We will deal with the Death Goddess. We've done it before."

"I appreciate that, but we can't have a war against the dead," I said.

"I think you need to tell us about these dreams you've been having," Carth said.

I turned to face my mates, who did not look happy—not at all. Erroh was scowling, Parin had his arms crossed, Zain's jaw was clenched, and Carth's usual flirty smile was replaced with a frown.

"I've been having dreams of only one man every night—a man I'd never met until now. At first, I thought he was my Earth mate, but then Parin came and set that to rest."

"You never dreamed of us?" Zain asked.

"No, only of him. I can't deny it—he is my mate, just like the four of you are."

"It's completely out of the question," Jasin, said. "He's the most wanted criminal in Soulspire. The Silver Guard has been trying to dig up something concrete on that man and the Quickblades for years. Every time we get something, there never proves to be enough evidence to charge him, and no one will speak up against him. He cannot be your mate."

"Besides, *we* are your mates," Parin said with a note of finality in his voice. "There are always four, and four alone."

"Not anymore." I sighed. "Believe me, I don't like this any more than you do."

Erroh took my hand. "I'll support whatever you decide, but my vote is to throw him in the dungeon."

I pushed at his shoulder. "That's obviously not an option."

Slade met my eyes, his face filled with fatherly disapproval. "He's a villain, Sora. A criminal."

"Yes, but he seems to be telling the truth," Auric said. "And I don't see the other Gods stepping in to stop the Death Goddess in this matter."

"This is going to be a disaster," Carth muttered.

"Agreed," Zain said. "But we're with you Sora, whatever you decide."

I turned away, my head spinning. Whatever I decided wouldn't just affect me, but my other mates too—and possibly the entire world. We were meant to be guardians, protectors, mediators...could a champion of Death serve those roles too?

"I need to think on this some more," I said with a sigh. "I'll make a decision tomorrow."

Mom nodded. "Only you know the dreams and what they mean. If this is what you must do, so be it. If not, we will stand beside you against the Death Goddess."

I gave her a weak smile. "Thanks. I have a feeling I'll need your help either way."

Mom would support me no matter my decision, and could help me figure out how to navigate being mated to such a man. But my four fathers were another story. They were likely to band together and try to force Varek to leave the city. Or arrest him.

Or kill him.

I went back to my room alone and then paced back and forth as I went over what happened. It was too early to sleep, and my mind was too restless for that anyway. I had to figure out what to do about Varek or the anxiety would eat me up inside.

I couldn't refuse him. Somehow I knew that deep in my core. Not only because unleashing the dead upon the world was a horrible idea that would sacrifice many lives, but because when I looked at Varek I felt... something. The same connection I had with my other mates, even though I'd never met him before. I didn't want to feel it, but I did.

He was one of my mates and I had to accept that, no matter how much I disliked it.

But accepting it wouldn't make things easier. My other mates I had feelings for, and I knew they cared for me. I could envision sharing many years with them by my side, and knew that love would grow between us. Varek, on the other hand, I could only feel apprehension about. We had no love for each other. Could I ever grow to love the champion of Death? Would he care for me in return?

Pacing back and forth in my bedroom would do nothing to answer these questions. It was time to take action. I hadn't really gotten a chance to speak with Varek because I'd been surrounded by my mates, my parents, and an entire audience of guards and palace staff. I needed to talk to him alone. Tomorrow I planned to go to the Air Temple, and I didn't want to put that off unless I had to. Which meant facing Varek tonight.

I changed from my evening dress into my fighting leathers, strapped on all of my throwing knives, and put my wild curls up in a high bun, out of my way. Then I donned my black cloak and pulled the hood over my head, before grabbing my sword.

Once I was ready, I opened the large window by my desk and climbed onto the tree, then slipped down into the darkness. Reven had taught me everything about stealth, and I used those skills now to easily maneuver around the patrolling guards and head outside the palace grounds. I was allowed to leave the palace by myself whenever I wanted, since who would dare attack me? But in this matter, I wished to be discreet. I didn't want anyone to ask me questions or try to stop me. Or worse, get my fathers or my mates. They'd all want to send someone with me for protection, and I needed to do this on my own.

Our palace resided inside the great city of Soulspire, located at the center of the four Realms—one each for Fire, Earth, Air, and Water. Soulspire was neutral and not part of any one of them, ruled completely by the Dragons and the Silver Guard. The palace loomed over the city with its shining arches and tall tower in the center, where my parents lived. They told me that in their day the palace had been dark, run-down, and imposing, but now it gleamed like a beacon of peace and stability that all residents of Soulspire could look upon.

I made my way through the dark streets under the faint moonlight, past taverns and cafes bustling with people. Drunken couples stumbled by me, but no one gave me a second glance as I searched for the place Varek had mentioned. I passed a bar filled entirely with elementals, and nearly collided with a water elemental as it came out of the place. Luckily I moved away from its giant watery body in time before I got soaked. It mumbled that I should be more careful in the elemental language, probably assuming I wouldn't understand. Few humans did, but I'd learned it from Auric as a child.

Finally I turned onto a dimly lit street and saw an image of a wolf on a tavern sign. As I got closer, I made out the name *Lone Wolf Pub* above the door. The windows were darkened so I couldn't see anything inside. No music drifted from the black door. No one stumbled out drunk and laughing. Was the place empty? Or closed?

I wiped my damp palms on my trousers, then felt annoyed at myself. I was the daughter of Dragons. Varek was my mate. I had no reason to be nervous.

I opened the door and stepped inside.

CHAPTER SEVEN

T he inside of the bar was only lit by a few candles around the room,
illuminating dark wooden tables and chairs, plus a few booths with
red leather in the back. A large man with a long moustache wiped down
the bar from behind the counter while giving me an unfriendly look. The
few patrons inside all had a rough edge to them—tattoos, muscles, scowls
—and glared at me for daring to enter their pub. Not a friendly crowd.

"I see the princess has come to play," a female voice said to my side.

I turned toward the sound, where a striking woman with long black
hair and gray eyes sat in the corner with her legs crossed, revealing thigh-
high boots. Her sneer didn't do anything to make me feel like I should stick
around another minute.

My fists clenched at the word princess, but I stopped myself from
responding. "I'm looking for Varek."

"Of course you are." She rose to her feet and I spotted a large dagger
at her waist. "Follow me."

She took me to a door beside the counter, past the scowling bartender,
and led me down a dark hallway. We passed two doorways, only one of
which was open. As I peered inside, I was shocked to see an enormous
room, which must have been built into the hill behind the bar. This place
didn't look this big from the outside.

Dozens of people stood inside in a circle, surrounding two huge,
sweaty, shirtless men who circled each other while everyone else cheered.
One of their fists flew toward the other, but I didn't see the blow land
before the door slammed shut.

"That's not for you," the woman said.

"Was that an underground fight club?" I asked, unable to hide the shock in my voice. Such a thing was forbidden by the Silver Guard. Then again, Varek was a known criminal, so I shouldn't have been surprised.

She shrugged and headed around the corner. "Didn't see anything like that."

"Of course not," I muttered.

She stopped at another door and knocked sharply, then waited for the deep, "Come in," on the other side before she opened it.

Varek was inside, sitting behind a large black desk. He looked up and met my eyes, and that little spark between us made me suck in a sharp breath. Why did the man have to be so damn handsome?

"Oh." Varek looked down at the open notebook on his desk. "It's you."

"That's the welcome I get?" I asked, my blood boiling.

"Better than I got earlier." His eyes shifted to the other woman. "Thank you, Wrill."

Wrill gave him a quick nod, then stepped out and shut the door behind her, after throwing me another sneer.

"She seems lovely," I said.

"She's my sister."

"That explains it then."

He slammed his notebook shut. "You're bold to come walking through the front door of my pub. I thought you'd be a bit more discreet, princess."

"I'm not a princess, and why should I be discreet? If I take you as a mate, everyone in the four Realms will know."

He steepled his long fingers. "I will admit, I'm surprised you came to me so quickly. I thought you'd debate and dawdle for a few days, before finally realizing this is inevitable."

I huffed. "I don't dawdle."

A slow grin spread across his face. "I do like a woman of action."

Something about the way he said it made me flush. What was it about this man that had me so out of sorts? I steeled myself and said, "I've decided to take you as my mate."

"Obviously."

His arrogance only enraged me further. "On one condition."

He arched a dark eyebrow. "Oh?"

"You have to give up your criminal lifestyle."

He tilted his head back and let out a laugh that sounded a lot like a roar. Then he cut it off short and asked, "Anything else?"

"You'll need to move into the palace, of course."

He waved a dismissive hand. "Thanks for the offer, but I'll pass."

"Excuse me? If you are to be my mate, you'll have to give up..." I gestured vaguely to the room around me. "All this and join me at the palace."

"No, I really don't."

My jaw dropped, even though I wanted to remain cool and collected. Who would turn down living at the palace and becoming a Dragon? "What other choice do you have?"

He stood, giving me a good view of his strong arms covered in black ink. "I'll be your mate, don't you fear, but I'm not giving anything up. I'll remain here in the city, while you stay in the palace with your other men."

"Do you even want to be my mate?" I asked, completely flabbergasted.

His eyes narrowed. "The Death Goddess chose me and I will serve her however she commands."

"And she commanded you to be my mate, with everything that involves!" Gods, why was he so damn frustrating?

"Was that all you came for?" He picked up the notebook on his desk and put it on a bookshelf behind him, then turned back to me. "I was hoping you wanted to sample the goods."

"What? No! Why would you possibly think that?"

"Too bad. I made the bed and everything." His eyes moved to something behind me, and I followed his gaze to a bed large enough for two. When I'd entered the room, I'd had nothing but eyes for him, and now I saw that this office also served as a bedchamber, probably a temporary one.

I was suddenly extremely aware that I was alone in a room with a criminal and a bed. I'd eventually need to have sex with this man, but he would not be my first. I'd kill him before that happened, Death Goddess be damned. I was more than capable of doing that.

"Go back to your palace." He walked around the desk and slowly approached me. I held my ground, unwilling to give him an inch. "You may be the princess of this city, but I'm the king. One day, you'll bow to me too."

"Never."

He was so close now I could smell him. Leather, mixed with something faint and spicy. Something dangerous. Our eyes were locked together, and I found myself breathing faster, my heart pounding. Even worse, his body called to mine. Heat from his chest ran across my breasts, making my nipples harden under my leather top. I wanted him to touch me, while at the same time I wanted to push him away.

His head tilted down and he seemed to breathe me in, and for a second I thought he would press his lips to mine. I held my breath, waiting to see what he would do. But then he stepped back and turned away.

"Run home, little princess, before your watchdogs realize you're slumming it here with us criminals."

Unbelievable. "If you won't come to the palace, I don't see how we can be mates."

"I'm sure we'll figure something out." He sat behind his desk again and leaned back in his chair, crossing his tattooed arms behind his head. "Come back when you're ready to head to the Death Temple for our bonding."

I grit my teeth, but I had nothing more to say to this awful man. I turned and stomped toward the door, ready to be far away from him.

As soon I touched the knob, he said, "Wait."

I turned back and saw him stalking toward me, his long black hair flowing behind him, making my breath catch. "Yes?"

He brushed past me and opened the door. "I'll show you out the back."

I rolled my eyes and followed him down the hallway. "Why, don't want me to see more of your illegal activities?"

"I think you've seen enough for one night."

He opened a door at the far end and a cool rush of outdoor air flew inside, along with the sound of many voices. As I started forward, Varek threw a large, inked arm in front of me. "Stop."

"What is it?" I asked.

"Something you should stay away from."

"Why?" I craned my head, trying to see out. "What's happening out there?"

I pushed past him and he sighed and let me go. I stepped outside and saw a large crowd gathered around a person in a featureless black mask standing on a crate beside a statue of my mother in dragon form. Other people in gray masks stood around in support, staring out at the people gathered there.

The person on the crate raised a fist. "For too long, humans have been powerless, while the elementals and the Dragons use their magic to control the world. We all know this peace with the elementals won't last. There are reports every day of elementals and shades attacking human settlements in the outer reaches, and where are the Dragons? In their lofty tower, lording over us. We can't rely on them to protect us any longer. They've sided with the enemy. We need to defend ourselves and rise up against the oppressors. It's time to put humans first again!"

My jaw dropped as I stared at the leader, but then Varek grabbed my hood and yanked it down over my head. "It would be best if you weren't seen."

"Why? Trying to protect me from them?" I hadn't expected that from him.

He gave me a dark glare. "I don't want to lose my mate before claiming her."

I shook my head at him and moved forward, trying to get a better look. I'd never heard this kind of talk before. The Dragons were the protectors of the Four Realms. Their while purpose was to keep humans safe. Did these people truly believe they were doing such a bad job of it?

"We are the Unseen, but we will not be ignored any longer!" The speaker on the crate spread their arms, and flames burst forth from their fingertips. I gasped and actually stumbled back. That wasn't possible. I could count on one hand the number of people with fire magic, and none of them would be saying something like this. For a second I wondered if this was some kind of prank and it was Zain up there, or my father, but that didn't make any sense.

Fists went up in the air with the chant, "Humans first!" I gazed around, shocked by the vehemence in their voices and the anger on their faces, as much as the leader's fire display. Varek grabbed my arm as the crowd started throwing bottles and rocks at the statue of Kira. He had to drag me out of there, and I was too stunned and horrified to do anything but go along with him.

"That was a trick, right? That person didn't really use magic?" I asked, as we turned a corner and went out of view of the crowd. I could still hear them in the distance, along with the sound of another bottle smashing. I cringed as I stumbled forward. "Do they really believe all that?"

Varek didn't answer me, but kept leading me down alleys and dark streets I'd never visited before, until the gates of the palace came into view. Only then did he stop.

He released the grip on my arm, and I absently rubbed the spot where his hand had been. I looked up at him, realizing that he'd gotten me out of a dangerous situation and escorted me home. Maybe he wasn't as bad as I'd thought.

"You know where to find me," he said. "Try to be a little less obvious next time."

My eyes narrowed. "I don't need to hide or sneak around. I'm the Ascendant."

His laugh mocked me. "Did you learn nothing from that rally? The streets of Soulspire are no longer safe for you."

I could only gape at him as he slipped back into the shadows and left me alone with my dark thoughts.

The guards didn't react as I walked through the gates. Nor did the guards at the door, or the two I passed going up the stairs to my wing of the palace.

When I walked into my chambers, though, my mates blinked several times at me. "Where have you been?" Erroh asked. "We thought you were in bed."

They sat around the living area, drinking what looked like ale. I shrugged off my cloak. "I couldn't sleep, so I went to talk to Varek."

"What?" Zain asked. "Why would you do that alone?"

I strode forward and took Erroh's drink from his hand, gulping it down. I needed it, after what I'd just been through. "To take him as my mate, of course."

"I thought you were going to make your decision in the morning," Parin said.

"I didn't want to delay our trip to the Air Temple, and besides, there was no real decision to make. I have to take him as my mate. Unleashing the Death Goddess upon the world is not an option."

"But—" Erroh started.

I held up a hand. "It's not just that. I feel it. The mate-bond. Just like I feel it with all of you. There's no denying the Gods' will. I have to do this."

The men glanced at each other with wary expressions, before Carth finally cracked a grin and said, "Well, the more the merrier, in my opinion. I'm just eager to get started."

"Is Varek even willing to be your mate?" Zain asked.

"He's going to be difficult," I said with a sigh. "He doesn't want to leave the Quickblades or move into the palace. But there's something else I need to tell you."

"What is it?" Parin asked.

"When I left Varek's pub, I encountered a crowd with all these people wearing gray masks that covered their entire faces. Their leader stood on a crate and gave a speech about how humans were oppressed by the elementals and the Dragons and it was time to put humans first again."

"Oh." Erroh nodded his head. "I've heard of them. The Unseen. They used to be a small human rights group, very anti-elemental, but otherwise harmless. They've recently been growing in numbers in Soulspire though and have become something more like a cult, so Jasin's had some of the Silver Guard keeping an eye on them."

"I didn't see any Silver Guard tonight when they were throwing things at the statue of my mother," I said, clenching my fists at the memory.

"They did that?" Zain asked.

"Yes, and there's more too." I sank into the only empty chair. The room had been designed to hold five of us comfortably. We'd have to rethink it if Varek joined us. "I saw the leader controlling fire."

Zain shook his head. "Not possible. Only Kira, Jasin, and I can control fire, along with the High Priestess of the Fire Temple. I strongly doubt any of them would be doing such a thing."

"He's right," Parin said. "Humans have never been able to control the elements. The Gods do not favor them that way."

"It could've been a trick," Erroh suggested. "They could've contrived something to make the crowd think they had magic to get a reaction from them."

"That's what I thought too, but it seemed so…real," I said.

"It can't be real." Zain reached over and stroked my arm. "I'm sure the rally was upsetting to witness, but you must put it from your mind and focus on what is important—bonding with us so that you can become a Dragon."

"He's right," Carth said. "Tomorrow you'll start going to the temples and we'll put all this from your mind."

I nodded slowly. Between Varek and the demonstration, my stomach was all twisted up in knots. We had to leave first thing in the morning, and me brooding over Varek or the human wielding fire wouldn't help me bond with my mates.

I said good night to my men and retreated to my bed alone, but no matter how I tried, I couldn't get what I'd seen off my mind. Sleep was a long time coming.

CHAPTER EIGHT

After some debate, we decided it would be faster and easier if only Erroh and I went to the Air Temple while everyone else stayed behind. There was nothing in the books that said all my mates had to be there for the bonding, after all. Additionally, the Air Temple was to the east, while the Water Temple—our next destination—was to the west, so we'd have to come back to Soulspire anyway. My other mates weren't thrilled about it, but the journey would take Auric, the fastest of the Dragons, a full day of flying as it was. He'd volunteered to take me, as the Air Dragon, and none of my other fathers had argued. Slade seemed relieved he wouldn't have to go, actually.

Just after dawn, we stood out in the courtyard with Auric already in his dragon form, his golden scales gleaming bright under the morning sunlight. I held up a hand to cover a yawn, wishing I'd managed more sleep last night. Or any night since my Ascension.

I was quickly saying goodbye to my other parents and my mates, while Erroh said farewell to his own family. Cadock and Faya took turns hugging him, then stepped back beside Parin.

Faya smiled at them both. "It's so incredible and…surprising that the Gods chose each of you for Sora's mates."

"Yes, it was a shock when we were both chosen." Parin cleared his throat and turned to his brother. "Good luck at the Air Temple."

"I'm not sure we need luck, but thanks," Erroh said, with a slight frown.

"We're very proud of you two," Cadock said, clasping a hand on both of his sons' shoulders. Although Parin was technically his adopted son, Cadock had never treated him any differently from his other children.

I turned away from them and hugged Carth next. "Enjoy yourself," he whispered, then pressed a kiss to my neck.

"Are you sure we can't come with you?" Zain asked. "Although I grew up in the Fire Temple, I've never visited the others."

Kira shook her head. "I'm sorry, but I need Sora's other fathers' help. We received reports this morning that the elementals on Divine Isle are demanding more land in the four Realms, and we need to travel there to speak with them before any fighting breaks out. Especially with the rumors of elementals going missing fueling their anger."

"Besides, none of us want to be there when *it* happens," Jasin said, wrinkling his nose.

Reven rolled his eyes. "Sora's a grown woman now. We knew this would happen."

"Doesn't mean we have to like it," Slade muttered.

"She'll be fine," Mom said, shaking her head with an amused smile.

I wanted nothing more than to escape this awkward moment where everyone was talking about me having sex without actually saying it out loud. Thank the Gods all of my parents weren't coming. Having one at the temple would be bad enough.

"Let's go," I said, taking Erroh's hand and practically dragging him toward Auric. We climbed onto my father's hard, scaly back, and then waved at everyone and shouted our goodbyes, as Auric lifted up into the air with a flap of his great golden wings.

Flying was my favorite thing in the world. My fathers always loved taking me for rides, soaring high above the city with the sunshine soaking into our skin. As a kid, they took me all over the four Realms with them, even to the elementals' Divine Isle, and I was completely comfortable riding on a dragon for long hours. But whereas I grew up with dragon-riding as my main form of transportation, Erroh and my other mates had not.

Erroh was probably the only one who had ever ridden a dragon before, actually. As kids, we'd sometimes gotten a quick ride from one of my dads, but it had been many years since then.

Erroh seemed to remember though. He wrapped his arms around me and let out a loud whoop as we ascended high into the sky and zoomed over Soulspire. His joy was contagious, and I found myself grinning as the wind buffeted my face and tugged at my tied-back hair. His arms squeezed me tight, and I leaned back against him. If it wasn't for the fact that we were sitting on top of Auric, I would've found the experience of finally being able to rest in his arms very alluring.

Since Soulspire was located at the cross point of all four Realms, we entered the Air Realm immediately and soared over forests that changed to rolling hills and then to sharp mountains. We stopped briefly for lunch on a rocky cliff, and while we munched on packed bread, meat, and cheese, Auric told us about what it was like when he traveled to the Air Temple to bond with my mother, from riding on camels to finding the temple destroyed and the priests killed to fighting two of the previous Dragons in the air. I'd heard the story many times before, of course, but Erroh hung onto every word. Then we set off again, flying over the barren desert of Sandstorm Valley while the relentless sun beat down on us.

A few hours later, after the sun had set, the Air Temple came into view —a large sand-colored tower that reached high into the clouds, surrounded by a small lake with palm trees. It was the only thing in sight for miles amid the endless, empty desert. During my parents' rule, the Air Temple had been rebuilt and a new High Priestess had been chosen. I'd been there a few times with my parents, but things were different now that I was coming here with a new purpose.

"Is that where we'll meet the Air God?" Erroh asked, shielding his eyes to peer at the temple's grounds.

"No, it will be on the roof," Auric's dragon voice rumbled.

After we bonded and I gained Erroh's powers, the Air God would come and speak to us. For my parents, they'd answered a few questions and gave some cryptic information, but I had no idea what they would say to me.

Auric landed in front of the Air Temple and kicked up some sand with his wings. High Priestess Blair, a dark-skinned woman in her fifties with gray-streaked black hair, approached us with a kind smile. She wore a loose yellow robe with bare shoulders, while her mates trailed behind her. Like me and my mom, the High Priestesses each got four mates to serve as their priests.

"Welcome Sora," Blair said, clasping my hands in her own. "We are honored to be the first temple in your travels." Then she turned toward Erroh and also took his hands. "And a fond greeting to our next Air Dragon."

"Thank you," Erroh said, as he glanced at the priests watching on. He had to be as overwhelmed as I was, but he was doing a good job of hiding it so far. "I'm very lucky to have been chosen."

"It's good to see you again," Auric said to Blair.

"Always an honor, Air Dragon," she said with a bow.

Auric waved a hand. "You know you don't need to do that. I had enough bowing when I was a prince."

"Of course. Please, come inside," Blair said. "We've prepared everything for your bonding. Would you like a meal or a bath first?"

Although I was quite dusty and hadn't eaten since lunch, I had no desire for either of those things. I'd waited for this moment for years and all I wanted was to get on with it, but I also didn't want to seem too eager in front of my father. "A meal would be lovely, thanks."

Blair and her mates led us into a large dining room, with big windows open to the cool night breeze floating inside. We shared a quick meal that lasted longer than I hoped, during which Blair asked Erroh about himself. I suppose it was important for the High Priestess to get to know her next Dragon, but I couldn't wait to be finished. Judging by the way Erroh's hand moved to my leg under the table and began stroking my thigh, I knew he felt the same.

When dinner finally ended, Auric kissed my forehead and gave me a warm smile. "I'm happy the Air God chose Erroh. He is a good man and I know he will treat you well."

"Me too." Somehow Dad knew exactly what to say to make me feel better about all this.

"You know, I was a virgin too when I came here and—"

I quickly held up a hand and tried not to gag. "Please stop right there."

Dad gave me a goofy grin. "All right. I just want you to know everything will be fine."

He gave me a warm hug, and then shook Erroh's hand, before going with the priests into the library, his favorite place.

Blair led us up a never ending spiral staircase, and even though Erroh and I were both in great shape, by the time we reached the top, we were both out of breath and needed a second to recover. Flying up here would have been so much easier.

It was worth it though once we stepped through the doorway onto the open-air platform at the top of the temple. Most of the clouds had disappeared, and from here all I could see was endless night sky, sparkling stars, and the thin sliver of the crescent moon. Oh, and the large bed waiting for us.

"Please let me know if you need anything else," Blair said, before bowing and then heading back down the stairs.

Erroh met my eyes. "Finally, we're alone."

CHAPTER NINE

I looked down at myself, suddenly nervous. I'd packed a light bag with a change of clothes and a silky tunic that would be more appropriate than my traveling clothes, but hadn't changed into them yet. I'd expected to have more time to prepare somehow.

I sucked in a sharp breath. "I'm dusty."

Erroh chuckled. "I can fix that."

With the sweep of his hand, a breeze swirled around me and sent the dust flying. It also undid my bun, loosening my hair, and we both laughed as my curls went wild.

He moved close and tried to smooth my hair down with a grin. "Sorry! I'm still learning."

I pressed my hands to his cheeks. There was no reason for me to be nervous, not when I was here with my best friend. "You're perfect."

With his hands still tangled in my hair, we moved together for a kiss. It started out sweet, but quickly turned deeper, as the magnitude of the moment settled upon us. After so many years wishing we could be together but fearing it was impossible, tonight we would finally be bound together as mates.

Erroh broke off the kiss to lead me to the large bed, where he began unlacing his shirt, then shrugged it off as I stared in amazement at his sculpted chest. I'd seen him shirtless before, and it had been like looking upon a dessert I wasn't allowed to eat.

Tonight I could devour him.

I began removing my own shirt as Erroh watched, and his eyes flew straight to my hands as they moved down my chest. The weight of his gaze excited me and made me want to keep going. When my shirt was completely undone, I left it on so it gaped in the front without exposing my breasts.

We both pulled off our boots next, and when I bent down, my breasts spilled out of my shirt. When I rose, the shirt slid off my shoulders to the floor behind me, leaving me exposed. Erroh's sharp breath told me he liked the sight. I'd never been naked in front of a man before, but I wasn't shy either, and the look on Erroh's face encouraged me to keep going.

He put his thumbs in the waistband of his pants and tugged down. I mimicked him, both of us kicking off our trousers simultaneously. And there it was. My first glimpse of the completely naked male form. I'd seen men fighting, sparring, swimming, but never this part of them.

His hard cock pointed at me as if it knew the direction it wanted him to move, and he stepped close, sliding his arms around my waist. I had to touch him too. I couldn't help myself. Lifting my hands, I placed one on his hard chest and the other on his neck as I stared at his lips, willing him to take the lead. His calloused hands slid down my hips while he pressed his lips to mine, and I gasped against him as his tongue pushed into my mouth. My body acted of its own accord, arching toward him, eager for his naked body to press against mine.

"Erroh," I breathed when he stopped kissing me to trail his lips down my neck.

"I'm sure you know this, but I've never done this before. Have you?"

He paused and then looked up at me. "Only a few times. When you made it clear we couldn't be together, I tried to use other women to forget you, but it never helped, not one bit. The only woman I've ever wanted is you."

My cheeks flushed at that, and he pulled me back against him and resumed his exploration of my body with his tongue. I ran my hands down his body, then lost myself for a moment as his lips closed around my nipple. Sensations I'd never experienced before shot through my body, right to my core, and I sensed I was growing wet. His hands on my naked skin only increased my desire, as did the feel of his hard body under my fingertips. Years of looking but not touching had finally ended in this moment, and I couldn't get enough.

Neither could Erroh. He sucked on each of my breasts while stroking my body slowly, then we floated together toward the big bed. He set me down upon it, then spread my legs wide as he hovered over me. I thought it would happen, his cock finally breaching me, but then his head dropped.

He grinned up at me. "I want to make sure you're nice and ready for me so there's no pain. Don't worry, I read all about this in a book."

It was such an Erroh thing to say that I laughed, but the sound quickly died in my throat as his mouth pressed to the aching spot between my legs. Pleasure like I'd never experienced before spread through me as his tongue danced along my folds and his fingers slid inside me, and then he did things that had me moaning so loud, I briefly worried the people in the temple might be able to hear us. I didn't much care though, especially when he sucked on me in a way that caused an orgasm to sweep through me like a tornado.

As my body twitched with warm pleasure, he slowly moved up my body, until he hovered over me. His eyes gazed into mine as his cock brushed against my thigh. "Are you ready?"

"Gods, yes," I managed, reaching up to wrap my arms around his neck.

"I love you, Sora. I always have."

"I love you too."

He captured my lips in a passionate kiss as his hard length slowly pushed inside me. The pressure was intense and I gasped, but then he paused and waited for me to adjust to his size. I had nothing to compare it to, but he felt huge inside me, and I wasn't sure how he would ever fit. But he took his time until he was all the way inside, filling me completely.

"Sora, this is incredible," Erroh said, pressing his face against my shoulder. "I dreamed of this moment for so long, and it's even better than I expected."

I wasn't so sure, until he began to slowly slide in and out of me, and then things quickly turned pleasurable again. Soon my body took over, instinctively knowing how to move in time with his body so that we rocked together, taking us to new heights. I dug my nails into his shoulders as he thrust inside me faster, and all I could do was moan and hold on to him as the pleasure built. He slipped one hand between us and began stroking me in time with his movements, and I threw my head back as another climax took hold of me. He let out a shout as he increased his pace and came at the same time, spilling his seed inside me.

As he did, a huge gust of wind swept around us, then lifted us into the air. Even knowing something about what to expect, it made me gasp and cling harder to Erroh. The air swirled around our entwined bodies and we flew high up among the stars, the cool night breeze kissing our naked skin. Power spread through me like crackling lightning, but Erroh only held me tighter, until we slowly floated back down to the bed.

The wind disappeared as quickly as it started, and Erroh and I gazed into each other's eyes. "Nothing has ever felt so right as this moment," he said.

I reached up to play with his dark hair. "We're mates now, for all time. Bonded together for the rest of our lives."

"It's about damn time." He grinned and lowered his head for another kiss.

We stayed on the bed like that for some time, just kissing and lazily exploring each other's bodies, before I remembered there was more to this bonding ritual. We reluctantly put our clothes back on, with plans to take them off again soon and return to bed, then made our way to the edge of the platform. Erroh glanced at me and squeezed my hand, with eager eyes and a nervous smile. This was where the Air God had appeared to my parents, and we held our breath while we waited for him to arrive.

And we waited.

And we waited.

And the Air God never came.

CHAPTER TEN

We had sex two more times that night, just in case that was the problem, but the Air God still never appeared to give us his blessing. Eventually we slept, tangled in each other's arms and legs, with sated smiles on our faces.

As dawn's bright light woke us, we made love again, just for good measure, but then we grew worried.

"This isn't normal," I said. "Not from everything I've been told. The Air God should have spoken to us."

"Can you use air magic?" Erroh asked.

"I don't know." I reached out a hand toward the bed, and to my surprise, the sheets began to moved a little. "Yes, I think so!"

"That's good. The bonding worked then."

"Can you turn into a dragon?"

"I'm not really sure how, but I can try." Erroh's brows furrowed in concentration, but then golden scales began to slide across his skin. His body grew larger, shifting and changing, until he grew wings and a long tail, along with sharp fangs and talons. He let out a roar and stomped his feet, swishing his tail around, and then gave me what I think was a toothy grin. "That was incredible!"

I laughed and rested a hand on his golden snout. "I guess the Air God isn't coming, but he gave us both his blessing anyway. I'll have to ask Auric what he thinks on our way home."

"Hopefully the Air God doesn't regret his choice," Erroh said, in his rasping dragon voice.

"Of course he doesn't. If he did, you wouldn't be a dragon right now. Let me see your wings." He spread them wide, and I walked around him and stroked the scales. "Very nice. I can't wait to ride you."

He snorted. "I thought you just did that."

I rolled my eyes. "You'll probably need to practice flying, but maybe not. Auric got the hang of it instantly, while Jasin and Slade needed more practice. Either way, soon I'll be able to fly beside you."

"Get on," he said. "I want to see what it feels like."

"I'm naked!"

"After what we just did, I don't think that matters."

With a laugh, I climbed up and settled myself on his back, his hard scales pressing into my core. He walked across the platform, spreading his wings, and I enjoyed the feel of his muscles moving under my legs and excitable areas. Then I climbed off, and he shifted back into his human form. I could tell he wanted to try flying, but probably not from this great height.

Once we dressed, we headed back down the tower, where we met my dad outside the library. "How did it go?" he asked.

Erroh and I exchanged a worried glance. "Um…" I started.

Auric's face fell. "Oh no. Was it awkward? I know first times can be difficult but—"

"No! It's not that!" I said, my face turning red.

Erroh rubbed the back of his neck. "All of that was fine. Really good actually."

I had to quickly get us back on track before this became more awkward. "The Air God never visited us."

Auric's jaw dropped. "What?"

We quickly explained what happened, minus all the naughty parts, and confirmed the bonding worked. Dad said he'd never read about anything like that occurring before. We asked Blair and the priests about it, but they were just as surprised as we were, although they'd also not spoken to the God for some time either. That was pretty normal though—they often only appeared to choose a new High Priestess and after the Ascension bonding.

After a quick breakfast we set off for Soulspire, with Auric promising to show Erroh how to fly later and to give me some rudimentary air magic lessons. As we flew, it was hard not to feel disappointment though. I'd expected to meet a God, and he'd never arrived. Was I not worthy of his time? Or did this have something to do with the Death Goddess and my fifth mate? Hopefully once I bonded with Carth at the Water Temple we'd gain more insight into the matter.

When we arrived home that night I hoped to be able to speak with my mother, but she and my other dads had already left for Divine Isle to meet with the elementals, and there was a note requesting Auric join them the next day. My other mates grilled Erroh for details, but I was exhausted and wanted nothing more than to collapse in my bed.

Finally, I got a good night's sleep.

In the morning, I was excited to get to work. When I got outside, I found Auric and Erroh already in a nearby field in their dragon forms, and I watched from afar as my father taught my mate how to fly up into the air. Erroh caught on quickly, like he was born to be a dragon, and I laughed as he started doing flips in the sky. I laughed even harder when he crashed right into Auric, making them both fall a little, until their wings caught them.

They shifted back to human form as I approached. "That was fun to watch," I said.

"I got a little carried away there," Erroh said. "Sorry."

"It's fine." Auric smiled at us both. "I still remember how thrilling it was to be a dragon at first. Sora, I'd hoped to begin your air training today, but unfortunately Kira wishes me to visit Divine Isle to speak with the elementals. I'm sure Erroh can give you some tips though, and I can help you both some more when I return."

"I'd like that." I said, giving him a hug.

Soon he was flying across the sky as a dragon again, and Erroh started showing me a few of the things Auric had taught him. While we were training, my other mates joined us to practice their own magic. It was so easy being around them, joking and laughing as we'd done our entire lives, with the exception of Parin. He stood a little apart from us, solemn and stiff, like he wasn't sure he belonged there. I wasn't entirely sure either, although my pulse quickened when I looked at his handsome face.

Afterward, we all headed into the city to share a drink at a pub, although not Varek's one, of course. We stayed on the other side of the city entirely, though I distantly wondered if I should have invited him. No, he'd been clear he wanted nothing to do with this part of being my mate.

"To Erroh and Sora!" Carth said, as he raised his tankard of ale with a wink. "And to getting that over with, so we can head to the Water Temple tomorrow!"

We all raised our glasses and laughed, before chugging our ale down. Then Erroh wrapped an arm around my shoulders. "We had a pretty incredible night. Are you sure you want to follow that?"

Carth smirked. "I'm sure I can manage to top whatever you did."

Parin held up a hand, his face serious. "Wait. Have you noticed it's cleared out in here?"

I set down my ale and glanced around the tavern. Parin was right—when we'd entered, the place had been packed, but now only a few people in hoods sat at various spots around the room. The bartender and serving staff were gone too.

Then the people in hoods all stood and turned toward us, wearing those same blank gray masks as the protestors the other night.

I hastily pushed my chair back and stood. "We have company."

There were about twelve of them, and they didn't have any weapons. Then again, we'd left most of ours behind too. But we had magic.

"We are the Unseen, and we reject the rule of the Dragons," one of them said, wearing a black mask. Then she—I think it was a she, anyway—opened her hand and shot a ball of fire at us. We jumped out of the way, hitting the dirty, sticky floor as the flames engulfed the table where we'd been sitting. I could only gape at it, and at the person who must be their leader.

"Believe me now?" I asked the guys, as we all scrambled to our feet and summoned our elemental powers. Carth dumped a bucketful of water on the table, dousing the flames, just as the woman sent another burst of fire at us. This time Zain managed to gain control of it and throw it back at her, but then one of the other masked people used water to stop it.

That meant more of them had powers. Maybe *all* of them. How?

I didn't have time to find out, not when the elemental attacks came quickly. Floorboards ripped up and flew toward us in sharp, pointed stakes. Chairs and tables were blown into us, along with tankards and other glasses. Shards of ice shot toward us, along with balls of fire. The attack came from all sides, and we were totally surrounded and outnumbered.

"Shift into a dragon!" Zain called to Erroh, as he melted a shard of ice midair.

Erroh used his air magic to toss a chair out of the way. "I can't—there's not enough room in here!"

I tried to use my air magic to blast someone back, but I only made a light breeze. Damn, I needed more practice. Instead, I kicked one of the Unseen in the chest, then knocked them out with a quick move Reven taught me. One down. Many to go.

It was a good reminder that I didn't need elemental magic or weapons to take people down. I'd been trained by the best, after all. I moved through the pub room, using my combat and parkour skills to avoid attacks and knock the attackers down, while my mates handled the magic flying all around us.

Suddenly the tavern door burst open, and Varek stood in the doorway. He grabbed the nearest cultist by the throat and the life drained out of the screaming man, turning his skin black.

"Leave this place, or death will find you too," his voice boomed out, making everyone pause. I couldn't help but stare at him too. Darkness surrounded Varek like a cloak, and he looked absolutely terrifying.

And devastatingly handsome.

He wore a shirt that showed off his muscular, inked arms, and with his hands clenched he stalked forward toward another cultist. The masked person stepped back quickly, but they were too slow, and Varek grabbed them next. As death took the cultist, the other Unseen all stumbled and tripped and forced their way out of the building. By the time the cultist's body hit the ground, the tavern was empty of everyone except us, along with the people we'd already taken down.

Varek ripped the mask off the dead cultist and tossed it aside, then shook his head in disgust.

"What did you do?" I asked. "You killed those people!"

"I'm not the only one." He gestured at some other cultists we'd taken out in the battle.

I set my hands on my hips. "That was self-defense. And many of them are unconscious, not dead. You didn't have to kill them!"

"I was defending you," he snapped. "I'm the champion of Death. This is my way."

"I didn't need defending!"

"How did you know we were here?" Parin asked, as he stepped over a broken chair to approach us.

"I heard there would be an attack from my informants." Varek shot me an arrogant look. "Aren't you glad I have a criminal organization now?"

"We had it under control," I snapped.

"I'm not so sure about that." Erroh glanced down at his arm and winced at the burn there.

"You were right about the human with fire powers," Zain said. "We shouldn't have dismissed your concerns. It was just hard to believe without seeing it with my own eyes."

"And they had not only fire, but all the elements," Parin added.

"The Unseen are getting elemental magic somehow." I moved across the room and took Erroh's arm in my hands, then let out some of my healing life magic. The burn vanished and the skin repaired itself in seconds. "We need to find out how."

"We *need* to head to the Water Temple," Carth said, his voice serious for once. "We were outnumbered today. We need to finish bonding with Sora so we're all at full strength for the next attack."

I wished my parents were in Soulspire so I could talk to them about what happened tonight. With them gone, it was even more reason to become dragons quickly so we could defend ourselves and the city. Mother had told me not to rush, but what other choice did I have?

I sighed. "We'll leave first thing in the morning, though it might take longer without a ride from one of my dads."

"I'll fly you," Erroh said. "I just need a good night's rest first."

"I'll see what my people can learn about the Unseen and how they're getting magic," Varek said.

I bit my lip, but then forced out, "Thank you."

Varek moved close and looked down at me with smoldering intensity. My breath caught when it seemed as though he might kiss me, and try as I might to ignore the attraction between us, I couldn't. His very presence tugged at me and made me want to step into his arms and embrace his darkness.

"Try not to get killed before our bonding," he growled, and all the desire vanished.

Or so I told myself.

CHAPTER ELEVEN

I n the morning, Carth's parents met us outside before our departure. Brin was a nobleman from the Air Realm who'd disobeyed her parents' wishes and married Leni, Slade's younger sister. Since they couldn't have children of their own, they'd adopted Carth and his older sister, who was back at their estates.

Brin stroked Carth's sandy hair with pride and love in her eyes. "We're so proud of you, son. But couldn't you have been chosen by the Air God instead?"

Leni laughed and nudged her wife. "Carth was born in the Water Realm. It's in his very soul, even if we raised him in the Air Realm. Just like my heart will always belong to the Earth Realm."

"I know, I'm only teasing," Brin said. "I think you'll make an excellent Water Dragon."

"Thanks, Moms." Carth gave her a hug, and then did the same with Leni.

"Now you take good care of my niece," Leni said, pinching Carth's cheeks.

"I'll do my best." He winked at me.

Leni gave me a warm hug next. "Do try to keep him in line, dear. I know it won't be easy."

I laughed. Brin and Leni were my favorite relatives by far. "I'm not sure anyone can do that."

"We have faith in you," Brin said, as she took Leni's hand. "Now get going, I want to see Carth as a dragon already."

With those words, we said our goodbyes and climbed onto Erroh, then took off.

The Water Temple was the second farthest one away from Soulspire, and Erroh had only had a few hours of flying practice. Lucky for us, he was a natural at flying, which was probably normal for an Air Dragon, but he still wasn't used to going long distances. It didn't help that the Water Realm was mostly made up of hundreds of islands, so we couldn't exactly travel the distance by foot either.

I rode Erroh with Carth's arms wrapped around me. This experience was far different than when I rode on my fathers' backs. The feel of the powerful dragon moving under me and Carth's arms around me were powerful aphrodisiacs, and I was eager to get to the temple.

At midday, we stopped in a fishing village for lunch, and were able to board a small boat to give Erroh a few hours to rest. He passed out in the back of the boat with a blanket over his head to shield him from the sun. Then at sunset the boat docked, and we continued flying again until we found another island with an inn to rest in for the night.

We finally reached the island near the Water Temple by the next after-noon. Erroh's taloned feet crashed down on the sand, and he swung his large head around. "Are you sure this is the right place?"

I folded up the map and slid off his back. "Yes, this is it."

Neither one of them had been to the Water Temple before, but I'd visited a few times with my dads. The island we stood on had one lone palm tree and was about the size of my bedroom in the palace. Nothing about it indicated the Water Temple was below. Originally there had been another Water Temple, but after it was destroyed the High Priestess and her mates moved to this secret one. When the danger had passed, they simply decided to stay.

Carth jumped off of Erroh and peered into the water. "It's under there? How will we get down there without drowning?"

"With our magic, of course," I said with a laugh. "Erroh and I can wrap a bubble of air around ourselves, and you can keep the water away from you." Both guys looked skeptical, and I rolled my eyes. "Trust me, I've done it before. Well, I've seen it done, anyway. How hard can it be?"

"I'm not sure I want to find out while at the bottom of the ocean," Erroh said, after shifting to his human form.

"We can practice up here first." I slipped off my shoes, rolled up my trousers to my knees, and waded into the ocean. The two guys slowly followed me.

It took a lot more practice than we expected, but hours later we were continuing our journey underwater toward the Water Temple. Erroh was back in dragon form, and together we kept a bubble of air around us, keeping us dry and allowing us to breath, while Carth used water to propel us forward. We dove down into the clear blue waters, passing a few fish, and then Erroh paused at the sharp drop into the darker depths. I felt the same hesitation—if our magic failed, we would all drown—but then I stroked his shoulder and said, "We can do this."

He used his wings to dive down into the darkness, and although I expected this, it was still terrifying to be in the middle of the ocean unable to see anything, not knowing which way was up anymore. But then a light came into view, and we began to make out the beautiful, pale building of the Water Temple at the bottom of the ocean.

I directed Erroh on where to land, and we stopped on the ocean floor beside a large dragon sculpture before walking into the large dome of air that surrounded the temple. My skin tingled as we passed through, and then we dropped our air bubble. The Water God protected the temple so it's priests could live there safely.

A small woman with black hair and olive skin emerged from the stone door of the temple, wearing a sea-green robe. Wella was only ten years older than I was and had recently taken over from her mother as High Priestess. Now her stomach was round with her pregnancy, and she waddled out to us with a warm smile. Her four handsome priests followed after her, some of them looking on with concern.

"Welcome!" she said, and then gathered me in a friendly hug. "We weren't sure when to expect you, but we're so happy you're here now."

"Thank you. It looks like we came at a good time." I gestured at her round stomach. "When are you due?"

"Any day now," she said with a laugh. "Don't worry, we've prepared everything for you. Mostly my priests, since they won't let me do anything these days."

I laughed and gestured at my mates. "This is Erroh, my Air Dragon, and Carth, who will be my Water Dragon."

Carth stepped forward and took Wella's hands in his own and gave them a light kiss. "You look radiant. Your husbands are very lucky."

Wella blushed in a cute way. "An honor to meet you. Please come inside."

We followed Wella and her priests into the great temple, walking over shiny sea green tiles through sand-colored rooms. She showed us to our rooms for the evening, where we quickly freshened up, and then we all shared a quick meal together. Wella and I did most of the talking, catching up on how she's been and how her mother is doing in retirement. Then Erroh went to his room to collapse in exhaustion, and Wella led Carth and me to the bonding room.

My heart beat quickened as the door opened. Flickering candlelight revealed a raised platform in the middle of the room with a large bed on it, similar to the one at the Air Temple. However, this platform was surrounded by a pool of knee-deep water, with shiny seashells along the floor. On the other side of the bed there was an entire wall missing, opening the room to the ocean, although the dome of air kept us safe. I'd never been in this room before, and at first all I could do was stare in awe at the fish swimming just out of our reach.

Wella shut the door, leaving me with Carth. He gave me one of his flirty grins and offered his hand. "Alone at last."

I slid my hand into his much larger one, entwining our fingers together as we stepped forward along the raised path to the bed. Now that I knew something of what to expect during my bonding, it was hard not to rush forward.

"I've wanted to do this for a long time," Carth said, as we reached the bed. I'd changed from my traveling clothes into a long, silken dress in dark blue, and he took his time letting his gaze move down my curves. "You're gorgeous. I could look upon you for hours. Days. Years. And never grow tired."

"You're such a charmer." I stepped closer to him. "But is there anything real behind that flirtatious smile?"

He pressed a hand to his chest. "You wound me. I have never told you a lie."

"No, but I'm not the only one you flirt with, and I know you've shared a bed with many ladies before me."

"Only to practice for this moment." He slid his arms around my waist. "From now on the one bed I'll be sharing is yours."

Our lips met and his tongue danced inside mine, while his fingers slid across my breasts, making my nipples instantly hard. With a groan, he tugged the dress up and over my head, revealing my naked skin. I wore nothing underneath in anticipation of this moment, and was rewarded with a guttural sound in his throat as he looked at me.

"Get in the pool," he said, while he began removing his own shirt. "We'll save the bed for later."

While watching him undress, I walked over and put my toes in the pool beside the bed. It was just deep enough for me to sit down in, and as soon as Carth had his pants unlaced, I dropped down into it.

"It's so much warmer than I expected," I said as I sank into the pool.

Carth sat on the platform beside me and put his feet in the water. He was fully naked now, and I admired the body that so many women had coveted before me. Sculpted muscle, but different from Erroh's somehow. While Erroh had a soldier's body, Carth was leaner, his body developed from years of swimming, with the tan skin and sandy hair to match. The large cock jutting up between his legs was also quite impressive.

The water suddenly leaped up and washed over my shoulders, while Carth gave me a wry grin. His eyes roamed over my body, and wherever he looked, water rushed over me. It spent a lot of time on my breasts, and I couldn't help but moan as the water tickled, then squeezed, then ran in circles around my nipples. Even without touching me, Carth knew how to drive me wild.

I reached over and wrapped my fingers around Carth's hard cock, the long rod giving a different feel in my hands than Erroh's had. The soreness from my first time had passed, leaving excitement in its place. Our mouths met again, our kiss passionate and demanding, while I stroked his length.

Water rushed between my legs, caressing and teasing, but it wasn't enough. "Carth, please," I said with desperation.

He dove into the water toward me, pulling me into his arms while his mouth fell on my neck. Pressure between my legs made me part them, and as soon as I did, the water rushed around our naked bodies, pressing us closer together. I wrapped my legs around his hips, while his fingers cupped my bottom.

He guided his cock to my entrance, then rubbed it against my folds to make me moan in desire. As my fingers dug into his skin, he sank inside me slowly, with a sigh of great satisfaction.

"Gods, you are so snug," he said, as he filled me to the hilt. He felt different than Erroh, though I wasn't sure how exactly, but I loved the contrast anyway. A girl would never get bored with four lovers, that was for sure. Or five, for that matter.

The water pushed us together, holding me up and giving him leverage to move in and out of me. Waves rippled around us as our bodies rocked together. I threw my head back and held on to him while he pumped into my core. His mouth found my neck and discovered a spot below my ear that had me moaning hard.

Then his speed increased, to my intense delight. Every thrust made my body respond with passion and pleasure. The water surged around me, stroking my ass, between my thighs, around my nipples, hitting me everywhere, allowing Carth to touch me in ways I'd never imagined.

My release built slowly, with pleasure rushing through my body like a stream, and then a river, and then a waterfall.

"Carth, more," I moaned when the feeling of release eluded me.

He moved faster, then took one hand off of my hip to tease the little nub that evoked such strong orgasms, as Erroh and I had discovered. At the same time, water rubbed my tight hole in the back, in an area no man had touched before. I cried out, grasping at his shoulders to try to center myself as I came apart.

He pulled me close and thrust deep as he came inside me. As we both surged together, the water around us shot straight up in the air, and then ice began to form along our skin. It completely covered us, locking us together, while waves of pleasure spread through us. All we could do was kiss and ride it out.

After the water receded and the ice melted away, I wrapped my arms around Carth and breathed in his scent, committing our first time to memory—one I'd never forget. Making love in the water was certainly an exhilarating experience, especially when he used his magic at the same time.

"How did you learn how to do all that with the water?" I asked.

"I've been practicing—alone, mind you—ever since I got these powers." He gave me a sensual grin. "If they can't be used for sex, then why bother having them at all?"

I laughed, as he picked me up and grabbed a nearby towel, wrapping me up in it. Then he set me down on the bed and crawled up beside me, folding his arms under his head.

"The Water God should appear to us now, probably in the ocean there." I rested my head on his shoulder and gazed at the school of fish swimming by.

"Somehow I don't think he's coming."

"Me neither."

Carth wrapped an arm tightly around me. "That's all right. I'm sure I can keep you entertained." Then he paused. "Although I should have asked this earlier. Do we need to worry about pregnancy?"

"No. One of the benefits of being the Ascendant is there is no chance of a surprise pregnancy. I will have one daughter in ten years, like my mother did, and that girl will replace me when the time comes."

"Which means you can have as much sex as you want until then," he said, pulling me on top of his growing cock.

I laughed. "And you're obviously eager to provide it."

"It's my job to please the woman I love, is it not?"

"I suppose it is." I bent my head to kiss him.

The Water God never arrived, but we managed to find plenty of ways to keep ourselves occupied, until we finally fell asleep.

CHAPTER TWELVE

The journey back to Soulspire was faster and easier now that Carth was a dragon too. Erroh spent a few hours showing Carth the basics before we left the Water Temple, and then they took turns flying us until we reached the palace.

When we landed in the castle garden, Varek was waiting for us, along with Parin and Zain. My other mates did not look pleased that he was there, and I shared their sentiment.

Carth set down on the ground and let out a roar, spreading his blue wings wide, and Zain gave him an approving nod. I quickly hugged Zain and Parin, and then turned to my fifth mate. "What brings you to the palace you hate so much?"

Varek snorted. "Sorry to disturb you, princess, but I have news about the Unseen."

"It's the only reason we let him inside," Parin said, eyeing Varek with disdain.

I tried not to bristle at Varek's nickname. "Continue."

"As suspected, the rally you witnessed near my bar was a recruitment effort on their part. They've been holding them all over the city, and rumor is they're spreading outside Soulspire too."

"Do so many people hate the elementals and the Dragons?" Erroh asked.

Varek shrugged. "They make some good points about the inequality among humans and elementals, but I'm not going to stand back and let them attack us again. I know I run in some questionable circles, and many may think—" He shot my other mates a wry look. "That I'm only a criminal, but I have a line I won't cross. I'm pretty sure they do not."

I crossed my arms, feeling exhausted after our long journey. "Do you have any actual information?"

Varek clenched his jaw. "I was getting to that. I sent some of my people to join their cult to gather information. They say the Unseen have something planned, something big they want to show everyone."

"What do you suspect?" Parin asked.

"I believe the Unseen are somehow stealing elemental powers, but I'm not sure how."

"That should be impossible," I said, but then remembered what my mother had said. "Although you might be correct. We've had reports of missing elementals."

"If they are stealing elemental powers, we need to stop them immediately," Zain said.

"There's an Unseen meeting at midnight tonight at the old warehouse that burned down at the northern end of Soulspire," Varek said. "We can sneak in and learn more then."

"I know the place," Erroh said. "But can we trust a criminal?"

Carth crossed his arms. "I'm with Erroh, I'm not sure we should work with a man with his…connections."

"My connections saved you once already," Varek snapped. "While you've been off having sex in fancy temples, I've been investigating these cultists. You wouldn't know anything about them if not for me."

"Or maybe this is some kind of trap," Zain said.

"Believe what you want." Varek spread his hands. "I'll be at the meeting. You can join me if you wish, or I can handle things on my own. Your choice."

"We'll be there," I said, the words slipping out of my mouth immediately. My mates didn't trust the man, and in many ways I didn't either, but I believed he was helping us. I felt it in my gut.

Of course, I'd seen him do some seriously heinous things in my dreams. He couldn't explain away cold-blooded murder. I wouldn't forget that either.

Parin cleared his throat. "We appreciate any accurate information you can give us."

"Come inside," I told my five mates. "We can speak more privately in our chambers."

"As you wish, princess," Varek said, but his inflection had changed. The offensive pet name didn't have the same level of vinegar in it this time.

We headed inside the palace and got many looks from the guards as

Varek walked with us to the other wing. Then we entered our communal dining room and sat down to a huge meal. I wanted to kiss the cooks for having food ready even though they didn't know when we'd return. My parents were still gone, and the responsibility of dealing with the Unseen was firmly on our shoulders. I'd be able to form a plan for infiltrating the meeting a lot better with a full stomach, and hopefully my mates would be less grumpy about Varek's presence too.

At least he was here in the palace. That was a start.

Varek didn't stay long. During our meal we sketched out a rough strategy, and then he headed back into the city with plans to meet us at the warehouse after dark. He said he would procure us some masks too.

We were relying on him a lot for this mission. I hoped it wasn't a mistake.

I borrowed a dress from a servant and donned my black cloak, before heading out. I was far too recognizable in Soulspire, but hopefully with a mask and my hair under a hood, I could avoid notice. My other mates were similarly dressed in plain clothes, including Carth, who had to borrow something from Erroh.

We split up into two groups to travel in different paths to the location. A woman with four men might be a little too obvious. Of course, my mates tried to talk me out of going, until we were standing outside the building that had once housed a large warehouse before a fire destroyed it years ago. A fire that was caused by elementals. The irony was not lost upon me.

As we moved down an alley toward the back entrance, a large man suddenly stepped out of the shadows directly in front of us. I jumped, along with Erroh and Parin at my back, all of us reaching for our weapons, but then I recognized Varek.

"Are you trying to get yourself stabbed?" Erroh asked.

"Put these on." Varek held out three gray masks toward us. "The password to enter is 'nameless.' We'll go in two at a time, or our number will draw suspicion."

"The others?" I asked. Zain and Carth had taken the shorter route to the warehouse.

"Already inside. The meeting is starting soon."

I donned the mask with a nod, then pulled the hood up to cover my hair. Parin stayed back with Varek, while Erroh and I approached the metal door and knocked.

A slat opened at the top of it. Eyes peered out. Waiting. Watching.

"Nameless," Erroh said.

The slat shut, and then the door opened. We stepped into a dark hallway with stale air, the walls blackened and charred in places. A large man grunted and gestured for us to move forward.

The hallway opened up to a big room filled with people, most of them wearing gray masks, though some didn't bother. A large wooden stage had been set up on one end, and more masked people waited there, along with something big and boxy that was covered by a black cloth. A large crate maybe?

I gazed around the room, sizing up the audience. So many people, a lot more than I expected, all crowded together and eager for this meeting to start. My mates were among them somewhere, but I couldn't pick them out with the masks on. At least I had Erroh at my side.

The masked people on stage suddenly clapped their hands three times, making the room go quiet as everyone realized the meeting was starting. One of them stepped forward, wearing a black mask.

"We are the Unseen, but we will not be ignored any longer," the person said in a booming voice, repeating a phrase I'd heard at the rally. The voice sounded vaguely feminine, but I recognized she was trying hard to deepen and alter her tone. Probably for anonymity. "We applaud your bravery for meeting us here tonight, for recognizing the inequality humans face every single day, and for being willing to put an end to it through whatever means necessary. It's time to put humans first again."

My stomach twisted as people in the crowd raised their fists and chanted, "Humans first, humans first, humans first!"

The leader raised her hands and flames burst forth from them, causing the audience to settle down again. "For years, we've been powerless against the elementals and the Dragons, but no longer. We've discovered a way to gain magic ourselves, and tonight we will demonstrate for you. Soon, we will be equal to the elementals…and then the Dragons themselves!"

The crowd surged forward in anticipation and I was shuffled along too, anxious to see whatever they were about to do to gain magic. As I watched, the leader nodded at some of the other masked figures, who yanked off the cloth. Underneath it was four cages, and inside them were elementals—one of each type. They were in bad shape too, the fire elemental's flames dim, the water elemental's body too thin, the earth elemental's rock body partly smashed, and the air elemental little more than a wisp. I couldn't help but gasp in horror at the sight, and quickly covered my mouth. Something terrible was about to happen. I needed to stop it, but I had to know what they were doing too.

"Do we have a volunteer?" the leader asked.

Dozens of people raised their hands, and she chose a young woman with red hair who wasn't wearing a mask, then asked her, "What type of magic would you like? Earth, air, fire, or water?"

The redhead glanced between the elementals with excitement in her eyes. "I think… air. Yes, air."

"A fine choice." The leader stepped toward the cage with the air elemental, who floated backward as she approached, but there was nowhere to go. "Step forward, initiate."

The redhead moved closer, and the leader took her hand, before reaching toward the elemental with her other one. Dark tendrils lashed out from her fingertips and sank into the air elemental's chest, causing it to scream, a sound like a whirling tornado. It struggled and fought, but the iron cage kept it contained and unable to use its magic.

"No!" I yelled, rushing forward.

A strong hand clamped down on my arm, holding me back. I glanced over my shoulder and saw black hair. Varek.

"Don't do anything stupid," he hissed.

"I have to stop this!" It was my duty to protect those elementals from the humans, and vice versa. I couldn't stand back and do nothing as they hurt it.

As I struggled to get closer, the leader's dark tendrils yanked out something from inside the elemental, a swirling vortex of glowing yellow air, and shoved it into the redhead's chest. The air elemental immediately dissipated, vanishing before our eyes as it passed away. A yellow glow surrounded the redhead for a brief second, before fading.

"You now have the powers of an air elemental," the leader said. "Try them."

The redhead looked uncertain, but she waved her hand and a breeze went through the room. The crowd erupted into a loud cheer, stomping and hollering, and the woman cracked a huge smile.

The leader gave her a nod. "You are one of us now. We will train you in how to use your new magic to defend humankind and take back the world."

"Thank you," the woman said, and another masked member led her away.

The leader gazed back at the crowd. "I need another volunteer."

This time just about everyone's hand raised. It made me sick. Did no one care that this was murder?

I wasn't going to stand around and let this happen. It was time to end this meeting and free these elementals. I shrugged Varek's hand off my arm and used my air magic to lift me up toward the ceiling, then used my newest elemental magic to spray water down on everyone, drenching the crowd. People screamed and looked up.

I yanked off my mask as I hovered over them. "What you're doing is murder and I won't let this continue! Free the elementals now!"

"It's the Dragon spawn!" the leader yelled. "They're here to stop us from gaining the power that should be ours, but we will not be stopped!"

She launched fire at me, and I stopped it with a blast of water magic. Erroh flew up next to me, while my other mates surged through the crowd toward the remaining cages. They knew what to do—freeing the elementals was our number one priority.

Most of the crowd screamed and fled in a panic, but many of the people on stage started fighting us back with their elemental magic. There was not enough space for Erroh or Carth to become dragons with so many people running around, so Erroh and I fought from the air, while my other three mates climbed the stage. Zain and Varek used fire and death magic to stop some of the cultists, while Carth ran to the first cage and freed the elementals.

It was total chaos in the warehouse. I didn't want to hurt anyone in the crowd who wasn't attacking us, but it was hard to know who had magic and who didn't. I tried to go after the leader, but she'd vanished into the crowd at some point.

Soon the warehouse was empty except for the five of us, a few cultists we'd knocked out, and the freed elementals, who I immediately began healing as best I could. The Silver Guard showed up, hearing the commotion, but by then it was over. The leader and most of the cultists had fled, but at least the other three elementals were safe.

And now we knew why they were going missing.

CHAPTER THIRTEEN

T he elementals were escorted back to the palace by the Silver Guard, where our staff began taking care of them immediately. The few cultists we captured were dragged off for interrogation, but I doubted they'd give us much information. Varek left to try and track down the Unseen's leader, while the rest of us returned to our quarters in the palace.

As we entered our communal area, I slumped down on the sofa, feeling defeated. Yes, we'd rescued three of the elementals, but we'd failed to save the fourth, and everything I'd seen and heard tonight had left me shaken.

"I need to contact my parents and tell them we know why the elementals are going missing," I said.

"I can't believe the Unseen would go to these lengths," Parin said, shaking his head. "It's barbaric."

Zain sat on the sofa beside me, moving stiffly. "People will do many things to gain power. Especially when they feel they have none."

"Are you all right?" I asked, noting the way he held his side.

"I'm fine."

"Let me see," I demanded. "If you're injured, I can heal you."

He moved his hand, and it came away bloody, but he shrugged. "One of the Unseen had a large knife."

Carth rolled his eyes. "That's why you use your magic to keep them away."

"I was trying not to burn the entire place down a second time," Zain said. "Fire is different from air or water or even earth. You need precise control. You can't just throw it around and hope for the best."

"He does have a point," Erroh said.

"Nice to see you've learned something in your training sessions," Parin muttered.

I rose to my feet. "Let's go into my quarters. The rest of you, get me some cloths and a bowl of water."

Zain stood and winced, and I took his hand and practically dragged him onto the bed, after setting down a towel underneath him.

"Off with your shirt," I ordered.

Zain leaned back on my pillows. "You're bossy when someone is injured."

When he unlaced his shirt too slowly, I grew impatient and reached over to help. Even though I was worried about him, I couldn't help but enjoy the sight as I bared his chest. He was exquisite, his body toned from being a guard at the Fire Temple.

As soon as I saw the cut on his side, my focus went entirely to it. He winced as I prodded it, but didn't make a peep. "It's long and deep. I bet it hurts a lot."

"I've had more enjoyable nights, it's true," Zain said in a clenched tone.

"Why didn't you say anything sooner?"

"It was more important for you to heal the elementals."

Pressing my hand to the wound, I sent healing life energy into it. While I did, Parin and Erroh returned with some cloths, while Carth brought me a bowl of water. I sent them away after that so I could concentrate.

Under my care, the injury slowly disappeared. When I was finished, I grabbed the cloth and carefully cleaned the blood off of Zain. "Here," I held out my hand. "Sit up, let's get this shirt off to be cleaned. It's covered in your blood."

"I can do it now." Zain sat up without difficulty and shrugged the torn shirt off his shoulders. "But the shirt is ruined."

"I can't heal it as easily as I did you," I told him with a smile.

"Thank you." Zain leaned forward and took the cloth from me, throwing it into the basin. He put his hands on my shoulders. His lips neared mine, and I couldn't slow the race of my heart.

My healing must've been effective because he pulled me close and rolled us, so I was suddenly on my back on the bed, with him looming over me. His mouth came down on mine hard and his tongue tangled with mine. When he pulled back, I was breathless and hot with desire. The evidence of his arousal was pressed into my core too. He pushed it harder against me, and I moaned and arched up against him.

"We can't do this until we get to the temple," I whispered.

He flexed his hips and his hard length rubbed against me, pressing into my little nub that was so eager for his attention. My moan turned breathy and I spread my legs, giving him more access to grind against me, even as I said, "This can't go any further. We don't know if the Gods would be angered."

"The Gods have deserted us, have they not?" he replied, then to my shock and delight, sank his teeth into my neck just enough to harden my nipples pressed against his chest.

I was seconds from giving in when the door was flung open. Carth bounded into the room. "Break it up, you two. No naughty business until we get to the Fire Temple."

The others followed him inside, and Zain and I reluctantly broke apart. My mates all draped themselves on my bed like they belonged there, except Parin, who stood apart with his arms crossed. He still didn't feel like one of us.

"We need to talk about your actions earlier," he said.

"What do you mean?" I asked, sitting up and trying to ignore the wetness between my legs.

"You were pretty reckless at the meeting," Erroh said.

"I had to stop them from killing another elemental!" I glanced between them. "Do you not agree?"

"Of course we do," Carth said. "They had to be stopped. But we were split up from you and couldn't protect you."

Zain took my chin in his hand. "If you ever do something like that again without a second thought to your own well-being again, I'll..."

I arched one eyebrow. "You'll what?"

"Yeah, what will you do?" Carth asked with a grin. "Turn her over your knee and give her a spanking?"

Erroh doubled over laughing. "No, she might enjoy that too much."

I rolled my eyes, even as heat flared between my thighs. Welcome to life with four mates. "I appreciate your desire to protect me, but don't forget I've spent my entire life training for this role under the current Dragons. I can handle myself in combat."

Parin cleared his throat and shifted like he was uncomfortable. "We need to figure out a plan for dealing with the Unseen."

"Varek is trying to get more information for us," I said. "He proved to be trustworthy tonight, so we have to believe he will continue helping us. I will send a message to my mother about the kidnapped elementals too."

"We should continue to the Fire Temple," Zain said, and gave me a heated look. "It's more important than ever for us to be at our full strength now."

I nodded, and swallowed my desire before it overwhelmed me. "We'll leave tomorrow."

CHAPTER FOURTEEN

I n the morning, we set off for the Fire Temple.
  Parin stayed behind to see what he could learn about the Unseen, to oversee the protection of the kidnapped elementals, and to fill in my parents if they returned before we did.

Carth and Erroh both stayed in dragon form for the entire trip, except for when we stopped to eat or take a break. The journey took most of the day, although the Fire Temple was the shortest distance from Soulspire, at least when flying. Zain and I alternated riding the two dragons, giving the other one time to practice flying maneuvers. We could have had a dragon each to ride, but out of an unspoken agreement we decided to sit together. I liked having his arms around me and his hard chest against my back. I also liked when his hands spread down to cup my breasts or idly stroke my thighs.

As the sun set, the land underneath us changed to a desolate expanse of earth turned black by previously spilled lava. The volcano, Valefire, loomed before us with smoke rising from its mound, and I glimpsed the ocean behind it. We flew over vents in the ground shooting up steam and boiling water, and as we approached, the air grew thick with heat and humidity, along with the smell of rotten eggs.

Zain's hands tightened around my waist. "It's good to be home."

We landed on the top of the volcano, which was flat and smooth before dropping off into a huge crater in the center. A glowing light came from within it, and Mom told me that was where the Fire God had appeared to them. I wondered if he would make an appearance for us, or if Zain was right and the Gods had abandoned us. Hearing him, my most devout mate, say such a thing had been disturbing…but I feared he might be right.

The Fire Temple stood before us and was made of glossy black obsidian and featured huge pointed towers. Two women emerged from the tall door at the front, both wearing black silk robes with red trim. One was Zain's mother, High Priestess Oria, and the other was his grandmother Calla, who had been High Priestess during my mother's Ascension. Oria had the same nearly-white hair as Zain, and Calla's hair had once been blond but had turned white with age. She held onto Oria's arm for support as they moved toward us.

"Mother, grandmother," Zain said. "I'm pleased to announce I am Sora's fire mate."

"We've heard." Oria held out her arms, and Zain hugged her. "We're so proud. I prayed you would be chosen, and I'm pleased the Fire God listened."

"I prayed as well," Zain said.

"Zain," Calla said with a giant smile as she embraced him. "I'm happy to see you on this joyous day."

"And you, grandmother. None of this would have been possible without you."

"Our family has always served the Fire God, and it pleases me that you will continue that tradition." She patted his cheek and then turned to me.

I bowed my head in respect. "High Priestesses."

Calla took my hand. "I'm so pleased things happened this way. You've always been the granddaughter of my heart, but now it's official."

My heart warmed at her words. She'd been like a grandmother to me as well, even though we were not related. When I was very small, if my parents needed to leave me to go on some diplomatic mission or another, they'd always left me with Calla, first in the Fire Temple, and then in Sparkport after she retired as High Priestess.

"We've prepared the bonding room for you," Oria said, as she led us inside to a large entry with a statue of a dragon. "Would you like to share a meal first?"

"No, thank you," I said, glancing at Zain. He nodded. Neither one of us wanted to wait any longer.

"We've already eaten, but we'd enjoy sharing a meal with you in the morning," Zain said diplomatically.

In the entryway, we briefly said hello to Zain's four fathers who all told him how proud they were, before they took Erroh and Carth to their own rooms.

We didn't have to go anywhere—the bonding room was just on the other side of a tall door in here, which was carved with two dragons. Oria and Calla both gave us knowing smiles and bowed their heads, as we stepped inside.

The bonding room had a domed ceiling, flickering torches, and the large bed I'd come to expect. But I barely had time to look around before Zain reached for me.

There were no nerves. No hesitation. No need to speak. I didn't care about the dust we'd picked up or how wild my hair was. As soon as the door closed behind us, we launched ourselves at one another, removing our clothes as quickly as we could.

"Later I will take the time to savor you slowly," Zain said, between passionate, hungry kisses. "Being the third of your mates has been torture. I can't wait any longer."

"I can't wait either. I've wanted to do this since we kissed a year ago."

His hand slid down to my breast, recreating the moment when we'd shared a forbidden kiss in the dark halls of the temple, only to never speak of it again. Until now—when we were finally allowed to be together.

We fell on the bed together, in the same position we'd been interrupted in the night before. Desire raced through me, this time hotter, brighter. I spread my legs and grabbed his hard cock. His girth was impressive, more than either Carth or Erroh, though not quite as long. As I guided him to my entrance, eager to feel him move inside me, I couldn't help but wonder what it would be like to be with all three men at once.

But when he pushed into me, all thoughts vanished. Throwing myself back on the bed, I moaned at the feel of him filling me, stretching me.

Zain moved fast, pulling me into his arms and thrusting into me over and over. I clenched around him when he slipped a hand between us to press against me, knowing exactly where to go and what to do.

Then he rolled us over on the silk sheets, putting me on top. After sleeping with two other men a few times, I knew what to do now, and I rolled my hips while he pinched my nipples. It felt good to take control and chase my own pleasure, especially when I could see how much it excited him too.

In the hot, humid room, sweat poured out of me, slicking my body against his so that each slide was an erotic massage. His hands clenched my behind and guided me faster, harder, urging me on while I threw my head back and let go.

My cry of pleasure echoed through the obsidian chamber as the orgasm burned through me. My inner walls clenched of their own volition, milking Zain and bringing his climax too. As we both came together, fire burst out of his skin and soon engulfed me, spreading through me like I was a dry forest full of kindling. I knew now this was how our bond was formed, and how I gained his powers, but it was still shocking to have flames rippling across my naked skin.

Then the fire died out, and we clung to each other while we caught our breath. The heat inside me slowly quieted until the sweat dried on my skin.

"I love you," Zain murmured against my ear, as he stroked my back.

"I love you too."

He sat up and reached for his clothes. "Come. Let's see if we can lure the Fire God from the volcano."

There was a door on the other side of the room that Zain opened, and it took us back outside, this time near the crater in the volcano. The heat grew more intense here, but the volcano was not erupting right now, so we had little to fear as we approached.

Zain stood before the glowing crater and raised his arms. "Fire God, we have come for your blessing. Please honor your devoted servants with your presence."

He was laying it on thick, but waiting around for the Gods in the other temples hadn't worked. Maybe this would. Mother had told me the Gods had just showed up, but things had changed since then. My Ascension was proving to be very different from hers.

"We beseech you," Zain called out. "Show yourself!"

Nothing happened.

I let out a long sigh. "He isn't coming. As you said, the Gods have abandoned us."

"I thought, out of all your mates, I would be the one who could summon a God." A heavy frown settled on his face. "I've failed, like the others."

"I'm sorry." I took his hand. "It isn't your fault. None of us know why they're not appearing, but the Fire God chose you for a reason. He knew you were my perfect mate. Focus on that."

He slowly nodded. "I can do that."

We went back inside the bonding room, and he focused on me for the rest of the night. It was enough to almost make my worries about the Gods vanish completely...but not quite.

CHAPTER FIFTEEN

In the morning we had a nice breakfast with Zain's family, and then we stepped outside so he could shift into a dragon for the first time. Everyone applauded and cheered as blood red scales covered his body and grew into wings, and then he launched into the air. He had a moment where he took a dive and nearly fell, but Erroh and Carth were there to lift him up with some wind magic and give him a few pointers.

We returned to the palace that evening, and Parin rushed out to meet us when we returned. His face showed obvious distress, and I quickly slid off Zain's back and asked, "What is it? Is something wrong?"

"I'm glad you're back so soon," he said. "We have a problem."

As my other mates returned to their human form, they gathered close. "Tell us," Zain demanded.

"A large delegation of elementals was supposed to arrive this morning from Divine Isle. They've been visiting each Realm, trying to continue to foster good relations between the humans and the elementals, as your mother requested."

"Let me guess," Carth said. "They never arrived."

"Indeed. No one has heard anything from them in days."

"Perhaps they're simply delayed," Erroh said, though he didn't sound like he believed that.

"Have any of my parents returned yet?" I asked, as my stomach became leaden with dread. We all knew what had happened to the elementals, even if we hoped that wasn't the case.

"Unfortunately, no," Parin said.

My mouth twisted into a grimace. "We'll have to handle this on our own then. Is there anything else you can tell us? How many there were? Where were they coming from?"

"They were coming from the Air Realm. I believe there were about twenty-five of them."

"That's twenty-five more people who could have magic soon," Zain said.

I turned toward my three bonded mates. "Do the three of you feel up to flying again?"

Erroh puffed out his chest. "I could fly all night long without a problem."

Carth rolled his eyes. "We'll be fine. We can investigate the elementals' journey, retrace their steps as best we can, and see if we find anything."

"Thank you," I said. "Are you sure you'll be all right?"

All three men swore they were fine and would leave immediately after grabbing some dinner from the kitchen. Flying made you very hungry.

My heart sank a bit as they walked away. I didn't like the idea of being away from them, but it was necessary to find anything we could about that missing delegation.

I turned toward Parin. "I'm going to visit Varek and see if he's learned anything new."

Parin's brow furrowed. "Would you like me to come with you?"

"No, although I appreciate you asking, instead of demanding you're going to protect me."

"You're a formidable woman, Sora. I've come to realize that over the last few days."

His words gave me a bit of hope. Maybe he no longer saw me as just a little sister anymore?

"Besides," he continued. "Although I don't approve of Varek's lifestyle, he has proved useful. We need whatever information we can get from him."

"I agree." I tentatively reached out and took his hand. "Thank you for taking care of things while we were gone."

Parin glanced down at our linked fingers, and then gave my hand a squeeze. "I'm happy to help however I can."

I leaned close and pressed a light kiss to his check. "Please stay here in case the elementals or my parents arrive. I'll be back as soon as I can."

675

I didn't waste any time rushing out to find Varek. An entire envoy of missing elementals was enough to make my blood run cold. If the Unseen took all their powers, we would be vastly outnumbered in a fight. The delegation had to be found immediately.

Remembering Varek's words about being discreet, I went to the back door of the Lone Wolf Pub, the one he'd led me out of last time. Once there, I knocked sharply, keeping my head down and my hood pulled low over my face. I couldn't risk getting caught alone by the Unseen.

Varek's sister, whose name I vaguely remembered was Wrill, opened the door with a sneer. I was starting to think that was her permanent expression. "The princess has returned."

"I need to speak with Varek."

She stepped aside to let me in. "We knew you'd come crawling back for more."

"He is my mate," I snapped. What was her problem with me? "I didn't choose him, but I have to make the best of it. As does he."

She tossed her black hair. "Go on then. You know where to find him."

Ignoring all the other doors, I headed straight for Varek's office. I considered going right in, but took a deep breath and knocked instead. Just because Wrill was rude and condescending didn't mean I needed to be too.

"Enter," he barked.

I stepped inside, and saw him standing beside his desk. He was shirtless and slightly sweaty, rubbing a cloth along the back of his neck, and I was momentarily stunned by the sight of all those muscles and tattoos. I had the strongest desire to run my hands down his chest and trace every dark line of ink.

When he saw it was me, a slow grin spread across his face. "A visit from the princess. Is it time for our bonding?"

"No, although I'm sure you wish it was." My gaze snapped back to his face as I tried to focus on why I was here. "A delegation of elementals went missing, and we suspect the Unseen have taken them. Have you heard anything about that?"

"I have not."

I sighed and tried again. "Have you learned anything new about the Unseen since we last spoke?"

"No, but my people are still working on it." He tilted his head and studied me. "That's not the real reason you came here though, and we both know it."

The way he said it sent heat to my core, but I refused to let him affect me that way. "It's time you moved to the castle and became one of my mates in more than just name. We need your help with the Unseen, and that will be easier if you're beside us."

He stalked across the room, until he was standing right in front of me, and I couldn't help but look at his naked chest again. "Or maybe you just want me near you."

"It wouldn't hurt for us to get to know each other better," I admitted.

"We know everything we need." His hand reached up and slid behind my neck, and I thought he would pull me in for a kiss, but he only gazed into my eyes. "I'll make you a deal. Fight me in the ring. I want to see if you're as good as the stories say. If you win, I'll move to the palace and be the good little mate you want."

That sounded too good to be true, considering it was unlikely he'd win. "And if I lose?"

"You get on your knees and suck my cock until my seed spurts down your throat. Then you call me your king."

My eyes widened at his vulgar words and shocking demands. His fingers tightened in my hair and his dark eyes roamed down my body, making it clear he planned to win. I tried not to show the way my body responded to his rough, demanding touch, and to the thought of wrapping my lips around his cock. I shouldn't have wanted him so badly, but I couldn't help myself.

"Deal," I said, my voice breathless.

A wicked grin crossed his lips as he let go of me. "Follow me, princess."

He led us to the door I'd peered inside the first time I came to his bar. The door opened into the massive room, where two men were fighting while a small crowd watched.

"Everyone out," Varek's voice boomed. No one argued or even hesitated. They grabbed their things and headed out the door, only pausing to give him nods of respect.

When the last person had exited and we were alone, we both stepped into the ring painted on the floor. Torchlight flickered across Varek's chest as he faced me. I loosened my shoulders and rolled my head, ready to fight. I couldn't lose this one.

"No weapons, no magic," he said. "We fight until one of us concedes defeat or is forced out of the ring."

"Agreed."

Varek went immediately on the offensive. He ran straight for me but was easy to dodge. We spent a few minutes going back and forth that way, each of us easily ducking and darting away from the other.

I spread my arms, taunting him. "We can't do this all day."

"Indeed." Without warning, he changed his tactic, rushing toward me with impressive speed and force. I barely managed to avoid his blow, but I was able to use his momentum to spin around and kick him in the face. He stumbled back, then wiped a tiny spot of blood on his lip with a grin.

Then it got interesting. He'd been toying with me before, but now he truly came after me. I had to admit, his abilities were a real test of my skills. I'd previously thought only the best of the Silver Guard was a match for me, including Erroh. Now I had to add Varek to that short list too.

As we moved around the ring, exchanging blows and occasionally grappling with our bodies pressed close together, I began to wonder if I was going to lose. Would I have to return to my mates knowing I'd sucked the cock of the city's number one criminal?

That couldn't happen, no matter how excited the thought made me. I redoubled my efforts, flinging Varek to the ground and landing on top of him as I tried to get a grip on his arms.

But he threw me off, and the next thing I knew, it was me on the bottom. His bigger size pinned me down, and his hard body pressed against mine. A slow smile crept across his face, and his lips came down to my ear. "I think you like this a little too much."

With a grunt, I swung my leg around and wrapped it around his neck, twirling both of us until I was on top again. Straddling his waist, I fought the desire that rushed through me as I held him down. "Submit."

"Never." He gripped my hips, rubbing his cock against me once, and then shoved me off him.

We both scrambled back to our feet, breathing heavily, and not just from the exertion. When we faced each other this time, it was with hunger in our eyes too. My gaze fell to the large bulge in his pants.

Maybe losing wouldn't be so bad after all.

He used my distraction against me and managed to grab my waist, lift me up, and nearly throw me out of the ring. I got away just in time, then launched a series of sharp kicks and blows against him. When he came at me again, I back up right to the edge and used a move Jasin had taught me, dropping down and sweeping my leg under Varek. He toppled over, knocking me down with him, but only he was over the line. We both saw it at the same time, and a huge grin spread across my face.

I stood and offered him my hand. "I win."

He stared at my hand for a second, before taking it and letting me help him to his feet. Then he yanked me toward him and captured my mouth in a rough kiss. His other hand gripped my behind and pulled me hard against him, while my heart raced. My fingers gripped his muscular upper arms, squeezing them, while he ravished my mouth. I wondered if he would do the same to my body when the time came.

"I let you win." He took my chin in his hand. "But one day you're still going to suck my cock and call me your king."

I stared back at him defiantly, even as my body arched toward his touch. "Not likely."

"We both know you want it as much as I do." He released me and called out, "Wrill!"

She stepped into the room and glowered at me. "Yes, brother?"

He wiped sweat off his brow and stalked toward the door. "I'm moving into the palace tonight."

"You...what?" She blinked at him.

"The princess needs my services." He rested a hand on her shoulder. "Though it pains me to leave the Quickblades, I'm placing you in charge of them."

"Brother, this is madness. You built this organization. You can't leave it now for some...woman."

"The Death Goddess chose me, and I have to accept my role as Sora's mate. I'll make sure no one questions your command, and I have faith that you will lead the Quickblades well."

She stammered, but then nodded with a grim set to her features. "I'll do my best."

Varek turned back to me. "I need to take care of a few things here tonight, but I'll have my things brought to the palace in the morning. Does that suit you, princess?"

"That's fine." I was shocked he was actually fulfilling his part of the deal, and going beyond it at that. I'd asked him to move into the palace, but hadn't said anything about giving up the Quickblades. Maybe he was finally starting to realize he had a higher purpose as one of my Dragons.

CHAPTER SIXTEEN

Varek moved all his things into the palace the next morning. Ever since we discovered I had a fifth mate the staff had been busy getting a room ready for him, even adding a new door so it connected to our main living space. They weren't sure how to decorate it—how did one represent the Death Goddess, with skulls and black curtains?—but I'd told them to leave it fairly plain so Varek could put his own touches on it.

Parin watched Varek move in with a tight-lipped expression, his arms crossed. I wasn't sure if any of my mates would ever be able to accept Varek, even after he gave up his criminal lifestyle. I wasn't sure I could accept him either. My body responded to him, but if we were going to be bound together for the rest of our lives, I needed more than that.

Varek didn't even have time to unpack his belongings before Carth and Zain returned. We had a balcony outside our communal area that was large enough for two dragons to land on at once, and we met them out there under the midday sun.

I rushed toward them and lovingly touched both their dragon snouts, relieved to see them unharmed. "Did you find anything? Where's Erroh?"

"We found the site of the ambush in the Air Realm," Zain said. "The elementals were smart and left scorch marks along the ground, leading to what we think is the Unseen's current hideout. It's an old barn on a farm that's long abandoned. Erroh stayed behind to watch them in case they move again."

"How far away?" Parin asked.

"Too far to walk," Carth said. "Are your parents back?"

I shook my head. "Unfortunately not."

"We'll have to do this on our own," Varek said.

Both dragons swung their heads toward him, their fangs flashing. "What are you doing here?" Zain asked.

Varek gave him an icy look. "I live here now."

"Varek's given up his position in the Quickblades and has moved into the palace," I said.

"About time you conceded defeat," Carth said, then snorted.

"I did no such thing," Varek snapped.

I pressed my palm to my forehead. "Enough. Carth and Zain, you should grab some food quickly to recover your strength, while the rest of us prepare to leave. We'll go as soon as we can to rescue those elementals."

We arrived at the location about an hour later, with me and Parin riding Zain, and Varek riding Carth. No one was pleased about the seating arrangements, but we had bigger things to worry about.

Since showing up as dragons would be a little too obvious, we stopped a short distance away and my mates reverted to their human forms. From there, we crept through the woods until we found the tree Erroh was hiding in, which had a good view of the barn. He did a doubletake when he saw Varek with us.

"Has anything changed?" Carth asked.

"No," Erroh said. "No one has gone in or out."

"Are we certain the elementals are inside?" Parin asked.

"No, but it's the only lead we have," Zain said.

I surveyed the barn. It was obviously abandoned and much of it had already collapsed, except for a large section on one side that appeared intact. That's where the Unseen had to be holding the elementals. "An ambush seems like the best option. Quick and fast."

"I have another idea," Varek said. "I can summon a group of shades and send them in to distract the people inside, and possibly cause them to run out in fear."

"You can summon shades?" I asked, horrified. Shades were minions of the Death Goddess who hungered for life. Like elementals, they could only be harmed by earth, air, fire, and water—weapons did nothing to them. They could also turn both invisible and intangible, making them especially deadly to humans. My parents had made it one of their missions to make sure there were none left in the four Realms. "Why didn't you mention that before?"

"I can do many things." Varek leveled an intense stare at me. "I knew this one would offend your delicate sensibilities."

"I don't like it," Parin said. "Shades are…unnatural."

"And creepy," Erroh added.

"Do you have an alternative plan?" Varek asked.

"We could shift into dragons, fly in, and tear the place apart," Carth said.

I debated it, but then shook my head. "Too dangerous. The elementals might get hurt. Better if the cultists don't know we're here at first."

Varek raised his chin. "Then we go with my plan."

I sighed. Sending in shades to do this felt wrong, but we needed whatever advantage we could get in this fight. "Yes, fine, summon your shades."

Varek stepped into the woods a short distance away from us and spread his arms, his eyes closed. As we watched, ten shades rose up out of the earth, floating into existence in front of us. They appeared to be made of shadow and were only vaguely human-like, with glowing yellow eyes and sharp claws.

A shiver ran down my spine. Varek may have been one of my mates, but that didn't make the shades any less unsettling. I wondered what Mom would think of me agreeing to such a horrible thing. Would she consider it worth it to save these elementals and prevent more humans from stealing magic?

Varek whispered something to the shades, and they headed for the barn. From our hiding spot behind some trees and bushes, we watched the shades float to the side of the barn and then glide through it, as if the walls weren't even there.

The screams started only moments later. Gods, what had we done?

We used the distraction to surround the barn's entrance. The door flew open and people began to run outside to escape the shades. As they did, Parin used an earthquake to knock them off their feet, while Erroh had the same effect with a huge blast of air. When Carth saw someone throwing fire, he blasted them with water. The next person that came out of the barn sent jets of water toward us, which Zain quickly extinguished.

I used the distraction to step inside the barn, which looked a lot better on the inside than the outside—it was clear they'd cleaned up in here when they'd made it one of their hideouts. The shades were attacking the cultists, but the humans were fighting back with magic. Everywhere I looked I saw flashes of fire and water, and many of the shades were already vanquished. Even worse, I spotted a dozen cages set up around the room, like the one at the demonstration the other night. They were all empty.

We were too late.

I didn't have time to mourn, because a piece of the fallen roof launched itself toward me, no doubt thrown by one of the cultists. I used air magic to redirect it, then turned to face the person who'd attacked me. The woman in the black mask. Before I could react, she launched a fireball at me, along with a shard of ice. I quickly used fire and water to stop the attack without hesitation, but then gaped at the cultist standing before me. Had she really used both fire *and* water?

"How?" I asked.

A harsh feminine laugh came from behind the black mask as she threw a blast of air at me. "Yes, I do have all four elements…and more."

After I dodged the air blast, a bolt of darkness snaked out from her hand toward me. It looked like the same shadowy mass that the shades were made out of, the same thing she'd used to steal magic from the elementals. I blasted it with fire, though I was still new to using the element, and my control was weak. I ended up spraying wide, setting the floor on fire beside her. The flames quickly jumped high, and I lost her in them.

Carth appeared beside me and quickly put out the flames with a spray of water. There was no sign of the woman in the black mask. We ran outside, where most of the fighting had moved. I expected my mates to be in dragon form taking people down, but none of them were. Most of the cultists had either fled, or were dead or captured. The shades were gone.

"Fly above and search for the leader!" I told them. "She can't have gotten far."

"We can't," Erroh said, as he held a few cultists in a hurricane-like whirlwind.

"Can't?" I asked.

"None of us can shift," Zain said.

I glanced between all of them to confirm. "How?"

No one had an answer. My mates continued to subdue the remaining cultists that fought us, and I stared as Varek reached out with that same shadowy power to grab three people in front of him and suck the life from their bodies.

I gazed out at the forest, cursing myself for letting the leader get away. She was damn good with her magic and she had more elemental powers than I did, since she also had earth. But she had something else too. Something I didn't have—but Varek did.

When the fighting ended, we began to investigate the barn and the area around it. Now that it was empty I spotted a lot more things I hadn't noticed before, like four strange pillars at each outside corner of the barn, covered in inky black ooze, with the four elemental symbols carved on the side and a skull on top.

"This is what is stopping our shifting," Erroh said with a shudder. "It feels horrible just being near it."

"The Death Goddess is involved somehow," I said. "That's her magic on these pillars, and I'm pretty sure the leader has it too."

All eyes turned to Varek, who shrugged. "I don't know anything more than you do."

"Is this some kind of trick?" Erroh asked.

"Yeah, are you double-crossing us?" Carth added.

Varek huffed. "I've done nothing but help you and fight by your side, and you still don't trust me. Enough. Figure this one out on your own."

He turned on his heel and stomped away, into the forest. I had no idea if he'd head back to the palace, or if we'd just lost any ground I'd previously gained with him.

I sighed. "The Death Goddess is obviously helping the cultists, but that doesn't mean Varek is too."

"We know that, but we need to be careful too." Parin gestured at the pillars. "Especially with things like this in play."

"Let's destroy it," Zain said.

He unleashed magic at the pillar, but it seemed to absorb it. Magic wouldn't work against it. Just like it prevented anyone nearby from shifting into dragon form.

"I'll send the Silver Guard to see what they can do," Erroh said. "For now, let's get out of here."

We moved back into the forest, until my mates claimed to not feel the effects of the pillars anymore. Then I sagged against the nearest tree. "The elementals are all dead. The Unseen's leader has all four elements. We failed."

Erroh leaned beside me. "We did the best we could, and we'll be better prepared next time."

"If it weren't for those pillars, we would have stopped them," Carth said.

I knew they were trying to make me feel better, but they were wrong. We'd never stood a chance today—and now we'd lost Varek too.

CHAPTER SEVENTEEN

W hen we returned to the palace, Varek was nowhere to be found. His things were still there, his bags half unpacked, but there was no sign of him.

We'd gathered up the few prisoners at the barn, but there were more dead than captured. The rest had fled. The cultists the Silver Guard imprisoned would be questioned, but we already knew from previous attempts that they wouldn't talk. They were too devoted to their cause.

My parents returned that afternoon from Divine Isle, and I was forced to explain everything that had happened while they were gone. Getting the words out was difficult. I felt like the biggest failure ever. How was I supposed to take over for my Mom when I couldn't even protect a few elementals?

When I'd finished, Mom surprised me with a tight hug. "You've done the best you could in a difficult situation," she said. "I'm proud of you."

"There's nothing to be proud of," I said, bowing my head.

"Of course there is," Slade said, resting a hand on my back. "You handled everything that happened just as we would have done."

I wasn't sure I believed that, but it didn't matter, because they were back now. It was such a relief to know they'd returned and could help with this problem. And to think only weeks ago I'd been eager to be the Ascendant, and believed I was more than ready to take on any challenge. Now I realized how foolish I'd been.

I wasn't ready. Not even close.

We were in my parents' living room, where I'd spent many days and nights with them before. Mom sat beside me on a sofa, with Slade standing beside us. Reven leaned against the nearest wall, while Auric sat in a nearby chair and Jasin paced restlessly.

"I'll have my spies try to uncover more information about the Unseen," Reven said.

Auric rubbed his chin. "We can't let those cultists murder any more elementals. Tensions are already high with the elementals at the moment."

"I'll set up extra guards around the city," Jasin said.

Kira nodded. "I'll speak with the elemental ambassadors and advise them to be especially cautious due to a radical human group."

"Is there anything I can do?" I asked. "Or my mates?"

Mom offered me a warm smile. "Thank you for the offer, but I think it's best if you continue your training and focus on growing closer with your mates. How are things going with them?"

"Things are good with Erroh, Carth, and Zain. I bonded with them at their temples and feel confident about them as my mates." I hesitated. "The other two...are more complicated."

"That's why it's especially important to spend some time with them now." She kissed my cheek. "Go and be with them. We'll take care of everything else."

"Thank you, Mom."

When I returned to my quarters, it was time for supper, but I found my three dragons passed out in exhaustion. They'd been doing a lot of flying and fighting, so I guess I couldn't blame them. I hoped to spend some time with Parin instead, but a member of the staff informed me he'd gone to visit his sister and her baby. I took supper alone in my room and went over some of the books we had about the Death Goddess, looking for any information that might help us.

A knock on my door made me jump, and I realized I'd fallen asleep with my face in a book. I quickly tamped down my unruly curls and went to open the door. "Yes?"

To my surprise, Varek stood on the other side. His long black hair was wet, as was his clothing, due to the soft rain outside. "May I come in?"

His unexpected politeness left me speechless, but I nodded and stood back. He swept into my room, his large masculine presence filling it completely.

"I wasn't sure if you were going to return," I said softly, surprised at how relieved I felt to have him here again.

"We made a deal, and despite what you think, I am a man of my word."

"I'm pleased to hear it."

He gave me a short nod. "I've been out searching for answers. I know your mates—and you, probably—don't trust me, but I have nothing to do with the Unseen."

I stepped closer to him, unable to stop myself. "I believe you. Do you know how their leader is using death magic?"

"I have my suspicions, but I'm not ready to share them yet. Not until I'm sure."

I bit my lip and considered pressing the issue, but then decided not to push him. We were already in an awkward place with each other, and I didn't want to make things worse. I needed him to become part of the team.

"All right," I said. "In the morning, we're going to begin training together. If we can't fight as a group, we're not going to be able to defeat the Unseen, and that includes you too. We can't always rely on the shades to give us an edge."

He arched a dark eyebrow. "I'm fine with that, but are your other mates?"

"They don't get a choice in the matter."

A wry grin split across his lush lips. "I like a woman who's not afraid to boss her men around. Just as long as you realize that won't work on me."

"Won't it?" I asked, with a challenge in my eyes.

"A king doesn't take commands, he gives them." He took my chin and kissed me hard, plundering my mouth with his tongue, until I was gasping with desire. Then he stepped back and headed to the door. "I'll see you tomorrow for training."

And just like that, he'd left me speechless again.

Training with all five of my mates began the next morning. As we stood out in the field, under a sky taunting us with the chance of rain, I sensed my bonded mates' apprehension. Now that we were mated, I could feel some emotions from Erroh, Carth, and Zain. It would only grow stronger in time, but for now it was more of a tingle and a clear sense they weren't all that happy about Varek being among us. I couldn't feel emotions from Varek or Parin yet, but their crossed arms, scowls, and stiff body language said they weren't best pleased either.

"I'm not sure how exactly you'd like me to train with the others," Varek said, gesturing at my mates. "If I use my magic on them, they'll die. That's the nature of it."

"Is there anything you can do that isn't, well...deadly?" I asked.

"No. Is there anything you can do with life magic that isn't healing?"

I sighed, but he had a fair point. "Fine, then you'll focus on combat training and deflecting the others' magic. Later, we can run the Gauntlet too."

We split up into pairs, with plans to rotate throughout the day. I was especially keen to work on my fire magic, but Zain was still a beginner too. If we weren't careful, we'd burn the palace down. I'd have to ask my fathers to join us tomorrow.

Instead, I practiced air against Parin and water against Zain. I'd grown up watching my dads using their powers, and even though I hadn't had any magic of my own yet, I'd studied every movement they made. Maybe it was because of that subconscious training that I picked up magic easily once I actually gained it. I felt like I'd been using it my entire life, and had only now unlocked my full potential.

Or almost full, anyway. I wouldn't be a dragon until I bonded with my other mates and gained their powers too.

Parin was next. I watched him spar with Varek, using his weapon of choice, a staff. He had been trained in combat, like we all had, but he was a diplomat, not a real fighter. Varek took him down easily, but as I watched, he reached out and shook Parin's hand after the match. Maybe there was some hope for them yet.

Erroh stood beside me as we watched them start another match. "I notice you haven't been pushing to go to the Earth Temple," he said.

"No, I thought we could all use some time together first." I turned toward him. "Plus, I needed to get used to the idea of Parin as my mate. Are you still upset he was chosen?"

"A little." Erroh rubbed the back of his neck. "Is it strange that my brother will share your bed, as I do? Yes. But I've started to accept it. I can tell he cares about you, in his own rigid way. It could be much worse."

I couldn't help but laugh. "High praise there."

He took my hand. "I want whatever makes you happy. If that's my brother, then that's fine. If that's Varek… well, I'll accept that too."

I pressed a kiss to his lips. "Thank you."

He grinned and stepped back, then created a tornado between us. "Now, back to work. See if you can dissolve this."

We continued practicing every day for a week against each other, trying to hone our skills so we could go up against the Unseen again. Next time we would be better prepared. My fathers came out to the field and gave us tips too, and by the end of the week, I could use fire without being a hazard to myself and others.

During meals, Erroh, Carth, and Zain joked around like the friends they were. Varek and Parin were still separate from them, not joining in on the fun, except one time I caught them rolling their eyes in unison when the other three were being particularly ridiculous. Progress.

In the evenings, one of my bonded mates came to my bed. It was nice not sleeping alone anymore, and I began to wonder what it would be like to have multiple men in my bed too. Would that ever happen?

On the last night of the week, Parin cleared his throat and said, "Now that we are confident about working together and your parents are here to continue the investigations into the Unseen, I think it's an appropriate time to make our way to the Earth Temple."

Carth nudged Zain with a huge grin. "I told you he'd bring it up first."

Zain grumbled and pulled out a coin, slamming it on the table. "Fine."

"You were betting on this?" I asked, my eyebrows jumping up.

"Just a bit of fun." Carth shoved the coin in his pocket, his eyes dancing. "I bet he'd crack by the end of the week, unable to resist Sora any longer. Zain thought Sora would demand to go first."

Parin looked away at that, as did Erroh. I wasn't sure how to respond either. Yes, I wanted to bond with Parin. I'd always been attracted to him. Plus I wanted to gain my powers and unlock Parin's true potential as a dragon. But I'd been waiting because I wasn't sure how he felt about me and didn't want to rush things.

Varek leaned forward with a grin and broke the awkward silence. "You made a bet and didn't include me? For shame."

The tension broke and Zain said, "Next time."

"None of you should be making bets," I said, rolling my eyes. "But yes, I do agree it's time to go to the Earth Temple. The Unseen could attack again at any moment, and it's best if we're better prepared for them."

I'd put off the next journey as long as I could. We'd hurt The Unseen with our attack, but as much as Reven's spies searched, not another whisper was heard about the cultists. If Varek knew anything, he was keeping silent.

But bonding with Parin meant bonding with Varek next. I wasn't sure I'd ever be ready for that.

CHAPTER EIGHTEEN

The journey to the Earth Temple was the longest of them all. It was a good thing my mates had been practicing flying. My parents offered to take us to the temple, but we declined, saying it would be better for us to do this on our own, and they were needed to defend the elementals against the Unseen.

This time, everyone came with me and Parin, except Varek, who said he still had business in the city. The dragons traded off flying to conserve their strength, and Parin held me stiffly the entire time. I tried to relax and enjoy being in his arms, but it didn't work. I was too nervous he was only doing this because he had no other choice.

As we flew, Parin pointed out places of interest. As a diplomat to the Earth Realm, he knew much about its history, even things my parents had never told me. At least our flight wasn't boring.

It took us three days to reach Frostmount, the tallest mountain in the Earth Realm, located far in the north. The air was freezing, especially up this high, but we'd all donned warmer clothes this morning in preparation. We glided over the snow-covered mountains until we saw Frostmount ahead of us, with the Earth Temple at the top.

Unlike the other temples, this one was not a building but more of a cave inside the mountain. It had been destroyed by my grandparents, led by The Black Dragon, much like they'd destroyed the Air Temple. Slade and the new High Priestess, Parin's aunt Stina, recreated the temple with their earth magic many years ago. However, they couldn't make up for the battle that had happened here—the one that cost Parin's father his life.

High Priestess Stina met us just inside the cave entrance. She had the same rich, dark skin that Parin had, along with thick dark hair touched by gray and big brown eyes. She threw her arms around Parin and laughed.

"How lucky to have my own grandson chosen by the Earth God! Ah, and Sora, always good to see you. And you too, Erroh, I swear you look bigger than when I last saw you." Stina gave another hug to Parin, then went to Erroh and patted his cheek. Her brother had been Parin's father, which meant she wasn't related to Erroh, though they had a good relationship. "I know you're probably eager for the bonding, but I made your favorite meal."

"I could never turn your beef stew down, Aunt Stina," Parin said.

"Good. You can tell me all about how the Gods chose two brothers for Sora's mates. I've never heard of such a thing before!"

The two brothers shared a look, before trudging forward. It was obvious they both had zero desire to discuss this topic. At least they were united on that front.

The Earth Temple had always been my favorite, and I tuned out their conversation to gaze around the great cave. The walls were unnaturally smooth due to earth magic, and embedded inside them were hundreds of glittering crystals. The flickering candlelight made them look like shimmering jewels, casting a rainbow of colors along the stone floor and the large jade green dragon statue we passed.

Stina spent the entire dinner digging for information, while her priests looked on with enjoyment. It was abundantly clear she was amused by the unconventional relationship that included both half-brothers. I humored her and explained that none of us really had much of a choice. The Gods chose for us, and she couldn't argue with that.

When supper was over, Stina and her priests stood, and she spread her arms. "And now we shall take you to the bonding chamber."

Erroh cleared his throat and looked away. "I think I'll head to bed early. Good luck, and all that."

Parin nodded to him with a pinched expression, and then we turned away and headed down a tunnel to the bonding chamber. Inside there were even more crystals, casting rainbows around the room like shadow. Otherwise the large room was pretty plain, with only a bed and some stone tables beside it.

"This room is beautiful." I ran my hands along the wall. Warm energy caressed my skin as I felt the power within the crystals. "I've always loved the Earth Temple."

"Me too." Parin sat on the edge of the bed, his movements stiff. He looked like he would rather be anywhere else. "Sometimes I like to imagine my father here, and what it was like for him to grow up within these walls."

Well, that made me feel like a total fool. I should've been more aware of how being here might affect Parin. His father died here, after all. A father he'd never even met.

Before I knew it, I'd crossed the room to put my hand on his arm. He studied it for several moments, then took my hand and pulled me down to sit beside him on the bed.

"How often did you visit here as a child?" I asked.

"About once a year. My mom always came to pay her respects and mourn my father, even after she married Erroh's dad. She also wanted me to have a good relationship with my aunt. Mostly for Stina. I'm the only thing left of her brother, after all."

"Does it bother you to be here?" I asked.

"Not at all." He tilted his head up and studied the crystals. "At first, I was shocked when the Earth God chose me. I didn't want such a position, not when it would take me away from my duties as a diplomat. Now I've decided it's the perfect way to honor my father and his sacrifice, while continuing to foster diplomacy in the four Realms."

"I'm sure he would be proud of you."

"I hope so."

When he looked at me with warmth in his eyes, I decided to try something. Scooting closer, I put my hand on his knee and leaned forward, pressing my lips to his. He stiffened before wrapping his arms around me, but his kiss was light and hesitant.

I pulled back, my cheeks burning up. "I'm sorry. I shouldn't have done that."

"No, don't apologize. It's what we came for after all."

"Yes, but…" I sucked in a sharp breath. "I know you don't see me that way, and that's okay. We just have to get through this once, and we don't have to do it again."

Parin's face softened. "That's not what I want. Yes, I used to see you as something like a little sister, but more than that, I always saw you as completely off-limits. You were Erroh's more than mine. It's taken me some time to adjust my thinking."

"I understand."

"Are you all right with this? I never asked before, but I am ten years older than you, after all. Does it bother you?"

"No." I ducked my head, unable to look at him. "I've always had something of a crush on you, even though I never dreamed being with you would be possible, for so many reasons. When you were chosen I was shocked, but excited too."

"Truly? I was never sure if you saw me that way."

I laughed. "I also wasn't sure how you felt about me."

"What a pair we are. Both of us wondering if the other wanted this or not."

"To be fair, our lives have been chaotic since we found out. We've barely had time to sit down and really talk."

"Then let's talk." He brushed the back of my knuckles with his thumb. "We don't have to do the bonding tonight. We can spend time getting to know one another. As equals."

"I'd like that."

We talked for hours, long into the night. He asked me questions about my wants and dreams. We discussed our favorite foods, colors, and hobbies. I learned he'd previously been with a woman for three years in a serious relationship, but she disliked how often he had to travel for work. She left him two years ago for a man in the Silver Guard, and he'd been alone since. In fact, he'd sworn off relationships, having decided they weren't for him, until the Earth God told him he had a different fate.

When I yawned, he looked at the pillows. "I will be a perfect gentleman if you'd like to settle in. I can sleep on the floor."

"I'm sorry. I didn't realize how tired I was. It's probably best if we get some sleep."

He averted his eyes as I took off my traveling clothes and put on the silky gown I'd brought to sleep in. When I was settled under the soft brown blankets, I sat up and looked at him. He'd removed his clothes and stood in his linen shorts and my mouth fell open. I'd never seen Parin shirtless before, and the reflected light from the crystals made his dark skin gleam, highlighting his frame. He wasn't as muscular as my other mates, but he was large and toned…and beautiful.

He was about to spread a blanket on the floor when I said his name. "Parin," I said softly. "Come sleep here."

He looked back and forth for a moment, then dipped his head. "Thank you."

I pulled the blankets up to my chin and tried not to obviously stare at him as he slid under them beside me. The heat of his body spread under the covers, chasing away the heavy chill in the air. I used air magic to blow out many of the candles in the room, covering us in darkness, and then we both said goodnight.

I kept waiting for his breathing to shallow and even out, but it never did. He shifted from his back to his side, facing me, and caught me looking at him in the dim light. Too late for me to pretend to be asleep.

Scooting under the covers, I shifted closer to him. Parin lifted the blankets so I could move my head to his pillow. My body wasn't pressed against his, but brushed against him in several spots, sending shivers of anticipation through me.

Something had changed during our conversation. I began to see him as something different. Not Erroh's brother. Not the older boy who always tried to keep me out of trouble. Not a forbidden crush.

A man. An attractive, virile man.

The tension had evaporated between us, and I pressed my lips to his again. This time they softened around mine, caressing and pressing, stealing my breath.

His large hand slid up my bare arm to my neck, changing the angle of the kiss. Parin's tongue slipped through the seam of my lips and I parted them, eager to see what he wanted to do with that tongue.

His tongue turned out to be my favorite feature of his. He kissed his way down my cheek, his hand still on my neck. Then he settled me back against the pillows as his lips and tongue made their way to my shoulders. He used his free hand to slide the flimsy strap of the nightgown down my shoulder. I pulled my arm out, but froze as his hand traced the collar of the gown. He pulled the other strap down, then tugged the material below my breasts.

I gasped when my nipples hit the cold air. Parin grunted and moved lower, his tongue circling one nipple, while his warm palm covered the other. He continued this amazing torment, slowly covering my breasts with his tongue, before moving to my belly, and then lower, lower, lower. Between my legs. Parting them wide.

His head moved between my thighs, and he showed me just how amazing his tongue truly was. Licking, sucking, teasing, until I was crying out his name and gripping the pillows hard.

"Parin, please," I cried. "I need you inside me."

He moved up my body and settled between my legs. The head of his cock pressed against me, inducing shivers of anticipation from me. His eyes met mine in the dim light, and he kissed me tenderly as his cock breached my entrance.

He sank into me slowly. I watched his face as he pushed in. He looked...content.

"Sora," he gasped.

"I feel it too," I whispered. The connection with him came quickly, and was deep and steady, like the earth. It wouldn't be shaken by any small force. Parin was my rock.

I allowed myself to close my eyes and focus on the connection with him as he moved in and out of me. Slowly at first, then faster and harder.

He ground into me, until an orgasm spread deep through me, making my body tighten around him. His hips rocked into me as he came too, and the ground around us rumbled and shook. Under my fingertips his skin turned to stone, including the hard cock inside me, but then the magic spread across my skin too. It held us there like a statue of a couple caught in the act of lovemaking, before fading away.

We both relaxed on the bed, sated and satisfied, and I rolled over and snuggled close. Parin looked at me in surprise, and then his expression turned pleased. We both knew the Earth God wasn't coming, so there was no sense getting dressed or waiting for him. He wrapped his arms around me and pulled me onto his chest.

I slept like a rock.

CHAPTER NINETEEN

I n the morning we decided not to rush back to the city, and instead to
take some time to practice our magic and give Parin space to learn to
fly. As the Earth Dragon, flying would be most difficult for him, at least
according to my father, Slade. Their deep connection to the ground made
it harder for them to embrace the sky.

After a hearty breakfast, we headed outside into the freezing air,
trudging through the snow on the mountain, and then began to practice
our magic. I reached for the earth and made it shake, then loosened some
stones and raised them in the air. I now had all four of the main elements
in my control. This was when I should have been able to ask the Life
Goddess for her blessing, except I'd been given a fifth mate. My own
dragon form would have to wait a little longer, unfortunately.

Erroh clapped Parin on the back. "Come on, big brother. For once I
can teach you a thing or two."

Parin grunted and then shifted into his dragon form. He was the
largest of all my dragons, with a stout body and dark hunter green scales
that looked almost black, until the sun hit them.

Zain, Carth, and Erroh shifted too, my four dragons all spreading their
wings before me. I couldn't help but smile, even as I felt a pang of jealousy.
More than that though, I felt a strong love and deep affection for them. I
could sense through the bond how happy they were and how close they felt
to each other too. Even Parin—he was truly one of them now.

With the help of my other mates, Parin managed to lift off the ground,
though it wasn't easy at first. His aunt and her priests whooped and

cheered as his wings stretched above us and he flew circles around the Earth Temple.

Now I only had one more mate to bond with...but he would be a challenge.

As we approached Soulspire a few days later, the smoke was the first sign that something was wrong. "Hurry!" I yelled to Erroh, whose back I rode. As the Air Dragon he was the fastest, even while carrying me, and he zoomed ahead of the others. Zain and Carth were just behind us, with Parin at the rear.

Thick plumes of smoke shot up from various parts of the city. We flew toward the nearest one, and saw it was a hotel specializing in hosting elementals, now on fire. The Unseen had attacked again. Except this time there were dead humans in the street too, including some of the Silver Guard. Carth let out a roar and sprayed water on the flames, dousing the building, but it was too late. The battle here was already over.

We flew across the city, over other places the Unseen had attacked, and a pattern emerged—every place had been one that catered to elementals. I spotted my fathers helping out at the various spots, and it was a relief to see they were safe. There was no sign of my mother, however. My dads would never be out there if she was injured though, so she was probably busy dealing with the aftermath of the attack elsewhere.

When we came to a spot near Varek's bar, we spotted him outside a café that had crumbled down like an earthquake had demolished it. He was speaking to one of the Silver Guard and pointing, but he turned toward us as we landed.

"What happened?" I asked.

Varek's face was grim, and I noticed exhaustion in his eyes. "The Unseen attacked locations around the city where the elementals were known to gather. There were so many of the cultists, the elementals and the Silver Guard didn't stand a chance. Your parents and I came out here to help, but by then it was too late. Many elementals and guards were already dead. Some elementals were kidnapped."

"How could they have done this?" Zain asked.

"I thought we'd weakened them a lot," Erroh added.

Varek shook his head and looked away. "Their numbers have grown considerably."

"Where is my mother?" I asked.

"She's set up an infirmary in the palace and is healing people there."

I nodded, since it was exactly what I'd expect. "I should go do that too. The rest of you, please see how you can help my fathers throughout the city."

"Wait," Varek said, raising a hand to stop us.

"What is it?" Parin asked.

Varek's jaw clenched. "Nothing. We can speak on it later."

"You know something, don't you?" Carth asked.

I took a step toward Varek. "You've kept a secret too long. It's time you told us."

"I think I know who the Unseen's leader is and how she has Death Magic." He drew in a sharp breath. "It's my twin sister, Wrill."

"You're twins?" I asked.

He nodded. "Born only minutes apart. I believe when the Death Goddess gave me her power, she bestowed it upon my twin too."

"She can't have two champions!" Zain said.

Varek shrugged. "I don't think the Death Goddess cares about playing by the rules. If it's true, then Wrill has all the same powers I do, but with no duty to become Sora's mate."

"Why didn't you tell us sooner?" Parin asked. "We could have prevented all this."

"I didn't believe it at first. I also knew if I told you before I was sure, you'd rush in and do something rash. I wanted to be certain."

"And you're certain now?" Erroh asked.

"Fairly. I've been trying to find Wrill for the last few days so I could talk to her, but she's gone into hiding."

"And you put her in charge of the Quickblades," I said, as the true horror of Wrill as the Unseen's leader settled in.

Varek's frown deepened. "Unfortunately, yes. Hence the bolstered numbers today. She's using them for her cause."

I sighed. "We'll discuss this later. For now we need to deal with the aftermath of these attacks and get the city back in order."

My mates agreed with me, and we split up to do our duty. My heart was heavy as I returned to the palace and found the infirmary. Tears sprang to my eyes when I saw the number of injured humans and elementals in the room. This was my fault. I should have made Varek tell me his suspicions instead of giving him space. I should have dealt with the cultists before going to the Earth Temple. I should have done a better job of being the protector of the four Realms.

I hadn't been the Ascendant for very long, and already I'd failed miserably.

I healed alongside my mother all through the afternoon and into the night. At some point I passed out in a chair in the corner, planning to only take a five minute nap, and I woke when someone picked me up. My eyes cracked open and I was startled to find myself in Varek's strong arms, cradled against his hard chest. He didn't look at me as he carried me through the palace, and he ignored my sleepy protests that I was fine and could continue healing.

Finally he set me down in my bed. "You need to rest."

I tried to hide a yawn. "You can't tell me what to do."

He spread his arms wide. "By all means, get up and walk out this door. I won't stop you."

I couldn't do it. Exhaustion had turned my limbs to heavy weights, and the thought of moving them seemed impossible.

I didn't know if I responded or not. I'd like to think I replied with some clever quip, but it was more likely I fell asleep immediately. Next thing I knew, it was morning, and one of the servants was quietly bringing me some food and water. I devoured both, needing sustenance after using so much energy to heal people. I wanted to get back to the patients immediately, although by the time I'd fallen asleep, everyone who was injured had already been attended to by myself or my mom.

After a quick bath, I received a summons from my parents, and met them in their living room again. All five of them looked weary. It was strange to see, as I'd always viewed them as unstoppable and indestructible. Now I was beginning to understand the pressure they'd been under my entire life.

Mom looked especially tired and was eating fruit from a tray when I entered. She patted the spot on the couch beside her. "I'm sorry to summon you like this, Sora, but it's important."

I sat beside her and stole some of the fruit from her tray. "What is it?"

"I think you should go to the Death Temple with all haste and complete your bonding."

If my mouth hadn't been full of melon, my jaw would've dropped. I hadn't expected her to encourage me to mate with Varek.

I swallowed. "Are you sure?"

"I do. Your fathers and I are not happy about the Death Goddess involving herself, but you've decided to accept him as your mate, and there's nothing we can do at this point unless we wish to start a war against the Realm of the Dead."

I settled back against her pillows. "No, we don't want that. We have enough problems at the moment."

"I saw Varek carry you to your room last night," Jasin said. "I appreciate that he seems to care for you, but you must be cautious. There was a reason I never could find proof about his criminal enterprises, and it's not that he was innocent."

"I know. I am. But he's given up all of that." I hesitated, but then decided not to tell them about Wrill. Not until we had more information. "He's helping us uncover the source of the Unseen's powers and we should know more soon."

"It's very disturbing that the Death Goddess is helping them," Auric said, rubbing his chin. "Especially since the other Gods have abandoned us."

"There must be an explanation for their absence," Slade said.

Mom stared out the window in thought. "Perhaps they've taken a step back from the world, entrusting us to handle things ourselves."

"They should at least give us their blessing." My head dropped. "I would have liked to meet them."

Mom wrapped her arm around me and gave me a squeeze. "I'm sorry. Perhaps they will come to you once all of the bonding is complete and the Life Goddess gives you her blessing. Even more reason for you to go to the Death Temple immediately."

Reven crossed his arms and spoke from his spot against the wall. "If she isn't ready, we shouldn't push her. Let Sora choose her own path."

I gave him a grateful smile. "Thanks, Dad. I think I'm ready, but I don't want to leave the city yet. There could be more attacks at any moment, and it's my duty to protect the people."

"We will be here to defend the city," Jasin said. "Don't worry about that."

Auric reached over and patted my hand. "You'll be able to help the people even more once you have your dragon form."

"I'm with Reven, there is no reason to rush this," Slade said. "Sora, go whenever you are ready. If it's tomorrow, fine. If it's a year from now, so be it."

"We only want whatever is best for you, of course," Kira said. "And we believe in you."

"I want to do my part to help the people," I said. "I'll speak with Varek and see if we're ready. If not, we will continue our training and help defend the city."

All of my parents seem satisfied with that answer, and I went to the infirmary to check on the patients still there. Most of them had recovered, and the rest I did some more healing on. When I was finished, I returned to my rooms and collapsed.

A tingle down my spine woke me sometime later, when night had fallen. The room was pitch black, except for a tiny sliver of moonlight, and silent except for the lightest footfall. I sat up quickly, just in time to dodge a blade made of ice. Above me, I saw a smooth black mask.

The leader of the Unseen had come to kill me.

CHAPTER TWENTY

The door burst open and Varek swooped inside, wielding a large knife. He immediately leaped forward and put himself between me and the attacker, then grabbed her by the arms.

"What are you doing?" he demanded, his voice angry.

Flames danced across the Unseen leader's skin and Varek was forced to let her go. I blasted her with water to douse the flames, then used air to circle her like a hurricane. When Varek got to his feet, he reached through the torrent of water and air and grabbed her mask, yanking it from her face.

I let my magic go with a gasp when I saw Varek's twin standing before him. We'd suspected it was her, but seeing the truth was still shocking. Especially since she'd just tried to assassinate me in my sleep.

"I knew it." Varek threw the mask aside in disgust. "I just hoped I was wrong."

Wrill looked up at her brother with an angry slant to her mouth, but made no move to attack again. "You shouldn't have stopped me."

"What were you thinking?" he asked. I'd never seen his face so raw, utterly stripped of all the walls and masks he put up to keep himself aloof. "Sneaking in here to try to kill my mate? How could you?"

Wrill's gaze moved from him to me, and murder glinted in her eyes. "I did it for you, brother. If she's dead, you don't have to mate with her and become the thing we hate the most—a Dragon. How could I? How could *you?*"

"The Death Goddess chose me. She set me on this path. I could not refuse." His eyes flicked to me. "Nor do I want to."

She lurched forward and took his hands in her own. "Varek, please. There's still time to change your fate. Walk away from this. Return to the Quickblades. Help me run the Unseen." Her eyes gleamed with hope and righteousness. "We're doing great work. Righting the balance between humans and elementals. You can be a part of that too."

He shook his head. "What you're doing is wrong. Yes, there is a power imbalance, but murdering elementals is not the way."

"We're changing things," she snapped. "You can either be a part of that change, or you can be the enemy."

"I am where I am meant to be."

Wrill glared at him and then turned it to me. "Then you've chosen to side with the oppressors. So be it."

She leaped out the open window into the night, and then used air to lift her up and fly away. Varek and I rushed after her, but then we stopped. Varek didn't want to go after his own sister, and even if I could catch her, what would I do? Kill my mate's sister? Lock her up?

All I knew was that this new development wasn't going to make our bonding any easier.

My bedroom door burst open and my other mates rushed in wielding weapons. They looked around, but saw only me and Varek standing there, and then relaxed.

"We heard a commotion," Zain asked. "Is everything all right?"

"Yes, we're fine," I said, though I was still a bit shaken by everything that had happened.

Varek's jaw clenched. "The leader of the Unseen is my sister. We've confirmed it now."

"She was here?" Erroh asked.

"She tried to kill Sora."

"She did what?" Carth asked, and the other men echoed his statement.

I held up a hand. "It didn't work, obviously. We stopped her and no one was injured. At least now we know for sure it is her."

"We need to double your guards," Parin said. "No one should have been able to get in here."

"My sister has control of all four elements, plus death magic," Varek said. "She is almost unstoppable. More guards won't help much."

He was right. Wrill was the dark version of me, with death magic instead of life. My equal, at least until I bonded with Varek, gained his death magic, and then became a dragon myself. Only then could I have any hope of defeating her one-on-one.

"I'd like to speak with Varek alone, please," I told my mates.

703

Erroh nodded. "We'll patrol the area in case other members of the Unseen are about."

My other mates headed out the door with him. As soon as it was shut, I let out a long sigh, feeling exhausted again. I sat on the edge of the bed and looked up at Varek, who stared out the window where his sister had vanished.

"I can't believe she came here to kill you." He shook his head. "I knew she was the leader of the Unseen and what she was doing, but I never thought she would go so far."

"Why does she hate the Dragons so much?" I was especially curious since she'd implied Varek hated them too.

"Our childhood did not leave us with much love for the Dragons. Or the elementals."

"Tell me."

"Very well, but it's not a nice tale." He pulled out a chair from my desk and sat in it, facing me. "Our father was a general in the Onyx Army. He was killed in the last battle against the Black Dragon."

That meant he was one of the men that fought against my parents— and lost. "I'm sorry. I had no idea."

"Wrill and I were only two at the time. When the new regime took over, my mother was left a widow with two small children. No one would help her, because of who her husband was and how he'd died. The Onyx Army was disbanded and disgraced. She tried to find work, and often took in sewing and laundry, but it wasn't enough. She even applied here at the palace, but was turned away."

My heart broke, imagining a tiny Varek coming to the palace with his mother, looking for help. "That's awful."

"She was young and pretty though, so she had one other way to make money. A way I preferred to pretend wasn't happening." He scowled as he stared off into space. "She got involved with some bad people and got hooked on alcohol. Wrill and I were on our own for the most part, growing up on the streets, and I did everything I could to take care of my mother and my sister."

"That must have been difficult for all of you," I said.

He shrugged. "There are many who went through similar things when your parents took over. It wasn't an easy transition for anyone who supported the Black Dragon."

I bowed my head. "I…I had no idea."

"Of course not. You grew up in a palace with everyone telling you how special you are." His voice was harsh, but then he paused and sucked in a breath. "As I was saying, things were tough for us, but we managed. Our mom took a new job with some elementals, helping them as an assistant in the warehouse. Then one of them lost their temper and burned the place down. She died from the smoke."

I gasped and covered my mouth. "That's horrible. Was it the same warehouse where the Unseen had their meeting?"

"Yes. That's when I began to suspect it was Wrill. We were thirteen when Mom died, and she never got over it. She blamed the Dragons for our father's death, and the elementals for our mother's."

"That does explain a lot." I sighed. "Do you blame us also?"

He gazed at me for an eternity. "No," he finally said. "Perhaps I did once. But not anymore. Otherwise I wouldn't be here now."

I let out a relieved breath. "Good."

"After my mother passed, I did whatever I could to take care of Wrill. Many of the things I did were...not exactly legal. Before I knew it, I had people working for me. I formed the Quickblades, with Wrill at my side. Though you think we're nothing more than criminals, we did have a code, of sorts. We didn't kill without being sure of guilt. We didn't steal from those that would be hurt by the theft. We didn't force anyone to join us. We tried to give back and protect those who were overlooked by the rest of society. Widows, orphans, the disabled."

"So there is honor among thieves after all," I said, feeling something almost like respect for him. How unexpected.

He leaned forward, his gaze intense. "Honor, yes. But your other mates are right. I was a criminal. I fought. I stole. I killed. I am no stranger to death. That's why the Death Goddess chose me as her champion."

"You've walked away from all of that now."

"I have, but it's still a part of me. That darkness will always live in my past, and in my heart."

"I'm not afraid of the dark," I said. "But I do need to know where you stand. Will it be a problem if we face your sister again?"

"No. She's gone too far. I always knew she'd gone to some human rights rallies, and I supported that, but not this."

"I feel like such a fool. I didn't even know there were rallies about this sort of thing until recently."

"I'm sure that knowledge was kept from you. Surely you must realize now there is inequality between Dragons, humans, and elementals. Humans are defenseless against the might of the elementals, and though the Dragons now are more just than the previous ones, many still remember the old days and worry this peace won't last. The elementals or the Dragons could enslave the entire human race all too easily."

"We would never do such a thing," I said, horrified at the very idea. "The Dragons exist to keep the balance between humans and elementals, and between the four Realms. My family has no interest in ruling."

"Your grandmother ruled for hundreds of years. I know you and your parents are different now that I've met you, but before that?" He shrugged. "Many just assumed you were another set of overlords."

"That's preposterous! My parents brought peace, freedom, and prosperity to the entire world."

"And yet, the elementals still are a threat. They want more land, and humans are defenseless against them."

"Which is why they need the Dragons!" I huffed.

Varek spread his hands. "I'm only trying to show you the imbalance of power in the world. I never said it was your fault. I know you didn't ask for this role either. But in order to stop the Unseen, we must understand their purpose and why so many people are joining their ranks."

I ran a hand through my curls, tugging on them. This sort of talk was upsetting because it made me rethink everything I'd believed my entire life. Yet at the same time, it felt good to open my eyes to the truth too. If humans were suffering, it was my duty to do something about it. Even if the Unseen's methods were wrong, their message resonated with a lot of people. The imbalance of power between the elementals, humans, and Dragons had to be addressed at some point, but not with violence and murder. If the Gods would give the humans powers, or at least some of them, they could protect themselves. It might balance the world out.

But the Gods had abandoned us.

"Thank you for telling me all this," I said. "I'm glad someone can speak honestly with me about these things, and I appreciate you telling me about your past. I feel as though I know you better now."

"And what do you think of everything I told you about my past?" His words were a challenge, but there was something vulnerable in his eyes. Whatever I said now would determine the fate of our relationship.

I stood and moved in front of him, so he had to look up at me. "I can embrace your darkness, if you will let me."

His large hands rested on my hips, sending heat to my core. "I felt it when Wrill was here, you know. I didn't hesitate coming to stop her. I couldn't let her kill you."

"Because the Death Goddess wants you to bond with me."

"Not only that." He pulled me down into his lap and rested his hand on my thigh. "Even if we weren't mates, I'd want to claim you as my own."

"Is that so?" I asked, stroking his rough jaw.

"You're smart, tough, and loyal. Not to mention, damn gorgeous. I'm too old for you, but I don't much care. You see me as a criminal and a villain, but I don't much care about that either. You will be mine."

His mouth captured mine, putting his words into action, while his fingers dug into my hips. A soft moan escaped my lips as his tongue plundered my mouth and our bodies pressed together. If I was worried about the bonding before, now all doubts fled my mind. We both wanted this, and there was no reason to wait any longer.

I pulled back and gazed into Varek's eyes. "Let's go to the Death Temple."

"Now?" he asked, as he slid his hands up my thighs.

"Do you want to wait any longer?"

"No." He set me down on the floor and stood. "No, I don't."

"Then let's get going."

CHAPTER TWENTY-ONE

The Death Temple didn't exist during my grandmother's rule. Neither did the Life Temple, for that matter. Instead, there was one place called the Spirit Temple, just south of Soulspire. That was where the battle between my parents and my grandparents was fought, and where many elementals and humans died on the field outside it. After the Spirit Goddess was split into the Life Goddess and the Death Goddess, it was decided two temples were needed. The Life Temple was built from the ruins of the old Spirit Temple, while the Death Temple was constructed on the battlefield, its powers fueled by the many lives lost in that spot. Including Varek's father.

The two temples faced one another, reflecting the twin goddesses and their never-ending rivalry. One could not exist without the other, and yet the Death Goddess had tried to take over before. She'd nearly succeeded during my grandparents' rule. My parents had sent her back to the Realm of the Dead, and she'd stayed quiet since then, at least until she demanded I take a mate to represent her too.

I'd been inside the Death Temple a few times and it had always made my skin crawl. I'd been blessed by the Life Goddess from birth, and every-thing about this temple was anathema to me. The building was covered in the bones of both humans and animals, and stood in the middle of the blackened and bloodstained field. Once, plants grew here and animals roamed freely, but no more.

The High Priestess Harga let us inside the temple, into a dark cavernous room lit by a single torch, which cast deep shadows across the walls. Like the exterior, the walls here were inlaid with bones of various shapes and sizes, including skulls, and in the center of the room was a statue of a huge dragon made entirely of bone too. I tried to focus on Harga instead, but her unnaturally pale skin, long black hair, and deep-set eyes only made me shiver even more.

"Welcome back, Sora. It's about time you accepted death as part of your life." Even her low voice was creepy. I forced a smile, and luckily she turned to Varek before I had to answer. "Welcome back, Varek. The Death Goddess awaits your service."

As she led us down somber, dark hallways with dry flowers, I whispered, "You've been here before?"

Varek nodded. "I came to pay my respects after being chosen."

We passed four open doorways, each with a priest standing in them, who all bowed their heads but said not a word. No food or drink was offered. No smiles were given. I felt like I was at a funeral and was vaguely worried I had not dressed for the occasion.

Harga stopped at two double doors and bowed. Then she remained in that lowered position, while we stood there. Varek opened the doors, and I followed him inside the bonding chamber, although I secretly wanted to see how long she would stay like that.

After the doors shut, Varek began to chuckle. "They're very serious here."

I blew out a long breath. "That's an understatement."

To my relief, this room didn't have any skulls or other bones on the walls. It was empty, save for a bed with black sheets and some candles. As we stepped closer, I ran my hand along the sheets. Silk.

"I have to admit, this temple managed to kill my mood from earlier, but this room is a lot better," I said.

"You said you wanted to embrace my darkness." Varek spread his arms. "Here it is."

"I didn't realize there would be quite so many skulls."

He let out a deep laugh, and then grabbed my waist and yanked me against him. When Varek looked at me, all the previous vulnerability was gone. In its place was pure lust. He kissed me hard, while his hands roamed across my body, feeling me through my long dress. He untied my cloak and let the fabric pool at my feet, while devouring my mouth like he wanted to show me he owned it.

Then he abruptly let go of me and sat on the edge of the bed, leaning back on his palms. I breathed harder, anticipation dancing up my spine.

"Now, princess..." His gaze raked down my body. "Now, you strip for me."

At first, I could only stare back at him. No one ordered me around. Not even my mates.

"Take off your clothes," he demanded.

I should have demanded he remove his own clothes. But I didn't. Something about his commanding tone made lust race through my veins. I was torn between defiance and desire. One of us had to surrender, and I realized in the Death Temple, it had to be me.

I reached up and untied the back of my dress, then slowly tugged it down my shoulders. His dark gaze devoured every inch of skin I revealed, until the fabric slid below my breasts, freeing them. Then it continued down my hips and my thighs, before pooling at my feet. I stepped out of the dress and the rest of my underthings and stood before him completely naked.

Surprisingly, it didn't embarrass me. The thought of standing naked before him excited me. Made me feel powerful even. Especially when he looked at me like the sight of my flesh was enough to drive him mad with lust.

"Aren't you going to undress now?" I asked.

"I will undress when I choose to. And you may address me as your king."

My eyes widened. Was he serious? "My king?"

"When we are alone in the bedroom together, you will call me your king." His voice left no room for argument.

I crossed my arms over my breasts. "I won't agree to that."

His lips quirked up at that. He liked when I challenged him. "You will."

Then he stood and pulled off his shirt, revealing a broad chest and strong muscles. I longed to run my hand over that skin, to feel every ridge and valley, to trace the dark hair trailing down into his trousers. Trousers which he slowly removed and slid down, revealing his perfect, very hard cock.

He rested a hand on it, knowing I was watching, then sat on the edge of the bed. "I let you win when we fought. Now I demand you fulfill your side of the bargain."

I tilted my head. "I'm not sure I believe you let me win."

"Get on your knees and suck my cock," he ordered, his eyes unforgiving.

His commands should have annoyed or infuriated me, but instead they only made me want him even more. He was the only man who could get away with saying such things to me.

I dropped to my knees, and found myself wrapping my lips around the head of his cock. I'd never taken a man into my mouth before, and though

I had no idea what I was doing, I'd secretly dreamed of this moment ever since my fight with Varek. He tasted salty and masculine, and he felt huge in my mouth.

One of his hands slid into my hair, while the other he used to prop himself up on the bed. He used the grip on my hair to angle me better, as his cock slid deeper along my tongue. "That's it. Take it all, princess."

My eyes fluttered up to him, wide and unsure, and met his dark gaze. I flicked my tongue along his shaft, tasting him, and Varek grunted. Though I wasn't sure what to do, he guided me up and down on his cock, moving his hips in time to thrust inside.

"Suck harder," he said, and I tried to obey. "Good girl. Such a perfect princess, even on your knees."

Everything he said made me want him even more. How was that possible? I was desperate to please him, and even more desperate to have that cock inside me.

"Enough," he said, but I disobeyed him. I found I quite liked it now that I was getting into it. I felt powerful, knowing I could make his face twist with pleasure and elicit low grunts from his throat. He couldn't stop me—he was too far gone. His fingers tightened in my hair and he threw his head back as I sucked him harder, and his seed spurted down my throat, just like he'd demanded during our fight.

"Gods, woman. You are exquisite." He pulled his cock from my mouth and used his thumb to wipe his seed off the corner of my lips. Then he picked me up as if I weighed nothing, spun me around, and pushed me down on the bed face first. I could've fought him off, as I'd proved in the back of his bar, but I didn't want to. I was very interested in what he would do next.

His cock slid between my back cheeks, and I felt it hardening again. "None of the others have taken you here, have they?"

I shook my head, too overwhelmed to speak as his cock brushed against my tight entrance.

"Good. Tonight I'm going to fill all your holes."

With that, he thrust hard into my folds, making me gasp. I was already so wet from desire, and his cock was already slick from my mouth, that he slid inside with ease. At the same time, his finger entered my behind, turning my gasp into a loud moan. No one had touched me there before, and at first it was rather shocking, but then I liked it. Especially as he began thrusting with both his cock and his finger, pressing me down into the bed. His body completely covered mine, and I could only grip the silk sheets as he dominated me. I wanted to complain, but Gods, it felt so good to let him use my body that way.

Then he suddenly pulled out and nudged his cock into my back entrance. I nearly screamed from the intense pressure as he began to fill me from behind. It hurt, but somehow it felt good too. I didn't understand it, but I bit my lip as he kept breaching that tight hole, making me stretch around his huge shaft.

"That's it," he murmured against my hair. "Relax and let me fill you. Gods, you're tight."

Then he was suddenly completely inside, all the way to the hilt, and I felt so full I could barely stand it. He groaned as he kneaded my buttocks, letting me adjust to his size. Then he yanked up my hips, getting a better angle, so he could begin moving in and out of me.

"You're all mine now," he said, as he thrust into me. "Every inch of you belongs to me tonight."

The pressure and pain soon gave way to immense pleasure unlike anything I'd experienced before. It got even better when he slid one finger inside me, and used another to rub that sensitive spot just above my folds. All I could do was let him control my body as I braced myself on the bed, taking everything he gave me. He was rough and demanding as he claimed me, but I loved every second of it.

My orgasm came quickly and violently, making my body tremble with pleasure while sounds came out of my mouth like I'd never made before. He didn't slow. If anything, he only pounded me harder, relentless in his need to make me his own. Somehow he teased another orgasm out of me, or maybe it was the same one that only got even more intense. His cock surged inside me as his climax came too, and then darkness surrounded us in a thick layer, turning everything black. Inky shadows crawled across our bodies, tying us together, as his magic spread into me.

As soon as the darkness faded away, Varek pulled out of me and wrapped his arms around me, rolling us onto our sides so he was spooning me from behind. His hands stroked my tender skin, as his lips brushed my ear.

"I own you now, princess," he said. "But you own me too."

"My king," I whispered. "I'm yours."

His arms tightened around me as I said the word, and then he rolled me toward him. His hands cupped my cheeks, and he pressed a soft kiss to my lips. My heart fluttered faster.

"Perhaps I should call you my queen now, for you've claimed my heart as surely as I've claimed your body." He kissed me again, longer, deeper. "I never thought I could love anyone, but I love you."

I stroked his rough cheek. "I love you too. I didn't think it would be possible, but I do."

A rumbling sound interrupted our tender moment, and we both sat up, confused. Darkness seemed to crawl across the floor like fog, gathering in one spot in front of the bed, before solidifying into a large dragon made of bones. I yanked the sheets up to cover my nakedness and gasped.

The bone dragon had eyes made of darkness and decay, and she reared up and roared, spreading her skeletal wings. Varek dropped into a bow on the bed, not caring that he was naked, and I did the same while trying to retain some semblance of modesty.

"You honor us, Goddess," Varek murmured.

Of all the Gods to actually appear before me, it had to be this one. The Death Goddess fixed her beady black eyes on us and bared fangs that dripped with venom, before letting out something like a cackle. "Good work, my champion. You have mated with the Ascendant and claimed your place as one of her bonded mates."

She ignored me completely, but I straightened up and faced her, while clutching the sheet to my chest. "Why did you demand I take Varek as your champion?"

"All of the other Gods have representatives in the world. Is it not fair that I should have one of my own?"

"I suppose it is," I said. I'd never considered it that way before. "But why did you give Wrill your powers too? No God has two champions."

"I made Wrill my new High Priestess. Harga is only a decoy."

"Why?" Varek asked.

The Death Goddess swished her tail, which made a horrible clacking sound. "You both serve a purpose. Wrill's is to sow chaos and spread death, while also bringing to light the problems of this world that the other Gods have caused. Your duty is to bring balance to that chaos and continue my legacy."

Her words made no sense to me. She wanted chaos and death, but she also wanted us to stop Wrill? My parents had told me the Gods were enigmatic, but I had no idea how true that was until now.

"Even now, you think me the villain," the bone dragon said with a sneer. "Yet while the other Gods have abandoned this world, I am here."

She made a fair point, even as my heart sank. My suspicious about the other Gods were proving to be true. They could have come to give us their blessings, they simply chose not to do so.

"We will serve you as best we can," Varek said.

"See that you do." She bared her fangs. "Give my regards to my sister."

With that, the bones of her body collapsed into a heap, and then they turned to dust before our eyes. She was gone.

CHAPTER TWENTY-TWO

W e spent the rest of the night alternating between sleep and sex, but in the morning, I was ready to get going. I couldn't sleep well in the temple, even if death didn't bother me as much now that I could control it—not that I planned to test that out anytime soon. More importantly, now that I'd mated with all five of my men, I could head to the Life Temple and become a dragon myself. Assuming the Life Goddess would give me her blessing.

Varek's dragon form was huge and his scales were shiny and black, like a dark lake under a moonless night. He practiced flying over the barren field around the Death Temple for a short while, before feeling confident he could fly us back the short distance to the palace.

As we approached Soulspire, we noticed other dragons flying over the city, both my parents and my mates. "A show of force?" I asked. Varek growled his agreement.

When we landed, we found the palace on lockdown, a safety measure put in place by the Silver Guard after the attacks on the city and the assassination attempt last night. My mother rushed out of the palace and glanced between me and Varek, who had already resumed his human form.

"Is it done?" she asked.

"Yes, I've bonded with all five mates," I said.

Kira then reached out her hands to Varek. "Welcome to the family. I know we got off to a rocky start, but you are one of us now."

Varek took her hands, though he looked uncertain. "Thank you."

"We want to go to the Life Temple immediately," I said.

Mom nodded. "I think that is a wise idea."

"Do you know what I should expect?"

"No. I'm sorry. Things were completely different for me. Hopefully your meeting with the Life Goddess is a lot easier."

My parents had gone to the Spirit Temple and fought my grandmother and her mates, while a huge battle was waged outside. When they'd defeated her, they'd released the Spirit Goddess and separated her into the twin Life and Death Goddesses. After banishing the Death Goddess back to her world, the Life Goddess gave Mom her blessing. I was grateful I didn't have to go through all that.

Kira wrapped me in a hug. "When you get back, we will celebrate. We're all very proud of you."

"Thanks, Mom." I gave her a squeeze and then stepped back. She nodded at us both, and then went to speak to some of the guard.

My other mates swooped down into the courtyard, returning from their patrols of the city. I embraced them all, and felt through our bond how relieved they were that I had returned.

"How did it go?" Erroh asked.

I exchanged a glance with Varek with a secretive smile. "It went well."

"Better than well, judging by her moans," Varek said with a smirk.

My cheeks heated and I cringed a little, worried the other guys would get upset. But Carth only chuckled and said, "She does get pretty loud sometimes."

The other guys grinned and I scowled at them all. "I do not!"

That only amused them more.

"You seem different," Parin told Varek. "Lighter, somehow."

"A night with the princess will do that to a man," Varek said.

"No more of that nickname," I said, but then paused. "Unless we're in bed, anyway."

They all laughed, and I couldn't help but be amazed at the change in the group from only a week before. Even with the threat of the Unseen looming over our heads, we'd become a team. Maybe even something more.

We all freshened up and had a quick bite to eat before leaving for the Life Temple. I rode on Varek's back, surrounded by my four other dragons like an honor guard. As we flew, I thought about how this would be one of the last times I would ride on the back of a dragon—soon I would be one myself.

It was a short flight heading south of Soulspire, and soon the Life Temple came into view. The temple had been rebuilt after it had been destroyed in the battle against the Black Dragon, and unlike the Death Temple nearby, this one was surrounded by vibrant plants and animals. The temple itself sat at the top of a hill overlooking the plains, and was nestled against the side of a mountain with a waterfall running down it, which turned into a river that ran through the valley and nourished life there. The building was made of gleaming white stone, with dark green ivy wrapped around its large pillars.

The High Priestess was outside when we arrived, tending to a garden of beautiful flowers with a rabbit watching her. Nelsa was in her fifties, with very long blond hair, sun-kissed skin, and kind blue eyes. She wore a simple white gown with no sleeves and her feet were bare.

Nelsa gave me a low bow and a warm smile. "Hello, Sora. We've been expecting you. We got word you were at the Death Temple this morning."

Her priests stood at the arched doorway and gestured for us to enter. They bowed as we passed through it into an open-air courtyard with a bubbling fountain in the center topped with a dragon figure made entirely from plants. A black and white dog ran up to us and wagged its tail, while brightly colored birds perched along different spots in the courtyard and squawked loudly.

"Do you care for some refreshments?" Nelsa asked, as she led us further into the temple, the dog happily trotting beside her.

"No, thank you," I said, as I drew in a deep breath of fragrant air. Being here felt so right to me, more so than any of the other temples. I'd grown up with the Life Goddess's magic, and this place was like home.

Nelsa led us to a door on the other side of the courtyard. "The Life Goddess awaits you."

We stepped through it and were outside again in a large garden full of flowers and plants, with butterflies flitting through the air. The waterfall could be seen above us, and a stream of water gurgled nearby. A small fire pit had been set up and danced with flames, while large, smooth rocks provided seating. All of the elements were represented in this place, and it resonated deep inside me. The only one missing was death—probably because no one had planned for this fifth element to become involved.

My mates fanned out behind me, glancing around. Parin touched one of the smooth rocks. "Impressive."

Varek scowled. "I shouldn't be here."

"Nonsense," I replied, while holding out a hand. A bright blue butterfly landed on my fingertips. "You're as much my mate as any of the others."

"We're here, now what do we do?" Carth asked.

"The Life Goddess needs to be summoned," Zain said.

Erroh's face brightened. "Oh, I researched this the other week. Auric gave me some old texts. Sora needs to prove that she has all the elements, and then the Goddess shall appear and give her blessing."

"I can do that." I sucked in a breath, then took a step forward. The elemental power inside me was still fresh and new, but it was easy for me to reach. First air, from my oldest friend, Erroh. I made it swirl around me, the wind rustling my hair and dress. Next, water, from my flirtatious lover, Carth. I gathered it from the stream and made a ball of it in my palm. Third was fire, from my devoted protector, Zain. I pulled it from the fire pit and made the flames dance in my other hand. Then it was earth, from my solemn mate, Parin. I made the ground under me rumble and thrust up, lifting me above everyone else on a piece of jutting rock.

That might have done it, but I couldn't forget my final mate, Varek, even if no one had expected him. I let out a burst of death magic, making the grass under my feet shrivel up and turn brown in a circle around me.

The sun overhead seemed to brighten until it was blinding, and we all had to throw up our arms to shield our eyes. When the light dimmed, a huge, shimmering dragon stood before us, seemingly made of light. Flowers bloomed at her feet and butterflies perched on her wings. She gazed down at me with a kind smile that filled me with warmth.

"Hello, my child," she said. "You have bonded with all of your mates and control all the elements. You are ready to become my champion."

I bowed my head, feeling breathless but also relaxed. It made no sense. "Thank you."

"I realize my sister threw in a complication, but you handled it well. I cannot fault her for wanting to be represented and worshipped as the other Gods are."

I hesitated, but then asked, "Forgive me, but where are the other Gods? We expected to meet them at their temples."

"Once your mother became the Silver Dragon, we decided to retreat from the world and let mortals control their own fates. We had so easily been corrupted and nearly led the world to ruin, we thought it would be better for our champions to guide humans and elementals into the future."

"There are many who no longer want the Dragons to lead," I said with a sigh.

"I'm certain you will find a solution to the troubles you face." She bent her head, touching my forehead with her snout like a kiss. "You have my blessing."

As soon as she touched me, she vanished. At the same time, shimmering scales rippled across my skin, while my body expanded and shifted into something much bigger. I grew claws, fangs, and a tail, then spread my sparkling wings wide. As I did, dozens of colors moved along my scales, refracting the light and forming rainbows. Pride and exultation filled my chest. I'd prepared for this moment every day of my life, and now I'd done it.

I was a Dragon, like my mother.

CHAPTER TWENTY-THREE

F lying was even better than I'd imagined all these years. Riding on the backs of other dragons was already incredible, but this topped even that. Feeling the air against my face, the strength in my body, and the power in my wings made me never want to turn human again.

I did flips and turns over the Life Temple, and my mates cheered me on while hovering beside me in their own dragon forms, while giving me a few pointers now and then. We danced in the air, chased each other around, and roared into the sky, before finally heading back to Soulspire. I couldn't wait to show my mother my new form, and to fly with my entire family.

When we arrived at the palace, I instantly knew something was wrong. Smoke filled the air, and the gate in front had been twisted and bent by someone who could control earth magic. Even worse, the bodies of slain guards were scattered across the courtyard, some blackened by fire. Other guards rushed around, shouting to one another, while palace staff tried to tend to the injured.

I shifted back to human form and grabbed the nearest guard I saw, shaking him a little. "What happened here?"

"They took them!" he sputtered, his eyes panicked.

"Who?"

"Your parents!"

Cold terror washed through me. "How? Where?"

The guard drew in a ragged breath and tried to compose himself. "Someone in the palace was working for the Unseen and poisoned your parents' meal. It knocked them out, and the Unseen attacked the palace gates and kidnapped them. We tried to stop them, but they had powers. I'm sorry."

"Where did they take them?" I nearly shouted, my heart hammering in my chest.

"I don't know!"

I turned to my mates, who had landed behind me. "We have to find them!"

"I'm the fastest," Erroh said. "I'll patrol the city while you help these people."

"I'll go too," Carth added. "I'm nearly as fast as you are, and we can cover more ground that way."

Parin nodded. "The rest of us will stay here and protect the palace and help however we can."

I wanted to protest that we should all go searching, but then I heard the moans of people in the courtyard and nodded, while choking back my fear and rage. I would be of most use here, and I trusted my mates to do the best they could to find my parents.

By the time Erroh and Carth returned, I'd managed to lose myself in the healing and block out everything else, and had done everything I could. I rushed toward my mates, eager for news of my parents.

"They're in the stadium across town," Erroh said, his voice panicked. "The Unseen are gathering a huge crowd there and they're going to drain your parents in front of everyone for all the humans to see, as soon as the sun sets. They have some elementals too. We need to go, now."

"They have those pillars up that are preventing your parents from shifting," Carth added. "Those need to be our first targets."

Gods, it was even worse than I'd thought. Especially since the sun was nearing the edge of the horizon now. I summoned water to wash the blood off my hands and then shifted back into my dragon form, enjoying the rush of power it gave me. "Let's rescue my parents and put an end to this."

"Is Wrill leading the Unseen?" Varek asked.

"Yes, she is," Carth said.

I swung my large head toward Varek. "Is this going to be a problem?"

His jaw clenched. "Not at all."

We devised a rough plan and then the five of us took off, soaring into the air as quickly as we could. This was not the time for stealth. We were going to show them that the Dragons were chosen to lead for a reason, and we would not be bullied by humans with stolen powers.

It was a short flight to the stadium on the other side of Soulspire, and we arrived just as the sun dipped below the horizon, turning the sky a deep indigo. As the six of us circled over the packed stadium, I released a loud, primal roar, laced with my anger and fear. My mates all chimed in and added their thunderous voices too, until we filled the night with the sound. Some people in the stadium screamed and began to run. Good.

The stadium was packed with onlookers, probably curious humans the Unseen had gathered to watch the event. We had to try to avoid hurting any of them. The Unseen stood in the center of the stadium, surrounding cages that held elementals and my parents, who were chained up and in their human forms. Those black pillars were set up in a circle around the cages, preventing them from shifting. Wrill stood beside one of them with her hands on her hips, gazing up at us with her face behind her black mask. I could practically feel her hatred for me even from afar.

We descended as a group, swooping down low over the crowd, sending terror throughout more people who bolted for the exit. Then we circled the center of the stadium, beating our wings rapidly. The Unseen began shooting fire, ice, and rocks up at us, while others tried to control the air around us to prevent us from flying, but we'd expected that and we fought back their attacks. Carth blasted away the fire, Zain melted through the ice, Parin defected the rocks, and Erroh soothed the wind. I helped as I could, using my elemental magic to catch anything they missed, while Varek summoned shades on the ground and ordered them to attack. We'd trained to work as a team, and even though we weren't as experienced as my parents, we were a force to be reckoned with as long as we stuck together.

While my four elemental dragons continued flying around and deflecting attacks, keeping the Unseen busy, Varek and I charged forward with our own mission. We each landed beside a pillar and placed our talons on the inky black stuff covering them, then drew out the death magic within them. The pillars collapsed, and we moved to the next ones.

"Sora!" my mother called out from inside a cage, which was also covered in that inky black stuff, probably to prevent her from using magic. My fathers were in identical cages beside her, with elementals in others behind them.

"We're going to get you out of there as soon as we can!" I roared to her, swishing my tail, then went to work on another pillar.

A huge blast of fire made me dart back. Wrill flew toward me, using air to propel herself through the sky. She attacked me with a combination of swirling air, rocks, and water, creating a hurricane that surrounded me. I threw up a shield of water and air to block it, then unleashed a massive column of fire at her. She threw out an arm and deflected the magic away from her, where it hit one of our shades and made it vanish.

She laughed as she summoned shards of ice, laced with darkness and death. "Is that all you've got?"

I let out a roar and slashed at her with my tail, but she dodged. I was about to charge her and tear her apart with my talons, but then I saw Varek behind her, back in his human form.

"I'm sorry," Varek said. "I love you, sister."

A shadowy bolt stretched out from his hand and hit her in the back, sinking into her chest. Her arms spread wide and her mask fell off as she screamed. It was just like when she'd taken the power from the elementals, but in reverse. Varek pulled out the elemental magic she'd stolen from the others with his death magic, a glowing ball of swirling colors laced with black, which dissolved into thin air before us.

When it was done, Wrill collapsed onto her knees and sobbed, then looked up at us with hateful eyes. She reached out and tried to use her magic against us, but nothing happened. She tried again and again, but it was gone. Even her death magic.

"What have you done?" she yelled.

Varek stood before her, looking down at his sister with harsh pity. "I took back what should never have been yours, and sent those poor elemental souls to the Realm of the Dead."

"You should have been one of us," Wrill said. "Our cause was just."

"Maybe so, but your methods were not." Varek tied her arms behind her, though it didn't seem like she was going anywhere now. "I believe in your cause, sister, and I will do what I can to help humans. But this is not the way."

"What other way is there?" Wrill asked, then glared at me. "If the Dragons can't help us, who will?"

Her words resonated in me, and I knew I would have to do something to address this problem soon, but not now. All around us the battle was ending, as the other Unseen members were either defeated or were surrendering to my mates. Varek and I destroyed the other pillars, then freed my parents and the other elementals.

Kira burst out of her cage and wrapped her arms around my large dragon neck. "You were incredible. And your dragon form—it's so beautiful!"

Her praise made me stand a little taller, especially as my fathers came out to hug me too. Now that they were free, it was easy to subdue the remaining attackers and throw them in the cages that once held my parents and the elementals.

Varek showed me how to remove the stolen magic inside each of the humans, and we went through them, one by one, freeing the elementals' souls. A few of the cultists might have escaped, but we'd be able to take them down if they caused any problems later.

The Unseen were no more.

CHAPTER TWENTY-FOUR

Peace was restored to Soulspire now that the Unseen were defeated, but I knew nothing will be the same. Those cultists were violent murderers and criminals, but they shed light on a real problem plaguing the world. Humans lacked the power of the elementals or the Dragons, and felt that their voices were not being heard and their lives were in danger. As the chosen representative of the Gods, it was my place to address this problem. If only I knew how.

Wrill and many of the Unseen were sent to prison. The Quickblades were disbanded. My mother called an assembly and gave a beautiful speech about change and acceptance, and though the city settled down again, I knew it wasn't enough. Real changes had to be made, or humans would rise up again to demand equality.

My mates and I settled into the palace, continuing to train together to become a stronger team, while our love grew every day. Even Varek was fitting in like a true member of the pack.

And then one night, they cornered me in my bedroom.

I had just donned my chemise when all five of my mates walked in. We had a rotating schedule set up so that I shared a bed with one man a night, plus had two nights free. This was one of my alone nights, which I often needed after being surrounded by so much masculine energy all day. However, tonight the men had other plans.

"What are you all doing here?" I asked, as they filled my room. It seemed a lot smaller with five large men inside.

"We think it's time we all took you to bed," Carth said, with a naughty gleam in his eye.

"Is that so?" It was something I'd wanted badly, but I hadn't been sure when the other men would be ready for such a thing.

"We've discussed it, and we think it would strengthen our bonds," Parin said.

Erroh rolled his eyes at his brother. "What he means is, yes, we want to do this. All of us. Together."

"Tonight," Zain said.

"Now get that chemise off," Varek demanded.

I cocked my hip. "Only if you take your clothes off too."

"I think we can manage that," Erroh said.

They were done talking then, and before I knew what was happening, they'd removed my chemise and pushed me back on the bed. For a few seconds they each took me in appreciatively, like I was the sexiest woman they'd ever seen. Then they removed their own clothing, and it was my turn to appreciate them. Five gorgeous men, all with different muscular bodies, but each mine.

I wanted to admire their bodies some more, but they had other plans. They moved in on me as one, each taking a different section of my body. Their hands were all over me, gentle yet firm, as they explored me. Zain's fingers roamed across my calves while Carth stroked my thighs, sending waves of sweet heat right to my core. Varek's rough palms covered my breasts, squeezing and fondling them, his callused skin brushing against my nipples and making me moan. Parin's hands went into my soft hair and his mouth found mine, and we kissed while Erroh's lips moved along my neck and shoulders.

When I was first given my mates, I hadn't thought I would feel anything for Parin and Varek like what I felt for Erroh, Carth, and Zain, but as Parin kissed me, I realized I was wrong. I loved all five of them. And I wanted all five of them inside me tonight.

I pulled Erroh up to my mouth and kissed him too, while Parin moved to lick and kiss my neck. As Erroh's tongue slipped into my mouth, Carth gripped my ankles and spread my legs wide. A second later, his lips traced a path up the inside of my thighs, getting closer and closer to where I needed him. I arched my hips, wanting more, but he took his time as he got a taste of me.

Finally his mouth moved to my core and when his tongue slipped inside my wet folds, I gasped into Erroh's mouth. Parin had moved to my breasts now, sharing them with Varek, their tongues flicking against my sensitive nipples, driving me wild. I had tongues on me and inside me, worshipping me, making me feel things I'd never felt before. I was in absolute heaven.

Then Zain shoved Carth aside and dipped his head between my legs too. The two of them licked and sucked me at the same time, and I cried out when one of them lifted up my leg to get a new angle. I felt the touch of a tongue on my back hole, and all new sensations shot through me. Then the men added their fingers, sliding one of them inside each hole, and I was totally gone. The orgasm shook through me, making me cry out and grab onto the guys around me.

"That's the first of many," Carth said, as he stood up. "Tonight's all about you."

"I need you inside me," I begged. "All of you."

Varek flashed me a devilish grin. "Patience."

"We should give her what she wants," Zain said.

"Yes, she deserves it," Parin agreed. "And I'm claiming her first this time."

"Do it, brother," Erroh said.

Parin stood up and pulled me to the edge of the bed, so my behind was almost hanging off. Then he lifted my ankles and set them on his shoulder, exposing me and stretching me wide. I was shocked at his boldness, but Parin had changed a lot during our time together.

"Beautiful," he said, as he gripped his cock and rubbed it against my wetness. Then he grabbed my behind and lifted my hips up as he pushed inside. "This what you want?"

"Yes!"

He pulled my hips flush against his, and he was buried so deep in me thanks to this angle. He held onto my ankles as he began sliding in and out, withdrawing almost completely, them slamming back inside in one hard thrust.

The other four men were watching with lusty eyes, and I knew they would want to get in on this soon. I reached for Erroh and he moved toward me, bringing that long cock right by my face. I took it in hand and brought it to my mouth, humming in approval as he slipped inside. I licked and sucked on his hard length, until he closed his eyes in satisfaction, while his brother pumped into me. Varek pinched my nipples at the same time, sending a touch of pain to mingle with the pleasure. I moaned around Erroh's cock and he dug his fingers into my hair, moving my head as he thrust between my lips. Then he surged against my tongue and his hot seed spilled down my throat. Parin pumped into me harder as he came at the same time, and seeing both brothers come apart sent me over the edge too.

"Our turn," Carth said.

I didn't have time to recover before Zain was lifting me up, wrapping my legs around his waist. He turned so he could lay back on the bed with me on top of him with his cock in me, nice and deep. I liked being on top and I began to ride him, my breasts hanging over his face. Carth moved behind and grabbed my cheeks, then spread them wide. I felt some oil being slid into my back entrance, followed by the pressure of his cock there.

"We're both going to be in you at once," Carth said, his lips by my ear. "Do you want that?"

"Yes!" I managed to get out, as the feeling became overwhelming. Carth pushed inside to the hilt, filling me completely, while his best friend filled me from the front.

Carth had his hands on my hips, and he guided himself in and out of me, which pushed me on and off Zain at the same time. Soon they found a rhythm and all I could do was give myself up to it, as the pleasure built quickly.

"I need to get in there too," Varek said, and then his cock was shoved between my lips so fast and hard I almost gagged. Somehow when Varek treated me roughly like that it only turned me on even more. I looked up at him with a challenge in my eyes as he pumped into my mouth, but I was helpless to do anything but let him own me.

Varek grabbed my chin and held me steady as the other guys pounded into me from behind and below. Their skin was touching me everywhere, and I didn't know where any one of us ended and the other began. We were one entity, writhing in pleasure together, racing toward our release.

It was too much though, and soon I was screaming around Varek's cock as the most amazing orgasm exploded through my body. That caused both Carth and Zain to climax into me with quick thrusts and rough groans, their fingers digging into my skin. I thought Varek might do the same, but instead he lifted me off the other men, wrapped my legs around his waist, and slid his cock into me. I was already weak from pleasure and could only hold onto him and enjoy the lingering effects of my climax as he came inside me too, while kissing me hard.

When it was over, we all collapsed in the bed, a mess of sweaty limbs and pounding hearts. I understood now why this bed was so large and smiled up at the ceiling. My soul was bursting not just with pleasure, but with love.

"That was incredible." I touched each of their faces softly. "I love you all so much."

"We love you too," Erroh said, and the other guys murmured in agreement as they curled up around me and pressed loving kisses to my skin.

Varek propped himself up on one muscular arm. "Now that we've all filled you with our seed, can we expect a child in nine months?"

I gave him a sad smile. "It doesn't work that way. In ten years, I will have one daughter, who will become the next Ascendant. No more, no less. Such is the price we pay as Dragons."

Erroh idly rubbed my stomach with his hand. "How do we determine who the father will be?"

"I'm putting in my claim now," Varek said.

Parin played with my curls. "I don't think that's allowed."

"No, we'll have some sort of contest when the time comes," Carth said.

"What kind of contest?" Zain asked.

"We're not having a contest," I said, but a pang hit my heart at the thought of not having a child with each of them. I wanted that, more than I could ever imagine.

Then I had an idea.

I untangled myself from my men and stood up, gathering my clothes. "Get up. We're going to the Life Temple."

Erroh sat up with a confused expression. "Now?"

"Why?" Zain asked.

"Because I know how to fix things."

727

CHAPTER TWENTY-FIVE

High Priestess Nelsa was very confused by our sudden arrival at the temple in the middle of the night, but she couldn't refuse us either. With a yawn, she led us to the outside area where we had met the Life Goddess before, and then bowed and left us alone.

Once there, I stood in front of my mates and centered myself. I'd never summoned the Gods before, but the old tomes all said it was possible. They were just vague on how exactly.

Focusing on my power, on the magic deep inside me, I pulled the elements out. The twin forces of life and death, along with fire, water, air, and earth. Tugging on each thread, they erupted from my fingers with a rush of color. Wrestling with them, I forced the colorful magical threads to comply, and weaved them around one another, moving my arms to help me focus my mind until they were braided together. Then I released the magic into the world.

"I call on the Gods to appear before us!" I yelled, as I pushed my power into the fabric of the realm, into the very source of it all. The primal essence of the universe.

My mates then released a burst of their own magic and called out to the Gods, and through our bond I felt their power surging and strengthening mine. We were all connected, with invisible chains tying us together, and through that bond I demanded the Gods appear before us.

And then, they did. First the Life Goddess, in her radiant glory, her dragon scales erupting with light. Beside her stood the Death Goddess, with her bones and poison fangs. Then the four male Gods appeared behind them, all of them in their dragon forms. The Fire God, with skin like shifting lava and flames on his breath. The Earth God, massive in size and made entirely of crystal. The Water God, composed of shifting waves with talons of ice. The Air God, with cloudy wings and lightning in his eyes.

"You have summoned us and we have appeared," the Life Goddess said. "What do you require, child?"

I glanced at my mates, and several of them nodded, giving me strength. I straightened up and faced the Gods. "You said the Gods wished to retreat from the world and let mortals control their own destiny. Is this still true?"

"Yes, it is," the Earth God said, his voice like the rumbling of a rockslide.

"We brought much chaos and pain to the world when we were corrupted," the Air God rasped.

The Fire God flexed his flaming wings. "We will not allow that to happen again."

"We have faith in our champions to lead the mortal world," said the Water God, whose tail swished, spraying drops everywhere.

"You made this world," I said. "And now you plan to abandon it?"

"No," the Life Goddess replied. Her smile sent hope and joy searing through my heart. "We'd never leave it. We will still be there, but more as silent observers."

"Including the Death Goddess?" I asked.

She snarled and bared her fangs. "I have done what was required to bring necessary changes to this world. Now I am content to rule the Realm of the Dead."

I bowed my head. "If you plan to remove yourself from this world, then I have a few requests for things that would bring balance to the world. That is my purpose, after all."

"Name them," the Life Goddess said.

"Give all mortals elemental powers and the ability to turn into dragons."

"That is too much power," the Fire God roared with a rush of heat.

"Agreed," the Water God said, his voice laced with frost.

Lightning crackled in the Air God's eyes. "Humans can be trouble-some and combative."

"If they all had magic it would lead to never ending wars," the Earth God rumbled.

I had a feeling they would say something like that, and I was prepared with an answer. "Then give the power only to a few select humans who embody the traits you each look for in your own champions. Bravery, wisdom, and so forth. Then allow the power to pass down to their children."

The Gods all glanced between one another, and I sensed they were communicating telepathically. Some time passed, and I shifted on my feet, nervous they wouldn't agree to my proposal. If this failed, I had no other plan for helping the humans.

"Very well," the Life Goddess finally said. "We will choose the humans who will become our champions, and the ability will be passed down through their lineage. But be prepared. As with other things, the humans may not always make the best choices with their magic."

"If we do this, it will mean the end of the Ascendancy," the Death Goddess said. "You and your Dragons will no longer be the only champions of the Gods. Are you ready to make that sacrifice?"

I sucked in a breath. "I am. As long as you allow me to have as many children as I wish, and promise they will be no different than any other of your other champions."

"Very well," the Life Goddess said. "You will be the last Ascendant."

She reached out with one of her claws and touched my chest lightly. I felt a shiver run through me. Otherwise, I felt no different.

"It is done." She raised her wings. "Our champions will be chosen by dawn. They will require your guidance. Be prepared."

I nodded and swallowed hard. This would be a new challenge, but one my mates and I would be ready to face—and it would bring balance to the world.

EPILOGUE

ONE YEAR LATER

I paced back and forth in the chamber, biting my nails, while the train of my long silver gown trailed behind me.

Erroh swatted at my hand. "Stop that."

I dropped it and clutched my rumbling stomach instead. "I'm going to be sick."

"You're going to be fine," Parin said, in his calm, firm voice.

Carth wrapped an arm around my shoulders. "Relax, Sora. This is your day. Well, all of ours, really."

"It's just so much responsibility," I said.

"Your parents wouldn't be doing this if they didn't feel it was right," Zain said.

Varek took my hand and pressed a kiss to it. "You're going to do great."

The door opened, and my four fathers stood on the other side. Like me and my mates, they were dressed in their finest clothes, each one in the color representing their element.

"It's time," Jasin said, before giving me a warm hug.

I stepped back, shaking my head. "I'm not ready."

"Yes, you are," Reven said, as he stroked my hair. "We've trained you for this since the moment you were born."

"I'm not, though," I said. "I have so much to learn still. What if I make a mistake?"

"You did a wonderful job dealing with the cult," Auric said, as he squeezed my hand. "And it's not like we're going to disappear. We'll always be here to guide you and advise you."

"True." I smoothed my dress, gathering my confidence, but it only returned when Slade wrapped me in one of his big bear hugs.

"We're very proud of you," he said.

Tears pricked my eyes as I pulled back and looked at my four fathers. Things might have been awkward with them and my mates at times, especially at first, but I could never have asked for four better men to raise me. Each one of them had given me the best parts of themselves and loved me unconditionally. I owed them everything—along with my mother, of course.

We stepped out of the palace and into the courtyard, which was filled with people as far as the eye could see, along with elementals. Kira stood in a silver gown of her own on a podium, with her sword in her hand, the one Slade had made her that was imbued with all the elements. My fathers moved to fan out behind her, and then my mates and I stood to the side.

Mom flashed me a warm smile, as the sunlight glinted off her beautiful red hair. Then she turned to the crowd.

"For thousands of years the Dragons have acted as guardians, protectors, and sometimes overlords of the world, but our time has come to an end. My daughter, the Rainbow Dragon, shall be the last of the Ascendants, and shall oversee the beginning of a new era. She has brought balance to the world, and has made a great sacrifice to ensure that equality shall flourish among all mortals."

The crowd watched with rapt attention, and my heart warmed at the sight of so many familiar faces. Erroh and Parin's parents, Faya and Cadock, along with their sister and her family. Carth's parents, Brin and Leni. All of the High Priestesses from every temple, including Calla. Even a few former members of the Quickblades, who had joined the Silver Guard at Varek's request.

Kira lifted up her sword and turned toward me. "Sora, you and your mates have proven yourselves ready to take on the peaceful oversight of our world. My mates and I formally step aside, and we charge you with keeping the harmony between humans and elementals, and maintaining balance in the four Realms."

I took the sword from her and bowed my head as I held its weight. "I take on this duty with pride and honor, with my mates by my side."

The audience erupted into cheers as I sheathed the sword, and my mother and I faced the crowd, our men behind us. Mom rested a hand on my back and gave me a proud smile that brought tears back to my eyes. Kira and her men were not only heroes, but amazing parents too. I could only hope to live up to the example they'd set.

The ceremony ended, and a banquet began. A small orchestra began to play music, and food and refreshments were served to the guests. The night quickly passed in a whirlwind of drinking, dancing, and delicious food. Everyone wanted to congratulate me and my mates, and ask us about the new school we'd founded just outside Soulspire, the Elemental Dragon Academy.

Ever since the night we summoned the Gods, humans across the four Realms had woken up to new powers. Most of the champions were young, below twenty, but a few of them were older. We sent out word that anyone with magic should come to Soulspire for training, and for weeks we flew around the world, looking for our new students and transporting them to their new home. My family built it from scratch using magic, and it would house hundreds of people. We asked the High Priestesses, both former and current, to help us with the training, along with my parents. So far, it was going well. The new dragons were smaller and less powerful than we were, but they gave the people hope. That was what mattered.

Our purpose now was to train the next generation of elemental dragons and to create a school that would continue after we had moved on. Especially since our own children would need to be trained there too.

I found my mates in my mother's garden, my favorite place at the palace. They all turned toward me and smiled as I approached, and I decided now was the time to tell them the good news.

"What are you doing out here?" I asked.

"Getting away from all the stuffy guests with a million questions," Carth said with a smirk.

"Yes, it's much quieter out here," Parin said.

"Wine?" Varek offered me, with a knowing gleam. "I noticed your glass has been empty all night."

"No, thank you," I said, as I sat on a bench. "There's something I need to tell you all."

Erroh's face lit up. "We already know."

"You do?" I asked.

"It's obvious from the way you've been acting," Zain said. "You're pregnant."

I laughed and placed a hand over my belly. "How could you tell? I wasn't even sure myself until Mom examined me this morning."

"No wine or ale was the obvious one, of course," Carth said.

"Additionally, you refused eggs for breakfast, and we know you love eggs," Parin added.

"And you kept complaining of being tired," Zain said.

Carth smirked. "I suppose that means we don't need to have a competition over who will be the father. This time, anyway."

"Do you know who it is?" Erroh asked.

I bit my lip, but then nodded, and my gaze landed on Varek. His eyes widened in shock, and then he let out a laugh. Next thing I knew, he was sweeping me up into his arms and giving me a passionate kiss.

"It's mine? Truly?" he asked.

"Yes, Mom confirmed it with her magic," I said. "A boy too. The first boy ever born to any Ascendant."

He pressed his forehead against mine and laughed again. "I can't believe it. We're going to have a son."

The other men patted him on the back and congratulated him, but I wanted to make sure they understood something important. I turned to my mates and said, "Even though Varek is the biological father, this child shall be son to all of you. As will any other children we have. Just like my parents raised me."

"I claim the next one," Erroh said, and everyone laughed. I rolled my eyes, knowing he wasn't serious. Probably.

We hugged and kissed and laughed until the party disbanded, and then we returned to our wing of the palace together. Tomorrow we'd head back to the academy to work with the students, but tonight we would relax. Satisfaction and happiness settled upon me as I climbed into my large bed with my five men. The four Realms were at peace again, and I was starting a family with the men I loved.

Though the time of the Dragons would soon be over, our legacy would live on. Forever.

LIGHT THE FIRE

A HER ELEMENTAL DRAGONS STORY

CHAPTER ONE

The giant brazier flared bright, beckoning me closer. I picked up a scrap of bark and a pointed piece of obsidian from the nearby pile as I considered the flickering flames, along with my future. While a man beside me debated what to write with a frown, I quickly carved my wish on the tiny bit of wood. When I was finished, I read the words once before sending the bark into the fire, where it blackened and curled almost immediately and soon turned to ash and flame. As the Fire God accepted my offering I bowed low and said a small prayer that he'd grant my wish and give me guidance, before I turned back to the celebration. Not that I expected him to answer, of course. But it *was* tradition.

The center of Sparkport was packed tonight with nearly everyone in the village crammed into its town square. Torches lit up the darkness, adults made wishes at the brazier, and children pranced across the dirt road flying red dragon kites in the air. Fire dancers performed on a stage nearby, their flames leaving trails of light as they twirled in time to the lively music. I moved through the crowd toward one of merchant stalls lining the road, brushing past people in their finest clothes who were dancing together or eating special treats.

The Fire Festival was one of the five celebrations in honor of the Gods and the Dragons, and here in the Fire Realm it was the biggest holiday of the year. My family had been preparing our bakery's stall for weeks, while my sisters and I had spent months sewing our gowns. Mine was a flame red dress with a black lace trim that hugged my body in a way that turned a few heads. An obsidian pendant that belonged to my mother rested between my full breasts, and my blond hair had been tied up with red and black ribbon, though some wispy hairs had already escaped it.

I approached my family's stall with its familiar scent of warm bread and baked sugar. My mother stood inside it, offering one of our signature mini volcano cakes to a child and her father. My older sister Krea was putting out more chocolate-coated flame cookies, while our youngest sister Loka was sneaking one of the fried crab cakes into her mouth. I arched an eyebrow at her and she wiped her mouth with an impish grin.

"Welcome back, Calla," Mom said with a smile. "Did you make a wish?"

"I did. Has it been busy?" I asked, as I stepped behind the stall to join them.

"Very," Mom said. "We're going to run out of those volcano cakes before midnight at this rate."

"All because of Krea's hard work," I said.

"Thank you," my older sister replied, ducking her head so her pale hair partially covered her face. "I had no idea they'd be so popular."

Krea was the one who had come up with the design for the tiny domed chocolate cakes filled with strawberry cream, then topped them with frosting to look like lava. She had true artistic talent, while Loka prided herself on finding the most delicious combinations of food—usually by tasting them herself. Together they would make my mother proud when they took over the bakery. And me? I could bake, certainly, but I didn't have the talent for making pastries beautiful like Krea, and I didn't have the knack for coming up with new recipes like Loka. I'd likely find myself serving customers in the front of the shop my entire life—or I'd be passed off to help my future husband with whatever his trade was.

I wished I had a talent like my sisters, but so far nothing had emerged. I was passably good at many things—sewing, baking, candle making—but an expert in none. Instead I preferred to spend my time reading, but books were in short supply in a small town like Sparkport and scholars were not exactly in demand here either. I had no idea what my future would hold, but now that I was twenty years old I supposed it was time it got started.

As I idly rearranged the boring cheese pastries I'd made—which no one was buying, since they could get them every day in the shop—a loud rumble sounded in the distance from the nearby volcano, Valefire. A moment later the earth trembled under our feet and the crowd murmured and paused until the ground stilled once more. After a few tense seconds, the music started up again and the festival continued on, as if nothing had happened.

"Another earthquake?" I asked, glancing at the tall, flat-topped mountain with its black slopes. Our town was situated in the shadow of Valefire, where the Fire God's temple stood. We'd always respected the volcano, knowing it could awaken at any time, but none of us truly believed it would. Until last month, when the earthquakes had started to increase in frequency and strength.

"It's simply the Fire God showing his approval for the festival," Mom said.

Loka rolled her eyes. "The Fire God hasn't been seen for hundreds of years."

My mother clucked her tongue. "And this is his way of reminding us he's still watching over us, even if we've forgotten him and abandoned his temple. This is why we must celebrate him on holidays like this."

"And pray the volcano stays dormant," I muttered.

"The volcano hasn't erupted in many lifetimes," Mom said, waving our concerns away. "We've always had earthquakes here in Sparkport. There's nothing to be worried about. In fact, you should all go enjoy the festival tonight. I can handle the stall by myself."

"Are you sure?" Krea asked.

"Yes. You'll make me happy by having fun tonight. The Fire Festival is for the young." She shooed Krea and Loka away with a smile. Loka skipped off immediately with a squeal, while Krea hesitated until her betrothed caught her eye and gestured for her to dance with him.

"I'll stay," I said, as Krea slipped away into the crowd.

Mom patted my arm. "That's kind of you, but you should dance too. Derel looks like he could use a break as well."

I followed her gaze to the stall across from ours, run by the local butcher. Mom waved her hand at Sucy, the wife of the butcher and my mother's best friend. Her son, Derel, stood behind the beef kabobs, lemon shrimp, and meatballs they were selling, which I had to admit looked delicious. Behind him, Derel's father tended a large pig roasting on a spit, which would be served at the end of the festival to the entire village. We had a giant volcano cake prepared to go with it, filled with strawberries and cream.

Derel's head turned toward me and he caught me staring at him. I quickly looked away and busied myself in the back of the stall, but the damage was done. It didn't help that Derel was distractingly handsome either, even if I hated to admit it. He had the rich dark skin of his grandparents, who'd moved here from the Earth Realm, with deep brown eyes and gorgeous full lips. Not that I'd spent much time staring at his lips before. Definitely not.

My mother nudged me with her elbow. "Go on, dance with him."

I groaned. "Do I have to?"

"Yes, you do." She clasped her hands together. "I do wish the two of you would get married already. It's all been planned out for you for years!"

"Yes, that's the problem."

"You're lucky. When I was younger I thought I'd never find a husband in this tiny village. If your father hadn't moved to town I'd probably still be alone. I tried to make it easier on you and your sisters by promising you to others as children. Krea and Parin will soon be married. Next it should be you and Derel."

I rolled my eyes. "I doubt Loka will want to marry the man you chose for her."

"Well, I had no idea she'd prefer women or I'd have chosen her a nice wife." She suddenly straightened up. "Oh, here he comes. Be nice." She shuffled away and busied herself at the stall next to ours by offering the chandler some cookies, leaving me to face Derel alone.

As he approached I felt a sense of dread, but also excitement. The Fire Festival made the night feel like anything was possible, even something magical. Like me and Derel getting along for five minutes.

"Care to dance?" he asked in the least convincing voice ever.

I gave him a sickly sweet smile. "With you? Not really."

"Trust me, I'm only here because my mother insisted."

I glanced at my own mother, who gave me a big smile and nodded eagerly. I could practically see visions of dark-skinned grandchildren dancing through her head. "Fine, I'll dance with you. Only because my mother will never stop pestering me until I do."

He took my hand in his strong grip and led me into the square to join the other dancing couples. This dance was an upbeat one, and we switched off clasping hands and spinning and twirling until my heart beat fast and I was almost—*almost*—having a good time with Derel. It didn't hurt that he was an excellent dancer either.

When the music slowed he clasped my hand and pulled me close against his toned body. "Is your mother pressing you to get married like mine is?"

"Always." Though arranged marriages had fallen out of fashion generations ago—much to my mother's dismay—from the time Derel and I were born we'd been promised to each other, whether we liked it or not. And trust me, we did not. The worst part was that if we hadn't been forced together at every opportunity and told how perfect we were for each other, maybe we would have gotten along and fallen in love in our own time. Now we would never know.

"Maybe we should just do it already to get them off our backs," he said, as his hand slowly smoothed down my back.

I let out a sharp laugh to hide how shocked I was at his words, and how much I didn't hate the idea when it came from him. Too bad I knew he wasn't serious. How could he be? We hated each other—always had, always would. "Is that your version of a romantic proposal?"

"I'm going for practical, not romantic. But if romance is what you want..." His smoldering eyes met mine in a way that made my breath catch, especially as he pulled me tighter against him. My gaze dropped to his sensual mouth and I thought, not for the first time, what it would be like to kiss him. As his fingers curled around my chin and he looked at me in the same way, I knew he was thinking about it too.

I shook my head to break the spell he'd cast over me. "Definitely not. I'm never going to marry you."

Was that disappointment flashing across his face before it returned to his normal, disinterested look? Surely not. "Probably for the best. We'd break poor Falon's heart."

"Falon?" I laughed. "Only because you'd spend less time with him if you were married."

He gave me a look dripping with disdain. "If that's what you think then you're more clueless than I thought."

My smile fell. "What is that supposed to mean?"

"Nothing." Derel shook his head.

Was he suggesting Falon had feelings for me? That was certainly news to me. Falon was our best friend, the one thing in common we had besides our parents, but he'd never been anything more—much to my dismay.

"This dress you have on is quite alluring," Derel said. "Are you sure you're not looking for a proposal tonight?"

"Maybe I am, but not from you." None of the men I wanted would propose to me tonight, so it didn't really matter. But I definitely hadn't worn this for Derel, of all people. "What did you mean about Falon?"

He idly touched the lace at my neck. "The quality is quite fine. Let me guess, Krea made it?"

"No, I did." I shoved against his chest, stepping away from him. I knew he was purposefully baiting me to change the subject, but he always knew exactly how to get under my skin and I couldn't help but respond. "Why are you always so impossible?"

His lips quirked up in a wry smile. "You just bring out that side of me, I suppose."

CHAPTER TWO

W hen the song ended, Derel took my hand and led me over to
Falon, who sipped something hot and steamy from a metal cup.
Falon was just as handsome as Derel but in an entirely different way.
Where Derel was lithe and toned, Falon was broad and muscular. While
Derel was dark, Falon was bright. When Derel was rude, Falon was kind.

"It's your turn," Derel said to Falon. "I'm done dancing with her."

"And so gracious about it," I muttered.

"Don't pretend you didn't enjoy it." He gave me one last smoldering
look before stalking back to his parents' stall.

"Shall we dance?" Falen asked with a smile, offering me his hand.

My nerves instantly calmed as I entwined my fingers with his. "I'd like
that."

Falon led me back into the square amid the other revelers. He rested
his hand on my waist, but kept his distance from me. I tried not to hide my
disappointment, especially after Derel had sparked the idea in my head
that Falon might have feelings for me. But that was ridiculous. Falon and I
had been friends ever since his family had moved to our village when he
was five, but there had never been anything more between us. Unfortunately.

Falon's family worked as carpenters, and his strong, rough fingers felt
good against my own. He was a large man, the kind who'd gained his
muscles working long hours, and I wished he would pull me against his
chest like Derel had done. I'd secretly harbored feelings for Falon for years,
but he'd never shown even a hint that he saw me as anything more than a

friend. If only he would give me a sign he wanted more, maybe we could ease the awkwardness between us. But he never did.

"You look beautiful tonight," he said, making my heart skip a beat. "That dress is lovely."

"Thank you. Krea designed it for me, although I all the sewing," I admitted. Unlike Derel, Falon didn't judge me or tease me. I could tell him anything.

"No doubt the Fire God will smile upon your efforts. Did you throw a wish in the brazier?"

"Of course. Did you?"

He nodded. "What did you wish for?"

I gave him a teasing smile as I played with the collar of his shirt. "You know we're not supposed to tell."

"Oh, come on. We're best friends. Surely you can tell me what you wished for."

There it was. Best friends. That was how he saw me, and that would never change. "Definitely not."

His blue eyes danced with amusement. "Let me guess. You wished for love."

"Love?" I said, with a short laugh.

"That's what everyone wishes for."

"Not me. I asked the Fire God to show me what my path should be. To give me a hint about my role in this town and what I should do with my life." I tilted my head. "What about you? Did you wish for love?"

"No, of course not," he said a little too quickly, before looking away. "I wished for the same thing as you, pretty much. To have a good future."

"Uh huh." I smiled at him. "Who's the lucky lady you have your eye on?"

"There's no one." He fingers tightened around my waist. "You're the only lady I ever spend time with, after all."

That was true. But if he'd wished for love and I was the one he wanted to be with, why didn't he just tell me so? Was he worried about Derel? He must know I could barely stand to be in Derel's presence, even if my body was physically attracted to him at times. Or was Falon concerned we'd ruin our friendship? Or that I didn't feel the same for him?

Maybe he needed a little hint as to my feelings. I pressed my lips to his cheek as the song ended. "It's okay if you did wish for love, you know."

He turned his head toward me, so that my mouth nearly touched his own. I felt both of us breathing heavily, locked in a close embrace that had somehow shifted from friendly to more. I slid my fingers up into his short blond hair while he looked at me in a new way and opened his mouth.

Hope rose up in my chest that he might finally confess his feelings, but then a hand landed on my shoulder and ruined the moment.

"My turn," a low voice said.

I looked up at Blane in surprise as he swept me into his arms in a lover's embrace, so different from the way Falon had been holding me and even more intimate than the way Derel had danced with me. I should have pushed him away or told him to stop, but instead I found my traitorous arms sliding around his neck and my heart racing as we began to dance. I glanced back at Falon, who gave me a friendly smile and a nod, before the crowd swallowed us up.

"When did they let you out of jail?" I asked Blane, mainly to distract myself from the way he felt. And smelled. And looked. Everything about Blane was irresistible, from the sexy drawl of his voice, to his dark tousled hair, to his tall, muscular body. And trust me, I'd tried to resist.

"Jail" was really the basement of the chandler's house, since Sparkport was too small to have an actual prison and Blane was the only person who was ever thrown into it on a regular basis. Usually by Derel and Falon, who acted as the town guard on most nights.

"This morning," Blane said, with a roguish grin. "Falon took pity on me. He didn't want me to miss the Fire Festival, after all."

"What was it this time?"

He lifted one shoulder in a casual shrug. "I appropriated some wine from that grumpy old merchant Carik. He had plenty, trust me."

I sighed. Carik was known to cheat people out of their money, but that didn't excuse Blane's theft. "I shouldn't even be dancing with you."

"Why not? Embarrassed to be seen in my arms?"

"Something like that."

"Too bad you like it so much." His lips brushed against my neck and sent shivers down my spine. The worst part was, he was right. Blane was the village bad boy, always getting into trouble, but for some reason I couldn't resist him even though I knew it was wrong. My family would never let me be with him, and Blane wasn't the type who'd want to get married anyway. But I couldn't stay away.

Blane was one of the two men I'd kissed in my life, and I knew he wanted more from me too, but I'd held myself back so far. It was difficult though because the man practically oozed sexuality. Just being around him made me damp between my legs. And his touch? It made me crave more every time.

"You wore this dress for me, didn't you?" he asked, his lips trailing down to the spot next to my pendant, dangerously close to my breasts. I gasped, worried about people watching us, though I was finding it hard to care at the moment.

"Don't be silly," I said, though my breathless voice gave me away.

"You look so very tempting in it. The only way you'd look better is with it pooled at your feet." His hand ran down my back to rest on my bottom possessively. "Will you meet me later tonight?"

"I can't."

"That's too bad." He took my earlobe between his teeth and I let out a gasp. "I can't stop thinking about you."

"Well, you should. Stop, I mean." Gods, Blane made me flustered in a way no one else did. "We both know we don't have a future together. My mother is pushing for me to marry soon, after all, and—"

He pulled back, his eyebrows darting up. "Why don't we have a future? Because I'm not good enough for you?"

"No! I just.... I mean... I didn't think you were the kind to settle down."

"I might surprise you. I could be convinced to settle down…with the right woman." He gave me a look that made me melt, and I thought for sure he would kiss me right there in front of everyone, and I imagined all the things my mother would say afterward and how we'd be gossiped about for weeks or even months, and I decided at that moment I didn't care one bit because it would be worth it for another kiss from Blane. But then he released me. "I've got something to do, but I'll find you later. I promise."

I nodded and swallowed, unable to speak. As he left, I told myself it was for the best that he'd walked away. I could never truly be with Blane, and I didn't believe he really wanted a serious relationship. Best to put him out of my mind entirely from now on.

But who was I kidding? I'd be counting down the minutes until he returned.

CHAPTER THREE

I looked for Falon again, but he was dancing with one of his sister's friends, and then my eyes caught sight of a dark man standing in the corner with his arms crossed. My mouth fell open at the sight. Roth was here! I didn't think he would come. How long had he been standing there? Had he seen me dance with the others? Was he jealous? Or did he no longer care?

I approached Roth in the shadows with a tentative smile. From this angle I could only see one side of his face, which was devastatingly hand-some, as if he'd been sculpted by the Gods themselves. High cheekbones. A perfect masculine nose. A strong jaw. And the rich, auburn hair that was so highly prized in the Fire Realm, which I desperately wanted to run my hands through again.

But when he turned toward me the rest of him became visible under the torchlight, revealing a horrible burn scar that ran down the other side of his face. I knew it bothered him, but to me it only highlighted how beautiful he was. If anything, the imperfection only made him look better to me. Especially since I'd been there when he'd gotten it.

"Calla," he said in a tone that made it clear he wasn't happy to see me. "Why aren't you dancing?"

"I was hoping you'd dance with me."

"You know I don't dance."

"You used to."

"I did." He look away with a scowl. "Before."

Roth had always been rather serious and quiet, but after the accident he'd turned downright brooding. Now I barely ever saw him, and when I did, he tried to push me away. The only times I ever spoke with him was when I found him working on the docks or on the rare occasions he brought crab to the bakery. I was tired of him avoiding me.

I gave him a hesitant smile. "Everyone is dancing. No one will stare, I promise."

"No."

I sighed. "All right. Then why don't we get something to eat? It's been ages since we talked." My voice dropped into nearly a whisper. "I miss you, Roth."

He ran a hand over his face, hiding his scars, a sure sign he was dismayed. "You're very kind, Calla, but I shouldn't have come tonight. I think I'll just go."

"No, please." I took his hand and sparks danced under my skin. Once I'd thought Roth and I might marry. We'd always been close, and two years ago it had flared into more. He'd confessed his love for me at that Fire Festival, and then invited me out onto his family's boat the next night.

When we were out at sea, we made love for the first time, and I'd never felt so happy before. I was certain he was going to ask for my hand, but then we were attacked by a water elemental. Here, in the Fire Realm, of all places.

The elemental covered my face with water and nearly drowned me, but Roth stepped in to defend me with a torch he'd lit. He managed to save my life and defeat the elemental, but the boat was set on fire in the process. While trying to put out the flames the left side of his body was badly burned, including his face. We were forced to abandon the boat, and I was so weak from nearly drowning he had to pull me back to shore, where he then passed out from the pain.

After that, he hid himself from the world—and from me.

I took a step closer to Roth. "I wish we could be friends again, at least. You know I don't blame you for what happened. If anything, I see you as a hero. You saved us both and—"

"I nearly got you killed and I destroyed my family's boat at the same time." He gestured at his face. "Not to mention, I got a nice reminder of my failure, which I have to see every time I look in a mirror." He turned to leave, but said over his shoulder, "Trust me, Calla. You're better off without me in your life. And now I must go."

"No one's leaving yet," Blane said, with a devious grin. Falon and Derel stood behind him, watching Roth with interest. "Not until I show you something."

Roth cast him a skeptical look. "What is it?"

"Come with me and you'll see. I promise it's worth your time."

Derel snorted. "Last time you said that we got so drunk we spent the next day vomiting."

Blane offered me his hand. "Fine, I'll take Calla by myself. We can have a romantic moment together while you three stay here with the crowd."

"Where are we going?" I asked, intrigued despite myself. Blane was always getting us into trouble, but we all secretly liked it. There wasn't much to do in a small village like this, but Blane always managed to keep things interesting.

"To the beach."

Falon sighed. "Well, now we have to go to make sure Blane doesn't get Calla in trouble."

"True," Derel said. "Or we could arrest him now and save ourselves the trouble."

Blane rolled his eyes. "You already arrested me once this week. And you let me off, too."

"I'm starting to regret that decision," Fallon said.

Together we all walked over to the docks at the end of town, where I saw Loka dart off with another girl, both of them holding hands and giggling. I smiled, hoping she'd find some happiness tonight.

Blane carried a torch and led us to the beach, where the dark waves were slowly lapping at the shore. I held up my skirt as we stepped into the sand, but then arms swept me off my feet from behind. I found myself in Falon's strong arms and let out a gasp.

"Didn't want you to ruin that pretty gown you'd worked so hard on," he said with a smile.

"Thank you." First the dance, and now this. I wasn't sure Falon had touched me so much in my life before this night. Not that I was complaining.

Blane kept walking through the sand until he reached a cluster of rocks, well away from the lights, sounds, and smells of the festival. He bent down to remove a hidden sack and opened it up to reveal a dozen long tubes with pointed ends. Fireworks.

"Where did you get these?" I asked.

"In Flamedale on my last trip." Blane was the only one of us who had ever left the village. His mother died in childbirth, and his father died ten years later after years of being an alcoholic. After that Blane took whatever jobs he could get in order to keep food in his stomach and a roof over his head. He was the best fighter in the village and often worked as a mercenary for traveling merchants or whatever else was required of him. Rumor had it he had joined up with some bandits at one point too. But he always came back to Sparkport.

"Did you steal these?" Falon asked, as he picked up one of the fireworks.

"It doesn't matter how I got them," Blane said.

Derel crossed his arms. "Do you even know how to use them?"

Blane shrugged. "You light this end with fire and aim it at the sky. How hard can it be?"

"You're going to get us all killed," Roth muttered.

"Then Calla had better kiss us first, just in case," Blane said.

My jaw fell open. "All of you?"

Blane grinned. "Why not?"

I was speechless as I glanced between them, though I couldn't help but imagine it. I knew how good it felt to kiss Blane and Roth, and I'd just been in Derel and Falon's arms while we'd danced. I pictured moving from one man to the other, or all of them surrounding me, their hands and mouths sliding across my skin...

The five of us had once been best friends and practically inseparable. When you grew up in a small village it was natural to form close bonds with the other people your age, and for me it was the four of them. But when we got older my feelings for each of them shifted and grew into more. We began spending less time together, especially as we all became busy learning our trades, though I wondered if there was more to it than that. Sometimes I wondered if it was because of me.

I had the opposite of the problem my mother had when she was younger: I had four men I could see potentially marrying, but my relationship with each one was complicated and in the end I was with none of them. Besides, how could I ever pick one when I had feelings for all of them? Yes, even Derel, though I hated to admit it to myself.

I'd heard that in the Air and Water Realms many people took multiple partners the way the Spirit Goddess and the Black Dragon did. Some considered it a way to honor them and believed it was normal to love more than one person. But here in the Fire Realm we were more traditional and it was almost unheard of—I certainly knew my mother would never approve.

"Now you've scared her," Falon said, snapping me out of my thoughts.

Blane picked up one of the fireworks. "Come on, the town will love it. Help me light one."

"I want no part of this," Roth said, stepping back.

"Nothing is going to happen, I promise. Besides, there's nothing here but sand and water."

"And us," Roth muttered. He threw an arm in front of me, as if to block me from the fireworks.

"Let's do one and see how it goes," Derel said. He was always the first one to jump on Blane's wild plans, despite being the town guard. After he joined in, Falon always did too, and then Roth would finally cave in. And me? I was always happy to be near them, no matter what trouble we were getting into.

I watched as the guys debated the best way to light the fireworks. Eventually they decided to prop one of them up in the sand right next to the water, in case it went wrong.

But then a huge rumble sounded in the distance coming from Valefire. The ground beneath us shook violently, making me lose my footing in the black sand. I clutched onto Roth for support as the world trembled and the mountain roared. We all stared as ominous white smoke burst from its peak in a huge plume, illuminated by an eerie light coming from inside of Valefire.

The volcano had awakened.

CHAPTER FOUR

B lane scooped up his fireworks while the rest of us rushed across the sand back toward Sparkport. Another earthquake swept through the land, this one so strong it made me stumble into Derel, who caught my arm to steady me. Fear made me scramble back up again, along with worry for my family. That rumble had been so loud and there was so much smoke rising into the sky, it made me nervous the volcano could erupt at any moment.

As we entered the village the crowd was screaming and running about, the mood changed from festive to chaotic. The music had stopped, the stage where the dancers had been was on fire, and worst of all, a crack had formed down the middle of the town square. Not large enough to truly injure anyone, but not a good sign either.

Derel kept his arm around me as people shoved and pushed against us in their frenzy, but we lost the other men in the crowd. He didn't let go until we found our family's stalls, where my mother threw her arms around me.

"Calla! I was so worried."

"I'm okay." I gave her a squeeze, and then hugged Krea next.

"Thank you, Derel," Mom said. Now she'd never let up on us getting married. He gave us both a nod, before moving to speak with his own parents at their stall. Mom turned back to me. "Have you seen Loka?"

"She's not here?" I glanced quickly through the crowd, but then remembered seeing her at the docks with that girl. "I think I know where she is. I'll get her quickly."

Mom grasped my hands tightly. "Please be careful, and head back to the house as soon as you find her."

"I will."

I slipped back through the crowd, which was quickly dispersing as people ran to their homes or found shelter in case the volcano began raining lava, rocks, or ash from the sky. We'd all heard tales of when the Fire God was displeased with his subjects and had nearly destroyed the entire Realm with his wrath, and how it wasn't just the lava that had taken so many lives but the poisonous smoke and the fiery rocks that descended on the land. We were close enough to the volcano that if it did erupt and the lava flowed in our direction we could lose all our homes—and possibly our lives.

Long ago, the five Gods had created this world, and each one represented the elements of earth, air, fire, water, and spirit. The Spirit Goddess was their leader, and took the other four Gods as her mates. Later they created the five Dragons to act as their representatives in the world, and then the Gods vanished. Now the five Dragons—Black, Crimson, Azure, Jade, and Golden—ruled over the different Realms and its people, but many people believed the Gods would one day return. I'd never thought it would happen in my lifetime, but now I was starting to change my mind.

I ran back toward the dock, but when I arrived I didn't see a single soul, only the fishing boats tied to the wooden pier. "Loka?" I called out. "Are you here?"

When I couldn't find her I headed down the beach in the opposite direction from where Blane had hidden the fireworks, hoping Loka and her girlfriend might be scared and hiding somewhere. I continued around the bend, calling her name, climbing onto the large rocks where she'd liked to play where we were kids. But I didn't see her anywhere.

She must have gone back to the town. I probably just missed her. Or so I hoped.

As I turned around to head back to Sparkport, I felt a blast of heat and smoke. I blinked it away and came face to face with a giant made of fire, who'd suddenly materialized in front of me.

I screamed and scrambled back, slipping on the wet rocks and falling on my behind with a sharp jolt. I couldn't get away fast enough, my fear causing me to stumble over the rocks and back onto the sand in a mad dash to escape the fiery thing in front of me.

At first I thought it was an elemental, but the one Roth and I had encountered looked like an upside-down teardrop made of swirling water, with arms and glowing eyes. But this was different—it clearly was male, at least in shape, but made entirely of flame and as tall as a house.

And it was coming right for me.

"Calla of the Fire Realm," a voice bellowed out of his burning mouth. He took another step toward me, his flaming feet turning the black sand to glass. "Are you willing to serve your God?"

I froze, panic making my throat clench up, as it slowly dawned on me who was standing before me. The Fire God.

Could it really be him? No one had seen or heard from the Gods in centuries. They were myths and legends, the Fire Temple had been abandoned years ago, and even though I prayed to the Fire God like a good daughter, I could hardly believe he was standing in front of me.

As the shock wore off I considered running and screaming for help, but then he let out a roar. A circle of fire burst up around us, blocking out the rest of the world. Heat coated my skin and terror consumed me, along with sheer awe. Was he going to strike me down?

The blazing eyes seemed to look deep into my soul as he spoke. "You asked for clarity. You wanted a path. You prayed for my guidance. Do you refuse it now?"

Somehow he knew what I'd written and thrown in the brazier. It truly was him. I dropped to my knees, my gown pressing into the sand, and bowed my head at the Fire God. As the terror faded away, I finally found my voice. "What must I do?"

"You will come to the Fire Temple and serve me as High Priestess. Bring four men to serve as your priests and your mates. Once you arrive, I will give you further instructions. Do you accept my offer?"

"I..." My voice trailed off as his words sunk in. I'd asked for a sign as to what my place in the world would be, but I'd never expected *this*. He was asking me to give up my entire life and walk away from everything I knew to live in the Fire Temple on top of the volcano and serve as his priestess. It was impossible to consider, but he was a God—could I even refuse? Would he strike me down if I did?

And why me? My mother was much more devout than I was. There were many days when I hadn't believed the Gods existed at all, or if I did, I'd cursed them. I had no idea what being his High Priestess even meant. Not to mention, he wanted me to bring four men with me and take them as my mates. I certainly knew the four I'd want, but I couldn't ask them to give up their entire lives for me.

Yet as the shock wore off, a sense of purpose and wonder filled me, like nothing I'd ever known before. I would serve one of the Gods— there was no higher calling than that, especially if they were awakening after all this time. But how would I ever convince the others to go with me? Derel would never leave behind his family's business, Blane was definitely not priest material, and Roth could barely spend a moment alone with me anymore. The only one who might do it out of loyalty was Falon, but I had a hard time seeing him going anywhere without Derel.

"Why four men?" I managed to ask.

"The Spirit Goddess has four mates. The Black Dragon has four mates. My High Priestess must also have four."

I supposed that made sense and, if I was honest, the idea of being with all four men excited me, assuming they would ever agree to it. But they would never consider leaving as long as Sparkport was in danger, and neither would I. "What of the volcano? I can't leave my family behind if there is a risk of it erupting—and I wouldn't be able to reach the Fire Temple if it does."

"Once you arrive at the temple the volcano will become calm again."

I glanced back in the direction of the village, though the rocks blocked it from view, and then sighed. This was my destiny, like it or not. "Yes, I will become your High Priestess."

"Then rise."

I pushed myself up on shaking knees and faced the God in front of me. He moved close, singeing my dress and my hair, and my skin felt like it was going to peel off me. Before I could pull away he reached for me, and then all I knew was fire and heat. It raced along my skin, tore at my flesh, and melted my bones. I was taken apart and reformed. I died and was born again. I was ash and flame, smoke and lava, sparks and coal, and then I was whole again.

As the fire faded away and vanished, I stumbled back—but the Fire God was gone.

CHAPTER FIVE

Somehow I found my way back through the empty town, past the abandoned stalls, discarded dragon kites, and the new crack in the road. I felt so odd, like I was watching myself from a distance, unable to comprehend what had just happened. The Fire God had done something to me—but what?

I was in shock, still in disbelief that I'd said yes to his offer, and now I had a journey ahead of me that I was both excited and nervous about. But first I had to talk to the four men in my life, along with my family. How was I going to explain what had happened on the beach? Would anyone even believe me? I certainly wouldn't.

When I made it back to our home, the door flew open and Loka dashed out. "There you are!" she said as she wrapped her arms around me. "Gods, your dress! What did you do to it?"

I glanced down at myself and saw my crimson gown, which I'd worked so hard on for months, had been torn, covered in sand, and singed in numerous places. I could only shake my head as she led me inside, where the rest of our family waited.

"Thank the Gods you're safe," Mom said, as she swept me into her embrace.

"I'm just glad Loka made it back," I managed to say.

"Yes, she arrived not long after you left to find her. You must have just missed each other." She wiped soot off my face. "Goodness, you look like you had a fight with a hearth and lost. Is the ash from the volcano truly that bad already?"

"No, I..." I sank down into a chair, still shaken. "I have to tell you something."

They sat at the wooden dining table and listened intently while I went over everything that had happened at the beach, which sounded even more unbelievable when I said it all out loud. When I was finished, my sisters glanced at each other skeptically.

"Are you sure you weren't dreaming?" Krea asked.

"Yes, maybe you slipped and hit your head on the rocks," Loka added. "Are you feeling all right?"

I shook my head. "I know it sounds impossible, but it was real. I wish there was a way to prove it to you."

My mother had remained silent the entire time, her mouth frozen in a permanent tight line. But now she said, "There is a way."

"How?" I asked.

"The High Priestess can summon her God's element." She reached for a candle and set it on the table in front of me. "Try it."

Now I was the one giving skeptical looks. "How do you know?"

A faint smile touched her lips. "My grandmother was also High Priestess, as was her mother, and her mother before that. They could control fire too."

"It's hereditary?" I asked.

"It was, at least in the old days."

"You never told us any of this," Loka said, her eyes huge.

"What happened?" Krea asked. "The Fire Temple has been abandoned for years."

"My grandmother Ara left the temple and married a man here in Sparkport. I don't know why exactly, but my mother believed perhaps Ara grew tired of serving an absent God that no one believed in anymore. Maybe all of world did stop believing, but now the Fire God is stirring, which means something is changing. And he's chosen you to be part of it. You can't refuse."

"But I don't have any magic," I said.

"Maybe you do now. You said the flames covered you, but you appear unharmed." She rested her hand over mine and gave it a squeeze. "Have faith. He came to you for a reason."

"I'll try," I said, but I didn't have any confidence it would work. My body felt no different than it had before meeting the Fire God. It was my mind that had been shaken.

I reached for the candle and thought of fire, but nothing happened, although I sensed...something. I closed my eyes and remembered how it had felt when the Fire God had touched me and infused me with flames, how they'd become part of my body. Maybe I could channel that out of me now.

The candle wick suddenly burst into a huge flame, so large it made me gasp. My sisters stared at me like they'd never met me before, while my mother had never looked more proud.

She clasped her hands to her chest. "I knew it. Praise the Fire God."

"It's true," Loka whispered. "You really are the High Priestess."

I waved my hand at the fire, and to my surprise, it went out. "Not yet. I still need to travel to the temple. Only then will the Fire God tell me my purpose—and stop the volcano." I swallowed. "And I need to bring four men with me to be my priests."

"Lucky you," Krea said, with a knowing smile.

"That shouldn't be a problem," Mom said. "I'm sure Derel will agree, and those other friends of his probably will too. They all seem to be smitten with you."

"For some strange reason," Loka added as she nudged me with her elbow, making me smile.

"This is such a large thing to ask of them though. They'd be giving up their lives here for one at the temple, and they'd have to all agree to be with me." I glanced at my mother. "Are you sure you're all right with that?"

"As I said, our family is descended from the High Priestesses of the past. My grandmother had four fathers. It's not common in the Fire Realm, but if the Gods demand four husbands for their High Priestess, who are we to argue with them?"

I nodded and ran my hand along the table, feeling the ridges and grooves that I'd known my entire life. "If I do this, I'll be leaving Sparkport forever."

"You can still come visit, I'm sure," Krea said. "The Fire God won't demand you stay in the temple every single moment of your life."

Loka squeezed my hand with a smile. "We can come visit you too. We'll make sure you have enough supplies. It's not far, after all."

I nodded. As she said, Valefire wasn't far—only about a two day walk or so—but the journey up the volcano wouldn't be easy, especially when it was active. I'd have to trust that the Fire God was not sending me to my death and that he would protect me and my men.

Emotion made my throat tight as I glanced between my sisters and my mother. "I'm going to miss you all so much though. And the bakery—will you be okay without me?"

"Of course we will." Mom wiped at her eyes and then gathered me in a hug. "We'll miss you too, but this is your calling. I'm so proud of you, dear."

I hugged my mother back, my eyes filling with tears. I'd wanted guidance, but I hadn't expected my entire life to change this night—or that I'd have to say goodbye to the people I loved.

"We'll take care of Mom," Krea said, as she and Loka hugged me next.

"Don't worry about us. When are you leaving?" Loka asked.

Another small quake rippled under our feet, reminding us of my duty. "Tomorrow. Assuming I can convince the four men to come with me."

Mom jumped to her feet. "I'll start preparing some food for you to take."

"I'll help you pack," Krea said.

I rose in a daze to begin preparations, but then a knock sounded on the door. Mom rushed over to answer it and smiled when she saw it was Derel. "What a lovely surprise."

"Mother wanted me to check on all of you." His dark eyes found me behind the rest of my family, almost like he was seeking me out, but then he turned back to my mother. "Are you well?"

"Yes, thank you. But Calla has something she must speak to you about."

"Is that so?" Derel asked, raising an eyebrow.

I took Derel's arm, leading him outside, away from my nosy family. I closed the door behind me and spoke in hushed tones. "Can you get the others and meet me on the beach in a few minutes? It's important."

His face changed from intrigued to worried. "Is something wrong?"

"No, but I need to ask all of you something. Tonight."

He nodded. "I'll get them."

CHAPTER SIX

I sat on the rock where Blane had hid the fireworks earlier and adjusted my ruined dress, wishing I'd spared a moment to change into a new one. I'd been too busy packing my things and debating how to explain all of this to the four men I hoped would come with me to the temple. If I couldn't convince them, what then?

The volcano had calmed now, perhaps because I'd accepted the Fire God's offer and was doing what he wanted. The four men stood in front of me on the sand, the moonlight illuminating their handsome features. I'd agonized for so long over which man I would marry and how I would ever choose, but now I wouldn't have to—assuming they said yes.

"Is everything all right?" Falon asked.

"When I said we should meet later, I didn't mean with these other guys," Blane muttered.

Roth crossed his arms, looking surly. "Why have you brought us out here in the middle of the night?"

I drew in a deep breath. "There's something I need to tell you. And more importantly, something I need to ask you. All of you."

"What is it?" Derel asked.

There was no easy way to say this, so I got right to it. "After the volcano awakened I went looking for my sister on the beach to the north. There I met the Fire God."

Falon's brow furrowed. "I don't understand."

"What do you mean, you met the Fire God?" Blane asked.

"He came to me looking like a giant flaming man. He said he's chosen

759

me to be his High Priestess and that I need to go to the Fire Temple to serve him." I glanced at the volcano, which still had a plume of smoke rising from it. "Only then will Valefire return to sleep."

The four men gave each other confused and skeptical looks, probably wondering if they should be worried for my sanity or if I was trying to play some kind of prank on them, like we did when we were kids. I sighed and held out my hand, hoping the magic would come to me again this time. A spark flashed and then flickered into a small flame dancing in my palm. Oddly enough, it didn't burn me at all.

"I know this is hard to believe," I said, as they all gasped and stared at the fire. "But it's the truth. I'm leaving tomorrow for the Fire Temple, and I'm here to ask if you will go with me and become my priests." I swallowed and lowered my eyes. "And my mates."

Blane raised an eyebrow. "Your *mates?*"

"You want us to become priests?" Falon asked, looking more baffled than ever. "And...share you?"

"How would that even work?" Derel asked.

"And how did you summon fire?" Roth added.

"I don't know," I admitted. "I'm still figuring all of this out myself."

"Did he tell you anything else?" Falon asked.

"No, but he said we would learn more once we arrived at the temple. All I know is that the Fire God chose me and he told me to bring four men with me." I closed my palm over the fire, snuffing it out. "I know this is a lot to ask of you, but I can't imagine choosing any other men as my mates."

"And if we say no?" Roth asked.

"I...suppose I'll have to find others. The Fire God demanded four." I shuddered at the thought of taking strangers as my mates.

Roth ran a hand over his scarred face. "Are you sure you truly want each of us?"

The hint of vulnerability in his voice made my chest ache. "Yes, I am." I met their eyes in turn as I spoke slowly, hesitant to admit the feelings I'd kept inside so long. "I care about all of you so much. For years I've wondered if one of you might become my husband, but I wasn't sure I could ever choose between you. Now I don't have to choose, as long as you all say yes."

None of the four men jumped on my offer, but each one seemed as though they were considering it. I didn't blame them—it was a huge decision that would impact the rest of our lives. Yet with each passing minute, my path became clearer and I began to accept that this was my true calling. I only hoped they agreed to be part of my destiny.

I rose to my feet. "Think on it tonight. I plan to leave at dawn."

"So soon?" Derel asked.

"The sooner I get to the temple the sooner the town will be safe from the volcano."

"What of your family?" Falon asked.

"I'm going to miss them terribly, but this is something I have to do. My mother agreed—she said our family is descended from the last High Priestess. Besides, we'll be able to visit now and then, and our families can come to the temple anytime too. I'll still see my family when I can."

Blane ran a hand through his dark hair. "This is a lot to take in."

"I know, and I'm so sorry. If you're outside my house in the morning, then I'll be honored to have you at my side on this journey. If you decide to stay, I completely understand and won't hold it against you." I gave them all a weak smile. "We'll always remain friends, no matter what you choose."

I stepped off the rocks and began the trek back toward my house to finish packing and try to get some sleep before my long walk to the volcano, though I knew sleep would elude me tonight. I'd be too worried over what the men would decide and what would face me in the days to come.

As I passed the men, Blane's hand shot out and caught my arm. "Wait." He pulled me back toward him, taking me in his arms so suddenly I lost my breath. "I'm going with you."

His mouth descended on mine and he stole a demanding, possessive kiss right in front of the other men. As always, my body melted at his touch and begged for more, even if I worried what the others would think.

When I managed to pull back, I asked, "You are?"

He ran his rough thumb along my sensitive lips. "I don't have anything tying me down here except you. If you leave, I'm going with you."

"I'm going too," Derel said, surprising me even more than Blane.

I spun around to face him. "What about your family? Everyone expects you to take over as the town butcher one day."

He shrugged. "They'll have to find someone else. Besides, my mother would never let me hear the end of it if I didn't go with you."

"Thank you," I said, sliding my arms around him. After a moment's hesitation, he embraced me back, his smoldering eyes staring down at me as if he wanted to kiss me. His hands skimmed down my back, getting distractingly close to my behind. Other than the dance earlier, it was the most intimate we'd ever been together. Most of the time we hated each other...but maybe we didn't. Not really.

"I'm in too," Falon said. "The temple is probably falling apart anyway. You'll need a good carpenter."

I moved into Falon's open arms with a smile. "Yes, we will."

761

His hug was friendly, though he held me tight against him. I found myself pressing my face to his neck, breathing him in, wishing I was bold enough to press my lips there. Would he kiss me back if I pulled him down to my mouth? Was he going with me because he cared for me too—or only as my friend?

I turned to Roth, the only one who hadn't spoken up, hoping he'd say he was coming too. It had to be the four of them, my closest friends, the men I'd always loved, but he shook his head. "I'm sorry, Calla. Like I said, you're better off without me."

He walked away as sadness dragged me down. I bowed my head, unable to watch him leave, knowing it meant the end for the two of us. For the past few years I'd held on to the hope that he would come around and we'd have a chance at happiness again, but now I knew that had been futile.

"Roth!" Blane called out, as Roth's form vanished in the darkness.

"Let him go," Derel said.

"Are you okay, Calla?" Falon asked, running his hands along my bare arms as if to warm them.

I forced a smile and blinked back tears. "Yes, I'm all right. I didn't really expect any of you to say yes. Especially so quickly. Thank you so much for going on this journey with me and everything that entails." I glanced between the three of them, thinking how lucky I was that they'd agreed to come with me. "Now we should get some rest—we leave at first light."

CHAPTER SEVEN

W hen I stepped out of my house, I was shocked to see a crowd already waiting for me. I'd always known gossip traveled quickly in a small town like Sparkport, but I had no idea just how fast until now.

"Oh my," Mom said, as she moved out from behind me and took in the throng of people before us. "It seems the entire town's come to see you off."

"How many people did you tell about this?"

She shrugged. "Only Sucy, of course."

I groaned. I should have known. Derel's mother was the town gossip. Then again, he would have to tell her why he was suddenly leaving town, so I supposed it was inevitable that all of Sparkport would soon know about the Fire God's visit and my destiny. Along with my upcoming relationship with four men.

I caught sight of Derel standing with his parents, who were giving him hugs and wiping at their eyes. Nearby, Falon was saying goodbye to his family too. I felt horrible for taking them away from the people they loved, who'd depended on them to take over their trades in a few years. Falon's brother could take over his family's carpentry business, but Derel's family would have to find themselves a new apprentice butcher now.

Blane, on the other hand, was alone. He leaned against the side of my house with his bag hanging off his shoulder, looking the total outcast. As an orphan and the town pariah, he had no one who would miss him here —but I was happy he'd be at my side for the rest of my life.

But then I caught sight of an unexpected face in the crowd, one that stood out with its mix of flaws and perfection. Roth pushed past people until he emerged in front of me, while people stared at his scarred face. It was rare for him to be out in public like this, especially in bright daylight.

"You're here," I said, breathless and afraid to hope that he'd changed his mind.

"I'm here," he said. "I couldn't let you choose some stranger to be your fourth. Though I'm not sure what use a fisherman will be at the Fire Temple."

I smiled at him, while resisting the urge to hug him in front of all these people, which I knew he'd hate. "Valefire is on the coast, and we'll still need to eat. Even if that weren't true, I'd want you with me anyway."

"I knew you'd change your mind," Derel said to Roth, who just scowled.

"We ready to get moving?" Blane asked.

"Don't rush her," Falon said.

Blane rolled his eyes. "I'm not, but if we want to make it to the temple by tomorrow night, we'll need to get on the road soon."

"I'm almost ready," I said, before turning back to my mother and sisters. Emotion clogged my chest and tears filled my eyes as I hugged them one by one.

"Good luck," Krea whispered in my ear.

"I'm going to miss you so much," Loka said.

My mother hugged me so long and tight I started to feel like she was never going to let me go. Then she pulled back to look at me. "This is your destiny and I'm very proud of you. Your father would be too. Take care of yourself and those four young men, and come visit whenever you can."

I sniffed. "I will."

"Remember, you're descended from a long line of priestesses." She patted my cheek. "Now get to the Fire Temple before the volcano tears apart our town."

I chuckled through my tears. "Yes, Mom."

I turned away and grabbed the bag that held the few things I'd decided to take with me. It was time to face my destiny.

My four men formed a circle around me as we moved through the town, parting the crowd like a wave. The people I'd known my entire life now looked at me with a mix of awe, fear, and hope. Many of them called out their blessings or wished us well, some even thanking us for protecting them from the volcano, while others frowned or turned away. Maybe they didn't believe the Fire God had truly chosen me, or maybe they didn't agree with me taking four mates.

"Whore," someone muttered in the crowd, and Blane lurched forward like he would strike the person down. Falon gripped his arm and held him back. I bowed my head, my face heating up and no doubt turning red, and picked up my pace. Though it was sad leaving my village and family, there were definitely some people I would not miss.

We kept walking and soon left the crowd and the town behind. I'd gone over the map with my mother last night, since she'd visited the Fire Temple once as a child, though she hadn't left Sparkport in many years. According to her, people in our village used to regularly visit the temple and leave offerings, but that fell out of practice. It was likely no one had visited for at least twenty years now.

As we followed the road, I hefted my bag higher on my shoulder. I'd only brought one, and it had been hard to leave a lifetime's worth of belongings behind, but for this journey I only needed the essentials. Plus a few books, of course. I would return and get the rest of my things once I was settled in the temple.

"Thank you again for coming with me," I said to the men, who had fanned out around me. "I know it was a lot to ask and on such short notice too. I mean, you had to give up your families, your professions, and your homes. I'm still in awe that you all said yes."

"You had to give up all of those things too when the Fire God chose you," Falon pointed out. "At least we had a choice."

"The Fire God did give me a choice, but it didn't feel like much of one. How do you say no to a God?" I smiled faintly as I remembered my fear upon meeting him. "Although I wouldn't have said no anyway. Though it was a shock at first, I truly feel this is my path. As if I'd been searching for myself my entire life and now I finally found her. And all of you are a part of that. Maybe there was a reason I felt so strongly for all of you..." I trailed off, stealing glances at the men, wondering if I'd said too much. I still didn't know if they felt the same for me. They were here with me, but was that because of duty, friendship, desire...or love?

"Anyway, I really appreciate that you're all going on this journey with me," I added quickly. "For the last few years I've been torn between each of you, unable to decide who I wanted to spend my life with. I'm so happy that now I don't have to decide. I can have you all."

Falon cleared his throat. "I can't speak for the others, but I'm happy to be here, even if it was unexpected."

"You know I'm always up for an adventure," Blane said.

"No kidding," Roth said. "Did you bring the fireworks?"

"Of course I did," Blane said.

Derel rolled his eyes. "You'll probably shoot off your arm with them."

Blane grinned. "If I do, we'll call it an offering to the Fire God. He'll love it."

I laughed and shook my head. If nothing else, I would never be bored at the Fire Temple with these four around.

It wasn't long before we had to diverge off the road to begin walking on the rough terrain. The volcano was almost directly north of Sparkport on the coast, and while there might have been a road leading to it years ago, it had all but vanished now. This journey would have been a lot faster and easier if we were all riding horses, but our village didn't have any that could be spared. I wasn't sure we'd be able to get horses up the volcano anyway—we were in for a bit of a climb once we reached it.

I glanced up at Valefire in the distance, which was still releasing a never-ending stream of white smoke into the sky. Journeying there seemed an impossible task, and no one in their right mind would ever want to live there. I could only trust that the Fire God knew what he was doing—even if it was hard to banish my fears and doubts about what was to come.

CHAPTER EIGHT

W e stopped for a quick lunch by a tiny stream that looked like it might dry up at any moment. How would we get water at the volcano anyway? People had lived there at one point so there must be a way, but it only reminded me I had no idea what to expect at the temple.

I sat with my back against a scraggly little tree which offered a tiny amount of shade. Derel sat beside me, taking the rest of the shade, while the other guys found other spots near the stream to try to stay cool. As we got closer to Valefire it would no doubt get hotter too.

"What do you think we'll encounter at the Fire Temple?" I asked, as I ripped apart a piece of the bread my mother had packed for us.

Derel brushed crumbs off of himself. "I don't know. Hopefully it's still standing."

"Were your parents upset about you leaving? They'll have to find someone else to help run the butcher shop now."

"Dad was upset, but luckily my cousin can step in and take my place at the shop. Mom was sad, but was also excited because I was going with you." He rolled his eyes. "Still hoping we'll get married and give her tons of grandkids, no doubt."

"Of course." Except…we kind of were getting married. Not officially, but in practice. Unless they didn't see it the same way I did?

"Are you sure you want to do this?" I asked, trying to ignore the tightness in my chest. "I know the two of us haven't always gotten along in the past."

He snorted. "Only because you're always picking fights with me."

I turned to face him. "Me? You're the one who is always rude to me!"

"Maybe because you deserve it."

I threw my last piece of bread at his head. "I do not. If anyone deserves rudeness, it's you."

He threw the bread back at me, his brows drawn together. "Gods, you make me crazy, Calla. You're stubborn and infuriating and so damn beautiful it nearly hurts to look at you sometimes."

"I…what?" I'd been so ready to argue with him more that his last words made my mouth fall open in shock.

He slid his hand into my hair and drew me toward him, capturing my wordless surprise with his lips. Twenty years of pent-up frustration and desire unraveled at his kiss and I found myself pulling at his shirt to draw him closer. When his tongue slid against mine it sent a rush of heat right between my legs.

"I'm shocked," I managed to say. "I had no idea you felt that way."

"Don't be ridiculous. You must know how we all feel about you."

"No, I truly don't." Although I was beginning to realize it. I probably should have known all along, but I'd been worried my feelings for them were mostly one-sided. Only once they'd agreed to journey with me to the Fire Temple did I realize they might care for me the same way I cared for them.

Derel ran his fingers through my blond hair like he couldn't get enough of it. "I've wanted to kiss you for years. I've spent long nights thinking about wrapping this hair around my fingers. And all the other things I want to do with you too…"

"If you had feelings for me, why didn't you ever tell me?

He shrugged. "I thought you hated me."

I softened against him and touched his face in wonder. "I never hated you, I just hated the circumstances we were in. Our mothers forced us together from the time we were born. We never had a choice in the matter and that made me frustrated. I guess I took it out on you. I'm sorry."

"I'm equally guilty. I was pretty horrible to you at times."

"Yes, like the time you pushed me in the ocean when we were five. Or when we were seven and you tricked me into sitting on those strawberries and ruined my dress. Or—"

He grimaced. "Okay, yes, I was quite awful. But I had to get your attention somehow." He let out a low laugh. "Wow, I'd forgotten about the strawberries. No wonder you hated me."

"I didn't hate you. Well, maybe a little…"

He pulled me close and kissed me again, and every time it was like a revelation. I'd spent my entire life thinking Derel was my nemesis. Now I looked on him with a whole new light.

"We should probably get going," he finally said. He helped me to my feet and we brushed dirt off ourselves, but then he paused. "There was another reason I was rude to you."

"What was it?"

He glanced over at the other guys, who looked like they were trying to watch us without being too obvious about it. "Falon."

"Falon only sees me as a friend."

"We both know that's not true of anyone in this group." He shook his head. "Like I said last night, you should talk to him about that."

With those words he grabbed his pack and walked away, leaving me with only my thoughts. I grabbed my things and hurried after him.

For the next few hours we traveled through the empty wilds, the volcano looming large in front of us. As I kicked up dirt, I went through my memories of Derel and saw everything he'd done—all the pranks, the teasing, the arguments—in a new light. It made me wonder what else I'd been wrong about all my life.

I slowed my pace to fall in line with Falon, who walked at the rear of the group. Last time I'd tried to talk to Falon about us it hadn't gone as planned, but his being here had to be a sign he cared for me as more than a friend...didn't it?

"I see you and Derel have worked out your issues finally," he said with a teasing voice.

"We did." While Derel had long driven me mad, Falon had a way of calming me. I always relaxed in his presence. "He told me to talk to you."

He ducked his head and rubbed the back of his neck. "Me? Why?"

"He said one of the reasons he pushed me away all these years was because of you." I glanced over at Falon quickly to gauge his reaction, but couldn't meet his eyes.

He blew out a long breath. "What a pair we are. He wouldn't do anything because of me, and I wouldn't do anything because of him."

"What do you mean?"

He stopped and turned toward me, allowing me to gaze into his clear blue eyes. "Gods, after so many years this is difficult to finally admit. I have feelings for you, Calla. I always have."

Warmth spread throughout my chest. "Why didn't you tell me?"

"You've been promised to Derel for our entire lives—how was I supposed to get in the way of that?"

"You knew that was what our parents wanted, not us."

"Trust me, Derel wanted it too. He pretended he didn't because he knew how I felt about you and he didn't want to get in the way. Which naturally was the same reason I never acted on my feelings. Maybe one of us might have told you the truth eventually, but then you became involved with Roth and it looked like you would marry him, so we decided to keep our feelings to ourselves."

"Yes, but my relationship with Roth didn't last long."

"True, but then you started seeing Blane…"

I shook my head. "That wasn't serious."

He arched an eyebrow. "Is that what you think? Because I'm pretty sure it's serious to him."

I bit my lip and looked over at Blane. I'd have to talk to him later to see if Falon was right. I turned back to Falon and sighed. "I wish I'd known the truth all this time. I thought you only saw me as a friend."

"I didn't know if you felt that way for me either. Not until last night." He took my hands in his and gave me a warm smile. "I was terrified if I told you I had feelings for you that you wouldn't return them and it would ruin our friendship. I couldn't stand the thought of that. I tried to tell myself your friendship was enough, and that I'd be happy if you married one of the other guys, but the truth was, I was miserable seeing you with them. I wanted it to be me."

"Are you going to be okay with this arrangement?"

"I think so. It's the perfect solution." He glanced over at the other three guys, who were still trudging along ahead of us. "The five of us were all so close when we were younger. We've each loved you for years. But we knew if we acted on it, it could tear our group apart."

"Roth and Blane acted on it," I pointed out.

"Roth was a selfish jerk before the attack," Falon said with a wink. "But we would have gladly let you marry him if he made you happy. Blane too, for that matter. But you probably noticed that once you became involved with them, the group stopped spending as much time together."

I nodded. "I know, and I realize that was partly my fault. I just hope this situation brings us closer together instead of tearing us further apart."

"It will. We may be hesitant at first to share you, but we'd rather share you than not have you at all." He took my face in his hands. "And now I'm going to kiss you, because I'm the only one who never has."

"Finally," I said.

He bent his head and touched his mouth to mine slowly, then gave me soft, teasing kisses, as though he was learning the shape of my lips. I slid my arms around his neck and pulled him closer, wanting more, but he was infuriatingly patient. I suppose he had to be, if he'd waited this long to kiss me. But then his tongue swiped across my lower lip and I opened for him with a gasp. As his tongue slid sensually against mine, he clutched me in his arms and made me feel cherished and adored, like he wanted to take his time kissing me and never let me go.

He pressed his forehead against mine. "Even better than I imagined it would be."

"Good, now you've kissed all of us," Blane called out. "We can finally move on to the fun stuff."

I laughed. "What makes you think that will happen?"

"A man can hope."

"That seems rather presumptuous," I said, as I hefted my bag onto my other shoulder and continued walking alongside Falon. Gods, why had I packed so many things? With each step the bag became heavier and heavier.

"Isn't that why we're here?" Blane asked with a wicked grin. "To serve you?"

"You're coming with me to serve the Fire God." A small smile played across my lips. "And to keep me company, I suppose."

"I think Blane has a specific way he wants to pass the time," Derel said.

Blane chuckled. "As if you aren't hoping for the same thing."

CHAPTER NINE

I thought about Blane's comment as we found a spot to make camp for the night. I had kissed all of them now, although I hadn't kissed Roth in years. Not since the night of the attack, when our lives changed forever. I wanted to kiss him again, but would he let me?

I'd tried to be supportive after his injury. I'd told him I didn't care what he looked like, that I loved him no matter what and still wanted to be with him—but he couldn't even listen to the words without going into a rage. He was in so much pain, both inside and out, and he said that seeing me only made it worse. He asked me to leave him alone, telling me he didn't want me anymore, and I foolishly listened, hoping he would change his mind once he healed. Now I wished I could go back and force myself to stay, no matter what harmful things he'd said to me.

It was warm enough that we didn't need a fire, but I drifted away from the group and began practicing my new magic on some weeds growing up from some rocks. The fire came easier now, though it still surprised me every time.

"I thought only the Dragons had magic," Roth said, his gravelly voice behind me.

"Me too. It seems the Gods can make exceptions." I tried to snuff out the flames, but when my magic didn't work, I stomped on the weeds with my boots. "I'm sorry. Does the fire bring back bad memories?"

"It's fine. We should get back to the camp though."

I nodded and began to follow him, but then stopped. I was tired of this distance between us. "Roth, wait."

He stopped and turned toward me, the moonlight highlighting both halves of his face. It made my chest tighten with emotion, and I found myself crossing the distance to him. When he didn't move away, I gripped his shirt in my hand and lifted on my toes to press my mouth against his. At first he didn't respond and I worried I'd made a fool of myself, but then he let out a groan and his arms went around me, hauling me against his muscular body. His mouth devoured mine like he was making up for the last two years.

My back pressed against the boulder behind me as Roth's lips trailed down my neck. Desire swept through me, hot and needy, and I fumbled for his trousers, wanting him inside me again. Gods, it had been way too long, and I'd never stopped aching for him since that night.

He tore his mouth from mine as my fingers rubbed against his hard bulge. "Calla... We shouldn't."

"Why not? We've slept together before."

"Yes, but not since *this*." He gestured at the burn marring his otherwise perfect face.

"I don't care about that. I loved you before your scars and I love you now too. If they took over your entire body I would still love you." He didn't say anything as I took his face in my hands. "Besides, this side of you is so pretty you need something to balance it out. Otherwise you'd make the other guys jealous."

That finally got one corner of his mouth to twitch up. "I *was* always the best looking one in our group."

I pressed a kiss to both of his cheeks. "I was so happy when I saw you in the crowd this morning. I couldn't imagine spending my life without you. And now we're here together, and I'm ready to go back to what we once had."

He let out a ragged breath. "I love you too, Calla."

My eyes widened. "You do?"

"I should have said it years ago. I just couldn't imagine you would still love me when I looked like this, especially when you almost died that night. I figured if I stayed away, you'd marry one of the other guys, who I knew also loved you."

"They were probably worried about hurting you by being with me."

"Maybe, though I did a pretty good job of pushing them away over the years. Especially Blane." He tangled his fingers in my hair. "I was both relieved and jealous when the two of you started seeing each other. I hoped you would be happy together."

"I didn't think it was serious with Blane, but now I'm starting to wonder. And I never slept with him, you know."

"No? What about the others?"

"You're my first and only."

His grip on my hair tightened, turning possessive as he looked down at me with hunger. "You're my first and only too. Although I suspect I won't be your only much longer."

"Does that bother you?"

"No. I lost my claim on you years ago." He glanced back at the camp. "And maybe we all knew, deep down, this was the only way for us to all be happy."

"I think I knew that too. I was just afraid to admit it, and I worried what people would think of us."

"Now you don't have to worry."

"No, I don't." I slid my hands into his thick hair to pull him close again. "But at this moment I only want you."

His mouth crushed against mine and he pressed me back against the boulder. I wrapped myself tighter around him and his hands slid down to cup my behind, lifting me up and against him. My skirts bunched up around my hips and I wrapped my legs around him, marveling at his strong shoulders, built from working long hours on the docks and on his uncle's fishing boat. I'd spent a lot of time at the docks watching him, both before and after his injury, staring at his shirtless body as he hauled on ropes and climbed the rigging of his uncle's ship, remembering what it felt like to touch that tanned skin. The same skin I was touching and tasting now.

Passion and desire made us desperate for each other. With one hand pressed against the boulder for support, he used his other hand to pull open his trousers. I gasped as the head of his cock pushed against my core, which was already so wet for him. I'd been waiting to feel him inside me again for years, and I tightened my legs around him, not wanting to delay another second. His fingers gripped my behind as he entered me nice and slow, filling me up completely and making me stretch around him. Gods, I'd forgotten how big he was and how good he felt inside me.

He began to move with deep, languid strokes that hit me in all the right places. I clung to his neck as his strong arms held us up, the hard stone digging into my back while he pumped into me. He captured my mouth again and the touch of his tongue against mine made me nearly come undone. I'd waited so long to be one with him again, and now I never wanted it to end.

But he demanded more, pushing me further, shifting me higher, until the angle of his movements was just perfect. I was close, so close, and as his lips trailed across my neck I let go, giving in to the sweet friction of our bodies and his hard length filling me. My head fell back as sensation washed over me and I pulsed around him, nails digging into his shoulders as I called out his name. He rewarded me by thrusting harder and faster until he released himself inside me with a throaty groan.

I pressed my forehead against his as we trembled together, overcome with the emotions coursing through us. Soon our lips found each other again, but this time we kissed slowly, our movements unhurried. As if we only now realized we had the rest of our lives to do this again and again. Now that we'd found each other a second time, there was no need to rush.

But then I remembered the other men back in camp. They probably had a good idea of what we were doing, and I couldn't help but wonder what they thought about it. Would they be jealous...or would they want to join in?

CHAPTER TEN

I woke to find a strong arm wrapped around me, holding me close. For a moment I simply reveled in the feeling of a large, masculine body at my back and the mystery man's even breathing in my ear. I wasn't sure who it was, but it didn't matter, because I would gladly wake up beside any one of my men...or all of them.

When Roth and I had returned last night, the other men had been quiet. Falon and Derel would barely meet my eyes, while Blane openly grinned at me. I'd completely exhausted at that point, and had practically fallen onto my bedroll and passed out immediately. It seemed someone had joined me in the middle of the night.

I must have stirred a little, because I felt his breathing change as he woke. Warm lips pressed a kiss to my neck and the arm tightened around me.

"Morning, beautiful," Blane drawled.

I should have known it was him. None of the other men would have been so bold. I turned my head just enough to catch his mouth and draw him into a kiss without a word. I'd wanted to sleep with Blane for a long time, but I'd always held back because I was never sure if what we had together was real. Once he'd volunteered to go with me to the Fire Temple, I'd realized I'd misjudged him, along with our relationship. And now that I'd had a reminder of how good sex could be, I wanted to experience it with Blane too.

Judging by the hardness pressed against my behind, he wanted me just as badly. I rubbed back against him and he groaned, then slid his hand down my chemise to cup my breast. His thumb flicked over my hard nipple, while his mouth found my neck and pressed a warm kiss there.

"You've tempted me for so long," his rough voice said in my ear. "Last night I heard your moans of pleasure with Roth, and now *I'm* going to be the one making you moan."

"Yes," I managed to whisper.

His fingers trailed down and down, reaching the bottom of my chemise, which he yanked up enough to gain access to my naked body underneath. His hand roamed across my skin as he explored me, and I wished I could touch him more too, but at the same time I loved the way he was in control. When that hand finally slid between my thighs, I cried out for more.

He traced my folds and made a soft humming sound of approval. "So wet for me already?"

"Blane, please," I whispered, trying to keep my voice down to not wake the others in the camp. I had a feeling that wouldn't last long though.

He hooked my leg back over his and then his cock nudged between my thighs from behind. With one smooth thrust he was inside, filling me up completely. Gods, he was huge and so thick too. His fingers dug into my hip while he slid deep, over and over again, and all I could do was gasp with each stroke. I spread myself wider, pushing back against him in time with his movements, trying to take as much of him as possible.

He claimed me with each thrust, and then his fingers slid between my thighs too. I turned my head back toward him and he took my mouth in a deep, rough kiss while he continued pumping in and out of me. Our bodies moved together in a delicious rhythm, faster and faster, until it became too much. Pleasure crept over me in rolling waves and I tore my mouth away from him to cry out his name. His fingers kept up their pressure and urged me into new heights, while he pinned me back against him. With a rough growl he pushed deep and held me there as his cock pulsed inside me with his release.

For some time we simply lay there, entwined together in blissful silence, until our breathing calmed. I turned back toward him with a smile, amazed he was here with me. Of all the men, I'd figured he would say no to my offer—but instead he'd been the first to volunteer.

"I can't see you being a priest somehow," I said.

"Yeah, me neither. Truthfully I don't care about any of that stuff. The Gods can rot for all I care. I'm only here for you." He pressed a kiss to my neck. "Besides, my family is gone and Sparkport never accepted me. I would have left years ago and never returned if not for you."

I rolled over to face him, surprised by his confession. "I was never sure if you truly cared for me in that way, or if I was just a temporary distraction before you went off on some adventure again."

"I always came back, didn't I?"

"Yes, but I figured you had women in other towns…" I shrugged.

"I did when you and Roth were together. When that ended, I decided I only wanted you."

"Why didn't you tell me?"

"Because I knew you'd never want to be with me, not like that. You worried about what people would think of us being together." I opened my mouth to protest but he silenced me with a kiss. "Admit it, you were."

"Only because I knew my mother would never let me marry you." My eyes dropped. "Maybe there is some truth to what you are saying. I'm sorry. I shouldn't have let that come between us."

"And I should have been clear that I wanted you for more than just a little fun on the side." He cupped my cheek and gazed into my eyes. "I've always loved you. I just never thought I would ever be lucky enough to have you. I certainly don't deserve you."

"I love you too," I said, before pressing another kiss to his lips. "And don't say that. You were the first to volunteer to go with me."

"The others have families and homes and professions to leave behind. I had nothing, except you." He drew me tighter into his arms. "You're all that matters to me."

"If you two lovebirds are done, it's time we get going," Derel called out.

Blane chuckled. "He must be jealous."

Was he? If the other men were jealous or upset, I'd have to find a way to fix that soon. We were going to spend the rest of our lives together, the five of us in one small temple, and I'd have to make sure we were all okay with that—and everything it entailed.

CHAPTER ELEVEN

The closer we got to the volcano the more desolate the landscape became. The ground under our feet became black from ancient lava now hardened, and plumes of steam and boiling water would sometimes burst up without warning. The air grew hotter too, and began to smell of burning weeds and rotten eggs. Valefire raged on without care, sending white smoke up into the air and making the land rumble beneath us, and all I could do was trust that the Fire God would keep his end of the bargain.

Once we reached the base of Valefire, we were all covered in a thin layer of ash and sweat, and now came the hard part—the climb. We took a quick break to drink water and eat some of the sliced pork Derel had brought, gathering our strength as best we could before the final part of our journey.

"Do you think it will erupt?" Falon asked, as he wiped sweat off his brow.

"Not if we make it there soon," I said, hoping I was right. I straightened up again and hefted my bag over my shoulder with a groan. At first it had seemed far too small considering all the things I'd left behind, but now it felt like a load of bricks on my back. I started to wish I'd been even more selective when I'd packed.

"Here, let me help you with that," Falon said, as he reached for my bag.

"Oh. Thank you." I rolled my shoulders with relief.

He threw my bag onto his back. "Gods, this thing must weigh a ton. What do you have in here?"

"My clothes and some other things."

"And a stack of books, no doubt," Roth said.

"I only brought a few!" It had made me sick leaving any of my books behind, but I couldn't exactly carry them all.

"How many is a few?" Derel asked.

I bit my lip. "Um, four?"

Falon laughed. "Four? No wonder this thing is so heavy."

"If we divide them up between all of us it won't be so bad," Derel said.

"All right, but I'm carrying my bag again after that," I said, as I took it back from Falon and opened it up. I handed each of the guys one of my small leather-bound books, and they slipped them into their own packs. Except for Blane, who stared at his.

"This is the one I got you," he said. "You brought it with you."

"Of course I did. It's my favorite." Blane had picked up the book on one of his journeys to the Air Realm, which was known for its amazing libraries and museums.

He opened his mouth, but no words came out. When he looked up at me, emotion flickered across his face. "Why?"

"Because it came from you." I leaned close and pressed a quick kiss to his lips, while the other guys watched.

Blane pulled me closer and pressed his lips to my ear. "I love you."

I nuzzled my face in his neck. I should have realized the true depth of Blane's feelings when he got me the book, but it was nice to have no doubts about them now. "I love you too."

We broke apart and began to ascend the mountain. The climb was grueling, especially when we were already exhausted. The hot sun on our backs didn't help, nor did the thick layer of smoke as we got higher and higher. I coughed constantly and felt like I would never be clean again, assuming I could make it to the summit without passing out. The men didn't seem to be faring much better, and would often stop to readjust their bags or wipe sweat from their brows. The relentless heat and the horrible smells only made it worse. Would we ever get used to this?

When we finally reached the summit, my knees were weak and I could barely find the strength to stand. But there, rising before us, was the temple of the Fire God in all its glory—our new home.

The temple was a large building made entirely of obsidian, the black volcanic glass so common in this part of the Fire Realm. In Sparkport we used it for many things—arrowheads, tools, jewelry—and many traders sold it in other parts of the world. But I'd never seen an entire structure made out of it.

Night had fallen sometime during our ascent, and the black temple was highlighted from behind by the eerie orange glow from the great open maw of the volcano.

"We're here," Roth said. "Now what?"

I hesitated. "I suppose we go inside and make ourselves at home."

Derel and Falon moved to the great temple door and tugged it open with some difficulty. As they did, a rush of dust fluttered out into the humid air. The room inside was pitch black, and I summoned a ball of flame into my palm as we stepped inside.

With the feeble light shining inside the expansive room, I caught sight of something. A flash of light and dark. A whisper of movement. A hint we weren't alone.

I gripped Blane's arm. "What was that?"

"I didn't see anything," he said, although he drew his sword anyway.

"It looked like a shadow," Falon said with a frown.

"Rats probably," Derel added.

I nodded and continued forward, tampering down my fear while moving across the stone floor. I made the flame bigger to illuminate more of the room, and gasped at what the light revealed.

Shadowy figures with dimly glowing eyes stood around the great hall. They looked almost like humans except for their long claws and the way their bodies tapered off near the bottom. As those glowing yellow eyes turned toward us, cold fear shot down my spine.

"Shades," Blane said, as he pushed me behind him.

Impossible. Shades were a myth, nothing more. They were stories parents told to their children to keep them from misbehaving. Shades were said to once have been friendly spirits, but were now twisted, deadly ghosts trapped between this world and the next. Worst of all, they were hungry... and nearly impossible to kill.

The shades rushed toward us, trailing across the floor with their insubstantial bodies, moving through anything in their way. Roth, Derel, and Falon all drew their weapons too, swiping at the nearest ones alongside Blane. Each of the men knew how to fight, while all I could do was stand behind them and pray. Except their blades went straight through the shades as if they were nothing but air.

"Weapons don't hurt them!" Derel called out.

"We need fire," Roth said, as one of the shades tried to claw at his arm.

Fire—of course. Like the elementals, shades could probably only be stopped by fire, water, air, or earth.

That meant I had to do something, but how? I wasn't a fighter. I'd never killed anyone before. But we were in danger and I couldn't let my men get injured. I summoned the Fire God's gift into my palms, the heat giving me clarity and strength. As the shade lunged for Roth again, I threw my ball of fire at it. The magic hit with a loud sizzle and flames flashed all over the shade, before the creature vanished in a cloud of black smoke. I felt a split second of triumph, before more shades crowded around us.

Now that we'd seen what my fire could do to the shades, I summoned even more of it. Blane grabbed a torch off the wall and swept it through my ball of flame, lighting it instantly. Falon picked up a discarded chair and broke it over his knee, splintering the wood into pieces. He tossed them to Derel and Roth, and they gestured for me to light their stakes as well. Roth hesitated as his stake lit up with fire, no doubt remembering how he got his injury, but then he guarded me from the shades with the others.

We backed up behind a discarded bookshelf and some tables, but the shades moved right through the furniture without slowing at all. Blane rushed the closest one with a roar, swiping his torch at it. The other shades surrounded us almost instantly, and I could barely summon fire fast enough to blast them before they got to me. The men fought them off with their improvised fiery weapons, although the shades' claws still managed to rip through their clothes and slash their skin.

As another of my men cried out, fear swelled within me and I prayed to the Fire God for help. We were in his temple, doing his work, why wasn't he helping us? Was this some kind of test? Were we on our own?

But he'd given me a gift, and even though I barely knew how to control it, I felt it flickering inside me. My fear and determination to protect my mates only made it flare hotter, and I let out a roar and spread my arms, calling forth the Fire God's wrath with power I didn't know I possessed. Each shade in the room suddenly burnt up with a piercing scream, turning to ash.

As the power left me, I crumpled to the floor, completely spent. Derel rushed over to me and asked, "Are you all right?"

I nodded. "Yes, although it seems I need a little more practice with my magic."

The other men were immediately at my side, though they were all bleeding from various minor cuts from the shades. I was just relieved we were still alive.

Blane brushed back a damp piece of blond hair from my eyes. "I think you did a damn good job with your magic already."

"You were incredible," Falon said, touching my cheek lovingly.

Roth suddenly swept me up into his strong arms. "Let's find you somewhere to lie down."

"Really, I'm fine," I said, though I didn't protest too much because I liked being held like this against his hard body.

He grunted and carried me through the dark temple, while the others lit torches where we could find them to brighten the dark halls. The room with the shades had been some sort of grand entrance hall, with tall ceilings and a huge statue of a fiery dragon in the center. Other doors led down hallways to more rooms, including kitchens, storerooms, bedrooms, and washrooms. Tomorrow I wanted to fully explore, but at the moment it took everything I had to keep my eyes open.

I barely remembered Roth setting me down, or the others tucking some blankets over me. All I knew was that each one kissed me goodnight, and I fell asleep wondering if this would ever feel like home.

CHAPTER TWELVE

In the morning I discovered I'd been placed in a bedroom that the men had prepared for me, although it needed more cleaning, as did the rest of the temple. Dim, murky light shone through the windows from the smoke-covered sky, reminding me that the volcano still raged on. We'd made it to the temple—would the Fire God speak to me soon and tell me my purpose?

I visited the washroom quickly, then began a more thorough tour of the temple. I barely remembered anything from last night after the shade attack, and now I surveyed the building with a more critical eye, making a mental note of everything I'd want to change or fix. Though the temple itself was all black volcanic stone and didn't need any repairs, everything inside it required straightening, repairing, or cleaning. If we were going to live here for the rest of our lives, we had a lot of work to do.

I stopped in the kitchen, where Derel was scrubbing down the counters. "I had a feeling you'd be in here."

He looked up at me with a wry grin. "Someone needs to cook for us. Unless you want to do it?"

I held up my hands in surrender. "I'll help with the baking if you'd like, but you're welcome to take over in the kitchen. That was more my sisters' area of expertise."

"Yes, I remember." He propped his hip on the counter and offered me a bit of bread, ham, and cheese. "You preferred to hole up in a corner somewhere with your books."

"That's true," I said, as I devoured the food. When was the last time

I'd eaten? Lunch yesterday, perhaps? "Unfortunately I couldn't turn reading into a profession."

"You can now."

"What do you mean?"

Amusement made his dark eyes dance. "Let's just say you're going to be very happy when you see the library."

My eyes widened. "There's a library?"

He nodded. "I'm pretty sure it has more books than all of Sparkport. It'll take you years to read them all."

I finished off his food and wiped my hands. "I'd better get started then."

"Not yet," he said, taking my arm. "There's another place I think you'll want to visit first."

"What is it?"

"I'll show you."

He led me out of the kitchen and down the halls. I spotted Roth and Blane arranging some furniture in another room, but Derel continued on. Soon we came upon a cave-like room filled with steaming water in a few different pools. Falon was already inside and turned toward us with a smile.

"What is this place?" I asked.

"A natural hot spring," Falon said, as he bent down to dip his fingers in. He brought them to his lips with a smile. "Freshwater. Nice and warm too."

"This is where we'll get our water to drink and cook with," Derel said, gesturing at one of the smaller pools, before turning to the largest one. "And this one can be used for bathing."

"Incredible." I wanted to fall to my knees and thank the Fire God for providing this for us. I'd suspected there was a way to survive up here, but this was better than I'd imagined.

Derel moved behind me and began sliding down the straps of my dress. "I think we should try it out."

"Do you?" I asked, my breath catching as he pressed a kiss to my neck.

Falon closed in on me from the front, caging me between his best friend. "You must be eager to wash off the dirt from our days of traveling." His hands slid along my bare arms as his mouth lowered to mine. "We can help."

"I am feeling quite dirty," I said, before our lips met.

Derel left a trail of kisses down my neck to my shoulder, then tugged my dress down, revealing one of my breasts. Falon immediately palmed it in his large, rough hand, and began squeezing my flesh. I moaned as Derel continued yanking the dress down, freeing another breast for his friend to claim. The fabric brushed against my hips as my entire torso was bared to the two men, who took their time exploring me with eager strokes and light kisses.

Their boldness surprised and thrilled me. Derel and I hadn't gotten along for most of my life, but the sexual chemistry had always simmered between us under the surface. Now that he'd admitted his feelings for me, it seemed he didn't want to hold back any longer. Falon, on the other hand, had always acted as though he was nothing more than a friend, but not anymore. As he took one breast in his mouth and ran his tongue over my nipple, I didn't have any more doubts that what we had was more than friendship.

"We know you've been with Blane and Roth, but now we're going to make you ours," Derel's voice said, as he nipped at my ear. His hard length pressed against my behind and sent a rush of wet heat between my thighs.

Falon ran his hand down my hips to continue easing my dress down, until it fell to the floor. "For years we held back because of our friendship, knowing we could never be happy if you picked one of us. But that isn't a problem anymore."

"I want you both," I said, pressing a kiss to Falon's lips, before turning to kiss Derel too. "I've always wanted you both."

"How about at the same time?" Derel asked, as he stroked my behind.

"Is that possible?"

"Oh yes." He gave my bottom a hard squeeze. "Now get in the water."

The two men watched as I moved toward the spring and stepped down into the water. Delicious warmth crept over me as I sank into it, making all my muscles relax. Before me, both men began to undress, tearing off their shirts and dropping their trousers, revealing their muscular bodies and jutting cocks. If this was going to be my life from now on, I couldn't complain.

Derel descended first into the water and took me in his arms, kissing me hard while his fingers slipped between my thighs. He stroked me in both my mouth and my core and I had to cling to him as pleasure swept over me. His wet, muscular body pressed against mine in the most sensual way, and I wrapped my legs around him to get even closer. His cock slipped inside me as we came together, like it couldn't help but find its way to where it belonged. I gasped at the sudden joining, but then his tongue was sliding against mine, matching his thrusts.

Then Falon's hands were on me too, his body fitted against my back. He was even more muscular than Derel from days spent working as a carpenter, and I enjoyed the feel of his hard ridges on my skin. Along with the other hard thing poking into my behind, which I knew wanted a taste of me too.

While Derel gripped my hips to pump into me, Falon's hands claimed my breasts and his mouth sucked on my neck. I arched back against him, taking Derel deeper, while turning my head to capture Falon's mouth. Derel leaned down to lick water off my neck, but then he pulled out of me and spun me toward Falon. With water churning around us, Falon took me into his arms and captured my mouth, then entered me with one smooth push. He filled me up just as well as Derel did, but it was different. Derel was longer, but Falon was thicker—and both of them were mine.

"I think we're clean enough," Derel said.

Falon nodded and lifted me out of the water, my body wrapped around him as he moved onto the black stone floor. He set me down on a long cloth the men had laid out, and then pumped into me from above a few times, like he couldn't help himself, before rolling us over so that I was on top. I took a moment to savor how huge he felt in this position, while Derel moved behind us. He picked up a bottle of oil, and I realized they'd been planning this all along. Waiting for me to wake up, so they could lay their claim to me...together.

Derel kneeled behind me and began stroking my behind, spreading my cheeks, sliding his oiled fingers along my back entrance. I gasped with each touch, especially as Falon slowly rocked underneath me. When Derel's finger eased inside, I let out a cry of pleasure and surprise. No one had touched me there before, and I was shocked to find how much I enjoyed it.

Derel spent a few minutes stretching me wide while I rode Falon, and it was hard to believe anything could be more pleasurable than this moment, but I knew it would be once Derel was inside me too.

Then Derel's fingers vanished, and were quickly replaced by something much larger, harder, and thicker. As he pushed inside my tight hole, a mix of pleasure and pain shot through me and I clung to Falon as I cried out. He held me in his arms and stroked my breasts lovingly, and when his mouth captured mine, Derel was able to inch deeper inside me from behind.

"That's it," he said. "Just relax and let me in."

"Oh Gods," I said, as he filled me up slowly, stretching me around him in impossible ways.

"You're doing great," Falon said, with a slight pinch to my nipples.

Suddenly Derel was all the way inside, his hips flush with my behind, and I drew in a ragged breath as the feelings swept through me. I was one with both men at the same time, all of us joined together in the most intimate way.

"Please," I dug my fingers into the light curls on Falon's chest and whimpered, not knowing what I asked for, only that I needed *more*.

Falon gripped my hips and began to thrust up into me, which made

Derel move too. Derel's hands found my breasts and he arched over me from behind as he sank deep inside. Together the two of them began to move in a smooth rhythm, which felt more incredible than anything I'd ever known before. I was pressed between them, joined with them both, and all I could do was let them take control of my body and bring us all to release.

The climax swept through me quickly, making me cry out again and again as pleasure shook my body. I tightened up around both men and they seemed to surge inside me, both of them groaning and exploding together. All of us succumbing at the same time to the unimaginable pleasure of being one with each other's bodies.

As satisfaction swept over us, the men wrapped me in their arms, squeezing me between them, while they whispered that they loved me and always would. I whispered that I loved them too as I snuggled close against them, my enemy and my best friend, and thought how lucky I was to have them here with me.

CHAPTER THIRTEEN

A fter my tryst with Falon and Derel I found the library, while the men continued working in other rooms of the temple. At first all I could do was stare at the bookshelves lining every wall from floor to ceiling, full of dusty old tomes I couldn't wait to crack open. Then I slowly stepped inside, examining a seating area on one side of the room and a small desk on the other with a giant flame carved into it. This was all for me, the High Priestess, I realized. Maybe I was meant to be a scholar of sorts after all.

A faded leather journal sat on top of the desk, covered in dust. I blew it off as I sat in the chair and then flipped the journal open, the pages making an audible crack as they moved for the first time in years. With my breath in my throat, I began to read.

My name is Ara and one day I'm going to be the next High Priestess.

Ara—my grandmother! Did she leave this here for me? No, she couldn't have known I would come to the temple…but maybe she knew *someone* would.

For years the Dragons have been pressuring all the High Priestesses to step down. They're scared of what we know. They're afraid of what will happen if the Gods awaken.

My mother refuses to leave, of course, even though the Gods remain as dormant as this volcano. I've decided to record my thoughts in case something should happen to us, in the hopes that one day a future High Priestess will find it.

My mother said she didn't know why Ara had left the temple and moved to Sparkport. Could this journal hold the key? Was it because of the Dragons?

I'd lived in fear of the Dragons all my life, as did everyone else with any sense. But the Dragons served the Gods alongside the priests—didn't they? Why would they be afraid if the Gods woke? I had much to learn, obviously. Yet the Fire God remained silent.

I intended to read the journal cover to cover to learn about my grandmother's life and my role here, but for now I skipped to the very last entry, desperate to know why she'd left the temple.

Once I turned twenty I was supposed to leave the temple and find four priests who would become my mates. Instead I let the Crimson Dragon seduce me, much to my mother's dismay. She says he did it as a way to ruin me, and I suppose she might be right. If so, his plan worked—because I am pregnant.

I sat back and rested a hand over my racing heart. Gods, was I the granddaughter of the Crimson Dragon? Sark was the most ruthless and brutal Dragon of them all, even though he served the Fire God and ostensibly protected the Fire Realm and led our armies. I'd only seen him a few times when he'd come to check on Sparkport to instill fear in us, and he had been quite handsome, especially for someone hundreds of years old. But I'd also heard rumors that he burnt down the houses of anyone he suspected of conspiring against the Dragons. How could my grandmother sleep with him?

I forced myself to keep reading the final entry.

Sark took advantage of me when I was young, lonely, and foolish…and now I'll never be able to convince four men to become my mates. Not when I am carrying another man's child—especially the Crimson Dragon's. I suspect that was his plan all along, to prevent me from becoming High Priestess, though now he has abandoned me, claiming the child cannot be his because he is loyal to the Black Dragon. No doubt she would punish all of us if she found out he had sired a child with someone else, which is why I must keep this secret to my grave.

My mother says that one day the Fire God will awaken and the next Black Dragon will be crowned. I'd hoped that I would be the High Priestess at the time, but Valefire remains silent and the Dragons continue to rule. I can no longer hold onto the hope that the Fire God will return from his slumber during my lifetime, and have decided to leave the temple and return to Sparkport to raise my child among my cousins. Perhaps it is for the best, as I find my faith lacking these days and have become a disappointment to my mother and those in the temple.

I can only pray that one of my descendants will find their way back to this temple when the Fire God awakens to carry out our divine mission, even though I have failed as High Priestess. If that is who is reading this, please accept my apology for not preparing you better. I had no idea if this day would ever come, but I trust you will make the Fire God proud.

And remember this above all else: we serve the Gods, not the Dragons.

I reread her words over and over as I absorbed everything she'd written. I was descended from both the High Priestess and the Crimson Dragon. I'd always thought the Dragons served the Gods, but it seemed there was some conflict between them. Now that the Fire God had awakened, would the Dragons become our enemies?

Falon appeared in the doorway, breathing quickly. "Calla, there's something you need to see."

"What is it?"

"The Dragons are coming."

CHAPTER FOURTEEN

I rushed to the front of the temple with Falon, where the other men were already waiting and watching the sky. As I lifted my eyes, I caught sight of four large reptilian forms with massive wings and terrifying talons descending toward us quickly. With his blood red scales I spotted the Crimson Dragon immediately, leading the charge to his own temple. Beside him was the Golden Dragon, who represented the Air God; the Azure Dragon, who spoke for the Water God; and the Jade Dragon, who was meant to serve the Earth God. The Black Dragon, the avatar of the Spirit Goddess, was the only one missing, for which I was thankful. She was their leader and the most powerful and terrifying of them all.

As the Crimson Dragon landed on the temple's shiny black steps, his body transformed back into a man, and I stood face to face with my grandfather. His hair was a shockingly pale color, almost white, and cut in a short military style. I recognized my own brown eyes on him, though his were harsh as they swept over me with a scowl. As we stared at each other, I could tell he knew who I was. But before either of us could speak, the other Dragons touched the ground and shifted back to their human forms.

I'd never seen the others before. Doran, the Azure Dragon, had long golden hair, a rugged beard, and tanned, weathered skin. Beside him, Isen, the Golden Dragon, looked completely opposite with pale, perfect skin and shiny black hair tied back. The final Dragon, Heldor, had a shaved head and tattoos running down his muscular arms, his massive body an imposing figure even beside the other large men.

"It's true then," Heldor said, his voice low and rumbling. "The Fire God is free."

Doran arched an eyebrow. "How can we be sure? All I see is a bit of smoke."

Isen snorted. "The volcano hasn't been active all this time. Why else would it suddenly stir now?"

I remembered Ara's words. *They're afraid of what will happen if the Gods awaken.* I stepped forward and said, "The Fire God remains absent, my lords. It is only us here at the temple."

From the corner of my eye I saw my mates shift and cast strange glances at me, but they didn't know what I'd found. They hadn't read my grandmother's journal, or seen her warning. *We serve the Gods, not the Dragons.*

I wasn't sure what was happening, but I knew in my gut that I must lie to the Dragons and protect the Fire God and whatever he had planned. He'd awakened and brought us here for a reason, and I had a feeling the Dragons wouldn't like it.

"Who is this?" Isen asked, casting a dismissive glance at me.

Sark pinned me with his cruel gaze. "The High Priestess."

"I thought this temple was abandoned," Heldor said, raising an eyebrow at Sark.

"It was."

I swallowed. "I'm trying to revive the old traditions in the hopes it will calm the volcano. It's been rumbling for some time, though my mother says that is normal."

"Has the Fire God spoken to you?" Heldor asked.

"No," I lied.

"Why should we believe you?" Isen asked, before his eyes fell on my mates. "Maybe we should make sure she's telling the truth."

"You think this girl could have awakened the Fire God?" Doran asked, with a haughty laugh. "Even if she did, the others are still bound. He is powerless on his own."

"I wouldn't call a God powerless," Isen snapped.

"We're wasting time here," Doran said. "I don't see any evidence of the Fire God. And Sark would know if he'd broken free, wouldn't he?"

Sark grunted in response, still staring at me in a way that made my skin crawl.

"This is your temple," Heldor said to Sark. "Find out the truth and deal with it. Or Nysa will be forced to come here herself, and you know how she'll feel about that."

With that, Heldor shifted back into his dragon form, his dark green wings glimmering under the sun as he leaped into the air. Though I was sweating, a chill ran through me at his words. Nysa, the Black Dragon, rarely left the city of Soulspire where she ruled, but when she did, destruction and death followed.

"Return when you have answers," Isen told Sark, before his golden scales flashed bright as he took off toward the sky.

Sark grumbled and pushed his way past me inside the temple, leaving me alone with the Azure Dragon. The golden-haired man gave me a quick nod, before shifting and flying off, his glimmering dark blue body quickly blending in with the sky.

"What was that about?" Derel asked, once they were gone.

"I'll tell you later," I said. "For now, just follow my lead."

The other guys nodded and we headed back inside the temple to find Sark. He'd opened the door at the back of the great room, which had been locked up until now. It led to another room with a large bed on a raised platform, almost like an altar. The room was coated in a layer of dust and I got the sense it was meant for some kind of ritual. How odd.

Another door on the other side opened to the outside, behind the temple. I stepped through it and was hit with a wave of heat coming from the mouth of the volcano, which was only a short distance away.

Sark stood over the edge of it, looking down into the smoking abyss. He spun around to face me as I approached. "Tell me the truth. Why are you here?"

I bowed my head. "I serve the Gods, as do you. Isn't that right?"

His lips pressed into a tight line. "Of course. That's why I must know if he's been freed."

I tilted my head. "I didn't realize the Fire God was imprisoned."

He grabbed my chin in his hand. "I can make you talk, you know. I'll burn off your limbs. Throw your mates into the pit. Turn your entire village to ash. Unless you tell me the truth."

"You would truly harm your own granddaughter?" I asked, keeping my voice sweet, even though I was more scared than I'd ever been in my life.

Behind me, my mates gasped, but Sark's eyes only narrowed. "You don't know what you speak of."

As his fingers tightened painfully on my chin, I met his gaze without flinching. "I wonder what the Black Dragon would say if she knew you had a child with someone else?"

He glared at me for a few more seconds, then shoved me away so hard I hit the ground, scraping my palms on the black rocks. Sark then turned to my mates and gave them all a dangerous look. They each stood poised to fight, even though there was no way any of them could win against Sark, the deadliest of the Black Dragon's mates.

"If the Fire God awakens, I expect you to send word to me immediately," he snapped.

I bowed low. "Of course. I live to serve the Dragons."

"See that you do, or everyone you love will suffer for it."

Sark's body seamlessly shifted into his terrifying dragon form before he launched into the air and flew over the mouth of the volcano. He let out a huge blast of fire as a warning, before he flew away.

Once he was only a tiny speck in the distance, my shoulders finally relaxed. The other men all surrounded me and wrapped their arms around me.

"Are you okay?" Falon asked.

I nodded. "I think so."

"What was that about?" Blane asked.

"Let's go inside," I said. "I have a lot to tell you."

But as we headed back toward the temple, the volcano began to rumble loudly and the ground shook beneath our feet. The air suddenly became much hotter, to the point where it became hard to breathe, and my skin tingled with awareness. As we turned back to the gaping maw, lava and sparks shot out from it as a monstrously large dragon reared up from inside it. This one was much larger and more incredible than the ones we'd just faced, and its skin seemed to be made from lava itself.

"Calla of the Fire Realm," the dragon's deep voice said, while it pinned me with its fiery eyes. "You have served me well."

"The Fire God," Falon whispered, while the ground continued to rumble around us.

"It's really true," Blane said, while Roth and Derel could only gape and stare in awe.

This must be the Fire God's true form, only seen here at his most holy place. I bowed my head low, while the volcano surged around us. "I've done everything you asked. I came to the temple and brought four men to serve as my mates. Will you calm the volcano now?"

In response, the glow from the mouth of the volcano dimmed and the ground stopped shaking. "Very well. But there is still more for you to do."

I swallowed and glanced at the men at my side, who nodded and gazed back at me with determined eyes. "What would you have us do?"

"You must prepare for the next Dragons to rise—the ascendants."

I tilted my head, unsure if I'd heard him correctly. "The next ones?"

"The Dragons were created to protect the world, and were meant to bring balance between the humans and elementals. Many years ago that changed and the current Dragons allowed their purpose to be corrupted. Now their time is at an end. The next Black Dragon has been born, and in twenty years she will visit this temple with her mates." His fanged mouth dipped low. "And you will be ready for them."

"But the Dragons have ruled for as long as anyone can remember," Derel said. "How can they be replaced?"

"The Dragons were only meant to rule for a short time, before passing the torch to the next generation. Nysa and her mates defied the Gods to gain immortality. Now their rule must come to an end."

I glanced at my mates again, the four men I loved, and knew they'd stand beside me no matter what we faced. If our purpose was to prepare for these ascendants, we'd be ready. If we had to defy the Dragons, we'd do it.

I stepped forward and gazed up at the fiery god. "We're ready to serve."

CHAPTER FIFTEEN

TWENTY YEARS LATER

I stood in front of the temple and gazed out across the barren landscape surrounding the volcano. Small figures approached in the distance on horseback, getting closer with every minute. Purpose and determination smoldered inside me, along with the Fire God's flames. I'd waited for this day for twenty years and it was hard to believe this moment was finally here.

I turned around and headed back through the temple, where my four mates waited for me. Blane, Roth, Derel, and Falon all wore the red and black robes of the Fire God's priests and I gazed at each of them with love nearly bursting inside of me. Even after twenty years together, we were still as much in love as when we first came to the temple, if not more so. Every day we'd spent together was a true blessing, and I was so thankful the Fire God chose me—and that these four men had agreed to become my priests.

"It's time," I said.

"The new Black Dragon?" Blane asked, arching an eyebrow.

I nodded. "She and her mates are approaching now. They should be here in a few hours."

"I'll start preparing a feast," Derel said. "They're going to be hungry after they climb that mountain."

"I'll prepare the bonding room," Falon said, glancing back at the room with the altar and the bed that we rarely went into, which had been waiting for the ascendants all this time.

"Thank you," I told them both with a smile.

"Any sign of the other Dragons?" Roth asked. "Sark?"

797

"Not yet." I glanced back at the smoke-filled sky. The Fire God had kept his promise and the volcano had been quiet for the entire time we'd lived here—until now. We all knew what that meant, and were prepared to leave on a moment's notice if needed. "But I'm glad we sent the children to Sparkport, just in case."

I'd been blessed with four children, one from each of my mates, which we considered gifts from the Fire God. Our oldest daughter would one day become the High Priestess after me, if she wished to take that role. For now, they were safe at the bakery with Loka and her wife. Once this was over, we'd be reunited again.

Though the Fire God had never appeared to me again, I knew he'd been watching over us, waiting for this day. He'd given me purpose, and over the years I'd devoured every book in the library and studied up on the Dragons, or what little was left about them anyway, while my mates and I prepared as best we could for the new Dragons' arrival. Change was coming to the four Realms, but if our plans were successful, we would no longer live under Nysa's oppressive regime. Soon the new Black Dragon would rise, with her four mates at her side. Only then would balance return to the world.

While the men took care of final preparations, I dressed in my ceremonial robes and waited for the ascendants to climb the volcano, much like we'd done years ago. Until, hours later, a young woman with red hair took the final steps onto the summit of Valefire, with her mates at her side.

It was time to meet the people who would save the world.

ABOUT THE AUTHOR

Elizabeth Briggs is a New York Times and Top 5 Amazon bestselling author of paranormal and fantasy romance featuring twisty plots, plenty of spice, and a guaranteed happy ending. She's a Stage IV cancer warrior who has worked with teens in foster care and volunteered with animal rescue organizations. She lives in Los Angeles with her husband, their daughter, and a pack of fluffy dogs.

Visit Elizabeth's website: www.elizabethbriggs.com